About [illegible]

Robin Porecky is of Polish origin but was born [illegible] p in England. For over twenty-five years he has worked in S[illegible]en as a writer and maker of customised knives. This is his sixth novel, following 'A Pathless Land', 'Fool's Island', 'Come Into My Arms', 'The Devil's Field', and 'Finished'. It is the fourth book in the Magnus Trygg series of Swedish crime novels.

Dedication

To Laurie and Tony who have given me such steadfast support.

Robin Porecky

RaRa's Last Fan Dance

Austin Macauley
Publishers Ltd.

A CIP catalogue record for this title is available from the British Library.

Royalties from the sale of this novel go to the registered charity The Camphill Village Trust Ltd.

ISBN 978 1 84963 644 5

www.austinmacauley.com

First Published (2015)
Austin Macauley Publishers Ltd.
25 Canada Square
Canary Wharf
London
E14 5LB

Printed and bound in Great Britain

ALSO BY ROBIN PORECKY

A PATHLESS LAND (2009)
978-1-90560-958-1

In 1897 Martin Janow sets out to rescue Tempest, a mad evangelist, from the wilds of Swedish Lapland. His motive is not entirely unselfish, for Mary Warmouth has promised herself to him if he succeeds.
But why is she so eager to save the priest, and is Tempest really mad? On the increasingly frightening journey homeward the layers of truth are gradually peeled back and Janow must fight for his own sanity and his survival.

CRITICAL ACCLAIM

"The plot resembles both Conrad's *Heart of Darkness* and Henry James' *The Ambassadors,* but is none the worse for it. The scenes in Lapland are superbly eerie; and what Janow finds at the end of his voyage of discovery suitably disturbing."

Alexander Lucie-Smith, *The Tablet*

"A gripping, erudite and highly original journey into the heart of Nordic Darkness. Porecky explores issues of spirituality, culture and fanaticism with the flair of a born storyteller."

Liz Jensen, author of '*The Ninth Life of Louis Drax*'

"There are echoes of the great Australian novelist Patrick White's *Voss*: the same epic feel and sense of inevitability. I felt plunged into a powerful place ... and was swept along."

Piers Plowright, *Triple Prix Italia winner and Radio 4's 'Saturday review' critic*

LONGLISTED FOR THE AUTHORS' CLUB BEST FIRST NOVEL AWARD 2010

FOOL'S ISLAND (2011)
978-1-84963-075-7

In 1759 the young and wilful Franulka leaves her castle home for Warsaw, where she attracts the attentions of the King's son. Eighteen months later, with her Fool and maid, she vanishes. A closed carriage in the early morning, with an armed outrider, suggests disgrace and exile.
But nothing is as it seems. Caught up in a deadly conspiracy, only the Fool can save her. But is the price too high?
Shifting between Poland, Russia, Venice and an Adriatic island, this is a gripping historical mystery, a passionate love story and a moving study of the painful growth of self-awareness.

"Here's a novel that grabs you by the ear and eye and plunges you into the life of 18th century Poland: court intrigues, love sacred and profane, jealousy, rage, adventure, comedy and danger. And your guide is that wisest of men, a professional 'fool'. The journey to his island is a thrilling one."

Piers Plowright, Broadcaster and Critic

"A born storyteller."

Liz Jensen, author of 'The Rapture'

"Powerfully written, impeccably researched."

Elizabeth Carter-Jones, Reviewer

COME INTO MY ARMS (2012)
978-1-84963-166-2

Magnus Trygg is a happy man. He loves his Swedish wife, his two young children and his home in the sparsely populated northern county of Jämtland. He is proud of his job as a junior policeman in the local force and, though half-Thai, he has always thought of himself as fully Swedish.
Then a young Kurdish girl is found in the forest, tied to a stake and shot. Magnus, waiting with the body throughout the long summer night until an Inspector is available, discovers the murder weapon. It suggests an honour killing, and he is ordered to bring in the father. But Magnus knows Hashmet Nazif, likes him, and is reluctant to believe he would harm his daughter. Unsettled by the sudden explosion of anti-immigrant feeling, he decides to use his local knowledge to uncover anything that may suggest a different truth. It is a very dangerous decision.

"Tremendous pace, a lot of tension and a thoroughly gripping climax."

Piers Plowright, Critic and Broadcaster

"A good and surprising read."

Bernard Krichefski, Television Drama Producer

THE DEVIL'S FIELD (2013)
978-1-84963-167-9

Magnus Trygg, temporarily in charge of the High Coast district, is called out to a body with a knife in its back. August Frisk, who alerted him, insists he's never seen the man before, and the others living there agree. The only suspect is Paulus, a Sami reindeer herder who flees to the White Sea where the Russian authorities prove uncooperative. Inspector Amrén suggests the case might be suspended until he can be questioned.

But Magnus, eager to prove himself, carries on probing. He's sensed hidden tensions at Frisk's and, his own marriage in crisis, he's powerfully drawn to August's daughter-in-law, Hanna. But putting pressure on already vulnerable people reveals other secrets, which have unwanted consequences for them all.

Set in northern Sweden, Poland and the crime-ridden Russian enclave of Kaliningrad in 2004, this is the second book in the Magnus Trygg series.

"A splendid piece of work."

Brendan Walsh, Literary Editor 'The Tablet'

"A powerful tale, grippingly told. I salute the author's energy and skill."

Piers Plowright, Critic and Broadcaster

FINISHED (2014)
978-1-84963-642-1

In the Swedish town of Sundsvall the female owner of a basement flea market is killed by a single hammer blow. Magnus Trygg is away on an Inspector's course and so the case is reluctantly given to his rival for the post of Head of Homicide, Lennart Havendal. An unlucky man, struggling to cope with the death of his wife, he does uncover one vital clue: although the murder weapon is beside the body, another hammer has been removed from a display unit.

Unable to make more progress with the first murder, he is soon investigating a second. Magnus, when he returns, volunteers to act as protection officer for the woman Lennart believes will be the next victim. Magnus has his doubts, but another hammer is missing and time is not on their side.

Set in northern Sweden and England in 2005, this is the third book in the Magnus Trygg series.

"The best yet. A cracking opening, highly page-turning, full of tension, and, ultimately, rather touching."

Piers Plowright, Broadcaster and Critic

CHAPTER 1

In the darkness, hours before dawn, he swayed above the road looking down at the occasional car which passed beneath him. The rock on either side of him had been blasted to form a pass through the height above the Indal River at Utanede, a cowboy canyon with a tarmac base. The cold was intense, and the crest of snow at the rocky lips was deep and pure. At intervals he moved slowly like a circling buzzard; but at other times he was as still as a pendulum in an unwound clock.

Below, coming out of the forest, a small hunched figure moved along the narrow track toward the split rock. He was walking very slowly, and it became apparent it was not an injury that was slowing him, nor exhaustion, but simply age. It had given him his stoop, and the plodding sedateness of his movement had become the natural rhythm of his body. In one hand he carried a fishing rod, and in the other he had a looped twig from which dangled two stream-trout. He may have been looking forward to eating them for an early breakfast, fresh from the water and fried in butter, for there was a look of contentment about the man despite the weight of his years. He picked his way along the barely visible path with the unerring precision of somebody who has used it all his life and has reached an age where he is largely indifferent to darkness or light. He was humming a tune as he went along, the fingers of his left hand moving on the rod as if it was the keyboard of a piano-accordion.

Above him the silent watcher moved more violently in a sudden gust of wind, and the rope creaked. The fisherman stopped, peering upwards. It seemed his sight was no longer as keen as it once might have been, for with an audible sigh which ended the *Dala* dance with a wheezy discord, he stooped to lay his rod and fish on a convenient tree stump, took out his torch and shone it upwards. Then he began to toil up the narrow ascent towards the top of the cutting. When he was about half-way, he stopped and turned to face what was now level with him. The morning breeze eddied, and the person on the rope approached him through the gloom. He came so close, if only momentarily, that the old man could see in the torchlight the noose around his neck, the dead-fish look of the skin, the absence of any sign of life. Above, on the crest of the rock, a sturdy birch had sunk its roots deep into the crevices of the granite and, over time, while still remaining firmly anchored, had leant lower and lower into the drop. The rope was attached to its upper trunk, and had then been passed over a strong branch somewhat further out so that the hanging man, in the stillness of his death, contemplated the empty road with equally empty eyes.

But there was no doubt that he was intended to be seen once the sun was up. There was a white placard tied to his chest by strings which ran around his waist and neck, and the black lettering on it would stand out clearly in the light of day. Though not as old as the man who scrutinised the message, he was not young. He was wearing a suit that, though dated, had been expensive, and his white shirt and narrow tie added to the appearance of professional elegance. His black shoes were lovingly polished and he had that calm demeanour of someone who has lived long enough to be beyond surprise. Even his own death, or so it seemed from his expression, had not surprised him.

CHAPTER 2

Four days previously Ragnar Amrén had set out southwards for the 2006 County Police Commissioners Conference in Uppsala. Medelpad was covered in fresh snow and for the first few hours he drove through traditional Norrland winter scenes, lacking only red-capped Christmas elves to turn them into childhood Christmas cards. But just above Gävle the snow became sparser, and a slight drizzle compelled him to use his windscreen wipers. He'd enjoyed having such beauty around him, and now he missed it, but he felt comfortable and secure in his well-heated Volvo. As head of the Sundsvall force he could have opted for a more daring car, flashier even, but it was typical of his caution that he'd gone for something safe, practical and unexciting. He was aware his colleagues smiled behind his back, and poked fun at him for his lack of adventure; and those who knew him best had probably won some money betting on his final choice of car. But he believed they were not unhappy to be led by someone whose qualities were personified by the vehicle he drove - solid and dependable.

The weather became increasingly dreary the further south he went, but it couldn't dampen his spirits. He was nursing a secret, hugging it to himself where it warmed him whatever the outside temperature. Nobody had seen it coming, least of all himself. Yet once it had taken place he'd experienced a sense of vindication, as if he was finally getting what he might justifiably deserve. More used to it himself now, he joyfully anticipated the astonishment of his colleagues when the public announcement was made and they discovered their placid, predictable leader was actually destined for higher things.

Wizelius, the police commissioner for Västernorrland, was dying. A man of few words and strong opinions, he'd been effective if not always popular. Amrén, who was mostly accommodating rather than contrary, had got on perfectly well with him, though he'd never been blind to his faults. When he heard the cancer had spread to an extent that made surgery pointless, his immediate reaction was one of genuine sorrow for Wizelius himself, followed by a secondary feeling of reluctant irritation that he would have to adapt himself to another overseer. At least Wizelius had interfered very little in Sundsvall's police affairs, but a new broom might feel the need to throw his weight around at first. Not once did he consider himself as a possible contender for the position. He had long ago decided that his present post was as high as he wanted to climb. Nor had he ever felt the least regret about that decision, or so, at least, he'd believed. But he had always been especially sensitive to any change in people's attitude to him, and it was not long before he picked up the early signals that others *did* see him as a suitable candidate.

He should, of course, have deliberately scotched his chances from the first, putting himself out of contention. At any time in the previous thirty years of his police career he would have done so. But something seemed to have altered in him, and, to his own surprise, he let it run. It was not that he did not know his real worth, but hitherto he'd been able to accept without resentment that many above him were less effective than he would have been in their jobs because he did not covet their jobs. But on this occasion, at the first indication that an eventual offer might be coming his way, he suddenly found he desperately wanted to seize his chance.

He felt uneasy at such an unpremeditated response, for he had never before reacted without his usual cautious appraisal of every possible consequence. But this urge was overpowering. Excitement ruled him and though he was shaken by the strength of this late-flowering ambition, he could not rein it in. When it became clear he was likely to succeed, it filled him with an exhilaration which was quite new to him. Ragnar Amrén was going to be County Police Commissioner for Västernorrland, with a budget of three million *kronor,* and responsibility for a population of two hundred and fifty thousand. It was intoxicating.

But that was not all. In the course of confidential conversation, away from Sundsvall, and with some very senior figures, it became clear the promotion might be a means to a very different end. In the not too distant future, or so he was told, another post would be coming up, and some of the commissioners already thought he might be the one to fill it. Though he hardly dared to think of it, it would be something much, much more. However he might discount it, he was considered, by several influential people, the right choice to become the highest ranking policeman in Sweden.

He wondered whether others had scented the change in him before he noticed it himself, and that was why the tentative approaches began. He did not know. But now he, who had never sought anything for himself, began to stalk the possibility of promotion. When important people unexpectedly sought him out, happening to come across him at meetings, or just passing through Sundsvall and taking the opportunity to look in, he welcomed them in a way he never would have done before. Instead of becoming reticent, pleading work or another engagement so that he could slip away as soon as possible, he put himself at their disposal, discussing his work, brushing aside his achievements but not so modestly that he did not make it apparent what they were. He allowed himself to speak of his ambitions where before no ambition had existed. After such a quiet life it was a heady experience, and perhaps it did go to his head. He'd never sought anything for himself before, and he convinced himself that he did not want more than his due - to be the County Police Commissioner. But when allusions were made to the present unsatisfactory state of the force, the possibility of a change of leadership not too far in the future, and the vital importance of having someone who had the trust and respect of ordinary policemen, he discovered that ambition, once spawned, is hard to contain. The day he knew he was to be Commissioner became the day he desperately wanted the highest rank as well.

Outside Uppsala, he slowed the car and turned it into the long avenue. Black, leafless trees dripped in the November drizzle, and in the ditches the vestiges of the last snowfall were grey and shrivelled. He stopped the car and lowered the window. It was bitterly cold, but here there was none of the beauty which had comforted him when he left Sundsvall, early that morning. Then there were white trees in a white landscape; here there was bleakness.

But at the far end of the avenue he could just make out the circular drive around the still-green grass centre, the large stone two-handled bowl high on its pedestal, filled with welcoming freshly planted dark-pink flowers. Beyond it spread the splendour of the pale-yellow *herrgård*, dominating the road, commanding a fine view over Lake Mälaren, its stone steps leading to the pillared portico, the impressive stately home that was the chosen venue of the 2006 Conference. It was there his promotion would be announced, and his unofficial anointment as a possible future National Police Commissioner would slip into the stream of consciousness of those in the force who really mattered.

He shivered in the cold, but as he raised the window he knew it was also a shiver of excitement. After so long, he was going to make something of his life.

He drove on, wanting to have a little time to himself before meeting Jörgen Bergqvist, Commissioner of the Stockholm Police and current chairman of the CPC, who had invited him to a pre-conference lunch here, before the other delegates arrived. He steered around the main building and coasted down between twin lines of ancient linden trees. He could see the lake at the far end, but had to turn off into the residential car park before he reached it. He checked into his room, unpacked and looked at his watch. He hated to be late, and for many years now it had been one of his principles to be on time for any engagement. He would not have liked to reckon up the number of hours he'd wasted hanging around and waiting just so that he could always arrive on the minute. But it was one of the ways he'd built a reputation for absolute reliability with much the same planned care as he was using now over his promotion. And not just reliability, but amiability too, a listener more than a talker, a man who never refused a task and never left it unfinished, who never shirked hard work, who never spoke ill of people behind their backs. A nice guy, a good man, sympathetic, loyal, and, though he didn't like to think about it any longer, an officer, in his younger days, with a proven track-record of reckless courage when the need arose.

He'd met Jörgen privately once before, and at that meeting the commissioner had shown he was not a man for niceties.

"Do you want to be County Police Chief?" he'd growled in the alcohol thickened voice familiar from countless television interviews.

"I do," he replied, as though he was answering a priest officiating at his marriage.

"You've never shown much bloody ambition before."

"I was waiting until I felt I was ready. I'm ready now."

Jörgen gave a grunt which sounded both sceptical and irritated by the prissiness of the answer.

"I've looked at your record, and it's impressive. You've risked your life to save others, you've taken difficult decisions, and on some operations you've gambled on your own instincts and been proved right. But at times, like now, you come across as a sanctimonious creep. Why's that?"

Amrén briefly considered this. "Perhaps it's because you and I are very different. We're unlikely to understand each other."

"Meaning that I drink? Everybody knows it, and I don't give a fuck about it as long as it doesn't interfere with my job, whereas you're squeaky clean and therefore holier than thou. Is that why you've never married, because you'd like to have been a monk?"

Amrén couldn't help laughing, though he understood this was the question Jörgen, in his own particular style, had been softening him up for.

"It was more bad timing than spiritual castration. I fell in love when I was quite young, but she was already married. Although I continue to live in hope, nobody else has ever matched her."

"I've done my research, and I was surprised to discover that, especially in your earlier years in the force, you were well known for a fan dance you performed at parties, during which you mocked politicians, do-gooders, and other police-critics."

"It was a long time ago."

"Yet it was known about in Sundsvall, so there must have been the odd little repeat performance?"

"I did it once at a small private party," Amrén conceded.

"In November the bloody talking-shop we call a commissioner's conference starts with a get-together with the press, and that's when you'll be introduced to the nation as the next Commissioner for Västernorrland. But the conference ends with a private party, and no prying journalists of any sort or colour are allowed at that. Someone always does a short turn, and this year I'd like it to be you. There are still some among us who think you're a bit of a dull dog, and before we start on any sort of move to get you considered for the highest post we need to wake people up to the fact that though you may be quiet, you're certainly not dull. Will you do it?"

He'd amazed himself by agreeing at once. His fan dance was something very intimate, to be performed among tried and trusted colleagues. The thought of doing it on a wider stage frightened him, but it tempted him as well. Dressing up, disguising himself, becoming a different person, so dominant, so critical, always had a strange effect on him, almost as if it was a powerful drug. It was certainly a sort of madness, the only time he lost control, handing himself over to some depth inside himself that embraced everything he normally abhorred. He would flaunt himself, savage all critics of the police, holding his audience helpless, leading them where he wished, working them up, forcing them to follow him, and leaving them emptied of their darkest thoughts and shameful prejudices and cheering the man who'd made their difficult job seem temporarily easy. It was an exposure of himself, but it was in private, and so he could accept it. But deep-down he was conscious that he longed to do it, relished the challenge and knew he could, and would, surmount it.

He'd been less happy about being introduced at the Press Conference, though he'd accepted that as well. Now, waiting to meet Jörgen again, he was much more confident, and did not doubt his ability to survive. It was true that previously he'd always shunned personal publicity, and avoided the limelight, however pale it might be. Now, at the new level to which he'd climbed so astonishingly quickly, it was probably important television and radio should take him into every home. He would be known, recognised, someone special, someone with power and, of course, someone to knock down as much as to revere. But he would be revealing to the cameras the new self-assured, forthright character he'd assumed; or could it be the real character he'd never previously permitted to appear?

"You've got a real chance to establish your qualities in front of the press," Jörgen now announced as soon as they sat down together, the wine had been poured and the food set before them. "They're getting together sample questions submitted by the public, and they'll fire them at you to test your mettle. It'll be the same old rubbish, but your answers will seem fresh because you're a new face."

He drained his glass and signalled to the hovering waiter to fill it up again. Once that was done the waiter looked expectantly at Amrén, but he put his hand over his glass. Jörgen, raising his bushy eyebrows but waving the waiter away, leant forward.

"Is there anything in your past, Ragnar? Is there anything at all that in such new circumstances might emerge and bite you? You'll be sticking your head above the parapet as a County Chief, and even more so as a contender for the top post. It'll allow the fuckers in the press corps open season on you. They'll hunt through your life with their dirty minds and discover every time you didn't wipe your arse properly. If you've got any secret, don't kid yourself they'll miss it. They won't, because they've got a better sense of smell for scandal than salmon scenting their home river while they're still at sea. Believe me, there's nothing they enjoy more than crucifying a public figure, especially a policeman. So if there's something hidden, anything at all, you'd really better tell me now."

Amrén looked at Jörgen without a vestige of doubt. He noted the tiredness of the face before him, the sag of the skin, the weary knowledge in the eyes. Embedded in every column written about him was the cruel implication that he enjoyed his drink too much, and although he never flinched, and never changed his habits, everybody knew that sooner or later a media onslaught would bring him down.

"Nothing," he answered quietly, confirming his status as a safe pair of hands, a dedicated officer with a solid reputation and an unblemished record. "Even so, do you really believe I've got a chance of going further than County Commissioner?"

Jörgen chewed his seared beef thoughtfully. "It won't be in my hands," he answered finally. "The drinking is catching up with me, and I'm on my way out. It may be several years, but when I do go, others will go too. That always happens, a sort of clear out at the top which allows changes in direction, new ideas, the fresh start so loved by our government hotshots. Some sort of consensus is already emerging that the next National Police Commissioner should be a practical policeman, not a political one. Of course the government believes it will make the decision, along with local politicians and various committees, and we're happy to let them think it. But it's still the old way that counts, a hand on the elbow, a quiet word in the corner, and then the really influential few make up their minds. A name starts to do the rounds and, unless something unexpected comes out of the woodwork, that same name gets chosen by our political masters."

He stared at Amrén as if he still didn't quite fit the picture he was painting. "This time there's likely to be a preference for somebody from a smallish or medium-sized county, so your promotion to Västernorrland, at this particular moment, will certainly ensure you'll be a contender. And if you do well, stick to your police guns but don't make any political enemies, you're likely to be just the sort of safe candidate the right people will go for. But remember the National Police Commissioner is not only Head of the National Police Board, with overall supervision of the county forces, the National Laboratory of Forensic Science, and all police training. Crucially, he's also in charge of the allocation of government funds to the counties, and you can take my word for it that it gives him a mighty lot of power and influence."

He paused to ponder the power and influence he would soon no longer have, then shrugged resignedly. "So you can understand why we want a dyed-in-the-wool policeman like you, someone who's done it all himself and so really understands our needs and problems. That's particularly important because the vexed subject of county reorganisation is coming up again, and this time the plan is to merge the 21 county forces into 9 larger regions. Only somebody fresh from the frontline can fight that one. The trouble is that not many potential candidates are liked by the police, the public *and* the politicians. But as you seem to have that rare knack of doing what you want without upsetting people, you'll have a good chance."

"Won't you have retired by then?"

"Yes, and that'll give you an even better chance. A lot of us already think you're right for the job, but I'm not one of them. And before you ask me to explain that, I want you to tell me again whether there are any secrets in your life."

Amrén laughed, shaking his head. "I don't think I'm the sort of person who has skeletons in his cupboard. I tend to be cautious, like to be in control. I often suspect I'm altogether too careful, that perhaps I ought to let myself go sometimes. But I wouldn't find that easy."

Jörgen sighed. "No, I don't think you would. And now I can tell you that's precisely why I don't think you're the right man for the top job. You're almost too clean, and puritans don't usually make the best leaders. Perhaps I'll change my mind about you after your fan dance. If you can make County Police Commissioners laugh, you're probably capable of anything. But we all deceive ourselves, Ragnar, and nobody knows that better than I do. The man a person lies to most is himself. We have an image of ourselves, and it's immune to logic, and to common sense. It deflects the truth so easily we don't even know what the truth is about ourselves. I thought I could control my drinking. You tell me there's nothing you need control, not in your past, not in your present. I hope to God you're right."

CHAPTER 3

It was still drizzling outside, and in the November gloom, unrelieved by any heavy fall of snow, the *Herrgård* had a secretive look. Amrén hurried back to his room to prepare himself for the press conference. He sat very still in the darkest corner, closed his eyes, and reviewed for the umpteenth time all the likely questions he might be asked. It wasn't very difficult to guess what they might be in broad terms, for he was well aware of public concerns over funding, manpower, reaction times, political interference and a suspicion of corruption in certain branches of the force; but he wanted to be certain no question on any aspect of these would take him by surprise. He would adopt a quiet, thoughtful manner, with short, unhesitating and sincere responses, though that would only be possible if he was prepared for anything. So he stayed there, motionless, until he was.

The press conference had been set up in the ballroom. There were defined spaces for local and national TV and radio, and a hosting area for the journalists, complete with a small bar and an attractive young female police press officer. At one end there was a table on a raised platform where he, Jörgen and their host, the Uppsala commissioner, would sit. They were told that a slight technical problem would delay the start, and as neither he nor Jörgen had anything further to say to each other, and the silence between them was becoming awkward, Jörgen broke it by going to the bar and ostentatiously ordering a cranberry juice. A nearby reporter made a jocular comment and Jörgen shrugged expressively, indicating that duty called; but Amrén guessed he would soon disappear for a moment and add some vodka from the small flask he carried in his pocket. Left to his own devices, Amrén wandered over to chat to the *Svenska Dagbladet* crime reporter, Göran Broselius, who'd started his career in the north. He'd first encountered him during an honour killing case in which the Sundsvall force had cooperated with the Jämtland police. Göran asked after Magnus Trygg, whom Amrén had also met during the investigation and who was now his Head of Homicide., They reminisced about the curious circumstances in which Göran, who had loved the dead girl, had briefly become a suspect. Then they talked about the other journalists in the room, and Amrén asked if there were any he should watch out for. Göran pointed to an overweight reporter with yellow and blue Swedish flag elastic armbands on his shirtsleeves. He was holding his mobile to his ear and, whereas most of the others were watching the new boy with good-natured interest, he kept his back turned, concentrating on his call.

"His name's Ryd, works for *Expressen,* and he's set himself up to be the scourge of the Stockholm police. He's damaged Jörgen Bergqvist, and I suppose it's possible that if he thinks you're his protégé he may have a go at you. Since Stieg Larsson's death a couple of years ago, he's tried very hard to fill his shoes, but he's not in the same league. He just reacts to what happens around him, but Larsson was the genuine article, a real investigative journalist."

Amrén looked at him with interest. "There have been so many conspiracy theories about Larsson's death it's hard to know what to believe. Did you know him well?"

"Well enough to be sure he wasn't killed by the right wing extremists he fought throughout his time as a journalist, despite the death threats. He wasn't knocked off by anyone else, either. He was a driven man, a workaholic, never took care of himself and smoked sixty a day. Just before the end he climbed seven flights of stairs to his office because the lift didn't work and, not surprisingly, died of a heart attack. Reality is never as exciting as newspaper headlines."

There was an announcement that the technical problem had been resolved and the press conference would commence in three minutes. Jörgen rejoined him, and they both sat down at the table. Lights came on, cameras were readied, the journalists shuffled into their places and microphones were aimed. At the last minute they were joined by a deliberately harassed-looking Leopold Krigsman, the Uppsala commissioner. He looked all round, running his fingers through his untidy shock of grey hair, shrugging apologetically and waving the large file he was carrying to indicate that pressure of business was the excuse for his late arrival. Since it was exactly the delayed entrance Jörgen had predicted, Amrén almost smiled, noticing the title on the file-cover was 'Pending'.

Then it all began. Jörgen and Leopold Krigsman did most of the talking, and it was at once clear to Amrén that there had been careful preparation beforehand, and so none of the questions they were asked flurried them in the least. Jörgen gave a moving and apparently entirely genuine tribute to Wizelius, stressing his devotion to duty and linking his tireless hard work to the ill-health that was now forcing his early retirement. As the session drew towards an end Krigsman introduced Amrén as the new Västernorrland commissioner, a rising star of the police force who'd started his career in Östersund and had subsequently managed to solve crimes in Poland and England while being paid to solve them in Sweden. It got the laugh he'd intended, and Amrén, not paying full attention, had to be quick to assume an expression of wry embarrassment which the press thoroughly enjoyed. One even called out, "There's lots of crime in Stockholm, try solving one there!", and as the mirth increased Krigsman flourished his hand in Amrén's direction, and welcomed him to the conference.

"He's not a pen-pushing administrator like Göran and me," he said, claiming their attention again, "he's a working policeman, and you'll get some real answers to your questions."

Amrén stood up, trying to look both relaxed and serious. He dealt easily with a question about crime figures, and then he began to enjoy himself. Out of the corner of his eye he watched the blue and yellow armbands, wondering whether Ryd, who was staring at his mobile as though he was expecting a text, would become involved. After a few more predictable questions, just as Krigsman was preparing to stand and bring it to an end, he did intervene, putting away his mobile and asking a question about police corruption. It was phrased in an odd way, querying whether, in Amrén's experience, officers ever used their position of authority to obtain favours from vulnerable people who might feel that they needed to placate them. A free cup of coffee, for example, an item from a shop without the need to pay for it, even sexual favours from a woman caught up in some minor misdemeanour?

Krigsman glanced across, and Amrén nodded, fielding the question with his usual skill. He didn't deny that in all walks of life there were bound to be temptations to break the rules, and the police service was not exempt from that. But in *his* experience, which was what he had been asked, he'd never come across it and was constantly surprised by the integrity of officers who recognised that effective policing depended on the absolute trust of the public.

It was a good note on which to end, and Krigsman neatly brought the whole thing to a conclusion. Magnus walked back to his room aware that he had come through, and that his confident performance would be repeated before the eyes of a large part of the population on the evening news.

Later, at the conference-opening dinner, he was made to feel very welcome and all the northern commissioners congratulated him and seemed glad to chat to him. Over the next two days the conference passed in something of a blur. He listened to the main lectures which were given by speakers from a number of countries. London introduced new techniques in crowd control, especially containment. At question time one of the delegates asked about toilet arrangements while they were being contained. The answer from the burly policeman was unofficially voted the quote of the 2006 Conference. His face showing a very English weary restraint, he replied, “We’re the Metropolitan Police, not a public convenience. If you have a small bladder you shouldn’t protest.”

Finland showed a video presentation of advances in prison building, and although there was some acceptance of the need to provide the prisoners with better access to technology-enhanced learning to improve their employment prospects, the hotel style comfort did nothing to convert die-hard listeners who still believed that prison should be a deterrent. Germany revealed astonishing developments in DNA tracing, and the lecture, given by an attractive and obviously very intelligent young woman, was unanimously rated the most compelling presentation and the most valuable to Swedish police. Norway explained ways of lowering re-offending rates in child criminals, but this was less well-received because it seemed to criticise existing methods in Sweden.

Even though all of them were interesting, whether he agreed with them or not, Amrén frequently found it hard to concentrate. He was in a sort of dream. He’d made it to the top forum, but it didn’t feel real yet, and he felt cautious about too much pleasure in case he woke up to find it wasn’t true. During the coffee and lunch breaks he wandered round the stalls which had replaced the journalists in the ballroom. These displayed, demonstrated and sold an array of equipment including stab vests, pepper sprays, stun guns, quick-lock handcuffs and extendable batons. In the setting of an oddly beribboned ballroom it became an eastern bazaar of restraint and disablement, though there were also more mundane items of uniform including summer boots that were light, comfortable yet strong, and even rugby jock-strap style underpants.

In the afternoons he joined the discussion groups and quickly detected the subtle difference between north and south. The former seemed generally committed and sincere, the latter ever so slightly disparaging of their colleagues' earnestness, as if they knew that any final decisions would be taken by the more numerous south, and it was right they should be. They seemed less content to leave things as they were, whereas the northerners listened politely to new ideas but did not take them too seriously. He realised this was a whole new world where the politics were below the surface, and would need to be studied with great care. If he was to be anything but a figurehead as eventual National Commissioner he would need to learn fast, and attract allies. None of that seemed real, though it did occur to him that he might have been set up to be a deliberately popular but ineffectual choice, and the real power would lie elsewhere.

As the last day passed, he could only think of his special evening, drawing so close. He'd started the fan dance as a young policeman, at a time when he'd been rather at odds with himself. It was as if he'd wanted to re-invent himself, or simply turn eyes away from the real man and onto the fiction behind the fans. It had been rather nerve-wracking at the time, and perhaps he'd moved too close to the false image so that it almost threatened to become the real one. But now, more than a quarter of a century later, he remembered those days as pleasurable, almost carefree. He'd been better known for his dance than his abilities as a policeman, and the best occasion of all had been in Poland, when he'd performed it for Inspector Jurek Bojanowski and his friends. They were all drunk, as he was, and they were celebrating a Swedish/Polish crime bust in which he'd somehow saved Jurek's life. After that incident, though still known for his mordant wit and his destructive criticism of all who dared to try to hinder police work, he was also recognised as an effective and dedicated policeman.

On the infrequent occasions when he'd still performed the fan-dance, twice in the last ten years, it was always at private gatherings, among his fellows, and he never failed to make them laugh at their worries and temporarily free them from their depressive belief they were not appreciated. He honed his gift for mimicry, enhanced the sense of theatre, and accepted within himself what he would not have admitted before, a love of dressing up and a delight in being somebody else. Now, just when he'd thought he'd put it all behind him, he had to do it again - and this time it would be before an audience who would hold his fate in their hands.

In the afternoon he skipped the last lecture and wandered through the park, letting his mind run free as the rain pattered on the taut skin of his umbrella. His performance was the prelude to the final dinner, and although some of the local delegates might slip away after that, most would stay the night and leave after breakfast. He went down to the lakeside where there was a ruined cloister. The spatter of the rain combined with the slap of the lake ripples to create an eerie sense of menace as he stood within the broken walls. The breeze, whipping across the lake, tormented the bare branches of the trees, forcing them to groan as they rubbed against each other. The whole atmosphere, however natural, seemed somehow contrived and theatrical. Though this helped to put him in the right mood for what was to come, it also worried him because it might be yet another indication that at times he couldn't distinguish his acting from reality. He was probably more involved when he was playing a part than when he was himself, and that in its turn led to the fear that, even when he was himself, he might still be playing a part.

He'd been preparing his programme for many weeks, constantly up-dating it as new controversies arose. Politicians would be an easy target, for they always put themselves before police needs. The media, too, had to be mocked for their campaigns against the liberalism of the police on one day and their howls of outrage at their brutality on the next. Do-gooders would be another quarry, though more gently treated; but he'd decided the compensation-culture would get a real roasting. He'd drag the cuts in manpower and resources into the uncomfortable limelight, and he'd tie it all into the final Gordian knot – society's wishes versus society's fears. Why didn't society free the police from the restraints they imposed on them and allow them to be fully effective, so that criminals would feel real fear and not dare to break the law? It was what so many wanted, more than would ever admit it. But there was this deep-rooted fear that the police, unshackled, might one day turn against them; and while they wanted strong action for the criminal classes, they did not want it for themselves. This created a tension they did not know how to resolve, and it left a vacuum which was in danger of being filled by gangs on one side and vigilantes on the other. He hoped his fan-dance might ease that tension, but it would be only temporary because it could not solve the problem itself.

Would he know how to solve it if he became National Commissioner? He shivered, feeling momentarily inadequate. But the future was never certain, and once it assumed its final shape he might, at that moment, discover the best way forward.

CHAPTER 4

It was over. He had not expected the standing ovation at the end, so that was the sensation that crowned all those he'd experienced since he'd pulled on the specially made one-piece blue silk suit that was and yet was not a policeman's uniform. The initial feeling, as the silk rippled across his skin, had been a thrill of anticipation. The second, as he finished applying the white make-up which rendered his face expressionless, was one of utter peacefulness. He was RaRa again, a different person; immune, cut off from his job, a dispenser of a different sort of justice, skewering the enemies of the police, exposing their absurdities and exaggerations, their hypocrisy and the sour jealousy which drove them to attack what kept them safe. That pallid layer was better than any armour, and the nerves which had been causing his stomach to tighten and his hands to tremble were replaced by a triumphant certainty. He could do this, and it would be well done.

From his place behind the curtain he heard Krigsman announce him, and that was followed by a brief buzz of speculative chatter. That excited him. To stand in the darkness, secure in a no-man's land where he could no longer be stopped whatever he planned to do, to know that whenever he wished he could burst out into the limelight and play the audience as though stroking the strings of a harp, that was true power. He made them wait for him, revelling in the sensation, holding back until the talking began to die.

Then he entered quietly and stood immobile in the spotlight, eyes meekly lowered, relying on the first shock of the shimmering silk, and its contrast to the impassive whiteness of his face, to still the remaining voices. He held the white ostrich feather fans at his side, one in each hand, prolonging the expectant hush until an element of uncertainty entered the audience. That was the moment he flicked the fans across his body, hiding the uniform, becoming a single white pillar, motionless, inscrutable, disquieting. Then he spoke, pitching his voice into a powerful whine which filled the room.

"Criminals are victims too, you know, and they have a right to compensation."

It was received with a roar of laughter and delighted applause, and from then on he could do no wrong. His voice was never quite his own, his shape never entirely true to life; for the silk suit could make him male and female, the loose trousers becoming a long skirt when he put one leg slightly behind the other. He could be anyone he wanted, but never himself. This neutralised him so that the burning anger, the pitiless lampooning of their critics, became the general voice of the police, speaking through him.

Social workers, prison reformers, psychiatrists, journalists, politicians - all were paraded before his audience, sometimes in voice alone, at others in movement too, caricaturing characteristic attitudes and solemn postures with mincing little dance steps, sudden flourishes of the fans, peering over one, hiding behind another, covering his retreat, accentuating his thrust, swirling his fury, dismissing each one with the tauntingly sarcastic 'Ra Ra' that had become his nickname.

Between the burlesque, the lampooning and the ridicule, he acted out two stories, both based on recent cases, suitably altered but clearly recognisable to his audience; and there was strong reaction to each.

In the first he held the fans jauntily as a teenage boy drinking with his mates. The drunker he became, the more aggressively he held the fans. Suddenly, in a furious flurry of feathers, he broke away, knocked down the imaginary driver who was just getting out of his car, seized the keys, jumped in, rejected the seat belt and began joy-riding round town. He crouched, surrounding himself with fans to indicate the car, their fluttering increasing with the acceleration, the jerking of his head and screams of fearful excitement revealing each time he struck a pedestrian, the peering over his shoulder, the shouted obscenity and the increase in speed revealing the fact that a police-car was pursuing him. A look of desperation appeared on his face, he swung the imaginary wheel and then his expression altered to one of horror. The sprawling of his body, one leg caught under him, and the unearthly scream marked the moment he ran into the back of a stationary lorry; and the fans became the slow, faltering, heart-beats of the injured boy.

He rose then, leaving the fans on the floor, a lonely figure with a white face.

"No father should go through the hell I did" he cried. "I wasn't there, I couldn't be; my new girl friend needed me. I never did see as much of him as I'd have liked, but that was my first wife's fault, daring to claim I was a bad influence on him. But he'd only had a few drinks like any fifteen-year-old, and no lad with any guts can resist a go with a fast car. The police should never have chased him, he'd have been all right if they hadn't made him panic." He suddenly raised his muzzle to the moon and howled, "They're the ones to blame. If it wasn't for them, my boy would be playing football, making money by it, instead of limping all his life. I won't rest until I've got the compensation it's his right to have."

Then he was the rich businessman who snorted recreational coke, quarrelled with his girl-friend, and started shooting at his neighbours with a shotgun. The fans were held to one side of him to represent the girl, swaying as he yelled at her, gradually moving in increasingly weird patterns as the cocaine began to work in him and the girl vanished. Suddenly the fans were pointed as the gun. He turned his blue uniformed back to represent the arrival of the police, and altered his voice to produce the metallic loud-hailer tone, insisting that the weapon be unloaded and thrown down from the window. He swung round, shouting a belligerent 'not fucking likely', pointed the fan to fire and then hurled himself backwards as he himself was shot.

"It is with great sadness we announce the death of this respected entrepreneur," he intoned from his prone position, "shot dead by an armed unit of police in circumstances that require the most rigorous investigation. There is considerable doubt whether such action was necessary, involving as it did a man well-known in business circles. Should it be proved, as we believe it may be, that the armed-response unit was over-zealous and acted beyond the limits of a rational interpretation of the operational guidelines, it is only right they should suffer the full rigour of the law."

Then he began to sing. Putting into his voice and posture all the helplessness of a force caught up in the blame-culture, he sang 'Damned if you do, damned if you don't' to the ABBA melody 'I have a dream'. Instead of the refrain 'I believe in angels', he sang 'I believe in fairness', but his expressionless white face reflected each policeman's lack of faith that such balance would ever be restored.

It had taken a bare ten minutes to cover all the areas which roused most bile, and there he stopped. Conscious of Jörgen's approving gaze, he disappeared behind his fans, bowed low, and let the applause reach its crescendo as the audience rose to their feet. Then he straightened himself and, as arranged, the lights went out. When they came up again the stage was empty.

He slipped away, hurrying down the empty corridor, carrying with him the final exquisite sensation of the evening, triumph. Patches of perspiration stained the blue silk, and runnels of sweat ran through his make-up. Then, quite suddenly, he felt completely empty, as if returning to his real self was almost a Gethsemane garden agony. It underlined the contradiction he'd never been able to understand, that onstage he never thought about himself, whereas offstage he could not escape himself.

Seeing a waiter in the corridor, he ordered a large whisky and a *carafe* of water, with plenty of ice. All he wanted to do was to reach the room they'd set aside for him as a changing area, throw down the fans, strip off the silk suit, wipe away the make-up, swallow the whisky, get into the shower and hope the full force of the cleansing water would finally restore him to reality. There was no hurry to return to the others, for they would be busy enjoying the final dinner. They had received all they required from him, onstage.

Inside the room, sitting before the mirror, he rubbed the cream slowly onto his face and began to remove the white make-up. He felt calmer, at peace with himself again, unhurried now, re-living his performance and anticipating the initial swallow of the whisky. He called 'yes' when there was a knock on the door, and eagerly took the glass while the *carafe* was placed beside him on the table.

"Thanks," he said absently, reaching for a note, realising there were no pockets in the silk suit, and feeling too tired to move and search among his proper clothes. "I'll leave something at the desk for you." He glanced at the man, noticing for the first time that he was old, and was not wearing the hotel livery.

"I'm not the waiter," the man explained, staring at him with his pale eyes. "I met him in the corridor and said I'd bring the tray in, as I was on my way to see you. I think he must have thought I was a retired policeman." He smiled at that. He was an upright man, probably well into his seventies, taller than Amrén, much thinner too, with close-cut white hair and a face full of controlled sadness. "I'm sorry to disturb you," he went on. "I'm Lilly's father, and I've been looking forward to meeting you for such a very long time."

CHAPTER 5

Amrén knew it was all over for him. He knew it at once, yet he felt no shock. He realised who had been phoning Ryd at the press conference, he understood why the question about police corruption had been phrased in such a particular way and how easily he had fallen into the trap that had been prepared for him. It was the unexploded bomb which had been ticking away beside him for twenty-eight years even though he'd never permitted himself to be aware of it. He supposed that, somewhere deep inside, he'd assumed that after so very many years Lilly was no longer a threat to him. That was why he'd suddenly freed ambition from the shackles he'd unconsciously imposed upon it. He'd successfully muffled the occasional danger signal. He'd been scrupulously honest when he'd said there was nothing in his past, because there wasn't any longer. All that was finally over, it was out of his life. But he'd been wrong. He'd disarmed himself of caution, and now there would be disgrace instead of promotion. From this moment, clad in his sweat-stained blue silk uniform, his police career was at an end.

He felt an overwhelming tiredness, and was thankful he was already sitting down because his legs would not have supported him. The relief that he had no wife or children brought home to him another truth he'd always hidden from himself; that it was precisely *why* he had no wife or children. The thought of what Magnus Trygg would think about him, when he knew, scalded him with such a reality of shame that he almost cried out. He had not only permitted himself to get close to Magnus, he had gradually let himself be drawn towards his family, at ease with the children, on rare occasions even confiding to his wife Sonja intimate revelations he could never have admitted to a man. Now they would all despise him.

That knowledge exposed to him why he had normally been so cautious about friendship. At some hidden level, he must have known he would be found out one day, and yet somehow he'd never allowed that awareness to surface.

It never occurred to him to deny he'd ever known Lilly, though it was what he should have done. He was a policeman, a powerful one, and this old man was an intruder, with no right to be present at the conference. He could simply order him to leave, tell him to make any complaint through the proper channels. But that was the weakness of his position. Though no complaint had yet been raised, he was convicted by the prior knowledge that there would be one. He'd been waiting for Lilly to make contact with him for twenty-eight years, and now her father was in front of him. At the thought of her, suddenly brought so close to him, his heart lurched with painful pleasure and he found it hard to concentrate on anything else. Scarcely knowing what he did, he took a gulp of whisky.

"I am not guiltless myself" the old man said in the same conversational tone. "I was too angry on Lilly's behalf, I may even have dominated her, and that has held me back from pursuing you. I was not certain I had the right, since my behaviour too was questionable. I watched you, of course, but it seemed you might have learned a lesson. You did not marry, did not have children, and you did not seem to seek a high position where you would be able to influence the many rather than the few."

Amrén bowed his head, seeing blue and yellow flag armbands and guessing what would follow.

"But then a friend who works for a newspaper, and knew I kept an eye on you, rang me to say you were going to be commissioner, and were even tipped to be a future National

Head. So, through him, I set you a little test, a question about police corruption, in the belief your answer would tell me whether you had truly changed. It gave you the opportunity to admit that you had transgressed once, but that remorse had changed you. You didn't take that opportunity, and so it was up to me to act, as I suppose it always has been."

He paused, watching Amrén with dispassionate curiosity as though studying a slide of some virus that was reacting oddly. Then he added, "I will not hide from you that it was something of a relief. At long last the waiting is over."

Amrén felt at such a disadvantage sitting there in his now ridiculous clinging silk, his face smeared with make-up and cream, his exhausted body rank. He drank more whisky, staring at the man who was going to destroy him. He was elderly, he deserved respect, he was Lilly's father and he couldn't hate him. He had tried to blot out the past, and thought he had succeeded. But now it was before him, as fresh as if it had never been buried.

"How is Lilly?" he asked, and he could not hide the emotion in his voice.

The man looked at him curiously. "I thought you might claim you couldn't remember her."

"It was such a long time ago," Amrén said, hearing the futility of the words but feeling he must take some sort of a stand. "She was helpful during an investigation, and I recall I liked both her and her husband."

The old man smiled, shaking his head in wonder. "You are in such deep denial, and I speak as a doctor who's had some experience of mental problems. Something happened to her husband."

"It was an accident."

"That was the conclusion of the internal police enquiry, but they were not privy to all the facts."

Amrén forced himself to rise. "I have to shower, and then return to my colleagues," he said with an attempt at firmness. He wanted to hold out his hand, to touch flesh that had been in contact with Lilly, but he was shaking too much. "I'll say goodbye now, but if you want to tell me more about Lilly I'll be happy to talk to you when I'm back in Sundsvall. Ring my office, and we can fix something up."

The man did not move. "Her mother died when Lilly was ten, and after that she and I were always close. After Olle's accident, as you call it, she came back to me."

His eyes were half-closed, and he seemed to be reminiscing, almost oblivious of Amrén's presence. "She was my only child, and she had nowhere else to go, but I like to feel she wanted to be with me. At first she told me nothing, beyond a few simple facts, but I knew that if I waited she'd tell me everything in the end. She'd been like that when things went wrong at school, or with her friends. She'd say nothing for a day or so, and then it would all pour out."

Amrén shifted uncomfortably, needing to delay these revelations until he was more in control of himself; and the doctor's eyes opened fully, the pale, disconcerting eyes fixing themselves on him. "Of course, you wanted to take a shower. You must forgive me, going on so, and I'm sure that even when she did finally break down Lilly didn't tell me everything. But she told me what you did to her."

"If Lilly has any complaint about me, she should tell me so herself. I'm not prepared to hear it from a third party."

"Quite right; and you mustn't let me stop you taking a shower and getting properly dressed. As a doctor, I'm quite used to human bodies, so just behave as if I wasn't here. But there are still things you need to hear, and this will be our only opportunity. I have commitments, just as I'm sure you do. But mine cannot wait, so I really must claim priority."

Amrén shook his head. "You must leave now, Doctor," he said urgently. "You have introduced matters concerning Lilly, and I will speak to no one about those except to Lilly herself."

"I am the only one who is able to speak for her," explained her father patiently. "Lilly is dead."

Amrén just made it to the shower, and retched, then retched again, and as he retched the tears poured from his eyes. He'd never loved anybody but Lilly, had never been able to love anyone but Lilly. She'd started his emotional life and she had ended it. After their parting he'd looked out for her wherever he went, convinced they would meet again one day, though he'd never made a conscious attempt to find her. He knew now his certainty she was living had kept him alive. If she was dead, nothing mattered any more.

He wiped his mouth with the towel, dried his eyes and removed the clinging cream.

"Was her death recent?" he asked from behind the half-open shower door when he felt he'd got some sort of grip on himself, though his voice still wavered.

"When were you transferred from Östersund?"

"I can't exactly remember. I think I did two years in my first post, so it would have been around 1984 or '85."

"Lilly died in February 1985."

Amrén turned away, pushing his forehead into the plastic shower wall and wishing it was more solid so that he could beat his head against it as he absorbed the shock. All those empty years, expecting to see her, feeling she was close, still thinking of him; all that belief that one day she would be with him once again and they would be man and wife. It seemed so terribly unfair.

"I think I recall she left the area shortly after her husband's accident," he mumbled automatically, as though the detail was more important than the all-encompassing fact that she was dead. "I was still in Jämtland then."

It was as if he was hypnotised. He knew there was more to come, things he didn't want to hear, but it was so difficult to break the spell. He was helpless to force the issue, to insist on the doctor leaving, because it seemed so trivial beside the tragedy of a daughter's death. But what about the tragedy of a loved-one's death, and its effect on him? Nothing might matter anymore, but why should he stand meekly by while her father told him what he'd surely come to say? With a barely controlled sob he stripped off the silk, pulled the door across and put the water on full blast, drowning out the words the doctor might be uttering. The water stung him as though it was his conscience, but he was careful to let his mind stay empty while he concentrated on the shampoo and liquid soap, mechanically washing away the odours and the make-up, ensuring he was presentable on the outside though the inward taint remained.

Stepping out, he began to towel himself vigorously. The doctor had fallen into a doze, and so had clearly not been bothering to say anything at all. But, once Amrén started to dress himself, he began to speak again as though he had merely put himself on hold, and now released the key.

"I never really liked her husband, always felt she'd made a mistake there, and it caused a breach in our relationship. So we weren't often in touch when she was in Jämtland, and it was only when she came back to me that we were close again. I was so happy, having her there with me, and I probably didn't see as much as I should have done, even when she'd told me what had happened to her. I could only think of how I'd punish you, and it blinded me. But I was a doctor, after all, and I still blame myself. I should have spotted the signs."

Amrén, fortified by his shower and proper clothing, finally dared to ask the question.

"How did Lilly die?"

"She killed herself. Of course she did it properly, to spare me as much as possible. Opened my medical cabinet, took the necessary tablets, went to sleep and didn't wake. I think she simply no longer wished to be alive."

Amrén swayed, wondering how many more devastating punches such a frail man could land. He grabbed the back of the chair, holding himself upright until his head stopped spinning, and then he sat, his head bowed.

"Do you blame me for her death?"

"Only you can answer that question. I imagine you buried your guilt along with the truth, but it will be harder for you now you know she's dead, and how she died. Guilt, unacknowledged for too long, can destroy you. That's why many people act in such a way that it's bound to be discovered, and only then will they find peace. The subconscious works in mysterious ways."

Amrén bent low to tie his laces, hiding his face, clearing his head and not caring that the position indicated, accurately, that the burden put upon his shoulders was too heavy for him to bear.

Lilly's father regarded him with a doctor's professional gaze. "For several years since my retirement I've kept myself busy poking about in and around Näverede and building a small dossier, now safely lodged with a lawyer. I talked to *Fru* Sjöman, who was your other neighbour back then, and although her house was some distance away she seems to have kept her eyes open, presumably with the aid of the telescope she had, for she admitted her sight was not too good even in her young days. She signed a statement for me. Pleasant woman, but you probably don't remember her?"

Amrén shook his head helplessly.

"It'll all come back to you over the next few days and weeks," the old man announced, now speaking as a doctor. "But you lived in Näverede?"

Amrén stiffened, and then shook his head again. "I lived in Östersund," he said.

"The police enquiry made the same statement, but of course it wasn't true. Confirmation of the real truth was yet another interesting fact I picked up during my little investigation."

He stood up and looked down at Amrén. "I got an insight into your sort of detective work as I started prying, and I'm glad I wasn't a policeman for the number of years you have been. I cannot help feeling the nature of what you do must inevitably have a debilitating affect on moral attitudes. Now I must be going, and we won't be meeting again. I'm sure you'll be considering whether you're really fit for promotion, or even staying in the police. But I can't just leave it to you. There needs to be a public debate, so I'll start the ball rolling. Now that I've seen you, I think the precaution my lawyer insisted on was probably unnecessary, but he wired me up so that there would be a recording of our conversation."

He stepped close, watching Amrén curiously, and with a certain professional pride he unbuttoned his shirt to reveal the hidden microphone taped onto his chest. For a terrible moment Amrén was tempted to tear it off him, and the miniature recorder. But immediately he saw where that was leading. It would only help him if there was no doctor alive to describe the conversation, to tell how the device had been forcibly taken from him, to produce photos of the marks where the tape had been wrenched from his skin and a signed statement from his lawyer describing how he had fitted him up with the equipment before the meeting. He could see the old man knew all this, yet he was seemingly offering himself as a sacrificial victim. He rose from his chair and almost took a step towards him. But a flash of triumph in the pale eyes warned him that this was no victim, he was a tempter, urging him to cross the final line and doom himself.

Appalled at what he might have done, remembering that Lilly's father had alerted Ryd and that a lawyer was also in the know, he dropped back into the chair, his head slumping in defeat.

The doctor smiled.

"I don't know how well you know your Aeschylus," he said, "but in 'The Libation Bearers' he writes, 'Frenzy goes through the guilty like infection, swarming through the brain.' From what I saw of many of my troubled patients, his description is extraordinarily perceptive. It makes me wonder whether you will be strong enough to survive. Lilly wasn't."

He went out as quietly as he had come in.

CHAPTER 6

Magnus Trygg was woken by the phone. It felt early, and his bedside alarm told him it was ten past five. Since the soft warmth of Sonja at his side remained unchanged, he felt relieved that she hadn't been disturbed, and he gave his number quietly as he eased himself from the bed.

A familiar voice from Jämtland chided him for not being out fishing, and asked him if Västernorrland was making him soft. It was Izidor, who was over eighty.

"The road from Sundsvall crosses the Jämtland border, goes uphill, and then passes through the gap they blasted in the rock. I'm waiting for you there, and I've got something to show you."

Magnus could not help smiling as he went softly downstairs. He and Izidor had often fished together in the years when he was growing up in Jämtland, and when he'd been a young constable in the Östersund force.

"I'm not driving all the way out there just to see a bigger trout than I've ever caught, or am ever likely to catch."

"I wish it was a fish," Izidor said soberly. "It's a man's body, hanging over the road, and he's got a notice round his neck that you need to see before anybody else does. It'll be light in a few hours, so get a move on."

"But I'm with the Sundsvall police now, so it's out of my area."

"I'm not in my dotage yet," Izidor replied tartly. "I know I should be calling Östersund, but I'm doing you a favour. Get up here as soon as you can, and bring a thermos of coffee. Mine's nearly empty and I'm shivering so much I may fall apart at the seams. Maybe a camera too, but you know the drill better than I do."

"Are you certain he's dead? Perhaps I'd better get an ambulance."

"In case you've forgotten, I drove an ambulance for years before I became a musician. I started doing it in the war as a protest against neutrality, driving for the Norwegians, and even though we often secretly carried resistance fighters to their *rendezvous,* I saw enough medical action to know a dead man from a live one."

Magnus left a hurried note for Sonja, listened to make sure neither Johan nor Angelica had woken, then took the thermos he'd just filled and went out to his garage. Everything he might need, including a camera, was neatly stowed inside the car, so he unplugged the engine from the external heater and drove off northwards, his studded tyres gripping the snow. He felt unusually excited, a young policeman on an early call instead of a respected Head of Homicide who would only be roused when others had done the legwork. The nearer he got, the more nostalgic he became. This was the wilder, emptier part of Sweden where he had been born, had grown up, and started his police career. It was where he had met and married Sonja, where both their children had been born and where they had spent their earliest years. An intense happiness filled him. In the rush of promotion and town-life he had not realised how much he missed the country, the space, the hunting and the fishing, the old stone churches, the summer music festivals.

Izidor was waiting for him, peacefully smoking his pipe and scratching at the steel plate let into his skull which, after a complicated operation, had given him back his hearing.

Though it was months since Magnus had seen him he seemed to get no older. He was, perhaps, a trifle more wizened, but with no sign yet of anything that might require him to alter his lifestyle. Never demonstrative, he nodded at the sight of the thermos, briefly shook Magnus' hand, and then pointed upwards.

Magnus strained his eyes, but in the darkness he could see nothing except, after a few seconds, a swaying patch of slightly darker darkness.

"How on earth did you spot him?" he asked, reaching for his torch.

"Just chance, like so much else in life. I'd been out early at a stream above here, determined to get something before the ice closes over. But, as well as the two trout, I got thoroughly cold, so I set off back along the forest path that comes out over there. My hearing's so good now after the operation that I heard a rope creak as I crossed the road and glimpsed something swaying above me. So I clambered up and there he was. Then I saw the placard round his neck, read it, realised it would soon be visible to any passing car, and so rang you. Whoever did this, Magnus, definitely wants it to be seen."

"What does it say?"

"I'd rather you went up and read it for yourself."

Following his directions, Magnus climbed up and got himself on the ledge. He always felt uncomfortable in the presence of death, as though it rendered his own abundant life-force unseemly. But this man, far from young, seemed quite at peace, as though dangling above the road had been a lifelong ambition. The notice round his neck was big, and it was shockingly easy to read the bold lettering.

'VÄSTERNORRLAND'S NEW COMMISSIONER IS A DOUBLE KILLER'

Magnus automatically shook his head. It was inconceivable that Amrén could be a murderer. It wasn't something he need consider in any way at all.

He went back down to Izidor. "I can understand now why you rang me," he said. "I can't tell you how grateful I am."

"It wasn't just so you could see it. It was because I can cast a triple hook from the ledge straight into his jacket and pull him over to the side where you can remove the placard. I know you admire your chief, and as no one but me has seen this, nobody else need ever know what was said about him. I'm not the sort of person who'd ever talk."

Magnus nodded. "I know that all right, and that's why the same thought about removing the placard went through my mind when I was up there, though I wasn't clever enough to work out how it could be done. But I'm not certain it's the way to go."

"Sometimes I think you're too scrupulous for your own good," grumbled Izidor. "If you leave that placard in place, it's going to be a messy business."

"There's more to it than just being scrupulous, Izidor. The placard is almost too obvious, as though it's tempting us to take it off. And that may be a trap. The killer has gone to so much trouble to draw attention to everything, even making sure the crime is not on our patch so Amrén's own force can't investigate it, that I'm convinced it's just a first step, and there's more information to be leaked. If this is an attempt to smear the police, there's nothing the perpetrator would like more than for us to be caught suppressing evidence."

He opened the thermos and poured two coffees. He knew Izidor would never ask the question, but he wanted to answer it anyway. "I've no idea what this is all about, but I've total faith in Amrén. He's a good man, and I can't think of a less-likely double murderer. It's absurd."

Izidor smiled. "You've always believed in people, Magnus. I just hope you don't get hurt. Are you going to bring in the Östersund police?"

"I have to. But I'm not letting you stay out in the cold any longer. Go off home, eat your trout for breakfast and then catch up on some sleep. I'll pass on your address, tell them you found the body, and they'll come and take a statement when they're ready. "

"If you're really sure," answered Izidor, but Magnus could see he was shivering again and was relieved when he set off at once with a grateful wave of his hand.

Magnus glanced at his watch. It was nearly eight o'clock, and he reckoned Inspector Widmark would be in her office.

They'd worked together before, and, although he never felt fully at ease with her, he respected her judgement.

"Pia, it's Magnus," he said when she picked up the phone. "I really need your help. I was called out early this morning because a body was seen hanging over the 86 by Utanede, but it's on your side of the boundary. There are, though, certain aspects which may require careful handling. Would you be able to meet me here as soon as possible, before it gets so light that lots of drivers see the body, people begin to talk and the press start swarming all over us. Maybe a squad car could follow you to divert the traffic."

"Sounds like trouble," she complained, "and bang goes my chance to catch up on my paper work. I won't even ask why it had to be you, the Head of Homicide, who was called out at what must have been a ghastly hour of the morning, because I probably wouldn't like the answer. I'm on my way."

Magnus was thankful it was an overcast morning, and as far as he could tell none of the sprinkling of drivers saw anything unusual. He could now see the body more clearly, and it was not hanging over the middle of the road, but more to one side where it was less visible than he'd at first feared. With any luck it would only be noticed by a driver who was especially alert.

As soon as Pia arrived, and he'd taken her up onto the ledge to see the placard, she briskly told the two officers in the squad car to divert all traffic through Utanede.

"This is a poisoned chalice, but I suppose I've got to accept it," she muttered as she walked Magnus to her car. She was older than he was, very short beside him but heavier in build, except for her head, which was small and neat, with the close-cut hair of a male Roman statue. She rolled her shoulders as though she was limbering up for a fight and said, "Bear with me as I get the investigation started, and then you'd better fill me in with all the details."

Magnus admired the efficient way she put a team together and got them moving. Then they sat in her car and she made notes as he explained about Izidor's call, and how she could get in touch with him. She was a good listener - not querying or commenting, but occasionally inserting question marks into what she was writing. But she never fully fixed her sharp eyes on him, and he realised that it was precisely because of this that he did not feel totally at ease with her. Something about him clearly unsettled her, and, though he came to the conclusion reluctantly, he was almost convinced it could only be his colour. He never thought of himself as anything but Swedish, but despite his Jämtland accent she seemed to see him as Thai. The Swedish half of him appeared in his big bones and his height; but from his mother he'd inherited his bronze colour, jet-black hair and high cheek bones. Looking at his face alone, he *was* Thai, and it was precisely his face that Pia seemed to find disquieting. Although he was certain she wasn't racist in any conscious sense, the colour of his skin apparently unnerved her.

"It's never good when another policeman is involved, especially such a senior one," Pia said as she got out of the car. "I'll try to handle it as tactfully as I can, and of course another force would have had to undertake the investigation even if it had been your side of the border, just to avoid the corruption smell of local police looking after their own people. Did you spot anything helpful while you were looking around?"

Magnus nodded. "There's something not quite right about it as a murder scene. He's a well-dressed elderly man, not the usual sort of victim of a publicly-revealed execution like this. The placard worries me too. If it represents some anti-Amrén crusade by the man who's wearing it, and he was killed for that, why was the placard left? And if the murderer wanted it to be seen, does that mean the victim was killed simply to be a hanging billboard above the road? Whichever way you look at it, it makes no proper sense."

"I'll bear all that in mind as the investigation proceeds, and I'll keep you fully informed," Pia said rather more warmly, though she was busy putting away her notebook and did not look at him. "If we were to find anything that seemed to implicate your chief, you can rest assured I'd tell you before anybody else. I saw him on television at the press conference, and I thought he spoke well. He's obviously being groomed for higher things, and that's good for all of us in the north. If this is part of a campaign to stop him getting the top job, I don't want it to succeed any more than you do. I'll bet you all gave him a good reception when he came back to Sundsvall."

For a second Magnus hesitated, but he knew it would be fatal to their relationship if he held anything back.

"He hasn't returned," he replied, and he could hear the worry in his own voice. "He was due back yesterday morning, but he sent me a text saying he was taking some leave that was owing to him."

Pia sighed, making a note of what he'd said. "Do you think there might be something in it?" she asked tentatively.

"No," answered Magnus. "It would be completely beyond him." Then, hearing the belligerence in his voice, he grinned sheepishly. "But it's a bloody bad time to go on leave."

"He may need good friends like you. You'll let me know the moment he surfaces?"

"I will. Now I'll get out of your hair. I know from bitter experience how infuriating it is to have outsiders around when you're starting an investigation."

He waited to see if Pia would hold out a hand in farewell, but she only gave him a nod. As he walked back to his car he considered her comment about Amrén needing good friends. It was certainly true, but he couldn't recall Amrén ever talking much about friends. He often mentioned colleagues in the police, especially ones he'd worked with in other countries, but he'd never been a man to talk about his personal life. Magnus counted himself as a friend as well as a colleague, but he couldn't immediately think of any others in Sweden.

CHAPTER 7

The snow-covered mountains brooding over Zakopane looked down at Jurek Bojanowski with as little interest as he looked up at them. He took exercise every afternoon because he was becoming plump with good living and his muscles were slackening, but he was neither a skier nor a climber and he despised the hordes of tourists who poured into the town, besotted by the Tatras, exclaiming over and over again that they were *real* mountains. Jurek scowled at the peaks. He'd been born in the north of Poland, in Gdansk where there were no mountains, and he'd spent his working life on the Baltic coast. Here, on the southern border, there was little enough to excite a retired policeman and throughout the first year he regretted he'd ever come.

Zakopane, dedicated to mountain life, was too slick for him, too smart, too false. The carefully retained dialect, the flaunted highland-costume and the shepherd's-crook street lights all seemed pretentious, and its new hotels, like the Orbis-Kasprowy on the slope of Gubalowka Hill, unnecessarily flashy. To his mind it was attempting to celebrate Poland's membership of the EU, which he'd opposed. With its big brand stores, its cappuccino cafés and its French restaurants, it was becoming European and not Polish at all. As a boy in the 1968 March Events he'd been beaten up by Gomulka's police for protesting about Russian control of Polish life. Now he'd been forced to watch his country joyfully hand itself over to a set of Brussels bureaucrats.

It had been his chief, Stachek, who'd suggested early retirement and a new life far away from Gdansk.

"You're like me, Jurek," he'd said as they drank vodka in his office. "You like the old ways best. You've always broken the rules, you've had your own morality, but you've been the most successful policeman we've ever had. You're tough, you're afraid of nothing and you've never licked an arse in your life."

"And never will," Jurek muttered, helping himself to another vodka.

"Then you must get out, now, while this very generous retirement package is still on the table. I'm going, that's what I called you in to tell you. They don't want people like us any longer. The new policing will be European policing, with a bloody great rule book to go with it. Conformity is the buzz word now and you haven't got a conformist bone in your body."

"And never will," repeated Jurek, re-filling his glass.

"I know that," said Stachek, scratching his stubbly chin which sagged more than it used to. "You've been beaten and shot and it's never stopped you getting your man, even if you had to cut a few corners and hurt a few low-lifes along the way. But they'll never understand your talents in the new regime and you'll never understand their pale-piss sanctity. If you stay they'll throw you to the wolves without, of course, meaning to or even understanding what they're doing."

"There are a number of wolves still hanging about round here who are very busy covering themselves with new, fresh-smelling skins," Jurek commented reflectively. "You know that as well as I do."

"And many of them will never forgive you for banging them up and they'll finish you off once you're no longer protected by being a policeman. So my advice to you is to pick up any favours still owing to you, and then get right away to somewhere you can enjoy your retirement."

"What about you?" Jurek asked curiously.

"Lithuania," Stachek replied briefly. "It's ten years behind Poland and there's a job waiting for me there. I should be able to make enough out of that to set myself up somewhere pleasant and law-abiding. I've a hankering for Sicily, but the Mafia might be a problem."

They'd both laughed then, and he'd followed Stachek's advice. One of the favours he'd pulled in was a well-paid job as a bodyguard to a high-flying politician building a little empire for himself in Zakopane, and that was why he'd ended up there.

But the job had lasted less than a year. By then he'd reached the stage where he bitterly resented protecting a man who so clearly deserved to die. He'd discovered that his activities included trafficking women across the mountains from Slovakia and using them as sex-slaves for those he wished to influence. A father who'd followed the trail was beginning to be a nuisance and he'd been told to deal with him. So Jurek took him into the forest and seemed to shoot him. He then went back to his employer, gave him photographic proof in the form of a bloodstained body, and resigned his post on the grounds that he'd not been hired as an assassin.

A few days later the politician was himself shot by somebody who may have resembled the father; and the police, tipped off anonymously, found the girls and sent them back to Slovakia.

It was such a successful and exhilarating adventure that it restored Jurek to his usual cheerful self. He'd made a few useful contacts during the year, he'd put some money into a couple of businesses that thrived, and he gradually became accustomed to his surroundings even if he never really liked them. By then he'd heard of Stachek's death in Lithuania, a nasty car accident with an even nastier smell to it, and it had made him realise when he was well off. Money was coming in, he never felt threatened and he'd become almost comfortable despite his occasional boredom. He was satisfied by good food and drink, and by a local woman he wouldn't have to marry. So he'd hung on, thinking about the past, re-living the dangers and thrills of his life, working at his various enterprises every morning, taking a lengthy and gastronomically discerning lunch break and then energetically working it off in the late afternoon.

Turning his eyes from the mountains he walked briskly down Krupowki Street and crossed the creek at the north end. He smiled now at the Tatra Mountain Museum, for its architecture, which he'd detested at first, had provided him with a good joke which he told to anyone who would listen to him. It looked, he proclaimed, like the result of an ill-matched mating between a Swiss chalet and a German cathedral, and, especially after a few vodkas, it was a witticism that always managed to raise a smile.

He turned south down Kasprusie Street, past the Villa Alta, and on until he was finally in the Strazyska Valley. Everyone around him was eagerly photographing Mount Giewont and the range of mountains that bore the same name. Though Jurek remained a man of streets and buildings, he acknowledged the wild beauty of the view with a glance, went on to the snow-covered tree that was his marker, turned round and went back the way he'd come.

The daylight was beginning to dim by the time he reached the smart new house he rented, just round the corner from the Giewont Hotel. Taking off his outer clothing and his snow-boots, he threw himself into his leather recliner and, feeling tired, fell into a doze. But before it could become a deeper sleep he was roused by the doorbell.

He wasn't expecting anyone and he took the sensible precautions that had become second-nature to him before he opened the door. The peephole showed him a small man, hunched, looking exhausted, and there was no one else in the vicinity. Unless he was a suicide bomber he would have no trouble handling him with his bare hands and, perhaps because Catholics believed so strongly that taking your own life was a sin, Poland was not yet affected by this terrible new method of multiple killing. So he thrust the pistol into the back of the waistband of his jeans, made sure his sleeveless fleece covered it, and opened the door.

CHAPTER 8

Amrén saw straight away that Jurek didn't recognise him.

"It's RaRa," he said quickly, speaking in English and wondering if it was just the gloom or whether his appearance could have changed so much in a night and a day. "I'm sorry I couldn't give you any warning, but it was a spur of the moment decision. I felt I had to get away for a few days, and I thought of you."

Jurek hid the sense of shock at how much his friend seemed to have aged and looked at him fondly, mangling his hand in his hearty welcoming grip. "Bloody right you should think of me. Many years ago you saved my life, and now I'll save yours with vodka because you look exhausted and vodka cures everything. Come on in, put down that silly suitcase and drink with me. I was getting very bored with my retirement, but your arrival changes everything. " He threw his huge arms round Amrén and hugged him. "It's so good, Ragnar, so very good, to have you here in my home."

After the second vodka Amrén began to wonder why on earth he'd come. He'd attempted to explain that something had happened, that he'd panicked and caught the early morning flight to Krakow, but Jurek wouldn't listen to him. He waved it all aside.

"Not now, RaRa. We'll go out to a little place I know, only one table, very trusty people, and there we'll eat our fill and you'll feel better. You can talk there, get it all out, wonder why you ever worried, then come back here and sleep like a baby. Now I just want to drink with you, enjoy having you with me again, feel good because you chose to come to me."

They clinked their glasses together and Jurek dared to hope that his treatment was working. He'd been dismayed by the deterioration in Ragnar, but he'd seen that shrunken greyness often before among his own officers. It would happen after a horrific traffic accident, the discovery of a murdered child, or the first time a policeman shot somebody. Over the years he'd learnt not to encourage them to discuss it too quickly, but to provide vodka and a good meal followed by a long sleep. In the majority of cases it seemed to do the trick. They could begin to talk about it after the food and drink, and when they woke from the lengthy sleep they could see it in a more reasonable light. He knew he wouldn't be able to stop Ragnar's explanation for too long and he doubted that in such a cautious man it would be the whole truth. It might be best to precipitate the issue before the end of the meal but he'd make sure Ragnar was pretty drunk before he did so.

After the third vodka the reason he'd left Uppsala and flown to Poland no longer seemed important to Ragnar; he was just so happy he'd come. Jurek was bulkier than he remembered him, and his belly protruded more. But his astonishing vitality had not diminished, and he surrendered himself to that dynamic exuberance which swallowed him up and squeezed the juice of forgetfulness onto his eyelids. He let Jurek's anger at the state of the world and his scorn for the softness of the present Polish police replace his own concerns, and he comforted himself with Jurek's easy Catholic faith where confession, when the moment came for it, would scour away all lurking guilt.

They went out and ate alone, as Jurek had said they would, a few guttering candles the only light. He guessed their waitress was the proprietor, and probably something rather more to Jurek who slapped her rolling rump with easy familiarity and twinkled his eyes at her whenever she served or cleared a dish. They started with *chlodnik*, an iced beetroot soup with sour cream, and followed it with *pierogi z miesem,* dumplings with a meat filling, accompanied by the famous *Goldwasser* vodka containing flakes of real gold.

Jurek encouraged Ragnar to agitate his glass to produce a golden snowstorm.

"Some idiotic Flemish merchant started this idea nearly five hundred years ago, in Gdansk of course. He just wanted to show off his wealth, but it became popular and at my request Magdalena always keeps a few bottles here for my most special guests."

He toasted Ragnar, and they both drank deeply, Jurek claiming he could actually taste the gold. Then they began to talk about the old days when Ragnar had been working with the Polish police in Gdansk, and Jurek was assigned to work with him. Jurek pulled open his shirt and showed him his scar again, and both relived the battle in which he'd been shot and Amrén risked his life to drive off the attackers.

"You were a madman, RaRa, completely crazy," Jurek told him nostalgically. "Afraid of nothing, and then you sang me filthy songs to keep me conscious until help came."

"They were Lutheran hymns," Amrén protested.

"To a Catholic, that is filth, and it made me so angry I wouldn't let myself die until I'd told you so."

"You were a good policeman, Jurek. Magnus Trygg couldn't stop talking about you after I'd sent him to you to get information about the Russian killed on our High Coast."

Jurek chuckled at the memories this dredged up.

"I'd hoped you'd come yourself, Ragnar, but he was a good man even if he was second best. He had such an inscrutable face it was hard to know what he was thinking most of the time, especially when I took him across the border into Russian Kaliningrad and faced a roomful of Mafia with him. I'd given him a gun and when that barman challenged him, he should have used it. He was a bit like you, Ragnar, too much conscience. But at least he kicked the barman's backside for him, and somehow he got away with it. I was nearly wetting myself, but he didn't seem to bat an eyelid. How's he doing now?"

"He's my right hand man, Jurek, Head of Homicide and good at his job. And he was absolutely right about you. You weren't just a good policeman, you were the best."

Jurek laughed scornfully. "You say so, I say so, but at the end I was embarrassing for them, one of the old school who didn't obey the new rules. So finally I told them where to stick their rules, took my pension and left."

"And came to Zakopane?"

"There were too many memories along the northern coast; and the memories some had kept of me were not nice and I might have ended up dead. It was crazy, really, coming here, because I hate mountains. How about you?"

"I like lakes better than mountains."

"Fuck the mountains, and the lakes too! How about your problems? I know you, Ragnar, and you're in the shit."

Amrén gave him a melancholy smile. "Unlike you, everything was going well for me in my career. A glittering prize was dangled in front of me, maybe the top job one day. And I forgot all caution, went on TV, even did my fan dance at the police chiefs' conference."

"I liked your fan dance. You really came alive then, forgot your Lutheran principles."

"Somebody recognised me. It was from my past, my first year in the police, before I met you, the father of a girl I fell in love with, the only girl I ever fell in love with. He's going to whip up a scandal that'll finish me, and show my bosses up as idiots for selecting me for higher things."

"Falling in love's not a crime. Tell the father to stick his head up his arse. He can't hurt you."

Ragnar laughed, and realised he was suddenly feeling better. He swallowed more vodka and felt better still. "You're good for me, Jurek. You make mountains seem like worm casts. But it's not as simple as that. The girl was married."

Jurek guffawed. "Magdalena," he bawled, "were you married when I first fucked you?"

"I am still married," was her dignified response from the kitchen, "and still you fuck me."

Jurek looked delighted. "You see, RaRa, a Catholic conscience is different from a Lutheran one. We sin, we repent, but then we sin again, it is our weakness. You try to be perfect, we know we can't be."

Ragnar felt he was really coming alive again, and it partially freed him from his inability to speak about the past.

"I was investigating a spate of robberies, and this girl's husband was the main suspect. That complicated things, and I behaved unprofessionally."

Jurek threw up his hands in mock horror. "You fucked the wife of a suspect! My God, RaRa, no policeman ever committed such an atrocity in the history of the civilized world. I can no longer be the friend of such a sinner."

"It gets worse," continued Ragnar earnestly. "The husband was involved in an accident. It was nothing to do with me, but it caused comment, fingers were pointed, and the girl moved away, wanting nothing more to do with me."

Jurek pretended to wipe away tears. "You're breaking my heart, RaRa. But what does the father blame you for?"

"Some time later the girl died. According to him she killed herself, and he blames me for her death."

"When did you meet the girl?"

"Twenty-eight years ago."

"And you think a poor crazed father is going to be able to hurt your reputation after so long? You're not thinking straight, RaRa. It's your bloody conscience; you always were far too ready to blame yourself for anything that went wrong, weighing everything you did with such ridiculous precision. Go home before your absence gives you a guilty look. Stop trying to be perfect, ignore this man and get on with your life."

"There's bound to be an internal police investigation."

"So? I've faced investigations like that almost as many times as I've fucked married women, but they've never nailed me. Deep down, they're always on your side. They know you're good at your job, they don't want to lose you, and they'll fudge it in your favour even if anything is found against you. I'll drive you to Krakow airport tomorrow morning, and you can take the first flight back. I'll make the booking for you as soon as we get home. When it's all over you can come and see me again, stay for some time, and I'll show you the real Poland, not tourist places like this. But now you need to be back in Sweden and fighting mad."

Ragnar swallowed some more vodka and nodded. "You're right, Jurek. I made too much of it. We'll laugh about it when I see you again."

They left the little restaurant happily drunk. Jurek felt pleased with the way it had gone so far, but he knew the next morning would show whether Ragnar had been able to throw off the guilt and hold his head high. He helped him to his room and was glad to see that Ragnar didn't have time to get his clothes off before he collapsed on his bed and fell into a profound sleep.

He woke late, and for a few precious seconds he felt the same dreamy reassurance that all was well. But it didn't last. He caught a sudden glimpse of himself as others would see him if they knew the truth about him; his heart began to race, his stomach turned over and he vomited into the basin.

Dully he cleaned up. It was not the vodka. His internal defences had been breached, and the acid of his shame burnt him. He'd been respectable for so many years, and hadn't realised how much he'd valued it. Now, knowing he was about to lose all respect, he felt naked and defenceless. He was in an entirely new land, where everyone's attitude to him would be different, and he would have to explore it, trying to avoid the unexploded bomb ticking at the heart of it. So much that he'd held at a great distance was starting to flood back and no dams were ever going to be effective again. Memories, once aroused, would just get sharper. Already the part he'd played was being bleached of its Technicolor glow, and was beginning to stand out starkly in black and white. No going back was possible. He could feel how the mental assaults he was experiencing were weakening his body and his mind, so that every normal act was slow and laboured. He was even forced to remind himself of proper sequences in such mundane acts as shaving and showering.

He faced Jurek across the breakfast table, the mask only partially back on his face. He found it difficult to sit still and kept getting up to fetch something or pretend to look at a picture on the wall, though he knew Jurek was watching him with concern.

"Did you make that flight booking last night?" he asked after he'd gulped down his coffee.

Jurek nodded, handing him the details he'd scrawled on a memo pad.

"That's good," Ragnar said. "We'll let it stand, in case I change my mind, and if it causes a bit of confusion, that's fine by me. But I'm not actually expected back quite yet. I told Magnus I was taking holiday time I'd built up, and I've been thinking I might go the long way home. I've never visited the Baltic States, so it'd be a sort of adventure, seeing fresh places. Maybe Russia, too, St Petersburg at least, and then renew a few acquaintances before flying to Sweden. It'll give me time to plan my moves really carefully, so when I get back I won't make any silly mistakes."

Jurek was looking at him sharply, and then his face softened and he gave a sigh. "Ragnar, my dear friend, this is terrible news."

"I think I probably simplified things somewhat last night," Ragnar conceded. "The vodka allowed me to see it all in a rather rosy glow. In fact, there are some problems I need to sort out in my mind before I can fully acquit myself of having wronged anyone."

"Then for God's sake let your common sense guide you through it all, and not that over-developed conscience which always seems to give you so much grief."

Ragnar smiled. "That's why I needed to come here, and why I'm so glad I did. You help to keep me balanced. But at the moment I feel as though I've never really known myself, and I have to work through that before I can face my accuser."

"You know you can stay on here if you like, for as long as you need."

"I do know that, and it's tempted me, but it wouldn't work. I'd be hiding, and to think properly I need to be moving and utterly alone. With enough time and space, among strangers in new surroundings, I'll be able to think about myself and my life, and I may be able to discover what I really am." He hesitated, and then he brought it out. "But I don't want to travel as myself."

Jurek nodded thoughtfully and went to a drawer. He looked through several worn passports then dropped one on the table in front of him. "It'll need your photograph, with the proper stamps, but we can organise that in an hour. The owner of this passport is dead, I took it off his body myself, so you can be quite certain nobody will pop up suddenly to claim it. Now that we're all European, I doubt if anyone will be interested in passports on your route anyway, but it'll cover your tracks just in case. I wouldn't advise trying Russia, but I suspect that saying you might go there was just throwing dust in my eyes." He smiled awkwardly. "I'm glad you'll be Polish once again."

"I'm glad too. It'll be a sort of certainty, because otherwise I really don't know who I am at the moment. I'm like a child, trying to grow up." He pulled the SIM-card from his mobile and handed it to Jurek. "Can you destroy that for me, and maybe on the way to Krakow we could stop and dump the mobile itself somewhere safe?"

Jurek nodded, put the SIM-card in his pocket, and then gripped Amrén's hand, not meeting his eyes. "You won't be able to keep me in touch then, but try to let me know somehow when you've found the answer. I've never been a good Catholic, but I pray God will walk with you in your wanderings, though I don't want to know where they'll be in case somebody asks me." He paused, cleared his throat loudly, looked him in the face and spoke in his usual rough voice. "Now let's sort out the photograph, and then we'll be on our way."

As they left Zakopane, Jurek swung off the main road and drove up towards the snowy peaks. After about ten minutes, when they were still travelling through forest, he stopped the car by a small waterfall which had not iced up. Ragnar got out and walked over to it, marvelling at the silence and the emptiness that reminded him of Lapland, though the mountains here made anything there look like small hillocks. He dropped his mobile into the clear water, and it disappeared from view. He hoped his own disappearance would be achieved just as swiftly and easily.

At the station they said an uncomfortable goodbye. Jurek put a hand on his arm, squeezing it, while Ragnar mumbled thanks. Then they parted and he was on the train, settling into a front facing window seat in the emptiest carriage he could find. He knew he should be feeling especial sadness at leaving Jurek, but all he actually felt was intense relief. The need to be alone had become overwhelming, blotting out all finer feelings, all emotions, leaving only the selfishness of self-preservation. He was teetering on the brink of something awful, where he might so easily fall into the abyss and, quite literally, lose his mind. Later he might let it all go, voluntarily, reaching the stage where he no longer wished for a past or future. But for now he had to cling on, and he could only do that if he was a stranger, moving through places he had never visited before, surrounded by people he did not know, could not know, and would never know. Then, and only then, he could allow his thoughts to drift across the twenty-eight years and discover what was there.

The train shuddered and rumbled on its slow departure, and views that were quite fresh to him began to move across the cinema screen of his window. Around him were the total strangers who knew no more of him than he knew of them. He sank back and fell into a sort of doze in which he was not bodily present though mentally he was dreamily aware of earlier times. He supposed he was spiralling down into the early stages of depression, but it was not uncomfortable and without anything familiar on the train or outside it, with a new nationality, nothing at all to remind him of the past, he was suddenly able to reflect upon it. The present slid away, leaving much earlier memories, and among those he slowly wandered. He thought about his mother who'd died unexpectedly from a massive stroke when he was just finishing his police training. She had never married and whenever she mentioned men there was always a note of disparagement in her voice. Male shopkeepers were little dictators, interested only in profit. Male bus drivers, and that was almost all of them, were boorish country-bumpkins. Doctors were stuck in a social time warp, quite unable to understand how a woman could bring up a son without a man to support her, and even less able to understand that it was something she'd chosen to do. Before Ragnar learnt to ask no questions about his father, which he did at quite an early age, he used to bring him into the conversation as often as he could. This was partly because he was fascinated by the thought of a father who had disappeared, and partly because his mother never mentioned him of her own volition. But her answers to his questions were terse and dismissive. He was a wastrel, charming of course, but he had no depth to him.

Ragnar gradually understood that he was expected to be a different sort of man. Charm was to be discouraged, depth was a virtue. He was always to respect women, and it was an expectation that made him rather fear them.

Although his whole thought process on this rumbling train had become sluggish, it was a slowing-down that was somehow soothing. He had so much time in front of him that there was no sense of urgency to panic him. His mind could simply drift, picking up memories as and when it liked. Fear was banished for the moment, but it still lurked just out of sight, with the memories still to come. Deep down he knew there would be nightmares in them.

CHAPTER 9

He'd gone to Östersund in March 1978, when he was twenty-four. He'd just completed his training and was about to start his first job with the Jämtland force. His immediate problem, finding somewhere to live, would probably not have been difficult for anybody else. Inspector Stenberg, to whom he reported, recommended a small flat near the Police Headquarters. But his personal sensitivity about houses and locations and the fact that he had not fully recovered from the shock of his mother's death, complicated any decision. He wanted somewhere near enough his job but not on top of it, somewhere that would be a retreat offering the privacy he needed to be able to think his often complicated thoughts and relax in comforting silence. He was still hesitating, because nothing on his list was quite right, when he was told about a house for rent in the secluded village of Näverede, just off the road between Hammarstrand and Östersund. It was small, a traditional red summer cottage recently upgraded to round the year use with effective insulation, wood-stove heating, running water and an inside shower and toilet. He fell in love with the thick hand-hewn timbers with their knots and age-cracks; and as it was slightly away from the single village street and close to the Indal River, it provided exactly the peaceful isolation he sought. So he took it.

As the first months passed, he found he did not mind how hard he was asked to work, secure in the knowledge that when the job was over he could retire to where he always felt at peace. He wasn't naturally sociable; he'd never had a gift for surface chit-chat; but now, at work, he learnt to pretend a sociability he did not really feel. He built himself a reputation for industry and for generosity with his free time, and he even acquired the ability to join the after-hours partying, staying until he could slip away home without attention being drawn to him. It was the happy start to a double life, the policeman and his private self.

In Näverede he lived undisturbed. His uniform made clear what he was, and people did not intrude. He was aware of distant movements around the house which was between him and the river, but he took care never to look up and risk the possibility of conversation. He was concentrating so hard on making a good impression at police headquarters, often volunteering for extra hours or willingly covering for his colleagues, that he was usually exhausted when he reached his cottage, and slept as soon as he had eaten. He was tidy by nature, and washing, ironing, cleaning and cooking took all his free time. But as the snow began to melt, the sun warmed the air, the days became longer and his confidence grew, he started to look about him a little more.

He noticed that his neighbour was as young as he was, and his wife was dowdy. He was an active man, often away during the day, even at weekends, but busy about the place when he returned, whistling as he worked. Then, early one evening, there was a loud and rhythmic rapping on his door and he was there, introducing himself as Olle Nyström and offering to sell him some wood for his stove. He was cheerful, almost cheeky, admitting he'd been keeping a watch on his neighbour's diminishing store of logs and seemingly amused at the idea of selling something to a policeman. When Amrén handed him some notes he said he'd bring the wood over in the next few days, which he did. After that they waved to each other whenever they happened to meet. Amrén even became curious about Olle's wife, because he never seemed to see her.

At least he never seemed to see her when he was engaged with Olle, whether they were merely waving to each other, or chatting. Occasionally, through his window, he did catch a glimpse of her when only Olle was near; but whenever he appeared on the scene, she vanished inside. He decided she must be very shy, or was afraid of policemen; but the explanation didn't entirely convince him and he began to keep an eye on the house before he left in the morning, and when he got home, peering at the lighted windows in the evening. On those occasions when he did spot her she never seemed to be still, and there was a startled look on her face as if she somehow sensed that he was watching her.

It occurred to him she might be lonely as well as shy, for Olle wasn't around much, leaving earlier as the days lightened and returning later. Amrén, so busy himself, wondered how she spent her time. From the distant look of her, which gave the impression of stiffness, he assumed she was older than Olle, and probably not much fun for a man who seemed so vibrant, so full of restless energy. Yet occasionally he was struck by a movement that was almost graceful, a tilt of the head that implied intelligent interest; for Olle's sake, he hoped there might be a little more to her than appeared on the surface.

At first Amrén was amused that he was even curious about her at all. He decided it was because he was settling into his new life, relaxing and beginning to feel a special sort of loneliness himself. He'd always been too shy to chase after girls, and too reserved, or so he supposed, for any girl to show an interest in him. But though he was utterly inexperienced, or perhaps because of it, he was conscious of a burgeoning eagerness to be with a girl, to get to know her mentally and, though he scarcely dared to think about it but frequently did, even physically as well. The other young policemen boasted of their experiences with married women who were often older, and they went into graphic, if probably exaggerated, detail about all they had learnt from them. Amrén was not at all attracted by such casual coupling, but he was increasingly conscious that he would very much like to meet an unattached girl his own age. He decided to stop thinking about Olle's wife and keep his eyes open for someone more suitable.

On his next free Sunday he went out to explore the immediate area, wondering if there were other houses on the far side of the Indal. It was a perfect early April day, cold, bright, sunny and invigorating, seeming to carry the promise of a fine summer to come. He walked towards the river, circling behind his neighbours' house, avoiding the deeper patches of melting slush and relishing the sunshine. Conifers, dripping the last of the snow from their needles, refreshed him as he strode along. The blood began to pump through him as he picked up his pace, revelling in the temporary freedom from any police work. He brushed the droplets from his hair, plunged into the thicker stand of trees through which he could just hear the rush of the river, and unexpectedly burst into a sun-filled clearing. Instantly he stopped and stayed very still.

Some trees had been felled there - birch and aspen of similar size to the sawn logs Olle had sold him, many of which had not required splitting. In front of him, at the far end of this glade, Olle's wife was asleep, sitting on a stump she'd covered with a woven shopping bag and resting her back against the smooth-barked slender stem of a silver birch. She was wearing a man's jacket, old, tattered, gaping open and ridiculously large for the small body it partially revealed. She had rubber boots on her feet, and above them her plain woollen skirt had been pulled up to let the sun get to her knees and lower thighs. Her head was covered by a peaked cap advertising Husqvarna chainsaws, but it had slipped sideways and made her look touchingly youthful.

He was about to retrace his steps as quietly as he could so he would not wake her, when it dawned on him that she didn't just look young, she *was* young, younger than he was, not more than twenty. She wasn't dowdy, either, despite the awful clothes, but rather sweet and almost pretty.

He took several slow and careful steps backward so that he was in the shadow of the trees. Then he bent, picked up a dead branch and snapped it. She woke with a little gasp and sprang to her feet, one hand going convulsively to her throat, her eyes swivelling round to see who or what was there. Only then did he move slowly forward into the sun so that she would recognise him and calm herself.

"I'm so sorry," she burst out, her voice almost cracking. "I wanted to get out of the house for a moment, to walk in the sun. I didn't know anybody else was near or I'd never have come."

It wasn't so much fear he heard in her voice, but acute embarrassment. It made him feel completely at ease with her, though he was usually the awkward one when he met any girl. The slight body and the nervous eyes made him feel protective, too, as though he, the stronger of the two, ought to ensure there was nothing at all for her to worry about.

"It's entirely my fault," he said soothingly, stepping closer and holding out his hand. "I'm your new neighbour, Ragnar, and I wanted to be out in the sun and fresh air just like you did. I was exploring, trying to find my way to the river bank, and I'm very sorry if I startled you."

She stared at him, studying his face as if that was the only way she could understand his words. Then she put her hand out, her cap fell off, she bent down to retrieve it, almost overbalanced and had to grip his hand hard to pull herself up.

"I'm Olle's wife, Lilly," she said, blushing to find she was holding his hand so firmly.

He noted the way she put her position before her name, as if being Olle's wife was more important to her than her own personal identity. But, before he could say anything more to reassure her, she noticed her clothes.

"I look such a mess," she whispered in horror. "I was in a hurry, and I grabbed the first things that came to hand just to get out while the sun shone. This is Olle's oldest jacket, and the cap's his. I don't know what you must think, and Olle will be ashamed of me when he knows. I'm never any good with visitors, I get so panicky."

Ragnar smiled. "I think you look fine. A little unusual, perhaps, but the cap suits you particularly well." He reached forward, tilting it a little and brushing back a loose strand of dark hair that was obscuring her face. "Now you look even better. And when I tell Olle I met you when we were both out for a walk, I shan't say anything about what you were wearing."

Lilly peered at him again, dwelling on his words, seeming in some way to examine whether they were genuine.

"You're very kind," she said, as if his words had passed her test. Momentarily she relaxed, but then she stiffened again. "Did you see me asleep?"

He knew she meant more than that, wondering whether he'd seen her with her skirt pulled up; and instinctively he decided to spare her additional discomfort by saying that he hadn't. But it was such a direct question he was momentarily flustered, and, with those intense brown eyes staring at him so trustingly, he found he couldn't lie.

"I came upon you suddenly, and you looked so lovely and peaceful in the sunshine I was afraid of frightening you. So I broke a stick to give you warning of my approach."

She nodded slowly, taking it in. "You've met Olle, haven't you? He sold you some wood."

"Yes. I liked him, and I should have come round to introduce myself to you, too. But I'm not very good with new people either. I needed time to settle, to get used to my job and fresh surroundings, so I put it off. But I know that's no excuse, and I hope you'll forgive my bad manners."

"You're a policeman, aren't you?"

He nodded. "But that doesn't mean I shouldn't have good manners."

It made her smile and he saw the brown of her eyes was flecked with green.

"You know that isn't what I meant, and I think you're teasing me to put me at my ease. I should have come with Olle to welcome you, but I've grown accustomed to leave it all to him. He's so good at it."

"Well, you've welcomed me now, and I hope we'll meet quite often."

Deliberately or not, she avoided a direct answer. "When you said you weren't very good with new people, I think you were just pretending to be like me, out of kindness. You seemed quite at ease with Olle."

"You're forcing me to admit something I'm ashamed of. I'm all right with other men, but I'm unsure of myself with girls."

"But you don't seem unsure of yourself now, with me."

"No," he said slowly, hearing the change in his voice but unable to do anything about it. "You're right, I'm not. But I've never met a girl like you before."

She clasped her arms round her, almost defensively, and lowered her eyes, and, as if to emphasise the change in both their attitudes, the sun clouded over.

"Is this your land?" he asked, trying to put everything back onto a normal level.

He saw her glance nervously at the freshly cut stumps, and she looked awkward again, her relaxed body suddenly becoming almost ungainly. "No, we have no land except where the buildings and the jetty are."

Though embarrassment was now affecting both of them, Ragnar tried to prolong their time together.

"I thought I might walk to the river. Do you want to come?"

She shook her head. "I must be going home now. I didn't mean to sleep and I've wasted nearly two hours. Olle says I spend too much time dreaming, and he's right."

"Would you like me to see you home?"

She shook her head again. "No, please, you go on to the river. It's beautiful there, you'll like it."

He was disappointed, but he nodded cheerfully and moved off, looking back once to see her scurrying away in the direction of the house. But he didn't walk far, and even when he reached the river he scarcely looked at it. He leant against a tree trunk and lost himself in his thoughts.

He'd met a girl, talked to her, touched her hair; and it had not been difficult at all. She reminded him of a baby female chaffinch he'd raised when he was a boy. She'd been so fearful at first, trembling in his hand, then gradually becoming warmer, calmer, allowing him to stroke her, accepting the flies and other insects he caught for her. She used to watch for him to come to her in the hay-filled box he'd given her, seemed to enjoy his gentle caresses, grew stronger until, one day, she flew away. But if Lilly was a captive bird and he set her free, would she fly to him?

For the next few months they circled round each other and he began to believe she was as conscious of him as he was of her. If they were close enough, though never very close, she'd give a little flutter of a wave and he'd return it. Each time it happened she seemed to smile, though she always kept her head down and it was hard to see her precise expression. But it contented him, for he was busy at work, gaining confidence as a police officer; and at home, as he now thought of the cottage, he experienced a deep and continuous happiness he'd never known before. Although they never spoke, he felt very close to Lilly, certain that he was in her thoughts, as she was in his.

But in the summer police business suddenly pushed him towards Olle - and towards Lilly too. There had been a spate of minor burglaries in all the villages along the upper Indal, and he was assigned to sort it out. Utanede had suffered, Västerede, Österede, Ede itself as well as Hammarstrand, Ammer and Stugun. He was kept busy taking statements, and he quickly came to the not-too-difficult conclusion that a boat was the most obvious link between the thefts. Then Näverede was struck when cash and a bottle of vodka were taken from his neighbours' house.

He received the report on a Monday as soon as he reached headquarters. Olle had rung in just before he arrived, and so he drove straight back. Approaching Olle's house in his official capacity he felt full of confidence. He noticed for the first time what a substantial house it was in comparison to his, with its two-storey timber construction, its long balcony with fretted decoration and a high double pitch roof with a permanent ladder climbing up each section to enable the snow to be easily cleared. But it had a neglected look, with flaking paint on the windows, and faded red walls.

He was so certain Olle would be at home awaiting him that he'd shut out of his mind any possibility of seeing Lilly. As a result, when the green door, which was as faded as the rest of the house, was opened by her, he was momentarily tongue-tied, staring at her in amazed wonder. Later he wished he could remember a bolt of lightning striking him, explosions of highly-coloured fireworks all around him. But though there was nothing as dramatic as that, there certainly was a desperate increase in the speed of his heartbeats. He tried to cling to his professionalism, looking down, frowning and telling himself he felt a slight annoyance; for if Olle was out, Lilly might be unable to answer his questions with any coherence and so he would have to return later.

"You'd better come in," Lilly said quickly, as though she felt it necessary to get him out of sight before anyone else in the village saw him at her door. But he also heard reluctance in her voice and, though he stepped inside, he wondered whether he was making a mistake. As soon as the door was closed she started to apologise.

"I'm sorry it's such a mess, I wasn't expecting anyone to come so quickly. Olle's out in his boat, so I don't know whether I'll be able to help you much. Maybe you should come back when he's here?"

Obstinacy took over, and he looked her full in the face, taking his time, refusing to be driven out but determined to be patient, kind and firm. But what he saw surprised him so much that for a moment he did not reply to her, standing quite still and trying to understand exactly what was there in her expression. It was certainly fear, but he did not think it was fear of him.

He held out his hand in formal greeting, and after surreptitiously wiping it on her blue denim skirt hers joined his, lying quietly against his enclosing fingers as though she had surrendered in her brief struggle to keep him away from her.

"I'm sure you'll be able to give me all the information I require," he said reassuringly, and he wondered if her hand was clinging to his a fraction longer than was strictly necessary.

When he took out his notebook and walked into the living room towards the worn sofa, she gave a gasp of dismay and whisked away the washing drying over the back of it. He sat down, feeling the dampness when he leaned back and hoping he wouldn't have too obvious a wet patch on his uniform when he stood up again.

"When did you first find the money and the vodka was missing?" he asked, resting his pen and pad on his knee.

She sank down onto a small chair opposite him, unconsciously smoothing her skirt over her legs and straightening her worn white blouse as though official questions couldn't be answered unless she was tidily dressed. But the effect on him was again one of surprise. In that interior light, momentarily unselfconscious, she was almost beautiful.

"First thing in the morning," she answered breathlessly, and he was sure she'd noticed his eyes on her. "I was going to take the car and do some shopping, and I'd put the housekeeping money Olle gives me in the kitchen drawer, to have it ready for an early start. But when I came down from the, well, from upstairs, the drawer was open and the money was gone."

"Any sign of anybody breaking in?"

"The door was locked, but the kitchen window was open."

He looked up and found that her eyes were glued to his face. She seemed utterly open to him, defenceless, as though she was desperately trying to draw some strength from him because she no longer had that strength herself. He was profoundly stirred, feeling for the first time in his life that he was actually needed by a woman. He experienced a whole new sense of potency that was disturbingly sexual as well as social; and, as though she glimpsed something of that in his expression, she suddenly dropped her gaze and stood up awkwardly. But there was no rejection in it, only an embarrassed awareness of how he might be feeling towards her, and how she herself might be reacting to him.

She led the way into the kitchen and he followed her, watching the way she moved, taller, straighter, more confident in response to some uncanny knowledge that he was looking at her as an attractive woman, not a witness.

"That's the drawer, and that's the window beside it," she explained, but her voice trembled slightly as if she was saying something much less mundane.

"Was the window properly closed overnight?"

She shook her head, looking as though he'd caught her out in some misdemeanour, yet not reacting with quite the automatic shame she'd shown in her earlier apologies. This time, though not denying her fault, she seemed to be more interested in what his reaction would be and, when he did not seem critical of her, she added in a firmer tone, "It was only open a tiny bit, to let some air in because Olle said there was a cooking smell. He doesn't like that, so I always put a teaspoon between the window and the frame and hook that loop of string over the catch to hold it almost shut."

"Was it still like that in the morning?"

"Yes."

"But somebody could have unhooked the string, reached in, opened the drawer and taken the money, then closed the drawer and put the loop on again so that it looked as though nothing had happened?"

He realised his tone had taken on the deliberate severity of the police interrogator and at once she shrank, almost as though she was about to cry. "You're right; it's what must have happened, so it is my fault."

"What about the vodka?" he asked more gently.

"I don't really know about that. Olle kept it in the outhouse nearer the river. That's where he works, doing bits of carpentry for people."

"Does he lock that door at night?"

"No. People are honest round here; we've never had trouble before."

There seemed to be nothing else to say, but neither of them moved. Finally she asked, "Did you reach the river?"

"Yes."

"Did you think it was beautiful?"

"I thought it was very beautiful, just as you said it would be. Did you get back home all right?"

"Yes. Olle wasn't home by then, so he never knew I'd been out."

She flushed as she realised her words implied a secret between them. He saw her breasts rise and fall as her breathing quickened, and he forced himself to look away, staring instead at the kitchen drawer. "Did anybody touch that this morning?"

"I opened it, which was when I noticed the money was missing. Olle was sure the notes had just gone to the back of the drawer, so he pulled it out and searched it." She suddenly realised what that meant, and looked disheartened. "We've messed up the fingerprints, haven't we?"

"The thief probably wore gloves, so it doesn't really matter. How much was there?"

"Two hundred *kronor.*" She seemed to feel it required some explanation, and she blurted out, "We're not rich, it's a lot of money for us."

He went outside, but he found no footprints. He looked at the outhouse, still seeing her in front of him though she was no longer there. He recalled the trembling of her hand in his as, at their first meeting, they'd stood together among the trees, the sunshine warming them. He remembered the green lights he'd discovered in her brown eyes and how, a few moments ago, as he'd noticed her rapid breathing, he'd longed to stretch out his fingers and trace the dark eyebrows down to those neat ears where her hair curled enticingly. She was so unsure of herself, so timid, and yet she was protective of a husband who seemed to keep her down. But she'd shown no trace of guile, for she'd told him Olle owned a boat without understanding that it might link him to the robberies. He'd certainly need to speak to him.

He went back to the house, knowing she was watching him from the porch.

"Did Olle go into the outhouse this morning?"

She winced, as though he'd made an accusation.

"It's where he works," she explained. "It was only then he discovered the bottle of vodka was missing. He didn't think about fingerprints, and nor did I. We were just so worried about somebody stealing from us."

He wondered if she always overreacted, or whether she too thought Olle might be involved. He didn't tell her that two hundred *kronor* and a bottle of vodka would not justify the cost of a fingerprint technician, or even much working time from a new young police officer. The other robberies had all been small: a chainsaw, tools, cash, alcohol, a fishing rod, items for which conclusive ownership might be hard to prove.

"Would you like to come in and have some coffee?" she asked suddenly, her voice throaty with nervousness. It was as if she'd overcome some huge block to get the question out, and he nodded, not trusting his voice. Uncertainty as to whether it was compatible with his official standing was swept aside by the sudden charge of excitement. This was how so many of the stories he'd heard began, with some sort of invitation when the husband was away. Until now he'd always been a listener to such narratives. Now he almost began to believe he was on the verge of something extraordinary, not the kind of quick-roll episode his colleagues told, but the fulfilment of a romantic dream he'd never thought attainable.

They sat together at the kitchen table, and neither spoke. He was certain she knew how he felt, and he was equally sure she felt the same. She seemed to be stunned by her own daring, her hand shaking as she passed him a cup and saucer. To do nothing might humiliate her; to rush anything would certainly frighten her.

He watched her pour his coffee and found he was imagining things better banished from his mind. Desperately he took the sugary white biscuit she offered him, tasted it and automatically told her how delicious it was. He was amazed to discover he could go on acting normally when his thoughts were in such turmoil. Sure she had made the biscuits herself, he ate several more to please her, although they were not as tasty as they looked. He hoped it wasn't the fact he was a policeman that was opening the way for him. If she just saw him as an authority figure, and she was already used to doing whatever her husband told her, she might do whatever he wanted, too. But that was not the way he wanted it. He needed her to like him for himself; and the recollection that all this had begun near the river when he'd not been wearing uniform renewed his hope.

But that thought of her husband's influence over her disturbed him. If Olle was out rowing or paddling there would be no engine noise to warn him when he returned, and the river and the outhouse were too far away from the house for him to be certain of even hearing him pulling the boat onshore or unloading it. The worry of it inhibited him and he was relieved when she broke the silence.

"What will you do next?" she asked. She was calmer than he was now, the anxiety gone from her face as if a decision had been made. As her face and body relaxed she became younger, more like her real age, and he believed she might be aware he was attracted to her, was pleased by it and curious how this new experience might develop. She rose to fill his coffee cup, no longer stiff and awkward but pliant and unhesitating. She stood behind him as she poured, her body touching his, and he felt the warmth of her, inhaled the smell of fresh soap and was overwhelmed by a new sensation that was not erotic at all, a longing for her that was filled with love and contentment, a desperate wish that she was not Olle's wife, but his.

"I shall certainly need to talk to you some more," he said, suddenly needing to know he would be seeing her again, even if something was to happen between them now. "And I must speak to Olle, too. Perhaps he could come round to my place this evening and sign a statement? What time do you think he'll be back?"

She put down the coffee pot, but she stayed behind him where he couldn't see her face. "He's not usually back before he's ready to eat, and that's around five-thirty. Would an hour after that be all right?"

"Fine," he said, draining the coffee she'd poured in one long swallow and beginning to rise. He didn't know whether he was getting up to kiss her, or to leave and try to sort out the contradictory thoughts that were filling his mind. But he felt her hand on his shoulder, surprisingly firm, keeping him in his seat.

"Why would you need to talk to me again?"

He panicked, at a loss for an answer, feeling the insistent pressure of her hand and unable to speak.

"Is it really about the case?"

He felt they had changed roles. She was the authoritative one, and he was full of nervous hesitation.

"It's not, I suppose, really about the case. Of course I'd like to keep you up to date about developments, but it's not strictly necessary. Don't you want me to speak to you again?"

Her fingers tightened on his shoulder. "Of course I want you to speak to me again. But I'm not clever like you; I want you to be honest with me so I know where I am."

He bowed his head, his manoeuvring undone by her simplicity. Then he turned in his chair and buried his head in the waistband of her skirt, wincing as he grazed his nose on the metal buckle of her belt. "I'm mad about you," he whispered into the denim.

She stroked his hair and sighed. "You've only just met me. Go home, please, drive to Östersund, get right away from me, and then you'll feel differently. Please, go now, please."

He stood up, faced her, and took her gently by the arms. "I'll leave, of course. You're married, I'm an investigating officer in a case where you're a possible witness, all this is complete lunacy. But what if I still feel exactly the same tomorrow, and all the days after that?"

He would never be able to forget the smile she gave him then, shy, tender and completely confident. "If you ever reach that stage, however long it takes, come and tell me. I'll be waiting for you."

They were so close together it seemed natural to kiss her, but she stepped away from him and quietly opened the door, no longer looking at him. It was a gesture which compelled him to leave unsure of her reply to the question his kiss would have asked her.

CHAPTER 10

That evening, Olle came to see him. Uneasily conscious of what had transpired in the kitchen, Ragnar watched him with particular attention for any sign he might have discerned something from Lilly's attitude. He couldn't imagine she was good at pretending, and she seemed so cowed by Olle that her very nervousness might have revealed more than she intended. But Olle seemed just as he had been when he'd sold him the firewood, a cheerful blond muscular man with a cocky attitude and a sly smile. For a dreadful moment he wondered whether that very slyness indicated some secret knowledge, not unwelcome because it put a policeman in his power. But he rapidly realised it was just part of Olle's whole approach to life. Whoever he met, whatever their station in life - and that clearly included policemen, Olle always knew he'd be able to run rings round them. They might be powerful or clever, but he was sharp, as sharp as a whetted blade, and the knowledge shone delightedly through him. Ragnar had already discovered that he could have got firewood at a lower price than Olle charged, and so he was immediately on his guard when Olle began to peer professionally at his little cottage. Before he could start pointing out any weak points that might need attention, Ragnar quickly asked him about the items taken from his house.

With complete assurance, Olle told him exactly the same story as Lilly, his blue eyes twinkling as though he dared anyone to disbelieve him. While Ragnar prepared a statement for him to sign, he was happy to let him talk in the hope he might be careless and contradict himself, or even say something about Lilly that would indicate his feelings for her. But he never mentioned her at all, and though he chatted happily about fishing and the jobs he did around the nearby villages, he said nothing that might indicate an involvement in the petty thieving. He signed the statement without reading it through, and then offered to give Ragnar's house a fresh coat of red *falurödfärg* and repair two of the window frames.

"It'll cost you, of course, but it's never sensible to let a house go off."

Ragnar reminded him he was just the tenant, but he said he'd think about it, conscious that he would certainly not want Olle to be working so close to home, but aware that he ought to keep up good relations with him. He watched him walk away, ambling towards his house as though he hadn't a care in the world, leaving him somewhat shamed that already his attitude was being controlled by his feelings for Lilly. It was only when he saw a movement in the upstairs window that he realised Lilly had been watching them together, and he wondered whether she'd felt the same discomfort he did.

He thought of her all the time, but his thoughts had become more tangled. Alone, separated from her if only by a short distance, he wanted her increasingly desperately; and he let himself believe she might eventually let him have her. But he loved her too, wanted to take her away from Olle, live with her, marry her. It had to be possible, things like that happened all the time. Over the months he'd become certain she didn't really love Olle, and he showed no sign of loving her. But everything was happening at such a bad time, just when he was settling into his job. It would have been so much easier if he could simply consider seducing her, a one-off affair. Yet, whatever his body wanted, his mind didn't work like that. Making love meant being in love, and that meant being together all the time, for all time, which in its turn meant marriage.

He was astounded at himself. He had never thought of himself as a particularly sexual person, and certainly not a passionate one. Now, without warning, he was overwhelmed, behaving just like other young men of his age when he'd always considered himself different. He'd been proud of that difference, but meeting Lilly, and realising the opportunity the thefts gave him, reduced him to an everyday anybody. It seemed as though in the space of two cups of coffee he'd moved from the possibility of a kiss and some sort of sexual encounter to a decision to break up his neighbour's marriage, steal his wife, and take on a commitment he couldn't afford. But it was worse even than that, because Olle and Lilly weren't just neighbours, they were victims in the crime he was investigating. Worst of all, he couldn't hide from himself the suspicion that Olle might well be the culprit.

It was all much too complicated. He was in an emotional mess, and yet he'd never been so happy. Lilly would be waiting for him whenever he chose to go to her, and perhaps everything would be simple then. He knew he loved her, and he was almost convinced she loved him too. Perhaps what still made him different was that he wasn't just going to dream about the outcome, he would make it happen. Shunning the easiest option, to satisfy his own needs, he would go the whole hog, love, marriage and a future together, whatever the difficulties.

Remembering her loyalty to a man he was sure she did not love, it occurred to him that everything might be easier if he could show her that Olle really was the thief. It would mean he'd have to delay seeing Lilly while he continued his investigation, but she might be pleased if he seemed to be taking several days to consider all the ramifications of their feelings for each other, and to be certain what it was he wanted from her.

That night he extinguished his lights as though he'd gone to bed, and then slipped out of the window farthest away from Olle's house. He circled round through the trees until he reached the river upstream of the outhouse, and then moved cautiously down until he could see the tiny inlet beside it. That was where Olle moored his rowing boat and his canoe, and it was there he might start to betray himself. He settled himself to wait in a tight clump of hazel bushes, controlling his excitement so that his concentration was not affected, and thankful that the summer nights were still so light. His field glasses and his camera were within easy reach of his hand, and they would provide the necessary evidence.

Nothing occurred on the first night. On the second, well before dawn, he saw Olle paddle out into the river in his canoe, a fishing rod jutting prominently from the stern, but although he watched until the sun was quite high in the sky, he never saw him return. The next night there was still no sign of him. But, patiently keeping watch the night after that, he spotted him paddling back up river. The field glasses showed him that the canoe seemed to be riding lower in the water, and the fishing rod was no longer visible; but to his frustration he couldn't see what might be in the canoe now that had not been there before. He used his camera anyway, and continued to take pictures as Olle unloaded. But Olle did this crouching down, and although he got a good shot of him with a load in his arms when he entered his outhouse, whatever he was carrying was covered with an old tablecloth.

Ragnar went back home, slept for a couple of hours, drove to Östersund, and picked up the reports that had come in about stolen items along the Indal. He smiled when he saw the list: two chickens, a trowel, a sledge hammer, a scythe blade, a Mora knife in a plastic sheath, a Sandvik saw and a felling axe. It was hardly in the Mafia crime league. But the axe was from the 100 year old Gränsfors Bruks, hand-forged, expensive, unlikely to be common along the Indal, and quite out of the economic reach of a somewhat feckless odd-job man. Receiving permission to make an official visit to Olle's house, he drove back to Näverede in a state of elation.

Just before he reached his house he passed Olle driving away, and they waved to each other. It was after nine, and once he'd had a quick shower he went straight over. There was no reply at first, and then Lilly opened the door to him, clutching her dressing gown tightly around her.

“Thank goodness you’re in uniform,” she gasped, closing the door quickly behind him. “I’m sure Ingalill was watching the house through her telescope.”

“Who’s Ingalill?” he asked in bewilderment.

“Ingalill Sjöman. She lives in the house across the road from you.”

“But why would she be interested in watching you?” he asked her with a smile, hoping to calm her.

“I don’t think she likes us much, not Olle anyway, and because she’s almost housebound she spends her time spying on us with her dead father’s telescope. I saw the flash of the sun on the glass when your knock woke me and I opened the curtains a fraction to see who it was. Her father was a sea captain.”

“I’m sure she’s just bored, and looks at all her neighbours.”

Lilly stared at him as though her mind wasn’t really on Ingalill at all. “I overslept, you see, I wasn’t expecting you, didn’t think you’d come back so I must have fallen asleep again when Olle left.” She glanced at the clock on the wall, and gave a little wail.

“I don’t know what’s the matter with me. I never usually behave like this. I’m so ashamed, I must look awful.”

He went close to her then, and put his arms round her, inhaling her warm sleepy odour. “Every time I think of you it will be like this, all tousled and half-asleep. You’re so tempting I might gobble you up for breakfast.”

She relaxed against him, and then stiffened again. “You probably *do* want breakfast, and I haven’t got anything ready. There’s some tea I made for Olle, but it’ll be cold by now, and anyway you probably want coffee. I could make you some after I’ve got dressed, but it feels so slovenly being with you in my night clothes, as though I’m inadequate, and can’t cope properly, and if I went near the window Ingalill would spot I was entertaining you in my dressing gown.” She looked at him anxiously, half turning towards the stairs. “I’ll be very quick, I promise.”

"Be quick, then," he said laughing. "I'm here partly because there've been more robberies. Have you noticed if anything more has gone missing?"

She shook her head. "I don't think so, and I know Olle would have told me if he'd found anything had been taken, even though he was in a hurry. He had to get to the Brunflo market to sell some tools he doesn't need any longer."

"While you go upstairs I'll just look around and make sure there are no signs of a break-in."

As soon as she'd left, he opened the fridge. Two plucked chickens were inside, and he didn't doubt that the expensive axe and the other tools were being quietly sold beside some stall in Brunflo. He supposed he ought to leave immediately, follow Olle and try to catch him in the act, but he would probably be too late and only alert Olle to his suspicions. He wanted to avoid that at all costs, and meanwhile the knowledge that Olle was almost certainly the thief made him feel powerful. He would catch him red-handed the next time, and as he listened to Lilly moving in the room above, imagining her slipping on her clothes, he felt the thrill of a suddenly surging anticipation.

Lilly was as quick as she'd said she would be, scampering down the stairs looking flushed and pleased with herself, pushing her short dark hair into place by running her slender fingers rapidly through the thick waves. She bustled about the kitchen making fresh coffee, and putting out several breads, cheese and some cucumber which she neatly sliced. She looked fresh and at ease in blue jeans and a turquoise blouse which he guessed was her best. When she noticed he was staring at her admiringly, she met his eyes with none of the startled-rabbit anxiety that had characterised their first meeting. Now there was a new certainty about her and she smiled at him, showing her pleasure in his attention. It occurred to him that nobody might ever have looked at her in that way before, and that led him to consider whether anybody had even seen her as he saw her, as she really was.

"There's no sign of any break-in," he told her. "And I think I'd better have a little milk with my coffee this early in the day."

She went to the fridge, and he moved behind her as she opened it. "You're well supplied with meat, then," he remarked. "Do you keep chickens?"

He already knew she didn't, and he was relieved when she shook her head. "Olle brought them in, as a surprise for me this morning. He'd swapped them for some trout he'd caught. I'll roast one of them tonight and give him a good meal as a thank you. He's so thoughtful, he knows I like chicken more than fish."

She poured the milk into a small jug which was marked Stockholm, and had a picture of the royal palace on it. She passed it to him and sat down opposite him at the table, looking preoccupied.

"Olle's been very good to me; I want you to know that. I don't love him, but he was there when I needed somebody." She shifted uncomfortably, seeming to find it difficult to talk about herself, and yet driven by a need to be honest with him. "My mother died when I was fourteen, and my father, who's a doctor, isn't an easy man. He's not unkind, nothing like that, and it was probably mostly my fault, but, without my mother there, he became very protective, almost possessive. He kept saying I was all he had, which was a great responsibility for me; and he saw me as somebody I wasn't. I'm not very clever, but he wanted me to be a doctor just like him; and he had very clear ideas about the sort of man I should marry."

"He sounds very difficult indeed," he said encouragingly. "He was probably determined not let you become independent of him."

Lilly nodded thoughtfully, seeming to draw strength from his interest, settling back more comfortably in her chair before she went on.

"Over the next few years I really tried so hard to please him, but everything I did, everything I was, disappointed him. I felt myself shrivelling up; becoming a failure even though I knew it wouldn't be like that if only I could be myself. In the end I panicked. I had a school friend who lived up here, and I persuaded her to invite me to stay with her for a while."

Timidly, but with a little smile as though it was somehow wonderful to do it, she reached across, took his coffee cup, and drank from it.

"It was so peaceful here, and I met Olle. But then my friend, Lise, who'd been applying for jobs, was offered one as an *au pair* to a family in Minnesota, and they wanted her to start at the beginning of the next month. I was desperate, I didn't know what to do, and when Olle found me crying, and proposed, I accepted him. I suppose it was a terrible thing to do, to marry him without love just to escape and be myself, but in a way it's worked."

She got up, pushing the chair back clumsily and walking aimlessly about the little kitchen. Ragnar watched her, sure it was best if he kept silent.

"I haven't ever talked like this before," she burst out. "I never could explain things to my father and Olle isn't a man who questions anything. He just takes each day at a time, busy with his own life. I know he likes being looked after, and I like looking after him, but he doesn't want to know what I think, or what I do, and after my father that sort of space is like freedom after prison. Can you understand that, or does it sound silly, as though I've never grown up?"

"I've always been a bit of a loner myself, because I'm not good with people."

"You're good with me. You listen to me, and you take me seriously."

"I have a very special reason for that."

"I know. I shouldn't have let you put your arms round me the other day, it was wrong of me. But I'm glad I did, though I'm beginning to wonder if I have a thing about uniforms." Her face lit up then with a smile of such utter relaxation that he was amazed at her quiet confidence in a situation he'd have expected to paralyse her. "I'm glad, too, that I sent you away to think about it, because it's given me time to think as well. That's why I've just told you about how I came to marry Olle and what I feel for him, because if we do something I want to have been absolutely honest with you." She twisted her fingers awkwardly together as she added. "Olle and I don't make love very often, and when we do it's quite quick, for his satisfaction. He doesn't seem to mind that I'm not very involved, although I like him doing it because it makes him so happy. It's a way I can give him something in return for providing me with a safe place to be."

He was so moved by her simplicity he felt he had to be equally open.

"I've thought a lot about it, too, especially what we might do if, by some miracle, you felt as I feel about you. I've never had very much to do with girls. I think I found their giggling threatening; and their way of hanging around together, seeming so sure of themselves, rather frightened me. But I was still attracted, wanting to make love to them, though I never have. But when I saw you I felt calm, almost at peace, and when I noticed how lovely you really are I admit I was desperate to make love to you straight away. I think the fact that you were married made it seem somehow safer."

He saw her lean forward and open her mouth, but he hurried on before she could interrupt him.

"Then I began to feel much more deeply for you, beginning to fall in love with you, and I was happy to delay the love-making as long as I could kiss you, hold you, feel you, look at you."

He got up, came round the table and kissed her, pulling her upright out of her chair, holding her against him though there was no resistance. At first it was just a kiss, and he was overwhelmed by the softness of her lips, the warmth of her body, the extraordinary sense of two people fusing into one. He had never known such contentment and for a long time they simply stood entwined together, their naked mouths, one upon the other, the only necessary expression of their love. But eventually it wasn't enough, and he explored her body a little with his hands, moving them over her hips and thighs. He felt her hands stroke his back and without releasing her lips he slowly raised his to the front of her dress. At once she pushed them away and stepped back. She did not seem annoyed at all, but awkward and embarrassed.

"Olle won't be back until this evening," she said. "When he goes to the market he hangs out with a lot of friends and they have some beers together, so he's never in a hurry to get home. But all this, you and me, it's so sudden. You say you love me, and I believe you, and I feel the same about you, but you'll move on, you'll soon forget me, and that's how it should be. But if I was to be with you, just once, I must be certain I can trust you never, ever, to say a word about it. Nobody must ever know."

He gave her his solemn oath, wild excitement coursing through his body. He assured her it was something deep and special, his voice thickening as he said it, and he would never, ever, betray her. In his own mind he knew it would not be only once, because he would marry her and have a lifetime with her. But that would follow naturally once she'd given herself to him.

"Don't come up until I tell you," she whispered, and she went up the stairs.

He prowled the kitchen, overwhelmed by the feeling she had given him that it was really going to happen. He tried to quell his agitation, telling himself that he could and would perform, and that a new stage in his life was opening.

He heard her soft call and ran up the stairs. The door to the room above the kitchen was open, and when he looked in she was standing by the bed, the green dressing gown covering her to the chin. The curtains were closed, and the dimmed daylight made it excitingly intimate. He went up to her, put his hands on her shoulders, and felt her trembling.

"Because I overslept I haven't had my bath this morning, and I want to do that first if you'll let me. I hope it doesn't make you angry, keeping you waiting like this?"

"I need a bath too," he claimed. "Can I come in with you? Then you can just relax and I'll soap your back."

She laughed, surprised. "Would you really want to do that? I'm sure I look awful in the bath, and I don't think Olle has ever seen me completely naked. I'm too thin, I'm almost skinny."

"I want it almost as much as I want to make love to you. You'll probably have to stop me taking you right there, while the bath water sloshes all around us."

She laughed again, happily, seemingly increasingly at ease with herself, and with him. "I'm protected; I've got a coil. So if you did get carried away there wouldn't be a risk except to your knees, because the bath isn't comfortable at all. I'll go and run it, and you can get undressed here. Olle's dressing gown is hanging on the back of the door, and you could borrow that."

He took his clothes off hurriedly, pushing his uniform so far under the bed that it was completely out of sight. He hesitated over the belt which held his baton and holstered pistol, guiltily aware that by leaving it unattended in an empty room, not securely locked away, he was breaking a fundamental rule of policing. Finally he took the pistol out of its holster, hid it under the mattress, and then thrust the rest after his uniform. It was crazy, he knew it, but he felt almost mad, totally out of control, able to think of one thing only, and that was Lilly, naked in the bath. He wished he was taller and less plump about the middle, and that his face was more heroic instead of round and smooth and pink. But, astonishingly, she appeared not to mind what he looked like, concentrating on the sort of person he was. She seemed to have lost her fears and anxieties, and was acting more naturally with him than ever before, almost as though he was an old friend and making love was simply a nice way to welcome him.

The bathroom was very plain, the paint grey and peeling, and there was a deep basin with old-fashioned taps. The high bath dominated the space, on clawed legs and clearly as uncomfortable as she had said. But Lilly was lying in it, protected by scented bubbles she must just have stirred up to hide herself. He could only just make out her shape, and she seemed so innocent lying there awaiting him that for a moment he feared he might be taking advantage of her. But, then everything was transformed by her smile when she saw him.

He threw the dressing gown over the square cork-topped laundry box and as she sat up to give him space, he climbed in behind her, putting his legs either side of her and pulling her back so that her dark hair tickled his chest and his hands covered hers. It wasn't a posture he'd be able to hold for very long, for, although the bath was long, it was quite narrow and his knees were crushed against the side; but he was deeply stirred by the feel of her against him, both inwardly and externally.

"Are you going to wash me now, before the water gets cold?" she asked him after an interval when she had lain so still and so totally relaxed against him he thought she might have fallen asleep.

She sat up again, the water and the bubbles streaming off her, and he soaped her back. She wasn't skinny, though her arms were thin and her shoulders narrow. He slipped his hands under her wrists and soaped the flat stomach and then the small waist, gradually moving his hands upward. Recalling her instinctive withdrawal when he'd reached towards her breast when she was dressed, he touched so gently that he felt little but the subtle contours. They did not seem as large as certain magazine photographs had led him to believe; but when he took them in his hands he was thrilled by their weight and fullness. He wondered if she would recoil again, but she seemed to have lost her shyness with her clothes, welcoming his hands wherever they ventured; and it encouraged him to dare even more.

"Kneel up," he urged, "I can't get at the rest of you."

She shifted, tucking her feet under her as she raised herself and knelt with her back to him. The water cascaded down the pebbly protrusions of her spine, streaming over the fleshy whiteness below; and she, the first live girl he'd ever seen naked, delighted him with the curving shapeliness of her hips, so different to his own. Peering down over her shoulder he saw the bathwater trickling down the front of her, the soap bubbles decorating the springy curls, and his excitement rose.

Tentatively he touched her there, lathering and rinsing, almost dying of desire, his fingers teasing out the hair as he had seen her do earlier to the curls behind her ears. With assumed familiarity masking the daring thrill, he gradually moved his hand backwards, skimming the skin's surface, gently using his soaped fingertips to stroke, explore, circle and fractionally intrude. She gave what was almost a giggle and commented that he was certainly washing her thoroughly. The acceptance in her voice, the obvious enjoyment of everything he was doing to her, roused him to such a pitch that he knew he would have to enter her soon or he would burst. He eased her further apart, then let his fingers dance and flicker, forward and back, testing, seeking reaction, allowing Lilly to take the lead, to respond to his touching wherever and whenever she wished, maintaining the pretence of washing, splashing away the soap as soon as he put it on so that the water caressed her too.

She began to press down to meet his fingers, leaning more forward to open herself, starting to sway in time to the stroking, panting with rising pleasure, surrendering herself, allowing a finger to slide inside and moulding herself to it, then shifting as the need took her so that she could take in more to raise the level of her ecstasy. He was tiptoeing to a joy he'd never expected to experience, where nothing was forbidden, where she was giving him her body and taking his so that she, and he, could share the explosion that was building to its crescendo. He wondered whether he would get her to the bed in time, or if he would have to take her on the bathroom floor.

She began to shudder, and he thought it was her budding desire. But then she froze, called out in a hoarse voice 'no, no', scrambling out of the bath, head bowed, arms hanging limply at her sides, eyes on the ground, stooped, ugly, like a pitiful pierced rag doll whose stuffing is falling out of her. She did not attempt to cover her nakedness, she made no sound nor did she move at all. But he knew he'd been rejected.

"I'm sorry, so sorry, but I can't do it, I really can't," she whimpered finally. "It's wrong. I didn't realise how it would be, it wasn't what I expected. I'm such a fool, but you'll have to go."

She began to sob then, and he saw that her whole body was shuddering. He was completely stunned, no longer the rampant lover but a flaccid fool, kneeling in the water, alone in the large bath, gasping with the humiliation of it. He climbed rapidly out, wrapped himself in a towel, and turned away so he would not have to see her. "You can dry me, if you like," he heard her say in a timid placating voice somewhere behind him, and she seemed to be squeezing the words out. "And I'll dry you," she offered desperately. "But we can't go any further."

She sobbed even harder then, great choking sobs, and he realised that somehow he'd disgusted her, that she was forcing herself to be kind to him, and it would never be the same again.

CHAPTER 11

He set the trap with care. Bo was in a police car at Krångede, facing down the road to Hammarstrand where Stefan sat in the other police car, pointing up towards him. Amrén was on the river in a borrowed inflatable with a powerful outboard motor. He had the camera case attached to his belt and he'd put a loudhailer in the boat's storage pocket beside him. All three of them were in radio contact, and each of them was young and eager, dreaming of a first arrest.

He'd been watching Olle for days, and he had begun to understand that the dam at each power station was the key to the way he worked. If he left home in his canoe, very early in the morning, he would be taking what pickings he could from the local area. But if, even earlier in the morning, he put the canoe in his van and drove off, he would be going further afield, on the river between a pair of the lower dams. On this occasion, at three in the morning, he had parked out of sight, below the dam at Krångede power station; so Amrén knew he would be pillaging the riverbank down to the next dam at Hammarstrand. He alerted Bo and Stefan, who drove off to the positions that would ensnare Olle between them. Then he launched the inflatable, taking great care not to make a splash, and followed Olle at a considerable distance, keeping the motor inboard and using the oars as silently as he possibly could. He kept close to the bank, and at each bend he turned into the edge and gripped an overhanging branch until Olle, who was clearly visible in the early morning summer light, had almost rounded the bend ahead. Even so, he quickly learnt to be particularly cautious because Olle would suddenly slow the canoe, drift in to the side, moor up, clamber out and slip into sheds and outhouses. Each time Amrén painstakingly photographed him going in, coming out, and returning to the canoe with his spoils.

The river was beautiful at this early hour of the morning. While he waited for Olle to complete his little thefts he watched the duck with their young and saw deer drinking at the water's edge, perfectly lit by the early sun. He observed the rings where fish were feeding, shivered at the doom-laden call of the black-throated diver, heard the splash of a marauding pike and unsuccessfully prayed that the osprey beating up the river would plunge into the water and come up with a fish in its beak right in front of him. He assumed it had taken Olle years as a jobbing handyman to build up the local knowledge of what would be unlocked and what would contain something he could use or sell, but would be very hard to trace. Observing him at work, he became more and more certain it was the adventure and excitement that was at least as compelling as the small profit or the chance to surprise his wife with an unexpected gift.

Since the last bitter occasion, he and Lilly had kept their distance from each other, and never made any attempt to speak of what had occurred. He was too mortified, too full of anger, and he did not care to know her thoughts. Occasionally he noticed her on the porch, and once she might have offered a desultory wave, but he pretended not to see. It was an impossible situation, especially while he was pursuing Olle, and it was best they remained distant from each other. Once Olle was arrested and shown up to be a thief, his wife might take a different view. She might even feel in need of his help.

Olle did not stop very often, and he was moving fast. Shortly before five o'clock, while the sun was still quite low in the sky, he was below Ammer and nearing Hammarstrand - where the river ran for a stretch beside the road. He spoke into his radio, warning Bo and asking him to drive slowly down from Krångede and be ready to move up rapidly in support once the trap was sprung. Then he alerted Stefan at Hammarstrand so that he could get into a good position, out of sight, just below the lowest part of the riverbank where he assumed Olle would try to beach the canoe and run for it as soon as he realised he was pursued. He pressed the release button and gently lowered the outboard motor into the water, hearing the satisfying clunk as it latched in place. He shipped the oars, made sure the camera with its damning pictures was safely tucked into the case at his belt, and then he drifted silently.

The moment Olle was at a diagonal with the low bank he started his motor with a roar, took up the loudhailer in one hand and spoke into it, his metallic voice reverberating off the rocky heights behind Hammarstrand as he said "Police, stay where you are." Then he sped towards him.

Exactly as he expected, Olle paddled furiously, heading for the side; and Amrén, knowing the unseen car was waiting for him, kept contentedly behind, driving him into the ambush. But then, still in deep water, Olle suddenly overturned the canoe, depositing the evidence in the river. Amrén hesitated, then slowed his boat and tried to grab some of the stolen goods while shouting into his radio to Bo to go full speed to prevent the suspect escaping.

Olle swam strongly for the bank, clambered up it and came face to face with Stefan beside his police car which had been creeping forward, invisible to him while he'd been in the water. Realising he was caught between the boat behind him and Stefan in front of him, he swerved to the left along the riverbank. Then, unable to see any southbound traffic because of a sharp bend in the road but gambling on its usual infrequency, he ran out across it towards the cover of a barn on the other side, straight into the path of Bo's car accelerating to cut off his escape. Amrén, hanging on to a plastic box of Volvo car-light bulbs he'd recovered from the water, shuddered at the scream of tyres, the acrid smell of scorched rubber, the dull thud of something hard colliding with something soft. And as he reached the bank he saw exactly what he knew he'd see, a sprawled and broken body, no movement in it except the spurting blood.

He told himself a criminal, attempting to evade arrest, had run under the wheels of a police car. It was an unfortunate accident, just one of those things. The driver of the car was not to blame, and surely no blame at all could be attached to the young organising officer who, by chance, had been the neighbour of the dead man's wife. He must never, not even for a moment, recall the tenth commandment, nor consider whether covet was the word that best described all he'd done with Lilly. Whatever his feelings, whatever his intention, God had intervened, looking down, taking action, making it all impossible. It was so much easier to blame God than himself.

Inspector Stenberg, to whom Amrén was responsible, took it even further than God. He was large, loud and shaking with rage.

"You cocky little creep," he shouted. "You've landed me in the first police enquiry of my career, and all because of a few chickens, some Volvo bulbs and your own determination to make your first arrest. I gave you permission to follow him, to have two cars at the ready, but I said nothing about telling one of them to drive like a maniac and kill the poor bugger."

Seeing that Amrén was about to speak, he raised his hand and glared at him. "Don't utter a single word or I won't be answerable for the consequences. You'll listen to me, I'll tell you what's what, and then you'll sign the statement like the chubby-faced little Christmas angel you resemble and pretend to be. And pretend is the right word, because I keep my ears open, and there's a story going its whispery way round this police station that doesn't make you sound very like a Christmas angel, or any sort of angel at all, and I really don't like the sound of it. You've been fucking the dead man's wife, that's what the story says, and, if that were true, any enquiry would finger you for having a very good motive for getting the husband out of the way. And, I may add, that motive might have been very strong indeed as it seems he may have known exactly what you were up to, which was up to your pubic hair in his wife's cunt."

He took a threatening step forward. "Are you following what I'm saying? Because you've gone all white and clammy and your eyes are rolling; I want your full attention."

He hissed the words right into Amrén's face, spattering him with spittle, and the shock drove away the horrified faintness that was gradually engulfing him, leaving him cold and trembling but alert to what was being said.

"Fortunately you've just denied that unfounded and disparaging rumour, not only because it's untrue, but because it isn't possible. You know, and I know, and by the time the enquiry opens, all this force will know, that you've been living here in Östersund since you joined us, in a little apartment in Rådhusgatan. You've got the keys in your pocket...," and he passed them to Amrén, "you haven't got any key to any cottage in Näverede...," and he took the key obediently held out to him, "and all your stuff will be in the apartment by the time you go to it tonight. Of course the husband knows you were in Näverede, but he's conveniently dead, isn't he? And his wife knows it, but she's hardly in a position to speak up after the positions she's been in with you. As for the owner, he's a very good friend of a very good friend, so he knows you weren't there either. So, as it's an internal police enquiry, nobody else in the village will get a word in edgeways and our efficient records will demonstrate that, from the day of your arrival, you've been living in Östersund. None of your colleagues will say any different, I shan't say any different, you won't say any different, and the enquiry will reach the conclusion it was an unfortunate accident, which I actually believe it probably was; and so no blame will be attached to any officer here."

He walked over to the basin in the corner and ostentatiously washed his hands. "Get out now, and stay out of my sight for as long as possible. Maybe you'll learn from this and become a competent officer or maybe you'll fuck up again and be out of this force quicker than a champagne cork out of a bottle at a wedding. But whichever it is, never forget this one very important fact. This hasn't been done for you, nobody cares a shit for you; it's been done to protect the reputation of the Jämtland police, and I happen to care a great deal about that."

As Stenberg had predicted, the police enquiry, after taking evidence, found that Olle's death was a tragic accident, and no officer was to blame. A few weeks later Amrén heard from a colleague who had a cousin who lived near Näverede that Lilly had left the house and nobody knew where she had gone.

CHAPTER 12

Magnus waited patiently for Pia Widmark to ring him from Östersund, though after a few days he did begin to wonder whether she really intended to keep him informed about developments in what the press were now calling 'The hanging road-man case'. But then she phoned him and suggested they met halfway, at Bräcke.

"My mother lives there, and I don't visit her anything like as often as I should. If you could make it by ten tomorrow, I'd have time to see her afterwards and still get back to tackle everything else that's piling up in my office. Lena's Café is on the right as you come from Sundsvall, and I'll meet you there if that's OK with you. I've got quite a lot to tell you."

Magnus agreed without hesitation, though he knew it would mean re-arranging a number of meetings. Since he'd been sitting in Amrén's chair as Sundsvall's temporary police chief, the amount of administration and the frequent committees he was required to chair had appalled him. His own job as Head of Homicide was either frantic when there was a murder, or slow-paced when there was not; but he'd never realised the constant burden that must have been on the shoulders of the uncomplaining Amrén. Fortunately the Sundsvall region was passing through a relatively peaceful phase at the moment, and he was just about managing to do both jobs.

Bräcke was so small he had no difficulty in spotting Lena's near the railway station. Lena herself was a youngish woman with a belief in healthy food. Despite the snow and freezing wind a salad bar dominated the room, and there were a large number of different yoghurts stacked on the counter. But there was also a hot pot of coffee from which he could help himself as often as he liked, and he took a blueberry and oat bar as well to please Lena. Pia joined him a few minutes later and ordered a plate of hot dogs and chips, with a low-alcohol beer.

"After you'd left the crime scene we found a blue Volvo" Pia told him. "It had Uppsala plates and it was parked up a little sidetrack leading to a derelict farmhouse."

"On the left as you drive south, just after the first turn-off to Utanede?"

"That's right. You know it?"

"I grew up near there. I think I know almost every centimetre of the area."

"Then you won't have any difficulty following what we discovered. There were clear tracks leading from the car to the crime scene, but of one person only. The dead man was a doctor, Näslund by name, and it didn't take us long to establish that the car was his. Since there was no sign of any other participants, it began to look more like suicide than murder, and it still does."

"It seems pretty extreme, hanging yourself in order to point the finger at Amrén. I can't see any normal person doing it. Maybe he was round the twist?"

"The same thought occurred to us, but the whole thing was meticulously planned. He must have known in advance there was a tree leaning over the chasm, which indicates he'd scouted the terrain beforehand. He'd also worked out that, after attaching the rope to the trunk, he'd need to throw it over a higher branch so that when the noose was round his neck and he launched himself into space, his weight would bend the tree even more. That way he'd be further out towards the centre of the road and more certain to be seen."

"He doesn't seem too mad, then, but how else do you explain it?"

"The autopsy explained it for us. It showed he was in the final stages of incurable pancreatic cancer. So he was dying anyway, and he'd also swallowed a lethal dose of pain-killers before hanging himself. From the look of the marks around the top of the rock, he set everything up, put the noose round his neck, attached the placard, and then lay on the side until the very last moment before pushing himself off. He was probably unconscious almost immediately, but the cold is likely to have killed him before the pills or the noose."

"And maybe he died happy knowing that he'd used his last moments to stage a bizarre revenge. He must have really hated Amrén to try to ruin him in such a dramatic way. If Izidor hadn't found him so early, the media would have had a field day right then."

"They still will have, I'm afraid. It's only been delayed."

Magnus, who'd been just about to get up to replenish his coffee cup, stayed where he was and looked at her questioningly.

"As soon as we identified the body I tried to contact the next of kin, and there didn't seem to be any. But there was a note in his wallet, giving details of an Uppsala lawyer who should be informed in the event of his death. So I did that, and he rang me before I'd even had time to issue the briefest press release."

"Looks as though it was even better planned than you'd thought."

"I think you're right. It seems Dr. Näslund, a widower, had been building up a dossier of evidence against your chief over many years, beginning just before the death of his only child, a daughter. The lawyer, Bredenberg, wasn't giving much away, but I felt that at this early stage, he was really just warning me."

"What about?"

"Something he felt I needed to know before I put out a press statement, which was actually very considerate of him. On his dead client's instructions he will be placing evidence before the Uppsala prosecutor that will almost certainly lead to charges being brought against Amrén."

“What sort of charges?”

“He wouldn’t go further than that they were serious charges. But, in addition to a sworn witness affidavit from a neighbour, Ingalill Sjöman, he claims to have a signed statement from Lilly Nyström, the deceased married daughter. So I think we can assume she is the key to whatever it’s all about.”

“Do you know anything about her?”

“Oddly enough, I do, and it may explain why the father came all the way up north to Jämtland to kill himself and so have an investigation by the local police. Twenty-eight years ago, when Amrén was just starting his police career, he was with the Jämtland force, based in Östersund. At exactly the same period Lilly was living nearby.”

Magnus groaned. “You’ve obviously been very busy,” he said warily, “but it’s not so good for Amrén. Did you find out whether they were involved together?”

“Our police records are pretty coy about anything like that, but there is one link. Lilly’s husband Olle was under suspicion for a series of burglaries, and Amrén was the investigating officer. But there was an accident when they were trying to arrest him, and Olle died under the wheels of a police car.”

“Then I’m sure there must have been an enquiry.”

“There was, and no officer was blamed, neither the driver, nor Amrén who was in charge.”

“So he’s in the clear? Nothing can be made of an ancient case like that.”

Pia shook her head. “I don’t think that’s what it’s about; though I’m sure the placard accusation that Amrén was a double killer refers not only to Olle, but to Olle’s wife Lilly as well. The census records show that shortly after his death she went back to live with her father, and she was still living with him when she died.”

“Do we know what she died of?”

“It was recorded as accidental death, the accident being mistakenly taking too many anti-depressants. But considering her father was a doctor I would guess this was a generous medical cover-up for suicide."

Magnus needed more coffee and a moment to think, so he got up and filled his cup. He was increasingly impressed with Pia. She seemed to have no bias against Amrén, and she was certainly shrewd.

"What do you think this is all about?" he asked her frankly as he sat down again.

She replied without hesitation. "I think it's something sexual. Twenty-eight years is so long ago, yet the lawyer seemed to have no doubt the press will be extremely interested. A scandal that old only gets newspapers jumping when there's sex involved. Does that fit the Amrén you know?"

Magnus laughed. "Not in the slightest. I've never seen him take much interest in women, and he certainly wasn't interested in men."

"Did he ever mention an early love-affair?"

Magnus studied her expression, but it was inscrutable. "He didn't talk much about himself, and he usually shied away from discussing emotions, but he did once tell me he'd fallen desperately in love when he was young, and though she'd rejected him he'd never been able to forget her, and that was why he'd never married." He paused, and then he added, "If only he had, he could have been as happy as I've been with Sonja, and he might have been spared sexual accusations like this which are so easy for people to make especially if they're not in a proper and satisfying relationship themselves."

Pia started, and for the first time he could remember she looked him full in the face, but it was a far from pleasant look. "Is that a hit at me?" she asked bleakly.

Magnus stared at her in blank astonishment. "I don't understand" he said, shaking his head in perplexity.

"I think you understand very well. From the beginning I've felt there's some sort of barrier between us. I always knew you'd have heard things about me, but I never expected you to throw it in my face like that. Is it really such a problem for you that I share my life with a woman?"

Magnus was appalled she should think such a thing, and instinctively he reached out and grasped her wrist. "Pia, I knew nothing at all about it. I never seem to hear gossip and that may be because I'm not the slightest bit interested in it. But what you've told me makes no difference whatsoever. Sexual orientation isn't meant to be an issue in the police, and it certainly isn't with me. Oh shit, this is awful! Please, please, tell me I haven't got a reputation as a bigot. That really would upset me."

Pia shook her head, smiling at his concern. "No, but you've got a terrible reputation as the most happily married family man in the police force, and I suppose that made me especially sensitive. Married bliss, the sort you have, can be very awkward for people like me, especially as I *was* once married, to a man, and it was an utter disaster. As for the official policy of the police, the reality among my colleagues is far less understanding, especially as my husband was a policeman too. I suppose it's all made me very touchy. Didn't you notice I was a little ill at ease with you?"

Magnus nodded. "I thought you were disturbed by my colour," he confessed rather sheepishly.

Pia sighed. "There you go, then. We're just two people with chips on our shoulders, and both wrong, because I'm happy with almost all colours except green. My husband used to punch me sometimes, and when the bruises changed from blue to green it used to turn him on. But you'll be relieved to know I'm happy enough with brown." She patted the dusky hand that was still holding her wrist and they both laughed with relief.

"It was a stupid, generalised and tactless remark to make in any circumstances, and I apologise," Magnus said. "The truth is that I'm ridiculously over-protective of Amrén, and I keep looking for explanations for his apparently self-imposed loneliness. Because I've been so lucky with my marriage I keep harping on the fact that he's missed out on that. If you knew him, you might more easily understand, because there's something about him that makes you feel he doesn't quite live in the real world, and so one must try to help him towards a more interesting social life. If it's any comfort to you, my attitude to him drives Sonja mad as well."

"Is all that another way of saying that he doesn't find human relationships easy?"

"I don't think he goes in for human relationships much at all. He's an extremely private man."

"Maybe he just finds them so difficult that he avoids them. Now we're being honest with each other, you'd better know I'm not finding it easy living with a woman either, so I do understand any difficulties your chief may have had with relationships. They're full of pitfalls, especially for the police. You're just the infuriating exception that proves the rule."

"My marriage only works so well because Sonja somehow manages to put up with me, my moods, my late hours, my obsession with my work and, as we're talking about it, my obsession with Amrén's happiness. I'm very conscious that many women wouldn't stand for it. Why did you ask me about any early love affair Amrén might have had?

"The records of the police investigation into Olle's death were too clean. We both know the police always look after their own, and that's how this one read. So I talked to a man I know, who was with the force at that time, though he's retired now. He seemed to remember there was some cover-up over an address, and I think it's likely Amrén didn't live in Östersund, as the record showed, but probably in the village where Olle and Lilly lived. It would explain why he was always on the spot when he needed to follow Olle, and how he knew the area so well."

"You think he fell in love with Lilly?"

"It's the only explanation for the cover-up. If that had come out, it would have been a clear reason for Amrén arranging Olle's death."

"He may just have had an affair with her."

"It's possible, yes, though the other explanation fits what he told you about his first love. It also suggests why Olle's death could have been the reason why she would have nothing more to do with him."

"It might also explain why, when she went back to her father, she signed a statement accusing Amrén. She may have believed he killed Olle deliberately, so he could have her."

Pia looked at him doubtfully. "Is he the sort of man capable of arranging a killing?

"No," said Magnus unhesitatingly. "But I don't see why he's done a runner if it was just an accusation he could so easily refute."

"Is that what you think he has done?"

"Officially I'm denying it for all I'm worth, but, deep down, yes, I fear he's bolted."

"Then I think we've got as far as we can go today." She got up, loaded her tray and put it in the rack. "You'll soon know more. The lawyer questioned me about you, and he wants to meet you. He asked me to tell you he'll be in touch. His full name's Mikael Bredenberg."

When Magnus got back to his office, there was a message waiting for him. The Chairman of the Commissioners of Police, Jörgen Bergqvist, needed to speak to him urgently. He rang him, and he was put through immediately.

"I understand you're in charge in Amrén's absence?" The abrupt voice raised his hackles to such an extent that he had to get a firm grip on himself.

"I am, but it's only temporary. He'll be back soon."

"I'm not a fool, and I hope you're not. He's running, caught a plane to Poland, booked his return flight a day later, and never showed. He's a professional, one of us, and, if he doesn't want to leave a trail, he won't. Has he been in touch with you?"

"No, not since he sent me a text saying he was taking a few days holiday that was owing to him."

"Did you know he'd gone to Poland?"

"No."

"Do you know who he might have gone to see in Poland?"

"He's my chief. I don't know much about the people he knows."

"I'd heard you two were closer than the two sides of a clam shell; that he latched onto you when your first case took you into Sundsvall, offered you a temporary post working for him out on The High Coast, recommended you for promotion to Inspector and then took you on immediately as his Head of Homicide. That's what I'd heard, and on the basis of that I'm guessing he went to see a retired Polish policeman, Inspector Jurek Bojanowski. Since you went to Poland and worked with exactly the same man on the Savchenko case, I do hope you're not playing silly buggers with me."

"I still think he'll be back soon."

"And you know nothing about an Uppsala doctor who hanged himself from a tree leaning over a Jämtland road? The placard round his neck accused your chief of a double killing?"

"Inspector Widmark is keeping me up to date with any developments."

Jörgen suddenly chuckled.

"I'll bet she is, because I happen to know you were up there before she was, even though it's not your patch any longer, and that you wanted her to keep it from the press. For Christ's sake, Trygg, stop stonewalling me. We're on the same side and I'm sure we want the same outcome - to avoid any scandal. Have you talked with this lawyer chap who seems to have the goods on Amrén?"

"I haven't, and I don't believe for a moment it can be anything substantial."

There was a pause, and, when Jörgen spoke again, his voice was more sympathetic. "I admire your loyalty, Trygg, but don't go down with a sinking ship. Before the good doctor topped himself, he went to talk to Amrén at the conference, just after he'd finished his fan dance thing. I assume you didn't know that?"

Magnus felt his faith in Amrén waver. "I didn't, and I have to say I think I should have been informed about that immediately."

Jörgen whistled, nearly damaging his eardrum. "That's really a case of the pot calling the kettle black. You've told me nothing at all, and I'm the one who made contact with you, you're just ringing me back. If you had any choice in the matter, I have no doubt you'd try to do everything yourself and be answerable to nobody. But that's not the way the cards have fallen. Amrén disappeared in Uppsala, and the commissioner there, understanding what was at stake, asked me and my Stockholm force to handle that part of the case. The doctor decided to end his life in Jämtland, so the force there is working on that strand. You've only got a peripheral interest because Amrén was your chief. You may have taken over that post for the time being, but I've been instructed to take his place as acting commissioner for the area. So don't you get high and mighty with me, because I've got a legal right to instruct you what to do. On the other hand, you seem to be the only person who knew him well, and that could give you a central role. So do you want to listen to what I'm going to propose, and stop being so bloody prickly, or do you want to be left on the outside?"

Magnus thought about the valuable information Jörgen had already given him, and reacted in an appropriate way.

"You're entirely right, Sir, and I apologise. Amrén is held in very high regard here, and his disappearance has made us all jumpy, though that's no excuse for me as senior officer. I'll behave myself from now on."

Jörgen snorted. "I trust you even less when you pretend to crawl than when you bite. But we're going to have to work together, so it's best we don't get off on the wrong foot. I assume you saw the coverage of the conference, and the press ballyhoo about Amrén being tipped for higher things?"

The question sounded an alarm bell in his head, a vague memory of someone very different saying something very similar, but he couldn't get a grip on it.

"I did see it, yes, but I don't take much notice of media predictions. In my experience, they're usually wrong."

"This time they got it right. I spoke to Amrén myself, before the press conference, told him our plans for him, and asked him very particularly if there were any skeletons in his cupboard. He said there weren't, conveniently forgetting an enquiry into the death of a suspect."

"He's a scrupulously honest man, so I'm sure he'd forgotten events in his first year as a policeman, which is hardly surprising considering how long ago it was. But now you tell me this doctor came to see him, and that visit may have brought it all back to him. It would certainly explain why he might have needed time to consider his position. He's so correct and upright he may decide that even being the exonerated subject of a police enquiry twenty-eight years ago debars him from further promotion, and he'll withdraw. It would be just like him."

"It'll be too late. He's been in the public eye, and a withdrawal alone would have the press digging into everything. But with a dead man hanging over a road, an accusatory placard about two deaths, and the man himself vanished, there'll be a media frenzy, and it won't do the police any good at all. So we've got to act fast."

"Amrén will be back, or at the very least he'll be in touch. Until then we don't really know what we're dealing with."

Jörgen sighed. "We know enough. I had an unofficial word with this lawyer, and luckily he's not a fool. He has to follow his client's instructions, but he understands it wouldn't help society if the police as a whole were caught up in one man's disgrace. And before you start defending your friend again, you'd better know that there's the additional scent of a sex scandal now; and once it gets out it'll have editors salivating all over their front pages. It seems the documents the lawyer has now opened after the death of his client, consist of a statement from a woman who lived in the Östersund area in the late 1970's, making a serious charge of a sexual nature against a police officer, Ragnar Amrén; and a witness statement from a telescope wielding neighbour corroborating the charge and affirming that Amrén lived close to the complainant, not in Östersund as their police records purport to show."

Magnus was shaken and reacted unguardedly. "In the press conference he was asked about officers using their position of authority to obtain sexual favours. They must have been setting him up even then."

"Exactly, and he gave a good answer which will come back to haunt him. But the worst aspect of it is that an *Expressen* journalist, Ryd, the one who asked that question, knows a hell of a lot more about this than we do, presumably tipped off by the good doctor. So if we're going to contain it we'll have to act very swiftly indeed. The lawyer has agreed not to move at a faster pace than usual, which for lawyers is always like a constipated snail, so at least we've bought some time."

"If it ever comes to trial, Amrén will be acquitted, I'm certain of it."

"It mustn't come to trial. Innocent or not, the damage will have been done by then. Amrén has to face the fact, and you do too, that his career is finished whatever he does. But as long as he remains a senior officer who's disappeared, and can't be found, we, the police service, have a chance to play it down. There'll be a whiff of scandal, of course, but it's all so long ago that without the two main accusers, the doctor and his daughter, and without the accused, the story will almost certainly be a short-term wonder. But there's only one person who can make this work, and that's you. You know him, and he trusts you. So I want you to put somebody else in as temporary chief of police in Sundsvall, and you spend all your time and energy finding Amrén."

Magnus felt his stomach muscles tense with anticipation, but he remained cautious. "What makes you think I can succeed if none of your people have?"

"I've talked to people about you, Trygg, and you'd be surprised what I know. First and foremost, nobody, nobody at all, knows him as well as you do, and that gives you an edge. I happen to know, too, that you're a fine policeman, dogged, shrewd and able to think outside the loop. As for Amrén himself, he's a loose cannon now. He may come back at any moment, or issue a statement, or confess and throw himself on the mercy of the courts. So you have to be the first to find him, explain the facts of life to him and make bloody sure he co-operates. He has to stay invisible, and that's where another quality of yours will come in handy. I hear from everyone, and it's been apparent throughout this phone call, that you're tough and nobody bullshits you."

"However tough I may be, I still haven't got the power to authorise the extra salary for whoever takes my place."

"I have, and it's already agreed by my committee. A letter will reach you tomorrow. This is an emergency, and I have an emergency fund."

Magnus knew he must live up to the reputation he'd been saddled with, and so he didn't hesitate. "I'll do my best to find him, though it won't be easy. He's a very private man, he doesn't confide in anybody, and that includes me. If I find him, I'll try to talk to him. But you have to understand he may just listen, then not respond. He's his own man, something of a loner, and he takes his own decisions. So he may just go his own way regardless of anything I say to him. All I can do is try."

"That's not quite all you can do, Trygg. You can persuade him to act in his best interests."

"Which means the best interests of the police?"

"It means both. But since policing has been Amrén's whole life, and in his own way he's an honourable man, I like to believe he won't want to harm the service."

"You're convinced he's guilty?"

"It points that way, and by running he's made it seem certain. But guilty or not, it's still my job to protect the reputation of the police. It's the same with any major corporation or with the government. Once someone's reached the stage of potentially harming the firm, then it no longer matters whether he's truly guilty, you just can't support him. The decision between possibly damaging one man or certainly damaging the whole organisation is not a difficult one to take."

"I seem to recall Ryd is particularly gunning for you, and you won't come out of this very well. Doesn't it worry you that it might look as though you were especially protecting yourself?"

Jörgen chuckled. "You don't mind what you say, do you, Trygg? But you're wrong there. We'll look like a set of incompetent idiots as soon as the facts leak out, but I retire soon anyway, and I haven't got much reputation left to lose. But I am defending the police, and oddly enough I think I'm defending Amrén too. I hope I got to know him well enough to understand what he'd go through if he's thrown to the lions. Do you really believe such a sensitive man will be able to stand up to the glare of publicity in a public trial? And how do you think he'd cope in prison, a senior policeman with a sex conviction round his neck? It takes a special sort of thick-skinned toughness to survive in circumstances like that, and I don't think he's got it. What's more, I don't think you believe he has either."

"You think he should do the decent thing?"

"Since you ask, yes, I do, but then I'm old-fashioned. But even if we put that aside for a moment, I do think that sooner or later he'll need to talk to somebody, and that somebody will be you; and when you've heard it all I know I can rely on you to give him the right advice."

"And if he doesn't take it?"

"Whatever the truth of the charge, the doctor has set this up in such a way that Amrén is done for. Has he got so much else in his life that he can handle that?"

No, thought Magnus. No family, few close friends, he'd never cope with the trial and the media, and even less could he survive prison life. I'm being told a sick dog needs to be put down.

He hardened himself against any emotion in his voice. "You haven't answered my question. What if he doesn't take my advice?"

"You know the answer already, Trygg. He's probably armed, and he may very well turn against you if he doesn't like what you tell him to do. Normally I'd be very concerned about any man I sent into such a situation, but I happen to know something else about you. You're a crack shot. That's why I'm ordering you, in my capacity as your acting county commissioner, to be armed when you meet him and take whatever appropriate action is necessary."

With that, the line went dead.

CHAPTER 13

The train crossed from Poland into Lithuania, drawing closer to Vilnius where he would have to stay the night. Ragnar, momentarily roused from his semi-comatose state, realised he'd been obsessively studying his skin to see if it was visibly thinner than other skins he furtively peered at in the carriage.

He was not entirely sure what was wrong with him, but it was overwhelming, depriving him of physical strength and any ability at all to face the present. He shuddered at the very thought of meeting anybody he knew, or anyone who knew him. He supposed it must be a type of depression, brought on by guilt. But it was grief, too, a terrible debilitating grief. The knowledge that Lilly was dead, given to him in such a cruelly casual fashion by her father, had destroyed the basis of his life. He'd lived in the belief that one day she would return to him, forgive him, stay with him, and then, finally, he could have a proper life. He'd dreamed they might even meet by chance. Every day he'd felt her watching him, thinking about him, weighing up what he had done to her, gradually coming to terms with it, pardoning it and, above all, discerning the love for her that had always been within him. That scenario, that intense faith that sooner or later she would seek him out, had governed his life, coloured his life, given purpose to his life, provided him with hope. The shock of the discovery that all that time she had been dead, and that she'd killed herself, had, almost literally, blown him apart. With that knowledge there was no possibility of ever putting himself properly together again.

He snuggled into the fuggy atmosphere of the train, anonymous, lulled by the motion of the carriage and soothed by the companionable conversations around him in languages which did not intrude because he couldn't understand them. In his mind he lived entirely in the past, filling himself with all those memories of Lilly that sustained him, carefully skirting what might trigger the guilt he'd always carried within him. Early on, he'd delicately pruned his memory, disposing of the clippings in a rather special way. He'd heard a psychiatrist talking on the radio about the box method of keeping destructive memories at bay until you were strong enough to deal with them; and, realising this was the only way he could get on with his life, he followed his advice. He took an old brass snuff box, opened it, threw the worst of his guilt into it and quickly shut the lid. Each time such a recollection tried to surface he thought of the closed tin, saw it before him in all its detail, the Royal Arms of Gustav V engraved on the top, the poem extolling snuff on the underside, the strong hinges, the tight-fitting lid. Firmly he would tell himself the moment to open the lid had not arrived and the haunting scene within would be banished yet again.

Now, thinking so constantly about the past, this was becoming increasingly difficult and soon it would be impossible. But he had set himself a moment. When he reached his final sanctuary, ever creeping closer, he would raise the lid.

By the time he reached Vilnius, once a renowned university city within the ancient borders of Poland, he was at the point of collapse, an all-enveloping lethargy invading him. He could hardly manage his suitcase despite the wheels and extension handle, and, seeing a building-site skip, he threw into it the feather fans, the blue silk costume and the box of theatrical make-up. It seemed to lighten the case, if only because he was shedding a portion of his past. He took a room at a cheap hotel and collapsed on the bed, a desperate sickness of the soul prowling through him.

But he knew that if he was to survive, to finish his journey, he must walk and eat. He forced himself to get up, splash cold water on his face and go out. He wandered in the Old Town, finally eating in a bar which beckoned him because it was called the Gates of Dawn, which it overlooked. The last surviving portal through the original city wall was a shrine now, containing a revered miracle-working icon of the Virgin and he wanted to be close to it so that a little of its potency might spill into his soul. So, as he forced down the food he had ordered, he sent his desperate petition out across the short space to the icon, begging the Virgin to keep him safe that night.

As he left the bar he caught sight of himself in a mirror, stopping in surprise and scarcely recognising the stranger who looked back at him. His face had sagged; he looked gaunt and unkempt, seeming to have become the worthy owner of such a worn and faded passport. Behind him, in the mirror, a man reading a newspaper looked up and stared directly at him. He kept his eyes down as he turned, not daring to meet his gaze in case he saw some recognition in his eyes, some dawning knowledge of who he was and what he'd done. He did not believe a photo of him would have been circulated to the papers, not yet at least, but the man might know him and even if he didn't he felt the terror that other people might be able to see the guilt and shame in his own eyes. He slunk out and hurried to his hotel, where he only managed to sleep in snatches.

The next day a train took him on towards Latvia. He'd been so utterly exhausted in the morning he'd found it hard to move at all. He'd had to revert to childhood, playing cars around his bedroom, only able to move forward when he put the lever of his imaginary vehicle into first gear, making the grumbling engine noise himself, then changing up until the engine snarled, settled to a purr, and finally he was moving freely.

As soon as the train was in motion he fell into the same trance-like state as the day before, where the past was more real than the present. But this time he got beyond the need to recall the past; he needed, now, to understand it. Only then, once the last piece of the deliberately fractured puzzle fell into place, would he know for certain what the solution to all this had to be.

Understanding of one issue came quickly, without equivocation. He'd loved Lilly, had always loved her, and he still loved her. Whatever had happened between them, whatever its consequences, he could hold on to the fact of love. She'd been the love of his life, his only love, for he had never succeeded in replacing her. He had loved her from that first moment he'd seen her asleep among the trees; and despite everything he'd made her suffer later, despite the fact he'd driven her to her death but had not known it, the sole aim of his life thereafter had been to make himself worthy of her once again, to make her proud of him, so that one day, even in old age, they could be re-united.

It was the only good side of his new knowledge. The rest was guilt and shame and cowardice, the special thinness of his skin which seemed peculiar to him alone. He deliberately opened his ears to the tyres and the sodden thud on the road beside the Indal River, and after all these years he shuddered and clasped his head in his hands, trying to shut it out. Then he allowed himself to hear the stinging scorn in Inspector Stenberg's angry voice, and to experience again the shredding of his innate modesty by the brutally crude exposé of what he'd done with Lilly. The recollection, so clear that he could hear Stenberg's scathing tone and feel the spittle spraying his face, forced him to confront the underlying implications. His treasured secret life with Lilly had been no secret at all, but the basis of casual gossip and crude innuendo. Even Olle, it seemed, might have known what he was doing, possibly preparing to have him in his power; and though the interval was so many years, he still cringed now in humiliation.

Jurek had a thick skin; he did not notice pinpricks and so he always had the confidence to face a critic and defend himself with unhesitating vigour. But it was also why Jurek could not help him, why nobody could, except himself. What he had experienced with Lilly, so briefly, was too precious to be exposed to others who could not understand his vulnerability. One wrong word from them, however sensible, might destroy what he must now protect at all costs, hugging it to him, jealously guarding it: the love he and Lilly had shared, if only for a time. Without that he was nothing, and so he must withhold the very details necessary to explain his actions. It was why his love could never be exposed in court or internal police enquiry, for it would leak out to the press who were the modern Furies. They would belittle it, without understanding it or caring that they did not understand; and they would transform it into filth. Even Magnus, the one man with whom he felt at ease, the one man he trusted absolutely, the one man he had to meet before it was all over, even to him it would be difficult to tell the whole of it, though somehow he would manage it.

He was jolted into reality as the train which, unnoticed by him, had crossed the Latvian border, now pulled into Riga. An icy wind was blowing from the sea and his smart coat was powerless to keep the cold out. He wandered into an evening Christmas market and bought himself a paper cup of hot, spicy *glögg.* He downed the whole lot before it could cool, feeling the heat and the alcohol speed up his blood and increase his confidence. On the fringes of the market he found the everyday stalls, and one sold second-hand clothing. There he was able to part-exchange his coat for a salt-stained seaman's reefer jacket and a jaunty naval cap. Then he opened his case and handed over his expensive spare suit, and more money, in return for a pair of old ski trousers, a jacket, thick socks, gloves and a ski cap. Finally his expensive handmade shoes became a battered pair of snow boots.

The stall-owner pointed out a nearby bar beside a rooming house, and as soon as he'd swallowed a plate of steaming seafood, washed down with several beers, he went to bed and thought of the different levels of truth in his life. There was the official story he'd told to Jurek, true as far as it went, but leaving out much that was not to his advantage. There was the underlying story he told himself, which ended with the death of Olle, and Lilly leaving the area, with no word where she'd gone.

But below these there was another truth, one he didn't like to tell himself. As the years had passed, and a forgiving, loving Lily did not materialise, he could, at that stage, have searched for her. He was stronger by then, more in command of himself, and he should have done it. But gradually he had become accustomed to his life without her, though he still longed for the moment, distant perhaps, when they would be reunited. The fact that he had loved once, and, for a time his love had been returned, had become the bower anchor of his life, a glowing memory, an acceptance that it was a once and forever love. There was always the hope she would return, which was his kedge, and the two anchors together secured his life, however fierce the storms. If he were to search and, by some miracle, to find her now, after so long, an unforgiving confrontation might destroy even what he had, the memory of love, a future hope, the life he'd painstakingly constructed. So he had never dared to risk it, and using the fact that he did not know where she had run to because she hadn't told him, he never sought her out. Telling himself that any contact initiated by him would only make matters worse, and secretly and shamefully clinging to the belief she would be lonely and so desperate that one day she *would* forgive him and find she could love him after all, he conveniently left to Lilly the task of making contact if she ever wanted to see him again.

When he woke next morning he could not remember falling asleep, could not even be certain he had slept. He opened the window, stared out over the choppy Gulf, breathing the brackish tang of the air and hearing the shrill cries of the gulls. He glanced at his watch, realised he had little time and just caught his train to Estonia.

It was, he imagined, like going into regular therapy where, once you were used to the routine, you could commence the session almost instantly. By the time the train started, he was hunched in his corner and an interior review had begun. This time his mind considered what Lilly's father had revealed, that she had gone home to him. Though he'd carried this knowledge with him for several days, it was only now he began to think about the implications. At the time he'd assumed she'd simply punished him by her departure. Now, after all these years, he faced the likely cost to Lilly of being driven to return to her father. She'd told him enough about his overpowering protectiveness to understand why she had married a man she did not love just to get away from him. Now he had actually met the father he could imagine with frightening clarity how living under his care might eventually make life unendurable. Was that really why she'd taken her own life?

It was so tempting to believe it was nothing more than that, for then he could shift the blame onto the father. But he could not do it. It was he who'd caused Olle's death, he who'd then abandoned Lilly, and so, though he hadn't known it, he was the one who'd forced her back to her father. He thought about the desperation that must have driven her to the medicine cabinet, and he seemed to bleed inside. Inspector Stenberg had ordered him to leave Västerede, but, and he did not deny it any longer, he would have deserted Lilly anyway, at least until the dust storm he had raised had blown itself out.

That desertion was such a cowardly act that as the years passed he tried to blot it out by risking his life to save others. It was not just to prove his courage to himself, but also because the contempt he often felt for himself made him long at times to die a hero, atonement for the wrong he'd done to Lilly. Physical courage, he found, was so easy, especially in those circumstances. But moral courage, to admit his faults, to throw himself upon the mercy of someone else and have to listen to the lacerating truths that would rightly be cast in his face, that was a form of bravery he did not have. So in the end, though he'd risked death, Lilly had been the one who'd died.

He was only too aware that his whole adult life was being torn into strips and he was doing the shredding. Lilly's father had let loose the Furies, but even he wouldn't have guessed the Furies would be the victim himself, feasting on his own flesh. Now, once again, he was doing exactly as he had in

Näverede, acting in a precipitate fashion that prevented any possibility of rescue. By disappearing, running, he was making sure there was no way back. It was an admission of guilt, without the need to make it.

By the time he reached Tallinn he was very weak. He could not even recall leaving the train and station, or finding somewhere to sleep. He woke in the morning, staring bewilderedly round the strange room; but as he drank a coffee and chewed a piece of dark bread spread with slices of tomato, cucumber and cheese, he knew a decision had been reached. He would not be going back to face whatever charges Lilly's father might choose to bring against him. In the midst of all the searching of his soul he'd passed judgement on himself.

That evening, having crossed the narrow sea to Helsinki, he followed the pattern of the previous days and climbed aboard a train. He was heading north, through Finland.

CHAPTER 14

Magnus, who was normally afraid of nothing, sat in his car staring at Amrén's house, but he could not bring himself to get out and walk towards it. It was on a rise at the end of a *cul-de-sac*, overlooking a wintry Baltic and with a side view of the Njurunda church spire pointing the way to heaven like a giant altar candle. It gave the house an air of chastity which might be sullied if he entered it uninvited. Despite the fact that it was Ragnar himself who had given him the key 'in case of emergency', the distaste he felt at the prospect of invading his privacy was very powerful. His closeness to him, the respect he had for him and the consciousness that he owed most of his successful career to him, made it almost impossible for him to rummage through his personal and possibly secret life.

In desperation he checked his watch, but Sonja would not be back from the Day Nursery for another two hours. With her beside him he would have felt a little more at ease, a little less dirtied by what he had to do.

After Jörgen's call, he had sat and thought for many minutes, sorting out the implications and deciding what was for the best. Then he'd rung Lennart Havendal and made him a very happy man. Lennart had been a Detective-Inspector in the force when he'd first joined it, a decent and competent policeman broken by his wife's death, and a subsequent series of failed cases. Amrén had given him a last chance with what later became known as the Midsummer Revenge Murders, and to everyone's surprise he'd not only caught the killer, but he'd then insisted on resigning over some minor mistakes. But Magnus knew that disappointed hopes had played a part as well. Lennart not only dreamt of succeeding Amrén, he'd also coveted, as a stepping stone, the post of Head of Homicide; and he must have seen it as a final humiliation when it went instead to a newcomer, Magnus himself. Now, at least, he'd been able to make amends by offering Lennart the consolation of finally becoming Sundsvall's Chief of Police, if only temporarily; and he'd seized it with the confidence of a man who'd found new happiness in his marriage to his colleague on his final case, Annica Sundin.

Lennart had made only one condition: that he brought with him Lars Svedlund, the officer blinded in one eye during the Midsummer Revenge case and who had been on sick leave ever since. Magnus, a friend since their days together in the Östersund force, agreed at once. Often wild in the past, Lars was now happily settled with Annette whom he'd met just before he'd been shot-blasted in the face; and Magnus was confident he would make a shrewd and efficient assistant to Lennart.

With that problem out of the way, Magnus felt able to turn his attention to the mystery of where Ragnar might be. He sought inspiration from a large scale map of Northern Europe, putting a marker in Zakopane and then trying to plot the various routes he might have taken. But it was an impossible task, for he could have gone across the mountains into Southern Europe, west to the United Kingdom or America, or east to Russia. The only direction that seemed out of the question was north back into Sweden; but he did not even rule that out, for Ragnar was perfectly capable of doing the unexpected. The one certainty was that he would only be found if he wanted to be found.

As he pondered that certainty, he realised the key Ragnar had given him was his only lead. If he did want Magnus to come to him, some clue would have been left in his house.

Sighing, still uncertain whether he was doing the right thing, Magnus let himself in and sank down in the nearest armchair, trying to absorb the atmosphere. It was quiet, soothing, small but comfortable, clean and tidy, and quite unlike his own home which was full of the scattered paraphernalia of his two children and his wife, to say nothing of his own. There would be the smell of Sonja's cooking, the sound of Angelica practising the piano, Johan's noisy footsteps as he rushed up and down the stairs and in and out of the front door, working off the tireless energy of an eight year old. This house was very different, and the word antiseptic slipped into his mind. He hoped he was not being unduly influenced by all Jörgen had said to him, for he'd formed the distinct impression he hadn't really liked Amrén. That was partly why he'd not told him that the lawyer, Bredenberg, wanted to see him. He'd also felt the pressing need to keep a few aces tucked away, for there seemed to be a conspiracy to isolate Amrén, to keep him guilty but out of sight and speechless; and now even he had agreed to join the hunters.

He comforted himself that this was not the usual search of a suspect's house, where anything at all might be important; for as far as the Sundsvall police were concerned Amrén was not suspected of any crime. This was something much more specific, to discover where he might have gone, and so he began the search where he was, looking around the living room from the armchair. He'd sat in the chair often before. Together they'd discussed cases here, policy decisions, internal aggravations, and in so many ways it had become an extension police office. Now he must look at it differently, as a *living* room, where Amrén spent his private life, where he recalled the past, considered the present, dreamed his unexpectedly ambitious dreams for his future. But even that was difficult, because it had also been a social room where he and Sonja sipped their drinks before moving to the dining room for the wonderfully tasty dinners Ragnar cooked for them. He hadn't thought about it before, but now he wondered whether they'd been the only couple ever to be invited, and perhaps he was the only officer to attend extension meetings in this private house. Did Amrén trust them both in some special way, or were they really his only friends?

He remembered how suspicious Sonja was of him at first, and her simmering jealousy of Amrén's influence over him. It had begun when he persuaded Magnus to leave the Jämtland force and join him in Sundsvall, a decision he'd taken without consulting Sonja. It caused their first major quarrel, almost deep enough to split them apart, and she had never entirely forgiven Ragnar for it. But after the move from the country to the town proved unexpectedly successful, her deeper anger was replaced by a series of smaller irritations, largely revolving around her husband's apparent inability to say no to Ragnar whenever he needed him to stay late, sacrifice time-off or take on extra responsibilities.

"He's not married, for God's sake," she would say in exasperation, "he's never been married, he doesn't understand that your family needs you too. Why should he be more important than Johan, Angelica or even me? They need a father, I need a husband, but that man only seems to need you."

She never actually said she thought he might be gay, and that his need for Magnus might not be entirely a police matter; but he sensed it, and Ragnar, whose emotional antennae were finely tuned, must have divined something too. He asked them both to dinner, showed a genuine interest in Sonja and the children, and gave her every opportunity to get to know him. It was a turning point, confirmed when Sonja unexpectedly suggested he should come for a meal and crowned when she even asked him to spend Christmas Eve with them.

"It's the loneliest time of the year for someone without family," she explained to Magnus, who treasured his time with them all on such an important day and, in his turn, was not happy about the suggestion. But he went along with it, suspecting it was not just compassion, but a wish to imprint herself upon him as a woman with a family, to reveal what for Ragnar was probably an entirely alien way of life and if necessary rub his nose in it. But he'd been relaxed and amusing, he'd given shrewdly chosen small gifts, and Angelica and Johan were entirely at ease with him. The next day, on their way to church, the children asleep on the backseat, Magnus was amused, though secretly relieved, when Sonja confessed she'd been entirely wrong about him.

"There's a sadness," she said, "a sort of block, but he's a woman's man, that's definite. Maybe he lost someone he loved, maybe he was badly hurt by a woman, and now he'll never commit himself. But the instincts are there all right. Poor, poor man."

From then on the two of them established the peculiar closeness that can exist between a wife and her husband's best friend, and it was the turn of Magnus to feel an occasional jealous twinge.

He brought his thoughts back to the room. There were no personal photographs on display; and although he found a camera in one of the desk drawers he could not discover any photo albums. He was careful to avoid the phone in case it had been tapped already, and the phone bills, which he found correctly filed under 'Bills – phone', revealed nothing out of the very ordinary. The other files were equally bland. The one marked 'Property' contained only items referring to the house he was in, and the tax returns gave no indication he owned another. There was no personal correspondence, and it did not worry him too much that he did not know the password that would let him read his emails. Ragnar's intense distrust of computers and their lack of security was a source of amusement within the police station. Eventually he might have to bring in a technician, just so that he covered every area, but at this stage he certainly wasn't going to give any such public indication that his chief was under suspicion.

As he remembered from earlier visits, the four pictures on the living room walls were very different from the amateur but gently reassuring local country landscapes so typical of most Swedish homes, including his own. Here, they were all still-life, small oils in gilded frames, old and, to Magnus, very dull. One showed fruit against a dark background, with a wasp settling on the apple which had begun to rot; the others were close-ups of vegetables, then flowers and finally a loaf of bread beside a slice of meat. None provided a clue as to his whereabouts. The books were not typical either, but they were equally unhelpful. They confirmed the intellectual side of Ragnar's life that he'd suspected but most others were probably unaware of. He'd once admitted to Magnus an interest in poetry, and here on the shelves were volumes of Swedish verse ranging from Bellmann to Tomas Tranströmer, and anthologies from many countries. There was an English one which opened at Coleridge's 'Kubla Khan', instantly taking his mind back to the first time he'd worked with Amrén and the poetic clue that had enabled him to find the hidden body near the memorial to King Chulalongkorn. Another, 'Evening Brings Everything Back' by the Estonian poet Jaan Kaplinski, had a marker in it, and, after staring at the page, Magnus hurried back to a desk drawer he'd already opened and realised that part of the pile of hand-written notes was an unfinished attempt to review those poems. The other notes were in English, so he went back to the shelves and found another marker by a late Karin Boye poem, the title translated in the notes as 'Never was the wood so joyful as now'. From the number of times Ragnar had made different attempts to render one particular line into English, he could only assume he was using translation in an attempt to reveal the underlying meaning. Despite this, his final and so, presumably, his best attempt, 'Inaccessible is the room where the day's crop gently ripens' still didn't mean much to Magnus.

There were only a few novels, all classics like Selma Lagerlöf's 'Gösta Berlings Saga'; a number of books about Swedish history; and one on comparative religion. But, apart from the poetry, the majority of the books were works by great thinkers, ranging from Confucius and Aristotle to Thoreau and Primo Levi. With his new knowledge, Magnus imagined the years Ragnar might have spent searching for a religion or a philosophy to help him carry the burden of the past, and he wondered whether he'd ever found it. Although there was a TV, he found no DVDs and no player; but there was a shelf of CDs filled with Sufi songs and poetry, Dervish dance and other forms of mysticism. On another shelf there were three fine antiques. The painted Russian icon of the Virgin and Child looked very old, the medieval pilgrim token depicted an Archbishop on horseback and it was only the walnut tea caddy that might contain something. When he opened it, however, there was only the faint aroma of English tea.

But there had been a dull clink when he'd moved the metal-bound caddy and tucked in behind it was an old brass snuff box. He picked it up and, feeling a momentary excitement, opened both compartments. But there was nothing inside at all. He even read the verse inscribed on the underside in case that contained a clue:

'Many a wise man takes a pinch-
It uplifts your mind, improves the memory.
This box contains a treasure
Which your nose will glory in.
Take a pinch when your conk freezes;
Snuff is good in so many ways!

He turned it over several times and even shook it, just in case it *did* contain a treasure; but in the end, as with everything else so far, he had to admit defeat.

Several hours later he'd still found nothing that could conceivably be a message. There was nothing hidden behind the pictures, and there were no loose floorboards. Everything was exactly where it should be, even to the extent that there were no books lying on his bedside table. Whatever he read in bed must have been returned to the bookshelves the next morning, for there were no gaps in the lines of volumes, or anything secreted behind them. The kitchen was the only extravagant room, with all the latest equipment, as though it was only there he could forget his painful memories, and that it was cooking that provided precious periods of freedom from his mental struggles. But he found nothing that provided any clue to where he might be now.

Despondently he gave up and went to brief Lennart. He'd only known him after he'd begun to fall to pieces, and so he was surprised and relieved by his quick grasp of detail, his relaxed confidence and, most surprising of all to him, his new authority. He had always admired Inspector Sundin's police work, but what she had done for Lennart as his wife was beyond praise.

He was home in time to help Angelica with some schoolwork, and spend a happy hour in the workshop with Johan who was trying to construct the oval-shaped toboggan he'd invented. After the evening meal, when the children had gone to their rooms - ostensibly to get ready for bed - he was able to do what he liked best at this time of the day, to sit in the kitchen with Sonja and discuss what they'd done that day. It was never a fair division of time, because Sonja would be brief and amusing about the Day Nursery, and then he would pour out the frustrations he never showed at work.

"I can't find anything to help me in Ragnar's house," he complained. "It's like searching a monk's cell, there's no sign of an outward life there."

"What else did you expect?" replied Sonja with a laugh. "Ragnar's not like you. He's a very private man, he doesn't like mess, and he tidies everything away."

"But I've got to find him, and I haven't got long before the media get hold of everything. But I couldn't discover a single clue to where he might be."

"Maybe it's best you don't find him," Sonja suggested soberly. "I don't like the implications of what you've been asked to do."

Magnus looked at her questioningly, because he had not been entirely frank with her, saying nothing about the order that he should be armed.

"How do you mean?"

"You know perfectly well what I mean. They don't care about Ragnar, they just want to avoid any scandal. And they want to avoid it at any cost. You've been told to find him, talk to him, explain his position as if he wasn't already desperately aware of it, and then make sure he's never seen again. We both know what Ragnar's like, his sensitivity, his dislike of publicity, his need for privacy. Wherever he is, he must be desperate, suffering like a wounded animal, and it's as if you're being despatched to put him out of his misery. I think you should have refused to take it on, because to all intents and purposes you're being asked to drive him to his death."

He stared at her in secret admiration. She always had the extraordinary ability to see the truth beyond the facts. He tried to explain it to her without revealing the crux of Jörgen's instruction. "I know that's how it seems, but surely it's better I go than anybody else. Ragnar needs someone to talk to, someone he can trust, or he may lose the will to live. I can't turn my back on him when everybody else has, and once I've heard what this lawyer has to say to me I won't be so much in the dark. But first of all I have to discover where Ragnar is."

"Wouldn't he have found a way to tell you where he is, if he really wanted to see you?" Sonja asked.

Magnus shook his head in perplexity. "That's the awful part of it. I think he has told me, has left some clue in the house and expects me to find it. But I can't, not so far, anyway."

Sonja glanced at her watch. "Do you want me to come over with you to the house? Two pairs of eyes may be better than one, and a woman's eyes always see more."

Magnus grinned. "You'll probably spot it straight away, which would be irritating in the extreme. But I need to move fast, so I'd be very, very grateful if you would come... What about the children?"

"I'll give Ingrid a ring, and she'll keep an eye on them. I saw her when I went out with the rubbish, so I know she's there."

While she rang, Magnus went up to the children and told them what was happening.

"Is Mum going to be a detective?" asked Johan solemnly.

"She'd be a jolly good one," Angelica added. "She can always find my socks, and she always knows when we've been naughty."

"You make sure you're on your best behaviour, both of you, OK? I don't want to hear that Ingrid had any trouble with you."

Angelica yawned. "You always say that, and we've never played Ingrid up."

Magnus kissed them both, wondering for the umpteenth time what he'd done to deserve such wonderful children.

Sonja looked round Ragnar's house with eager curiosity, moving from room to room, peering here, there and everywhere but touching nothing.

"I think I already know where to look," she announced, "but I want to get a real feel for the place before I say anything."

Magnus left her to it, knowing she was shrewd about people and quick to spot what he'd often not noticed. He returned to the books, and stared at them. He'd read none of the ones by great thinkers, and doubted if he ever would. He pulled out the Confucius, and it fell open at Book 13, where Amrén had written out Analect 13 on a slip of card. 'The Master said, "If a man manages to make himself correct, what difficulty will there be for him to take part in government? If he cannot make himself correct, what business has he with making others correct?"

Magnus could imagine Ragnar reading that, and then debating with himself whether he was really fit for promotion. If it ever happened to him, at such a high level, Magnus knew he would just accept the promotion, and then try to do the new job as well as he possibly could. He felt relieved he was not given to intellectual anguish, but it saddened him that Ragnar probably approached everything in his life with the same soul-searching. If he'd had a wife and children there would have been no time for it, and it might have made him a happier man.

"Stop reading books and pay attention to the great detective," said Sonja, coming into the room with a satisfied smile. He returned Confucius to his proper place on the shelf, and went to stand beside her.

"You say you've looked at everything, so I want to cross-examine you about the pictures on the walls, all over the house.

Magnus sighed with relief. "They're just what I hoped you'd go for. You're artistic, you paint so beautifully on wooden bowls and spoons, and I know almost nothing about art except what I like and don't like."

"What do you notice about the pictures, generally?"

"There are no people in them," he answered at once.

Sonja looked impressed. "That's very good. Now, what do you notice about the sets of pictures in each room?"

He thought about this one. "On the ground floor, each set is quite different?"

"Different in what way?"

"Different techniques, different subject matter?"

She nodded, pleased with him, but a glint in her eye made him suspect she'd catch him out in the end. "Classify them, room by room."

"From memory?"

"If you can."

He sighed, knowing she'd got him. "Still-life oil paintings in here, old prints of Stockholm in the dining room, flower prints in the hall and up the stairs. But I can't exactly remember what's in the two bedrooms, though they're all abstract and I hated them."

"So upstairs he's broken his rule about having different sorts of pictures in each room?"

Magnus thought about this. "Maybe the technique is a bit different, and I didn't spot it because I'm not interested in pictures like that. I remember those in the spare room were bright blotches, so they might have been acrylic."

"And in his own bedroom?"

Magnus shrugged, almost defeated. "I've no idea, so they can't have made any impression on me." He thought harder, and suddenly he had his answer. "I remember now. There was only one, just a daub, jumbled, almost hallucinatory, and it would have given me nightmares."

"What's the technique?"

"I don't really know. It wasn't nearly as colourful as the ones in the spare room, so could it be crayon?"

"And are you sure it was truly abstract?"

"It had that sort of look, but I'm obviously wrong or you wouldn't have asked the question."

"And are you certain it didn't have any sort of figure in it?"

Magnus smiled. "I'm not sure I'd recognise a figure in a picture like that. It would probably have a hole where its face should be and a swollen lump for a body."

Sonja sighed. "You are so set in your ways, as though art stopped with the Impressionists." She led the way upstairs and allowed him a quick peep into the bedroom.

"Damn," said Magnus. "It's a watercolour, but it's still a mess. So where is all this leading?"

Sonja kept him on the landing and closed the bedroom door. "I want you to think about a few things before you go in. If you were a man, living alone, a man who often found it difficult to sleep at night, where would you hang your most comforting picture?"

Magnus stared at her, and then said, almost accusingly, "He never told me he couldn't sleep at night."

"He probably didn't tell you either that at moments of special stress he found relief in watercolour painting. That's why I was struck by that one immediately." She put her arms comfortingly around him. "He was a desperately lonely man, darling, and he felt he could say more personal things to a woman. So he'd often let little details slip to me that he probably wouldn't to you. You and he talked police work. With the children he became the sort of jolly uncle he'd have liked to be if he'd really been part of a family. I think I became the only person to whom he could confide small truths about himself. It probably enabled him to believe for a short time that he actually *belonged.*"

It was hard for him to accept the fact that, at an emotional level, Sonja had understood Ragnar better than he had, and had sensed his sadness. Then he was glad, glad that for a few minutes, two or three times each year, Amrén had experienced the comfort he himself enjoyed every day; and he hugged her tightly.

"You're wonderful," he exclaimed. "But why didn't I find his brushes and watercolours here?

"I'm sure he carries them with him wherever he goes. His sketchbook is probably the nearest thing he has to a diary. Now I think you should go in and look at that picture again."

Inside the bedroom he began to see what Sonja had spotted at once. The picture was so placed that it was immediately before Ragnar's eyes as he went to sleep, or when he woke in the night; and it was not truly abstract, for there *were* sketchy pieces of scenery, all mixed up together, part of a Christmas scene, some roofs, tiny bits of houses and even part of a dwarf-like figure. It was as though a number of landscapes had been exploded and different bits had fallen in different places.

"It's like a puzzle picture," he said finally. "There are lots of jigsaw pieces that could, perhaps, be re-assembled."

"Do you recognise any of the pieces?"

Peering at them again, so closely, he did suddenly see something he recognised. Part of a half-timbered building had a projecting porch supported on carved wooden posts. It was Jurek Bojanowski's summer house on Poland's Vistula Spit.

"I was there," he told Sonja in awed tones. "I slept there the night before Jurek and I went across the border into Russian Kaliningrad. But I'd never have seen it if you hadn't led me to it so cleverly. It's very well disguised."

"Rather like Ragnar himself," Sonja commented. "You ought to recognise another one as well. It's the bit that struck me at once."

He searched, but at first he found the different pieces hard to sort out. Then it dawned on him that the colours, though pale, might be the key. Jurek's house was essentially brown, and when he looked for other pieces with some sort of brown wash, he discovered sections of forested sand dune that could only be from that special Polish area. At first glance neither the red nor white sections recalled anything; but there was a verdant wash which covered scattered elements from the Christmas scene of a hunched green-coated gnome feeding the birds by an emerald-coloured dovecot shaped like a miniature house. It was a typical enough scene, reminiscent of Jenny Nyström, but the visible part of the tiny house was extraordinarily detailed. The drainpipe was so small it must have been added with a mapping pen using Indian ink. It sloped down at an awkward angle, not properly parallel to the edge of the house; and it caught his eye at once.

"That's exactly like the drainpipe I repaired so badly just before Ragnar spent Christmas with us."

"It certainly did stick out," Sonja said, laughing at him, "and Ragnar would have noticed it immediately. And it was the time he dressed up in green as *Jultomten* to give the presents out."

"So it represents our house and that occasion?"

"I think so. I think it's a memory picture of four places where he was truly happy."

"In the same way most people frame their wedding photo, pictures of the children and holiday snaps," Magnus added thoughtfully. "But these were just for him to see, painted in a disguised way, showing only a part of the whole but enough to recall pleasant memories. And it's certainly true he was happy with Jurek, and perhaps he was with us, too. "

"I'm certain he was, and if we can sort out the rest we'll find the other two places he liked to be, and that may help you find him."

"I can't see anything at all I recognise," Magnus said dubiously, "but I'll take it home with me and work at it there."

He took it off its hook and after locking the front door they set off home. At first they were silent, busy with their thoughts, and then Magnus heard Sonja sigh. He put his right hand on her comfortingly familiar thigh and squeezed it reassuringly. "I couldn't have done it without you. You're amazing."

"I don't feel so wonderful," Sonja replied. "Ever since I heard about Ragnar going for promotion and appearing on TV, I've been wondering what made him suddenly so daring, rash even. Before that, caution was a way of life for him. Then, when I was describing to you the little intimacies he'd revealed, and his relaxed behaviour with the children, it suddenly dawned on me that we might be the ones to blame. Last Christmas Eve he felt so at home with us he was happy to dress up as in that picture; and after it was over, and he'd been such a success with the children, I caught a glimpse of his face. He looked transfigured, as though he'd finally proved something to himself and a long spiritual Lent was over. Now I'm afraid that by bringing him into our family we made him feel he belonged at last to something bigger than himself, and it may have awakened long-buried ambitions which have ended in disaster."

"Your talk of promotion and ambition reminds me of something I'd completely forgotten. When I was in Kaliningrad two years ago, that Russian gang leader boasted he was close to some senior policemen in Sweden. He mentioned they were considering Ragnar for high promotion and implied he would be expected to repay the Mafia for such preferment."

"Did you tell him what was said?"

Magnus shook his head. "I feared it might imply that I believed he was corrupt in some way, so I persuaded myself it was just intended to sow dissension and said nothing. But now I wish I had, because it might have alerted him to the possibility of criminal elements already knowing there was something in his past they could use to manipulate him."

"Do you think he'd have heeded the warning?"

"If he had got something in his past, as it seems he probably had, he might have realised it would end badly."

"Will it end badly?" Sonja asked him, but Magnus didn't answer.

When they reached home, Johan was asleep but Angelica was still awake. Sonja went in to talk to her while Magnus, suddenly exhausted, put the picture beside his bed where he could stare at it and quickly dozed off. He woke at four in the morning with Sonja slumbering beside him, but no picture on his bedside table. He went down to the kitchen, made himself a cup of coffee and carried it into the living room. Angelica was sprawled over the table in her pyjamas and striped towelling robe, flaked out beside the picture. Crayons were scattered everywhere and there was a large pad of artist's paper under one of the arms that pillowed her head, partially obscured by her long curly blonde hair which spilled out across it. Magnus prepared to scoop her up and take her back to bed, a little irritated that Sonja must have told her about the picture puzzle and allowed her to use the artistic gifts they both recognised in her to try to solve it. But then he paused, staring at her as she slumbered. She wasn't a little girl any longer, she was nearly eleven, and if she really wanted to do something to help him, did it matter if she missed a bit of sleep? Perhaps she'd been looking for another opportunity to show she was an individual to be reckoned with within the family, someone with her own ideas, her own gifts, her own right to be involved. He kissed the unruly pale gold ringlets which were such a contrast to Johan's straight black hair, and as he did so he remembered the incident a few weeks before when he'd returned from work to find her confronting him with straight hair. He'd always had a special relationship with her, rather different to his unthinking rough and tumble one with Johan. They'd been precious to each other, seeming to read each other's mind and opting for mutual support instead of confrontation. As a result, they'd never had a cross word. But now, for the very first time, he felt anger rise up in him, and he noticed her blue eyes were watching him with a hard determination he'd never seen in them before. Fortunately, just in time, he caught Sonja's warning glance, and forced down his anger, saving himself from what might so easily have been a destructive clash.

"You haven't been pressing your hair on Mum's ironing board, have you?" he asked lightly; and at once her stubborn look changed to amused derision.

"You are *so* out of time, Dad. We have plug-in tongs now, and all my friends are going straight."

"What about your straight-haired friends? Are they going curly?"

She gave a groaning sigh. "Just *nobody* has curly hair now, Dad, it's not the thing."

He rubbed his hand over his close-cropped hair. "Can I keep my hair like this?"

She shrugged expressively. “You’re old, Dad, fashion doesn’t apply to you.”

“I’m glad to hear it,” Sonja broke in, giggling. “Think what he might have looked like if it did apply.”

Then they were all laughing, the crisis was over and a week later the curls were back because the straightening tongs were just too much trouble.

He stooped and picked her up without waking her, and there, on the table underneath her, were two beautifully executed pictures, one with a reddish tinge, the other with a great deal of white.

He carried her upstairs, wondering whether this had been a sort of thank you to him, a re-establishing of the special relationship at a more mature level. As soon as he’d laid her gently in her bed and covered her with the duvet, he came down again and began to study the pictures.

One showed a section of a cottage half- buried in snow, and there was something over the door which at first he thought might be elk horns. There was not too much detail, even on the original, but finally he decided they were too thin and spiky and were meant to represent reindeer antlers. In the background was the roof of another building with a tall chimney. The other also showed two houses, but only a small part of each. The more distant one was larger, with a balcony and the glint of water and forest beyond; the nearest was the end of a typical red log cabin.

“I hope you’re proud of our daughter,” Sonja said from behind him. “I refused to allow her to do it, but she stood up to me and overruled me, saying she had every right to help you and she was better at art than I was. And she was right, just look at the result.”

“I am,” answered Magnus, “and I think the red one is in Norrland.”

“It is,” said Sonja with certainty. “But where?”

“It’s possible I may know, but I’ll have to check it out.”

“You think it’s the house where that girl lived, the one he claimed to love,” guessed Sonja.

"It seems likely, and, if I can be sure of that, it leaves the last picture as our one clue to where Ragnar may be now."

"It's quite far north," said Sonja.

"No spruce or birch to be seen, so it may be above the tree line; and if those are reindeer horns, then it's probably Lapland. As it's the least likely direction for him to take, it might be exactly what he'd do."

"You didn't say whether you were proud of our daughter."

"I think she's remarkably gifted, like you, and I'm very proud of her. But..."

Sonja raised her eyebrows and waited.

"But she's got a will of her own and she's going to be a real handful when she's a teenager. Do you think we'll get through it somehow?"

Sonja took his hand. "If we stand together and present a united front we might just make it. We've both got strong wills too."

Magnus kept hold of her hand and pulled her into the kitchen. "I'm too excited to sleep any more, and I'm suddenly ravenous. Let's have an early breakfast."

CHAPTER 15

Later that morning Magnus drove up to see Pia in Östersund, and he took Angelica's Norrland picture with him. She looked at it with interest, then even more intently.

"It's either an extraordinary coincidence or my eyes are deceiving me. I think I really need to show you something, if you don't mind doing all the driving," she said, and she stared balefully at the snow swirl outside the window. "It's in Näverede."

He agreed at once, excited by their destination and sensing he was about to have his hunch confirmed.

"I've been digging into the past," she explained on the way. "I get a bit manic when I'm involved in something, and there's a detail I still don't know. Even though it may be a very small one, it really niggles me until I can get at the truth, and that's how it's been with the question of where exactly Amrén *did* live at the time Olle was killed. I don't mean just which village, but the actual house."

"Did you find something?"

"Yes, I think so, and that's why I'm taking you there. If your picture fits, we'll know for certain."

They were driving out of Östersund on the same road Magnus had come in by, but at the roundabout Pia told him to swing off east towards Sollefteå. After a few kilometres, it was left again onto a much smaller road which went down to the River Indal. Passing the turning to the hydroelectric power station dam, they circled round to a scattering of houses on either side of the road and Pia told him to pull in and stop there.

"This is the beginning of Näverede," she explained. "I want you to have a look around, and see if you can find those two houses that are partly shown in the painting. I'm not budging from the warmth of the car, so I'll try to judge from your expression as you walk back whether you've succeeded or not."

It didn't take him very long. He spotted the balcony first, and then dropped his eyes to the small red *stuga* in the foreground. Although there was no real doubt in his mind, he took out Angelica's picture, holding it under his coat to protect it from the steadily falling snow. He was interested to get the angle right, and once he'd lined up the two houses in exactly the way they appeared in the picture, he realised that the painting wasn't an entirely accurate representation. Rather more of the near-side of the big house and its balcony was visible than could be seen in reality, including an upstairs and a downstairs window. But when he walked round to the other side of the cottage, he realised the painting showed the view that was actually visible from its window. It was clearly a double memory picture, combining a partial study of the exterior of the cottage where he'd lived with the view he himself had of the neighbouring house when he was looking at it through his cottage window. Like the picture of Jurek's house, and his own, it was inaccurate in real terms because it was recalling particular memories; and he would have to keep that in mind when he was searching for the location of the final picture. As for this one, it seemed to indicate that those two windows, or the rooms inside them, held a particular significance for him.

He went back to the car and got in, trying not to sprinkle Pia with snow.

"You found the two houses," she declared triumphantly.

"You can't know that. I deliberately kept a miserable expression on my face."

"But you couldn't disguise your walk, which was eager and excited."

Magnus grinned. "I ought to have known I wouldn't be able to trick you. Yes, they were both there right enough, though the painting didn't show them exactly as they really are."

"That explains why I couldn't be absolutely sure and wanted you to see it for yourself. Did Amrén paint the original?"

"I'm certain he did, yes. It was in his house, and he painted in his spare time. Did he rent that cottage?"

"I can't be absolutely sure of that because it's been carefully covered up. But I know Lilly and Olle lived in the house with the balcony, and so your painting makes it virtually certain they were neighbours, probably right up until the day Olle was killed. Given all that we know now, that raises interesting questions; and the fact that he made a painting of the two houses together, and it was on his wall twenty-eight years later, that's pretty suggestive too."

Magnus told her about the windows that were in the painting even though they couldn't really be seen from that angle. "Do you think he caused Olle's death?" he asked bluntly.

Pia shook her head. "Although I wouldn't attempt to justify what my force did back then in hiding his real address, I think it was to protect a young officer from a suspicious coincidence that might have ruined his career, nothing more than that."

"You think he was carrying on with Lilly, went after the husband because he was implicated in the thefts, and then Olle was killed in a genuine accident?"

Pia looked at him sombrely. "I think most of that. But though I appreciate your loyalty to your chief, I worry you may be letting it blind you to reality. I have to tell you I suspect his relationship with Lilly was rather more shameful than just 'carrying on' as you express it. It would account for the allegations and the fact that Amrén has run."

Magnus felt his blood quicken. He didn't mention what Jörgen had told him about a serious charge of a sexual nature, but, feeling the need to utterly reject it, he overreacted. "And you think it right he should be hounded for something he did when he was just a young officer?"

Pia put a soothing hand on his arm. "That's your anger talking, Magnus, anger and friendship. But suppose it had been your daughter? I think you'd feel very differently then."

"Yes, I would. But I don't believe he's capable of doing anything very terrible."

"Then he has nothing to fear if he faces whatever the charge turns out to be. How long have you known him?"

"Five years."

"He may have been very different twenty-eight years ago, when the testosterone would be peaking. A young man would find it much less easy to control himself than the older Amrén you know now. If he fancied her, and she refused him, anything may have occurred."

"I realise what you're implying, Pia, but it just doesn't fit with what I know of him."

"But do you agree that breaking the law must always be punished, however much time has passed and regardless of subsequent events like a successful career or acts of kindness? If not, why do police officers like us exist?"

"We don't punish, we don't even prosecute. All we do is discover the facts and find the supposed perpetrator. The rest we leave to others."

"You know what I'm trying to say, Magnus. Life isn't simple, not for me, not for you. But a crime *is* simple. If it's been committed, we have to act. I think you're stalling until you find him and talk to him, and I can understand that. But when you do talk to him, make sure you speak as a policeman as well as a friend."

"Ouch!" said Magnus, but he managed a smile. "Somehow I don't think it'll be that simple. But I do appreciate your frank speaking, and I probably needed to hear it. I'm praying I'll know more when I've met that lawyer this afternoon."

He drove her back to Östersund, and then returned to Sundsvall. It was snowing much more heavily, and he was glad the road was so familiar to him. Even then, he had to drive slowly, and as the whiteness swirled around his car, his mind, sharpened by Pia's comments, turned to Ragnar. In particular he concentrated on those who'd known him in his younger days, and whose sign of lasting friendship was the use of his nickname, RaRa.

Jurek was probably his greatest friend, not least because Ragnar had saved his life. He'd heard the story from Jurek himself, and he remembered how surprised he'd been then by Ragnar's casual bravery, throwing himself at the man who'd shot Jurek just as he fired again, making him miss his target and allowing Jurek to get in a fatal shot before he collapsed. Certainly the devil-may-care man described by Jurek bore little resemblance to the one he knew, so perhaps Pia had been right in saying that he couldn't really judge what the young Ragnar had been like. This led on to other, gloomier, considerations, not least the fact that Sonja had known more about Ragnar's innermost thoughts than he had. He reminded himself he didn't even know the origin of the RaRa nickname, apart from the obvious link to the name Ragnar. Jurek had explained he'd understand it if he ever saw the fan dance. Axel Burman, the retired police doctor who'd also been close to Amrén, had told him teasingly he was too young to know about the nickname. Lennart, now comfortably settled into his temporary role as Sundsvall police chief and reminiscing about cooperation with the English police, had recalled how Chief Inspector Ford had reportedly described Ragnar as soft on top, hard underneath, and fearsome when he confronted a killer. That seemed to tie in with Jurek's description, though it in no way chimed with his own view of him as morally courageous but cautious in action. But all three men had clearly held him in extraordinarily high regard.

He was left with the feeling that not only had he not known the real Ragnar at all thoroughly, but that their rather formal friendship had prevented him from asking the obvious questions that might have revealed more. He'd assumed Ragnar did not care for closeness, and certainly not the intimacy of prying questions, and so he hadn't enquired. But now he worried he'd been wrong, that he'd shown a lack of interest and missed the chance of knowing him as well as he should have done. Shamefully he felt it might have been a 'man' thing, the need to set the clear boundaries that marked the two of them out as friendly colleagues, and nothing more.

He was due to meet Mikael Bredenberg at two, and he didn't want to be late. In his experience, lawyers tended to be sticklers for punctuality, and he was anxious not to get off on the wrong foot by keeping him waiting, especially as he was bracing himself for another moral lecture to underline the one Pia had already inflicted on him.

But it was Mikael Bredenberg who was late, by nearly an hour, and he was a surprise in other ways as well. In place of the impeccably dressed city dweller he'd envisaged, he was confronted by an overweight middle-aged man with thinning hair whose suit was as worn as his wet suede shoes.

"I'm starving," he boomed in what Magnus assumed was his courtroom voice as he shook hands. "Is there any chance of adjourning to Knaust? The food there, or so I'm told, is of quite a decent standard."

"Don't expect me to have much more than a cup of coffee," replied Magnus cautiously, well aware that Knaust was the most expensive hotel in Sundsvall. "I try not to overdo the eating in the middle of the day."

Mikael laughed, and Magnus noticed that his eyes, in contrast to his shabby appearance, were bright and alert. "As long as I can eat, I'm perfectly content to let you starve yourself. We'll talk as I gulp and you slurp."

Magnus drove him from the police station to the hotel, where the waiter instantly spotted Mikael as an epicure, and they discussed the possibilities of the menu and the wine list in reverentially hushed voices while Magnus searched for something simple among the hors d'oeuvres. Mikael finally settled on the reindeer steak with morels, berries, and roast potatoes sprinkled with parsley, to be partnered with a fine burgundy. Magnus chose the herring surprise and a glass of beer.

"I thought it best that our conversation should occur away from your workplace" Mikael remarked after he'd sampled the wine and the food, and given a great sigh of relief. "Everything I've heard about you suggests you are a man of principle, so you will understand at once when I say I am not in a position to answer any of the questions you are doubtless burning to ask. But there are other matters and I felt privacy on neutral ground was best."

Delicately he placed a morel on a section of reindeer, popped it neatly into his mouth, chewed with dedicated thoughtfulness, swallowed with obvious delight, paused for the after-taste, and then said, "I'm always nervous of travelling away from Stockholm and Uppsala; and coming north always seems especially daunting, almost as though one is leaving civilization behind. But really, you know, now that I've done it, it's not as bad as one fears, and this is very good food indeed. Even so, I find it hard to understand how you can have spent all your life here, as my research shows, but then I'm not in any sense an *outdoor* man."

He gave a small shudder at the very thought, fortified himself with another mouthful and a reflective sip of wine, and then resumed, briefly putting a surprisingly well-manicured hand on Magnus' arm to indicate there was nothing personal in what he was saying. "You must understand that my responsibility is entirely to my client who, before his dreadful death up here, gave me clear instructions which I shall carry out without fear or favour. Anything that could be revealed, at this early stage, I have already mentioned either to the young lady in Östersund or to Police Commissioner Bergqvist who believes he has succeeded in slowing me down." He addressed his food and wine again with more relish, it seemed to Magnus, than he had spoken about Bergqvist. "Needless to say, I am in fact moving at precisely the same measured pace as is my wont, but since he clearly enjoys believing he is very powerful, I saw no reason to disillusion him. I know you will have heard there is a sworn statement accusing Ragnar Amrén of an unlawful act, which, though it will have upset you, is true. So, for the moment at least, there is nothing more I am able to tell you."

He returned to his eating and drinking, and Magnus felt it would be best not to interrupt an activity that was clearly of the greatest importance to him. He felt somewhat dismayed though, for he had often found lawyers loved the sound of their own voices, enjoyed flaunting their sense of power by demonstrating how much they knew, and so often became indiscreet. But Mikael, by flaunting only his eating, clearly felt no temptation to give away secrets; and Magnus swallowed his disappointment with his excellent herrings and the pale beer that was fashionably over-chilled.

But once Mikael had finished his food and drained the last of the wine, he reached into his pocket and withdrew an envelope. "There is, however, one implied instruction from my client that I shall *not* carry out. He did not actually specify that I should read this letter, but the fact he left it with the other papers suggests that it was what he intended. But, like you, I try to be a man of principle, and this letter, written by his daughter Lilly, is clearly addressed in her own handwriting to Ragnar Amrén, and has a postage stamp for the correct amount attached to the sealed envelope."

Mikael paused, almost as though he was gathering his strength to do something that went against the innate caution of a lawyer. "I can only suppose that my client assumed a father's right to intercept it in order to prevent it being posted; but I do not accept that, in law, he had that right. She was of age, and though she was living in his house, he had no legal authority over her. I consider, therefore, that as he, in this instance, acted improperly in hindering a postal delivery, it is my duty, even after so many years, to hand it over, in its original state, to the proper recipient. And as nobody appears to know the recipient's whereabouts, I now pass it into your safe-keeping, as the person most likely to find him. It is, as you will see, unopened, which may suggest, though I could not possibly make such a deduction myself, that my client had a bad conscience about what he had done and could not bring himself to go beyond it by actually reading what he took."

He held out the envelope to Magnus, let him take it and watched him put it into his inside pocket. Then he said briskly, "Please sign this receipt for my records."

Magnus thought he should at least offer to drive him to the railway station. But the lawyer, after collecting payment for what Magnus had eaten and then settling the bill, asked the waiter to order a taxi.

As they stood together waiting for it, Mikael studied the hotel's famous arched and pillared baroque staircase. "Very fine, very fine indeed," he murmured, though Magnus felt his mind was not really on architecture. He was not entirely surprised therefore, just as the taxi drew up, that the lawyer turned to him, formally shook his hand and said, "I know he is your friend as well as your chief, and anybody else in your situation would have badgered me to give my professional opinion. You, as I expected, asked me nothing, so I will tell you what I think. As matters stand at present, on the written evidence I have in my possession, Amrén will at best face enforced early retirement, with his high reputation damaged beyond repair."

"And at worst?"

Mikael turned at the door. "You will be well aware there are various ways of compelling an unwilling victim to have intercourse, but they all constitute rape. The penalty for that is prison." Then he set off on his way back to civilization.

Magnus, deep in gloom and very conscious of the envelope in his pocket, drove back to his office, locked it in his safe, sat down at his computer and began to trawl through the lists of owners of properties in Lapland. As he'd expected there was nothing under Amrén, but he was disappointed when there was nothing under Jurek Bojanowski either, for he'd banked on Ragnar using his friend's name. He drew a blank with his last remaining hope, Axel Burman; but he was desperate enough to try the English surname, Ford, equally without result.

He closed his eyes and thought back, not concentrating on friendship this time, but on any name Ragnar might have mentioned. He could only think of one, the collector of Sami artefacts, Finn Jonsson, and that produced nothing either. But it took him back to the High Coast killing and another name surfaced. Amrén had specifically recommended the pathologist Hillevi Zander, so drunkenly wayward, so technically perceptive, and now deceased. But that name failed too and he seemed to be faced with the daunting prospect of personally looking at every house in Lapland until he found the one that matched the picture.

It had stopped snowing, and so he went up to *Norra Berget*, one of the two hills which flanked the town. There he did what had been effective before in moments of puzzlement, walking about briskly, breathing deeply, and trying to remember everything Ragnar had ever said to him about Lapland. But the more he thought, the more he became convinced that Ragnar had never mentioned Lapland, and that in itself was suggestive. Then he did recall something that had been said, though it was not Ragnar who'd said it. The use of Hillevi Zander's name during his computer search had stirred the memory, for suddenly he was back on his first visit to her, standing outside her ghastly pink front door while she threatened to pour a bucket of kitchen waste over his head. He'd told her Amrén had sent him, and she'd paid what he subsequently understood was her highest compliment when she'd commented that Amrén was 'all right'. She'd added something odd about reindeer, but he'd been far too preoccupied with her formidable size, angry threats and alcoholic breath to take much notice of it at the time. But later, after he'd come to appreciate her skills, if not her amorous advances, he'd thought about the words and been vaguely intrigued. Now, because they did form some sort of fragile link to Lapland, he recalled them. She'd said Amrén had used her forensic skills in an unusual reindeer dribble case.

He hurried back to his office, rang Sanfridsson, Head of Forensics and asked him if he had any idea what had happened to Hillevi Zander's records.

"As a matter of fact I do," Sanfridsson answered in his usual dry and somewhat pedantic manner. "They were all sent to the *Statens kriminaltekniska laboratorium.*"

"SKL? Isn't that in Linköping?"

"It is. They have an archive there, and since her papers have been properly sorted and catalogued there's been a greater awareness of just how groundbreaking much of her forensic work was."

"I'm very anxious to discover anything I can about a case she mentioned to me involving reindeer dribble."

He expected one of Sanfridsson's well known impatient outbursts, but instead his reply astonished him.

"I can probably help you with that. As it happens I know many of the staff at SKL. Was there anything special you wanted to know?"

"The name and address of the man she helped with whatever it was she discovered."

"I should be able to get that for you tomorrow. I assume it's urgent?"

"Yes."

"And confidential?"

"Yes."

"Then it's to do with Amrén and I really hope it helps. Whatever's being said, we're all on his side. And since I know you can't comment, I'm ringing off."

Magnus got the information at 10.36 the next morning and he immediately rang Kiruna. He made his request and was passed over to a girl who sounded young enough to be in school, though she was a Dr. Utsi. She listened quietly, seemed interested, asked him to send a photo of the picture as an email attachment, promised to ring him back if she found anything, and did so four hours later.

The next day Magnus caught the early flight to Swedish Lapland.

CHAPTER 16

As soon as he was in the evening train heading north from Helsinki, Ragnar felt a slight shift, a fractional lightening of his spirits. He was back on Scandinavian soil, he'd faced his past with Lilly, and both he and his love for her still survived. For a brief time, at least, his future was settled and he knew now he had the physical courage to do what subsequently might be necessary.

Whenever he opened his eyes he could see nothing beyond the train window but vast eerie moonlit stretches of snow-wrapped forest, which offered him a crumb of comfort. Unless he wanted it, nobody would find him in such a landscape.

His way of coping with his grief and shame had always been to run away. He'd run away from Lilly, he'd run away from the truth about himself and, after sufficient time to restore, at least in part, his reputation as a policeman, he'd run away from Östersund, applying for a transfer to the Västernorrland police in Sundsvall. In the interval between the two jobs he'd taken some leave and run away again, away from anyone who might remind him of those times, running as far away as he could get, to Swedish Lapland, near the Finnish border, not far from Karesuando. And it was there he first met Einar Ruong.

He was a Sami reindeer herder, about his age, who offered board and lodging through the tourist office, though he had only room for one. That attracted Ragnar, and so did the fact Einar was a man of few words, as was his wife Asa and his young son, Nisse. But once he was living there with him, he was particularly struck by his patient acceptance of whatever came his way, which seemed to make him mentally as strong as he was physically powerful. To Ragnar, prey to constant emotional turmoil, this calm endurance was an attribute he longed to acquire; and so he stayed all his free month with him, working voluntarily beside him, eating the same food, living the same life, helping with the reindeer, in the desperate hope that something of Einar would rub off on him and he would begin to heal.

He liked to think it did. At least if he did not get close to the stoicism of his host, he gained a little patience; and, although it was only at a superficial level, he acquired some slight control over his feelings. Physically he became stronger, fitter and he regained some confidence. So, at regular intervals as his police career developed, he returned there, to Einar, Asa and Nisse, and they became a family of sorts for him, a fixed point in his emotional wilderness. It became the one place where he could find peace. As a visitor he was always accepted without fuss; and no one ever bothered him, for Einar lived his life in exactly the same way whether Ragnar was there or not.

Twenty years after that initial visit, for the very first time, Einar phoned him to tell him he would not be there to greet him, and neither would Asa.

"Nisse will look after you," he announced. "I'm going to be arrested for murder."

It seemed so unlikely that for a second he thought it must be some sort of joke, but that would be almost as alien to Einar as murder.

"Who are you meant to have killed?"

"Asa."

"Your wife's dead?" he asked, appalled.

"Yes. I found her in the reindeer corral yesterday."

"What had happened to her?"

"She'd been trying to cure a sick *hiergge.* She can't have had a proper grip to stop it tossing its head, and one long tine of the antler went through her eye."

Einar showed no emotion, but Ragnar knew that was simply a reflection of his normal stoicism. A *hiergge* was a castrated bull used as a draft animal, and normally it would be fairly docile; but that wouldn't necessarily be so when it was ill, especially if it was in pain.

"But I don't understand why you should be blamed, and why anyone should think it was murder."

"The young policeman who came first said it was an accident. Then an older policeman came and searched my house and workshop. I don't like him, he doesn't like me, and he's going to arrest me for murder."

Ragnar knew it was going to take time before he got the full story, but Einar was not a man who could be hurried.

"Why would he do that?"

"In my workshop he found a reindeer antler. I was saving it for a knife hilt and it had blood on it. He asked me whose blood it was and I told him it was Asa's. As he is a fool and wants to harm me, he thinks it is the murder weapon."

"Why was Asa's blood on it?"

Einar answered in a surprised voice, as though the reason was so obvious he could not understand why the question should be asked. "She was holding it for me while I was measuring the *madda*, the straight, thick base section I could use for the hilt, but she'd cut her finger on a chisel while she was picking up the antler from my workbench and some of her blood must have got onto it."

Ragnar thought about this, jotted down a note, then asked him, "What's between you and this policeman? Why don't you like each other? Why does he want to harm you?"

He could imagine Einar's shrug. "He wanted to marry Asa too. Then we had reindeer trouble. Every few years he'd say I'd cut my ear-mark on some of his herd. There was pasturing trouble, too. Now he thinks he's got his chance. Once he's had the blood tested to make sure I'm not making a fool of him and the result shows it came from Asa, he'll arrest me. He says he doesn't believe my story because Asa was so experienced with reindeer, and a *hiergge* is not difficult to handle."

"Had you and Asa quarrelled?"

There was a long silence, emphasising that this was a personal question which should not be asked, even by a friend.

"The policeman had been hanging around, as he did at intervals. Asa smiled at him, and I spoke to her about it."

Ragnar, knowing there was only one way he might be able to help, asked the crucial question even though he expected to be disappointed. "Did you slaughter the reindeer after it killed Asa?"

"Why would I do that? Einar replied, astonishment in his voice. "He's a good beast, and Asa should have held his head more firmly."

Ragnar sighed with relief. "Take a sample of his saliva on a swab, or an absolutely clean piece of cloth. Do it as soon as you can, put it inside a new plastic box or bottle, one that's never been used, then post it to me at once. It may be too late already to test it, but I know someone who is very clever at it, so we'll try. If we can find out what illness the reindeer was suffering from, it may help."

"I'll do it now," Einar said, and he rang off.

By the time it arrived Ragnar had received a call from Nisse, now grown up, telling him that Einar had been arrested. Ragnar took the sample to Hillevi Zander who cursed him for the delay, told him he was, as always, asking the impossible, listened to brief details of the case, was overtaken by interest and even before he left she was already absorbed in working out possibilities. By the time Einar came up for trial she'd discovered the reindeer had eaten *Amanita muscaria,* the Fly Agaric fungus which, though not poisonous to reindeer, acted on them as a powerful hallucinogen and intoxicant. This enabled the defence lawyer to maintain that this was the 'illness' the animal had been suffering from, making it unpredictable even with humans it knew well. Primed by Hillevi, the lawyer also raised the subject of the stains on the antler in the workshop. When they had been tested, he asked, proving that it was Asa's blood, had they also established how fresh the bloodstains were? At first the prosecution said no; but, when the defence lawyer got permission from the judge to have it re-tested, it was conceded, with some fudging, that it was not in fact entirely fresh.

Einar was acquitted, and from that moment Ragnar was no longer a visitor, but an adopted member of the Ruong family. A cottage was set aside for him whenever he wished to come and, understanding how he felt about his privacy, his visits were not mentioned outside the family. Although he never asked for it, he was also aware that, when he was there, the extended family, which included Einar's brother, his wife, and four of Nisse's cousins, watched over him, keeping other visitors away and watching out for any strangers in the vicinity. It gave him a sense of complete security, and he went there whenever his life became too much for him or he needed absolute peace to think. It was where he'd decided to accept the chance of promotion; and it was to there he was fleeing from the consequences of that decision.

Early the next morning, ten hours out of Helsinki, he borrowed a mobile from a friendly-looking Finn and made a brief call. He handed the phone back with real gratitude, for the gruff answer had been entirely sufficient to reassure him that the end of his long journey, running away again, was really drawing closer.

He had told no one of the existence of such a refuge, nor had anyone ever made a chance discovery of him there. But all the time he'd been crossing northern Europe fleeing in shame from anyone who knew him, it had been constantly in his mind, a secure sanctuary where he could finally face the memory he'd hidden until now. For too long he'd been a soldier stepping around a minefield, a sane man keeping away from a memory that might make him mad. Now, once he was alone in his cottage, he would open the snuff box and face the consequences.

At Pello, as the scenery slowed, he recognised the battered four by four, seemingly the only car waiting for the train to stop and a passenger to alight. Once the train door unlocked, he went down onto the step, gasping involuntarily as he was struck by the icy cold. Then he was on the deserted platform, stumbling slightly after sitting so long but gaining strength as he walked to the car park, hurrying more and more to get away from the bitter blast. He grasped Einar's hand, climbed in, sank back against the worn seat and felt himself relax, the tension draining out of him, his heartbeats calming, his mind letting go of the images that had been haunting him. He was safe.

In the past, on arrival, his comment to Einar had always been 'no visitors'. But on this occasion, staring round at the familiar buildings of the tiny settlement, he varied it by making an exception for Magnus Trygg, as long as he was alone, unarmed, and no one was trailing him.

In his cottage, on his own, he ate the food they had prepared for him and found his thoughts stayed on Magnus. He was the one for whom he'd left the only clue, and he was certain he *would* come. And that had a special importance for him.

Magnus, he had increasingly come to believe, was the man he might have been if his life had followed the path he had intended and he had married Lilly. He'd recognised something of himself in him the first time they'd met, and from then on he'd manipulated events to keep him close to him, finally achieving exactly what he wanted. Magnus was now a close colleague, a cautious friend and, unknowingly, especially through his family, a mirror of all that might have been possible in his own life. He was the Ragnar he might have become if he had not made such a terrible mistake early in his emotional life and at the start of his police career. Magnus was straightforward, as he should have been. Like him, Magnus had met a girl early in his life and fallen in love with her. Then he'd married her, had two children with her, a boy and a girl, just as he had dreamed of doing with Lilly. So, whenever he looked at Magnus, he saw himself and all he'd lost; and if he could only bring himself to confess the whole truth, Magnus would be able to speak for him to those very few for whose opinion he still cared, to Jurek, Sonja, Angelica and Johan, pitting the truth, poor as it was, against the media dirt that would otherwise be his only epitaph.

That night, for the first time since the fateful meeting after his fan-dance, he slept peacefully without the aid of drink or pills. He woke refreshed, knowing what lay before him and accepting it.

He took out his snow-scooter and set off into the white wilderness. He went slowly, automatically looking out for any wildlife. But, in his mind, he was taking the brass snuff box from behind the tea caddy, and he was opening it to confront his final meeting with Lilly.

He tried to become the young man he had been then, thinking his thoughts and smarting with the pain of her rejection of him; and with no difficulty at all the past came back to him. He insisted to himself that he was not angry with her. But he did feel a bitter sense of deprivation, the sullen ache of injury; and the more he brooded on it, the more it seemed the only cure was to obtain what she had offered him, and then snatched away. This need to set it right, to start, as it were, all over again, became, as each day passed, an obsession.

He spent little time considering the possible causes of what had happened. She might have despised him because he could not match the tree trunk-sized organ he had once seen in a Japanese *shunga* print, depicting a Samurai having his way with a female prisoner. She might have led him on for her own satisfaction, only to watch him squirm when the finale was denied him. But neither scenario fitted Lilly in any way at all. It was just possible her last minute scruples had been intended to make him forceful, overwhelming her hesitation and allowing her to offload her moral guilt on him, but she had never evinced any scruple or moral guilt at all. Indeed, it was her admission that she did not love Olle, and her calm acceptance of him and all that they were doing, that had roused him to such a pitch.

He found that thinking of it as a case made it easier for him, and as a policeman he could find only three pieces of evidence that might point to her sudden withdrawal. When, in the kitchen, facing each other, both of them fully dressed, he had reached out to touch her breast, she had cringed away from him as if some lurking physical antipathy had suddenly risen to the surface. When they had gone upstairs she had arranged it so that they were in separate rooms and she would not have to see him undress. And she had been the first to mention a bath, the first to enter it, not demonstrating any modesty about herself, for she had been completely revealed. But it meant that he got in behind her, when her back was turned, and so she did not have to see him as exposed as she had been; and all their subsequent actions had transpired where he could see her, but she could not see him. It was only at the very end that she had twisted away from him, avoiding a face to face union of such ultimate intimacy.

He concentrated on that moment, recalling exactly what he'd done that might have led to her outburst. He'd been close to coming, he'd decided he would have to take her on the bathmat and he'd started to stand up. But how could it have been the sight of him that disgusted her, for he was still behind her?

Then he remembered the mirror over the basin, recalled the movement of her head in that direction immediately before her horrified reaction; and all became clear to him. She was attracted by his authority as a policeman, she responded to his kindness, was softened by his genuine interest in her; but he was short and plump and homely, probably ridiculous in his sexual arousal, and at the last moment that had outweighed all else she liked about him.

It was a conclusion that encouraged him to believe that all might not be lost. If he could somehow weight the balance more on the side of all she seemed to like about him, everything she respected in him and responded to, she might find it easier to accept the oddity of his looks. So he had not been defeated. He was only walking-wounded and, if he was clever enough, he would be able to recover the position.

Looking back on it with honest eyes, from such a distance of years, he realised that this was the moment he took the fateful decision that ruined both their lives. He convinced himself, so easily, that at the very least he should be fair to her and gently indicate that disappointing him would have inevitable consequences for Olle. So he tipped the scales in his favour, using the combination of his authority as a policeman and her own desire to do as much as possible to help her husband.

He stopped the scooter, dismounted and stared out over the snow. As soon as Lilly's father had spoken, as soon as he'd learnt that she was dead, he'd known it was all over for him and instinctively he'd run. Although he'd never faced it, although he'd almost succeeded in obliterating it from his conscious memory, he was aware what Lilly would have sworn that he had done to her, and it would not have been a lie.

CHAPTER 17

Lilly seemed pleased to see him when he went back to her three days after she'd rejected him, and that strengthened his belief that all was not lost. In fact, she acted as if it had never happened, as if she'd never cried out and pushed him away. But this time he was careful to ensure there'd be no misunderstandings. He'd seen Olle leave earlier that morning, and knowing they'd not be disturbed greatly increased his confidence.

He smiled at her, accepting her offer of coffee.

"Do you trust me, Lilly?"

"Of course," she answered wonderingly.

She brought the coffee, and sat down opposite him. Again he had the feeling she was waiting helplessly for something to happen. He loved her, he would always love her, and that love was driving him forward. As before, her timidity still made him feel strong, and the memory of her subsequent ease and confidence when they'd come together, so much greater than his, continued to delight and encourage him.

"I know about Olle," he said quietly.

Her hand went to her throat, where he could see her fingers trembling. She stared down at the table, but she didn't say anything.

"I saw the chickens in your fridge. I've been noting when he leaves in his boat, the direction he goes, the time he gets back. I can't prove anything yet, but I know he steals and I wanted to tell you that I knew."

The brown eyes with their green flecks fastened on his again, though for a moment the thin fingers continued to writhe in an agony of dismay. Then she asked him the question he knew had to come, but which now he almost dreaded. “Why? Why did you want to tell me that you knew?”

“I don’t think you like what he does; I don’t think you have anything to do with it. I need you to know that.”

He felt the now familiar surge of power the authority of his uniform generated, knew he could use it in any way he wished.

“Why are you being so kind?” she asked with a bemused lack of understanding. She seemed so baffled by what she obviously took to be his generosity that he felt she must in some way be feeling remorse for the way she’d treated him, and that spurred him on.

After a deliberate hesitation, feeling the blood beat through his body as the awareness grew that this was make or break, he blurted it out.

“I think you know why, Lilly.”

She squirmed awkwardly in the kitchen chair, and he thought how gawky she appeared compared to her grace when she was naked.

“Please don’t say that,” she replied beseechingly. “It’s all so difficult for me. Aren’t you afraid I’ll tell him you know what he gets up to?”

“Did you tell him about the bath?” he answered softly, and it was as though it was a sort of lovers’ dialogue, not moral blackmail at all.

She shook her head. “He’s a good man, he looks after me, and it was wrong of me to be so weak. Are you going to arrest him?”

He hadn’t expected her to be so direct, and for a moment he was floored.

“If I get the evidence, I’ll have to,” he said finally.

“I can’t stop him, I’ve tried before. I don’t think he’d stop even if he knew you were on to him. It’s like some silly game, and since you started to live here I really believe it’s like a challenge, to see who can win.”

"Maybe he'll be clever enough to stop me catching him in the act," he suggested, but he deliberately sounded unconvincing.

"Will he go to prison?"

"Has he got a record?"

"No."

"Then much will depend on the report of the arresting officer. He hasn't used violence, he hasn't taken anything terribly valuable and so he might get away with a caution."

"You'd help him?"

He made no reply, but concentrated on his coffee; and again she surprised him with her quickness and directness, instantly putting her finger on the dominant emotion he'd told himself he didn't have.

"You're angry, aren't you? You're angry about that last time." She gave a sigh of sad resignation. "I was afraid you wouldn't understand."

He still remained silent, sensing he was on the brink of gaining what he wanted, though realising that it was making him act in a way that was not natural for him. He longed to go on talking to her, listening to her, asking her why she'd thought he wouldn't understand, discover how she felt about him, tell her how he felt about her. But he'd chosen his path, and so he said nothing, putting everything on her.

"Would you help Olle if you weren't angry with me any longer?"

"I'd really like to," he said, but he made sure there was a lot of doubt in his voice.

She got up and cleared the table. Her movements were agitated, and he could see her in the kitchen, standing still and leaning her forehead against the edge of the cupboard. She was walking slowly when she came back to him.

"Suppose we pretend the last time never happened?" she said, holding out her hand to him. "Couldn't we imagine the clock's stopped and this really is the first time?"

His pulse beat more quickly, and when he spoke his voice had thickened. "Last time didn't have a very happy ending."

"But it won't be quite the same this time, because I won't stop you, and then you'll help Olle, won't you? He's not really bad; he's just, I don't know, he can't seem to do the right thing. He says nothing ever really happens round here, and he needs a little excitement."

She led him upstairs, and everything began to repeat itself. She still wouldn't undress in front of him, and she still seemed more at ease with him when he was behind her in the bath. Now that he was less hurriedly nervous, more certain of what he was about to achieve, he could study the extraordinary contrast of her clothed body and her nude one. Dressed, she appeared unformed, nervously hunched, clumsy and slow; unclothed she was quick, slender and graceful, smooth-skinned and, in a minor key, shapely. She was like a badly wrapped present, the exterior of which gives no inkling of the wonder of the gift inside. He'd been presented with this unlikely gift the last time they were together and he should have held on to what was so very precious however sudden and unexpected the problems that arose. But he hadn't done so; he'd let his injured pride take precedence; and shame lurked in the corner of his mind. However much it seemed she'd offered him this second chance, he was conscious of the shabby truth. She was doing it to save Olle, and he'd forced her into it. It was an acknowledgement he simply couldn't keep at bay, and it so altered his perception of the event, that on an emotional level it wasn't in any way a repeat of the earlier one. She allowed him do whatever he wanted, and he did all those things he'd achingly, wondrously, done before; but it didn't feel the same. On that occasion, until she'd stopped him, she'd been a part of it, as obviously excited as he was excited, feeling the pleasure he felt, the same unbelievable gladness filling them both. Now she did it for Olle, a man she didn't even love, and not for him at all. There was no mutual curiosity, no mutual astonishment, and, as he now realised much too late, no mutual love either. However gentle his words, he'd compelled her to do it and it had become a form of rape.

This time it was he who dared not face her. So he soaked a folded towel and laid it under the water where it would cushion their knees. Then he began to soap her, becoming more and more aroused, and the Japanese *shunga* woodprint came alive. He found he was imagining himself as the warrior, massively endowed, while the real Lilly faded to a captive in a war. It helped him to avoid the truth, that this time she was merely passive, letting him have his way, because it was the price he'd made her pay to save her husband. He watched the water run down her pale skin and felt he was near the peak. He pushed her forward so she had to grab the taps, came up close, and found he was inside her without knowing how he'd got there. He took her by the hips, pulled her even closer and lost all control. Unable to hold back the rising tidal wave, he cried out, not in speechless ardour but in wordless anguish as he achieved what he thought he wanted at the price of losing what he'd always really sought.

He longed to tell her that he loved her, wanted to spend his life with her, have her as his wife as well as lover, knowing with frightening certainty he'd never find another like her. But spent passion, rising reproach, remorse and shame prevented him from saying anything at all.

He returned to the spare bedroom where he'd concealed his uniform as if it was sullied by his use of it to get his way with her, leaving Lilly standing by the bath, not bothering to cover her nakedness, head down, hands hanging, turned away from him. There was no offer to let him dry her, no suggestion of her drying him, and this time she acted differently to the way she had before. She locked the bathroom door, he heard the slight splash as she re-entered the bath, and he understood that she was washing him away.

He got dressed quickly, wondering what he would say to her when she too was clothed again. But there was, after all, nothing left to say. She'd fulfilled her side of the bargain, and now he must honour his. It was the only way to try to make amends, to still the ever-rising feeling of disgust, to have a chance, however slender, to somehow put it right between them. Then, and only then, would he be able to speak the words he'd longed to say as he had climaxed.

He heard himself groan as he struggled to do up his buttons. For the bitter truth was that he couldn't do very much for Olle. He was too young, too junior, too unimportant. No one would take any notice of what he said, the prosecutor least of all. Olle would have to take his chance like everybody else. The bargain he'd made with Lilly was a fraudulent one, and she'd given herself to him for nothing. Had he known, then, that instead of saving Olle he would cause his death, he might finally have found the courage to rush back to the bathroom, shout his real feelings through the door, break it down if she did not open it, hold her and make her understand his love. But the future is always hidden, and instead, once he'd covered himself with his uniform again, he did what was to become a habit. He ran away, scurrying out of the house, into his car and driving to police headquarters in Östersund. There he outlined his plan for catching Olle; and when it was accepted he had to follow it, make the arrest, and Olle died under the wheels of the police car he'd urged to get up speed.

In exactly the same way as he'd crept from her house that day, so his continuing cowardice prevented him from speaking to her afterwards. He concentrated so hard on his own shame that he never considered what her suffering might be like, nor wondered whether there was any way in which he might alleviate it. In such a funk himself, envisaging her scorn, her righteous anger and her open pain, he'd simply covered his ears and eyes and hidden from it, deadening his brain so effectively and selfishly with his own suffering that he never once considered hers. His conscience made him craven, and even if subsequent events had not occurred, he wondered if he would ever have found the courage to speak to her again. But of course the other events did occur, and that enabled him to pile excuse upon excuse. How could he commiserate with her about Olle's death, when he had caused it? No woman accepts comfort from the guilty party, and so he did nothing at all, but ran away again, using his enforced removal into town as the excuse for avoiding her altogether.

Give it time, he told himself with sanctimonious glibness, let things die down, let raw emotions settle and grow a skin again; the time will come, but just not yet. In his devious mind he even began to shift responsibility onto Lilly. If she wanted to talk to him, then she would let him know in her own good time. If she wanted to hear from him, she would give an indication. It was not for him to force himself upon her.

Silently he screamed now as he traced those thoughts, out in the clean snow, clutching his head in an agony of remorse. The false piety of it almost made him vomit. Forcing himself upon her was exactly what he *had* done, in the bathroom, and then he'd abandoned her in her grief. What he was finally confessing to himself made him a monster. It was far worse than he'd ever allowed himself to believe. And it was even worse than that, because, though he hadn't known it but certainly should have realised, he'd driven her back to the very father he knew she'd married Olle to escape from. He understood now why he'd never before permitted himself to see it all so clearly, never before admitted the selfish cruelty of his actions. How could he have lived his life telling himself he'd loved her? No wonder she'd ended hers with such a desperate act. He was responsible for that as well, the blame was his alone. It was as if he'd murdered her, blow after blow, while comforting himself over the years that when she was ready she would find him, and so come back to him. He'd so often despised himself, without believing it with any sincerity at all. But now he loathed himself, his skin crawled at the true horror of what he'd done to her. It was unpardonable, and there was no way he could or should forgive himself. He was so loathsome, someone should crush him underfoot, as one might step upon a mosquito, without thought or hesitation, putting an end to something that should have no place in nature.

But at least he finally understood the way the Furies worked. It is the perpetrator of the evil who himself releases them; and by allowing Magnus to find him so that he could be confessor to him, he might also have enabled him, under pressure from above, to be the Furies' ultimate agent, bringing down the final curtain on a life that could no longer justify a moment's more existence.

CHAPTER 18

Magnus Trygg stared down at Kiruna as the plane began its descent. The mine had always dominated the town, usually rising over it like a darkly brooding presence. But now, smooth and pure in its winter clothing, it seemed almost benevolent despite the fact that soon it would devour the town itself.

It was the largest iron mine in Europe. A kilometre beneath the surface its voracious machines were burrowing ever further into the ore and now they were close to undermining the houses on the western edge. LKAB, the owners of the mine, officially warned the inhabitants that, by 2015, subsidence would cause the railway station and the other nearby buildings to slide into the excavations; and that if mining were not to be abandoned the whole town would have to move elsewhere. To outsiders it seemed the inhabitants were being confronted with a stark choice between the mine and the present location of their town. But in reality it wasn't such a difficult decision. Kiruna, the most northerly town in Sweden, was generally agreed to be the ugliest as well. Magnus, who'd visited it several times, agreed wholeheartedly with a recent description of it as 'a dirge to the misbegotten 1960's socialist love of concrete housing blocks as the acme of functional renewal'.

In such a wilderness, where iron ore ruled supreme, no mine meant no town; and once that harsh fact was accepted there was little option but to agree to the gradual removal of

Kiruna north-west to a new site near the hill of Luossavaara. Concessions were offered. The old timber buildings, worthy of preservation, would be dismantled, piece by numbered piece, and then carefully re-erected, as would a handful of interesting buildings which included the spiky wrought iron town hall and the church. After that, all at the mine's expense, and Magnus was not surprised it was the offer which clinched the deal, the rest of the town would gradually be demolished and a new and more attractive Kiruna would arise.

The plane landed and Magnus, shouldering his backpack, waited patiently to be released. But once he was on the tarmac, breathing the icy air, he used his long legs to stride past other travellers and get out as soon as possible to where the taxis waited. He spotted the man who'd been sent to meet him at once, even though he'd never seen him before. He was sitting backwards on his snow-scooter, away from the cars, relaxed but too watchful to be a casual observer. He'd guessed the ever-cautious Amrén would need to be assured he'd come alone; not just that he'd brought no others with him, but that no one had managed to shadow him without his knowledge. That was why Magnus had deliberately suggested being picked up at the airport, why he hadn't booked into a hotel, why he'd moved so quickly from the plane and why he'd been expecting a snowmobile, not a car. If, despite all his checks, a very clever tail was still on him, he or she would be easily lost when they travelled cross-country.

He went straight up to the man on the snow-scooter, held out his hand and said, "I'm Magnus."

The man was about his age, dark, almost as broad as he was tall, and he was wearing two Sami knives, one short with a decorated reindeer horn hilt, the other large and plain, a *huggare* used as an axe. "Nisse, Einar's son," he said with a cheerful grin, and Magnus felt his fingers crunch as they were compressed in a powerful grip. "You spoke to me on the phone." He looked disparagingly at the skiing outfit Magnus was wearing. "I've got proper clothes for you a few kilometres away, but until then you'll be cold." He swung to face the right way round, Magnus got on behind him and just heard the words “Hold tight” before the engine roared and they shot forward straight at the snow piled along the edge of the road. They hurtled up and over, momentarily losing contact with anything, then landing with a jolt that almost unseated Magnus. They pounded forward across the snow and he rapidly felt the truth of Nisse’s prediction about the cold. It was icy on his face, and the wind seemed to blow straight through his clothes. Even so he revelled in the speed and the adventure of skirting trees, slithering across a narrow bridge, and finally reaching the River Torne. Nisse went straight out onto the ice and then downriver for a time, maintaining his high speed while turning to stare backwards over Magnus’ shoulder.

“Is anyone following?”

Nisse laughed delightedly. “No chance,” he shouted. “I’m the best damn reindeer herder round here, nobody can keep up with me. But now, in the season, I’m a guide, leading snow-scooter trips to see the Northern Lights, and it drives me crazy. I have to go slow all the time so I don’t lose the tourists. It pays better than reindeer, but I’m so happy when I can drive like this for a bit.”

Magnus remembered the phone call he’d made to Nisse. Dr. Utsi had found the house in the painting without too much difficulty after studying the details of all the cottages close to Einar Ruong’s address. The Ruong family was a tight-knit group, living together in a small settlement near the river, and the building Magnus sought was close, but not so near that it did not offer privacy. She’d given him the number of the son, Nisse, and he’d rung him on his mobile in case his office and home phones were no longer secure. He spoke briefly, giving his name, saying he wished to get together with his friend, giving the time his plane would land at Kiruna and saying he needed to be met and taken to wherever it would be convenient for them to talk. He’d liked the voice at the other end, confident, not unfriendly, even more sparing with words than he’d been, asking no questions, ringing off quickly. Magnus was compelled to accept the risk he was just being politely fobbed off, and so he’d been greatly relieved to find anybody at all actually waiting for him, and even more relieved to recognise the voice.

They'd been going so smoothly for the last kilometre he'd relaxed his grip, and when the snow-mobile suddenly tilted sharply as it went up on a ridge of snow and Nisse seemed to lose control, he was pitched off, unhurt but almost buried. Nisse got to him quickly, slithering across the surface like a crab, throwing himself at him and almost wrestling with him as he got the backpack off him and turned him face upwards. Then he towed him back to the scooter, heaved him up onto the seat with extraordinary strength, rid his backpack of the snow that had got inside it, handed it back to him, pulled himself on board and drove off again.

"You could have just asked me," Magnus complained.

"Asked you what?"

"If I was armed."

Nisse chuckled. "I didn't know if you'd tell me the truth. This way I could search you and your backpack, and be sure. I hope you're not mad at me, but my father gives the orders."

"And Ragnar is a very careful man, and all of you are bodyguards."

"We are friends," corrected Nisse. "And we do as friends should, we keep Ragnar safe."

A dog sledding centre came into view and Nisse pulled up beside a large barn. Around them, in their caged enclosures, the huskies gave tongue, the one nearest to Magnus fixing him with his extraordinarily vivid blue eyes. Nisse shouted and at once the dogs were quiet. The variety of colours was remarkable, some almost pure white, others entirely black, some of several shades of grey or brown, and the majority mixed, with patterns of tan and cream, jet, charcoal and fawn, fudge, pepper and salt, and ochre on gesso. A woman appeared at the door of the small timber house, waved to Nisse and then went in again.

"Why are some smaller than the others?" Magnus asked. "It's not females and males."

"Siberian huskies are smaller than Alaskan," Nisse replied. "As you will see, we prefer Alaskans at this centre."

Inside the barn were boxes of protective jackets with fur-edged hoods, bib-trousers, heavy gauntlets, goggles, thick boots and balaclavas. Tourists, and now Magnus, could choose, as with the earliest Ford cars, any colour as long as it was black. Nisse unerringly chose the sizes for him, gave him an empty box where he could store his own clothes until his return journey, then left him to change.

Magnus felt clumsy but warm in the new outfit, and he felt the difference when they were travelling again. Now the chill wind seemed to be deflected from the surface of the clothes, his hands and feet were warm and his face much better protected. Although he still looked around him all the time, Nisse appeared more relaxed, as though he knew no one was following them. He began to point out anything of interest, including, in the distance, Sweden's highest mountain, Kebnekaise, bulky but not at all impressive in height. Magnus prided himself on being observant, but it was only when Nisse told him where to look that he saw the statue-still mother elk standing over its calf, then a solitary reindeer, and finally a white, fluffy-footed ptarmigan not moving till they passed.

After a quarter of an hour, Nisse stopped at the top of a rise. It was becoming dark in the way it did above the Arctic Circle, very suddenly, when the afternoon was scarcely over. Magnus walked about, finding he was stiffer than he'd expected, and that the cold was even colder now. Nisse had thrown himself down in the crisp snow, flat on his back, staring at the sky which, as it blackened, became festooned with bright stars. Magnus stared round at the horizon, but nowhere could he see the familiar artificial light pollution he was used to near Sundsvall. This was the night sky he would have seen a thousand years ago.

"What are you looking at?" he asked Nisse.

"I'm praying," was the entirely unexpected answer. "Praying to Rádienáhttje, the Sami Creator, praying that I won't see a police helicopter, realise you are betraying Ragnar and have to do something about it."

He lapsed into silence, and the two of them stayed still, listening. But no sound of civilization interrupted the sighing of the freshening breeze, or the groan of the increasing cold tightening the surface of the snow and ice.

"Ragnar is very much changed," Nisse said suddenly. "He has a sickness."

"Can it be cured?"

"It is a sickness of the soul. In the old days a Shaman might have given him back the will to live, but the Swedish Lutherans destroyed our beliefs, along with the Shamans' drums and finally the Shamans themselves. My Grandfather was one of the last, and though my father has some gift, I have only a vestige of it. Instead we have to rely on doctors and their hospitals. They can treat many illnesses, but not what Ragnar suffers from. My father and I believe that only Ragnar can decide the proper cure. "

He stared up at Magnus, studying his features and his colour. "Ragnar told us nothing about you except you were his friend. So I was surprised when I first saw you, and hopeful too. It was then I decided to speak to you about him, which I would not usually have done. I had this strong sense you might be able to understand my meaning. Like us, you are from a different culture, not really Christian, not really Swedish."

Magnus shook his head. "I am Swedish," he answered automatically, "and I'm a Christian more than anything else, though not a very good one."

Nisse stood. "I hope for your sake that is true, Magnus, and not just what you would like to be the truth. There is always danger in hiding what you really feel. It is perhaps what Ragnar did, and now he finds his life is not upon a firm promontory, but on a bog."

"I think you're probably right," Magnus said thoughtfully. "He does seem to have built on dreams of the past more than reality. A house built on sand is how the bible puts it."

Nisse waved a dismissive hand. "We Sami use our own land to describe things, not Israel and Palestine. I always found that strange in Christianity, that it wasn't Swedish, or even European, but based on the Middle East. We don't have much sand in Lapland, but we have an awful lot of bogs."

He went back to the snow-scooter, and in silence they both got on and set off again across the snow. Oddly, Magnus felt much closer to Nisse now, and he suspected that Nisse might feel the same. It was so rare nowadays for anyone to speak directly to him of matters of the heart and soul without acute embarrassment, and it might be true that there were issues for him to face about his mixed Thai and Swedish heritage. But all he could think of at this moment was the intuitive understanding Nisse showed about Ragnar's complex problems.

Eventually, as they topped a rise, he saw below him a small group of wooden buildings, huddled together in the snow, not easily visible until you came in close to them and the light of the snowmobile picked them out. They were near the river, and they had doubtless been built upon a rocky promontory. Nisse stopped outside a small cabin which stood somewhat apart from the others, waited until Magnus had dismounted, and then drove off with a brief wave of his hand. Shouldering his backpack, Magnus walked to the door, noticing there were no other tracks in the snow. Unexpectedly nervous, he knocked and the door opened almost instantly, as though his arrival had been watched.

"I've been waiting for you, Magnus," the familiar voice of Ragnar said, but it was a physically altered man who spoke. The smooth-skinned youthful plumpness, which had always so successfully masked the sharp intellect, had entirely drained away. Ragnar was gaunt now, and the mental suffering he'd so obviously endured had given him the uncertainty of a frail elderly man. It was nothing like his previous diffidence, which had been attractive and misleading, allowing criminals to believe he was unsure of himself, until, having revealed a little too much, they were suddenly trapped against a polite but steely will. Now there was no sign of that will. Whatever memories he'd been facing, they'd reduced him to someone who'd lost all faith in himself. But looking into those exhausted red-rimmed eyes, which met his only briefly and then scuttled away to fasten on anything less threatening than a fellow human being, he understood that it was more than this. The new Ragnar was ashamed; and he was also apprehensive, almost as though he was expecting to be fatally attacked.

CHAPTER 19

Ragnar began speaking as soon as he closed the front door, the words flooding out of him through a dam-breach triggered by the arrival of Magnus. He did not spare himself, but spoke almost as though he was giving evidence about someone else entirely. He was so chronologically lucid, the facts so carefully marshalled, that Magnus was in no doubt that he was hearing what had been dredged from his subconscious during his emotional exile between Poland and his refuge here in Lapland. As he listened he tried very hard to keep in mind Pia's sharp reminder that he must weigh up the facts and respond as a policeman as well as a friend. Breaking the law, she'd said, must always be punished. A crime is simple. If it's been committed, a policeman has to act. But just as he'd predicted, it wasn't turning out to be that simple.

He was moved by the obvious love Ragnar revealed each time he mentioned Lilly; but he found it harder to countenance the immaturity with which he'd behaved and the unconscious cruelty of his actions. The real problem, he realised, was that Ragnar was talking about a time so far in the past that it meant little to him. He'd been a five year old child then, and remembered almost nothing of that period in his life. He had no personal experience of the prevailing attitudes at that time to draw upon, and so nothing Ragnar said felt totally real. Yet there were sufficient links to the Ragnar he was familiar with to accept that it was the truth as he remembered it. He recognised his distaste for strong emotion, his lack of inherent understanding of the opposite sex, his extreme sensitivity. He could understand his fear of public ridicule, too, and so it was perfectly possible that he was hearing what the youthful Ragnar might have done. He could even comprehend the way Ragnar's fear led him to abandon Lilly when she needed him most, though he could not excuse it. He was, of course, relieved that the rape turned out to be scarcely rape at all, but then he'd never wavered in his belief that Ragnar would never have acted with such criminal abandon. But, his conscience pricked by Pia's matter of fact realism, he was compelled to admit to himself that a crime *had* been committed. Ragnar had deliberately and corruptly used his authority as a policeman to obtain a sexual favour from Lilly; and, although he could accept that Olle's death had been a tragic accident, the subsequent police enquiry had been flawed, protecting Ragnar when he probably should have received a reprimand. These were matters that could not be overlooked, that had to go before a police tribunal if not a court, with the inevitable result that it would leak into the media and the journalists would crucify him. At the very least his career would be stalled and early retirement inevitable.

Yet none of it had any reality for him and he could hardly stay awake. Johan had not been well last night, coughing and keeping them awake. He and Sonja had made him a hot drink which helped to soothe him; but no sooner had they finally got him settled than Angelica had a nightmare, shouting out and needing to be comforted before she dozed off again. That was his reality, and now he was hearing an old story, a confession from the past, and he wished he could shut his ears to it. He would *do* whatever was necessary for Ragnar. He was always good at doing. But he neither needed nor wanted to hear the detail which embarrassed him and unnecessarily diminished Ragnar.

Eventually, perhaps noticing his weariness, his eyes half-closing as he fought off sleep, Ragnar prepared some food for him; but he went on talking as he did so, as if he was afraid that once he paused he would be unable to continue. He talked as they ate, and when he showed Magnus the guest room. He sat on the bed while Magnus unpacked the few necessities he'd brought with him, explaining how he had lived his life in expectation that Lilly would one day return to him. It was only when he reached the Uppsala conference, and his meeting with Lilly's father, that it began to dawn on Magnus that what he was hearing was in fact some sort of tragedy, and that it was the more tragic for being entirely self-inflicted.

"When he told me Lilly was dead, and had been dead for most of the years I'd been dreaming of her return, I no longer wanted to defend myself. I saw myself for what I was, and I wasn't worth saving. "

For the first time he paused, seemed lost in thought, and Magnus took Lilly's letter from his pocket and handed it to him.

"The lawyer, Bredenberg, found it among the father's papers. It's a letter Lilly wrote to you, after she'd gone home. It's ready for posting, sealed and stamped, and Bredenberg believes her father must have intercepted it, without Lilly's knowledge, though how he did it we'll never know. But though he didn't open it, he carefully kept it, so he may have thought it would contain evidence against you that would justify the retribution he wanted to exact. Again, we'll never know the truth of it, except that it was revenge he wanted, and he was prepared to go to extraordinary lengths to try to get it."

Ragnar was staring at the letter, bewildered, turning it over and over in his hand and raising it as if to recover any lingering scent of Lilly.

"Why did Bredenberg give it back? Why didn't he open it and use it?"

"He believes in the law. Lilly was of age, she prepared this letter for the post, and therefore the father had no legal right to prevent it being sent. Even at this very late stage Bredenberg was not willing to condone his client's illegal act, let alone benefit by it. So, however lengthy the delay, he wanted it to be delivered to you, the intended recipient."

"I don't think I want to open it," Ragnar said, still staring at it as if a sense of what it said might materialize through the envelope and on into his mind. A visible shudder shook him and he held the letter out for Magnus to take back. "I know what she thought of me after what I did to her, and it would be too disturbing to read such condemnation in words from beyond the grave, for that's what they've become."

Magnus felt exasperation fill him and he shrugged, trying to control it. "It's up to you. It's been delivered to you, it's your property, so you can do whatever you like with it. But I'll tell you this; I won't take the letter back. And in fact you *don't* know what she thought of you, because you never gave her the opportunity to speak. You ducked out, putting the whole burden of meeting and speaking onto her. Now you've been offered that chance again, to hear her even though she's dead. Maybe you should think carefully before you run away from the letter, just as you ran away from her."

He had not realised how irritated the combination of exhaustion and Ragnar's recital had made him, but he knew it had shown in his voice. It wasn't entirely fair, because he was such a different character to Ragnar, and lived at a later time. If Sonja had rejected him during their early courting, he'd have tried to charm her into a gradual change of mind. He would never have forced her, never given up on her, and if she'd moved away he would have followed her. It was true that Sonja had not been married to someone else, and he'd not been about to arrest the husband, but even so he would have acted totally differently, and Ragnar's present feebleness frustrated him.

Ragnar was watching him thoughtfully, and when he finally spoke he seemed to have recovered something of his usual manner.

"So you think I should read the letter and then go back and face what I did?"

"Yes."

"But I rather doubt if that's what you were instructed to do. Jörgen would have realised very quickly that you were the only one who would be able to reach me, and I can guess what his instructions were, putting the needs of the group firmly before those of the individual. Jörgen will have told you, directly or by implication, that in order to protect the greater good of the police force, I must remain 'missing'. I'm intrigued to know whether he actually told you to shoot me, or just to put a pistol in my hand."

"Was that why you had me searched?"

"Partly, yes it was. But more than anything else I feared you'd do the right thing, and take me back with you to face what I deserve."

"And you thought I would force that on you?"

"You would have had to. Because I see everything very differently to you, and for me there can be no going back. Jörgen is no fool, and he's right." Ragnar smiled, but as he did so Magnus was relieved to see him tuck the letter into his pocket. "I'm sure you were asked to ensure there was no scandal, which there would be if I returned to stand trial. He and those he represents want an end to it, neat and clean, and he thought you were just the man to do it. You'll probably get my job, and I've no doubt there was an indication that you've got remarkable prospects, that you're a man of promise as I was, an officer who will not be forgotten."

Magnus smiled in his turn. "I'm sure all that was in Jörgen's mind, but he doesn't know me very well."

"Why did you come then?"

"Better me than somebody else. I needed to know what you wanted to do, and I had to ensure the letter was delivered."

Ragnar nodded, looking at him earnestly. "Before you brought this letter I knew exactly what I had to do. But opening this envelope terrifies me, Magnus. I'm being asked to face Lilly herself, and I don't know if I can do it. This isn't the Lilly I dreamed of meeting, a Lilly who, over time, had been able to accept the past. This is the raw and suffering Lilly, driven back by my cowardly selfishness to the father she believed she'd escaped from, a Lilly already contemplating death as her only way out. How can I bear to read what she says to me? Suddenly it isn't my own measured judgement I have to face, nor even yours or Jörgen's. It's her judgement on me, and it will hurt me so much more. The most shameful fact I've discovered about myself is that I've always been a thin-skinned moral coward; and this letter makes me an even greater one."

"What will you do?"

"I don't know yet. But I shall have made a decision, right or wrong, by tomorrow. Will you allow me that much time?"

Magnus nodded, not knowing what to say, but it seemed to satisfy Ragnar who fetched more coffee and suddenly relaxed. He swallowed a great gulp and began to talk again, his eyes fixed on something in the distance, and Magnus guessed it was only his presence that was necessary, not his real self.

"Running was instinctive, but in a way it was a decision. I had to sort out the real story, facing all the bad things that I'd done. When I was a little boy, I loved to whittle wood, shaving the bark away, slowly stripping off the outer layers of the birch until I saw the pale gleam of the inner wood, revealed to human eyes for the very first time, untouched, pure in its perfection. On my journey I've been whittling myself, and I've finally reached the inner layer, the truth of my love for Lilly. That's all I want preserved, my only legacy. So it was important to me that you should know it, too."

He fell into deep thought again, and the silence startled Magnus out of the sleep that had overcome him. Luckily Ragnar was so deep in his own reflections he hadn't noticed Magnus had dozed off and suddenly he said, "I was re-reading Proust's 'In Search of Lost Time' yesterday, and there's a passage about Monsieur Legrandin which spoke directly to me in a way it never had before. He hates snobs, but he cannot see, as all others can, that he is one himself. And it made me realise how true that is of me. We humans can see faults in others, but a defensive mechanism prevents us from seeing the whole truth about what is bad in ourselves. That's how I was, and I'm almost relieved I've been freed from those comforting but distorting illusions. Perhaps humour should be the proper antidote to such self-delusion, but I've never really been comfortable with humour. I avoid funny books, comedy films, and I've recently realised I don't laugh at myself. If I'd been able to see the funny side of what happened in the bath with

Lilly, if I hadn't lacked a sense of the ridiculous, we might have been able to smile about it, talk about it, and our lives would have been quite different. But I'm frightened of laughter, I don't like being laughed at, and so laughter has never come easily."

He looked across at Magnus and saw he was asleep. He walked quietly over to him, settled him more comfortably, placed a cushion beneath his head, found a rug to lay over him, put out the lights, and quietly left him to his slumber. Magnus, he realised, was not really very like him. He was so much younger, living in the present, not the past. He'd not been particularly interested in his great confession. It had not shocked him, it might even have bored him, and he'd probably dozed through some of it.

As he walked along the corridor to his bedroom he recalled the solemn, sleepy look on Magnus' face and he managed to laugh a little. Oddly, the unexpected way in which Magnus had responded encouraged him, reminding him that he was often wrong about other people's reactions. He reached into his pocket and took out Lilly's letter. Then he went into his room and shut the door.

CHAPTER 20

Magnus woke the next morning to the sound of singing. Someone was enjoying himself in the shower, and, since it couldn't be Ragnar, he assumed it was Nisse. Perhaps his own shower was broken and Ragnar had let him use his. But the song, despite the burbling under the water jet and the lack of discernible words, was still recognisable as '*Pepita Dansar'*, and somehow that seemed an unlikely song for Nisse even to know, let alone to sing.

Later, when he'd had a shower himself, and gone downstairs to have some breakfast, he was confronted by a rejuvenated Ragnar, almost his old self, smiling, assured and even capable of an early morning song. He came across to Magnus and hugged him. He'd never done it before, and it was totally out of character for someone who normally shunned any form of physical intimacy. Yet he performed it in an entirely natural way, expressing his delight at having Magnus as his guest.

"It's meant so much to me to have you here, Magnus. Just the fact you took the trouble to travel so far to seek me out was a remarkable act of faith, even if you were pretending to follow orders. But your presence here has changed everything for me, and though I've got to leave you on your own today while I take the snowmobile and sort out a few matters, tomorrow we'll do whatever you want, go anywhere, see anything."

Magnus longed to ask him whether he'd read Lilly's letter, but he was afraid of any action that might reverse the almost miraculous resurrection of the real Ragnar. Instead he asked a more practical question.

"Will you be coming back with me?"

"When do you have to leave?"

"The day after tomorrow."

"It's certainly possible. It's as though a huge weight has been lifted from me, and I can see myself positively again and face anything. It's an extraordinary feeling. I've been singing since I awoke."

"I heard you in the shower," replied Magnus ruefully. "I hope it'll be the only time I'm woken by my chief carolling forth about Pepita dancing the tango in Panama, in a vain attempt to imitate Evert Taube."

Ragnar laughed and put his hands up in surrender. "I'll never do it again," he assured him. "It was a once and for all special occasion. By the way, if you'd like to go out skiing, or maybe see the reindeer, Nisse will find you all the equipment and accompany you."

He waved cheerfully, went outside, and shortly afterwards Magnus heard the chatter of his snow scooter receding into the distance. It was a beautiful day, crisp, cold and sunny, and Nisse suggested he should take the opportunity of accompanying him to the reindeer rather than skiing which he could do round Sundsvall. Magnus agreed enthusiastically especially as Nisse said he would be happy to sleep behind him on the snowmobile, and Magnus could do the driving. The sun on the snow was so dazzling he was glad he had good goggles, and apart from a terse instruction or two from his passenger, he was able to imagine he was alone in this white vastness. It was as though the day of Ragnarök, the end of all things, had finally arrived, and the world was empty, buildings and human beings replaced by snow and scattered dwarfish trees. Apart from the throb of his own engine, he drove through silence. It was an uncanny experience, cleansing his mind of small matters and irritating worries, and filling it instead with a sense of wonder and a feeling of the closeness of divinity. Out here it did not seem strange to have such a thought, for it made it possible to accept one's own lack of importance in these surroundings. He felt his usual self draining away, replaced by an acceptance of his frailty in such a wilderness; and, diminished as he was, he drew comfort from the sense that some benign power was watching over him. Death seemed very close as well, of course, because, so far away from human habitation, the snow and the cold could easily swallow him up and kill him. But, despite Death breathing at his shoulder, he didn't feel at all unsafe, though that might be because the idea of oblivion was quite natural here. It was accepted as a part of life, and so there was no fear in it. In fact he felt ecstatically happy, renewed, and eager to face whatever the future might hold for him.

Nisse told him to pull up on a height, and below him he saw the huge herd of reindeer, busily scraping away the snow with their hooves, digging down to browse on the succulent lichen below. Some had antlers, others hadn't, and he could see at once that those with them had a considerable advantage, driving the others away from the best feeding areas.

"We males always seem to have an unfair advantage," he said teasingly to Nisse.

"If you're human, maybe yes," answered Nisse. "But reindeer organise things better. It's the cows who have the antlers at this time of the year, because they're pregnant and have a greater need of food. The bulls lose their antlers in the winter, so they're the ones at a disadvantage down there."

"When do they grow them again?"

"They're fully grown by the time of the rutting season next September. Bulls need them at that time because they have to fight. It's all based on utility. The cows drop them in spring when they start to migrate to the summer pastures, because food is getting plentiful then, and they no longer need to compete for it."

"There must be a reindeer god then, because that's very cleverly worked out."

"Everything about reindeer is amazing," Nisse said seriously. "You always know when it's time for the annual migration because the old cows move to the west side of the herd, indicating the direction they need to go to reach the summer pastures in the mountains. And did you know reindeer can only eat lichen when it's beneath the snow?"

Magnus nodded, a piece of knowledge from one of his cases flitting into his mind. "Isn't it because it's too tough to eat unless it's softened by the snow?"

Nisse nodded, looking surprised, and as they made their way down to the herders' camp Magnus told him a little about the murder on the High Coast committed with a Sami knife, the initial suspicion of the herder and the knowledge of reindeer he'd gained while eliminating him.

"Were you working with Ragnar then?"

"Yes, even though I was still with the Östersund force. But I'd met Ragnar when I was a young constable dealing with my first murder, and he arranged for me to be loaned to the Sundsvall police so I could take temporary charge on the High Coast."

"You liked him straight away?"

Magnus hesitated. "I was young, very full of myself then, and I think at first I liked him because he seemed to like me and thought I was a good policeman. It was only gradually that I came to appreciate his thoroughness, his fairness, his apparent calm, and especially his sense of decency if that doesn't sound too sentimental."

There was no one at the camp as the herders were with the reindeer, but Nisse drew his long knife, split some wood, and in no time at all he had a fire going in the open-topped *kåta* tent while Magnus sprawled on a reindeer skin thrown down on top of the birch twigs strewn over the floor. Nisse took a metal bowl, cut some reindeer meat into thin strips, added a little oil and cooked them over the fire, and they both devoured them with hunks of bread. It was delicious, and Magnus realised how hungry the journey had made him. Nisse brewed coffee, and while they were drinking it black, hot and sweet, he reverted to the earlier subject.

"What do you think of Ragnar now you're here?"

"When I arrived he was so terribly changed I almost found it hard to recognise him. It shocked me, and I don't think I was as understanding as I should have been. I don't know how much he told you, but I'm sure you're aware he's in some trouble, and he's made himself ill over it. But I couldn't help feeling he was exaggerating it, worrying too much about things that happened twenty-eight years ago. I think he's always had too much of a conscience, weighing everything up and blaming himself for tiny faults the rest of us would just shrug off. But this morning he suddenly seemed himself again, as though he'd put it all behind him, and with any luck the worst of the crisis is over."

"Perhaps it's because you came. We were suddenly lost when my mother was killed, and it was only when Ragnar took a hand and got it all sorted that we could think clearly. At the time we were caught up in a sort of terrible panic, and maybe it was the same with him. Then you came, he was able to talk about it, you didn't seem too fussed, and he suddenly began to think straight. All we can do is wait and see. When do you have to go back?"

"The day after tomorrow."

"Will he go with you?"

"As you said, we can only wait and see."

They got back just before the light failed, but Ragnar had not returned.

"Were you expecting him back?" Magnus asked worriedly.

"We never expect anything of Ragnar. He's his own man, he does what he likes and we never assume he will tell us anything or explain anything. That's the way it's always been, the way my father wants it, and the way Ragnar wants it. Whatever he does is all right by us, and we never interfere in his life. We live our life, he lives his, and it's the only way it can work."

"I understand that, Nisse, but I'm still worried."

"If it puts your mind at rest, he does often stay out at night, sleeping in a *kåta*, and he knows how to look after himself. My theory is that he enjoys pitting himself against the elements. It's a sort of challenge, and each time he succeeds he feels better about himself. Maybe it's a good thing to do when you start to doubt yourself. Maybe it's the way you find yourself again."

"I think I ought to go and look for him," Magnus said stubbornly.

"At night? And in which direction will you go to look for him? How will you survive if you run out of fuel? It's a huge empty area round here, you can't just go out searching for people as easily as you could where you live. And what will you say to him if you do find him? That you thought he was so useless he needed a nursemaid? We don't live like that up here, Magnus. Ragnar's a man, a friend, and we have to give him space. We have to trust him enough to believe he knows what he's doing. Otherwise you make a child of him, or an old man who's lost his marbles."

Magnus nodded slowly, went back inside the house and shut the door. But once there he became more and more concerned. He knew he shouldn't interfere, but his conscience wouldn't leave him alone. However much he reminded himself of Ragnar's happiness in the morning, and the seemingly magical change that had come over him, he felt he should be taking some action. He went outside again, and found that Nisse was still there, staring into the increasing darkness. It was so bitterly cold he found he could hardly speak, but after swallowing several times he asked Nisse if he'd tried to ring Ragnar's mobile.

"He hasn't had a mobile with him since he's been here this time."

Magnus felt a fool. He still couldn't get used to the fact Ragnar was on the run, in hiding, and he wasn't going to carry a mobile which would enable him to be tracked.

"Are you worried about him?"

Nisse didn't answer the question directly. "I've spoken to my father. You and I will go out as soon as it's light tomorrow morning. I'll have two scooters ready, with plenty of fuel. Now you'd better get what sleep you can."

Magnus left him, made himself a hot drink, picked desultorily at some cold food, and then got himself as ready as possible for a quick start the next morning, including putting out a thermos for hot coffee and placing a pocket first aid kit with his outer clothing. He dozed fitfully, scenes of his time with Ragnar jumping through his mind like an early silent movie show. He was meeting him for the first time in Sundsvall as he followed up clues to the killer of Hazal Nazif, tied to a stake and shot; being debriefed by him at the airport after his meeting with the Russian Mafia in Kaliningrad; nodding his head when he asked him to guard an old lady who might be the next victim of a hammer killer; and raising his glass to him as he handed round the Christmas presents to Angelica, Johan and Sonja, looking fat and rubicund in his *Jultomten* costume and trying to blow his white beard and moustache away from his skin when it tickled him. Imperceptibly Ragnar had become an intrinsic part of his life, and Magnus hoped he'd be able to find a way to save him.

He woke hours before the dawn, but he got up, made himself ready, and then wandered aimlessly round the little house until he saw Nisse outside. By the time they were on the two snow scooters, and the engines had been started, the sun was above the horizon, and they set off into the glittering solitude. Nisse led the way, and Magnus could sense that he was using his knowledge of Ragnar's usual movements to probe successive areas. Gradually they moved further and further away from the house, into more isolated places. Sometimes, while Nisse seemed to pursue a scent that only he could distinguish, Magnus sat still on his machine, methodically covering the ground with his field glasses, searching for any alien sign.

After nearly two hours Nisse angled down off the heights, out of the bitter wind to more protected areas where there were scattered stands of conifers, a number of them quite substantial for the area, with thick trunks and dense branches. Aware of the danger of fallen boughs or concealed stumps, they moved more slowly, taking their time to search. Often they moved apart, each stopping to sweep the area with their field glasses. It was quieter where they were, there was less light, and it was not easy to see beneath the low growing limbs of the Norway Spruce.

It was only because he was focussing the glasses so carefully as he searched the ground beneath one of the bigger trees that Magnus spotted a snowy hump, close to the base of the trunk. It looked too large to be a rock, the wrong shape for a dead animal, and where a shaft of sunlight touched it there was a reflected gleam. He signalled to Nisse, and as soon as he had his attention he moved closer, Nisse following him. His heart lurched when he saw it was a crumpled snow scooter which had smashed into the trunk of the spruce. The crash helmet that must have been torn off by the branch was lying by it, the dangling straps showing they had not been properly tightened. A short distance away, just where it would have been hurled off by the force of the collision, something was lying beneath the snow, covered by the early morning fall. Nisse pulled up beside him, took it all in with a glance, looked away and tactfully motioned Magnus, as friend and colleague, to go forward on his own.

It was Ragnar, and he was dead. Brushing away the snow revealed no obvious sign of injury except a cut and bruising on his forehead where he must have been struck by the lower branches as the helmet was ripped away; but if he had been unconscious it would not have taken long for the intense cold to kill him. He looked at peace, almost serene, as though he'd fallen asleep at a moment of intense happiness, when all his fears and guilty worries had left him. One pocket of his ski jacket was unbuttoned, and reaching carefully inside Magnus withdrew a clear plastic cover containing a letter. The handwriting was the same as that on the envelope he had received from Mikael Bredenberg, and which he'd brought to Ragnar. As he'd urged him to do, Ragnar had opened it and read it, and then he'd carefully protected it and carried it with him as he drove out into the wilderness where he could be utterly alone.

Magnus slipped it into his own pocket for later perusal. Only then would he know what to do with it; only then would he know what forces had been driving Ragnar at that moment when he left the open snow and went among the trees. Neither he nor Nisse had commented on the move from infinite space above to the more hazardous areas lower down, and he knew it would never be referred to. But Nisse would have had his own reasons for supposing it might be an area worth searching; and Magnus would have to draw his own conclusions.

He beckoned to Nisse, and for a moment both men crouched silently in the snow beside Ragnar's body.

"It's over then," said Nisse bluntly. "You can't bring a case against a dead man. He's found peace at last."

They both stood up, and Magnus faced him. "I shall have to make a report," he said in his official voice, studiously keeping it without any emphasis. "What do you think happened?"

"He must have lost concentration momentarily, crashed, and been thrown off unconscious into the snow where he froze to death. It's a fairly common winter accident. Maybe he was tired and dozed off for a second. It's all it takes, and he hadn't been sleeping well. He'd been taking pills, too, to calm him, and that's never good when you're out on a snow scooter, especially if you're driving fast."

"Do you think he was driving fast?"

"From the look of the damage to the snow scooter, it hit the tree at speed."

Magnus nodded. "That matches my conclusions, though I wondered whether he might have been so deep in his own thoughts that he might have failed to take enough care and lost control."

Nisse thought about this. "It's possible," he admitted, "though Ragnar was a very careful man. I think falling asleep is more likely."

"I shall need you to make a statement when we get back. If I type it out, and you're happy with it, will you sign it?"

Nisse nodded. "I know you're police, but don't you think you should ring the local officer?"

"There's no signal out here. You should ring him when we're back at your place, but meanwhile I'm assuming the responsibility for not leaving the body here where wild animals may get at it. We'll mark the place where it lay, leave the snowmobile here, but we'll take Ragnar home. He was a very senior officer, and he deserves special respect. Will you help me get him onto one of the scooters?"

"I'll take him on mine," said Nisse. "I'm more experienced with snow scooters, and I know every bump and hollow."

Magnus suddenly seemed to relax and Nisse did too, understanding that the official interlude was over. So it was that Ragnar came home to the place he loved in a funeral cortège of two snowmobiles, accompanied by his best friend and the son of the man he had saved from a miscarriage of justice.

CHAPTER 21

Dear Ragnar,

It seems strange to use your name when I've usually thought of you as Officer Amrén, but it didn't seem right to put that at the top of a personal letter. I've done something bad and you will be angry with me. I was very unhappy when I had to come home, and as each day has passed I've become more and more miserable. My father is convinced you did terrible things to me, and he's been on at me the whole time to tell him the details. You must believe that at first I defended you, and said it was all a misunderstanding between us, and that Olle's death had been an accident. But when I heard nothing from you I became quite ill, and in my mind I suppose I must have begun to blame you a little. He went on and on at me, and I cried a lot, and finally, when he began to question me in a nasty way, suggesting horrible things, I did say you had said you would help Olle if I would let you make love to me. But when he typed it all out, and told me I must sign it, it was all different, like rape, and it made it seem as if I thought you'd had Olle killed to stop him finding out what you'd done to me, and that had never occurred to me. For a long time I wouldn't sign it, but I became more and more ill, and a colleague of my father said it was depression and a form of post–traumatic shock which I didn't understand. But in the end, when I believed you would never take me away from my father and I would never see you again, I lost all hope, and I signed just to keep him away from me.

It was so weak of me, but I think I've always been weak, never really able to do things properly. Although I didn't love Olle I liked being with him as his wife because life was simple with him and I could do it and didn't make mistakes, and the other didn't matter because it wasn't often and not for long, and letting him was a way of thanking him for giving me a home and a sort of happiness. But then I met you, and you were different, kind and gentle and shy, and I felt at ease with you, and it was the first time, when I saw you look at me, that I felt I might be able to give as well as take. I was still a fool, of course, because I fell in love with you straight away although I'd never known what love was before. It seemed you might love me a bit, and you even seemed to find me a bit attractive, and that made me feel pretty. I didn't think it through, I sort of forgot I was married because my marriage wasn't really to do with love, but much more practical, like cooking and washing and cleaning. I must have thought I could have love with you and marriage to Olle, because I didn't feel wicked or anything, just happier than I'd ever been in my life.

But I never thought I might be peculiar in other ways, and that I'd upset you when I never wanted to, but didn't think enough. I've always known one of my breasts is smaller than the other, and I was teased about it at school though I don't think it's really much smaller, just a little. But I was so ashamed, feeling it was some sort of deformity, that I bought a bra padded on one side. I was never teased again and I've worn one ever since but it's a secret and I've never let anybody see it, not Olle or my father or anybody, I just couldn't do it because it's silly and shameful but I must have it. That's why I wouldn't let you touch my breast through my dress even though I was so glad you wanted to. It's why I wouldn't let you see me undress, but had to go in to the other room. You must have thought I was so peculiar, but I couldn't explain it's not my breasts I'm ashamed of, it's my need to wear the padded bra. I wanted you to see me naked because I hoped you'd like it, and you did seem to, and you didn't seem to notice anything wrong with my breasts which was so nice though it didn't stop me needing the bra, though I expect if we'd ever been able to live together I would have done because I'd have been so proud of you loving me that I wouldn't have felt ashamed of anything anymore.

I wish I could say I can't forgive myself for not letting you love me that first time, but I was as taken by surprise as you were. I didn't know it was going to happen, had never thought it possible, so I do forgive myself even though I wish a thousand times every day it had never happened. I don't know much about sex, and never used to think about it before I met you. It was so lovely when you held me, and it was even better in the bath when you were washing me. I felt you loved me and I knew I'd never stop loving you from that moment on and I haven't. Things were happening inside me that I'd never experienced before and although I didn't understand it I didn't want it to ever stop. I became happier and happier, and I'd never been really happy before. By the time you began to touch me I was in the power of something wonderful, which was you and yet something in me and something outside us both as well. Then I seemed to burst, I was taken over, and it terrified me, not because it wasn't nice but because it was too nice, and I knew that if it went on I would never be able to let Olle touch me again, I would not be able to stay with him, I would have to be with you, and you hadn't said anything about wanting to be with me forever, or even marrying me if I was free, and I didn't dare think it was even possible. So I panicked, I pushed you away, and in that moment I saw I'd destroyed whatever it was you felt for me.

And I had, hadn't I? You kept away from me, and, the next time I saw you, you were different, harder, almost as though you wanted to take some sort of revenge on me. Stupidly, knowing I'd behaved badly to you, though I truly hadn't meant to, I thought that if you did it you would feel better and we could start again. And I wanted you to do it, because even though I'm not clever about some things, I'd thought everything over and understood I must have had my first ever orgasm, and was probably about to have more. So by the time you arrived I knew my own mind. Whatever the consequences, I wanted you to make love to me again. I longed to have those orgasms even if you didn't love me, and never would, even if it meant my leaving Olle and living alone. I wanted you so much, and I couldn't wait to give myself to you.

Perhaps that was the sort of sin of lust my father talks about, because you were so different this time, and I didn't feel as I had before. You seemed ashamed of what you were doing, and though I pitied you for all you were feeling, and loved you still, and wanted to make it good for you, it was as though you'd become Olle, and I felt nothing at all.

It was as though we were fated, and maybe we were, because I was a married woman. You left hurriedly, Olle was killed before you could arrest him, and I never saw you again.

I shall wait for your reply to let me know whether it's possible you might be able to meet me and maybe even take me away. Please don't be too long because I feel I'm on the edge of a dark pit and one day soon I'm afraid I'll fall into it. If you don't reply at all I'll know you feel nothing for me, and I've misunderstood as I often seem to do. But I will understand the silence. Why should you feel for me? At least it'll set me free to make my own choice, with nobody to influence me but me.

I cannot talk to my father, he speaks and thinks like a doctor, too clever for me, full of knowledge of symptoms but without any understanding of human weakness which seems to disgust him. I've so surprised myself by being able to write so easily to you about all these things. I never could have done it before I met you, not to my father, not to Olle. I even believe if you'd been here I just might have been able to say it to your face. I begin to believe we went wrong because we both found it so hard to tell each other our real feelings.

After what I signed, and in case my father, who seems to hate you, tries to use it against you, I must put in writing that you did not rape me, or force me in any way at all. I wanted you to make love to me, wanted it so very much. It had nothing to do with what you said about helping Olle. On that I knew you better than you knew yourself. You'd have helped him anyway. Nor did I ever believe you wanted him dead. That was not possible for somebody as sensitive as you.

I understand, not perfectly but enough, the shame and horror you must have felt after his death, and the need to move away immediately in case you were accused. I fear you thought too that I would suspect you, or hate you, but that never happened. Time has passed now, so much time it seems, and if you are reassured by what I write I pray you will be brave and come, or write to me to tell me your feelings as I have tried to tell you mine.

Warm greetings,

Lilly

CHAPTER 22

Magnus was so busy over the next few hours he was able to prevent himself thinking too deeply about Ragnar's death. Tying up the loose ends with his customary efficiency and despatch enabled him to hide behind his position as the senior policeman on the spot, and so the official temporarily masked the personal.

A search of Ragnar's bedroom revealed a briefcase containing his will. It named Magnus as his executor, and almost everything was left to support the foundation of a scholarship for children of reindeer herders at the Jokkmokk Technical High School, which specialised in the many forms of Sami art. The only exception was a small bequest to Angelica and Johan, 'the family I never had', to help them with their higher education. A sealed letter addressed to Magnus expressed the wish to be cremated locally in Lapland, as quietly as possible, and his ashes to be scattered, during the summer, in the small garden he had made beside his cottage here.

Nisse, meanwhile, got in contact with Spiik, the Kiruna police officer with special responsibility for the area where Ragnar had died. He arrived on his snow-scooter shortly afterwards and Nisse brought him to Ragnar's house. He was a quietly spoken middle-aged man with a calm manner and an observant gaze. He shook hands with Magnus, showing no sign of subservience to his higher rank. He listened silently to the story he and Nisse told, and considered the marks on

Ragnar's face when he was shown the body, now lying on his own bed.

"Why did you move him?" he asked, but with no implied criticism in his tone. Magnus explained, Spiik pondered what he'd said, and then he nodded. "I'd like to see the place where the death occurred so that I can study the tree and the crashed motor-scooter."

As they left the house he suddenly looked searchingly at Magnus. "I understand he was under some pressure."

"A lot of pressure," Magnus admitted without hesitation. "It had just been announced that he'd been made Police Commissioner for Västernorrland, but shortly afterwards he was accused of a crime that happened twenty-eight years ago, when he was starting his police career in Jämtland."

"And what crime would that have been?"

"No charge has been made yet, but I understand from the lawyer representing the accuser that the alleged crime was rape."

"And why would you be singled out to receive that sort of information?"

"Amrén was my chief in Sundsvall. I'm Head of Homicide, and in his absence I took his place for a while."

"He must have been very depressed."

"He was. But yesterday he got good news, and the change in him was startling. He was singing in the shower, full of sudden energy and seemingly bursting with happiness."

Spiik swung round on Nisse, who was following them and Nisse nodded. "He was quite his old self, maybe even a bit more-so."

"Good news about his case?" Spiik asked, turning back to Magnus.

"Yes. He was shown a letter in which the girl he was accused of raping, withdrew the charge just before her death and completely vindicated him."

"Who had made the accusation?"

"Her father, who recently killed himself."

"That's rather a lot of death."

"Yes."

"And being so happy suddenly, so relieved, you feel it's unlikely your chief also killed himself?"

"Personally I think it is extremely unlikely."

"Then let's see what the tree and the snow-scooter tell us."

Nisse led the way, with Magnus up behind him, and Spiik followed on his snowmobile. At the scene he squatted down and painstakingly studied the crashed scooter, the tree and its branches.

"If he was so lively and happy, why did he crash?" he asked finally, and he was watching both Nisse and Magnus as he did so.

"He hadn't been sleeping well, not for days," Nisse replied, "and he'd been taking pills to help. I think it all caught up with him when he could relax at last, and he simply fell asleep while driving. You know as well as I do how hypnotic crossing kilometre after kilometre of snow can be; and when your body's exhausted it's easy for your eyes to close momentarily of their own accord. If you're driving fast, as he usually was, it may be fatal."

"I wonder why he suddenly left the open heights and came down among the trees?"

Nisse shrugged, though Magnus was certain he'd tensed inwardly at the probing question, just as he had. Although Spiik waited expectantly, Nisse did not let the silence unsettle him and wisely, Magnus thought, added nothing to his shrug.

Spiik glanced at Magnus. "Have you a different view?"

"Falling asleep is probably the most likely explanation, though I was so surprised by his sudden euphoria that I worry he may have gone over the top with relief, taken risks, driven dangerously, felt he was immortal and lost control."

"But either way it would be an accident?"

Both men nodded, waiting while Spiik stood immobile beside the tree, deep in thought.

"If he had still been depressed I would have decided he brought about his own death," he said finally, "though he was careful to make it look like an accident. But that's not usually the action of a happy man. So my conclusion is accidental death, and that is what I shall say in my report. In due course I'd be grateful for a copy of the letter of vindication, to attach to the report."

"I can give you a signed statement that it existed, that it was seen by Amrén the evening before he set out on his snowmobile, and I will include the relevant sentence in which the writer withdraws the charge she made and vindicates Amrén," Magnus replied decisively. "But it is a private letter, a very personal one, and now that Amrén is no longer accused of any crime I cannot, as his Executor, give you access to more than I feel is necessary to support your conclusions. If you really feel you require the full letter you will have to get a court order and apply to the lawyer to whom I shall be returning it."

"That won't be necessary," Spiik said. He shook hands formally with both men, got on his snowmobile and set off back to his office. Nisse took Magnus to Ragnar's house, and neither spoke a word during the drive, each busy with his thoughts. Magnus, who was afraid of emotion catching up with him, and desperate to keep it at bay, called Sonja as soon as he was alone. He needed to hear how she reacted to what had happened, believing it would help to shape his own eventual response and the succeeding grief.

"I can't be too sorry," she said. "It'll be harder for you, but Ragnar did what he felt was best for him, and as his friends we can't really argue with that. Will it be recorded as an accident?"

"Yes, Nisse and I made sure of that. But I don't think I'm too sad either," and he read her Lilly's letter.

"Poor foolish man," she murmured. "He was never much good at close relationships, and he had no gift at all for emotional communication. But, discovering finally that he really *had* been loved, I'm certain he'll have died happy."

"I think he probably did."

"As soon as you told me he'd fled I somehow felt death was the only solution he'd find, though I did wonder whether he'd finally baulk at doing it just to escape his past. Now I want to believe he did it because, for him, it was a perfect ending. After that letter nothing in the future would ever equal such a moment, so he just stopped living. I presume this will end any case against him."

"I'll talk to Mikael Bredenberg next, but yes, I think it will all be over. Lilly was very clear, and everyone involved is dead. But I've got to tell you I'm not particularly happy with the way I handled things. I wasn't very understanding when he began to tell me everything, and that must have hurt. I even fell asleep while he was still going on about it."

"You cared enough to go to him. That's what mattered most."

"And you know how to help and support me," he replied gratefully. "It's a comfort Ragnar never had."

There were no surprises in his call to Bredenberg. Magnus read Lilly's letter over to him, and his immediate verdict was emphatic. "There's no longer any case to answer, nobody to bring any charges and nobody to be charged. You can't proceed beyond such a full stop."

"I'm flying home via Arlanda after the funeral and I'll bring you the letter. It's too important to be put in the post."

"Let me know your arrival time and I'll meet you at the airport. To be absolutely safe, make a copy of the letter and put that in the post to me as well. I shall look forward to hearing more details when we meet."

After a call to Pia to bring her up to date and thank her for her cooperation, Magnus rang Jörgen Bergqvist.

"It's Magnus Trygg, and I thought you'd be glad to know it's all over," he said, choosing his words with great care. "There'll be no scandal."

"Amrén's dead?"

"Yes. He was involved in an unfortunate snowmobile mishap. The local policeman has completed an on the spot investigation and his report will confirm that it was accidental death."

"I see."

"You should also know that a letter has been found, from the dead girl, and it completely exonerates him."

"That's even better. You've done very well, Trygg, and from all I'd heard about you I expected no less. It won't be forgotten, and you can rest assured you'll go far in the force."

"Like Amrén?"

There was a pause. "It's understandable that you're upset, even entirely natural in the circumstances," Bergqvist finally conceded generously, though his voice was braced as though he'd sucked a lemon. "But you must remember that I see the bigger picture. That's my responsibility, and this is how I want things organised. We'll have a big funeral in Sundsvall. I'll attend it myself, and I'll make sure a number of the other commissioners do too. I may even be able to get a government minister, though that's not always easy at short notice. But you can rest assured we'll do him proud, and it'll kill any unfortunate rumours."

"I've arranged a quick cremation up here," Magnus replied quietly, "and a service restricted to two families. That was Amrén's wish, recorded in his will, and I'm his nominated executor. It's essential we do it that way."

He was ready for a battle. But Bergqvist, firmly attached to the conspiracy he believed he'd set up with Magnus, gave way at once.

"I understand entirely. And you're quite right of course. Get it done with as quickly as possible. I should have realised you'd know precisely what's required. Over to you."

There was such a knowing tone to his voice, and he'd rung off so quickly, that Magnus realised Bergqvist believed he had arranged Amrén's death and needed a quick cremation to hide the evidence.

He felt momentarily stunned. Was it really possible that Bergqvist thought he'd acted so ruthlessly? In that case, he probably believed he'd fixed Lilly's letter too, so that it removed any blame from Ragnar. He pondered that. In theory, he could have done it; for he'd had the letter in his possession for long enough to read it and alter it if necessary. And the fact was that he himself hadn't told Bergqvist the whole truth. To make Ragnar's death seem less an admission of guilt he and Nisse had persuaded Spiik it was an accident rather than the suicide they both believed it to be. But he'd failed to mention that to Bergqvist.

He sighed. Once you started moving away from anything but the truth, however virtuous your motives, you got tangled up in your own deceit. Now it seemed he might be looked on with favour, and promoted, because Bergqvist thought he'd followed his instructions. It was all so ridiculous he couldn't help smiling, though it occurred to him that others, too, might put two and two together and make five. He was pretty confident none of his colleagues in Sundsvall, nor Pia, would think him capable of such an act, and it would not even cross the minds of his friends and family, least of all Sonja. But, more generally, inside the police, especially those high-ranking enough to know the background details, it would be remembered that he'd searched for Ragnar and, once he'd been found, he'd died in a fatal accident. This conveniently put an end to a potential scandal and, a timely letter having vindicated Ragnar, he'd then arranged a quick cremation. It was a scenario that might well raise suspicions, and would certainly cause gossip, but he wasn't worried about that. It was one of the inherent dangers of the job he did, and he was confident enough not to bother to look over his shoulder at past events he couldn't do anything about. But if, not long afterwards, he was suddenly promoted, stepping into Ragnar's vacated shoes, suspicions might become certainties.

He was powerless to protect himself. If he insisted on a post mortem the conclusion might indicate suicide rather than accidental death, and would re-open the belief that Ragnar had done something so wrong he'd felt the need to kill himself. It seemed the price of whitening Ragnar might be some blackening of himself; and it was a price he'd just have to pay.

CHAPTER 23

The funeral was not as small as Magnus had at first assumed it would be. Since the nearest crematorium was at Kiruna, the service was held in the main church there which had been designed so that it did not represent any particular religion. Nisse and his father Einar came with all their family and friends. Sonja insisted on attending, and she brought Angelica and Johan with her. Lennart Havendal, in his new role as acting head of the Sundsvall police, thought it proper to be there, and Annica Sundin accompanied him. Pia Widmark came to represent the Jämtland force, and to the great surprise of Magnus, Jörgen Bergqvist, as the acting commissioner for Västernorrland, slipped into the service a little late and left a little early as though fearful that too close an association with Magnus might contaminate him.

Word had spread through Kiruna, and dignitaries of the town and representatives of the mine felt it would be correct for them to be there too, and the inquisitive and the press swelled the number even more. But the biggest surprise and the greatest joy to Magnus was the sudden sight of a towering bulky Polish ex-policeman, Jurek Bojanowski, with unashamed tears in his eyes and a great big hug for Magnus Trygg.

It was a simple service, the priest speaking the eulogy from in front of the altar. Magnus, flanked by Sonja on one side and his children on the other, was satisfied that Ragnar was getting a bigger send-off than he would have expected, and he thought he would be pleased. He would doubtless be intrigued, too, that his final appearance was in a church bizarrely shaped as a neo-Gothic interpretation of a Sami tent. The only embarrassing moment was when Johan leaned towards him and in a piercing stage-whisper asked him whether he would now be Head of the Sundsvall police instead of Uncle Ragnar. There was nothing he could do about it, so he just looked stolidly ahead without dignifying the question with a reply. But in his head he did give an answer. He would not push Lennart out until he wanted to go or reached retirement age in nine years time. Nobody at the funeral, unless you counted Jörgen, showed the slightest indication that they believed he'd had anything to do with Ragnar's death. But in his own mind he knew that, if promotion was to come his way, it would be best to delay it for a while. He loved his present job, he was unsure whether he was ready for more responsibility, and so it would be no hardship to wait.

After the service was over, people began to gather in groups to await the taxis which would drive them to Ripan, the restaurant on *Campingvägen*. Magnus wandered off a little way where he could be alone with his thoughts. Perhaps it marked the start of his grieving, for he finally faced the fact that he would never work with Ragnar again, never see him, never sit down to discuss cases with him, never feel better for inviting him into his home and family and seeing the happiness it gave him. Unexpectedly tears filled his eyes and a few rolled down his cheeks. Ragnar had been a larger part of his life than he'd admitted to himself, and he was only appreciating him now that he was dead.

His mind filled with the memory of the white church at Fors which he'd attended as a boy, once every two weeks. His father had explained to him that a farmer had responsibilities to his animals one week and his church the next, and a God who had been responsible for the creation of beasts as well as humans understood that. Magnus, on the alternate Sundays when he was not at church, and his father was in the fields, joined his mother as she performed the Thai Buddhist ceremonies he loved so much. Now, grieving for Ragnar as he had once mourned his father, it occurred to him that his father had deliberately arranged a system of church attendance that allowed his son to have the benefit of worshipping in both his parents' cultures. It had been typical of his quiet kindness that he never made any reference to it, for he was a man of few words, and he never even indicated that he was aware what happened at home on those Sundays when he was out on the farm. Magnus had always loved his mother unconditionally, and that had never altered. Now it seemed that as each year passed he came to appreciate his father more and more, to understand him better and to grasp all he had done for him. He did not doubt that it would be the same with Ragnar, for he could now admit that he'd first been drawn to him because he had something of his father's quiet and kindly manner.

Surreptitiously, Magnus wiped away his tears, breathed in the chilly air, and knew he no longer needed a father-figure. He was a father himself, with a father's responsibilities; and in these last few weeks he had become battle-hardened. Since Ragnar's death and his decision to refuse promotion and leave Lennart as Head of the Sundsvall police, he'd begun to comprehend the importance of his family to him. Sonja, Angelica and Johan were worth so much more to him than any advancement could ever be. Ragnar's last gift had been to show him the danger of over-ambition and any attempt to be somebody other than his real self.

"I'm happy you finally shed some tears," commented Jurek, coming up to him. "As you saw, I cried too, but as a Polish Catholic I'm not afraid to show emotion. You Swedish Lutherans can be too stiff, even when you lose somebody you love so much. Maybe you learnt something about loosening up from your time with me in Poland, just as Ragnar did."

Magnus smiled. "I learnt more than that, Jurek. I learnt to value your friendship, even though you nearly got me killed."

Jurek winked. "I knew you could look after yourself, even though I had a nasty moment when the waiter came at you with a knife. But that's in the past. Now it's the time to stop feeling sad about Ragnar, but rejoice as we remember him in food and drink. We'll sit together, you, me, that lovely wife of yours, your wonderful children and everybody else who loved Ragnar. We'll say farewell to him in a more noisy way than is possible in church. We'll sing, raise our vodka glasses to him, and I'll tell the story of how he saved my life, performed his fan dance and acquired the name of RaRa."

Magnus smiled and let himself be swept up in Jurek's vitality. He took a last look at the bleakness of the snowy landscape on all sides of the mine. Then he put an arm round Jurek's shoulders and set off back to Sonja and the children who were frantically waving at him to draw his attention to the waiting taxi.

END

COMING SOON
THE FIFTH AND FINAL BOOK IN THE MAGNUS TRYGG SERIES

'BENIN BRONZE'

In 1953 English infantry officer Johnny Callin is seconded to The Royal West African Frontier Force in Nigeria. Obsessed with rare Benin bronzes, he exploits his position to obtain them. When his term of service expires, he decides to drive home across the Sahara with all he has acquired; but over the border men are waiting for him...

In 2012, in Sweden, Magnus Trygg, struggling with the effect on his heart of an earlier gunshot, investigates the horrific death of a Nigerian boy at an isolated lake. The murder weapon, a military flamethrower, indicates the involvement of a ruthless Stockholm gang; and near the body he finds a *ju-ju* figure which suggests witchcraft. Warned that, if he discovers too much, the perpetrators may act against him or his family, Magnus doggedly perseveres. Soon he has uncovered a carefully-hidden link between the killing and events in Nigeria fifty-nine years before.

Robin Porecky's 'BENIN BRONZE' will be published by Austin Macauley in 2016

Vermeer

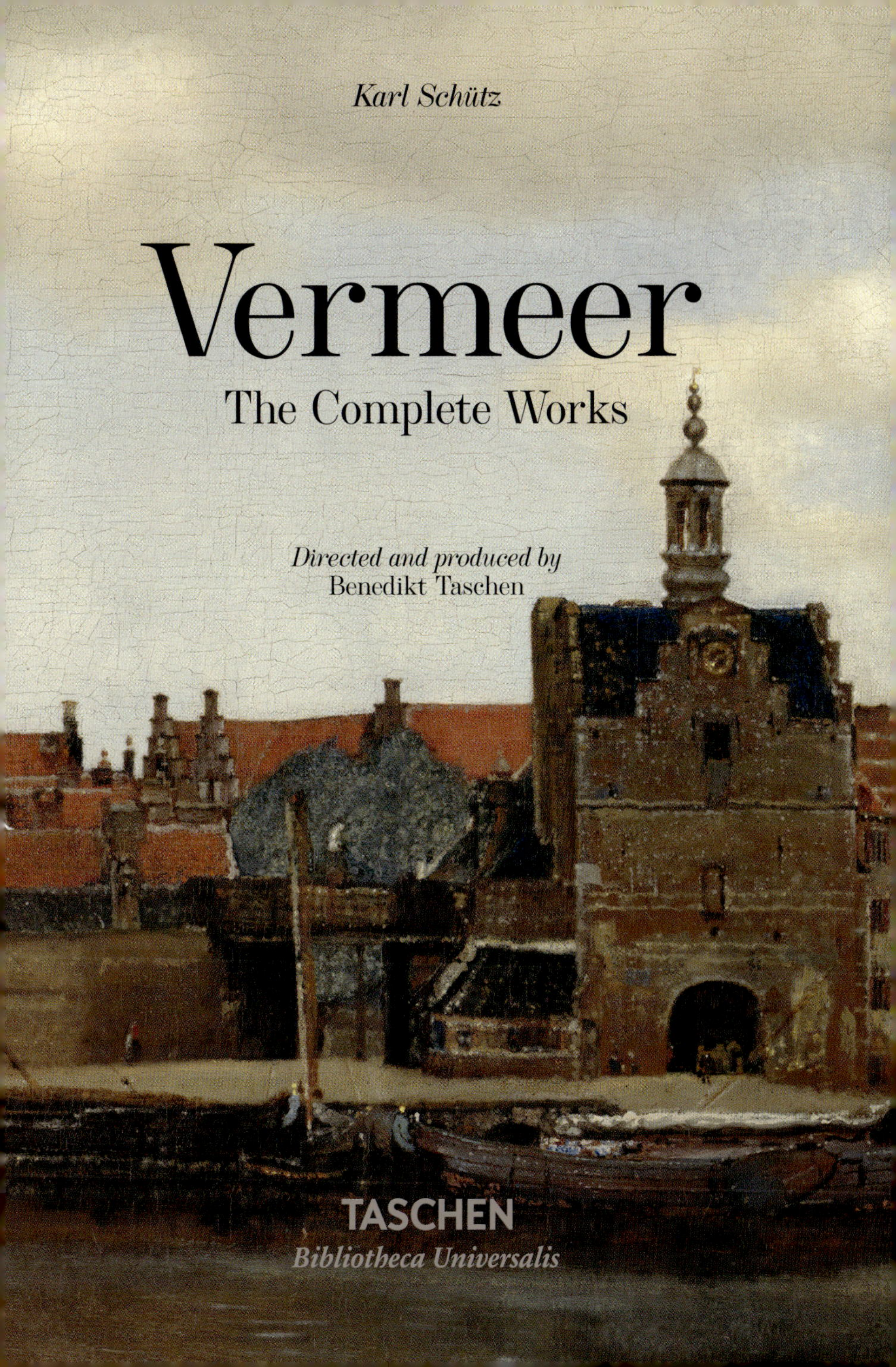

Karl Schütz

Vermeer

The Complete Works

Directed and produced by
Benedikt Taschen

TASCHEN
Bibliotheca Universalis

i·VMeer

Perspectives on Vermeer

Holland's Golden Age – the incomparable artistic flowering that occurred there in the 17th century – is today associated, above all, with the work of the two great painters seen as its most celebrated and significant representatives: Rembrandt (1606–1669) and Johannes Vermeer (1632–1675). They embody their era in exemplary fashion, their work uniting everything that we feel to be characteristic and outstanding in the Dutch art of their period: a sense of reality, precise observation and a break with every sort of idealization. Over and above this they are linked by an illusionism in the rendering of the visible world that testifies to supreme technical mastery and raises their work far above that of their contemporaries.

Yet the difference between the two artists could hardly be greater. Rembrandt was regarded, even within his own lifetime, as the most important painter of his era; and over the following centuries his work was both consistently valued by art lovers and reverently admired by other painters. Rembrandt ran a substantial and successful workshop, and his 40-year career resulted in a correspondingly large and diverse oeuvre comprising paintings, drawings and etchings. Vermeer's fame, by contrast, even within his own lifetime, barely extended beyond his native Delft and a small circle of patrons. After his death his name was almost forgotten, except by a few Dutch art collectors and dealers. Outside Holland his pictures came to be erroneously attributed to other artists. It was not until 1860 that Vermeer was rediscovered; but within a few decades he was enjoying quite spectacular posthumous renown. Vermeer died at the early age of 43, and from the output of his 22-year career we are now familiar with only 35 primarily small and middle-sized paintings – by any definition a small body of work, most of which is, moreover, limited to a few themes drawn from the contemporary life of the Dutch bourgeoisie.

After producing three early works in rapid succession – one mythological theme, one large religious subject and one moralizing genre scene (pp. 80/81, 83, 85, Cat. 1–3) – Vermeer painted almost exclusively domestic interiors. His calm scenes, usually featuring one, two or sometimes three figures, are invariably set in a series of similar, albeit always slightly varying rooms. The range of the action depicted is similarly limited: we encounter young women playing musical instruments, ladies receiving or writing letters, and couples either playing music together or conversing over a glass of wine. In spite of, or perhaps precisely because of, such thematic limitation, Vermeer is regarded as the most important witness to the life of the wealthy bourgeoisie during the Dutch Golden Age. With pictures such as *The Milkmaid* (p. 173, Cat. 8), *A View of Delft* (pp. 176/177, Cat. 12) or *Girl with a Pearl Earring* (p. 217, Cat. 21), Vermeer not only succeeded in producing pictorial archetypes that have stamped the visual memory of our entire culture; he was also able thereby to create an image of the Dutch nation, in which the Dutch recognized themselves and in which the world recognized them. Like almost no other work of art, Vermeer's *Milkmaid* may be said to epitomize the Dutch character; and the overpowering illusion of reality achieved here through pure painting both guarantees the truthfulness of the depiction and prevents it from becoming a cliché. It is not only since the success of the 2003 film indirectly inspired by Vermeer's *Girl with a Pearl Earring* that this has been the artist's best-known picture: just a short time after its rediscovery, in the late 19th century, it was hailed as the artist's masterpiece, the "Dutch Mona Lisa".

Vermeer's only surviving townscape, his *View of Delft*, shows his native city, but at the same time it evokes the very essence of a Dutch city: located on the water, traversed by a network of canals and overarched by a sky full of racing clouds that throw on to the roofs of the houses below a pattern consisting of dark shadows and bright light. It is a picture that powerfully conveys the impression of continuity and duration and yet also captures, in an almost impressionistic fashion, a fleeting state that in a few seconds will have changed. In a spirit of poetic solidarity Marcel Proust (1871–1922), in a letter to his friend Jean-Louis Vaudoyer (1883–1963), called Vermeer's townscape "the most beautiful picture in the world".[1] In an episode in his novel *À la recherche du temps perdu* the writer Bergotte visits an art exhibition to see *A View of Delft*. Suffering a fatal seizure in front of this very painting, he at last recognizes what it has to show him about his own creative endeavours: "That's how I ought to have written."[2]

Both *The Milkmaid* and *A View of Delft* have always been in Dutch collections and have always been recognized as the work of Vermeer. But it was only thanks to the efforts of the French critic and writer on art Étienne-Joseph Théophile Thoré (1807–1869), whose pen name was William Bürger, that Vermeer came to be acknowledged as one of the greatest Dutch artists of all time. Around 1860, starting with a knowledge of only seven or so paintings by Vermeer, Thoré-Bürger saw in this artist a painter of genius, and conjured into being the notion of Vermeer as the "sphinx of Delft", as the great unknown master who had emerged out of nothing and then, just as mysteriously, disappeared, leaving little trace of his earthly existence beyond a few paintings. By this means Thoré-Bürger created a myth that was to add a new facet to the 19th-century cult of the genius. The fascination of this myth endures, indeed, to this day. Even though we now recognize it as a myth, we are still entranced by the notion of Vermeer as a painter, of whose life nothing is known and the mystery of whose paintings remains impenetrable. It is, in fact, true that Vermeer's paintings are almost the only testament to his existence: no notes or letters from his hand have ever been discovered. The few documents that do throw some light on the environment in which he lived suggest that he was an artist much respected by his colleagues: we know, for example, that he was twice elected to serve as head of the Guild of Saint Luke, the professional association of painters in Delft. He also acted as an art dealer and was regarded as a well-informed connoisseur: we know of at least one occasion when he was called upon to deliver a verdict on certain pictures, a role demanding both professional expertise and a large degree of self-confidence.

Shortly after the appearance of Thoré-Bürger's publications, Dutch scholars, anxious to know more about one of their greatest painters, embarked on a search for relevant documentation. It was, in particular, Abraham Bredius (1855–1946), the leading Dutch connoisseur, collector and museum director of his era, who between 1880 and 1920 systematically combed through the Dutch archives. However, the greatest advance in research, above all, into Vermeer's family and social milieu, was achieved between 1975 and 1989 by the American economic and social historian John Michael Montias (1928–2005). While researching the economic situation of Dutch 17th-century painters in surviving records of the Delft Guild of Saint Luke, Montias came across numerous previously unremarked documents relating to Vermeer; these enabled him to provide a detailed and informative context for numerous pieces of earlier information and thereby to bring out the full significance of these. As a result it was not only the life and the achievements of Vermeer himself that assumed a new, three-dimensional reality; this was also true of the family into which he had been born and that into which he in due course married, and of the entire way of life in a Dutch city during the nation's Golden Age. As a result of these findings we know that Vermeer's father was not only a silk weaver, but had also worked as both a tavern keeper and an art dealer; and we now know a good deal more about the artist's self-confident and resolute mother-in-law, Maria Thins. The most important discovery to be made by Montias was that Vermeer produced most of his paintings for a single patron: Pieter Claesz. van Ruijven (1624–1674). Montias published the outcome of his ground-breaking work in the volume *Vermeer and His Milieu: A Web of Social History*.[3] All subsequent publications on Vermeer, including the present volume, owe their coverage of Vermeer's biography to the results of Montias's fundamental research.

While the social setting within which Vermeer pursued his career has thus only relatively recently become much better known, there has for several decades been general agreement on the size of his surviving oeuvre. Thoré-Bürger proposed the addition of a long series of works that he himself attributed to Vermeer (incorrectly, as it was to prove) to the few pictures that he knew for certain to be autograph. As a result Vermeer's artistic profile remained for some time very far from distinct. Over the following decades, up until the turn of the 20th century, pictures in private collections and on the art market were, one by one, identified as the work of Vermeer rather than, as previously assumed, that of Pieter de Hooch (1629–1684), Gabriel Metsu (1629–1667) or Eglon van der Neer (1635/36–1703). As these paintings were attributed to him, Vermeer's fame steadily grew, both in Holland and internationally, until he came to be regarded not only as one of the greatest Dutch painters but as one of the foremost figures in the entire history of art. The discovery, around 1900, of what were deemed to be two early works (Cat. 1, 2), and the fact that these were formally and thematically so distinct from the genre scenes with which Vermeer had been associated, caused a sensation in the art world. A similar effect was achieved 40 years later, with the sudden emergence of what appeared to be further pictures by Vermeer on religious themes – until the pictures in question were unmasked as forgeries by Han van Meegeren (1889–1947). For some time now the number of pictures generally deemed the work of Vermeer has remained limited to 35. A few of these have not been accepted by some art historians; and the more recent attempts to attribute further works to Vermeer have not been successful. All of the aforementioned 35 paintings are now in public collections; not one remains in private hands.

Since the time of Vermeer's "rediscovery", 150 years ago, the number of publications on the artist, on the predecessors he especially admired, on his style and, above all, on the meaning of his pictures has continued to grow. An enormous variety of interpretations is to be found within these publications. On the one hand there is the assumption that the illusionistically perfect rendering of scenes from the daily life of the Dutch bourgeoisie holds no deeper meaning. On the other hand there is the supposition that these images carry within them a deep, philosophically or religiously inflected symbolism. The earlier theory positing the essential "meaninglessness" of Vermeer's pictures, such as is still expounded in the writings of Pieter Swillens, has gradually ceased to be convincing. The publication, in particular, of Eddy de Jongh's research has brought about a general reappraisal of the semantic content of Dutch genre painting; and over the past few decades the notion of hidden meanings within Vermeer's pictures has found widespread acceptance.

Of considerable impact on the ever-increasing awareness and appreciation of Vermeer's work have been a number of large exhibitions. The monographic show mounted in 1995 at the National Gallery of Art in Washington, D.C., and at the Mauritshuis in The Hague attracted hundreds of thousands of visitors; and the findings published in its catalogue by its two curators, Arthur Wheelock and Ben Broos, gave new impetus to art-historical research in the field. A similar outcome was achieved by the 2001 exhibition curated by Walter Liedtke, which was presented at The Metropolitan Museum of Art in New York and at The National Gallery in London. This show sought to place Vermeer's own work within the artistic and cultural-historical context of the city of Delft.

Even more recent publications and exhibitions have focused on individual Vermeer paintings from particular points of view; have considered his career in the context of broader developments in the Dutch society of his time; have attended to the philosophical thought of his contemporaries Descartes (1596–1650) or Spinoza (1632–1677), to natural sciences or religion; or have addressed phenomenological issues such as the representation of time in Vermeer's work. In the past few years two themes, in particular, have attracted the attention of many scholars: the often hotly debated question as to whether Vermeer made use of any optical apparatus, such as a camera obscura, as an aid to composition; and the issue – arising in the context of gender studies – of the central role of women in his pictures and of what his works have to tell us of the position of women in 17th-century Dutch society. Unlike these specialist studies, however, the present book is intended as an all-embracing monographic account.

Pages 2–5
A View of Delft (details), *c.* 1660–1663
(see ill. pp. 176/177)

Page 6
The Little Street ("Het Straatje")
(detail), *c.* 1658–1661
(see ill. p. 175)

The Little Street ("Het Straatje")
(detail), *c.* 1658–1661
(see ill. p. 175)

I.

Delft and the Origins of Vermeer

"In the work of Vermeer the subject of the picture becomes – for the first time in the history of art – the object that is contemplated."

ANDRÉ MALRAUX, 1951

Johannes Vermeer's Origins and Family

Johannes Vermeer was baptized, as "Joannis", at the Nieuwe Kerk in Delft on 31 October 1632. He was the only son of Reynier Jansz. Vos, also known as Vermeer (*c.* 1591–1652), and his wife, Digna Baltens (*c.* 1595–1670).[4] The precise date of the child's birth is not known; but in the Reformed Church, to which Vermeer's parents belonged, it was usual for a child to be baptized when one or two weeks old. At the time of Vermeer's birth his parents had been married for 17 years, and his elder sister, Gertruy, was already 12. As was often the case with a first-born son, Vermeer was baptized "Jan" in memory of his paternal grandfather, Jan Reyersz., a tailor, who had lived in a house on the Beesten Marckt in Delft and who had died in 1597. The child was, however, given the name not of Jan, but of Johannes – or, more precisely, Joannis. This form would have been thought more refined, and it would have been preferred, above all, by Catholics and by Protestants of the upper classes. It was, indeed, this form of his name that the artist himself employed throughout his life. Art historians have also generally tended to employ the form Johannes, however, the painter is still erroneously referred to, even in the titles of books, as Jan Vermeer.

The social milieu to which Vermeer's parents belonged was petit bourgeois, which chiefly comprised craftsmen. Most of these would not have been able to read or write. The only surviving written documents relating to their lives are entries in the baptismal, marriage and burial registers of the parish churches overseeing these ceremonies; formal contracts drawn up when they sold or inherited houses or pieces of land, loaned sums of money or were declared insolvent; and records of judicial proceedings in the case of disputes that were brought to court. Such records tell us more about the crises and difficulties these people had than about what typified their day-to-day existence, their professional activity or their successes.

The information to be derived from such sources is, however, all the harder to evaluate on account of the fact that, in the Netherlands, even up to and beyond the turn of the 17th century, the uneducated still tended not to employ surnames. One indicated the relationship between a man or a woman and his or her father by adding the Christian name of the father to that of the son or daughter. Vermeer's grandfather Jan, the son of a certain Reyer (or Reynier), was thus called Jan Reyerszoon, usually abbreviated to Jan Reyersz. Vermeer's grandmother, who was called Cornelia, from which was derived the affectionate short form

Page 15
Gerard Houckgeest, **The Choir of the Nieuwe Kerk in Delft with the Tomb of William of Orange**, 1650
Oil on board, 125.7 x 89 cm / 49 ½ x 35 in. Hamburg, Hamburger Kunsthalle

Leonaert Bramer, **Allegory of Vanity**, *c.* 1640
Oil on board, 80.3 x 61.3 cm / 31 ⅝ x 24 ⅛ in. Vienna, Kunsthistorisches Museum, Gemäldegalerie

Neeltge, was called Gregorisdochter, after her own father, Gregory, abbreviated to Goris, the resulting name being Neeltge Goris. Vermeer's father was baptized Reynier after his own grandfather, and was called Reynier Jansz. It was sometimes the case, as with Johannes Vermeer, that one or more additional surnames might then be added. It appears that these were more or less freely chosen, but they might also be inherited; and, in due course, they would themselves become the surnames of descendants.

At the time of his death, in 1597, Johannes Vermeer's grandfather, Jan Reyersz., left behind three small children: Reynier, Anthony and a girl by the name of Maertge. It is probable that Reynier, born around 1591, was the oldest of the three.[5] The widow of Jan Reyersz., Neeltge Goris (*c.* 1567–1627), remarried within a year, her new husband being a tavern keeper and musician by the name of Claes Corstiaensz. (*c.* 1548–1618), who had an adolescent son, Dirck, from his own first marriage. Around 1599 a daughter, Adriaentge, was born to the couple, so becoming the new family's fifth child. Claes Corstiaensz. kept the tavern at the house called "De Drie Hamertgens" (At the Three Hammers) on the Beesten Marckt in Delft. Like his own father, who had moved to Delft from Flanders, he was a *speelman*, a musician who would play both to entertain the customers at his own and other taverns and, when required, also at weddings. Unlike their father or stepfather Claes Corstiaensz. (who in 1610 was able to sign, when witnessing a will, only with a cross), the three brothers Dirck, Reynier and Anthony had attended school, as is evident from their elegantly written signatures to the same document. But the two daughters, Maertge Jansdr. and Adriaentge Claes van der Minne, both signed in a clumsy manner, from which we may conclude that they had had very little schooling.

In 1611 Reynier Jansz. was sent by his parents to Amsterdam in order to train as a *caffawercker*, or silk weaver. By this date he was already 20 years old and thus far beyond the age at which an apprenticeship would typically begin, which was between the ages of 12 and 14. The reason for this delay is unknown. It is possible that the young man was unable, or unwilling, to follow in his stepfather's footsteps and become a musician; or he may already have embarked on training as a silk weaver while still in Delft. In the 17th and 18th centuries the term *caffa* was used with reference to a variety of textiles – silk, wool, linen or cotton – that were usually patterned but of a single colour. The manufacture of such textiles was introduced into the Netherlands by craftsmen from Antwerp. Amsterdam soon became their chief place of production, but a number of weavers could also be found in Delft. The term *caffa* derives from the Italian form of the name of the Crimean port city that was a Genoese trading colony from 1266 to 1475 (now, after the name of the original Greek city, known as Feodosiya). As in the case of damask, *caffa* reveals the Near and Middle Eastern origins of weaving, which spread throughout Europe from Italy. Qualified weavers had to be proficient draughtsmen in order to design patterns. One *caffa* weaver in Delft is recorded as

Jan van Goyen, **View of Delft from the North**, 1654
Oil on panel, 68 x 99 cm / 26 ¾ x 39 in. Delft, Museum Prinsenhof

having received instruction in drawing before 1600, from a certain "Master Jacob" (who is understood to have been the Delft painter Jacob Willemsz. Delff [*c.* 1550–1601]).

On completion of his training, the now 24-year-old Reynier Jansz. married the 20-year-old, Antwerp-born Digna Balthasars, known as Digna Baltens. The wedding ceremony, which took place on 19 July 1615, was led by the esteemed Calvinist preacher Jacobus Triglandius (1583–1654), one of the leading figures of the orthodox faction of the Gomarists, the followers of Franciscus Gomarus (1563–1641). These found support, above all, among the uneducated, whereas the wealthy bourgeoisie tended to favour those liberal Calvinists who, as Remonstrants, were ultimately to be excluded from the Calvinist Church.

The father of Digna Baltens, Balthasar Claesz. Gerrits (*c.* 1573–*c.* 1630), came from Antwerp and had moved to Amsterdam with his wife and daughter shortly after 1596.[6] He had originally trained as a craftsman working with some sort of metal, perhaps as a clock-maker or as a goldsmith, but had, in fact, practised many trades, and had on occasion also resorted to shady dealings in order to amass a fortune swiftly. Even while he was still working as a *lichterman*, unloading ships, he made money as a broker, speculating in plots of land that lay outside the gates of Amsterdam. The rapidly growing city suffered from a lack

Gerard van Honthorst, **Merry Society**, 1622
Oil on canvas, 130 x 195.6 cm / 51 ⅛ x 77 in.
Munich, Bayerische Staatsgemäldesammlungen, Alte Pinakothek

of space and there were already plans to expand it. Through his association with a group of merchants from Antwerp, Balthasar Claesz. Gerrits was able to join the Groot Compagnie, albeit only as a subordinate accessory. By short-selling property (which was later declared illegal), this association sought to manipulate the stock-market price of shares in the Dutch East India Company, which had been founded in 1602. By 1620 Balthasar Claesz. Gerrits, together with his son, Reynier Baltens, had become embroiled in a counterfeiting scandal. This also had a political dimension because it had arisen in connection with the acquisition of the Duchy of Cleves by the Elector of Brandenburg. The Elector had received a large loan for this purchase from the Dutch States General, which he was then unable to repay. While Balthasar Claesz. Gerrits, who had apparently produced the counterfeit coins, was more or less able to extricate himself from this affair, its two instigators, one of them the Elector's diplomatic representative in The Hague, were sentenced to death and beheaded. Reynier Baltens himself spent several months in prison before being bailed out by his family, a resolution in which the persuasive capacities of Neeltge Goris, his sister Digna's mother-in-law, doubtless played a crucial part. Reynier Jansz., Vermeer's father, would later complain that he had had to sell his own bed in order to fund his contribution to the sum required to buy his brother-in-law's freedom.

Shortly after their marriage in 1615, Reynier Jansz. and Digna Baltens settled in Delft, initially living in the house of his stepfather, Claes Corstiaensz. On 15 March 1620 the couple's first child was christened Gertruy. During the course of a not entirely transparent financial transaction between Reynier Jansz. and his father-in-law Balthasar Claesz., who had by this time moved to Gorinchem, the couple's household effects were recorded in a 1623 inventory,[7] and valued at 693 florins, a sum including a number of paintings to the value of 53 florins. Among these pictures were portraits of the Stadtholder, Maurice of Orange, Count of Nassau-Dillenburg (1567–1625), and of his brother, Prince Frederick Henry (1584–1647), in addition to two scenes from the Old Testament, which would appear to indicate that the owners were loyal members of the Reformed Church. Among other listed pictures were one of an Italian piper, a night scene and a so-called *bordeeltje*, probably all works by Utrecht followers of Caravaggio.[8]

In the 1620s Reynier Jansz., while continuing to work as a silk weaver, looked for other sources of income, and he took out a lease on a Delft tavern, "De Vliegende Vos" (The Flying Fox), in Voldersgracht. It is possible that he was thereby following the example of his father-in-law, Claes Corstiaensz., who had died in 1618, and who had been both a tavern keeper and a musician. The year 1627 brought the death of his mother, Neeltge, and her house on the Beesten Marckt, in which her son had spent his youth, had to be sold at auction, so that all outstanding debts might be paid.[9] Voldersgracht, close to the city's central Groote Markt, was in any case a better area than that around the Beesten Marckt, where the uneducated lived. In a document dating from 1629,[10] Reynier Jansz. is for the first time designated a tavern keeper (*herbergier*); and in another document, dated 1628,[11] he is for the first time referred to as Reynier Jansz. Vos. The incidental discovery that this tavern keeper Reynier Vos, who later worked as an art dealer, was none other than the father of Johannes Vermeer, was made in 1925 by the Dutch historian L. G. N. Bouricius, and it signified a great advance in the research into Vermeer's family history.

It is striking that the name of the tavern should be identical with the surname of its owner. However, we do not know for certain whether Reynier Jansz. assumed the surname Vos in allusion to the name of his tavern, "De Vliegende Vos", or if, on the contrary, he called the tavern after himself. In all probability, the tavern already had this name when Reynier Jansz. acquired it. It was, in any case, an obvious move for someone called Reynier to call himself a fox (quite apart from the matter of the tavern and its own name), after the French medieval fable *Roman de Renard*, which from the late Middle Ages was also widely known in the Low Countries as *Reynaerd de Vos*. The confusion of names is, in fact, even greater in as far as Reynier Jansz. Vos was, on occasion, called Reynier van der Minne and later Reynier Jansz. Vermeer. The name Van der Minne derives from the ancestors of his stepfather, Claes Corstiaensz., both of whose own children, Dirck and Adriaentge – the step- and half-siblings of Reynier Jansz. – were themselves so called, whereas Reynier's brother Anthony also used the surname Vermeer. We do not know, however, whether their father, Jan Reyersz., himself used the surname Vermeer.

Vermeer, which is a very common surname in Holland, is an abbreviated form of "van der Meer", meaning "of, or from, the lake" (the Dutch term *meer* generally referring to an inland body of water, as opposed to the Dutch term *zee*, referring to the open sea). During the time when art historians were just "discovering" Johannes Vermeer of Delft, two painters who were his contemporaries, but were not related to him – the landscape painter Johannes Jansz. Vermeer of Haarlem (1628–1691) and the Utrecht portrait and genre painter Johan van der Meer (1630–1695/97) – were frequently confused both with each other and with him. In Delft there was an apothecary and natural history collector by the name of Jan van der Meer (1616–1683), who was likewise not related to Johannes Vermeer.[12] From around 1630 Reynier Jansz. would use both surnames, although most frequently calling himself Vos. In 1631, when he became a member of the Delft Guild of Saint Luke, he was registered as "Reijnier Vos or Reijnier van der Minne".[13] In a document dated 6 September 1640, in which Reynier Jansz. is recorded as testifying as a witness for the still-life painter Jan Batista van Fornenburgh (*c.* 1590–1649), he called himself "Reijnier Jansz. Vermeer";[14] and on the following day Fornenburgh received a payment, as witnessed by the still-life painter Pieter Steenwijck and by "Reynier Jansz. Vermeer alias Vos".[15]

Between 1629 and 1631 we know of Reynier Jansz., above all, through documents relating to his friend Willem de Langue (1599–1656), a notary, poet and amateur calligrapher, who also collected pictures, for whom Reynier Jansz. frequently testified, being largely designated on these occasions as a tavern keeper, and not a silk weaver. A 1645 reference to Reynier Jansz. as a *caffawercker* is something of an exception to the rule by this date. From 1631 Reynier Jansz. also had another profession: on 13 October of that year he became a member of the Delft Painters' Guild as a "Mr. Constvercoper" [Master Art Dealer]. In as far as tavern keepers in 17th-century Holland frequently acted also as art dealers, this was not an unusual development. Artists at that time had little opportunity to mount public exhibitions of their work, and most pictures were sold directly from an artist's studio. Putting them on sale in a tavern offered a reasonable likelihood of finding a buyer. It is possible that it was Willem de Langue, who collected pictures and enjoyed a close connection with artists in Delft, who alerted Reynier Jansz. to this possible source of further income.

Exactly a year later, in October 1632, Johannes Vermeer, the future artist, was born to Reynier Jansz. and Digna Baltens. He was the second child of parents now aged 41 (his father) and 37 (his mother). On account of their decision to baptize their son Joannis, so unusual a form of the name, scholars have speculated that Vermeer, who was thought to have converted to Catholicism upon his marriage, may, in fact, have been baptized a Catholic. His baptism took place, however, in Delft's principal church, the Nieuwe Kerk, a Reformed institution; and all signs point to his parents, and, indeed, the entire family, being Calvinists. Pastor Taurinus, who we may assume himself baptized the one- or two-week-old child, was also called Joannis. In 1640 the building in which Reynier Jansz. kept his tavern "De Vliegende Vos" was sold. His lease was not extended, and on 23 April 1641 he bought a tavern of his own, the "Mechelen", on the north side of the Groote Markt and practically next to the Nieuwe Kerk, for the considerable sum of 2,700 guilders.[16] With its seven chimneys, this 16th-century property was a stately building excellently positioned within the city. Reynier Jansz. was, however, able to pay only 200 guilders of the sale price from his own funds. To cover the remaining 2,500 guilders, he had to take out two loans. A brewer in Haarlem loaned him 2,100 guilders; and Arent van Pijnacker, the brother-in-law of Willem de Langue, made a loan of the remaining 400 guilders. It would appear that, with the purchase of the tavern, Reynier Jansz. began to find himself in financial difficulties. It is known that in 1652 he owed a single wine merchant 250 guilders, and that it was only five years later that his heirs were able to pay off the last instalment of this debt.[17]

Reynier Jansz. died in the autumn of 1652 and was buried at the Nieuwe Kerk in Delft on 12 October. The entry in the Register of Burials reads "Reinier Jansz. Vermeer on the Marketplace".[18] Notably, no donation of clothing was made on this occasion to the public charity for the poor (the Camer van Charitate), an indication of the poverty at this time of the bereaved family members. Johannes, son of the deceased, was then 20 years old and had almost completed his training as a painter. After the death of Reynier Jansz., his widow, Digna Baltens, probably with the assistance of her daughter, took over the running of the tavern, or it was leased out. In 1669, when Digna Baltens tried in vain to have the tavern sold at auction, neither of the loans with which the house had been encumbered since its acquisition had been redeemed.[19] But it would seem that the financial situation of the Vermeer family was not altogether catastrophic: its members had, after all, been able to hold on to the tavern for all those years without being either forced out of business or constrained to sell up. In 1670 Johannes Vermeer's mother, Digna Baltens, died at the age of around 75, and was buried at the Nieuwe Kerk on 13 February.[20] Only a few months later came the death of her daughter, Gertruy, the painter's older sister. She was buried on 2 May, likewise at the Nieuwe Kerk.[21] On this occasion a donation of six guilders and six stuivers was made to the public charity.[22] From Gertruy's widower, Vermeer received the sum of 148 guilders as the final instalment of his sister's share in the inheritance. He was now the sole owner of the "Mechelen" tavern, which was still encumbered with the unredeemed loans.[23] In 1672 he leased it out.[24]

Delft and its Painters: Johannes Vermeer's Artistic Environment

With the political consolidation of the seven northern, and primarily Calvinist, Dutch Provinces that had, in 1579, formed the Union of Utrecht, there began to emerge, in each of the financial and cultural centres, the beginnings of a distinctive new Dutch tradition in art and in painting. Owing to the political situation and the emigration of Protestants from the southern, and still Catholic, Spanish Netherlands, above all, from Antwerp, the leading cities of Holland grew rapidly in both size and prosperity, while evolving local specialities in their artistic production, and not least in painting.

This was particularly true of Haarlem, where there was a strong tradition of late Mannerism, widely disseminated through the work of printmakers. This was the native city of Karel van Mander (1548–1606), whose *Schilder-boeck* (Book of Painters), published in 1604, comprised artists' biographies and was also intended to provide the painters of his time with a theoretical basis for their work. During the first decades of the 17th century Haarlem saw the production of the portraits of Frans Hals (1580/85–1666), the genre scenes of Adriaen Brouwer (*c.* 1605/06–1638) and Adriaen van Ostade (1610–1685), and the landscapes of Salomon van Ruysdael (*c.* 1600/03–1670), all of whom have had a decisive impact upon our conception of Dutch painting.

It was, however, the old bishopric of Utrecht that, in this respect, evolved the strongest local speciality. It was through Utrecht that every sort of italianizing art made its way into the northern Netherlands. After Karel van Mander had drawn attention to the work of Michelangelo Merisi da Caravaggio (1571–1610) – observing in the *Schilder-boeck* that:"There is also a certain Michael Agnolo from Caravaggio, who has done wonderful things in Rome, and has achieved fame, honour and a great name through his work" ("Daer is oock eenen Michael Agnolo van Caravaggio, die te Room wonderlijcke dinghen doet [...] Desen heeft alree met zijn wercken groot gherucht, eere en naem gecreghen") – many Utrecht artists became so-called *caravaggisti.*[25] Van Mander places particular emphasis on Caravaggio's naturalism, claiming that every single one of his brushstrokes was made in accordance with his own direct observations from life. As Dutch artists already prided themselves on looking to the model of nature, the readiness of Caravaggio's reception in Holland is not at all surprising.

On completing their training, the most notable Utrecht *caravaggisti* – Hendrick ter Brugghen (1588–1629), Dirck van Baburen (*c.* 1595–1624) and Gerard van Honthorst (1592–1656) – spent several years in Italy. Between 1600 and 1610 they returned home, profoundly

Hendrick ter Brugghen, **Saint Sebastian Tended by the Women**, 1625
Oil on canvas, 150.2 x 120 cm / 59 x 47 ¼ in.
Oberlin College, Ohio, Allen Memorial Art Museum, R. T. Miller, Jr., Fund, 1953

influenced by the new trends in Italian painting, subsequently depicting in Utrecht both tavern scenes and biblical episodes that were remarkable for their chiaroscuro effects. The oldest of this group, ter Brugghen, had travelled to Rome at the age of only 15 and may even have met Caravaggio. After ten years in Italy he returned, in 1614, to Utrecht, but his earliest surviving works date from as late as 1619/20. These point to the influence on his style of very diverse models: in addition to Caravaggio, these include much earlier artists, such as Albrecht Dürer (1471–1528). The unifying factor here was, in all probability, precision in the imitation of nature. This, in turn, points to the influence of ter Brugghen and the other *caravaggisti* as models for Vermeer, both as regards the evolution of his personal style and with reference to the subjects he chose to treat (p. 26). Dirck van Baburen, who was in Italy from 1612 to 1620, and who died only a few years after his return, painted scenes set in taverns and brothels, such as *Loose Society* (p. 59) or *The Procuress* (p. 182), but also pictures that were to be of significance for the work of the young Johannes Vermeer, above all, those incorporating half-length figures playing music, which could be interpreted both as genre scenes or as studies of particular social or emotional types, and which thereby constitute (notwithstanding their great difference in stylistic terms) a parallel to Vermeer's own pictorial inventions.

Amsterdam, however, was Holland's emergent metropolis: the fastest-growing city in the Netherlands and its largest centre of trade. Between 1600 and 1625 its population more than doubled, growing from some 50,000 to around 120,000. Amsterdam was a magnet for all those Dutch artists who sought greater success than their respective home towns could offer, among them Rembrandt, who after working for a few years in his native Leiden moved, in 1631, to Amsterdam, where he established a large workshop. His first pupil, Gerard Dou (1613–1675), remained in Leiden, founding there a tradition of "fine painting" that later came to be seen as that city's speciality. The genre scenes from the life of the well-to-do bourgeoisie painted by Gabriel Metsu and Frans van Mieris the Elder (1635–1681) offer striking thematic parallels with the work of Johannes Vermeer, and they will have served as an important impetus for his own output (cf. pp. 120, 154, 210, 252).

Art in The Hague – the traditional residence of the Counts of Holland – was, by contrast, made to meet the requirements of the Stadtholder, a member of the House of Orange, especially after Maurice of Orange had again moved his court there. His return necessitated the embellishment of the various palaces there with painted decoration and scenes from history and mythology, but also the addition of portraits. The most important surviving monument to courtly painting of this sort is the so-called Oranjezaal at

Hendrick ter Brugghen, **The Concert**, *c.* 1626
Oil on canvas, 99.1 x 116.8 cm / 39 x 46 in. London, The National Gallery

the palace known as the Huis ten Bosch in The Hague. In 1647, after the death of the Stadtholder Frederick Henry, this was converted by his widow, Amalia zu Solms-Braunfels (1602–1675), into a memorial chamber, and was decorated with history paintings by Flemish and Dutch artists (for more on this, see pp. 50 f.). The style of those who supplied this decoration, so distinct in character from the usual qualities of Dutch painting, is frequently referred to as "Dutch Classicism".[26] The work of these artists was to be of particular importance for the first surviving paintings of Johannes Vermeer (pp. 80/81, 83; Cat. 1, 2), at a point when he was still in search of a style of his own.

Delft, only a few kilometres distant from The Hague, had for a while endeavoured to compete with it. In 1572 William I of Orange (1533–1584), known as William the Silent, who had masterminded the Dutch Revolt against Spanish rule, established his own court in this well-fortified city, which could be far more effectively protected than could The Hague. Lacking fortifications, the latter had suffered greatly from the assaults of Spanish troops. The Prinsenhof in Delft, a former monastery, which became the residence of the Stadtholder and the point of assembly for the States General (comprising representatives of all the northern provinces), was for several years the focal point of the new state. In 1584 William of Orange was assassinated by a Catholic fanatic. The magnificent tomb that the States General erected for William, between 1614 and 1622, in the Nieuwe Kerk in Delft, created by the sculptor Hendrick de Keyser (1565–1621), became a major attraction for visitors to the city and the chief focus of commemoration for supporters of the Orange dynasty.

In the 17th century Delft was renowned for the excellent products of its craftsmen. François Spiering (*c.* 1549/51–1631), who had emigrated from the southern Netherlands, the old centre of the art of tapestry weaving, had in 1592 introduced this craft to Delft. His descendants carried on the business until the mid-17th century, but their products were so expensive that only the richest citizens in the land, and the Stadtholders themselves, could afford to buy them. Very soon widely disseminated were the products of the Delft ceramics industry, which had been established in the 1620s. Within a decade or two Delft was supplying most of Holland with painted vessels and wall tiles, while much of its output was intended for export.

Today, the artistic fame of Johannes Vermeer outshines that of any other artist born or active in Delft. Yet during the several decades before Vermeer's birth, and in those of his own lifetime, a number of painters were active in the city whose work was so outstanding that it is with every justification that one may speak of a distinct "Delft School",[27] even though its representatives are not obviously linked by qualities their work shares and, on the whole, remained only briefly in the city.

Two history painters – Leonaert Bramer (1596–1674) and Christiaen van Couwenbergh (1604–1667) – worked in Delft in the second quarter of the 17th century, that is to say, in the years of Vermeer's childhood and youth. To these may be added the genre and portrait painters Anthonie Palamedesz. (1601–1673), the landscape painter Pieter van Asch (1602–1678) and the still-life painter Balthasar van der Ast (1593/94–1657). Bramer and Couwenbergh looked primarily to Italian models. While still young, Bramer had spent 14 years in Italy, frequently moving on from one city to the next, although with long sojourns in Rome, Venice and Mantua, and came to know the Italian painter Domenico Fetti (1589–1624). Bramer returned to Delft in 1628 and, unique among Dutch artists, carried out large, frescoed murals, which have sadly not survived, primarily commissioned by the House of Orange for the palaces at Honselaarsdijk and Rijswijk. He also produced small history paintings that recall the work of Rembrandt's youth, painted in the 1630s. Bramer frequently depicted night scenes, and he loved dramatic light effects (p. 16). The Delft-born Couwenbergh, a later all-but-forgotten and still little-known artist, was the son of a Flemish silversmith, engraver and art dealer. It was once assumed that he, like Bramer, had spent years travelling in Italy, but this has since been called into question. In his genre scenes set in taverns one can detect the influence of the Utrecht *caravaggisti*, who were in turn a decisive influence upon the young Vermeer (cf. Cat. 3). Couwenbergh's social standing greatly improved through his marriage to the daughter of the Mayor of Delft. This apparently also enabled him to obtain many commissions from the Stadtholder Frederick Henry. He was employed in the embellishment of several palaces, including that at Honselaarsdijk and, ultimately, from 1651, in the painted decoration of the Oranjezaal at the Huis ten Bosch in The Hague. It is in both the context and the proximity of these campaigns of palace decoration that Vermeer's first surviving painting, *Diana and Her Companions* (pp. 80/81, Cat. 1), was created.

Couwenbergh and Bramer, who were both around 30 years older than Johannes Vermeer, may be said to have supplied thematic, rather than formal, inspiration for his early work. With regard to Vermeer's conception of art, his illusionism, his approach to the rendering of space and his interest in perspective, a number of other, somewhat younger Delft artists were to be of importance. Among these were Carel Fabritius (1622–1654) and the group of architectural painters in Delft that included Gerard Houckgeest (*c.* 1600–1661), Hendrick Cornelisz. van Vliet (*c.* 1611/12–1675) and Emanuel de Witte (*c.* 1610–1691/92). Around 1650 these architectural painters embarked on depicting in particular the two most prominent churches in Delft, the Oude Kerk and the Nieuwe Kerk, employing complex methods of perspective construction to produce strikingly persuasive images (pp. 15, 40, 94). The Delft School of Painters, in the strict sense of the term, which distinguished itself from that of other Dutch cities mainly through its achievements in painterly illusionism, comprised Fabritius, the architectural painters with their views of the interiors of Delft churches, Pieter de Hooch and Johannes Vermeer.

Apart from Vermeer, Carel Fabritius was probably the most talented of this group. Although he died at the early age of 32, and his surviving oeuvre is consequently small, his outstanding skill as a painter is evident in these extraordinarily diverse pictures. Fabritius came from Middenbeemster, a small village north of Amsterdam. Between 1641 and 1643 he was a pupil in this city of Rembrandt, thereafter returning to his birthplace. It was only in 1650, upon marrying for the second time, that he moved to Delft, which was his new wife's home city. Becoming a member of the Delft Guild of Painters in 1652, he died only two years later, on 12 October 1654, in the devastating Delft Gunpowder Explosion. In this accident, in which the Dutch state's central munitions store exploded, the fabric of almost half of the city was destroyed, and many people lost their lives. Numerous views of Delft painted after this event – for example that by Egbert van der Poel (1621–1664; p. 44) – record the extent of the destruction.

Carel Fabritius's particular talent lay in the rendering of light by capturing, in a most naturalistic fashion, the effects of illumination. During his last years in Delft he departed increasingly from the style of Rembrandt. His pictures became brighter in their colouring, spatial recession being suggested through delicate tonal gradations of grey, pale green and ochre. The atmospheric image of *The Sentry* (p. 35) beautifully demonstrates his gift of keen observation and of translating the effects observed into the language of painting. This idyll, in its archaizing architectural setting, is less reminiscent of the Dutch painting of the artist's own era than of the paintings of 19th-century Romanticism. Characteristic of the fruits of his observation of nature is the well-known picture *The Goldfinch* (p. 31), a small *trompe l'œil* painting on a wooden support, intended to cover a wall niche, or something of that sort, and to deceive the viewer into believing he has seen a real bird tamed into a domestic pet.

Fabritius's own contemporaries lauded his outstanding talent in devising perspective constructions capable of bringing about a high degree of illusionism. Notable among the few surviving works of this sort is the small *View of the Nieuwe Kerk in Delft* (p. 43), which was probably painted to be observed in a peep show. The picture was originally mounted on a curved support in its own case, and it could have been viewed through a small aperture, thereby delivering the striking illusion that, through this aperture, one was gazing at a square that extended into real, three-dimensional space. While the square with its view of the church, as depicted by Fabritius, corresponded with the view one might encounter in reality at this period, the table shown to the left, with its musical instruments, is imagined. Stringed instruments, with their rounded forms, were especially favoured by painters

Carel Fabritius, **The Goldfinch**, 1654
Oil on board, 33.5 x 22.8 cm / 13 ¼ x 9 in.
The Hague, Koninklijk Kabinet van Schilderijen Mauritshuis

C FABRITIUS 1654

engaged in perspective representations, because they offered artists a great deal of scope for demonstrating skill in foreshortening. Vermeer, too, repeatedly included perspectivally foreshortened stringed instruments, shown lying on the floor (cf. p. 285).

This masterpiece of perspectival painting linked Fabritius with the aforementioned painters of church interiors then active in Delft. Gerard Houckgeest, the oldest of these, devoted several decades to painting architectural fantasies: entirely imagined monumental palaces, pillared halls, Renaissance churches. But in 1650 he suddenly changed tack, painting a number of accurate views of the interiors of Delft churches. This would point to some form of external motivation, perhaps in the form of a commission. Houckgeest's innovative achievement in such work was the introduction of oblique views, with at least two, and often more than two, vanishing points. He would take up a lateral position, from which to record the view as observed, and he would then depict the view as it altered with each of a series of very slight shifts of position. By this means, and in changes introduced through the varying effects of illumination, startling insights and lively contrasts were obtained; but space as rendered became less distinct, and the actual extent of any particular segment of it is by no means easy to estimate. In 1650, in one of his most imposing compositions, Houckgeest depicted *The Choir of the Nieuwe Kerk in Delft with the Tomb of William of Orange* (p. 15). The view from the left nave runs diagonally towards the Choir, into which the tomb appears to fit rather snugly. As the view of the tomb is inevitably interrupted by columns, the architectonic structure of the sarcophagus itself is only partly visible. The composition is dominated by the receding sequence of monumental rounded columns, each with its high polygonal base, which divides the Choir itself from the ambulatory. The result, accordingly, is a series of effectively discrete views: on the left, further into the ambulatory; straight ahead, into the Choir with the tomb; and to the right, to the other end of the ambulatory.

Never before had the interior of a church been depicted so persuasively suggestive of truth to reality, and at the same time, through the most subtle gradations of shadow within a light-flooded space, in so illusionistic a manner with regard to light and colour. It is likely that Houckgeest, in his perspectival rendering of the architectural elements, relied on the assistance of a drawing frame, of the sort recorded by Albrecht Dürer in 1525. It has been assumed that the architectural painters also made use of other optical tools, such as the camera obscura, whose wonderful images were praised by Constantijn Huygens. This is, however, in all probability, not the case, just as it is unlikely that Vermeer employed a camera obscura in elaborating his own compositions (for more on this see pp. 105, 109).

Not long after 1650 the Delft architectural painters were to be found very frequently painting the interior of the Nieuwe Kerk with the free-standing tomb of William I of Orange in its Choir; and this may well be one of the reasons for the particular efflorescence of architectural painting in this city. But it is also possible to detect an additional, political context accounting for the popularity of this particular subject. In 1650 a dispute arose between the young Stadtholder William II of Orange (1626–1650) and the assembly of the Dutch States General. After the end of the Eighty Years War, marked by the 1648 Peace of Westphalia, the States General wished to radically reduce the Dutch state's military expenditure. The Stadtholder found this to be an unreasonable request and vehemently opposed it. His sudden death only shortly thereafter, in November 1650, gave the States General an unprecedented opportunity: notwithstanding the efforts of William's widow, to have her son, William III (1650–1702) – born eight days after his father's death, and thus a "minor" by any reckoning – installed as Stadtholder, they refused to permit this. They then sought to use the ensuing period in which there was no Stadtholder as an opportunity to force the House of Orange out of its governing role. During the course of this dispute, which divided Dutch society into two opposed camps, those who commissioned pictures depicting the tomb of William the Silent, hero of the Dutch Revolt and founder of the new Dutch state, would have been thereby affirming their own political allegiance to the House of Orange.

In 1651 Houckgeest left Delft and moved to Steenbergen in northern Brabant. Only one later Delft interior painted by him is thought to survive. This then opened the way for the younger painter Emanuel de Witte, who lived in Delft from 1640, and in 1642 became a member of the Delft Painters' Guild, to follow Houckgeest's example. Around 1651 he began painting interior views of both the Oude Kerk and the Nieuwe Kerk. These pictures adopted the compositional model established by Houckgeest in his own treatment of these subjects; but the results differed from the older artist's painting on account of their use of strong chiaroscuro effects and the dramatic impact of the varying illumination (p. 40).

The pictures painted in Delft shortly after 1650 by Fabritius and by Houckgeest, combining, as they did, a particular sense of proximity to reality with the undreamt-of illusionistic effects achieved through a virtuoso mastery of perspective, may be said to have demarcated, within a narrowly defined time and place, an exceptional artistic situation. Johannes Vermeer was then between 18 and 20 years old and on the point of completing his training as a painter.

Johannes Vermeer's Training

Vermeer's childhood and youth are not recorded in any reports or documents that would allow us to draw any conclusions as to the reasons for his choice of profession. Notwithstanding the decades of intensive archival research that got underway immediately after the artist's "rediscovery" by Étienne-Joseph Théophile Thoré (Thoré-Bürger), and culminated in the publication, in 1989, by John Michael Montias, of his own findings, which caused a sensation in the world of Vermeer research, not a single document has ever been found relating to events occurring between the entry of Vermeer's name in the Register of Baptisms for October 1632 and that in the Register of Marriages in April 1653. We can, however, be almost completely certain that Johannes Vermeer grew up in his parents' house in Delft, initially in the tavern "De Vliegende Vos" in Voldersgracht, and from 1641 at the "Mechelen" tavern on the Groote Markt. But we remain entirely in the dark as to why, as an adolescent, he chose to become a painter. We know only that Johannes Vermeer grew up within a wider environment that may well have fostered an inclination to art (see pp. 17–22). Nor have any documents ever been found, either in Delft or in any other Dutch city, relating to Vermeer's training as a painter, although we may reasonably assume that this training took place between *c.* 1645 and 1653. On 29 December 1653, at the age of 21, Vermeer was enrolled as a *meester Schilder*, that is to say, as an independent master, in the Guild of Saint Luke in Delft. The document concerned, an entry in the Register of Newly Enrolled Masters and Shopkeepers (*Register van alle de nieuwe meesters en winckelhouders*), was first published in 1877.[28] Membership of the Guild was open to painters and other artists, but also to craftsmen, such as makers of glass and of faience, to embroiderers and, until 1620, also to tapestry weavers, and moreover to art dealers and those engaged in the sale of glass. According to the rules of the Delft Painters' Guild, all painters applying for membership had to provide proof of at least six years of training before they could be admitted as independent masters. Only then was a painter permitted to append a signature to his own work and to offer it for sale. All painters enrolled in the Guild had, in addition, to pay an admission fee of six guilders. In the case of the sons of Guild members, this fee was halved, on the understanding that at least two years of the new member's training had been with a master who had himself been enrolled in the Guild. Vermeer was registered at the Guild as a citizen of Delft, and was required to pay the admission fee in full. He, in fact, paid only one and a half guilders upon enrolment, undertaking to pay the rest later. It was not until three years later, on 24 July 1656, that he was able to pay the remaining four and a half guilders.[29]

If Vermeer had, in fact, become a member of the Delft Guild of Painters immediately after completing his training, he would have embarked on this training at the end of 1647. But it is equally possible that a year or two elapsed between the end of his period of training and his admission to the Guild. We know that other painters active in this period, who moved to Delft after completing their training elsewhere, allowed some time to elapse before seeking enrolment in the Guild. Emanuel de Witte, for example, is recorded as resident in Delft from 1640, but was not admitted to the Guild until 1642; and Carel Fabritius, who arrived in Delft in 1650, became a member of the Guild only in 1652. It is also possible

Carel Fabritius, **The Sentry**, 1654
Oil on canvas, 68 x 58 cm / 26 ¾ x 22 ⅞ in. Schwerin, Staatliches Museum

that Vermeer lived for a while outside Delft. Wheelock has proposed the notion of a stay in Italy.[30] Although this is entirely hypothetical in view of the lack of any relevant documentation, the evidence to be found, in Vermeer's early work, that he already possessed a good knowledge of Italian painting, does point to such a possibility.

Further questions are raised by the matter of the admission fee. It remains to be determined whether the rules regarding who might be allowed to pay the reduced fee related only to the sons of painters or to the sons of all members of the Guild. In order to resolve this point, further archival research would be required, and it would be necessary to compare Vermeer with other painters in a similar situation. Vermeer's father was, of course, a member of the Guild, but he was enrolled in his capacity as an art dealer, not as an artist. If the reduction of the admission fee related to the sons of all pre-existing members of the Guild, this would indicate that Vermeer, who had to pay the fee in full, had received his training not in Delft but in another city, or even – as has on occasion been proposed in all seriousness – that he had received no formal training as a painter.

Over the past 150 years, during which art-historical research has addressed the subject of Johannes Vermeer, the most diverse assumptions on the identity of Vermeer's teacher have been voiced, and practically all the stylistic tendencies current in the Netherlands in the mid-17th century have thereby been taken into account. Yet no truly convincing answer has yet been found. Thoré-Bürger initially assumed that Johannes Vermeer had received his training alongside Nicolaes Maes (1634–1693), under Rembrandt in Amsterdam,[31] a hypothesis that MacColl was able to refute over a century ago in the course of examining the then newly discovered picture *Christ in the House of Mary and Martha* (Cat. 2).[32]

Even without our present knowledge of the many documents relating to members of Vermeer's family, published by Montias in 1989, it nonetheless seems probable that Vermeer trained in Delft, the city in which he had been born, in which he grew up and in which he ultimately spent the rest of his career. In the light of what we now know, the artist most likely to have taught Vermeer is Carel Fabritius, whose work of the 1650s has features in common with later works by Vermeer. In a poem on the death of Carel Fabritius, Arnold Bon described Vermeer as the deceased's reborn successor, who had risen like a phoenix out of Fabritius's ashes. The work of Arnold Bon was published by Dirck van Bleyswijck (1639–1681) in 1667, that is to say, within the lifetime of Vermeer, in his *Beschryvinge der stadt Delft* (Description of the City of Delft), an exhaustive exercise in local patriotism. The last, and eighth, verse reads:"Soo doov' dan desen Phenix t'onser schade / In 't midden,

Gerard ter Borch, **A Woman (Wiesken Matthys) Spinning**, *c.* 1652/53
Oil on board, 33.6 x 28.6 cm / 13 ¼ x 11 ¼ in.
Rotterdam, Museum Boijmans Van Beuningen, Stichting Willem van der Vorm

en in 't beste van zyn swier, / Maar weer gelukkig rees' er uyt zyn vier / VERMEER, die meesterlyck betrad zyn pade." (Thus expired this Phoenix [Carel Fabritius] to our loss / In the midst and in the best of his powers, / But happily there rose from his fire / Vermeer, who, masterlike, trod his path.)[33] In a somewhat later edition the first and last lines are altered. These read:"Dus bleev' dien Phenix op zyn dertig jaren" and "VERMEER, die 't meesterlyck hem na kost klaren", which can be translated as "Thus died this Phoenix, when he was thirty years of age" and "Vermeer, who, masterlike, was able to emulate him."[34]

In a history of Dutch painters, both male and female, *De groote schouburgh der Nederlantsche konstschilders en schilderessen*, published between 1718 and 1721, Arnold Houbraken (1660–1719) quoted extensively from Bon's elegy, albeit without citing Johannes Vermeer, who is mentioned only at the end of Bon's text, apparently because he simply neglected to leaf through the Bleyswijck volume and thus failed to see the passage mentioning Vermeer, which is printed on the next page.[35] As Houbraken's history remained, for several decades, the chief source of information on Dutch painting, his failure to mention Vermeer has been seen as one of the reasons why the artist appears to have been forgotten in the 18th and 19th centuries. The stylistic proximity between Vermeer's pictures and those of Fabritius does not necessarily presuppose that the relationship between the two artists was that of pupil and teacher. This would, moreover, have been difficult to achieve purely in terms of time, for Fabritius would not have been permitted to take pupils before he had himself qualified as a master, in 1652. In view of Fabritius's early death, in 1654, this would have left little more than a year in which any such training could have taken place. But there is no doubt that the work of so extraordinarily gifted an artist had a decisive influence on the later work of Vermeer. The fact that three paintings by Fabritius are to be found in the bequest of Vermeer testifies to his appreciation of the work of this predecessor.[36]

The second Delft painter to have been mooted as having perhaps been Vermeer's teacher is Leonaert Bramer. Yet, even apart from the fact that, in this case, too, there appears to have been no reason for the young painter to have paid the full admission fee upon enrolment in the Delft Painters' Guild, there are neither stylistic nor thematic similarities to be found between Bramer's history paintings with their picturesque light effects and the works of Vermeer. At the same time there does appear to be evidence of a close personal relationship between Vermeer and Bramer, for the latter served as a witness at the signing of Vermeer's marriage contract.[37]

In addition to this personal contact with Leonaert Bramer, Vermeer also appears to have known Gerard ter Borch (*c.* 1617–1681), whom he may have first encountered through his own father's art-dealing business. On 22 April 1653, two days after Vermeer's wedding, he and Gerard ter Borch acted as witnesses, before the Delft notary Willem de Langue, for an assurance sworn by a captain in the service of the States General.[38] Beyond this, however, there is no record of contact between Vermeer and Gerard ter Borch, who is known to have worked around this time in his home town, Zwolle, as well as in Amsterdam, The Hague and perhaps also in Kampen, and was in any case only fleetingly in Delft. It has been argued that Gerard ter Borch's presence in Delft in April 1653 was no coincidence, and that he had come from Zwolle, over a hundred kilometres away, for the express purpose of attending Vermeer's wedding. Were this true, it would presuppose a closer relationship with Gerard ter Borch, who was 15 years Vermeer's senior. In general, however, Gerard ter Borch has not been viewed as Vermeer's teacher, even though his genre scenes, with their restrained tranquillity, are close in mood to Vermeer's later works (see p. 110), and it would appear that the younger artist found much of interest in the themes treated by the elder.

Apart from Bramer, other Delft artists have been posited as Vermeer's teacher. Egbert van der Poel, who specialized in *brandjes*, night scenes lit by conflagrations, and also painters of Vermeer's own generation who were not from Delft but were there at some point during the 1650s, among them Jan Steen (1626–1679), who ran a brewery in Delft from 1654 to 1656, and Pieter de Hooch, whose presence in Delft is documented between 1653 and 1658, who in 1655 was admitted to the Delft Painters' Guild and who was in all probability still working in the city after 1660.

As Vermeer, on his enrolment in the Delft Painters' Guild, was required to pay the admission fee in full, it has been assumed that at least part of his training had taken place not in Delft, but in another city. On account of certain aspects of the character of Vermeer's early paintings that recall the work of the Dutch *caravaggisti* who worked in Utrecht, it has been supposed that Vermeer's teacher may have been one of them. Amsterdam, too, has been posited as the city in which Vermeer may have trained. Montias, calling in evidence a number of biographical facts and further relevant considerations, conjectures that Vermeer had his first lessons in drawing and mathematics, while still a boy, with Cornelis Daemen Rietwijck (*c.* 1590–1660), who lived in Voldersgracht in Delft, was admitted to the Guild of Saint Luke in his capacity as a portrait painter and ran a sort of private art school for the young.[39] In that case, Vermeer might have embarked on his training as a painter under the still-life specialist Evert van Aelst (1602–1657), who had commercial connections with Vermeer's father in the latter's capacity as an art dealer. According to Montias the rest of Vermeer's training would then have taken place in Amsterdam or in Utrecht. It is here perhaps significant that Vermeer's father had himself trained in Amsterdam. And in Utrecht Vermeer could have trained with Abraham Bloemaert (1566–1651), the leading Utrecht painter of the older generation. Around 1650 Bloemaert would already have been rather old, but he was still running a workshop in which he trained young painters. He died two years before Vermeer qualified as a master. Montias takes issue with the view that Bloemaert's death in 1651 excludes the possibility of his ever teaching Vermeer, but in any case regards as far more significant

the fact that Bloemaert was related to the family of Vermeer's future wife: Bloemaert was a distant relative of Vermeer's future mother-in-law, Maria Thins (*c.* 1593–1680). Her older cousin, Jan Geensz. Thins, who not only owned the house in which she lived in Delft but was also personally close to her, was a friend of Bloemaert and was related to him through marriage.[40] Montias suggests that it was in Bloemaert's workshop that Johannes Vermeer first came into contact with Catholicism, Bloemaert himself being a Catholic, and also that it may have been through Bloemaert that Vermeer met his future wife.

For the sake of thoroughness, we should also mention the entirely speculative thesis of Begheyn: that Vermeer may have been trained under the Jesuit painter Isaac van der Mije (1602–1656), who taught at the Jesuit College in Delft from 1650 to 1656.[41] Yet there is little to be said in favour of this supposition, except for Vermeer's later conversion to Catholicism and the close contact between his future mother-in-law, Maria Thins, and the Jesuits in Delft. Vermeer's own connection with, and conversion to, Catholicism is documented only upon his marriage to Catharina Bolnes in April 1653, by which point his training had long been completed. Montias also assumes that the additional cost of sending Vermeer away to be trained outside Delft was a cause of his father's financial difficulties. Liedtke, on the other hand, makes the very good point that the family's financial difficulties had begun as far back as 1641, with the acquisition of the "Mechelen" tavern and the loans taken out to cover its purchase, and argues that this situation in itself renders it improbable that Vermeer trained as a painter outside Delft.[42] Liedtke's supposition is that Vermeer received no regular training as an apprentice in the workshop of any particular master, but lived at home and was there trained by a painter friend of his father's who provided this service in return for free food and lodging at the "Mechelen". There are, in fact, other examples of such an arrangement. Emanuel de Witte, for example, undertook to train the 15-year-old nephew of the brewer Rocus van der Vin for a year in return for the use, over this period, of three rooms in Van der Vin's house: one in which to live and two in the attic to serve as his studio.

Vermeer must have learnt a great deal without the aid of a teacher. And it is in this respect surely significant that even his earliest known paintings point to the influence of no single artist who might have acted in such a role. This would lead to the conclusion that Vermeer, in fact, had no teacher; or, had he had one, that this teacher specialized in a particular type of work that did not become a speciality of Vermeer's, for example, landscape painting. It would, indeed, be difficult to reconcile our sense of Vermeer as ever open to diverse tendencies and models with a connection to a single teacher. As further, albeit not entirely

Emanuel de Witte, **The Oude Kerk in Delft during a Sermon**, 1651
Oil on board, 59 x 43 cm / 23 ¼ x 16 ⅞ in.
London, The Wallace Collection

convincing, evidence that Vermeer did not complete a regular programme of training as a painter, Liedtke cites four documents dating from April 1653.[43] In none of these documents is Vermeer designated a "painter". While it is true that at this date he had not been enrolled in the Guild of Saint Luke as a "master", we know of comparable cases in which painters recorded their profession as "painter" even before having completed their training as such.

In conclusion, then, we may say that a series of surviving documents and established facts relating to Vermeer's youth may be interpreted to mean that he received no regular training under a master, but was trained more informally and learnt a good deal without the aid of a teacher. To begin with, there is the matter of his father's precarious financial situation after the purchase of a tavern of his own on the Groote Markt in Delft, which would in itself have precluded the cost of formal training for his son, let alone the cost of sending him to train in another city. Secondly, no recognizable style of any one teacher can be clearly linked to Vermeer's early paintings. Thirdly, no documents have been found in which the young painter is designated as such. And lastly, Vermeer is recorded as having been required to pay the full admission fee upon enrolment in the Delft Painters' Guild (although this requirement indicates only that formal training, if any, had not taken place in Delft).

Such an interpretation of the facts nonetheless leaves a great deal still in doubt. Whoever provided Johannes Vermeer with some sort of training, and wherever this training took place, the excellence of the artist's later work – if one is not to account for its brilliance entirely on the basis of innate artistic genius – strongly suggests that the teaching must have been outstanding, even to the extent of not inducing the young artist to work, in future, in only one particular style. Is it conceivable that the Delft Painters' Guild, an institution so conscious of social standing, would have admitted to its ranks, as a "master", a painter only 21 years of age, also permitting him to owe for over two years the greater part of his admission fee, if this painter were not able to provide proof of having completed a regular course of training? Were this the case, it would presuppose that Vermeer had a number of powerful champions within the Guild. Johannes Vermeer's own father could not have been one of these, given that he had died more than a year before the artist was admitted to the Guild. It is, of course, possible that Vermeer's father had made provision for his son's enrolment in the Guild. And it is possible that a number of Guild members were indebted to Vermeer's father in his capacity as an art dealer, and would have been prepared to support the ambitions of his son. That Vermeer was readily welcomed and accepted by other painter members of the Guild is demonstrated by the fact that, in 1662, nine years after his admission, he was elected to head the Guild for a period of two years. In 1670 he assumed this role for a second time, again for two years.

Whatever sort of training Johannes Vermeer may have received, his earliest surviving paintings already attest to the fact that he possessed an astonishing inner artistic

Carel Fabritius, **View of the Nieuwe Kerk in Delft**, 1652
Oil on canvas, 15.4 x 13.6 cm / 6⅛ x 5⅜ in.
London, The National Gallery, presented by the National Art Collections Fund, 1922

independence, that he had an impressive knowledge of contemporary painting of diverse thematic and stylistic tendencies (which he may well have acquired through familiarity with his father's activity as an art dealer) and that he was able to draw, with cool confidence, upon diverse models. Vermeer's independence is equally manifest in his mastery of the techniques and materials of painting, which in itself reveals his remarkable individuality. Vermeer was clearly well-versed in various methods of paint application and in the use of glazes and varnishes, techniques that were distinct from those regularly and widely employed, and which other artists never mastered. The all-conquering illusionism in Vermeer's rendering of the surfaces of objects is owed to the velvety lustre of paint applied in minute dots, a technique already termed *pointillé* by Thoré-Bürger, who drew attention to it as one of the characteristic marks of any work by Vermeer. It is, not least, to this distinctive technique that Vermeer's paintings owe their extraordinary radiance, and their strong impact upon the viewer as unmistakably the work of this painter (see pp. 106–112).

Johannes Vermeer's Marriage to Catharina Bolnes

The year 1653 was to be of considerable significance in the life of the then 21-year-old Johannes Vermeer, not only on account of his admission to the Delft Guild of Painters, but also because of his marriage. His bride, Catharina Bolnes (*c.* 1631–1688), came from a well-to-do Catholic family. The wedding, conducted according to the Catholic Rite, took place on 20 April 1653 in Schipluy, now Schipluiden, a small village with a substantial Catholic

Egbert van der Poel, **View of Delft after the Gunpowder Explosion of 1654**, 1654
Oil on board, 36.2 x 49.5 cm / 14 ¼ x 19 ½ in. London, The National Gallery

population. The couple were married by a Jesuit priest who had a close connection with the Delft chapter of the Jesuit Order.

The bride's mother, Maria Thins, lived in a large house in the Catholic district of Delft, the so-called Papists' Quarter, around the Oude Langendijck. She came from a wealthy Catholic family in Gouda, a little more than 20 kilometres from Delft. Her father, Willem Thins, had died in 1601, leaving behind a widow and five children. The widow, Catharina von Hensbeeck (d. 1633), married for a second time, her new husband being Gerrit Camerling, a citizen of Delft. While the four siblings of Maria Thins appear not to have married and produced children, she herself married Reynier Bolnes, a Delft brick-maker, in 1622. This marriage produced three children, of whom the youngest, Catharina, later married Johannes Vermeer. Maria Thins's marriage was, however, not a happy one: her husband, Reynier Bolnes, was violent, and he beat his wife and his daughters. In 1641, after 20 years of marriage and two failed attempts to leave her husband, Maria Thins succeeded in obtaining a formal separation from him and, together with her two daughters, she left the marital home. The couple's son, Willem, however, remained with his father.[44] Some 20 years later, after 1660, diverse misdemeanours and high debts drove Willem into a correctional institution. The annual fee for residence there, 310 florins, was paid by his mother.[45] Maria Thins, in fact, possessed a large personal fortune, estimated in 1649 at the value of around 15,606 florins, over and above a considerable income from leasing out properties she owned and from investments. After the death of her brother, Jan Willemsz. Thins, in 1651, and of her sister, Cornelia, in 1661, she also had access, as the only surviving member of the family, to its entire fortune, which provided an annual income of around 1,500 florins. Her new son-in-law, by contrast, upon his enrolment in the Delft Painters' Guild, was able to pay only a quarter of the six-guilder admission fee, settling his debt three years later.

As mother of his prospective bride, Maria Thins refused to sign a document attesting to her formal consent to the marriage, as the two witnesses present – the painter Leonaert Bramer and the army captain Bartholomäus Melling – were to swear, on the day after the formal proposal, before the notary Johannes Ranck. Maria Thins had, in fact, declared that she had no objection to raise at the time of the publication of the marriage banns.[46] On account of the refusal to give formal consent, it has been erroneously concluded that the wedding took place against the will, and without the agreement, of Maria Thins. Her reservations would seem, rather, to be explained by the large difference in social standing between the two families, a difference underlined by the precarious financial situation of the bridegroom, and by the fact that one family, that of Vermeer, was Calvinist (like most of the Dutch population) while the other, that of the bride, was Catholic.

Given the Wars of Religion raging in much of Europe during this period, the religious situation in the northern Netherlands was unique. It is a credit to the progressive tolerance of bourgeois society in the Dutch Republic that the Calvinist majority enjoyed a largely peaceful co-existence with minorities such as the Catholics or the Remonstrants. Distinct tensions did, however, exist between the Calvinist majority and the Catholic minority. Even during the prolonged Revolt of the Netherlands the latter had not abandoned the Old Religion. In Delft they accounted for a quarter of the population, and in other cities even more. The rights of Dutch Catholics, with regard both to the exercise of their beliefs and to their lives as citizens, were narrowly restricted: they were not permitted to occupy public office, and they were allowed to hold their own religious services – which, strictly speaking, were forbidden – only in the concealed churches that had been installed in the houses of well-to-do Catholics, the so-called *schuilkerken*. The municipal authorities were regularly bribed to allow the Catholic Mass to be said in these concealed churches. This payment of protection money gradually evolved into an unofficial tax.[47]

This situation of tolerated freedom of religion had been preceded by a long period of acrimonious altercation between the liberal and the more orthodox Calvinists as to whether the struggle against Spanish rule was primarily about political freedom or about religious freedom (*libertatis sive religionis ergo*). Along with their concern for political independence, the liberals wished to do away with the imposition of any particular form of religious worship and, above all, to be rid of the Inquisition. The orthodox Calvinists, on the other hand, wished more than anything to see the Reformed Church established in Holland. At the 1618 Synod of Dordrecht the orthodox Calvinists, that is, those who believed absolutely in the doctrine of Predestination, enjoying the support of Maurice, Prince of Orange, held out against the Remonstrants, who as a political force were led by Johan van Oldenbarnevelt (1547–1619), a pre-eminent figure within the States General, and by the legal scholar Hugo Grotius (1583–1645), and whose supporters were largely drawn from the educated, wealthy urban bourgeoisie. Oldenbarnevelt was arraigned and executed. It was only around 20 years later that the suppression of the Remonstrants was relaxed: they were now permitted to hold their own religious services, but they were still excluded from occupying public office.

In Delft only two Catholic *schuilkerken* existed. One was on the Oude Langendijck, very close to the house of Maria Thins and her daughters, Cornelia and Catharina. It was a Jesuit institution, although those belonging to the Jesuit Order were not allowed to hold religious services there. The second was on the Oude Delft, in a former *begijnhof* (a semi-monastic community of women). Those in charge here were lay priests, who were close in their beliefs to the Jansenists, which made a conflict with the Jesuits more than likely. This conflict was not least among the factors that brought the Catholics into disrepute among the city's Calvinist majority.[48] We know of no documents attesting to Johannes Vermeer's conversion to Catholicism in order to secure the consent of Maria Thins to his marriage to her daughter; but there are several indications that a conversion, and for this very reason, took place. It is known that Johannes Vermeer enjoyed increasingly good relations with his mother-in-law, in whose house he and his wife lived from the late 1650s and whose financial support they enjoyed. It is also apparent that Vermeer's relations with his own family began to cool. This is reflected, for example, in the naming of Vermeer's sons: one was called Johannes (after his father), the others were called Ignatius and Franciscus (after the two pre-eminent saints of the Jesuit Order). None of his sons was given the name of his grandfather, Reynier, as would have been customary at the time, and usual for the Vermeer family. Nor should we overlook the evidence of Vermeer's unmistakably Catholic late work, *Allegory of Faith* (p. 297, Cat. 34).

Pieter de Hooch
Woman Drinking with Two Men and a Servant Girl, *c.* 1658
Oil on canvas, 73.7 x 64.6 cm / 29 x 25 3/8 in.
London, The National Gallery

II.

The Young Vermeer

1654–1659

"There is so much mystery in each painting, in the women he depicts, so many stories suggested but not told."

TRACY CHEVALIER, 2014

The Three Early Works

The artistic career of Johannes Vermeer opens with three pictures that are in every way distinct from the work he produced later and are also utterly unlike each other. Each of these three paintings stands on its own, each signifies a new start, without awaking the sense of a continuous line of artistic evolution. At the same time each of these pictures represents the "cutting edge" of contemporary style, yet each belongs to a distinct artistic category, almost as if the young artist were probing his own abilities in several fields and, at the same time, providing evidence of the sheer artistic talent that would, in time, prove capable of developing in opposed directions. This beginning has, accordingly, been regarded as a period in which Vermeer carefully sought to explore his options and determine how his works might be received on the art market.

The key work among the three early pictures is *The Procuress* (p. 85, Cat. 3). It is the only one of the three to bear a date (it is, indeed, one of only three dated works in the whole of Vermeer's surviving oeuvre), according to which it was painted in 1656. This was three years after Vermeer had been admitted to the Delft Painters' Guild, and it establishes a precise starting point for the chronology of his output. It has generally been assumed that the two other pictures of this group are earlier in date, and were painted between 1653 and 1656. But there is no secure basis for these assumptions. Moreover, each painting is in its own way very far from evincing the weaknesses of a beginner, even though the attempt has been made to discover in each of them awkwardness and errors of the sort that would betray a young artist.

One of the two undated pictures is a medium-sized mythological scene, *Diana and Her Companions* (pp. 80/81, Cat. 1), the other a much larger depiction of a New Testament subject, from the Gospel According to Saint Luke, *Christ in the House of Mary and Martha* (p. 83, Cat. 2). It may be of significance that both works are history paintings. As such, they belonged to the pictorial category that, in classical art theory, was more highly esteemed than genre paintings, that is, scenes drawn from everyday life, such as Vermeer later favoured. The high regard in which history painting was held reflected the recognition that it required the artist to address thematically and formally more complex subjects than were to be found in those taken from everyday life, that it challenged his capacities for invention and that it tested every aspect of his mastery in rendering the human figure, in particular, the nude. We can only speculate as to why Vermeer seems to have begun by producing history paintings. It is possible that he received commissions for paintings on these two subjects and simply supplied what was required. It would, however, seem more likely that these works reflect the young artist's ambition to establish his capacity to create complex compositions. This is something that we can find in the early careers of other Dutch painters of this period, who subsequently made their names chiefly as painters of

Jacob van Loo, ***Diana and Her Nymphs***, *c.* 1650–1655
Oil on canvas, 162 x 199 cm / 63 ¾ x 78 ⅜ in. Brunswick, Herzog Anton Ulrich-Museum

Page 49
A Young Woman Reading a Letter (detail), *c.* 1657
(see ill. p. 95)

portraits, landscapes or still lifes: among these are the landscape painters Aelbert Cuyp (1620–1691), Nicolaes Berchem (1620–1683) and Paulus Potter (1625–1654), the architectural painter Emanuel de Witte and the painter of genre scenes Gabriel Metsu.[49] In this respect it is significant that Vermeer incorporated several full-length figures in both compositions, thereby putting his capacities as a history painter to the test.

It is possible that Vermeer produced other history paintings that are now untraced, as is, indeed, indicated by a number of entries in the inventories of early collections.[50] In the 1657 inventory of the collection of the Amsterdam art dealer Johannes de Renialme (*c.* 1600–1657) there is an entry for a picture called "Een graft besoeckende van der Meer" ("Visitors to a Grave by van der Meer"), perhaps a reference to the biblical subject of the

Three Marys at the Grave of Christ.[51] And in 1761 a painting with a mythological subject from the collection of the distinguished Van Berckel family from Delft was sold at auction as "Jupiter, Venus en Mercurius door J. ver Meer".[52] It is also conceivable that, in addition to his early history paintings, Vermeer produced a much larger group of paintings from other categories, including landscapes and genre scenes, which are now untraced.[53]

Following Thoré-Bürger's "rediscovery" of Vermeer, from 1860 to 1866, and his recognition that *The Procuress* (Cat. 3) was, according to its signature and date, the earliest of the Vermeer paintings then known to him, it was quite some time before the two other early pictures were accepted as his works. His rendering of the subject treated in *Diana and Her Companions* may be considered within the larger context of "Dutch Classicism", a movement that is far less central to our current conception of 17th-century Dutch painting than are landscapes painted after nature, portraits, still lifes or genre scenes. "Dutch Classicism" is associated with the sort of history paintings that were initially, around 1610, produced as a response to Mannerism, and were later, around 1630, intended as a reaction to the work of the Dutch *caravaggisti*, whose own style had, in fact, evolved as a countermovement of Mannerism. The term "Dutch Classicism" is itself somewhat misleading in that it does not, as one might reasonably assume, refer to a style with rather severe formal characteristics closely derived from the theory and practice of Classical Antiquity.[54] The invocation of "Classicism" here primarily signals a counter-reaction to the Mannerist preference for all that was formally extreme and eccentric, a "normalizing" endeavour that favoured distinct and clearly illuminated forms, bright colours and subjects that were noble rather than crude or base. Setting out to provide a thorough and accurate account of his theme, it was argued, would ensure that an artist achieved the highest quality in formal and painterly terms.

The Princely Household of the Stadtholder Frederick Henry of Orange in The Hague was to become a focal point of this stately style; and, owing to the artistic interests of the Stadtholder's learned secretary, Constantijn Huygens (1596–1687), it evolved into a true centre of art and architecture. Under his guidance and supervision, palaces and palatial country houses were built in the environs of The Hague and Delft, and each was supplied with appropriately painted decoration. The preserved Oranjezaal in the Huis ten Bosch in The Hague, with its 30 large paintings executed between 1648 and 1652, serves as the most important monument to this mid-17th-century style. The Huis ten Bosch was planned, in 1645, as a small country house for Amalia zu Solms-Braunfels, the consort of Prince Frederick Henry. It was proposed that the "seven or eight best painters in the land",[55] under the guidance of Jacob van Campen (1596–1657), should depict subjects suited to the memory of the Prince, who had died in 1647. Contributing to this decorative scheme alongside Antwerp artists such as Jacob Jordaens (1593–1678), who supplied most of the paintings, Theodor van Thulden (1606–1669), Thomas Willeboirts Bosschaert (*c.* 1613/14–1654) and Gonzales Coques (1614–1684), who worked in the Baroque stylistic tradition of Peter Paul Rubens (1577–1640) and Anthony van Dyck (1599–1641), were the leading Dutch history painters, the true representatives of "Dutch Classicism": Pieter Soutman (*c.* 1580–1657), Caesar van Everdingen (*c.* 1616–1678), Pieter de Grebber (*c.* 1600–1652/53) and Salomon de Bray (1597–1664) from Haarlem; Jan Lievens (1607–1674) from Leiden, a close companion of the young Rembrandt; Christiaen van Couwenbergh from Delft and Gerard van Honthorst from Utrecht.

Another site of this campaign of painted decoration, which has, however, not survived, is the Huis Honselaarsdijk, in the environs of The Hague and to the west of Delft, which had been acquired in 1612 by Prince Frederick Henry. Decorated so as to resemble a hunting lodge, with motifs drawn from the mythology of Diana, Goddess of Hunting, this may well have supplied a direct thematic model for Johannes Vermeer. The Banqueting Hall contained large painted hunting scenes with Diana, of which the central image, above the fireplace, was a *Coronation of Diana*, the work of Rubens and his workshop and of Frans Snyders (1579–1657). In 1740 this was inherited by the King of Prussia, and it is today in the large picture gallery at Potsdam-Sanssouci. Couwenbergh supplied for the Huis Honselaarsdijk a large hunting scene with Diana and her nymphs, for which the pendant, a scene of Diana hunting with falcons, was the work of either Jacob van Campen or Paulus Bor (1601–1669). Neither of these two works survives. During the 17th century a great many pictures depicting Diana and her nymphs were executed for the court in The Hague. In 1644 Couwenbergh painted a picture of Diana, which had been commissioned by Prince Frederick Henry for the palace in Rijswijk, the Huis ter Nieuburch, halfway between Delft and The Hague.

For a young artist in Delft eager for commissions, subjects drawn from the mythology of Diana were an obvious thematic choice. Vermeer would also have found relevant models in his immediate surroundings. The works that offer the closest parallels to Vermeer's *Diana and Her Companions* are two paintings by Jacob van Loo (1614–1670), a "Classicist" active in Amsterdam. The subject afforded the artist the opportunity to depict the female nude, which was generally regarded as his forte. One painting, which offers a possible source of Vermeer's motif of the nymph washing Diana's feet, was painted in 1648 (p. 80). A second, which may be dated to *c.* 1650–1655 – thus exactly contemporary with, or perhaps even slightly later than, Vermeer's picture – shows Diana and her nymphs partially or entirely unclothed (p. 51). It is, above all, between the earlier of the two pictures by Van Loo and Vermeer's own composition that we can find notable similarities. Neither painting depicts one of the frequently treated episodes from the mythology of Diana, such as the discovery of Callisto's pregnancy or the transformation of Actaeon into a stag. Rather, Diana is shown entirely at rest and surrounded by her nymphs.

Vermeer's picture, on the other hand, is infused with a mood of subdued festivity. One nymph kneels before Diana, who is identified by her diadem with a crescent moon, and washes her feet with a sponge, while a second nymph is shown washing her own feet. The emphasis here on the element of water in itself alludes to the stories of both Actaeon and Callisto. It is possible that the later painting by Van Loo is intended to show the prelude to the revelation of Callisto's pregnancy: as recounted in Ovid,[56] the nymphs gather at the forest pool and disrobe in order to bathe. It is by no means certain that Vermeer intended the figure of the nymph standing to the right against a dark background to be Callisto, here attempting to conceal her pregnancy, as Liedtke was the first to conjecture.[57] But the most recent restoration of this painting, which has recovered the dark background, has given the composition a new character: on account of the now more evident pose of the figure in question and the way it is lit, an identification with Callisto seems altogether reasonable (see the entry for Cat. 1).

Also contributing to the festive mood of Vermeer's picture is the not only mythological but also Christian motif of cleansing, here recalling the iconographic model of Christian foot washing at the Last Supper or the anointing of Jesus by Mary Magdalene – in both cases the action of cleansing serving primarily as a gesture of humility. The bowl of water and the cloth in the foreground are themselves linked, as accessories to the Lamentation of Christ, with the History of Salvation, just as the thistle at the bottom left corner recalls God's curse upon Adam (Genesis 3: 18). Commentators have also pointed to similarities between Vermeer's figure of Diana and that of Bathsheba in Rembrandt's eponymous composition of the same period (Paris, Musée du Louvre). The subdued atmosphere of Rembrandt's painting, its relative lack of "action", and the treatment of both composition and illumination, as if in the creation of a still life, recall the later interiors of Vermeer.[58] Moreover, in both paintings the identity of the figures depicted and the nature of the activity in which they are absorbed remain ambiguous.

The second history painting, *Christ in the House of Mary and Martha* (p. 83, Cat. 2), quite openly belongs, as a religious work, to the painting tradition of the Catholic Counter-Reformation. Its large size – it is larger, in fact, than any other surviving work by Vermeer – and the way in which the biblical episode is depicted point to a picture intended for a church and commissioned by a Dutch Catholic community.[59] Moreover, we know that Johannes Vermeer, upon his marriage to Catharina Bolnes in April 1653, had at least a close connection with the Catholic Church, if he had not already joined it. It is possible that the picture was painted for one of the concealed Catholic *schuilkerken* installed within private houses, for these were often richly decorated. It may even have been intended as an altarpiece. Both the choice of subject and the way the scene is depicted do, indeed, make this probable. The picture meets all the criteria stipulated by

the Counter-Reformation for a religious composition. All three of its figures are unambiguously characterized with regard to role and, in each case, are illuminated so as to be easily identifiable. Vermeer effectively eschews any superfluous accessories that might divert attention from the essence of the event depicted. The interior itself is treated with extreme simplicity, and in the very plain clothing there are no echoes of the fashions of Vermeer's own era.

Rendered in diverse shades of dark brown, the background opens on to a corridor or neighbouring room, where a little light enters through a window to the side. In his handling of the illuminated interior, apparently informed by careful observation from nature, Vermeer was also adhering to a tradition established by painters in nearby Rotterdam, above all, Ludolf de Jongh (1616–1679) and, among the latter's followers, Pieter de Hooch. Both artists had by this point further developed their approach to rendering structures viewed as if receding sharply into the depth of the depicted space.[60] Vermeer's arrangement of the pictorial planes, which are linked and articulated by means of horizontal and vertical forms, anticipates the type of composition found in the artist's later interiors; and the carpet here covering the table, of which we see only a narrow strip, was to be a frequent motif in his later pictures.

The biblical subject of Christ in the House of Mary and Martha (Luke 10: 38–42) had been well established in Dutch painting since the 16th century. From it derived a Dutch pictorial tradition of market and kitchen scenes, in which the biblical story was increasingly pushed to the side or into the background of the composition, and pride of place given to the depiction of the preparation of the meal. One of the best-known treatments of this subject, a work of 1552 (p. 60), was painted by Pieter Aertsen (*c.* 1508–1575). At first glance it appears to show a vanitas still life; only gradually does one recognize that the subject is, in fact, drawn from the Bible. Aertsen's picture is one of the most

Matteo Rosselli, **Christ and the Woman of Samaria**, *c.* 1620
Oil on canvas, 241 x 194 cm / 94 7/8 x 76 3/8 in.
Vienna, Kunsthistorisches Museum, Gemäldegalerie

important early examples of what was then a nascent pictorial genre: that of the still life. Christ and the two women appear only as subsidiary elements. Most of the composition is devoted to a still life with a leg of mutton, bread and butter, folded napkins, a bunch of flowers and an open cabinet containing a pouch of money. In combination with the other objects shown, food prepared for a feast becomes a symbol of transience, thereby underlining Christ's words in the biblical parable: "Martha, Martha, thou art careful and troubled about many things: But one thing is needful: and Mary hath chosen that good part, which shall not be taken from her." This Flemish tradition of combining a large kitchen still life with the biblical subject of Christ in the House of Mary and Martha was still current in the mid-17th century, as demonstrated by the work of the Antwerp painter Erasmus Quellinus II (1607–1678). An earlier work by this artist, produced *c.* 1640–1645, has repeatedly been identified as the probable model for Christ's pose in Vermeer's picture (p. 82). Quellinus places Martha, viewed from the back, to the left of his composition, surrounded by the elements of a typical kitchen still life. Closer in composition to Vermeer's picture is a later work by Quellinus (p. 63). The group of Christ and the two women here correspond in many respects to Vermeer's arrangement of these three figures, even though Quellinus retains the large still life as the dominant feature.

In comparing Vermeer's picture with the last example, one is struck by the extent to which he plays down the usual contrast between Mary, seated on the ground and listening to Christ's teaching, and Martha, busy in the kitchen. In Vermeer's composition Martha seems just as calm and contemplative a woman as Mary. The practical activity in which she is absorbed is limited to laying upon the table a basket containing a loaf of bread, here simultaneously serving as a symbol of the Eucharist. Within the classical triangular composition, it is, indeed, Martha whose head occupies the centre, although the principal figure is, of course, Christ, at whom Martha looks. He speaks to her while pointing to Mary seated at his feet. The scene therefore illustrates the precise lines within the biblical passage (Luke 10: 41–42). By this means Vermeer places greater emphasis on the spiritual content of the scene, thereby restoring the original meaning to the narrative and transforming a secular genre scene into a sacred image once again.

Christ in the House of Mary and Martha is not only a stylistic anomaly within the context of Vermeer's own later work; it has also proved difficult to place the picture in the larger context of the Dutch painting of its time, or to identify what might have been the models for its stylistic qualities. Commentators have generally considered Vermeer's picture in connection with the work of the Dutch *caravaggisti*, who are associated with

The Procuress (detail), 1656
(see ill. p. 85)

Utrecht, particularly the paintings of Abraham Bloemaert and, above all, of Hendrick ter Brugghen. Vermeer's picture has been seen to share both formal and thematic qualities with works by Ter Brugghen: this is, for example, true of Vermeer's treatment of Mary's face shown in profile against the pale background of the tablecloth, or of the semi-shaded physiognomy of Martha. Reference is made, in this context, to the work viewed as Ter Brugghen's masterpiece: his *Saint Sebastian Tended by the Women* (p. 25). However, by contrast with Ter Brugghen's compact composition of interlaced bodies, the positioning of figures in Vermeer's painting can be comprehended at a glance. The use of chiaroscuro modelling for the figures is also far more restrained in Vermeer's composition. Commentators have also mentioned the possibility of the influence on Vermeer of Dirck van Baburen, a picture by whom was in the collection of Maria Thins. Liedtke also sees this early painting by Vermeer as incorporating Van Dyck's emotional treatment of pose and movement, on the one hand, and Ter Brugghen's emphatic use of light in modelling figures, on the other.[61]

Blankert identifies Jan Liss (*c.* 1597–1630) as a possible model for Vermeer's relatively loose and thick application of paint, regarding this as the only true parallel to what we find in Vermeer's picture.[62] He refers, in particular, to a rendering of *The Temptation of Paul* (Berlin, Staatliche Museen), a picture that in the 17th century was in the collection of the Reynst brothers in Amsterdam and that, in Blankert's view, Vermeer may have seen. Yet the stylistic and technical similarities between Vermeer and Liss are rather slight. Liss has a freer and more agitated manner of painting. The parallels between the two artists lie, rather, in their shared awareness of, and apparent regard for, Italian models and in the individuality of their approach to drawing on these, as is apparent, for example, in the explanatory gesture of Christ's hand (p. 55). We know, furthermore, that Liss spent the greater part of his career in Italy. We can still do no more than speculate that Vermeer may himself have travelled there.

There is general agreement among commentators that Vermeer's two undated pictures *Diana and Her Companions* and *Christ in the House of Mary and Martha* were produced before *The Procuress*, which bears the date 1656. The question, however, as to which of the two undated pictures is the earlier has been much discussed. Blankert believes *Christ in the House of Mary and Martha* to be the earlier picture because it is the more superficial of the two, a quality that he claims can be detected through careful examination. He points, for example, to the way in which the emphatic drapery folds disguise the bodies of the figures beneath, which, accordingly, have rather less physical presence. In some passages the execution is unclear: Christ's hands, for example, might be said almost to lack structure by comparison with the hands of the nymphs in *Diana and Her Companions*. In the latter, by contrast, Blankert detects an overall gain in Vermeer's artistic capacities.

Dirck van Baburen, **Loose Society**, 1623
Oil on canvas, 110 x 154 cm / 43 1/4 x 60 5/8 in. Mainz, Landesmuseum

Wheelock essentially agrees with this view, although he argues that *Saint Praxedis* (p. 393, Cat. 36), which he holds to be an autograph work by Vermeer, was painted even earlier than *Christ in the House of Mary and Martha*. Liedtke, on the other hand, believes *Diana and Her Companions* to be the earlier picture. He argues that, although the composition with Diana anticipates the general structure and the calm mood of Vermeer's later genre paintings, a comparison of the two early pictures leaves no room for doubt that *Christ in the House of Mary and Martha* – with its superb grasp of composition and far greater ambition in terms of both conception and execution – was painted after *Diana and Her Companions*. In as far as the temporal distance between the two early works is rather slight, the question of which picture is the earlier seems relatively unimportant, particularly because these works represent distinct genres. Both evince the beginnings of development in two entirely different directions.

The third of Vermeer's early works, which is dated 1656, is *The Procuress* (p. 85, Cat. 3). While thematically anticipating Vermeer's later work, it appears to strive, on account of its size and the emphatic presence of its protagonists, for the qualities of a history painting.

Pieter Aertsen, **Christ with Mary and Martha**, 1552
Oil on board, 83 x 121 cm / 32 5/8 x 47 5/8 in. Vienna, Kunsthistorisches Museum, Gemäldegalerie

In that respect it is closer, formally and probably also chronologically, to *Christ in the House of Mary and Martha* than to *Diana and Her Companions*. Here, for the first time, we encounter Vermeer in his capacity as a painter of genre scenes, the category with which his work as a whole is associated. Yet *The Procuress* is not really comparable to Vermeer's later genre scenes on account of its narrative content. The setting is a brothel, and the picture is both thematically and formally closer to a particular group of much earlier paintings: those of *c.* 1620–1630 by the Dutch followers of Caravaggio. The leading Dutch *caravaggisti* were Hendrick ter Brugghen, Dirck van Baburen and Gerard van Honthorst. They had a penchant for subjects seen up close, the protagonists featuring as half-length figures placed against dark backgrounds and in raking light, resulting in powerfully modelled forms and strong contrasts of light and shadow, so as to achieve highly dramatic effects (p. 20). Thematically, too, they preferred the lowlier subjects of genre painting: scenes from taverns with musicians, tricksters, prostitutes, procuresses and fortune tellers. This preference accorded with what had been, since the mid-16th century, a Dutch tradition of depicting examples of "loose society". Originally derived – as observed by Renger – from the biblical parable of the Prodigal Son,[63] who squandered his inheritance, such subjects increasingly eschewed illustration of the relevant biblical passage, under the influence of Calvinism, and so evolved into contemporary moralizing subjects.

It would not have been necessary for Vermeer to spend time in Utrecht in order to become familiar with paintings of this sort. Tavern scenes by the Dutch *caravaggisti* were to be found all over Holland; even the small collection of paintings owned by Maria Thins included a work by Dirck van Baburen depicting a procuress gesturing vigorously to demand the fee owed to her ("Een schilderije daer een coppelerste die in de hand wijst").[64] Vermeer knew this painting very well: it recurs in the background of several of his own later genre scenes, first in *The Concert* of the 1660s (p. 183, Cat. 19), then in the late *Young Woman Seated at a Virginal* (p. 285, Cat. 35). It is apparent that Dirck van Baburen's composition existed in several versions, one of which is now in the Museum of Fine Arts, Boston (p. 182). A second work by one of the *caravaggisti* to be found in the possession of Maria Thins, and which Vermeer was also to employ in his own compositions, was a version of the tale of Cimon and Pero, the so-called Caritas Romana ("Een schilderije van een die de borst suyght" / "a picture of a man sucking at a woman's breast"). In Delft there were probably many collectors who had acquired works by the Utrecht *caravaggisti.* We know, for example, of such works in the collection amassed by Boudewijn de Man.[65] Uta Neidhardt has drawn attention to the parallels between Vermeer's *Procuress* and a *Loose Society* of 1617/18 (Brunswick, Herzog Anton Ulrich-Museum) by Louis Finson (before 1560–1617), who was an early Flemish follower of Caravaggio; and she emphasizes in particular the formal rhythms set up within the tightly packed groups of figures and the similarities between both artists' treatment of the old woman in the background with her head covered.[66]

Vermeer seems, however, to have found more inspiration for his *Procuress* in the work of Dirck van Baburen and of a follower of Caravaggio then resident in Delft, Christiaen van Couwenbergh. It has been suggested that one of the reasons Vermeer looked to the example of Dirck van Baburen is that his pictures were at this time very much in demand on the Dutch art market, and sold at relatively high prices.[67] Vermeer's *Procuress* is closest, in terms of the treatment of specific motifs, to Dirck van Baburen's pictures of the 1620s and, above all, to a *Loose Society* painted in 1623 (p. 59). Like Vermeer's composition, this includes four half-length figures, albeit aligned, from left to right, in the exact reverse order: a half-naked prostitute with a fiddle in her hand, her suitor, behind them a procuress and, at the right, a musician who observes the depicted action but is shown smiling at the viewer. The musician, moreover, holds in his left hand a cittern, while with his right hand he pours wine for the suitor. As so often in paintings by Baburen, the faces are of a vulgar crudeness, and the mood is more relaxed than in Vermeer's tavern scene, which by comparison seems imbued with elegant restraint. Both Vermeer's picture and Dirck van Baburen's tavern scenes in general share the strong sense of figures crushed together and viewed so that they partially overlap each other, the consequent frequent juxtaposition of bright colour on dark foreground, and vice versa, and the suggestive play of the hands at the centre.

A significant point in which the compositions of Dirck van Baburen differ from Vermeer's *Procuress*, however, is in the relative importance imputed to the procuress herself. In Baburen's pictures she plays an active, demanding role; in Vermeer's painting the pose suggests that she is merely a passive observer. Initially, however, Vermeer approached this subject rather differently. During the restoration carried out in 2004, X-rays revealed where he had altered his composition while painting the picture. In an earlier state the old woman's right hand was visible next to the right hand of the young woman, which lies open to receive the glinting coin. The old woman, therefore, did not merely observe: she intruded into the action. The facial type of Vermeer's old woman, however, corresponds to what would at this time have been the recognized pictorial type of the sympathetic old woman, as featured in the work of Gerard ter Borch or Gerard Dou.

In addition to Dirck van Baburen, there were other artists in whose work Vermeer may have found inspiration for his treatment of the musician with his gaze fixed on the viewer, as what has been termed a "fictional narrator".[68] Such figures feature, for example, in a brothel scene by Couwenbergh. And they recur repeatedly in pictures by the Dutch *caravaggisti*, in which they are shown observing the action, drinking or playing a musical instrument. Each of these figures enters into communication with the viewer, commenting on the disreputable goings-on through hand gestures or facial expressions. The aforementioned X-rays revealed that Vermeer changed this figure's overall form and its distinctive clothing. The headgear seems to have originally been a much smaller feathered beret, of the type worn by lutenists in the paintings of Gerard van Honthorst, but it was then greatly enlarged, and the lace collar, initially absent, was added (p. 56). Vermeer's musician, as regards his clothing, bears a slight resemblance to the later figure of the painter viewed from the back in *The Art of Painting* (p. 265, Cat. 26). For this reason commentators have repeatedly proposed that the musician may have been intended as Vermeer's self-portrait. He is wearing a doublet, a black jacket with decoratively slashed sleeves and back, a very wide collar with Flemish lace trim and a large black beret.[69] He is, in fact, dressed in the fashion of the 1620s and 1630s, whereas the short and even more extensively slashed jacket of the painter in *The Art of Painting* – a so-called "innocent" – was in fashion when that painting was produced, in the 1660s. The possibility that Vermeer's musician may be intended as the artist's self-portrait seems especially likely on account of the figure's positioning at the extreme edge of the composition, and the fact that his glance is directed at the viewer. A parallel instance is to be found in the self-portrait of the young Jacob Jordaens, seen as a "mediating" accessory in the group portrait of the Van Noort family that he painted around 1615/16 (Kassel, Gemäldegalerie Alte Meister).

Erasmus Quellinus II and Jan Fyt, **Christ in the House of Mary and Martha**, *c.* 1650–1660
Oil on canvas, 112.5 x 163.5 cm / 44 ¼ x 64 ⅜ in. Lille, Palais des Beaux-Arts

It may well have been from a model known to him in Delft that Vermeer derived the compositional motif of the balustrade that separates the four protagonists from the viewer, albeit here it is all but invisible beneath the Ushak medaillon carpet draped over it (p. 84; see also the text of Cat. 3) and, to the left, the musician's black cloak draped over that. Liedtke has pointed out that at Huis Honselaarsdijk – where Christiaen van Couwenbergh was employed on the decorative scheme – a *trompe l'œil* gallery, painted in 1638, probably by Pieter de Grebber and Paulus Bor, once ran around the Banqueting Hall, and that it incorporated figures positioned behind a balustrade, over which carpets were draped.[70] This has not survived, but we do still have a number of related drawings by Pieter de Grebber, now in the Rijksprentenkabinett in Amsterdam.[71] Comparable illusionistic effects are to be found in paintings by Jan van Bijlert (*c.* 1603–1671) and Jan Gerritsz. van Bronckhorst (*c.* 1600–1661; p. 64), in which a number of figures are gathered to play musical instruments and perhaps also to sing, in a space incorporating a carpet draped over a balustrade.

In Vermeer's composition the four protagonists, three of them constituting a closed, interrelated group, the fourth somewhat apart from the rest on account of his

Jan Gerritsz. van Bronckhorst, **Merry Society**, *c.* 1645
Oil on canvas, 141 x 205.7 cm / 55 ½ x 80 in. Brunswick, Herzog Anton Ulrich-Museum

relationship with the viewer, are all depicted as half-length figures, confined within a narrow space around a small table behind a balustrade. The initially persuasive indication of spatial recession is interrupted by the sudden shift, around the centre of the composition, from the impression of looking up at the figures to the impression of looking straight at them and, for example, down on to the tabletop. The edge of the tabletop closest to the young woman supports both a wine jug and the wine glass in the young woman's hand.

We may assume the white cloth thrown over one part of the tabletop to be the apron worn by the young woman. By becoming aware of this abrupt shift in our implied spatial relation to what is depicted, we begin to recognize that other aspects of spatial relationships within the composition are not what they may at first have seemed to be. If we attend more closely to the Westphalian stoneware jug, for example, we will notice that it almost seems to hover rather than to stand. Unlike the care that Vermeer was to take in employing perspective construction in the persuasive rendering of space found in his later paintings, here he relies upon other, rather less successful means.

Compositionally, *The Procuress* is divided into lower and upper halves: the lower half is filled with the carpet, which is gathered in heavy folds towards the right, and with the black cloak thrown on top of it to the left, while it is entirely in the upper half that we find the figures and the action in which they have a part. At the same time the picture may be seen to have distinct right and left halves: on the right, rendered in powerful, radiant colours, we find the subject's true protagonist; on the left, both in dark clothing, the secondary figures: the procuress herself (the picture's nominal subject), old, emerging from the background and still partially masked by the two male figures, and the observer, who looks out at the viewer but whose own face is entirely in shadow, except for the light that just catches his chin and right cheek. There is also a difference between the female figures, whose faces are both clearly visible, and the male figures, whose faces are largely obscured by shadow. The heads of the male figures also mark the upper curves of the undulation that emerges within the figural sequence, the headgear in both cases notably being cropped by the upper picture edge. In Vermeer's original scheme all four heads were equally illuminated; only later was that of the suitor drawn back into shadow, this shift in turn resulting in the suppression of any evidence of direct eye contact between him and the young woman.

At this early date *The Procuress* anticipates aspects of Vermeer's later mastery in his treatment of light, as signalled in his attention to the "melting" quality of the slightly blurred contours of lit edges, and his characteristic illusionism in the rendering of surfaces, here, for example, in the depiction of the blue-and-white-glazed stoneware jug, set in contrast to the softness of the carpet's folds. It is, however, in the overall calmness of its mood that this scene anticipates what we find in the later work, and this in spite of a potentially raucous setting. *The Procuress* thereby differs fundamentally from the above-mentioned earlier pictures by the Dutch *caravaggisti*.

In short, what is innovative in *The Procuress* is to be found not in the subject matter, or in Vermeer's more general turn towards genre painting, but in an entirely new approach to the painterly appropriation of observed reality. It is here for the first time that Vermeer experiments with a particular sort of painterly illusionism and – especially in his treatment of the figure of the observer – the visual impact of light and shadow. Each of his four figures is convincingly individuated and appears to have been studied from a model. And the young woman, be it in her physiognomy or in her simple but radiant dress, may well strike us as an anticipation of the later *Milkmaid* (p. 173, Cat. 8). Vermeer's particular attention to such aspects of the figure is revealed in the evidence of the changes he made while working on the painting. In the final version of *The Procuress* the young woman's white bonnet is pushed so far back as to reveal most of her forehead (in *The Milkmaid* it is pushed even further back and uncovers her hairline; p. 129). In an earlier state of *The Procuress* the yellow bodice is entirely closed, as is that of the figure in *The Milkmaid.* Both of these young women are shown with their gaze lowered.

Neidhardt observes that, during the course of his work on this picture, Vermeer was, in fact, altering, in a very distinctive way, a composition of the type associated with a conventional brothel scene in the style of the Dutch *caravaggisti.*[72] He did this by picking out the young woman as the principal figure, through both colouring and illumination; by more intently disguising the picture's nominal subject; by adding an altogether greater refinement; and even by bringing the subject up to date through details such as the suitor's elegant hat and the beret and collar of the "narrator" on the left. Alterations of this sort anticipate the elegant and morally upright scenes of Vermeer's later career and thereby establish a connection between this work and those. In this respect, then, Vermeer's *Procuress* may be understood as functioning, in the development of the now 24-year-old painter, like what Blankert has termed a "hinge" between the early history paintings and the later genre scenes, in which individuals from a better class of the Dutch society of the day divert themselves in elegant interiors with conversation, music and wine.

Early Genre Scenes

The Procuress is Vermeer's first genre painting, albeit one in which he depicts figures in a setting that he has clearly invented, rather than actually observed. With the only slightly later picture *A Maid Asleep* (p. 87, Cat. 4), he for the first time embarked on genre painting in the strict sense of the term: the reasonably accurate depiction of scenes from the daily life of the Dutch men and women of his own time. This sort of painting was to occupy Vermeer almost exclusively throughout the rest of his career. Genre painting was, in fact, so designated only in the 18th century. As so often in the history of art, the term for a particular type of painting emerged long after the category itself had evolved.[73] The French term *genre*, which initially had the meaning of "category","type" or "manner", but also "fashion", was first used, in an art-critical context, by Denis Diderot (1713–1784) in his 1766 *Essais sur la Peinture*, to distinguish between the sort of work he designated *peinture d'histoire* and that which he called *peinture de genre*. From the point of view of the 18th century, *peinture de genre* embraced painting that was not already categorized as portrait, landscape or still life. The term was used, above all, to refer to scenes of everyday life such as were associated with the work of Jean-Baptiste Greuze (1725–1805). As it was recognized that artistic invention was required in genre painting, just as in history painting, it was allotted second place in the hierarchy of artistic categories. It was now also noted that there were qualities shared by Dutch 17th-century painting and the work of the then contemporary French genre painting exemplified by Greuze and by Jean-Antoine Watteau (1684–1721).

Genre paintings had, of course, effectively existed as far back as the 15th century, both north and south of the Alps, if not yet in great quantities. In the Netherlands genre paintings were frequently found in the second quarter of the 16th century, in the form of scenes set in markets or kitchens. This makes genre painting a quintessentially bourgeois art form; and in the Dutch "Golden Age" of the 17th century it attained a true efflorescence and became a readily recognized and fully accepted pictorial category. Dutch genre painting, however, was notable for its degree of realism, a quality that was, indeed, characteristic of Dutch painting in general. When Dutch writers of this period spoke of what we now understand as genre painting, they referred to the type of subject depicted, rather than employing a collective term. It was thought regrettable that an artist such as Vermeer should be constrained to waste his enormous talent on lightweight material rather than produce history paintings in which his artistic capacities would have been better able to evolve.

In reality, the Dutch painters of the 17th century often invested their pictures of everyday life with a deeper symbolic or moral significance than such later critics saw in them. This is apparent in their particular love of depicting characteristic situations, such as a housewife at work or a mother concerned with the care of her children, or scenes that also had a comic, as well as moral, dimension: peasants brawling in a tavern, or an old man hopelessly enamoured of a young girl. What may at first appear to be a situation accidentally observed will, in fact, have been carefully considered and meticulously composed. On occasion, the deeper meaning may be entirely clear, but often it is hidden and difficult to decipher, very frequently playing on figures of speech, on devotional literature or on emblem books. Such contexts were, of course, far more intellectually accessible to the 17th-century viewer than to those of later periods, so that much in the pictures in question may now be all but incomprehensible.

Gérard de Lairesse (1640–1711), a Dutch painter who was a few years younger than Vermeer who later became established as a writer on art and a champion of Classicism, suggested in his *Groot Schilderboek* (Great Book of Painters) of 1707 that a distinction should be made not, as was later to be proposed, between history painting and genre painting, but between the painting of themes drawn from Antiquity and the painting of themes drawn from modern times.[74] While the former category, which he himself preferred, would remain both thematically and formally constant, the latter would perforce respond to the perpetual shifts of fashion, and would thus inevitably come to be valued less and less as time went by: "The modern, contrarily, is so far from being free, that it is limited within certain narrow Bounds; and is of small Power; for it may or can represent no more than what is present, and that too in a Manner which is always changing: What is past and to come is without its Power; as also Histories, Fables and Emblems, as well poetical and philosophical as moral."[75] In Lairesse's view the painter should always strive to perfect the treatment of modern subjects so that this might be brought as close as possible to the treatment of subjects from Antiquity, as stated in the second chapter of Book III, which is entitled "Method for representing what is City-like or elegant Modern" ("Aanwyzinge om het burgerlyke of cierlyke Moderne wel uit te beelden").[76] In a later edition of his book, published in 1740, Lairesse cites "Mieris, Metzu, van der Meer" as exponents of this "elegant Modern".[77]

Other 17th- and 18th-century sources that comment on the painters of bourgeois life in modern times – in the present instance, in addition to Vermeer, there are references to Gabriel Metsu, Gerard ter Borch, Caspar Netscher (*c.* 1636–1684) and Eglon van der Neer (1635/36–1703) – describe their work as depicting "zaletjes vol jonkertjes en joffertjes" ("little rooms full of young men and young women").[78] Elsewhere it is observed of the pictures of Christoffel van der Laemen (1606–1652) that he "pinxit malle jonkertjes" ("paints foolish young men"). The diminutive Dutch forms "jonkertjes" (for "jonkers") and "joffertjes" (for "juffers"), which are also to be found in descriptions of paintings by Vermeer, are certainly not references merely to the small scale of the depicted figures,[79] but are also intended as a characterization of their carefree and frivolous youth.

Pictures to which such descriptions might apply had, in fact, been painted in Delft since around 1630, by Anthonie Palamedesz. His work shows relatively bare interiors in which groups of relaxed young people are seen enjoying themselves with a glass of wine and by playing music. Notable among the Dutch painters who, around 1650, in ever increasing numbers, turned to modern subjects, thereby exerting a strong influence on Vermeer, were Gerard ter Borch and Nicolaes Maes. These tended to show, in very different ways, two or three figures engaged in some sort of calm activity. They also worked in other genres, including portraiture. There is documentary evidence that Vermeer met Gerard ter Borch at least once (see also, p. 38). At the time Ter Borch was living in Delft only temporarily. Nicholas Maes, on the other hand, had lived and worked since 1653 in nearby Dordrecht. The domestic interiors painted by this artist date from between 1654 and 1659.

Vermeer's *A Maid Asleep* (p. 87, Cat. 4) has generally been dated to *c.* 1656/57. With its half-length female figure, *A Maid Asleep* has an evident connection to *The Procuress* (p. 85, Cat. 3). Also common to both works is the presence of a Turkish carpet dominating all or some of the lower half of the picture. The carpet found in *A Maid Asleep* extends into the left foreground, and covers foremost edge of the table. At its far end we experience a sharp shift in perspective that provides a view from above, rendering the sense of spatial

Christ in the House of Mary and Martha (detail), *c.* 1655
(see ill. p. 83)

recession beyond this point unclear (a further parallel with *The Procuress*). The depicted scene includes many individual objects and motifs that are to recur, in a similar form, in Vermeer's later work. The still life in the left foreground is notable in this respect for its white earthenware wine jug and a Chinese porcelain bowl containing fruit. There are also two wine glasses, one lying on its side next to the jug (which has rather suffered during earlier cleaning of the picture and can now only vaguely be made out), and a second, upright glass, which is almost empty, next to the fruit bowl. It is apparent in the X-ray that this glass was added by Vermeer only after he had overpainted a vine tendril originally depicted here. Equally recurrent in later work is the motif of the large chair pushed into the foreground and there serving as a *repoussoir* motif.

Especially notable throughout the composition is the treatment of space. Both the table and the empty chair are placed exceptionally close to the viewer, and the sleeping girl occupies the apparently very narrow space between the far table edge and the wall behind her, thereby producing a sense of spatial compression. All the more significant, then, is the available view, through the half-open door, into a narrow corridor, and then on, through a second open door, into a larger, neighbouring room. Virtually every aspect of the picture's background comprises forms made up of vertical and horizontal lines, and a geometrical sequence of discrete, bright and dark rectangular planes. It seems that Vermeer first grasped this possibility of combining clearly planar forms so as to call forth an illusion of three-dimensional space when he employed planes in graduated tones of brown to evoke a sense of space in the background of *Christ in the House of Mary and Martha* (p. 83, Cat. 2). Vermeer may well have found a model or a parallel for this type of pictorial structure in a series of contemporary interiors painted by Nicolaes Maes, in which the artist similarly employs, and to the same end, a series of elements set parallel to and at right angles to the picture plane. There are also connections between Vermeer and Maes in terms of the subjects treated in these structurally similar compositions. However, in the work of the Dordrecht painter Maes, greater emphasis is placed on the didacticism so favoured by the Reformation, with a particular concern for the moral instruction of the viewer.

The X-ray examination of Vermeer's *A Maid Asleep* has revealed numerous alterations made during his work on the painting. Little by little he may thereby effectively have altered the originally intended meaning of this work. For, as initially arranged, the composition was much closer to that of the picture by Nicolaes Maes repeatedly cited in comparison: *The Indolent Maid* (p. 79). There, we see a domestic servant who has fallen asleep in front of a huge pile of dishes that she was supposed to have washed. Next to her stands a second maid with a wine jug in her hand, who smiles as she points at her sleeping companion. Beyond the two figures, we can see, through an open door in the background, into a neighbouring room, with people around a table. Vermeer, too,

Gerard van Honthorst, **The Procuress**, 1625
Oil on board, 71 x 104 cm / 28 x 41 in. Utrecht, Centraal Museum

initially planned to include a second figure in his composition, in this case, a man wearing a hat, visible in the neighbouring room. This figure was later partly masked by the mirror hanging on the back wall. There was also to have been a dog, itself placed in the corridor but looking at the man: this then disappeared behind the back of the diagonally positioned chair added to the foreground. It is thus apparent that Vermeer intended to indicate some form of charged connection between the sleeping maid and another, male figure, whom we might imagine to be a visitor, or perhaps the gentleman of the house, about to surprise the sleeper.

Hanging on the wall above the sleeping woman is a framed picture that was originally smaller. It shows a naked Cupid, a motif that recurs in several other pictures by Vermeer, most notably in *Young Woman Standing at a Virginal* (p. 283, Cat. 33), painted around 15 years later (see also p. 121). Here, however, a theatrical mask is present, placed next to Cupid's cropped foot. Such a motif might symbolize the discovery, or the unmasking, of love. Regarding the intended significance of the principal figure in Vermeer's composition – the young woman whom we find sleeping, or perhaps simply absorbed in her thoughts –

it has proved much harder to reach agreement. In the first documented mention of the painting, on the occasion of the sale at auction of the collection of Jacob Abrahamsz. Dissius of Delft, in 1696, its subject is described as "a drunken sleeping maid at a table, by the same [i. e., Vermeer]".[80] The presence of a wine jug and of two wine glasses would seem to indicate pleasure found in alcohol and the drunken state to which such pleasure may lead. The girl supports her head on her right hand: a pose employed to signify melancholy as well as indolence. Sloth (accidie), one of the traditional Seven Deadly Sins, was interpreted as the outcome of inebriation, and was portrayed accordingly. Commentators have disagreed as to whether the young woman depicted is a servant or, in fact, the lady of the house. The earliest surviving reference to the depicted figure as "een dronke slapende Meyd", the roughly contemporary parallels with *The Indolent Maid* by Nicolaes Maes (p. 79) and, more generally, the ubiquity in Dutch literary and pictorial tradition of the figure of the negligent and idle domestic servant, would encourage us to assume that Vermeer's young woman is also a maid.[81] Yet, as both Wheelock and Schneider[82] point out, her well-groomed physical appearance, her elegant clothing and her pearl earrings are less characteristic of a maid than of her mistress, who may herself have intended to see to the housework, but has instead fallen asleep. On the other hand, as Liedtke also notes, there are written Dutch sources contemporary with the painting in which domestic servants are denounced for their finery; and, for this reason, too, he argues that the young woman, however well dressed, might be merely a maid. In Amsterdam in 1681, moreover, a sumptuary law prohibited domestic servants from wearing dresses made of silk or any form of jewellery.[83]

The possibly intended allusion to an amorous relationship as the subject of the young woman's dreams or to sad thoughts, far more emphatically present in Vermeer's original composition, could apply equally to a domestic servant or to her mistress. In this respect, this early picture already points to a characteristic of Vermeer: this is an artist who avoids committing himself. The secret of the elegance of his compositions lies in the fact that there is much about the relationships between the depicted individuals that remains ambiguous. Vermeer may first have learnt the art of the gentle hint from Gerard ter Borch, who captured moods and conveyed emotions that could not easily be communicated through the poses and gestures traditionally recorded by painters. In encountering these compositions, the viewer effectively becomes a secret voyeur.

It is probable that *A Young Woman Reading a Letter* (p. 95, Cat. 5) was painted a little later than *A Maid Asleep*, and dates from *c.* 1657. Yet again, a balustrade or, in this instance, a table covered by a carpet dominates the foreground, which serves to render depth in the composition, but also to separate us from the figure of the protagonist, here, too, shown as a half-length figure. As in the case of *A Maid Asleep*, the bunching and folding of the carpet and the diagonally positioned bowl of fruit introduce an almost surprising element of weight and three-dimensionality. The here very precisely rendered oriental carpet can again be identified as an example of the western Anatolian Ushak medallion type with a red background, made *c.* 1600 (cf. Cat. 3, 4).

A Young Woman Reading a Letter is the first picture in which the artist may be said to have found the subject that, more than any other, he would go on to make truly his own: the depiction of a young woman in an elegant, contemporary interior. Vermeer brings to this subject all the artistic means at his disposal, above all, his skill in the very precise perspective construction of depicted space, and his newly complete mastery of subtly differentiated techniques for applying paint. Here, Vermeer employs for the first time a type of pictorial composition that we will find recurring, in ever new variations, in much of his later work. Viewers are invited to look into the corner of a domestic interior. To the left is a window, the sole source of illumination; the back wall, always pale, runs parallel to the picture plane and serves as a foil for the calmly preoccupied figure standing or sitting in front of it and at a table. Here, bright sunlight falls, through the open window, into a high-ceilinged room, in which we discover a young woman, shown in profile and engaged in reading a letter. The picture is exceptionally tall, but the ostensibly "empty" space that constitutes its upper third or so adds greatly to the calm it radiates. Vermeer was to depict young women engaged in either reading or writing a letter in five subsequent paintings (cf. Cat. 16, 20, 24, 30, 31). These were subjects he would have encountered in the work of Gerard ter Borch.

This picture is especially notable for its heightened degree of illusionism. This is found in individual motifs such as the *trompe l'œil* effect of the pale green curtain in the right foreground, which "frames" the composition rather than forming part of it. We are easily persuaded to imagine that this curtain has just been pulled aside, allowing us to gaze at the true subject of the picture. The use of drapery in this way is frequently found in the work of Delft painters in the mid-17th century, and it was especially favoured by architectural painters such as Gerard Houckgeest (p. 94). However, whereas in his work a curtain in the foreground and a view beyond of the church interior with its tiny figures would effectively represent two distinct levels of reality, in Vermeer's picture the curtain and the figure beyond are rendered on the same scale. It is this that allows Vermeer to alert us to the unresolved ambivalence as regards the curtain's position, which does nothing to dispel the power of the illusion. We may assume that it hangs in front of the frame, and thus outside the picture.

Those of Vermeer's contemporaries who were well-versed in the literature of art may well have seen in his painted curtain an allusion to the episode from Antiquity recorded by Pliny the Elder (AD 23/24–79) in his *Natural History*,[84] in which Zeuxis and Parrhasius agree to compete with each other. Zeuxis, the most celebrated Greek painter (*fl. c.* 425 BC), had painted a bunch of grapes in so naturalistic a fashion that the birds flocked to this mere depiction, convinced that the grapes were real. His rival, Parrhasius, had painted a remarkably life-like curtain. Zeuxis, already convinced that he had won the day with his grapes, demanded that Parrhasius finally pull aside the curtain and reveal what he had painted. When Zeuxis realized that he had been tricked by his opponent, he shamefacedly accepted that Parrhasius had won the competition.

The now enhanced illusionism of Vermeer's representation, a quality also to be found in the contemporary work of the Leiden "fine painters" Gerard Dou and Frans van Mieris the Elder, is manifest in the subtly varied treatment of light, which defines the space through diverse degrees of brightness and is also to be detected in the many details that serve to differentiate between diverse textures and types of surface. For the first time the artist here employs a very individual painting technique, based on the rather pastose application of small, bright, luminous dabs of paint, which he brought to perfection only a little later, such as in *The Milkmaid* (p. 173, Cat. 8, see also pp. 108–112).

Vermeer created his *Young Woman Reading a Letter* in several stages and he carried out many corrections.[85] It has frequently been observed that neither the pose of the young woman, nor her hairstyle, nor the shape of her white collar correspond precisely with the reflection in the window, which is itself a brilliant example of Vermeer's skill in illusionism. As X-rays have revealed, Vermeer originally made the figure of the young woman smaller and had her turning away from the viewer so as to show a "lost profile". In altering her size and position, he seems not, however, to have altered her reflection. The curtain to the right was also a later addition.

The most far-reaching alteration was made with regard to the large, empty plane of pale wall in the background. Vermeer would have been able to study the compositional effect of large wall surfaces in the work of other Delft painters, among them, Carel Fabritius and Emanuel de Witte. As X-rays have revealed, Vermeer initially intended to place a large, black-framed picture here: this would have occupied a substantial portion of the visible wall surface, with part of its frame overlapped by the head of the young woman. Such a strong emphasis on vertical and horizontal elements would have made the composition much more like *A Maid Asleep* (p. 87, Cat. 4), and, indeed, the works by Nicolaes Maes in which Vermeer may have found his initial inspiration. The picture that was to hang on the back wall showed Cupid holding aloft a playing card. The outline of the picture is today clearly visible. Vermeer used this particular "picture within a picture" three times. It is initially seen, albeit on this occasion only in a small detail, in the background of *A Maid Asleep*. It occurs a second time showing the entire composition, albeit very dark and not clearly recognizable, in *Young Woman Interrupted at Music*,

Quiringh van Brekelenkam, **A Tailor's Workshop**, 1653
Oil on board, 60 x 85 cm / 23 5/8 x 33 1/2 in. Worcester, Massachusetts, Worcester Art Museum

pp. 168/169, Cat. 11). And it is found a third time, much later, in *Young Woman Standing at a Virginal* (p. 283, Cat. 33). The image of Cupid is derived from an emblem devised by Otto van Veen (p. 282): "Perfectus amor non est nisi ad unum" ("Love is perfect only if felt for one"). This comes from his *Amorum Emblemata*,[86] which describes sincere love and overcoming deception, and would, therefore, seem to relate to the letter reader and the possible contents of the letter she holds in her hand.[87] In overpainting the "picture within a picture" in this case, Vermeer not only introduced a new calm into the composition on account of the now large empty space, but at the same time opened the inner meaning of his scene with the letter reader to a much wider range of possible interpretations. He made further alterations to the foreground of the composition. To the original collection of three large fruits, he added further pieces, distributed across the table, and he overpainted both a large rummer, as well as a chair that had initially stood here.

Cavalier and Young Woman (p. 91, Cat. 6) was painted at more or less the same time as *A Young Woman Reading a Letter*, or perhaps a little later. In Vermeer's first two genre scenes in the strict sense of the term, female figures are shown on their own, and absorbed

in their own thoughts. In *Cavalier and Young Woman*, however, we see a couple, the man placed in the foreground in the form of a dark semi-silhouette with his back to the viewer, and the cheerful young woman facing him. The marked contrast between these two figures, be it in their respective size, the light and shade, the colouring or the distinctively male or female forms, strikes us immediately and dominates the overall impression made by this picture.

Vermeer used here the same simple spatial scheme as we find in *A Young Woman Reading a Letter*; this would become the standard compositional form of his paintings. Our gaze is directed into the corner of a room, the visible space being delineated by a back wall, which runs parallel to the picture plane, and a wall to the left, in which there is a window. This type of composition first emerged in Dutch depictions of domestic interiors around 1650, above all, in the work of painters who were active in the south of Holland, such as in Leiden, The Hague, Rotterdam and Dordrecht.[88] In the interiors shown in earlier Dutch painting, three walls were usually visible. This earlier tradition had first been adapted by painters such as Quiringh van Brekelenkam (*c.* 1620–1667/68) of Leiden (p. 75) to show the interior as it would have looked if viewed from a closer position, with the resulting disappearance of one of the three walls, and a sense of looking into one corner of the room. It was, above all, Pieter de Hooch, in the pictures he painted in Delft between 1655 and 1660, who enjoyed success with this particular compositional scheme (p. 90).

It would be hard to establish with any certainty how well Vermeer and Pieter de Hooch – both at work in Delft at the same time – may have influenced each other in this aspect of their work. The probable date of Vermeer's painting does, however, depend to a large extent on how one rates the influence on Vermeer of de Hooch. Liedtke,[89] who believes that de Hooch's influence on Vermeer was slight, dates *Cavalier and Young Woman* to 1657, while Wheelock – thinking it likely that de Hooch did have an influence on Vermeer – believes it to be somewhat later, *c.* 1658–1660.[90]

The large figure of the cavalier, viewed from the back, leads the viewer's eye into the picture. Our sense of the figure's scale is significantly enhanced by the emphatic foreshortening and by its semi-silhouetted appearance. The marked foreshortening is achieved through the slight discrepancy between the vanishing point and the distance point that Vermeer has selected for his perspective construction.[91] The male figure's large hat is the darkest part of his silhouette because it is positioned, as observed by the viewer, in front of the bright light entering the window. The motif of a large foreground figure shown entirely in shadow was first employed in the work of the Dutch *caravaggisti*. It

A Maid Asleep (detail), *c.* 1656/57
(see ill. p. 87)

can be found in compositions by Van Honthorst (p. 71), and it was also taken up by Couwenbergh.[92] The motif of two figures seated facing each other across a table corner is derived from Haarlem painting of the 1630s[93]; it is also to be found in the work of Gerard ter Borch and Pieter de Hooch. In Vermeer's composition both of the chairs share the same vanishing point and are positioned parallel to each other. The chair in question is yet another item of furniture that is to be found in many of Vermeer's pictures (Cat. 4, 5, 7, 15, 20, 23, 25). In his early genre scenes Vermeer frequently adds variety to his relatively limited number of themes by introducing many of the same motifs and objects in ever new combinations. This enabled him to draw with great facility on the work of numerous contemporary Dutch painters whose pictures treated similar themes.

As to his illusionism in rendering a variety of surfaces, Vermeer looked to the "fine painting" tradition of Leiden, to the pictures of Gerard Dou, Frans Mieris and Quiringh van Brekelenkam, and his own paintings recall their work both in their small size and on account of the technical aspects of how they are painted. Vermeer, however, outstripped all other painters with the powerful illusion of reality that he was able to achieve. This has led a great many commentators over the years to suggest that Vermeer must have relied upon the aid of a camera obscura for assistance in devising and executing his compositions. In the case of many of Vermeer's pictures, as, indeed, in *Cavalier and Young Woman*, a small hole is still visible on the picture surface. This marks the central vanishing point, and it is a sure indication that Vermeer made use of the traditional method of establishing the chief vanishing lines in any composition, using a thin, tightly stretched cord stained with chalk dust or powdered paint, which would be fixed to the canvas with a needle (for more on this see p. 111f.).

Just as crucial in establishing the persuasive illusion of reality as a compelling sense of space is the representation of light. As has already been noted, Vermeer rapidly gained in his ability to render the effects of illumination, and, indeed, light itself through the painterly means at his disposal. In *Cavalier and Young Woman* he uses the juxtaposition of bright and dark planes to structure space. In order to bring about the effects he was seeking to achieve, Vermeer made several alterations to the composition while at work on the painting: the young woman was originally wearing a white shawl, which Dutch women might wear in bed but also while at home during the day. This item was, however, eventually overpainted by Vermeer. Through his treatment of motifs such as the chair's carved lion's head finials with their glinting highlights or the gleaming wine glass, he increases the illusion of reality. The map on the back wall is not only of thematic significance, but also has an important formal function. The surface of the map, which is enlivened by the folds and creases thrown into relief by the play of light across it, is a further stupendous example of Vermeer's illusionism. This is a real map of Holland and

Friesland, produced in 1620 by Balthasar Florisz. van Berckenrode (*c.* 1591–1645) and published by Willem Jansz. Blaeu (1571–1638), of which only one surviving example is now known. Vermeer depicts, however, a version that is coloured in a most unusual way, with the land marked in pale blue. It has been assumed that Vermeer did not here record a version of the map that ever existed, but, rather, selected the colouring to accord with the composition as a whole.

It is impossible to overlook the erotic tension that exists between the man and the woman in Vermeer's picture, even though he has expressly left us uncertain as to the exact nature of their relationship. Much attention has, therefore, been paid to their respective poses, gestures and facial expressions. Slatkes, for example, believes that the presence of a wine glass and the young woman's hand held open in what might be seen as a demanding gesture indicates that she is, in fact, a woman of easy virtue, the map on the wall symbolizing her "worldly" attitude.[94] A more specific connection with the allegorical figure of "Lady World" has also been mooted.[95] Vermeer's map is not, however, a map of the world, and neither the young woman's clothing, nor her pose, nor her open hand (here surely shown in a gesture accompanying speech) can be interpreted as hints that love is here for sale. Wheelock sees in the juxtaposition of the young woman and the map a distant reflection of the personification of the Netherlands, the *Nederlandse Maagd*, here receiving strong military support in the figure of an officer.[96] Liedtke remains sceptical concerning all far-fetched interpretations of this sort.[97] In his view, Vermeer, like other Dutch genre painters at this time, here simply shows an officer and a young woman who happen to be conversing beneath a map of the Netherlands, where peace had only recently been restored.

Nicolaes Maes, **The Indolent Maid**, 1655
Oil on board, 70 x 53.3 cm / 27 ½ x 20 in. London, The National Gallery

Jacob van Loo, **Diana and Her Companions**, 1648
Oil on canvas, 136.8 x 170.6 cm / 53 7/8 x 67 1/8 in.
Berlin, Staatliche Museen zu Berlin, Gemäldegalerie

Diana and Her Companions, *c.* 1654
Oil on canvas, 97.8 x 104.6 cm / 38 1/2 x 41 1/8 in.
The Hague, Koninklijk Kabinet van Schilderijen Mauritshuis

Erasmus Quellinus II
Christ in the House of Mary and Martha, *c.* 1640–1645
Oil on canvas, 172 x 243 cm / 67 ¾ x 95 ⅝ in.
Valenciennes, Musée des Beaux-Arts

Christ in the House of Mary and Martha, *c.* 1655
Oil on canvas, 160 x 142 cm / 63 x 56 in.
Edinburgh, National Galleries of Scotland

Ushak medallion carpet, *c.* 1600
Wool, 208 x 410 cm / 81 ⅞ x 161 ⅜ in.
Vienna, Österreichisches Museum für angewandte Kunst

The Procuress, 1656
Oil on canvas, 143 x 130 cm / 56 ⅜ x 51 ¼ in.
Dresden, Staatliche Kunstsammlungen, Gemäldegalerie Alte Meister

Samuel van Hoogstraten (attrib.)
The Slippers, 1660–1665
Oil on canvas, 103 x 70 cm / 40 ½ x 27 ½ in. Paris, Musée du Louvre

A Maid Asleep, *c.* 1656/57
Oil on canvas, 87.6 x 76.5 cm / 34 ½ x 30 ⅛ in.
New York, The Metropolitan Museum of Art,
Bequest of Benjamin Altman, 1913

Pages 88/89
Cavalier and Young Woman (detail), *c.* 1657–1659
(see ill. p. 91)

Pieter de Hooch
Soldiers Playing Cards, *c.* 1657/58
Oil on board, 50.5 x 45.7 cm / 19 7/8 x 17 in.
Private collection

Cavalier and Young Woman, *c.* 1657–1659
Oil on canvas, 50.5 x 46 cm / 19 7/8 x 18 1/8 in.
New York, The Frick Collection

Pages 92/93
A Young Woman Reading a Letter (detail),
c. 1657 (see ill. p. 95)

Gerard Houckgeest
The Interior of the Oude Kerk in Delft, *c.* 1654 (?)
Oil on board, 49 x 41 cm / 19 ¼ x 16 ⅛ in.
Amsterdam, Rijksmuseum

A Young Woman Reading a Letter, *c.* 1657
Oil on canvas, 83 x 64.5 cm / 32 ⅜ x 25 ⅝ in.
Dresden, Staatliche Kunstsammlungen, Gemäldegalerie Alte Meister

III.

The Years of Vermeer's Maturity

1660–1665

"This strange painter's palette is blue, lemon yellow, pearl grey, black, white... the arrangement... is as characteristic of him as the black, white, grey, pink is of Velázquez."

VINCENT VAN GOGH, 1888

Living and Working in Delft

Very little documentation has been discovered relating to the life of Johannes Vermeer after his marriage to Catharina Bolnes and his enrolment, as a master, in the Delft Painters' Guild. We do not know where and under what circumstances the young married couple at first lived, nor where Vermeer had his first studio. It has been posited that the view shown in his painting of around 1660, *The Little Street* (p. 175, Cat. 9), is what could be seen from a window on the second floor of the "Mechelen" tavern on the Groote Markt, and that this is where his studio could be found at the time. It is also conceivable that his studio was in the house of his mother-in-law, Maria Thins, on the Oude Langendijck, which was close to the Groote Markt. We know that the Vermeer family was living here from at least December 1660, when "een kint van Johannes Vermeer aen den O. Langedijck" ("a child of Johannes Vermeer on the Oude Langedijck") was buried at the Oude Kerk in Delft.[98]

It appears that the painter had rather little money during the first years of his career. We know, from the evidence of the first will drawn up by Maria Thins, in 1657,[99] that Vermeer had received a loan of 300 florins from his mother-in-law. The aforementioned document divided Maria Thins's fortune among her daughter, Catharina Bolnes, the wife of Johannes Vermeer, the couple's eldest daughter, Maria Vermeer (who was also the goddaughter of Maria Thins), and Maria Thins's son, Willem Bolnes, who had remained with his father in Gouda after his parents had separated, and who in 1660 had been admitted to a privately run correctional institution.[100] Willem Bolnes was still an inmate there when he died in 1676.

In all, only four documents bear witness to Vermeer's presence and activity in Delft in the time between his marriage, in 1653, and the aforementioned burial of his child, in 1660.[101] In January 1654 he is registered as a *meester Schilder* (master painter) when testifying, before a notary, alongside a military captain from Cleves.[102] Montias conjectures that it may have been through his mother's brother, the military contractor Reynier Baltens, that Vermeer had access to military officers, who served as models for the cavaliers featuring in several of his genre scenes.[103] A second notary's document, drawn up in April 1654, likewise names Vermeer as a witness; and in December 1655 he served as a witness in another legal transaction, on this occasion being referred to as "Sr. [*seigneur*] Johannes

Page 97
Girl with a Pearl Earring (detail), *c.* 1665–1667
(see ill. p. 217)

The Girl with the Red Hat (detail), *c.* 1665–1667
(see ill. p. 221)

Vermeer", a respectful form of address, indicative of high social standing, such as was never granted to his father.[104] Vermeer's established position within the Delft community of painters is reflected in his being appointed *regerende Hooftman* (headman) of the Guild of Saint Luke. He held this position for two years, from autumn 1662.[105] In each such period the Guild had six headmen in total: two painters, two glassmakers and two fayence artists. At the age of 30, Vermeer was the youngest person to have held such a position since the Guild's reorganization, in 1611. This, however, has been seen not so much as an indication that Vermeer's contemporaries recognized his outstanding significance as an artist than as a sign of the gradual cultural decline of Delft, for the Guild now encountered difficulties filling such positions.[106]

The last of the four documents relating to Vermeer concerns a loan of 200 guilders, repayable within a year at an interest rate of 4.5 per cent, which Johnnes Vermeer and his wife received in 1657 from the wealthy Delft patrician Pieter Claesz. van Ruijven.[107] This document was discovered in 1885 by Abraham Bredius, but its far-reaching implications were recognized only much later, by Montias.[108] Montias put forward the thesis that, from 1657, Vermeer worked almost exclusively for a single patron, Pieter Claesz. van Ruijven, the documented loan marking the start of this collaboration and being, in all likelihood, the advance payment for pictures that Vermeer had undertaken to supply.

From the time of his work on *The Procuress*, dated 1656, a painting in the spirit of the Dutch *caravaggisti*, and the early genre scenes of the following years until around 1658/59 (Cat. 4–6), Vermeer devoted himself, with only a few exceptions (both of which are cityscapes), to the production of further genre scenes. Scholars have repeatedly wondered about the reasons for this. One explanation might be that Vermeer did, indeed, work for a single patron, and, therefore, produced paintings that suited this patron's desires and preferences or complied with the subjects and settings specified in his commissions.

Surviving documents relating to contemporaries of Vermeer indicate that many painters during this period did not produce work for the art market, but in response to commissions received from collectors. The two most important representatives of the Leiden tradition of "fine painting", Gerard Dou and Frans van Mieris, painted their especially labour-intensive, and therefore expensive, small genre scenes for specific collectors, to whom they were contracted. From these they received regular annual remuneration for all the work they had produced, although the respective patrons retained the "right of first refusal". It was only the "refused" paintings that the artists were then permitted to offer to other interested buyers. In this respect, the situation of painters in 17th-century Holland was fundamentally different from that of those in other parts of Europe, such as the Catholic countries, where the enduring dominance of ecclesiastical patronage ensured a prevalence of religious art. In Vermeer's Holland we encounter, to our surprise, a situation that appears to resemble the

Daniel Vosmaer, **View of Delft from an Imaginary Loggia**, 1663
Oil on canvas, 90.5 x 113 cm / 35 5/8 x 44 1/2 in. Delft, Museum Prinsenhof

modern phenomenon of artists producing work in the spirit of *l'art pour l'art* (art for the sake of art) – a concept primarily associated with the late 19th century.

It is highly likely that most of the pictures that Vermeer painted from 1657 onwards entered the collection of Pieter Claesz. van Ruijven (see Cat. 4, 6, 8–10, 12). However, as no list of the works in his collection or any recorded reference to it has been found, Montias was able to refer only to the catalogue of the 1696 sale at auction of works from the collection of Pieter van Ruijven's late son-in-law, Jacob Abrahamsz. Dissius (1653–1695).[109] Van Ruijven was so wealthy that the sum he spent on paintings only minimally reduced his fortune. Most of this, as also that of his wife, Maria Simonsdr. de Knuijt, had been inherited. He seems not to have pursued any sort of career; and the brewery that his father once ran was closed down around 1650. As a Remonstrant, and thus a member of a religious minority, he would not have been permitted to hold public office. The only post that he did occupy, from 1668 to 1672 – as had his father before him – was that of Director of the Delft Camer van Charitate, the public charity set up to ensure the welfare of the poor.

Pieter van Ruijven and his wife, together with a daughter born in 1655, lived on the Oude Delft, the city's most elegant street, in a house with a value estimated at 10,500 florins. In 1665 Pieter Claesz. and Maria van Ruijven drafted a joint will. This document has in part survived, although a codicil containing a list of his *schilderkonst*, the collection of paintings, and the provision formally made for its disposal, has been lost.[110] In a separate will drawn up by Maria van Ruijven, which would have taken effect only if her husband had predeceased her, specifies bequests to a number of relatives, to charitable institutions and to the Remonstrant Church, but also to Johannes Vermeer, who was to receive 500 florins.[111] Except for persons related to the couple, Vermeer is the only individual to be listed here as the intended recipient of a bequest, although it was specified that he alone was to be the beneficiary and not any of his heirs. Montias posits that, as a Remonstrant, Pieter van Ruijven was thereby seeking to prevent the sum bequeathed by his wife to Vermeer from later passing, through Vermeer's own wife, to the Jesuits in Delft. The evidence of this bequest has encouraged the conclusion among commentators that Vermeer and his most important patron were linked not only by a commercial arrangement but also by the bonds of a close friendship.

In 1669 Pieter van Ruijven acquired, for the sum of 16,000 florins, the domain of Spalant, comprising 21 acres of land. He used the accompanying title of Lord of Spalant when, in 1670, he served as a witness for, and a legal adviser to, Vermeer at the formal reading of the will of the latter's sister, Gertruy, and her husband, Anthony van der Wiel, in which Vermeer was left 400 florins.[112] In 1674, when Pieter van Ruijven reconfirmed the will he had drawn up earlier, he specified in a codicil that his only daughter, Magdalena van Ruijven (1655–1682), should inherit the title to the domain of Spalant. Pieter Claesz. van Ruijven died that year, and in 1680 his daughter married Jacob Abrahamsz. Dissius. The latter, while from a distinguished family, was entirely without financial means of his own. Upon his marriage, he was formally put in charge of the printing concern previously run by his father, presumably in order to overcome the large disparity between the personal wealth of the bride and the groom.[113] Magdalena died, however, without issue, two years later, in 1682, at the age of only 27. Jacob Abrahamsz. Dissius was constrained to borrow 400 florins from his father in order to be able to cover the cost of the funeral. In 1681, however, after the death of his mother-in-law, Maria de Knuijt, he had become the sole heir to the Van Ruijven family fortune, including the domain of Spalant, the income from the properties the family owned in Delft and the collection of paintings.

In April 1683 an inventory of the property owned by Jacob Abrahamsz. Dissius and inherited by him from Magdalena was drawn up and certified by a notary.[114] This list included 39 paintings, 20 of them by Vermeer. Eight of these, in addition to three pictures in cases (*kasies*), were to be found in the stately *voorkamer* of the house; in the back room there was a total of 12 paintings, of which four were by Vermeer, two were views of church interiors, two were *tronies*, that is to say, studies of heads of the sort seen in *Girl with a Pearl Earring* (Cat. 21), and two were night scenes. In the kitchen, which apparently served as both a living room and a bedroom, there were seven pictures, one of them by Vermeer, and two *tronies*. Two pictures by Vermeer were to be found in the basement (*op de kelder kamer*); and two further pictures by Vermeer were mentioned, albeit without any hint of their location within the house. Before Montias had realized the connection between Vermeer and Pieter Claesz. van Ruijven, it was long believed that Jacob Abrahamsz. Dissius had been the most important collector of paintings by Vermeer, if not his actual patron. It was, however, always noted that the large difference in age between Dissius and Vermeer – the former being only 22 when Vermeer died – made this rather unlikely.

On 16 May 1696 134 paintings, of diverse provenance, were sold at auction in Amsterdam. The accompanying sale catalogue was published by Gerard Hoet, in 1752, in a volume recording Dutch sales of works of art and the prices obtained for these; it has, therefore, long been familiar to scholars. Twenty-one paintings by Vermeer are included in the 1696 sale catalogue.[115] The descriptions of the subject of each picture are succinct and informative, allowing us easily to identify most, if not all, of the works that have survived. Twenty pictures by Vermeer are probably to be identified as those that, 13 years earlier, had been listed in the inventory of the collection of Jacob Abrahamsz. Dissius. Two pictures of church interiors in the inventory of 1683 are probably the works of Emanuel de Witte featured in the sale catalogue of 1696. The four *tronies* on the 1683 list correspond with three studies of heads by Vermeer and one by Rembrandt in the 1696 sale catalogue. A picture with houses mentioned in 1683 corresponds to "Een Gesicht van een Huys staende in Delft, door denzelven" ("a view of a house in Delft, by the same", i. e. Vermeer) recorded in 1696.

It is highly likely, therefore, that those works by Vermeer that were sold at auction in Amsterdam in 1696, deriving from the collection of both Pieter Claesz. van Ruijven and Jacob Abrahamsz. Dissius, entered the art market by this means. Of the 21 Vermeer pictures sold on this occasion, it is thought that 15 have survived and that six have since been lost, among the latter, a self-portrait, an interior with a man shown washing his hands, a couple playing musical instruments, a view of houses in Delft and two studies of heads.

The prices attained at the 1696 sale are especially instructive in the case of the pictures by Vermeer. The most expensive picture, which sold for 200 florins, was *A View of Delft* (Cat. 12). The next most expensive was *The Milkmaid* (Cat. 8), sold for 175 florins, while *Woman with a Balance* (Cat. 18) – a picture that was in a case (*kasie*) – sold for

155 florins. The remaining genre scenes were sold for between 30 and 80 florins each, and the studies of heads for between 17 and 36 florins each. An interior view of the Oude Kerk in Amsterdam by Emanuel de Witte, by comparison, was sold for 74 florins; a large landscape, much praised in the catalogue, by Simon de Vlieger (1601–1653), went for 26 florins; and a study of a head by Rembrandt sold for only 7 ¼ florins. Of the 35 surviving pictures that are today generally accepted as the work of Johannes Vermeer, 15 in all probability come from the collection of Pieter Claesz. van Ruijven. While this does not allow us to conclude that Vermeer produced paintings exclusively as commissions received from this patron, we can nonetheless state with certainty that Pieter van Ruijven was the most significant buyer of pictures by Vermeer.

On the basis of the number of the Vermeer pictures sold at auction in 1696 and the number of these that have survived, Montias endeavoured to calculate the size of Vermeer's overall output, arriving at a projected total of between 43 and 60 pictures.[116] For an artistic career lasting 19 years, that is to say, from 1656 (Montias regards this as starting with the production of *The Procuress*, dated to 1656, rather than with Vermeer's enrolment in the Delft Painters' Guild, at the end of 1653) to Vermeer's death in 1675, this would mean an average of two or three pictures per year. Such a slow rate of production is, indeed, what one might expect in the case of an artist working without an assistant and in view of Vermeer's highly complex and refined manner of painting. Montias also attempted, on the basis of this projected production rate, to estimate Vermeer's annual income and hence the financial basis of his ability to support his family. Further relevant evidence was to be found in the prices that his pictures fetched at the 1696 auction, in addition to information from other sources, and a comparison with the prices attained by the work of other artists. In 1657, for example, a now untraced depiction of *Women at a Grave* by Vermeer from the estate of the art dealer Johannes de Renialme was valued at 20 florins.[117] In 1661 a picture from the estate of Cornelis de Helt, a Delft tavern keeper, described in the inventory as "Int Voorhuys / In den eersten een schilderye in een swarte lyst door Jan van der Meer",[118] was sold at auction for 20 ½ florins.[119] A study of a head by Vermeer from the estate of the sculptor Johannes Larson in The Hague, who died in 1664, was described as "een tronie van Vermeer" ("a face by Vermeer"), and was sold for ten florins.[120]

In January 1676, only a few weeks after Vermeer's death, his widow sold to the baker Hendrick van Buyten (in order to clear the as yet unpaid bill for several years' worth of bread deliveries) two works by the painter: a picture with two figures, one of them a woman shown seated and writing a letter, and a picture of a woman playing a guitar (these may be identified, respectively, as Cat. 31 and 32), for a total of 617 florins and 6 stuivers. According to the notary's document drawn up to record the sale, Catharina Bolnes maintained her right to buy back these pictures, although she was, in fact, never able to do so, for 25 years later, they were still to be found in Hendrick van Buyten's possession.[121] For just two pictures to be sold for a figure in excess of 600 guilders was at this date remarkable, even allowing for the fact that Vermeer's widow knew the buyer well and that this may have induced him to be especially generous.

On the basis of all the information of this sort available to him, Montias calculated that Vermeer's average annual income from the sale of his pictures must have been between 200 and 600 florins.[122] Montias also estimates that, on account of Vermeer's growing recognition as an artist in the 1660s, he would have been able to charge higher than usual prices for his pictures, at least until the economic crisis triggered by the war with France brought about a collapse in the market for works of art in the 1670s. Montias calculates that Vermeer would have earned between 100 and 200 florins per year through the sale of his work on the open market, although relatively few pictures would have been disposed of in this way. Montias's chief source of information regarding this is the sale by Catharina Bolnes of 26 pictures from Vermeer's estate to the Haarlem painter and art dealer Jan Coelenbier (*c.* 1610–1677) for 500 florins.[123] This equates to a sale price of around 19 florins per picture. Montias assumes that Vermeer's widow sold off the entirety of her deceased husband's former collection.

This allows us to conclude that, without the financial contributions of his wife and his mother-in-law, Maria Thins, Vermeer would not have been able to feed his family.[124] The income from the bequests of Jan and Cornelia Thins (the brother and sister of Maria Thins, who had died, respectively, in 1651 and 1661) amounted to between 350 and 400 florins per year. In addition, there were the direct allowances and loans that Maria Thins made to her daughter. We do not know the full amounts concerned in any particular case, but in each of six consecutive years she loaned her 167 florins.[125] It was also doubtless the case that Vermeer and his family were not required to pay rent to his mother-in-law

Johannes van der Beeck, called Torrentius
Still Life with Pewter Jug, Glass and Bridle: Allegory of Temperance, 1614
Oil on board, 52 x 50.5 cm / 20 ½ x 19 ⅞ in. Amsterdam, Rijksmuseum

in return for being able to live in her house, and this would have saved them between 80 to 100 florins per year. On the basis of these, admittedly to some extent hypothetical, calculations, Montias arrives at a figure for the annual income of Vermeer and his wife of between 850 and 1,300 florins. With such an income Vermeer would by no means have been impoverished. By contrast, his mother, Digna Baltens, as we know from her unsuccessful attempt in 1669 to auction off the "Mechelen" tavern, was having to pay out 125 florins a year in interest on the loans taken out to cover its purchase.

Two art connoisseurs and collectors who visited Delft during their travels have left us a record of their encounters with Vermeer. In 1663 the French diplomat Balthasar de Monconys (1611–1655) made a journey through the Netherlands, not least in order to establish contacts with Dutch Catholics. A native of Lyons and educated by the Jesuits, he spent a long time in The Hague, making two short trips from there to Delft. On 11 August 1663 he made his second visit to the city. On this occasion he was accompanied by a certain Père Léon, probably a Carmelite from Brussels, and a military officer by the name of Gentile. The latter is perhaps to be identified as the painter Louis Cousin, also known as Luigi Gentile (1606–1667), who had long been based in Rome and who, from 1661, was a member of the Brussels Painters' Guild. On this occasion Monconys visited Vermeer in his studio, but the painter was unable to show him or to sell him any of his work. Instead, he advised his visitor to call on a certain master baker, whom we may assume to be Hendrick van Buyten (see also p. 104), who had recently acquired, reputedly for the enormous sum of 600 florins, a genre scene by Vermeer. In his notes, Monconys records that he saw a genre scene containing only a single figure and found the price to be more than ten times what it ought to have been: "In Delft I saw the painter Vermeer, who had none of his works to hand, but at a baker's we saw one, in which there was only one figure, which had been sold for 600 livres, and for which I myself would have thought six pistoles to be payment enough."[126] Two days later Monconys had the opportunity to see another single-figure painting, this time by Gerard Dou, which was reported to have been sold to Johan de Bye, Dou's chief patron, for the same sum as had been asked for the Vermeer.

In 1669 Vermeer was visited in his studio by another man with an interest in his work. This was Pieter Teding van Berckhout (1643–1713), a member of the circle that had formed around the Regent in The Hague, who travelled to neighbouring Delft in the company of other members of that court, one of whom may have been Constantijn Huygens. His diary records that, on 14 May, he saw "an outstanding painter by the

A Lady Writing (detail), *c.* 1665–1667
(see ill. p. 199)

name of Vermeer","who showed me a number of remarkable works of his own". Several weeks later, on 21 June 1669, he again visited Vermeer, of this encounter reporting that he had met "a celebrated painter by the name of Vermeer, who showed me some examples of his art, the most extraordinary and most curious aspect of which consists in the perspective".[127]

Vermeer's Technique

Since the time of Thoré-Bürger, all commentators on Vermeer have placed particular stress on the technical aspect of his work, which differed from that of other Dutch painters of the time. His aim was to achieve a perfect illusion of reality. He did not depict objects and space as they actually were, but exactly as they would have appeared to a spectator observing them from a particular vantage point under particular lighting conditions. Gleaming metal and reflecting glass, for example, lose something of their detectable form in the light, and the optical impression we receive consists, rather, of a system of light and dark colour spots. In order to achieve this illusionistic effect Vermeer devised a special way of painting, which involved the pastose application of small dots and dabs of paint, a method characterized by Thoré-Bürger as *pointillé*. Among more recent Vermeer specialists, it is, above all, Wheelock who has devoted particular attention to investigating the artist's painting technique and to supplying an exhaustive account of it. He embarked on his research in 1973 with a thorough study of the Vermeer pictures in the collection of the National Gallery of Art in Washington, D.C. Subsequently he conducted similar investigations in further museum collections, where he was able to study the Vermeer paintings in the respective restoration workshops. The accumulated results of these studies were published in the technical details included in the catalogue of the Vermeer exhibition presented in Washington, D.C., and The Hague in 1995/96, and in the simultaneously appearing volume *Vermeer and the Art of Painting*.

Several decades earlier, the optical effects that Vermeer succeeded in rendering had been compared by commentators with the slightly blurred images produced by a simple camera obscura. In 1964 Seymour juxtaposed photographs made using a camera obscura with details of paintings by Vermeer, and ascertained that there appeared to be an astonishing similarity between the two.[128] Seymour, however, like those who subsequently argued along the same lines – from Schwarz (1966) and Fink (1971) to Steadman (2001) – may be shown to have drawn the wrong conclusions from this discovery. At no phase of the work on any of his paintings did Vermeer make use of a camera obscura. The fact that some artists in the 17th century did, indeed, imitate the optical effects that might be achieved with the aid of such an optical apparatus by no means signifies that Vermeer himself made use of one or that he had any need to do so in making his own paintings.[129]

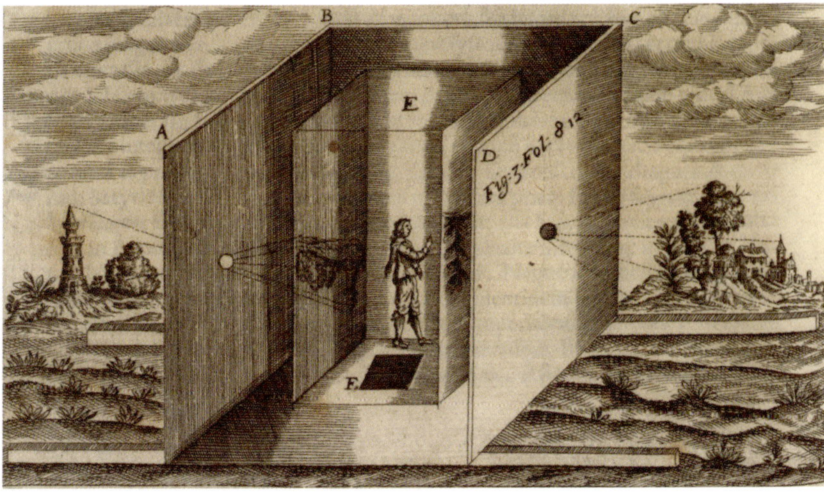

Athanasius Kircher, **Camera obscura**, in *Ars magna lucis et umbrae*, Rome 1646, plate 28

It is, of course, possible that Vermeer was familiar with the camera obscura, and that he may have been interested in the images it could produce. Dutch 17th-century society, which by comparison with much of the rest of Europe, was characterized by its tolerance, was notably open towards new discoveries in the sciences that posed a challenge to well-established notions.

The principle of the camera obscura had been familiar since Antiquity, although until the 17th century the term was used only in connection with its literal meaning: a dark room (p. 109). Through a very small hole in one of the walls of such a room bright daylight enters, thereby projecting on to the opposite, white-painted wall, albeit upside down, an image of what can be seen outside. As was observed by the German mathematician, astronomer and physicist Johannes Kepler (1571–1630), a portable camera obscura, in the form of a tent, might be used to advantage by those engaged in map-making and land-surveying.[130] It was Kepler who first recognized that the human eye functioned in exactly the same way as a camera obscura. This insight brought about a paradigm shift in the science of optics, for it had previously been thought – as had been the assumption since Antiquity – that the eye emitted active "seeing rays", and not, as now became apparent, that it, in fact, received rays of light. There are very few references to painters having used a camera obscura to make their pictures. The Nuremberg artist Hans Hauer (1586–1660) is known to have painted a panorama of this city with the aid of a portable camera

obscura equipped with a lens that could be turned.[131] By the 18th century, as demonstrated by the practices of the Venetian *vedutisti*, the camera obscura had become a small portable instrument, and the images it produced were projected on to a specially prepared surface, such as ground glass or a sheet of paper soaked in oil, and thereby rendered translucent.

Two Dutch sources from the 17th century make mention of the use of a camera obscura in connection with painting. Constantijn Huygens had encountered the camera obscura when in London in 1622. In his diary he describes a demonstration of a such an apparatus taking place before 1630 at the house of his father, in which the painters Jacques II de Gheyn (*c.* 1565–1629) and his son Jacques III (*c.* 1596–*c.* 1641), along with Johannes van der Beeck, called Torrentius (1589–1644), took part.[132] Huygens, by his own account, was suspicious of Torrentius for posing *faux-naif* questions regarding the demonstration, for this painter was certainly already familiar with the workings of a camera obscura "which nowadays everyone knows". We are familiar with only one surviving work by Torrentius: a still life entitled *Allegory of Temperance* (p. 105), which captivates with its extraordinary illusionism. The second 17th-century Dutch reference to artists making use of a camera obscura comes from the pen of Samuel van Hoogstraten (1627–1678), who in his treatise on painting recommends that young painters observe the images produced by a camera obscura to attain a knowledge of nature and to study the projection on to a plane of the contours and the colours of three-dimensional objects.[133] At no point, however, does he state that painters were making use of a camera obscura as a direct aid to drawing, by copying a projected image so as to achieve an exact reproduction of correct perspectival foreshortening without having to construct this themselves. Investigation has, indeed, shown that it would have been impossible, using a camera obscura with lenses of

Gerard ter Borch, **A Cavalier Offering a Lady a Glass of Wine**, *c.* 1660
Oil on board, 41.3 x 32.1 cm / 16 ¼ x 12 ⅝ in.
London, The Royal Collection, Her Majesty Queen Elizabeth II

the sort available in the 17th century, to transfer, in the supposed fashion, an interior such as those that Vermeer depicts on the scale of his painted images.[134]

The presence, moreover, in a total of 13 of Vermeer's surviving paintings of pinholes, in each case marking the composition's central vanishing point, attests to the fact that the artist did not transfer these compositions from an image projected by a camera obscura, nor even from a separate drawing made earlier, but that he constructed them directly on the canvas with the simplest of means.[135] On to a needle, which would be stuck into the canvas at the position intended as the central vanishing point, the artist would attach a thread that had been stained with chalk; this thread would then be drawn taut across the already grounded canvas so that, on its being snapped back on to this, it would leave a trace on the painting surface, which could then be reinforced with the brush. This would serve as the central vanishing line. It was by this means that the compositional layout of a picture was created directly on the painting surface. The lateral vanishing points would be fixed on the horizon line – which was itself established by reference to points lying beyond the canvas to left and right – and the degree of foreshortening required by the implied depth of depicted space thus established. In Vermeer's earlier paintings the distance between the central and lateral vanishing points was such as to produce a large viewing angle. In the case, by contrast, of a work produced in the late 1650s, *Cavalier and Young Woman* (p. 91, Cat. 6), the lateral vanishing points are to be found close to the central vanishing point, and the resulting viewing angle is thereby reduced to 53 degrees. The foreshortening is accordingly very abrupt, as is readily apparent in the seemingly exaggerated size of the figure of the cavalier positioned in the foreground and viewed from the back.[136] In such pictures, as also, for example, in *The Glass of Wine* (pp. 166/167, Cat. 7), the pattern of tiles on the floor exhibits an unnatural distortion in both the left and the right foreground. It was only with further practice that Vermeer was able to resolve such unsatisfactory passages, by means of a less elevated horizon line and more distant lateral vanishing points, an arrangement that would automatically produce a narrower viewing angle. In his paintings produced in the mid-1660s, such as *The Concert* (p. 183, Cat. 19), such distortions in the pattern of the tiles is no longer to be found.

Champions of the camera obscura theory like to emphasize that the perspectival arrangement in Vermeer's paintings is both so complex and so precise that it is improbable that he achieved it using a traditional method of construction. In response to this argument it has to be observed that, for a painter sufficiently familiar with the rules and methods of perspective construction, the precise composition of a picture presented no insuperable difficulties. For all the interiors he depicted, Vermeer chose a simple compositional arrangement: there is always only one central vanishing point, the entire composition is built around a system of horizontal and vertical forms, the back wall of the depicted room always lies parallel to the picture plane, and the alignment of the side walls is always in keeping with the lines running towards the central vanishing point. It is Vermeer's illusionistic rendering of surfaces that convinces us absolutely that we are looking at the "real thing", be it the glinting of metal, reflections in glass, the soft sheen of certain textiles or the play of light and shade. It is precisely on account of the tranquillity that pervades Vermeer's spatially simple compositions that the viewer can concentrate fully on the objects depicted.

Images of Courtship and Seduction Involving Wine and Music

In all his genre scenes painted between 1656 and the early 1660s, Vermeer treats, in its various aspects, the theme of seduction in pictures involving wine and occasionally accompanied by music. This group of pictures comprises *A Maid Asleep* (p. 87, Cat. 4) and *Cavalier and Young Woman* (p. 91, Cat. 6), in addition to three works painted in rapid succession in the artist's early maturity: *The Glass of Wine* (pp. 166/167, Cat. 7), *The Girl with the Wineglass* (p. 161, Cat. 10) and the so-called *Young Woman Interrupted at Music* (pp. 168/169, Cat. 11). The three last-named pictures are, in addition, all alike in terms of compositional structure; in each of them the protagonists are to be found in a suitably arranged domestic interior; and in each case a cavalier stands directly next to a young woman who is seated.

As was the case in Vermeer's first two pictures, the mythological *Diana and Her Companions* (Cat. 1) and the biblical *Christ in the House of Mary and Martha* (Cat. 2), so, too, in *The Glass of Wine*, he depicts his protagonists as full-length figures. At the same time *The Glass of Wine* marks the start of a distinct new series of comparable pictures, of which, in formal terms, it is an outstanding example. With this group of pictures Vermeer may be seen to progress from the phase of his early work to that of his mature style. In addition to a heightened illusionism – owing to Vermeer's increasingly confident mastery of his painterly means, his choice of colours and his subtlety in the various ways that paint might be applied, all qualities that may be seen to increase with every picture – Vermeer here achieves a new freedom in his perspectival rendering of space. He no longer relies upon those devices he employed in his early works to develop the viewer's sense of pictorial space, such as a balustrade or a table occupying the foreground so as to obstruct the viewer's gaze, and thereby guide it only gradually into the implied depth of the composition. Vermeer now eschews the use of such simplistic foreground motifs in favour of achieving far greater overall compositional clarity. He now shows us a much larger segment of the domestic interior that is his setting, and the protagonists, objects and pieces of furniture appear to be positioned much further from the observer. They occupy the middle distance of a now deeper space, thereby becoming far better integrated into the rooms they inhabit. Our impression of these depicted spaces no longer derives primarily from the way the figures are placed within them, but is formed independently of this.

In devising the construction of *The Glass of Wine*, Vermeer followed precisely the rules of linear perspective, disregarding the resultant unnatural distortion – evident, above all, in the patterning of the floor – that results from an implied viewing position towards the right foreground. The treatment of the floor plays a decisive role in determining a sense of spatial recession: on account of the seemingly immaterial surface of the evenly painted pale back wall, the precise extent and depth of the depicted space is not immediately clear to the spectator, and it is only on account of the foreshortening in the floor pattern that we are able to "read" this. The dominance of the colours green and red, established in the clothing of the two protagonists, is repeated in the floor. And the distribution of light and shadow is just as carefully calculated as the colour scheme. The light entering the nearest window picks out the surface of the bench, the back of a chair, the sheets of music, the wine jug and the young woman herself.

The domestic interiors painted by Pieter de Hooch at about the same time, that is to say, from around 1658, and which are created entirely through the architecture of the depicted spaces, provide an informative comparison with Vermeer (p. 47).[137] While De Hooch evolved his approach to this compositional form gradually, over many years, within Vermeer's oeuvre the corresponding evolution appears to have occurred very rapidly. In his *Glass of Wine* this sudden advance has produced a work that far surpasses the achievements of De Hooch, not only in its consummate perspective construction and treatment of light, but also in its subtle psychological rendering of the depicted scene. The relationship between Vermeer and Pieter de Hooch, who had been enrolled in the Delft Painters' Guild in 1655, was by no means merely a matter of the older artist (De Hooch) exerting his influence on Vermeer, who was three years his junior; it was, rather, an instance of fruitful reciprocity.

In *The Glass of Wine* Vermeer affords us a glimpse into the life of the upper stratum of Dutch 17th-century society. An exquisite elegance is a feature not only of this domestic interior and its furnishings but also of the two protagonists. Integral to this is also their behaviour: while this evinces a certain uncomfortable tension, it remains within the bounds of dignified and refined restraint. In *Cavalier and Young Woman* (p. 91, Cat. 6) Vermeer had already depicted a lady drinking a glass of wine in the company of a gentleman. In that composition the two figures, both sitting at a table, were shown facing each other, conversing and smiling. Here, by contrast, the man stands beside the seated lady, wrapped in a cloak that is thrown back across his shoulder, which seems to betray a certain dismissiveness. While an empty chair stands ready to receive him, a cittern has been placed upon it. For the 17th-century observer this would have served as a symbol both of harmony and of a dissolute way of life, and general dissipation, in as far as music outside the Church had a dubious reputation in Calvinist Holland. While the cavalier waits for the lady to drain her glass so that he may at once offer to refill it, her own tense pose indicates a feeling of unease. The cavalier clearly plays the dominant role here: both his hat and the cloak draped back over his shoulder give the impression that he has only just arrived, and his firm grip on the handle of the wine jug becomes a gesture of dominance within the composition, precisely calculated by Vermeer, who positions the voluminous white shirt cuff in such a way that it frames the jug on all sides. So assertive a presence in the room forms a stark contrast to the lady, who, with her partly covered face, appears to retreat behind her own wine glass. On account, however, of the essential stillness of both figures, Vermeer avoids any suggestion of an intimate relationship between them. While the musical instrument and the musical scores are lying there ready to be used, they remain untouched. We seem to be witnessing a moment of embarrassment in which the tension will remain unbearable until a new turn of events comes to pass.

Couples shown drinking wine were a common subject in Dutch genre painting of this period. Pieter de Hooch also frequently depicted them, albeit without the psychological penetration that characterizes Vermeer's composition. De Hooch comes closest to Vermeer in his treatment of the domestic interior itself, but it is the work of Gerard ter Borch that offers parallels with Vermeer's subtle grasp of conveying the protagonists' states of mind. In *A Cavalier Offering a Lady a Glass of Wine* (p. 110), Gerard ter Borch creates a scene which comes very close to that of Vermeer's picture in terms of its mood. Vermeer, however, goes further in retaining the element of ambiguity: he devises pictures that take contemporary attitudes to morality as their subject, yet without pointing to any one conclusion, permitting a wide range of interpretations. The 17th-century Dutch public took pleasure in multilayered symbolism and the variety of interpretations that this afforded. It has been observed that, in the moralizing Calvinist poetry produced at this time in Holland, ambiguity was much in demand, as in the case of *Zinne- en Minnebeelden* (1618) of Jacob Cats (1577–1660), a collection of emblems, each of which offered three possible interpretations.[138] "We learn from experience", writes Cats in another text, "that many things are much improved if they cannot be clearly recognized, but are encountered by us somewhat cloaked and shaded".[139] Similar views were expressed by Dutch art theorists, such as Karel van Mander and, in particular, Samuel van Hoogstraten, Vermeer's contemporary, who in 1678 wrote that paintings should be "clothed with one or another instructive meaning".[140]

Study of a Young Woman (detail),
c. 1665–1667 (see ill. p. 219)

We may, accordingly, seek out symbolic significance in further details within Vermeer's picture: the landscape painting hanging on the back wall, for instance, or the coat of arms incorporated into the window pane. In the case of the exceptionally dark wooded landscape, in the style of Jacob van Ruisdael (*c.* 1628/29–1682), Vermeer was perhaps intending to compare the perils of the wilderness with the uncertainties of a romantic entanglement.[141] As for the brightly lit and artful coat of arms set into the pane of the open window (a motif we find again in Cat. 10), it is possible that this is intended to stand, by contrast, for history and civilization, for family honour and comparable traditional values, such as may establish the acceptable parameters for the expression of human emotions. The alliance coat of arms depicted here was identified some time ago by Neurdenburg.[142] It belonged to a married couple in Delft, Jannette Jacobsdr. Vogel and Moses Jansz. van Nederveen, who had wed in 1589 and were both long dead by the time Vermeer painted his picture. They had lived in a part of the city inhabited by the well-to-do, in the Oude Delft, the address of Vermeer's patron Pieter Claesz. van Ruijven, a coincidence that may in itself supply the possible explanation for the repeated use of the same coat of arms. The ribbon-like forms have been interpreted as reins, and the figure therefore as an allegory of Temperance, the Virtue of Moderation, by analogy with a widely familiar emblem of Temperance devised by Gabriel Rollenhagen (1583–1619?),[143] with the motto "Serva modum" ("Observe moderation").[144] This interpretation was, however, conclusively refuted by Weber.[145]

The Girl with the Wineglass (p. 161, Cat. 10), which is generally assumed to be slightly later in date than *The Glass of Wine* in Berlin, nonetheless has much in common with it: the pattern of the flooring is identical and the window, similarly half-open, although lit rather differently, incorporates the same coat of arms. In other respects, however, the two compositions are distinctly different: the interior depicted in *The Girl with the Wineglass* has only one window, the shorter stretch of visible left wall suggesting a closer back wall, an impression that is, however, countered by the evidence of the expanse of the floor. The two chief protagonists appear much closer to the viewer's implied position and the composition is vertical rather than horizontal. The table is here placed much closer to the back wall, although there remains just enough space to accommodate the second cavalier seated at its far side, who rests his head on his right hand and appears to doze, oblivious of his companions. Spatial ambiguity pervades the composition. The young cavalier, who gallantly offers his lady a glass of wine, appears to stand behind the foremost edge of the table, which is covered by a white cloth, whereas he should, in fact, be standing in front of this.

Girl with a Flute (detail), *c.* 1665–1670
(see ill. p. 223)

In both *The Glass of Wine* and *The Girl with the Wineglass* one can find compositional connections with pictures of the same period by Pieter de Hooch, such as the painting *Woman Drinking with Soldiers* (p. 119), dating around 1658. There the situation is made clearer through the presence of a fourth figure: a procuress, who urges the cavalier to pour wine for the lady. De Hooch's composition offers the viewer a further unmistakable hint: the picture of the biblical story of Christ with the Woman Taken in Adultery hanging on the back wall. Vermeer, by comparison with Pieter de Hooch, moves his figures further into the foreground, making them the centre of attention, and he eschews details that are too unambiguous in their significance. Vermeer's composition is also generally more elegant than that of De Hooch, even though the figures found in *The Girl with the Wineglass* are, by comparison with those in *The Glass of Wine*, less profound and not so subtle and multilayered. Thoré-Bürger, nonetheless, writing in 1868, called this picture "La coquette", declaring it Vermeer's most attractive work. *The Glass of Wine* cannot be identified as any of the pictures listed in the catalogue of the 1696 Amsterdam sale. It is, therefore, probable that it was not in the collection of Pieter van Ruijven; and its provenance has so far been traced no further back than the second quarter of the 18th century. It is, therefore, all the more astonishing that *The Girl with the Wineglass* could come from the collection of Pieter van Ruijven, even though none of the descriptions in the 1696 sale catalogue corresponds precisely to this picture and could just as well refer to other works by Vermeer.[146] At the same time, this was the first painting by Vermeer to enter a princely collection, for by 1710 it had been acquired by Anthony Ulrich, Duke of Brunswick-Wolfenbüttel (1633–1714) for his own picture gallery.

In *The Girl with the Wineglass* Vermeer also approaches the work of the "fine painting" associated with Leiden, while distancing himself from Gerard ter Borch. The poses of Vermeer's figures and their implied way of moving is suggestive of the influence of Frans van Mieris; one may compare Vermeer's picture, for example, with the depiction of the "gallant" couple in *A Meal of Oysters* (The Hague, Mauritshuis).

The splendid dress of red silk, which seems just a little too gaudy to be counted as truly elegant, is the first aspect of the composition to attract the viewer's eye, and it characterizes its wearer as a girl of easy virtue. She appears to succumb to the seductive wiles of her cavalier more easily than does the demure lady of the Berlin picture (Cat. 7). It is no coincidence that ladies associated with unseemly conduct were in the 17th century almost always shown dressed in either red or yellow. According to the *Iconologia* of Cesare Ripa (1555–1622) personifications of drunkenness should take the form of a smiling woman dressed in red. The foolish and yet embarrassed smile with which the young woman in *The Girl with the Wineglass* turns to the viewer was in earlier accounts interpreted as a sign of inebriation; but her morally abject conduct may have appeared in times of

stricter behavioural norms as excusable on that account. Here, too, however, Vermeer leaves his composition open to several interpretations.

While the melancholic pose of the cavalier seen in the background suggests indifference to what is taking place, it remains to be established whether this is the result of his being rejected or merely on account of indolence. As in the case of Vermeer's composition *A Maid Asleep* (p. 87, Cat. 4) a broad range of symbols, derived from the Christian doctrine of the Virtues and Vices, could be invoked in relation to accidie, the Sin of Sloth. The portrait of a man, hanging on the back wall, in the style of Frans Hals (p. 160) or of Michiel van Miereveld (1567–1641), an artist active in Delft, may point, in connection with the coat of arms in the window pane, to the significance of family tradition or to the elevated social standing of the assembled individuals. This would then constitute almost a counterweight to their own dissolute conduct. It is also possible that these particular props, together with the wine jug and the silver tray with expensive fruits from the south of Europe, were intended as symbols of luxury, and perhaps also as an implied criticism of this. As in his other genre scenes, Vermeer reflects the social mores of his own era and comments upon them; but it is never entirely clear as to whether this commentary is intended as critical, from the point of view of a moralist, or as ironic, and voiced by a derisive observer.

Young Woman Interrupted at Music (pp. 168/169, Cat. 11) is the third in the group of works painted between 1658 and 1661 (see also Cat. 7, 10) that are closely related in both composition and subject matter. It is, however, not only much smaller than the two other pictures; the scene depicted also shows a much smaller segment of the domestic interior that is its setting. Both in its overall spatial arrangement and in the positioning of the table and the chairs, the picture seems like a smaller and simultaneously more closely viewed variant of *The Glass of Wine* (Cat. 7). The viewer directly faces the young woman seated at a table, who is depicted as a half-length figure. Notwithstanding the horizontal format, the width of the depicted space appears to have been reduced so that the distance

Pieter de Hooch, **Woman Drinking with Soldiers**, *c.* 1658
Oil on canvas, 68.6 x 60 cm / 27 x 23 5/8 in. Paris, Musée du Louvre

between table and window seems to be smaller than in the Berlin composition.

As is the case in the Berlin picture, here, too, we encounter a scene in which gallant conversation consorts uneasily with an attempt at seduction. A cavalier wrapped in a cloak has passed a sheet of music to a young woman, which she holds with both hands. The lady is not dressed so as to draw attention to herself. Her clothing is of the sort that such a woman might wear at home: a deep red jacket and a so-called night shawl, which covers both head and shoulders. On the sheet of paper she holds one can just make out both musical notes and text; and it does not require much of the viewer's imagination to interpret this as possibly a love song composed by the cavalier and dedicated to the young woman. Desiring greater physical proximity to her, he has placed his left hand on the back of her chair. The title by which this picture has traditionally been known, *Young Woman Interrupted at Music*, throws only a very incomplete light on the scene depicted and its meaning. Any such interruption can only have been brief, while the real subject of the composition is the young man approaching the young woman under the pretext of handing her a sheet of paper, while she turns, with a questioning glance, to the viewer, as does her counterpart in *The Girl with the Wineglass.*

The pictorial invention to be found in this group of paintings may be considered in the larger context of a substantial group of Dutch genre scenes of this period in which a male figure is shown establishing contact with a woman in a more or less demanding fashion. *Young Woman Interrupted at Music* reveals very clearly Vermeer's ability to select and then rework motifs taken both from his own earlier work and from the work of other painters, and to devise new compositions with them.[147] One of these painters was Judith Leyster (1609–1660), whose *The Proposition* of 1631 (The Hague, Mauritshuis) shows a man attempting to distract from her work a woman seen sewing by candlelight. Gabriel Metsu employed a similar motif in his *Lacemaker* (p. 120). Vermeer's young woman, for

Copy after Gabriel Metsu, **The Lacemaker**, second half of 17th century
Oil on oak board, 35.4 x 29 cm / 13 ⅞ x 11 ⅜ in.
Vienna, Kunsthistorisches Museum, Gemäldegalerie

her part, appears quite aware of the cavalier's real intentions, and their potential meaning for her own situation, by contrast, for example, with the lady seen in *The Music Lesson* by Frans van Mieris (1657–1660),[148] or the girl featured in the 1655 composition of the same name (Copenhagen, Statens Museum for Kunst) by Gerbrand van den Eeckhout (1621–1674). In Vermeer's painting the presence on the back wall of a picture of Cupid – notwithstanding its present unclarity on account of the poor state of preservation of this part of the composition – leads us to the same conclusion regarding the young woman. Vermeer included the same picture in the background of his *Young Woman Standing at a Virginal* (p. 283, Cat. 33), where it is much more clearly visible; he initially intended to depict it in *A Young Woman Reading a Letter* (p. 95, Cat. 5), before eventually painting over it; while a small strip of its right edge appears in *A Maid Asleep* (p. 87, Cat. 4). The motif of Cupid in this case derives from the aforementioned motif of an Otto van Veen emblem (p. 282). In this original form the figure of Cupid, or Amor, holds aloft a card inscribed with the number "1" and tramples underfoot another card inscribed with the numbers "2–9".[149] The significance of this image is spelt out in the motto "Love is perfect only if felt for one." In the version depicted by Vermeer, as a "picture within a picture", however, the figure of Cupid holds aloft a card that is blank. It is possible that, interpreted in the context of the scene being played out in the foreground of *Young Woman Interrupted at Music*, the image of Cupid is intended to mean that love is here "in play", or rather that love is always "a game of chance".

Pictures of Dutch Life

In the years between roughly 1658 and 1661, when Vermeer was producing his formally and thematically interconnected paintings with scenes of courtship and seduction involving wine and music, he also painted pictures showing motifs from everyday life in the city of Delft. Three of these works have survived, and they will here be considered as a group. They are pictures that now count among Vermeer's most celebrated works, on which his fame as "the painter of Holland" rests. In these pictures Vermeer effectively created archetypal images of the Dutch landscape, the Dutch city and the Dutch people. As such, they have left their mark on the collective memory of European culture and they constitute the basis of our mental image of how a Dutch city and its inhabitants looked during the country's "Golden Age".

At the same time each of these three pictures may be seen as an exception within Vermeer's entire surviving oeuvre. As far as we know Vermeer painted only one genre scene in which he did not depict the life of the well-to-do, but that of a hard-working, uneducated person: *The Milkmaid* (p. 173, Cat. 8). Likewise, only one street scene painted by Vermeer has come down to us (although we know from the 1696 sale catalogue that there were once at least two such compositions): *The Little Street* (p. 175, Cat. 9). And we know of only one cityscape painted by Vermeer: *A View of Delft* (pp. 176/177, Cat. 12). All three of these pictures are described in the Amsterdam sale catalogue of 1696, and it is therefore highly probable that they were once in the collection of Pieter Claesz. van Ruijven. Two of the three, *A View of Delft* and *The Milkmaid*, were sold for the highest prices attained on that occasion, 200 florins and 175 florins, respectively. That is to say that only a few decades after their creation, these pictures were not only considered to be of central importance within Vermeer's oeuvre, but were also regarded as being of great significance within the wider context of Dutch painting.

As a depiction of a woman absorbed in a particular activity, and the sole occupant of the room in which we find her, *The Milkmaid* belongs to a large group of genre paintings by Vermeer that spans his entire career. Together, these pictures reveal the rich variety of his ideas regarding composition and his growing skill in their formal realization. The earliest picture of this group is *A Young Woman Reading a Letter* (p. 95, Cat. 5), in which the protagonist, shown in profile, appears astonishingly small, a mere slip of a girl in relation to the composition as a whole. By comparison, the young woman seen in *The Milkmaid* is possessed of quite a different degree of corporeal presence. While she, too, is alone in a room, and a room which in itself is much emptier than that depicted in *A Young Woman Reading a Letter*, she nonetheless fills and dominates this empty space through her statuesque appearance. Prompted by the still life so central to this composition, we may well come to feel that time itself has stood still, that what we here encounter is taking place in an eternal present. Vermeer gives the figure a monumental quality through the low horizon line of the picture. This clearly runs below the level of the young woman's shoulders, giving the viewer the impression that he or she must almost look up into her face. The three-dimensional plasticity of the figure is created by means of powerful chiaroscuro modelling. This is especially clear in the young woman's face, lit from the left, with its rounded forehead and rosy cheeks, and in her muscular lower arms, but also in her heavy clothing, made of thick, rough material.

Everything in *The Milkmaid* is subordinated to a scheme of chromatic reduction. In addition to the white and grey tones of the room itself, the composition is chromatically reduced to the intense blue of the apron, the lidded earthenware jug and the cloth draped over the table in the foreground, the blue-green of the tablecloth, a few touches of yellow or reddish ochre tones and the deep red of the skirt. All the objects surrounding the figure seem as if selected primarily on account of their own colour, from the pale yellow of the basket hanging on the wall and the gleaming brass bucket, to the reddish earthenware of the milk jug and the brown bowl. Moreover, Vermeer here achieves illusionism of a new quality. This delivers the immediate impression of an overwhelming sense of reality, of a sort no other painter was able to attain. The material existence of the large white wall surface is conveyed by the precise rendering of its many small blemishes: stains, holes, protruding nails and chipped surfaces. By this means the artist prevents the wall being perceived as a mere foil for the figure of the young woman. The brightness of the wall is likewise subtly differentiated: to the right the figure of the young woman stands out as a darkly silhouetted form against a pale background, while to the left the brightness of the yellow jacket and the white headscarf is set off against a passage of wall that is somewhat darker.

The high point of Vermeer's illusionism is achieved in the still life on the table, comprising the blue-green earthenware lidded jug with its raised surface decoration, the other jug with its earthy brown glaze, the bread in the basket and the pieces of bread on the table (p. 170). These objects are possessed of an elemental presence, and in the perfection of their rendering it is clear that Vermeer can be counted among the greatest still-life painters of 17th-century Holland, comparable in this aspect of his art to a contemporary, Willem Kalf (1619–1693), who specialized in this genre.

In describing the achievement of such illusionism through a particular method of painting, Wheelock writes, for example, with reference to the various layers of paint that Vermeer applied when working on the blue jug: "In the dark blue jug at the back of the still life [...] Vermeer used a light gray paint in the initial blocking-in stage. He then indicated the placement of the raised highlights on the body of the jug with small dots of a light gray paint. This decorative pattern was defined and accented with opaque black paint, followed by the application of white accents along the top and ridges of the jug. He subsequently gave the jug its bluish tonality by applying small dabs of blue paint selectively across its surface, primarily over the black layer. Finally, he added smaller white dabs of paint to emphasize the circular highlights of the raised decorative pattern on the body of the jug."[150]

There are no parallels in Dutch painting for this approach – with the possible exception of Rembrandt, who evolved a similarly subtle painting style, albeit one that employed entirely different means to achieve such illusionistic effects. Liedtke's bold conjecture that Vermeer had had no formal training under an established master, but had taught himself most of what he knew, finds at least here justification.

Vermeer's technique of using small dabs or dots of paint has repeatedly been associated by commentators with his supposed use of a camera obscura (see also pp. 109f.); yet this assumption is refuted in this particular painting, as in others, by the evidence of a small pinhole in the picture surface, which indicates the vanishing point. Traditional perspective construction has clearly also helped Vermeer in his treatment of the edge of the table; for this, as was discovered by Gerhard Gutruf, is not square but, in fact, octagonal.[151] On closer inspection, a further, almost totally concealed edge of the table next to the maid's apron can be made out as a narrow strip of green tablecloth between several pieces of bread.

The rendering of kitchen scenes, with maids and often extensive still lifes comprising foodstuffs and kitchen utensils, has a long tradition in Netherlandish painting, going back to the 16th century.[152] Statuesque individual figures of kitchen maids, predecessors of our *Milkmaid*, are initially to be found in the work of Pieter Aertsen and his follower Joachim Bueckelaer (*c.* 1533–1574; p. 172). In the work, for example, of Frans Snyders and his own followers the Flemish kitchen still life enjoyed a second period of great popularity in the early 17th century. While the paintings of such artists were notable, above all, for the wealth and diversity of the objects they displayed (p. 125), Vermeer's composition is of a rustic simplicity, in which respect it is an exception both among his own genre paintings and among Netherlandish kitchen scenes. There is an elemental presence about the unadorned rural appearance of the maid's jacket of crudely sewn leather and her heavy clothing made of rough cloth, and about her concentration in pouring the milk. Over and above its art-historical derivation from Netherlandish kitchen scenes of the 16th century onwards, commentators have repeatedly speculated on the significance of Vermeer's image. Wheelock observes that Vermeer's painting is, in fact, neither a genre scene nor a portrait, but comes closer to the character of an allegory.[153] Yet there is no known allegorical meaning associated with the pouring of milk. The significance of Vermeer's figure can, therefore, be only of a metaphorical nature or lie in her embodiment of human dignity, here encountered in a moment of calm, unobserved practical activity.

Scholars have also repeatedly engaged with the question as to how realistic a depiction this is. A similar kitchen would have existed in the Vermeer household. In the inventory of household items drawn up on 29 February 1676, two and a half months after the artist's death, four kitchens are mentioned.[154] There was an "inner kitchen", which was furnished as a living room; a small kitchen at the back of the house; a kitchen reserved for cooking (*koockeucken*), in which, however, there was a bed; and a "kitchen" used for washing (*waskeukentgen*). It has been posited that Vermeer, in *The Milkmaid*, intended to depict the neglected kitchen of an impoverished household. Used only to prepare a simple mixture of bread and milk casserole, the room has no source of heating except for the small foot-warmer visible on the floor behind the maid.[155]

As X-rays have revealed, Vermeer originally intended to place a clothes basket where the supposed foot-warmer now stands. Another late addition was the row of tiles, decorated with small figures of Cupid, that runs along the base of the wall. These new motifs are not only better matched in terms of their scale to the rush basket and brass bucket hanging on the left wall; they also shift the import of the image in a particular direction. The miniature stove filled with glowing coals is a *mignon des dames* ("favourite of the ladies"). During the coldest months of the year women, when seated, would place these under their voluminous skirts as a welcome source of warmth. In both illustrations and

Circle of Frans Snyders, **A Kitchen Maid**, *c.* 1630
Oil on canvas, 97 x 126 cm / 38 ¼ x 49 ⅝ in. Brussels, Musées Royaux des Beaux-Arts de Belgique

texts of the 17th century this source of warmth was often employed as a symbol of female lust, as in the case of a moralizing emblem from the *Sinnepoppen* (p. 126), published in Amsterdam in 1614 by Roemer Visscher (1547–1620). If Vermeer's picture is understood not merely as a rendering of what is visible, captured with painterly illusionism, but is also thought to reflect the reality of life as a whole, then we might well be justified in seeing his paintings, taken all together, as the detailed record of life in a bourgeois house in Delft. While in the *voorkamer* the lady of the house entertains a visiting cavalier (see Cat. 7), in the kitchen a *Milkmaid* is busy preparing a dish of white bread and milk or cream. The *mignon des dames* that stands ready in the kitchen is intended not for the maid – notwithstanding the old Netherlandish iconographic tradition of ascribing loose morals to serving girls – but for the lady of the house. The maid would first have had to light a fire and to tend it, and only when it had burnt down a little would she be able to collect the glowing coals, fill the foot-warmer with them and take it to her mistress.

In *The Little Street* (p. 175, Cat. 9) – a title derived from the affectionate Dutch term for a small street, *het Straatje* – Vermeer took on a subject that was, as far as we know, entirely new for him: the view of a street in a Dutch city. It has been conjectured that this choice of subject was, in fact, not that of the painter, but of his patron and most significant source of commissions, Pieter Claesz. van Ruijven. At the 1696 Amsterdam

sale mention is made of a second such picture, which would seem to have resembled the one with which we are familiar: "32. A view of a house standing in Delft, by the same [that is, Vermeer], 33. A view of some houses by ditto."[156] That is to say that Vermeer painted at least one further picture of this sort; and Pieter van Ruijven perhaps had a liking for such scenes of the city, for he was also the owner of *A View of Delft* (Cat. 12).

Vermeer depicts the façades of two 16th-century houses, which are linked by a shared wall that has two entrances leading to their respective back yards. Both houses are cropped by the corresponding picture edges to the left and right, leaving visible only some of the chief features of the façades, which run parallel to the picture plane. This arrangement emphasizes the ostensibly random character of the segment of the street we are here shown. This is clearly not the record of a certain house or even of a particular street in Delft. It is, indeed, probable that, for compositional reasons, Vermeer has not even depicted two houses that in reality stood next to each other, but has devised a composite view, drawing on studies of several buildings.

In the earlier literature on Vermeer there was much debate over whether he had here depicted an actual location in Delft and, if so, where this was. It was erroneously assumed that the painting showed the actual view obtained from the "Mechelen" tavern in Voldersgracht, which would have made it a record of houses that were to be demolished in 1661 in order to clear the ground for a new building for the Delft Guild of Saint Luke.[157] Pieter Saenredam (1597–1665), for example, painted the former Amsterdam City Hall (Amsterdam, Rijksmuseum) before this was demolished. In fact, however, no houses were demolished to make way for a new building for the Guild of Saint Luke. Its Assembly Hall was, rather, transferred to a building that had once been an Old Men's

Roemer Visscher, **Mignon des Dames (foot-warmer)**, 1614
in *Sinnepoppen*, Amsterdam 1614, p. 178

Home, and had had its interior reconstructed and a new façade added. Wheelock nonetheless believes it possible that Vermeer used the view from his studio, on the second floor of the "Mechelen" tavern, as a basis of the left half of the composition of *The Little Street*, supplementing this with the building seen to the right.[158] Kaldenbach conjectures that, in the house to the right, with its stepped gable, Vermeer recorded the appearance of a building to be found in another Delft street, the Nieuwe Langendijck, and hence near the house of Maria Thins.[159]

Comparable to Vermeer's painting are the pictures of back yards in Delft and of their inhabitants produced by Pieter de Hooch just before 1660 (p. 174), which similarly combine architectural elements derived from various sources. These scenes are, however, generally viewed from relatively close quarters, while Vermeer depicts his town houses from a greater distance. At the same time Vermeer far outshines his contemporaries in the extreme illusionism of his picture, be it in the rendering of diverse types of surface or the weathered structure of the variously coloured, closed or open shutters.

Of particular importance for the tranquillity that Vermeer sought to convey in his image is the simple arrangement of the façades, which are aligned parallel to the picture plane. This system of vertical and horizontal orthogonals familiar to us from Vermeer's domestic interiors. This is, above all, the case of the larger house, to the right, with its high ground floor and the two lower storeys rising up above this, of its window frames and sills, and in the details of the filigree latticework of the window leading. Vermeer even incorporates within this system the perspectivally correct presentation of the protruding parts of the façade and the bench located to the left of the front door, so that he can correctly accommodate several horizontal elements, one above the other.[160] The viewer's sense of spatial recession in Vermeer's composition is assisted by the gables visible in the background and, above all, by the scene that can be viewed through the open door leading to the inner courtyard of the larger house. Here, we see a woman bending over a water barrel. A drainage gutter leads the eye back through this passage along the side of the house to where it meets the irregular grooves of the cobbled street. Carefully observed and precisely rendered details, such as the whitewashed walls of the lower part of the house walls, also play an important compositional role, in this case, serving both to ensure an optical separation of the immediate foreground comprising the cobbled surface of the street and the walls made of brick, and to create a foil for the figures. Other details, however, which are not so apparent at first glance, serve to alter reality as it would have been observed in the interests of pictorial construction. The open front door stands slightly to the left of the central axis of the façade of the house as here depicted; the sections of brick wall between the central entrance and the two large windows to either side of it have different widths (that to the right being clearly broader) in order to create enough space for the opened red shutter, at the lower right, which is crucial to the chromatic arrangement of the composition.

For the early 21st-century viewer the true subject of such a picture cannot but seem to be the encapsulation of the peaceful mood of a calm street in a city from the past, and the tranquil activity of its inhabitants: a woman working on some needlework while seated in the open front door of a house, a maid in the passage leading to the back yard busying herself with a task and two children playing at the side of the street under one of the benches that run along the house wall. Such a retrospective glimpse into a supposedly happy past, transfigured by the glow of nostalgia, creates so strong an emotional value that it still ensures a direct connection between the extant old houses in the tranquil corners of Dutch towns resembling those shown here and the present day.

A View of Delft (pp. 176/177, Cat. 12) occupies a special place in Vermeer's oeuvre in several respects. We have reason to believe that this work is not only the single surviving cityscape produced by Vermeer, but also in all probability the only such work that he ever painted. Most 17th-century Dutch painters tended to specialize in the production of one, or at the most two distinct pictorial categories, with which they then successfully made a name for themselves. Thus, there were established landscape painters, such as Jan van Goyen (1596–1656) or Jacob van Ruisdael, portrait painters such as Frans Hals and specialists in still life and painters of genre scenes, among whom Johannes Vermeer himself can be counted. Rembrandt was an exception to this rule in that he was primarily a history painter who also produced portraits and landscapes. *A View of Delft* is such an exception within Vermeer's oeuvre that it has been supposed that it would only have been painted at the special request of a patron.[161] As is revealed by a series of copies made in the 18th century, the composition was always highly regarded. In 1822 it was described, in the catalogue of an auction in Amsterdam, as "the most important and most celebrated picture by this master."[162] It is the highly individual approach of Vermeer that distinguishes his city panorama from similar pictures produced by contemporaries who were specialists in this sort of painting. Vermeer's picture has the character of a snapshot, and on this account retains to this day its timeless, and accordingly "modern", quality. It is no coincidence that it was precisely this picture that served as the starting point for Thoré-Bürger's rediscovery of Vermeer,[163] at a period when painters throughout Europe were beginning to produce landscapes *en plein air*, and no longer exclusively in their studios. Through the work of Marcel Proust, moreover, *A View of Delft* entered the realm of literature. In a letter to his friend Jean-Louis Vaudoyer he pronounced Vermeer's painting to be the most beautiful

The Milkmaid (detail), *c.* 1658–1661
(see ill. p. 173)

Hendrick Cornelisz. Vroom, **View of Delft from the North-west**, 1615–1634
Oil on canvas, 71 x 162 cm / 28 x 63 ¾ in. Delft, Museum Prinsenhof

picture in the world, and in the fifth volume of his monumental novel *À la recherche du temps perdu*, published posthumously in 1923, he has one of his chief characters, the writer Bergotte, die after encountering it in an exhibition and having the revelation: "That's how I ought to have written."[164]

Even though Vermeer's *A View of Delft* represents a completely new interpretation of the cityscape, a widespread pictorial category in the 17th century, and with its origins in printmaking, his painting nonetheless adheres to this tradition in its subject matter. We first encounter such city panoramas in the small images that often frame large wall maps, for instance, that featured in the background of Vermeer's *The Art of Painting* (p. 265, Cat. 26). Examples of painted city panoramas from the first half of the 17th century include *View of Zierikzee*, dated 1618, by Esaias van de Velde (1587–1630; Staatliche Museen zu Berlin, Gemäldegalerie), or the two well-known views painted in 1615 by Hendrick Cornelisz. Vroom (*c.* 1566–1640): *View of Delft from the South-west* (p. 133) and its pendant, *View of Delft from the North-west* (p. 130), produced as a private commission, then donated in the 1630s to the city and now in its Museum Prinsenhof.[165]

Such painters of city panoramas always strove to offer as complete an image as possible with regard to both topographical accuracy and distinctive character. Such panoramas usually featured a body of water in the foreground, and a cloudscape that often took up as much as half of the picture surface. The city's buildings would be viewed at some distance, and therefore appeared relatively small, while structures such as church spires or city gates would convey what was distinctive about the city in question. A few years before Vermeer painted his own *View of Delft*, Jan van Goyen, in his 1654 *View of*

Delft from the North (p. 19), had striven for topographical exactitude and, at the same time, a painterly effect.

Vermeer, however, took a decidedly different approach in his cityscape. On the one hand he appears to observe his subject very closely and to render it with compelling naturalism and illusionism. On the other he is highly subjective, conveying a fleeting impression of particular lighting conditions by highly sophisticated illusionistic means. Vermeer shows a very particular optical manifestation of the city – we see, for example, all the irregular surfaces of the brick walls and the roofs, but we also note the gently rippling surface of the water in the harbour, which is caused by the rapidly passing clouds and will, accordingly, remain as it is for only an instant. He also emphasizes the city's lively silhouette, which demarcates the buildings against the sky, and reiterates this in the dark reflection in the water. While the city's fortifications with their gates and the houses lying directly behind these are in the shadow of the dark clouds, the more distant part of the city is rendered in bright sunlight, not least the tower of the Nieuwe Kerk that soars above the other buildings. No painter of topographical views of the usual sort ever produced this particular painterly effect. The compelling impression of reality is achieved through a number of painterly devices that were characteristic of Vermeer: in addition to the powerful chiaroscuro contrasts, these include individual highlights consisting of thick dabs of lead white, thin shimmering strips of light, and the persuasive rendering of the surfaces of the roofs and the weathered walls through the distribution of dots of paint.

Vermeer shows Delft viewed from the south, with the harbour – known locally as the *Kolk* (pond) – assuming a roughly triangular shape. It linked the canals leading to Rotterdam, Schiedam and Delfshaven, and it was, accordingly, the city's bustling centre. The city wall directly beyond the harbour, as viewed in Vermeer's picture, featured a series of architecturally striking city gates. At the centre of the picture we find the massive Schiedam Gate, crowned by a small bell tower, and at the extreme right, at the far end of a covered bridge, the twin-turreted Rotterdam Gate. The sandy stretch of shore in the immediate foreground is observed from a slightly elevated position. The motif of a closely cropped diagonal stretch of shore, suggestive of compositional depth, was introduced into Netherlandish landscape painting by Pieter Bruegel the Elder (*c.* 1525/30–1569).[166] The sun is in the east, so it is clearly morning. As yet only a few people are to be seen, and the harbour is empty except for a barge in the foreground, two herring boats in front of the Rotterdam Gate and a few sailing boats in the background. The men standing by the boat would appear to be members of the well-to-do bourgeoisie, whereas the women are dressed in simple, regional costume.

Vermeer's picture is so compelling in its illusionism that it has erroneously been assumed that he did not only draw the view from his chosen spot, but also actually painted it in situ, or that he relied upon the assistance of a camera obscura to obtain a view that he then transferred to canvas.[167] In response to such claims it has been observed that Vermeer, in fact, out of formal considerations, improved and altered the view he would in reality have obtained.[168] He simplified his view of the city by emphasizing the horizontal structures. In connection with this, one may compare, for example, a drawing by Abraham Rademaker (*c.* 1676/77–1735), which reveals how Vermeer has broadened the proportions (p. 139). Here, too, we find clear evidence of his penchant for a composition based on orthogonal lines. The stepped gables of the houses in Ketelstraat, which runs directly behind the city wall, rise above this wall and create a seemingly continuous sequence. The windmill at the end of this street, which is a notable landmark in many city views, is not to be seen in *A View of Delft*. The horizontal banding of the Rotterdam Gate, produced by its alternating layers of stone and brick, is rendered by Vermeer only as several rows of dotted highlights. It has been observed that the bright sunlight that picks out the tower of the Nieuwe Kerk and makes it especially prominent within the scene could be intended to have a symbolic significance in that it was in this church that the tomb of William of Orange was to be found. This particular church tower has, however, above all a formal significance within Vermeer's composition, as a counterweight to the bell tower of the Schiedam Gate. Both towers effectively frame the bridge that spans the canal leading into the centre of the city. Of the tower of the Oude Kerk, which lies some distance away, we see only the very highest point.

Scenes of Music-making

In the early 1660s, with two pictures of people making music, Vermeer returned to the compositional pattern that he had developed a few years earlier in the painting *The Glass of Wine* (Cat. 7), and had since used with great success on several occasions (Cat. 10, 11). The new compositions were *The Music Lesson* (p. 181, Cat. 13) and *The Concert* (p. 183, Cat. 19). It is probable that both of these pictures were in the collection of Pieter Claesz. van Ruijven; they largely coincide both formally and thematically; and they are virtually identical in size. It has, therefore, been assumed that they may well have been intended as pendants. However, as they differ slightly in the treatment of perspective construction and the rendering of space, and as a year or more appears to have elapsed between the production of one picture and the other, they were probably not conceived as pendants (see also p. 137).

The Music Lesson depicts a large room lit by two windows. More light penetrates the more distant of these, which, as is usual in Dutch houses, is flush with the rear wall (cf. the external view in *The Little Street*, p. 175, Cat. 9), so that the far end of the room, in which the two depicted persons are to be found, is better lit and the rear wall is the brightest part of the entire picture. Here, placed at some distance from the viewer, we

Hendrick Cornelisz. Vroom, **View of Delft from the South-west**, 1615
Oil on canvas, 71 x 162 cm / 28 x 63¾ in. Delft, Museum Prinsenhof

find the protagonists of the scene: a young woman with her back turned towards us, who stands at an opened virginal, and next to her a cavalier, whose right hand rests on the edge of the instrument and his left hand is supported by a walking stick.

The composition is striking on account of its ostensible lack of balance: both the action and the powerful colour accents are concentrated on the right side, while the left seems rather empty. The horizon line is low, running roughly just above the height of the keyboard of the virginal, implying that the viewer is seated while observing the scene. The central vanishing point of the composition is found in the young woman's left sleeve. The lower part of the picture is taken up by the striking black-and-white patterned floor and the large Turkish carpet on the table, with its stiff, heavy folds extending some way into the room. In the lower left corner of the picture the floor pattern appears unnaturally distorted on account of the perspectival foreshortening.[169] The viewer's gaze is quickly drawn into the composition, focusing first on the floor, then on the carpet and the wall with its windows. On its right side, however, the view is obstructed by the chair, which, at the same time, serves to link the two figures. This exaggerated, or "accelerated", perspectival foreshortening was also favoured by other painters in these years.[170] *The Music Lesson* may be compared with works by Carel Fabritius, such as his *View of the Nieuwe Kerk in Delft* (p. 43), the church interiors of Hendrick van Vliet, the architectural pictures of Cornelis de Man (1621–1706) and Johannes Coesermans, the illusionistic *trompe l'œil* wall pictures by Samuel van Hoogstraten (the best known of these, at Dyrham Park, Gloucestershire, dates from 1662; see also p. 244), and *View of Delft from an Imaginary Loggia* (p. 101) by Daniel Vosmaer.

Vermeer articulates his composition by means of its dominant horizontal and vertical forms, such as the rectangular lid of the box-like virginal, whose shape is reiterated in the form of the mirror, the painting and the chair, all of which are arranged around the main figure. Of particular note is the illusionistic rendering of the reflection in the slightly inclined mirror (pp. 178/179). The vertical segments of the mirror's frame serve to balance the dominant horizontal form of the instrument. Vermeer has, in addition, provided a self-referential motif within the image shown in the mirror's reflection: here he includes a small part of his own easel, thereby repeating the effect first introduced by Jan van Eyck in the reflected image in his *Arnolfini Portrait* of 1434 (London, The National Gallery).

Wheelock refers to the symbolic function of Vermeer's treatment of light here.[171] The very clear shadow on the rear wall beneath the level of the window corresponds to no comparable shadows above. As this reveals the treatment of light is not truly realistic: rather, it links both light and shadow with the form of the virginal. Although only the rear part of the room is fully lit, the wine jug standing on the table much further forward is brightly illuminated. Wheelock sees here a metaphorical parallel between the music being played and the composition of the picture, through thnotion of repetition building towards a climax. In this context the reflection in the mirror may be seen as a reprise, showing us not only the reflected image of the musician from a new perspective, but also recalling the painter, who is present here through the visible detail of his easel.

The traditional title of the picture, *The Music Lesson*, ensures the erotic element that is always just below the surface in Vermeer's work is here not explicit. Between the two people seen making music there exists a relationship that apparently goes beyond the music-making itself. But the fact that music is being played at all is not apparent to the viewer through the presentation of the supposed players; only the virginal and the viola da gamba lying on the floor serve as indications of this. The Latin inscription on the inside lid of the virginal, in large Classical Antiqua lettering, MVSICA LETITIAE CO[ME?]S / MEDICINA DOLOR[VM?] ("Music is the accompanist of joy, a remedy for sorrow"), reflects in its complexity the mood of the picture. Through the prominent inscription, the picture takes up a position against the prevailing doctrine of the strictest Calvinism, which generally abjured music, with the sole exception of sung psalms. It was, nonetheless, common for music to be played with enthusiasm in liberally minded Dutch society, as is indeed demonstrated by the frequent depiction of musical instruments and music-making in Vermeer's own paintings. The very character of the depicted setting, moreover – this is an evidently wealthy household, with expensive furnishings such as the valuable musical instruments and the large Turkish carpet – calls forth an atmosphere of discreet restraint that hints at no sign of moral criticism on the part of the painter.

Music, however, is also a symbol of vanitas, that is, of transience: not only in the sense of strict Christian morality, which took a sceptical view of the sensual pleasure associated with the enjoyment of music, but also on account of the sheer speed with which music as an art form literally disappears. Barely has a note sounded than it is already gone. It is possibly in this connection that we are intended to perceive the mirror hanging on the wall above the virginal. For a mirror is also a symbol of vanitas, in that the images we see in it are deceptive. In this case, at least, it serves to produce a masterly illusion. A further interpretation of the mirror in Vermeer's composition, as an emblem of love, which reflects the beloved, has been proposed by reference to an emblem to be found in Pieter Cornelisz. Hooft's 1611 volume *Emblemata Amatoria*,[172] although this interpretation has been widely dismissed as being too literary, and thus too unlikely for Vermeer. Like the painter, the spectator sees the face of the young woman reflected in the mirror, without him- or herself being seen. The thematic connection between the painting shown hanging on the wall and the couple we observe making music offers several possible interpretations. The "picture within the picture" is reminiscent of the work of the Dutch *caravaggisti* who were followers of Dirck van Baburen, perhaps especially the Ghent painter Jan Janssens (1590–after 1650), and is a rendering of Cimon and Pero, the so-called Caritas Romana. In addition to the outright lascivious implications of this, such as are addressed by Gowing,[173] this subject could also be understood in a more restrained fashion, as an allusion to Christ's commandment to "love thy neighbour". In that respect, it could be seen as being linked with the inscription on the lid of the virginal.

While thematically close to *The Music Lesson*, Vermeer's picture *The Concert* (p. 183, Cat. 19) is usually assumed to be somewhat later, dating from around 1663 to 1666. Not only is the overall mood in both pictures comparable; the compositions are also alike in many respects: the arrangement of the music-making group in the background of the picture, around a large musical instrument; the table covered with a carpet; a viola da gamba placed on the floor in a position that reflects almost exactly its equivalent in the earlier painting; the arrangement of the pictures hanging on the back wall, which very roughly echo that of the picture and mirror in the other painting; and the rectangular form of the back of a chair that is pushed into position in front of the figures. The underlying perspective construction is, however, not the same in both paintings, as is most easily detectable if one examines the pattern and the foreshortening of the floor with its black-and-white flagstones. The lateral and central vanishing points are further apart in the case of *The Concert*, and the tempo of the foreshortening is therefore less marked; the figures are larger and they appear to be closer to the viewer. The result is a more closely cropped composition, and we see only the brightly lit rear wall, not the wall to the left, the presence of which is here merely implied through the light clearly entering through its

windows. On this account it is no longer generally assumed that the two paintings were commissioned as pendants.

In this composition the harmonious music-making of the three protagonists is set in contrast with the subjects depicted in both of the pictures hanging on the rear wall. To the right we see a *Procuress* by Dirck van Baburen, and to the left a dark wooded landscape in the style of Jacob van Ruisdael.[174] The scene in the tradition of the Dutch *caravaggisti* is very much like one to be found in the house of Maria Thins, and with which Vermeer would have been intimately acquainted.[175] The connection between *The Procuress* and the domestic enjoyment of music-making has yet to be established. The viola da gamba lying on the floor is rendered in emphatic perspectival foreshortening. Carel Fabritius incorporated such a pronounced example of foreshortening within his remarkable *View of the Nieuwe Kerk in Delft* (p. 43), a *tour de force* that was perhaps intended to be viewed in a peep show.

Female Occupations

Between roughly 1662 and 1666/67 Johannes Vermeer produced a group of pictures that show women engaged in domestic tasks. These pictures are formally interrelated and similarly composed: in each case we find only one woman, usually presented as a three-quarter-length figure, standing next to a table, in a closely cropped interior. All these pictures are more simply arranged in terms of their spatial structure than are those compositions showing a larger interior incorporating two or more full-length figures. The group begins with *The Glass of Wine* (Cat. 7) and continues with *The Music Lesson* (Cat. 13) and *The Concert* (Cat. 19). The simpler works recall, rather, a compositional scheme found already in some of Vermeer's early works: for the first time in *A Young Woman Reading a Letter* (Cat. 5) and then again in *The Milkmaid* (Cat. 8). While the more spacious pictures evince compositional similarities, above all, with works by Pieter de Hooch and other painters active in Delft, the pictorial structure of the group here under discussion resembles that to be found in works by Gerard ter Borch and the exponents of the Leiden tradition of "fine painting", such as Frans van Mieris and Gabriel Metsu. It is, therefore, not at all surprising that *Young Woman with a Water Pitcher* (p. 187, Cat. 14) was until the late 19th century believed to be a work by Metsu. The small pictures painted by Frans van Mieris and Gabriel Metsu excel in their emphasis on the qualities of diverse material surfaces, as in the case of the masterly juxtaposition of glinting metal and velvety textiles with the aim of astonishing the spectator. Vermeer's painting is likewise marked by illusionistic

Mistress and Maid (detail), *c.* 1666/67
(see ill. p. 215)

effects, although these are not employed merely as an end in themselves, as is generally the case with the "fine painters" of Leiden.

The first five pictures of the group were painted in rapid succession between 1662 and 1664. The order in which they were painted is much disputed, and any proposed sequence is at this stage hypothetical. It is, however, generally assumed that *Young Woman with a Water Pitcher* and *Woman with a Lute* (p. 191, Cat. 15) were followed by *Woman in Blue Reading a Letter* (p. 195, Cat. 16), *Woman with a Pearl Necklace* (p. 211, Cat. 17) and *Woman with a Balance* (p. 205, Cat. 18). It is also possible that *Woman in Blue Reading a Letter* was painted before *Young Woman with a Water Pitcher*.

Gowing termed these compositions "pearl pictures", for in all of them pearls are to be found, either worn by the women depicted or shown lying on a table.[176] It is possible that the term "pearl pictures" was also intended in the broader sense of "pearl-like", with reference to Vermeer's style of painting in these works, which is apparent not only in the smooth lustre of his rendering of the pearls, but also in an inimitably subtle quality in the painterly rendering of diverse surface types.

Common to all these pictures is a careful and considered composition, a balanced distribution of planes giving rise to a sense of depth. The treatment of light is central in every case: repeatedly a large, dark motif is placed in the foreground and set in contrast to a pale wall in the background, this contrast in itself evincing a certain sense of depth. The clear and simple layout of these compositions complements their reduction in thematic terms to what is most essential. The realization of this goal is achieved with a confident mastery of, and great economy in, the painterly means now at the artist's disposal. In their perfection, these pictures may be counted as the classical high point of all that Vermeer achieved.

A comparison between *A Young Woman Reading a Letter*, painted *c.* 1657 (p. 95, Cat. 5), and *Woman in Blue Reading a Letter*, produced approximately six years later (p. 195, Cat. 16), demonstrates very clearly the artist's evolution over this period. The pose of both young women is almost identical: each looks down on to the letter that she is holding with both hands. The illusionistic detail characterizing the earlier painting has in the later work ceded to more classically austere solutions. The treatment of the domestic interior in the later painting could hardly be simpler: a pale wall with a map takes up almost the entire width, and much of the height, of the picture plane, constituting a large part of the background and simultaneously serving as a foil for the female figure and the irregular, dark silhouette of the table with a jewel casket in the left foreground. The figure of the woman in profile and the few objects surrounding her are set against the wall. At the same time the uncovered wall surfaces and the outline of the objects create a planar pattern, in which light and dark alternate. Large planes are juxtaposed with areas characterized by minute detail, such as the woman's hands with the letter held close to

Abraham Rademaker
View of Delft with the Schiedam Gate and the Rotterdam Gate, early 18th century
Pen and ink on paper, 66 x 108 cm / 25 x 42 ½ in. Delft, Museum Prinsenhof

her breast, which are on the same horizontal level as the black rod at the base of the map, or those objects strewn across the table: a pearl necklace and an unfolded sheet of paper, perhaps the second page of the letter that has just been opened. The young woman stands exactly at the centre of the composition, turned towards an invisible source of light, which also brightly illuminates the wall, while her own face and hair, softly modelled by the light, are fully integrated into the chromatic character of the map. Vermeer here altogether eschews local colour, and limits himself chiefly to tones of blue and ochre. A sense of compositional depth derives, for example, from the chairs occupying distinct segments of space. Our implicitly low viewing position accounts for the monumental character of the scene.

It is apparent that Vermeer's work has gained not only in the simplicity and clarity of the composition, but also in his method of painting, which is characterized here by an extraordinary economy of means. This is all the more surprising in that Vermeer was already fully in command of all the requisite technical skills, including his use of colour, from the time of his earliest surviving works, to the extent that a further enhancement of these capacities would have seemed barely possible. And yet, in his paintings of the 1660s, he goes much further. The almost pointillist application of paint in small dabs and dots,

as can clearly be seen in *The Milkmaid* (p. 173, Cat. 8), now gives way to a preference for the use of colour planes, which in turn allows a more fluid and rapid approach to painting. The highlights and the reflections in the silver bowl and the jug in *Young Woman with a Water Pitcher* (p. 187, Cat. 14) are created from small patches, which when observed at close quarters or through a magnifying glass evince an almost abstract pattern. At the same time, viewed from a distance, they convey a perfect illusion of reality, as shown in the faintly shimmering colour reflections of the carpet on the underside of the bowl. Vermeer's singular ability to depict not objects, but rather the optical impression they make in the eye of the observer, is here brought to perfection. The rendering of the impression of light in the treatment of the depicted objects often causes these to appear slightly blurred, as if surrounded by a halo. Commentators have sought to account for this newly appearing phenomenon in Vermeer's pictures by referring to his experience of painting the two earlier cityscapes (Cat. 9, 12). Liedtke cites the treatment of light in the work of other Delft painters, for example, Emanuel de Witte, who in some of his architectural pictures employs columns lit from behind.[177]

Vermeer, however, goes further than this in his abstract rendering of forms. A work such as *Young Woman with a Water Pitcher* is not only constructed from numerous small planes of colour; the figure itself seems to have been formed from large shapes or geometrical bodies. Contributing to this impression are, above all, the form and colouring of the young woman's clothing, the cone-like skirt, the close-fitting bodice and the large, white collar placed over the shoulders for the purpose of carrying out her toilette (pp. 184/185). The dress made of yellow and blue cloth recurs, with a variety of striped patterns, in several of Vermeer's compositions. A comparison with *A Young Woman Reading a Letter* (p. 95, Cat. 5), painted a few years earlier, reveals considerable differences in the rendering of the textiles' qualities. In the case of the voluminous silken sleeve in the

Caesar van Everdingen, **Young Woman Playing a Cittern**, *c.* 1645–1650
Oil on canvas, 78 x 63.6 cm / 30 ¾ x 25 in. Rouen, Musée des Beaux-Arts

earlier picture Vermeer emphasizes every visually fascinating detail, such as the gathering at the shoulder and at the cuff (pp. 92/93). By contrast, the right sleeve in the later picture resembles a hollow tube-like entity, just as the young woman's lower arm itself is rendered as a smooth, cylindrical form.

On the whole, this picture is brighter than are Vermeer's earlier genre scenes, the colouring being based, above all, on the primary colours yellow, blue and red, in addition to white. As usual, Vermeer had decided from the very beginning on the composition's distribution of colour, as underpainting in variously brown and grey tones reveals.[178] Notwithstanding the care with which Vermeer constructed his composition, he still made alterations during the course of his work. In *Woman in Blue Reading a Letter* (Cat. 16), for example, the chair on the left behind the table had originally been placed in the foreground, and the map on the wall was extended further to the left, so that it entirely surrounded the young woman's head. These improvements chiefly relate to the overall painterly impact of the image through their effect on the distribution of light and dark colour planes, of light and shade. Fundamental alterations of this sort, undertaken during the process of painting, show that Vermeer allowed the composition to come gradually into being while he worked, and that he may be presumed not to have planned out everything in preliminary drawings or sketches.

With his painting *Woman with a Pearl Necklace* (p. 211, Cat. 17), it was only during the course of his work on the canvas that Vermeer resorted to the use of a large, unbroken plane of empty wall as his background, a decision that fully altered both the character and the thematic content of the picture. As revealed by X-rays, an earlier state of the composition incorporated a map on the wall. In this form the picture in Berlin would have been compositionally closer to *Woman in Blue Reading a Letter, Young Woman with a Water Pitcher* and *Woman with a Lute*. The dark area in the foreground that Vermeer eventually retained is also a feature in common with the three cited pictures. Vermeer increased the effect of chiaroscuro contrasts, deriving initially from the illumination particular to this composition, through the sombre colouring of the objects we encounter. Darkness continues to permeate the foreground, manifest in the brown table cloth, the young woman's skirt and the chair placed very close to the observer and cropped by both the right and the lower picture edges. Vermeer here dares to attempt a radically new type of composition in which the picture is effectively divided into a lower half so dark that it is almost black and an emphatically bright upper half. It is clear that Vermeer was aware of the difficulty of making the bright figure stand out against the large, empty bright plane of the wall; but he masters this with bravura by subtly rendering the contours of the figure against this background. The brightness decreases from left to right, so that the lit face of the young woman stands out against a somewhat darker part of the wall, while her back, which lies in shadow, forms a dark silhouette against it. More emphatic colour is provided by the yellow curtain, which, in turn, draws out the colour of the young woman's yellow silk jacket. Vermeer dresses the elegant young women in several of his pictures in this same jacket with ermine trim (Cat. 15, 17, 20, 24, 32), and a similar jacket was included in the inventory of possessions in the Vermeer household.

Characteristic of Vermeer's mature works is not only their profound tranquillity, but also their reduction of all narrative elements, thereby minimizing the action. All the details that might encourage various interpretations are now omitted. In the case of *Woman in Blue Reading a Letter* we see a young woman who focuses on this one activity. Any further-reaching interpretation would be mere speculation, unsupported by evidence found in the picture. We cannot know whether or not it is a love letter; if we assume this, it is only by analogy with other such compositions. We do not know if the letter arrived unexpectedly, and it is on account of this that the young woman has interrupted her toilette. This could be inferred from the pearl necklace lying on the table. Equally unanswered remains the question as to whether the map and the empty chairs may be seen to allude to the absence of a person dear to the young woman.

The assumption that the young woman shown here is pregnant has been refuted. It appears that one of the first to suggest this was Vincent van Gogh (1853–1890), in a letter to his brother, in reference to the jutting form of the young woman's clothing. On this basis the picture was subsequently seen to contain a moralizing message. The depiction of a love letter being received and read was interpreted as an allusion to a secret or illicit relationship, behaviour that stood in open contradiction to the integrity of a spouse and, in particular, of one who was soon to become a mother. Quite apart from the fact that in none of the early descriptions of the picture dating from before 1800 is the woman described as pregnant,[179] she is wearing a type of garment fashionable in the 17th century, a so-called *beddejak*, worn at home.[180] Equally inappropriate has proved the assumption – arising from the attempt, characteristic of the earlier literature on Vermeer, to resort to the artist's biography for an interpretation of the paintings – that the letter reader could be Vermeer's own wife. The map on the wall shows Holland and West Friesland. It is a real map, made in 1620 by Balthasar Florisz. van Berckenrode, and published a few years later by Willem Jansz. Blaeu.[181] The same map is found in the background of Vermeer's earlier painting *Cavalier and Young Woman* (p. 91, Cat. 6), although there shown on a smaller scale and with different colouring, an example of how Vermeer readily adapted both the size and the colouring of the objects he depicted to suit the composition in hand.

Mistress and Maid (detail), *c.* 1666/67
(see ill. p. 215)

While in *Woman in Blue Reading a Letter* any action is restricted to the thoughts and emotions of the reader, in the case of *Young Woman with a Water Pitcher* (Cat. 14) Vermeer captures his protagonist in mid-movement. The young woman grasps the frame of the window with her right hand, as if in the process of opening it, and simultaneously the water jug with her left. The water jug and the bowl indicate the subject of this picture: the young woman is shown at her toilette, for the purposes of which she wears a broad collar and a bonnet of white linen, in order to cover her hair. On the table next to her we find an open jewellery casket with a pearl necklace on a blue ribbon. The possibility of a symbolic significance for any of these details does not readily arise.

Alongside the toilette, and the receiving, reading and writing of letters, music is the third great aspect of female occupation treated by Vermeer in the 1660s. The three aspects do, however, belong thematically together, and may be linked into a continuous narrative. The toilette has been completed, necklace and earrings put on, and love letters received, read and answered, and now *Young Woman with a Lute* (p. 191, Cat. 15), awaiting the visit of her beloved, is seen tuning her instrument. The compositional convention employed here was probably in keeping with the wishes and expectations of Vermeer's contemporaries and of those who commissioned and bought his pictures. With particular reference to this painting, commentators have emphasized that it apparently did not come from the collection of Pieter Claesz. van Ruijven, and from this probability have drawn far-reaching conclusions regarding the choice of subject and its treatment. According to these the picture was not intended to meet the refined taste of Vermeer's most important patron, but was aimed at the rather less demanding standards of the art market, and it thus owed rather more to the general taste of the time (which would have favoured a work such as

Jan Sanders van Hemessen, **Woman Weighing Gold**, *c.* 1530–1535
Oil on board, 44 x 31 cm / 17 3/8 x 12 1/4 in.
Berlin, Staatliche Museen zu Berlin, Gemäldegalerie

Caesar van Everdingen's *Young Woman Playing a Cittern,* p. 140) than did those pictures that were painted for Pieter Claesz. van Ruijven. It was Mirimonde who first put forward the notion that the young woman is, in fact, awaiting the arrival of her beloved, with whom she hopes to play music and to flirt.[182] Slatkes offered an alternative, additional interpretation, taking his starting point in an emblem of Jacob Cats on the theme of a second instrument resonating with the sound of the first.[183] Although this is a theme frequently treated in Dutch painting, its meaning is ambivalent, being employed in diverse contexts from the music-making of a courtesan, in the style of Gerard van Honthorst after 1620, to the tuning of an instrument as the embodiment of Temperantia, the Virtue of Moderation, a motif that might also suit the present case. A comparably ambiguous instance is to be found in *Young Woman Playing Music* (p. 190) by Bartholomäus van der Helst (*c.* 1613–1670).

The usual attribute of Temperantia is, however, a vessel of water, out of which moderation is understood to flow. It would therefore appear equally, if not more, appropriate to interpret *Young Woman with a Water Pitcher* as just such an allegory. If we consider the other pictures in this group with regard to possible clues to the intended symbolism of Virtues and Vices, one does not have far to look. *Woman with a Pearl Necklace* (p. 211, Cat. 17) might well be a symbol of Superbia, or Pride. She holds a pearl necklace at her throat and checks her appearance in the mirror. She has already adorned herself with pearl earrings and a hair band decorated with a red bow, and on the table a powder box, a comb and a shawl are laid out ready for her.

The subject of a woman at her toilette was a great favourite among Dutch genre painters. In addition to such pictures by Gerard ter Borch and Gabriel Metsu, there is, above all, a picture more or less contemporary with this one of Vermeer, and compositionally close to it, by Frans van Mieris the Elder (p. 210). Yet the dark setting, the pose of the young woman and her black maidservant induces an entirely different mood. More closely comparable are pictures by Gerard ter Borch, such as his *Young Woman at Her Toilette with a Maidservant* (p. 148).

The true subject of *Woman with a Pearl Necklace* is, however, the act of looking. The young woman's glance into the mirror penetrates the entire breadth of the picture, a distance emphasized by Vermeer through the large, empty plane of the wall. The mirror is a traditional vanitas motif, as are the pearls for adornment. For a contemporary Calvinist, or indeed a Catholic, observer, the image of the young woman adorned with pearls and looking at her reflection in the mirror would doubtless be regarded as a symbol of the Deadly Sin of Superbia, or Pride and Conceit. In the Flemish Baroque iconographic tradition of Mary and Martha, the former's repentance and reform is treated through the motif of her taking off her jewellery, as seen in the painting of Peter Paul Rubens

(1577–1640; p. 147). Even in the time of the early Christian Church Fathers, attempts were made to identify Mary of Bethany, the sister of Martha (Luke, 10: 38–42), with the Sinner who anointed Christ's feet and whose sins were forgiven (Luke, 7: 36–50). Since the time, moreover, of Pope Gregory I (*c.* 540–604), she was identified with Mary Magdalene, who is frequently mentioned in the Gospels. In the Jesuit devotional literature of Antwerp Saint Mary Magdalene's conversion is described in terms of her abjuring all worldly conceit and her rejection of jewellery and other forms of adornment.[184] One should also bear in mind Paul's First Epistle to Timothy (2: 9–10), in which he dispenses advice to women: "In like manner also that women adorn themselves in modest apparel, with shamefacedness and sobriety, not with broided hair, or gold, or pearls, or costly array: But (which becometh women professing goodness) with good works."[185]

The clearest instance of an allegorical character of a work by Vermeer is to be found in *Woman with a Balance* (p. 205, Cat. 18). Thoré-Bürger recognized the thematic link between the young woman holding a balance and the painting shown hanging on the wall behind her, which depicts the Last Judgement. The everyday activity of the woman is thereby placed in connection with this most universal of themes. The similarity between Vermeer's picture and a number of related images has led to the supposition that Vermeer here intended to depict a late 16th-century painting by the Flemish painter Jacob de Backer (*c.* 1555–*c.* 1585). Backer frequently painted the Last Judgement with the Judge posed, as here, with both arms raised. Astonishingly, however, it has so far proved impossible to identify a precise model for the Last Judgement seen in the background of Vermeer's picture.

For a long time uncertainty existed regarding exactly what the woman shown here is doing. The popular name by which the picture was long known – "Woman Weighing Pearls" – derives from Thoré-Bürger. In earlier inventories the picture was called a "Woman Weighing Gold", after the early Netherlandish pictorial tradition (pp. 144, 204). Thoré-Bürger took the metallic highlights in the weighing pan to be pearls, or he imaginatively linked the action of weighing with the pearl necklace on the table and in the open casket. Repeated investigations have confirmed, however, that the weighing pans are empty. It is, therefore, nowadays usually assumed that the woman is not engaged in weighing anything; she is, rather, testing the empty scales to assess their precision.

The numerous interpretations the picture has invited tend to recognize in this scene either a positive or a negative significance. The most reasonable seems a connection with the theme of Justice. Scales have always been the most important attribute of the personification of Justitia, the Virtue of Justice; and an allegory of the administration of justice for all humanity is what we find in the Last Judgement, which since the early medieval period has been depicted in this way, with Christ at the centre as the Judge. After the

souls have been weighed by the Archangel, it is Christ who will decide between the Elect and the Damned. Vermeer's picture can, then, be understood as an appeal, under the eye of the Last Judgement, to let justice prevail and to observe moderation in all things. The notion that the remaining details – the casket with the pearl necklace, the coins on the table and the mirror on the wall – characterize the composition as a vanitas picture is rather less convincing.[186]

At the 1696 sale of the collection of Jacob Abrahamsz. Dissius, this picture was not only featured as no. 1 in the catalogue, but was also sold for a considerably higher price than comparable paintings.[187] It is possible that this was on account of its subject matter, but perhaps also because of the special container in which the picture was said to be kept. This may have been a case of the sort often used for small pictures since the 16th century, and such as Gerard Dou regularly made for his own works, to protect the sensitive surface of his valuable "fine paintings". Alternatively, it could have been a peep show: this would have allowed one to view the picture in an enclosed case with special lighting and a consequent increase in its illusionistic effect.

It is assumed that it was slightly later than the series of "pearl pictures" that Vermeer painted two further depictions of young women that are dedicated to the theme of letter writing: *A Lady Writing* (p. 199, Cat. 20) and *Mistress and Maid* (p. 215, Cat. 24). In *A Lady Writing* Vermeer further evolves the compositional scheme of the single-figure pictures of women produced in the early 1660s. With its darkened interior setting and the dominance of blue and yellow in the still life, it is closest to *Woman with a Balance*, and it might, therefore, have been painted directly after that work. Commentators have in particular compared *A Lady Writing* with Gerard ter Borch's 1655 painting *The Letter Writer* (p. 153), which has much in common with Vermeer's picture. Gerard ter Borch's picture does, however, differ from Vermeer's painting very significantly in one respect:

Peter Paul Rubens, **The Penitent Magdalene and Her Sister Martha**, *c.* 1620
Oil on canvas, 205 x 157 cm / 80 ¾ x 61 ⅛ in.
Vienna, Kunsthistorisches Museum, Gemäldegalerie

the woman depicted does not look out at the spectator, but is entirely focused on her writing. Indeed, the subject gazing at the viewer is a motif that Vermeer adapted from a Netherlandish tradition of portraits of scholars, and that was widely disseminated in the form of prints. Liedtke draws the comparison with Rembrandt's 1631 *Portrait of a Scholar with a Book* (p. 198). Even earlier the motif was to be found in Flemish painting, for example, in Rubens's *Portrait of Caspar Gervartius* (*c.* 1628; Antwerp, Koninklijk Museum voor Schone Kunsten), or in Anthony van Dyck's *Portrait of Lucas van Uffel* (1623; New York, The Metropolitan Museum of Art). That is to say Vermeer employs a pictorial motif that was originally used to record the public, or at least the professional, activity of a man in order to offer an insight into the hidden, domestic sphere of a woman and, in so doing, bestows on this motif a new significance. On account of the young woman's gaze being directed at the spectator, the picture effectively oscillates between genre painting and portrait; and it has frequently been conjectured that Vermeer may have depicted his own wife here. Rather contradicting this point, on the other hand, is the woman's informal clothing. The yellow silk jacket with fur trim would only have been worn in the home. The young woman certainly evinces very individualized traits such as one might well associate with a portrait; yet her clothing excludes the possibility that this work is a portrait in the strict sense of the term.

In the painting depicted in the background one can make out a still life with musical instruments, among which is a double base. In the view of Boström the model for this still life was a picture by Cornelis van der Meulen (1642–1692).[188] In the inventory of Vermeer's estate a vanitas still life is listed – albeit without mention of the name of its artist – in which a double bass and a skull ("een bas met een dootshooft") were to be found, and it is possible that this may have served as his model.[189]

Gerard ter Borch, **Young Woman at Her Toilette with a Maidservant**, *c.* 1650/51
Oil on board, 47.6 x 34.6 cm / 18 ¾ x 13⅝ in.
New York, The Metropolitan Museum of Art, Gift of J. Pierpont Morgan, 1917

Vermeer's painting *Mistress and Maid* (Cat. 24) is distinct in various respects from his other pictures of women. It is substantially bigger, the figures are around three-quarters life-size, considerably larger than those found in the genre scenes Vermeer painted after 1656. In addition, two figures are shown. Here, then, Vermeer effectively returns to the type of his rather more narrative genre scenes of the period around 1660, such as *The Glass of Wine* (Cat. 7) or *The Music Lesson* (Cat. 13). It is possible that Vermeer's pictorial invention was spurred by Gerard ter Borch, even though the work by this artist that is most readily cited for comparison – his *Rejected Letter* of between 1655 and 1658 (Munich, Neue Pinakothek) – evinces few compositional similarities.

It is striking that the dark background of Vermeer's picture reveals no hint that it occupies three-dimensional space, except for the suggestion of the folds of a curtain. As we also cannot ascertain the source of the illumination, the scene gives the impression of being presented on a stage. This has led some to assume that Vermeer may have intended to depict here the biblical subject of Bathsheba receiving King David's invitation to join him (II Samuel 11: 1–5). Less in keeping with this possibility, however, are the shiny writing set and the box on the table – both indicative of an elevated contemporary social milieu – and, above all, the fact that the lady is not only receiving a letter but is herself writing one.

Studies of Heads

We do not know if, in addition to painting genre scenes with one or more figures, Vermeer also painted portraits. In any case no references to such works by him are made in inventories or early sale catalogues. Vermeer did, however, paint a number of so-called head studies, which in both structure and cropping resemble portraits, even though they differ decidedly from these in one point: they are not intended as records of the appearance of a particular individual; they capture, rather, a particular kind of face, suggestive of a certain type of character – hence the traditional term "character head". Like portraits, such studies of heads take their starting point from the facial features of the particular individual who serves as their model. But these features are then elevated to have a universal validity, and the original model remains anonymous.

Such studies of heads had been painted in the Netherlands since the 16th century. It was in the work of Frans Floris (1516–1570), an influential Antwerp representative of Classicism, that they first emerged as an autonomous painted art form. As drawings, however, studies of heads had a much longer tradition, although these would generally be made not as autonomous works of art, but as part of the preparation for the individual figures or heads destined for altarpieces or history paintings. Albrecht Dürer is one of the first painters whose drawn studies of heads, and also hands, have been preserved; in imitation of the practice of Venetian artists, he drew these on coloured paper, incorporating white highlighting. The studies made in 1505/06 for the *Feast of the Rosary* (Prague, Národní Galerie) and for the *Twelve-Year-Old Jesus at the Temple* (Madrid, Museo Thyssen-Bornemisza), in addition to the studies dated 1508, for the lost segment of the Heller Altarpiece, are today regarded as masterpieces of drawing, and are among the best known of all Dürer's works. In 17th-century Flemish art we also find both drawn and painted studies of heads, for example, in the work of Peter Paul Rubens and Anthony van Dyck. While these, too, were part of preparatory work for large-scale painted compositions, in 17th-century Holland artists such as Rembrandt had already started to remove such works from a merely preparatory role, taking them as the starting point for a broader thematic context. Alongside "character heads" intended to portray outstanding personalities from history, literature and folkloric tradition where the lack of any secure records of actual appearance allowed the imagination much room for manoeuvre, we find studies of heads from the realms of Antiquity and the Near and Middle East. This variety is also reflected in the diverse designations used for studies of heads in the lists and inventories of Vermeer's period.[190]

The term *tronie* was the usual Dutch designation for the "study of a head". The word is derived from the Old French term *trogne*, signifying "character head". Such depictions went beyond everyday contemporary life, transporting us to the remote past, or to distant and exotic lands. The faces depicted did not have to seem contemporary, but could correspond to how a fictional, historical or exotic person may have been imagined. Despite their precise rendering of physiognomic detail, such pictures often did not observe the pictorial conventions of portraiture. In addition to valuing the characterful depiction of a specific type of physiognomy, art collectors also prized particular aesthetic qualities of the work itself, such as its painterly facture.

We know of only four surviving studies of heads – all of young women – painted by Vermeer. In the catalogue of the 1696 sale of the collection of Jacob Abrahamsz. Dissius, three "studies of heads" by Vermeer are listed (nos. 38–40).[191] Scholars have repeatedly endeavoured to identify these in relation to surviving pictures; but as it is likely that Vermeer painted more such works, which remain untraced, this has proved difficult. The four surviving examples were probably painted between 1665 and 1670. This dating is based entirely on the evidence of comparisons in terms of overall technique and the application of paint, in which one finds the closest parallels with the single-figure pictures of women from the mid-1660s. If it was within this period that Vermeer did indeed paint all his studies of heads, then one would be able to detect an evolution from spacious interiors such as found in the Berlin picture *The Glass of Wine* (Cat. 7), by way of a series of closely cropped single-figure pictures (Cat. 14–18), to the studies of heads. It would be tempting to see here a gradual increase in concentration, from the interiors with several figures to the pictures of closely observed individual physiognomy. But Vermeer was, in fact, to return in due course to both his earlier compositional format with a single figure as well as to interiors with several figures.

Two of Vermeer's studies of heads, both of medium size, present young women in front of a uniformly black background without any indication of a spatial setting. *Girl with a Pearl Earring* (p. 217, Cat. 21) is one of the best known and best loved of Vermeer's works. By contrast, the formally comparable *Study of a Young Woman* (p. 219, Cat. 22) is now much less well known and has a less immediate appeal to modern tastes. Two further studies of heads, *The Girl with the Red Hat* (p. 221, Cat. 23) and *Girl with a Flute* (p. 223, Cat. 25), are much smaller than the others. In addition, they are painted not on canvas, but on wooden panels, as was usual in both Flemish and Dutch painting of this period for small or sketch-like works.

The reasons for the great familiarity and popularity of *Girl with a Pearl Earring*, which are by no means only a contemporary phenomenon, probably lie in the particular and timeless attractiveness of the depicted individual. This is owed to several factors: her physiognomy (the enquiring glance directed at the viewer, the moist glint in the eyes, the half-open lips) and her pose (the turn of the slightly tilted head over the left shoulder). The young woman seen here incorporates an ideal of beauty that is valid to this day. But the powerful impact of the image is dependant not only on an aesthetic impression, but, above all, on the deep emotional radiance that derives from the suggestion of youthful vulnerability. This impression is strengthened through the application of paint, which eschews clear lines and achieves its ends, rather, by means of numerous highlights in the eyes, and the slightly opened mouth. At the same time, the depicted girl has always been perceived as somewhat exotic. As this is indicated by neither her physiognomy nor her clothing, it can only be on account of her headgear that this impression has arisen. This does, indeed, recall an oriental turban. As for the "pearl" from which the picture derives its traditional title: the model for this was, in all probability, a glass bead. The impression of immediacy produced by this picture is also due to the fact that its subject lacks any attributes that might tell us more about her, or that would invite an allegorical interpretation. In all of 17th-century Netherlandish painting there are only a few studies of heads – works by the Flemish painter Michiel Sweerts (1618–1664) – that come close to Vermeer's picture in their fluid handling of paint and in their capacity to convey emotion (p. 216).

It is possible that the *Study of a Young Woman* was painted at approximately the same time, between 1665 and 1667. To modern eyes at least, the model here appears much less attractive than the one seen in *Girl with a Pearl Earring*. It is possible that her appearance was intended to recall that of a female figure from Antiquity, as was the case, for example, with Jan Gerritsz. van Bronckhorst's *Study of a Woman's Head in Profile* (*c.* 1645–1650; Coral Gables, Florida, The Lowe Art Museum, University of Miami), in which both the profile presentation, reminiscent of cameos, and the clothing appear to allude to Antiquity.[192] Vermeer's young woman wears a white or pale grey dress that is arranged in voluminous folds. It is suggestive of a heavy, gleaming silk material. The yellow cloth hanging from the hair somewhat recalls the headgear seen in *Girl with a Pearl Earring*. The *Study of a Young Woman* does, however, appeal through its subtle colouring, centred on the contrast between the warmth of the brown hair and eyes and the flesh tones, and the cool bluish white of the cloth. What we see here, then, is a young Dutch girl of the 17th century who wears a dress that does not accord with contemporary fashion but strikes us as somewhat alien and is perhaps intended to allude to Antiquity. In contrast to this timeless quality in the drapery, however, several aspects of the young woman's appearance – most notably her shaved eyebrows and her high hairline – correspond precisely with the Dutch fashions of the 1660s.

In the motif of the lower left arm supported on the lower picture edge, Vermeer takes up a convention in portraiture that had already been employed by Titian (*c.* 1488–1576) and was later used by Rembrandt, such as in his *Self-portrait* of 1640 (London, The National Gallery). However, what is there used to suggest self-confidence, through establishing a certain distance from the viewer, is here only hinted at; and, on account of the almost entirely concealed hand, of which only a part of the back protrudes from the sleeve, it seems merely perfunctory.

Vermeer's *Girl with a Pearl Earring* and *Study of a Young Woman* are not only the same size; they are also similar in many other respects. In both cases the head and shoulders of a young woman are viewed against a dark background; each young woman turns to look directly at the viewer across her left shoulder. In both pictures the light enters from the left, illuminating the right side of the young woman's face so that the cheek turned towards the viewer remains in shadow. Although the clothing and physiognomy differ, in both cases a pearl earring, picked out through reflected light, occupies a central position. The two pictures were probably not painted as pendants, although it is possible that both were part of a larger series of *tronies* depicting various women in a variety of clothing, albeit removed from any particular context.

Two further, smaller studies of heads by Vermeer, *The Girl with the Red Hat* (p. 221, Cat. 23) and *Girl with a Flute* (p. 223, Cat. 25), have much in common with each other, but are very different from the other pair. The difference in size is particularly striking, the painted surfaces of the two smaller pictures taking up around a quarter of that of the other two. Each of the smaller pictures looks like a compact detail and as if it might well have been extracted from a larger composition. In the case of *The Girl with the*

Red Hat, the upper edge of the chair back, the young woman herself and the tapestry that comprises the background, with its characteristically subdued green and ochre tones, appear as if compressed, and we almost have the impression of looking through a telescope. The chair with the now familiar carved lion's head finials features here, albeit this time turned towards the viewer. It is, therefore, clearly not this chair on which the young woman is herself sitting.

Especially striking in these two smaller pictures, and, above all, in the case of *Girl with a Flute*, is the precise observation of the impact of light and colour, and their rendering so as to vividly convey diverse illuminated surfaces. In the case of *The Girl with the Red Hat* those parts of the flesh that are in shadow, such as the chin and the right cheek, receive a greenish and bluish shimmer by way of the light reflected up from the gleaming blue silk of the drapery. The glossy dark wood surfaces of the carved lion's head finials are conveyed through an irregular pattern of bright spots. Vermeer has consciously selected every detail and has arranged it in order to achieve the most interesting effects of colour and illumination. He sets the dazzling red hat in contrast with the softly gleaming pale and dark blue patterned silk material of the loose jacket, which resembles the woven material known as *caffa*, which Vermeer's father, Reynier Jansz. Vos, once produced. Vermeer places a second luminous accent with the white scarf, rendered with just a few loosely grouped brushstrokes, which supplies the brightest point in the entire picture; and he gives individual highlights to the tip of the nose and to the lips. It is possible that the hat was a head covering that never existed, but was, rather, one of Vermeer's inventions in his striving for a sense of the exotic. This rather improbable headgear and the "reversed" lion's head finials of the chair back seemed, to Blankert, to call into question Vermeer's authorship of this picture. Liedtke remarks in this connection that the

Gerard ter Borch, **The Letter Writer**, *c.* 1655
Oil on board, 39 x 29.5 cm / 15 3/8 x 11 5/8 in.
The Hague, Koninklijk Kabinet van Schilderijen Mauritshuis

figure seen in Rembrandt's *Saskia van Uylenburgh in 16th-Century Costume* (1633/34–1642; p. 220) wears a similar hat.[193] Hats of this sort were derived from the 16th-century German *Tellerbarett* (platter hat), as found in pictures by Lucas Cranach the Elder. Rembrandt would have known of this motif through its reproduction in prints.[194] The tapestry seen in the background of Vermeer's picture was in all probability from the southern Netherlands. Behind the girl's head one can make out two large figures and an architectural form, and the ornamental stripe to the right was probably part of the border.[195]

It is surely the case that all the uncertainty expressed as to whether Vermeer was indeed responsible for these two small paintings must concede their sheer painterly quality: the masterly treatment of paint that Vermeer – and only Vermeer in this unmistakable manner – applies, now in large planes, now in dabs and dots and individual strokes, to evoke the perfect illusion of a brightly lit young woman suddenly turning round to look out of the picture. The loose and sketchy application of paint primarily corresponds to the pictorial type of a study of a head, which, as a pictorial category largely unhampered by rules and expectations, afforded much greater freedom than did the prescribed forms of history painting or genre painting. Vermeer depicts those objects that are implicitly closer to the observer in a less sharply focused manner. In doing so he links the several distinct degrees of implied spatial recession within the picture. According to a long tradition of scholarship, this approach to painting is to be explained – although not in the view of the present author – by Vermeer's use of a camera obscura.[196] Be that as it may, the result is in any case a masterpiece in the observation and painterly rendering of diverse surfaces, be it from the point of view of colour or from that of illumination.

In many respects Vermeer's *Girl with a Flute* is so similar to his *Girl with the Red Hat* that one might well have assumed the two pictures to have been painted as pendants.

Frans van Mieris the Elder, **Study of a Young Woman in a Feathered Hat**, 1658
Oil on board, 11.1 x 8.4 cm / 4 3/8 x 3 1/4 in. Frankfurt am Main, Städel Museum

They are almost identical in size, very similar in composition and in the articulation of depicted space against the background of an expansively patterned Flemish tapestry, and feature the familiar Spanish chairs in the foreground. It also appears that Vermeer may have used the same model on both occasions. By the usual standards of a study of a head, both young women are strikingly dressed and wear extravagant headgear. In contrast to what we find in almost every other known composition by Vermeer, the light in both pictures enters from the right. Brightly lit areas are set in contrast to those that lie in shadow, so that these two pictures may also justifiably be regarded as "studies of illumination", in which Vermeer was able to demonstrate the sculptural quality of a profile brought out by the light, or the effect of reflected colour, as in the greenish light thrown up on to the shaded parts of the face.

Notwithstanding these similarities with *The Girl with the Red Hat, Girl with a Flute* is, indeed, the most problematic of Vermeer's works, above all, on account of its state of preservation and what we must assume to be the complex process of its creation. While some passages seem to be executed entirely in Vermeer's manner, others are rendered in a rather ungainly fashion, and can surely not be autograph: for example, the girl's right hand in the lower left corner of the picture, and the forefinger of her left hand, which holds the flute. The work on the face, moreover, is incomplete. The most plausible explanation for these aspects of the picture is that it was not only left unfinished by Vermeer, but that it also, at a very early date, suffered serious damage and was then finished by an unknown artist. At a later date, moreover, the picture has suffered further damage through overenthusiastic cleaning and uninformed restoration. The blue glaze that once covered the back of the chair, for example, has disappeared, so that we now see little more in this passage than a red-brown underpaint. The complex structure of the composition is, nonetheless, a strong indication that it derives from Vermeer.

Both initiated and subsequently completed by Vermeer was the painting of the triangular hat and several parts of the blue jacket. It is also apparent that Vermeer himself undertook a number of alterations during his work on the picture. The two strips of fur attached to the front of the jacket, for example, were a late addition, and one that gives this item of costume a greater similarity to the jacket featuring in *Woman with a Balance* (Cat. 18). The hat with its fantastical cloth covering, which we may perhaps imagine to be made of velvet with stripes of grey and yellow, appears to be an invention of Vermeer's, and was doubtless intended to give the picture a particular flavour. At first sight it rather recalls a Chinese head covering, though in that case it would, strictly speaking, have been made of bamboo. Wheelock observes that such hats are often worn by shepherdesses in Dutch paintings and prints.[197]

Woman with a Balance (detail), *c.* 1663/64
(see ill. p. 205)

Pages 158/159
The Girl with the Wineglass, *c.* 1659/60
(see ill. p. 161)

Frans Hals, **Tieleman Roosterman**, 1634
Oil on canvas, 117 x 87 cm / 46 ⅛ x 34 ¼ in.
Cleveland, The Cleveland Museum of Art

The Girl with the Wineglass, *c.* 1659/60
Oil on canvas, 77.5 x 66.7 cm / 30 ½ x 26 ¼ in.
Brunswick, Herzog Anton Ulrich-Museum

Pages 163/164
The Glass of Wine (detail), *c.* 1658–1660
(see ill. pp. 166/167)

The Glass of Wine, *c.* 1658–1660
Oil on canvas, 65 x 77 cm / 25 ½ x 30 ⅜ in.
Berlin, Staatliche Museen zu Berlin,
Gemäldegalerie

Young Woman Interrupted at Music,
c. 1659–1661
Oil on canvas, 39.3 x 44.4 cm / 15 ½ x 17 ½ in.
New York, The Frick Collection

The Milkmaid (detail), *c.* 1658–1661
(see ill. p. 173)

Joachim Bueckelaer, **The Cook**, 1574
Oil on board, 112 x 81 cm / 44 1/8 x 31 7/8 in.
Vienna, Kunsthistorisches Museum, Gemäldegalerie

The Milkmaid , *c.* 1658–1661
Oil on canvas, 45.5 x 41 cm / 17 7/8 x 16 in.
Amsterdam, Rijksmuseum

Pieter de Hooch, **A Backyard in Delft**, *c.* 1658–1660
Oil on canvas, 69.5 x 60 cm / 27 3/8 x 23 5/8 in.
Washington, D.C., National Gallery of Art, Andrew Mellon Collection, 1937

The Little Street ("Het Straatje"), *c.* 1658–1661
Oil on canvas, 53.5 x 43.5 cm / 21 1/8 x 17 1/8 in.
Amsterdam, Rijksmuseum

A View of Delft, *c.* 1660–1663
Oil on canvas,
96.5 x 115.7 cm / 38 x 45 ½ in.
The Hague, Koninklijk Kabinet
van Schilderijen Mauritshuis

Pages 178/179
The Music Lesson (detail), *c.* 1662–1664
(see ill. p. 181)

E·T I T I Æ · C O
A· D O L O R

Johannes Ruckers, **Virginal**, 1640
Amsterdam, Rijksmuseum

The Music Lesson, *c.* 1662–1664
Oil on canvas, 74 x 64.5 cm / 29 ⅛ x 29 ⅜ in.
London, The Royal Collection, Her Majesty Queen Elizabeth II

Dirck van Baburen, **The Procuress**, 1622
Oil on canvas, 101 x 107 cm / 39 ¾ x 42 ⅛ in.
Boston, Massachusetts, Museum of Fine Arts, M. Theresa B. Hopkins Fund

The Concert, *c.* 1663–1666
Oil on canvas, 72.5 x 64.7 cm / 28 ½ x 25 ½ in.
Boston, Massachusetts, Isabella Stewart Gardner Museum, inv. P21w27
(present whereabouts unknown)

Pages 184/185
Young Woman with a Water Pitcher (detail), *c.* 1662–1664
(see ill. p. 187)

Young Woman with a Water Pitcher, *c.* 1662–1664
Oil on canvas, 45.7 x 40.6 cm / 18 x 16 in.
New York, The Metropolitan Museum of Art,
Gift of Henry G. Marquand, 1889

Pages 188/189
Woman with a Lute (detail), *c.* 1662–1664
(see ill. p. 191)

Bartholomäus van der Helst
Young Woman Playing Music, 1662
Oil on canvas, 138.4 x 111.1 cm / 54 ½ x 43 ¾ in.
New York, The Metropolitan Museum of Art

Woman with a Lute, *c.* 1662–1664
Oil on canvas, 51.4 x 45.7 cm / 20 ¼ x 18 in.
New York, The Metropolitan Museum of Art,
Bequest of Collis P. Huntington, 1900

Pages 192/193
Woman in Blue Reading a Letter (detail), *c.* 1663/64
(see ill. p. 195)

Woman in Blue Reading a Letter, *c.* 1663/64
Oil on canvas, 46.6 x 39.1 cm / 18 3/8 x 15 3/8 in.
Amsterdam, Rijksmuseum

Pages 196/197
A Lady Writing (detail), *c.* 1665–1667
(see ill. p. 199)

Rembrandt Harmensz. van Rijn
Portrait of a Scholar with a Book, 1631
Oil on canvas, 104 x 92 cm / 41 x 36 ¼ in.
Saint Petersburg, Hermitage

A Lady Writing, *c.* 1665–1667
Oil on canvas, 45 x 39.9 cm / 17 ¾ x 15 ¾ in.
Washington, D.C., National Gallery of Art,
Gift of Harry Waldron Havemeyer and Horace Havemeyer, Jr.,
in memory of their father, Horace Havemeyer

Pages 200–202
Woman with a Balance (detail), *c.* 1663/64
(see ill. p. 205)

Pieter de Hooch, **Woman Weighing Gold**, *c.* 1664
Oil on canvas, 61 x 53 cm / 24 x 20 ⅞ in.
Berlin, Staatliche Museen zu Berlin, Gemäldegalerie

Woman with a Balance, *c.* 1663/64
Oil on canvas, 40.3 x 35.6 cm / 15 ⅞ x 14 in.
Washington, D.C., National Gallery of Art, Widener Collection

Pages 206–209
Woman with a Pearl Necklace (details),
c. 1663/64 (see ill. p. 211)

Frans van Mieris the Elder
Young Lady before a Mirror, *c.* 1662
Oil on board, 30 x 23 cm / 11 ¾ x 9 ½ in.
Berlin, Staatliche Museen zu Berlin, Gemäldegalerie

Woman with a Pearl Necklace, *c.* 1663/64
Oil on canvas, 51.2 x 45.1 cm / 20⅛ x 17 ¾ in.
Berlin, Staatliche Museen zu Berlin, Gemäldegalerie

Mistress and Maid, *c.* 1666/67
Oil on canvas, 90.2 x 78.7 cm / 35 ½ x 31 in.
New York, The Frick Collection

Michiel Sweerts, **A Young Maidservant**, *c.* 1660/61
Oil on canvas, 61 x 53.5 cm / 24 x 21 ⅛ in.
The Kremer Collection

Girl with a Pearl Earring, *c.* 1665–1667
Oil on canvas, 44.5 x 39 cm / 17 ½ x 15 ⅜ in.
The Hague, Koninklijk Kabinet van Schilderijen Mauritshuis

Study of a Young Woman, *c.* 1665–1667
Oil on canvas, 44.5 x 40 cm / 17 ½ x 15 ¾ in.
New York, The Metropolitan Museum of Art,
Gift of Mr and Mrs Charles Wrightsman, in memory of Theodore Rousseau, Jr.

Rembrandt Harmensz. van Rijn
Saskia van Uylenburgh in 16th-Century Costume, 1633/34–1642
Oil on board, 99.5 x 78.8 cm / 39 ⅛ x 31 in.
Kassel, Museumslandschaft Hessen Kassel, Gemäldegalerie Alte Meister

The Girl with the Red Hat, *c.* 1665–1667
Oil on board, 22.8 x 18 cm / 9 x 7 ⅛ in.
Washington, D.C., National Gallery of Art, Andrew W. Mellon Collection

Johannes Vermeer and an unidentified follower
Girl with a Flute, *c.* 1665–1670
Oil on board, 20 x 17.8 cm / 7 ⅞ x 7 in.
Washington, D.C., National Gallery of Art, Widener Collection

IV.

The Last Ten Years

1666–1675

"Vermeer of Delft, master of intimacy, innermost stillness of unspoken exchanges, reveals to us, be it in his portraits or in his interiors, a silence that is palpable. He does so without resorting to chiaroscuro employing only the most delicate touches, and mitigatin the impression of solitude through the atmosphere of a setting in which we may already feel at home."

EMIL M. CIORAN, 1937

Since the time of his marriage to Catharina Bolnes, in April 1653, it appears that Vermeer had had no contact with his mother, Digna Baltens, or with his older sister, Gertruy. He was not present in 1654 at the christening of his sister's daughter, on which occasion the child's maternal grandmother served also as her godparent.[198] Nor is there any mention of Johannes Vermeer in connection with Digna Baltens's vain attempt, in early January 1669, to auction the "Mechelen" tavern.[199] A few weeks later she rented out the tavern, which was said to be "glass ende vloerdicht" ("in good condition"), for three years, at an annual rent of 190 florins.[200] It is only a year or so later, on 10 or 11 February 1670, when Vermeer's mother died, at the age of about 75, and Vermeer's sister and her husband drew up a joint will, that Vermeer re-emerges in the surviving documentation, firstly as a beneficiary of this will, and then indirectly, through the person of his patron, Pieter Claesz. van Ruijven, who here served as a witness.[201] Montias draws attention to the highly unusual circumstances in which the will was read: at around nine o'clock on a winter evening, 11 February 1670 – Digna Baltens had only just passed away – the notary Geraerd van Assendelft and the two witnesses were called to the house of Anthony van der Wiel and Gertruy Vermeer.[202] This childless married couple (a daughter, baptized in 1654, had died while still very young) were, by mutual agreement, joint heirs of the deceased; but they stipulated that the relatives of the first of the couple to die were to receive from the surviving partner a certain portion of the inheritance. Gertruy was in all probability already gravely ill at this point; she died only a few months later, in early May 1670. In 1671, when the estates of Digna Baltens and of her daughter were settled, Vermeer, accordingly, received 148 florins from his brother-in-law, Anthony van der Wiel. At the same time he became the sole owner of the "Mechelen" tavern,[203] which since 1669 had been rented out to Leendert van Ackerdyck. In early 1673, after the three-year rental contract had expired, Vermeer rented the tavern out again, on this occasion for six years and to his namesake, the apothecary Johannes van der Meer. The annual rent was now 180 florins; but after the deduction of the interest payable on the two, now over 30-year-old loans taken out to fund the original purchase, only 55 florins of the annual proceeds went to Vermeer.

In 1672 Johannes Vermeer is cited in surviving documentation in his professional capacity as an appraiser of paintings.[204] The well-known Amsterdam art dealer Gerrit Uylenburgh (*c.* 1625–1679) had offered 12 paintings and a number of sculptural works to the Great Elector Frederick William of Brandenburg (1620–1688) for the sum of 30,000 guilders. When the Elector's artistic adviser and representative, the painter Hendrick

Pages 225 and 226
A Lady Writing a Letter with Her Maid (details), *c.* 1670/71
(see ill. p. 291)

de Fromantiou (1633–1693), voiced his own doubts as to the authenticity and supposed monetary value of the paintings that were on offer, these were returned to Amsterdam. Uylenburgh, however, refused to take them back. Fromentiou, therefore, commissioned several appraisers to examine the works in question and reach their own conclusions. According to their assessments, the items said to be the work of Hans Holbein the Younger (1497/98–1543) and Michelangelo (1475–1564), or of the Venetian painters Giorgione (1478–1510), Jacopo Palma (*c.* 1480–1528), Titian (*c.* 1488/90–1576) and Tintoretto (1518–1594), were almost entirely copies and imitations. When the pictures were exhibited at the Painters' Guild in The Hague, Johannes Vermeer and his colleague Hans Jordaens (1555–1630) were invited to appraise them. They likewise doubted their authenticity, declaring before a notary in The Hague that the works in question were "not outstanding Italian paintings, but, on the contrary, great pieces of rubbish and bad paintings, not worth by far the tenth part of the aforementioned proposed prices". Vermeer's formal statement in this battle of the appraisers has repeatedly been cited as proof that he had always carried on where his late father had left off as an art dealer alongside his career as a painter and that, in contrast to other Dutch painters, he was an outstanding connoisseur of Italian art, an expertise that he is thought to have acquired, above all, during his supposed training in Utrecht in the circle of the Dutch *caravaggisti* (see also p. 39). It would be possible to draw this conclusion only if one considered Vermeer's activity as an appraiser in isolation. In the larger context of this affair of the disputed paintings, however, such assumptions are untenable. Not only was Vermeer just one among many Dutch painters to serve now and then as an appraiser; it also appears that it was chiefly on account of his position as head of the Delft Painters' Guild, rather than on account of his supposed experience as an art dealer, that he was asked, on this occasion, to state his opinion.

The Art of Painting

At around the time that Arnold Bon wrote his eulogy on Carel Fabritius, in which he also praised Vermeer (see also p. 36), the latter painter produced an extraordinary picture that may justifiably be regarded as his masterpiece: *The Art of Painting* (p. 265, Cat. 26). This is in many respects an exception within Vermeer's oeuvre. It depicts a domestic interior, but is considerably larger than any of Vermeer's other paintings of such settings. It does not depict an episode from the everyday life of contemporary Dutch society, in the manner of the artist's genre scenes. It is, rather, an allegory, that is to say, a work belonging to the most highly esteemed artistic category: history painting.[205] Vermeer here allegorizes the art of painting, as we infer from the title that he himself appears to have chosen, *De Schilderkonst*, the title under which the work also appears in the inventory of his estate (see also p. 258). We do not know whether the picture remained in Vermeer's studio because he had failed to sell it or because he kept it on display there in order to show to interested visitors as an example of his work and a proof of his capacities as an artist – a common practice at this time.[206] There is, however, no indication that this work was painted specifically for the Delft Guild of Saint Luke and was put on display on its premises, as had once been assumed on account of the picture's subject. Vermeer's widow did all in her power to ensure that the picture stayed in the family's possession. In order to keep it out of the clutches of Vermeer's creditors she formally transferred it, two months after the artist's death, to the possession of her mother, Maria Thins.[207]

What can we see in this picture and how should we interpret it? A tapestry, pulled to one side, reveals a light-flooded interior with a black-and-white marble floor, a dark-beamed ceiling and a gleaming white rear wall bearing a large map of the Netherlands. Daylight enters from the left through the windows, which are themselves concealed behind the heavy drapery. Our gaze is drawn, above all, to the two figures. One is a painter, viewed from the back, seated on a stool before his easel, at work on a picture. We perceive his figure as a dark silhouette against the background. The artist's model, who faces us, is the focus of our attention: a young blond woman wrapped in a large piece of pale blue drapery. She poses for the painter, wearing a laurel wreath, holding a trumpet in her right hand and a large book in her left. Below the blue cloth she has draped around herself, one can make out her everyday clothing: a floor-length yellow skirt falling in large folds. Between the model, who stands very close to the rear wall, and the foreground there extends an evidently long, but emphatically foreshortened, table with a massive tabletop and a variety of objects distributed across it: a large yellow and blue cloth, a book and, in particular, a male head, which appears to be either a mask or a cast made of a sculptural work (p. 263). Next to this can be seen a sketchbook with drawings. In the immediate foreground we find a chair, its back partially hidden by the tapestry.

Samuel van Hoogstraten, **Clio**
in *Inleyding tot de hooge schoole der schilderkonst,* Rotterdam 1678
Vienna, Österreichische Nationalbibliothek, Sammlung von Handschriften und alten Drucken

A second chair is visible beyond the artist's easel, against the rear wall. The aforementioned large map takes up most of this wall. The darkness of the foreground, with its chair and tapestry, sets off the brightness of the tapering wedge of wall seen directly next to it.

Vermeer's use of light and colour creates the impression that the image is a faithful rendering of the space, without the exaggerated illumination that is often resorted to in allegorical scenes. The artist chose nothing more than the setting and the quotidian objects it contains to depict the abstract subject of an allegory. We are, therefore, not shown an allegory in the strict sense of the term. Rather, we see a room serving as an artist's studio, in which an allegory of History, embodied in the figure of Clio, the Muse of History, gradually takes shape on the canvas. This allegory, when complete, will take the form of a half-length figure equipped with its attributes and posed against a neutral background – exactly as in the work of the so-called Dutch Classicists. Only once the viewer grasps the picture's various references that betray its significance does Vermeer's depiction of an artist at work itself become an allegory – an allegory of Painting. As noted by Arasse, Vermeer "de-realized" the painter and his studio by allegorizing both, and simultaneously "de-allegorizing" his allegorical figure by presenting her as a real artist's model.[208]

The scene that we at first take to be an ordinary depiction of an artist in his studio is, in fact, a double allegory. We observe the creation, on the artist's canvas, of an allegory of History within a broader context that itself represents a glorification of painting. It is only in the past few decades that this supremely thoughtful picture, in which every detail is replete with significance, has gradually been deciphered. *The Art of Painting* has preoccupied scholars like few other artworks. It is one of the few great works to have given rise to a multitude of interpretations and, accordingly, to have been the subject of innumerable publications. Around 50 years ago a clash between two opposed interpretations of Vermeer's painting – that of Hans Sedlmayr and that of Kurt Badt – culminated in a fundamental dispute between distinct art-historical principles and methods.[209] Sedlmayr, adopting a structuralist approach, proposed a sequential interpretation of the allegory. Badt, however, heavily influenced by the philosophy of Martin Heidegger, approached the picture as a phenomenologist, responding strictly to what can be observed and, accordingly, re-titling the composition *Painter and Model*.

Hultén was the first art historian of modern times to recognize the model, on account of her attributes, as intended to represent Clio (p. 229).[210] For an educated observer in Vermeer's day it would not, of course, have been at all difficult to reach this conclusion: Vermeer's young woman is dressed and equipped exactly as recommended by Cesare Ripa, in his *Iconologia*, to serve as a personification of History. Vermeer was doubtless familiar with this 16th-century Italian compendium of traditional personifications and allegories, a well-established reference work among painters, in its Dutch translation, published in

Amsterdam in 1644. Here he would have read:"Wy sullen Clio een Maeghdeken met een Lauwerkrans afmaelen, die in de rechter hand een Trompet houd, en mette slincker een boeck, alwaer boven op sal geschreven zijn THUCYDIDES" ("We shall paint Clio as a girl with a laurel wreath, holding a trumpet in her right hand and in her left a book inscribed with the name THUCYDIDES"; trans. Miedema 1998, p. 291). The Muse of History, that is to say, appears holding a work by that author who, on account of his *History of the Peloponnesian War*, was regarded as the greatest historian of Antiquity. Of the laurel wreath itself Ripa, in the Dutch translation, has this to say: "De Lauwerkrans druckt uyt, dat gelijck de Lauwer altijd groen is en lange tijd wordt onderhouden, dat oock alsoo, door te Historie, de verledene, als mede de tegenwoordige dingen, eeuwigh leven" ("The laurel wreath indicates that, through the writing of history, things of the past like those of the present shall live forever, just as the laurel is at all times green"). The laurel, since Antiquity a traditional symbol of fame and honour, with which both victorious military leaders and poets would be crowned, stands here, too, for the lasting fame that being included in the historical record entails: "The Muse of History is the Painter's Inspiration."[211] Vermeer, therefore, ascribes to the writing of history a quality that was also claimed by painting: the ability to preserve for posterity what would otherwise be transient. As formulated in Albrecht Dürer's succinct description of the mission of the painter, his portraits were to preserve "the image of people after they had passed away".

Upon the canvas on the artist's easel, which has earlier been prepared with a ground in a neutral tone, Vermeer's painter has lightly drawn or brushed in the main outlines of his figure. This was largely in accordance with the actual practice of the period, which Vermeer himself observed.[212] The ground would be made up of lead white, to which chalk, ochre, umber or a vegetal black would be added, in order to achieve a neutral middling tone, which would usually range between a warm, pale brown and a cool, bluish grey. In the case of Vermeer's work, the ground played an important role, even within the finished painting. For, by comparison with other painters of the period, Vermeer evolved a particularly economical approach to the practice of painting, which he was able to further refine over time (see also pp. 123f.). Sometimes, he used thin glazes when painting over the ground so that this showed through sufficiently to influence the final chromatic effect; in other cases, the ground might remain visible, as a separate colour accent between two patches of paint. The painter seated at the easel appears to have begun working on his allegorical figure by depicting the laurel wreath. While this procedure may at first seem odd, it does, in fact, reflect the traditional practice in painting with oils, which was to attend to one part of a composition at a time, with a newly prepared palette for each, and to start at the top of the canvas. It appears, however, that Vermeer himself did not adhere to this tradition, preferring to work on several parts of his compositions simultaneously, and not one by one.[213]

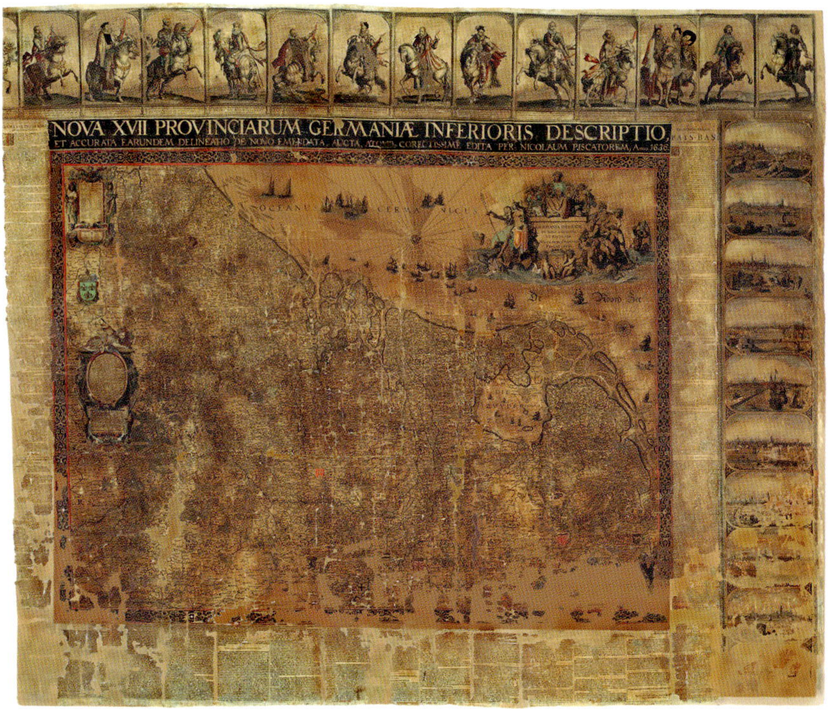

Claes Jansz. Visscher, **Wall Map of the Seventeen Provinces**, 1636
Coloured engraving, mounted on canvas. Håbo, Skoklosters Slott

In *The Art of Painting*, then, Vermeer depicts the traditional approach to creating a picture, not his own.

By thus "prioritizing" the laurel wreath, Vermeer's main concern was to emphasize its central significance for our understanding of the allegory.[214] Failing to grasp its role here, one might well mistake it for a merely ironic detail. The importance of history for painting, to which Vermeer's picture alludes, is in keeping with the exceptional role that history painting was accorded in art theory throughout the Early Modern Period, and in Vermeer's era by Karel van Mander, and among the latter's followers, by Samuel van Hoogstraten, who in 1678 affirmed: "den hoogsten en voornaemsten trap in de Schilderkonst, die alles onder zich heeft, geport en gedreven, welk is het uitbeelden der gedenkenwaerdichste Historien" ("the highest and most noble stage of the art of painting which surpasses all others, is the representation of the most worthy histories").[215] Important here was the desire that the painter himself might achieve lasting fame through his art, for painting would be sure to triumph over time. In the later, sceptical view of William Hogarth (1697–1764), however, Saturn would triumph over Art by bringing about its decay and destruction.

Vermeer's depiction of the posing model does not correspond exactly with artistic practice. The model has no need, for example, to hold a heavy book at this point, when the artist appears to be attending only to the laurel wreath.[216] The painter turns his back to the viewer, thereby retaining his anonymity and, with it, a timeless and generalized significance. There is no evidence that Vermeer intended the artist shown here to be himself, or the room being used as an artist's studio to be his own. Scholars have even endeavoured to identify the model seen here; and it has been proposed that she was Vermeer's eldest daughter, Maria, who was born in 1654, and was later trained as a painter by her father. But at the time Vermeer completed *The Art of Painting* Maria would have been, at the most, only 14 years old.

The depicted artist is not Vermeer. He is, rather, a figure embodying the art of painting. Hence, his clothing, which is remarkable, and thus not inappropriate for a history painting. He wears a short, tight-fitting black jacket, which is decoratively slashed across the upper back and lower sleeves, allowing the white of the shirt worn beneath to show through (p. 317). In addition, voluminous black leggings reach to the knee, and are worn over red silk stockings, with artfully sagging white over-socks, buckled black shoes and a black beret. As slashed clothing of this sort was a fashion primarily of the 15th and early 16th centuries, it was once thought that Vermeer had expressly dressed this figure in an archaizing costume. This was also thought to be "Burgundian" in its associations and, together with the map on the wall, which shows the entire Netherlands as an undivided territory, a possible allusion to the 15th-century origins of the fame of Netherlandish painting. In fact, this sort of dress enjoyed several revivals during the 17th century.[217] Slashed jackets had first come back into fashion in the 1620s and 1630s, as demonstrated by figures in the work of the Dutch *caravaggisti*; and they were enjoying a new revival around 1660, as evidenced also by references in literature. An artist shown at work in rather splendid attire was a topos deriving from the art literature of Antiquity, and was understood to be in keeping with the elevation of the artist's calling.

Vermeer's painter and his model occupy an illusionistically rendered interior that resembles, in its luxurious decoration, a good many of the rooms to be found in his earlier paintings, such as *The Glass of Wine* (pp. 166/167, Cat. 7) or *The Music Lesson* (p. 181, Cat. 13). This room is, however, clearly not to be confused with the actual studio used by Vermeer, in the *voorkamer* of the upper floor of the house in which the Vermeer family lived. Thanks to the detailed description found in the inventory, we know that this unadorned workroom contained two Spanish chairs and a rod with an ivory knob ("een rotting met een yvooren knop daer op"), which the clerk drawing up the list failed to recognize as the artist's maulstick.[218] This item is clearly visible in *The Art of Painting*, albeit here with a knob of red leather. Also to be found in Vermeer's studio were two easels, three palettes, six panels ("paneelen") and ten canvases ("schilderdoucken"), a number of prints and a desk, in addition to "further junk" – "rommeling" – "here and there a jumble of diverse items that are not worth listing separately" (see also pp. 258f.). Just as Vermeer supplied his painter with elegant clothing, rather than the sort of clothes in which a painter would usually work, his setting is an imposingly furnished salon rather than a painter's studio. Among the objects to be found here, the map, the tapestry, the chandelier, the table and the various objects upon it are of particular significance and merit further consideration.[219] The map, the tapestry and the brass chandelier were, moreover, extremely valuable objects, such as would have been found only in the wealthiest households. In the inventory of Vermeer's estate no mention is made of any such objects: evidently, as in the case of other items frequently appearing in his pictures, such as the virginal (p. 180, Cat. 13, 33, 35) or the clavichord (Cat. 19), he must have seen them in the houses of wealthy benefactors and patrons, who permitted him to study them, to draw them and, in due course, to integrate them into his compositions.

The map shows all 17 Netherlandish provinces: that is to say, those of the (later independent) north and those of the south. In the left and right borders are to be found ten cartouches, one above the other, each enclosing a view of one of the most important cities of the region. Along the top of the map Vermeer records, with great care, its Latin title: NOVA XVII PROVINCIARUM [GERMANIAE INF]ERIORIS DESCRIPTIO (the square brackets here indicate those letters masked by the chandelier; "A New Description of the 17 Provinces of the Netherlands"). In the left border we find depictions of the cities of Brussels, Luxembourg, Ghent, Berghen in Hennegau (now Mons), Amsterdam, Namen (now Namur), Leeuwarden, Utrecht and Zutphen. In the right border we see depictions of the cities of Limburg, Nijmegen, Atrecht (now Arras), Dordrecht, Middelburg, Antwerp, Mechelen, Deventer and Groningen. At the very bottom is a depiction of the courtly residences of The Hague (t'Hof van Hollandt), on the left, and of Brussels (t'Hof van Brabandt), on the right. The original of this map was the work of the Amsterdam cartographer Claes Jansz. Visscher (1586/87–1652), as is also indicated within its Latin inscription. Visscher had, in fact, prepared the map for publication by amalgamating nine individual cartographic sheets. Each of these had, in turn, been printed from earlier copper plates used, since 1587, by the Haarlem map engraver and publisher Johannes van Doetecum (d. 1605), which Visscher had acquired in 1630 from the estate of the latter's son and had extensively reworked. Visscher first published his combined wall map – to which he gave a new title, the aforementioned city views and an explanatory text – in 1636, re-issuing it in 1642.

A few years ago a complete, albeit poorly preserved, example of the second edition was discovered by Günther Schilder in Skoklosters Slott in Håbo, Sweden (p. 232). The Bibliothèque Nationale de France in Paris has an example of a later, posthumous printing comprising individual, unlined sheets. That is to say, as far as we know, there exist only two specimens of this particular wall map, an item of which several editions were published over a period of several decades.[220] Large maps of this sort, lined with canvas, were susceptible to damage, and sheets that had not been mounted in this way have only rarely survived.

Through its inclusion in Vermeer's painting, this map has remained famous. As such, it serves as an important testament to the outstanding achievements of 17th-century Dutch cartography. Of far more significance in this context, however, is the evident importance that the map assumes within Vermeer's composition – an importance that is immediately obvious from its prominent position. Commentators have always found of considerable significance the fact that the map records a period that was long past by the time Vermeer's picture was painted. It has been supposed that this might indicate that Vermeer and his contemporaries still essentially regarded the Netherlands as an undivided political entity and were unwilling to accept the country's political division into northern and southern provinces; and that Vermeer had deliberately alluded here to a political situation that was no longer current, to a period which may have seemed, or been nostalgically recalled as, better than that introduced by the followers of the House of Orange. There were many in Holland in Vermeer's day who felt this way, as is clearly revealed by the frequent occurrence, in maps of the Netherlands, of an outline form resembling a lion, accompanied by the inscription LEO BELGICUS. This was a means of alluding directly, if tactfully, to recent history. In Vermeer's picture it would seem that the positioning of the map, behind the Muse of History, is also to be interpreted in this way: painting had always brought fame to the Netherlands, and Clio

Foliage with a Peacock, a Turkey and a Deer, *c.* 1600–1630
Tapestry. Amsterdam, Rijksmuseum

Six-armed Chandelier, *c.* 1625–1650
Brass, height 65 cm, dia. 73 cm / height 25 5/8 in., dia. 28 3/4 in. Mechelen, Stedelijke Musea

now inspires the painter to strive for the fame that she may then trumpet forth and immortalize in the book of history. Quite apart from this, the map itself, as a physical object, is a true feat of painterly description. As the daylight entering from the left plays across its large, wavy folds and numerous small creases, it emerges not as a planar surface, but as an entity occupying three-dimensional space, and thus becoming all the more emphatic a presence within the composition. These visible traces of age themselves serve to remind the viewer that this is an old map and one recording an earlier political situation.

Equally masterly is Vermeer's rendering of the brass chandelier and of the tapestry in the left foreground. While the chandelier at first appears to be recorded in every detail (p. 236), on closer inspection, or inspection by means of a magnifying glass, it can be found, rather, to illustrate Vermeer's pre-eminence in the game of artistic illusionism. For the apparent graphic precision in the rendering of this item dissolves into a sequence of bright and dark brown dabs with bright yellow highlights created with a series of pastose spots and stripes (p. 239). On account of its prominent position, its elaborately projecting form and its radiance, the chandelier attracts the viewer's eye, thereby proclaiming itself an important element within the composition. Expensive brass chandeliers of this sort were very rarely to be found in private houses. They were a feature chiefly of the imposing Assembly Rooms of the city's Guilds, although also (often even larger and multitiered) of the interiors of churches. As the upper portion of the chandelier shown in Vermeer's composition takes the form of a clearly visible double eagle, similar to the heraldic symbol of the Habsburgs and thus of the Holy Roman Empire under Habsburg rule, it has been interpreted as an allusion to the (Spanish) Habsburg rule over the Netherlands – even though Vermeer's eagle heads (unlike those of the Habsburgs) are, in fact, not crowned. Were such an allusion indeed intended, it would be in line with the cartographic depiction of the 17 provinces of the Netherlands before their division into an independent north and a (Spanish) Habsburg south. The precise type of chandelier shown here may be associated with the city of Mechelen, which could itself account for the uncrowned double-headed eagle, which is to be found in that city's coat of arms. Biemond posits that a chandelier from Mechelen, the seat of the Primate of Belgium, the head of the leading archbishopric of the Netherlands, might well be a symbol of the religious unity of the territory within an as yet intact Catholic hierarchy, just as the map evokes an earlier political unity.[221] Another, rather less persuasive hypothesis holds that Vermeer's chandelier does not depict a double eagle, but a phoenix, and is intended as an allusion to the eulogy of Carel Fabritius (and Vermeer) by Arnold Bon (see also p. 36).[222]

The left half of the composition is taken up with the tapestry partially pulled to one side. This is a Netherlandish Verdure (or Garden) Tapestry (p. 235), of which part of the pictorial field and a strip of the framing border are visible.[223] Tapestries of this sort, with a foliage pattern, had been common since the late Middle Ages, and they were especially appreciated in the southern Netherlands in the 1550s. Invisible to the viewer, however, are the means by which the tapestry is attached to the beamed ceiling or gathered and fastened laterally at around mid-height. The tapestry makes up part of the depicted space, fulfilling here a similar function to the curtain placed outside the composition of *A Young Woman Reading a Letter* (p. 95, Cat. 5). Together with the chair, which is also to be found in the foreground, the tapestry serves as a kind of *repoussoir*, to create a sense of depth, an impression that is enhanced by Vermeer's treatment of light. Every art connoisseur of Vermeer's period, moreover, could be relied upon to make the connection between the tapestry here pulled to one side and a well-known anecdote from Antiquity, recounted by Pliny the Elder, about the contest between Zeuxis and Parrhasius (on which, in connection with Cat. 5, see p. 73).

The impression of the tapestry's proximity to the viewer derives from the blurred rendering of its pattern. At the same time, Vermeer emphasizes the soft yet rough character of the woollen tapestry, whose three-dimensional appearance is enhanced by means of superimposed dots of colour (p. 315). Proponents of the camera obscura theory (see also pp. 109–111) have seen this blurred rendering as a further argument in their favour. It is, however, significant that the tapestry is not to be found at the centre of the visual field. In as far as Vermeer effectively imitated the way the human eye perceives its surroundings, those aspects of the composition lying at the centre of the visual field – here, the painter and his model, in addition to the map – are rendered in sharp focus, whereas objects in the periphery or the immediate foreground are less detailed and partially blurred.

Among the objects on the table, the most prominent is the over-life-size sculpted head; though usually interpreted as a mask, it is more likely to be a cast of an indeterminate model, in all probability, one from Antiquity, as was then commonly used by painters and sculptors.[224] In addition to its role as a studio requisite, this has been interpreted as an allusion to the rivalry between painting and sculpture; or, in connection with the sketchbook lying alongside it, as a nod to *imitatio* and *disegno*, imitation and drawing. The large book behind it may perhaps stand for the upholding of principles in art.[225] Pénot points out the bright light that falls on to the head, believing this to be that of Apollo, the God of Light and of the Arts, and the Leader of the Muses.[226] As such, this would then embody either the union of, or the rivalry between, poetry and painting, and would serve as a symbol of Vermeer's own claim to be elevating painting to the level of the fine arts.

Geography and Astronomy

Geography and astronomy are interrelated sciences and were, accordingly, treated by Vermeer as companion pieces. With these two pictures he entered an entirely new thematic arena, although bringing to it familiar compositional forms and motifs. We know for certain that Vermeer's *Astronomer* (p. 269, Cat. 27) and *Geographer* (p. 273, Cat. 28) were painted as pendants, even though the two pictures bear different dates (*The Astronomer*, 1668; *The Geographer*, 1669) and are not directly related to each other in their respective compositions. The spatial arrangement and perspectival organization of the two pictures would seem to indicate that the later painting, *The Geographer*, was intended to be hung to the left of *The Astronomer*.[227] The large window and the open space to the right in *The Geographer* lead the viewer's gaze across to the earlier picture. Technical investigations have also confirmed that the two paintings belong together. Contrary to the claims of earlier scholars, they are identical in size. The signature on each is original, and this despite the striking and, unusually, double signature on *The Geographer* (p. 318).[228] The pictures

The Art of Painting (detail), *c.* 1666–1668
(see ill. p. 265)

remained together, even upon being sold, from the time they were first documented, in 1713, until 1797.

In addition to the formal congruence between the two pictures, there are also numerous thematic, symbolic and allegorical similarities. Astronomy and geography are two distinct approaches to investigating the earth. Both depicted scholars are absorbed in their work. The geographer, with a pair of compasses in his hand, leans over his map on the table, while gazing pensively into the distance (pp. 270/271). His pose, as Thoré-Bürger noted,[229] recalls that found in Rembrandt's etching *Dr Faustus*, of *c.* 1652 (p. 245). The astronomer considers the constellations marked on his celestial sphere, which he touches with his outstretched right hand (pp. 266/267). This motif recurs in a more or less contemporary picture by Cornelis de Man (1621–1706) showing geographers at work (p. 240). Both of Vermeer's scholars unite contemplation and empiricism. They both draw on teachings about nature sanctified by tradition, but also on the latest empirical findings.

It would appear that one and the same model posed for both pictures. For this reason there has been a tendency among commentators to see in the depicted individual the portrait of the unknown patron. Wheelock suggests that this may well be Antoni van Leeuwenhoek (1632–1723), who was later to serve as executor of Vermeer's estate.[230] He bases his view on the probability that the two men knew each other well, not only because Vermeer's father had been active as a silk weaver and Leeuwenhoek had trained to be a silk merchant, but also because they were united by their shared interest in optical phenomena. It was, however, in his capacity as an official of the city of Delft, and not as a former friend of Vermeer, that Leeuwenhoek was appointed executor of the latter's estate. And Leeuwenhoek's parallel involvement in scientific research is of no significance here. There would, then, seem to be no reason for regarding the individual portrayed in both *The Geographer* and *The Astronomer* as Antoni van Leeuwenhoek.[231] Liedtke believes that both pictures may have been commissioned by Adriaen Paets I (1631–1686), Director of

Cornelis de Man, **Geographers**, *c.* 1670
Oil on canvas, 81 x 68 cm / 31 7/8 x 26 3/4 in. Hamburg, Hamburger Kunsthalle

the Dutch East India Company in Rotterdam and, like his good friend Pieter Claesz. van Ruijven, a Remonstrant.[232] There are indeed grounds for believing that both pictures, when auctioned in 1713, were being sold from the collection of Adriaen Paets II (1657–1712).

The historical background of both pictures lies in the flowering of the natural sciences in Holland in the 17th century. Not only were diverse sorts of optical apparatus invented and produced there, but cartography also excelled: the Amsterdam publishing houses of Hondius, Blaeu and Visscher were at this time Europe's leading producers of maps and globes. Welu emphasizes that terrestrial and celestial globes were usually issued in pairs.[233] The terrestrial globe produced in 1618 by Jodocus Hondius (1563–1612), which sits on top of the cupboard seen in the background of *The Geographer*, has its counterpart in the celestial globe featured in *The Astronomer*. Of the geographer's terrestrial globe we are shown not the section with a decorative cartouche, but the Indian Ocean. This is an indication that Vermeer neither regards nor depicts the globe as a decorative object, but includes it to underline the scientific character of the depicted individual and his setting.[234] Nonetheless, the very same globe, albeit without its stand, was to recur in Vermeer's *Allegory of Faith* (p. 297, Cat. 34). It has also been possible to identify the framed map shown on the rear wall in *The Geographer*, thanks to its detailed depiction.[235] This is an example of the *Pascaarte van alle zee-custen van Europa*, a maritime map showing all the coasts of Europe, published for the first time in 1600 by Willem Jansz. Blaeu.[236] In the window hangs a Jacob's staff, a simple device made out of movable wooden rods, in use since the 14th century, with which distances could be measured and the relative position of the sun and the stars calculated.[237]

The book lying open on the astronomer's table is the guide published by Adriaen Metius (1571–1635) on the practical uses of astronomy and geography: *Institutiones Astronomicae & Geographicae, fondamentale en grondelijcke Onderwysinghe van de sterrekonst ende Beschryvinghe der Aerden door het Ghebruyck van de Hemelsche ende Aerdtsche Globen* (Amsterdam 1621; Astronomical & Geographical Instructions: Fundamental and Thorough Instructions in Astronomy and Geography by Means of Celestial and Terrestrial Globes). This offered, among much else, "brief and clear guidance in the art of navigation".[238] The book is shown opened at the first two pages of the third chapter, which treats the investigation into, and observation of, the stars, with an illustration of the "Wagenrad-Astrolabium" ("Cartwheel Astrolabe") invented by Metius. And, as if in further illustration, Vermeer depicts an astrolabe, leaning against the globe on the table. In the aforementioned section of the text Metius cites an author of Antiquity, Flavius Josephus (37/38–after 100), as having stated that the descendants of Seth discovered the knowledge of the heavens and the science of the stars.[239] There is also, therefore, a possible further connection with the picture hanging on the rear wall, which depicts the Finding of Moses: for in the Bible it is claimed of Moses that he was educated "in all the wisdom of the Egyptians". The same picture, rendered on a much larger scale, is to be found in a quite different context, in the background of Vermeer's painting *A Lady Writing a Letter with Her Maid* (p. 291, Cat. 31).

Pictures of Women around 1670

In a series of pictures probably painted between 1669 and 1672, Vermeer returned to familiar territory. These pictures show young women engaged in domestic tasks: at work, as in the case of *The Lacemaker* (p. 275, Cat. 29); receiving and answering letters, as in the so-called *The Love Letter* (p. 279, Cat. 30), and *A Lady Writing a Letter with Her Maid* (p. 291, Cat. 31); or playing a musical instrument, as in *The Guitar Player* (p. 281, Cat. 32) or *Young Woman Standing at a Virginal* (p. 283, Cat. 33). In terms of their composition, these works belong to several different pictorial categories. *The Lacemaker* recalls the earlier small studies of heads (Cat. 23, 25); the two pictures on the theme of letters further develop Vermeer's treatment of scenes set in spacious interiors, which opened with *The Glass of Wine* (Cat. 7) and continued with *The Music Lesson* (Cat. 13) and *The Concert* (Cat. 19), reaching its culmination in *The Art of Painting* (Cat. 26). *The Guitar Player* and *Young Woman Standing at a Virginal* are successors to the single-figure depictions of women from the 1660s (Cat. 14–18).

The Lacemaker gives the impression of being a closely cropped detail of a larger interior scene. The emphatically close view simulates the direct optical impression of a sharp focus on one plane with less sharply focused areas in front of it and behind it. Especially impressive here are the abstract foreground forms made up of colour spots, used by Vermeer to evoke the white and red threads spilling out of the sewing cushion on to a table carpet. It is only upon closer inspection that this tangle of colour and forms can be made out for what it is. The production of bobbin lace had long been established in the Netherlands; and, in both literary and artistic tradition, the activity was seen as the epitome of domestic virtue. Like other forms of skilled needlework, it was accordingly a frequent subject in genre painting (p. 37). To make lace with bobbins and pins one required a cushion, or a box with a lid that incorporated a cushion, the box also serving as a container for the bobbins (cf. Nicolaes Maes, p. 251). As a support for the lacemaker's box and cushion, Vermeer depicts a small table, which takes the form of a base with a turned wooden knob and a sloping work surface equipped with a tray. Regularly aligned holes allow the work surface to be positioned at the desired height.[240] As far as we know no such piece of 17th-century furniture has come down to us; nor are depictions of such tables to be found in other paintings. There do, however, exist illustrations of these in pattern books, for example, *New Modelbuch von Allerhandt Art Nehens und Stickens* by Nicolas Bassée, published in Frankfurt am Main in 1568.[241]

In Vermeer's picture a small wooden box, with a relatively flat cushion, covered by a pale blue cloth, lies on the work surface. The pink strip laid across this is a lace-making pattern (*patroon or kantbrief*) with a drawn, or more probably printed, diagram, into which the pins would be stuck, then held in place by the threads, which were wound around the bobbins, so producing the pattern of the lace. A second table, in the left foreground, is covered with a heavy carpet. Upon this lies a so-called sewing cushion (*naaikussen*): a dark blue container, in the form of a cushion with a pattern of white stripes and with tassels at its corners, out of which we see white and red threads or small ribbons hanging, these last rendered with a high degree of abstraction, notwithstanding the overall detailed precision of this picture.[242] Next to this lies a small book, tied with ribbons, which is either a pattern book for lace,[243] a prayer book or a small Bible, here intended as a token of domestic virtue and piety.[244]

It is probable that *The Love Letter* (p. 279, Cat. 30) was painted around 1669/70, that is to say, more or less at the same time as *The Lacemaker*. However, it represents an altogether different type of picture. As if positioned in a dark anteroom, we look through an opened door into the neighbouring room, in which the actual scene unfolds. The housemaid, who appears just to have arrived, has interrupted the elegantly dressed lady of the house at her lute by giving her a letter, which the young lady takes only hesitantly and with a questioning glance. A few years earlier Vermeer had painted a rather similar scene in *Mistress and Maid* (p. 215, Cat. 24). There, the figures appear to be close to the viewer, and the space they occupy is not in itself described, the emphasis instead being placed on the psychology of the depicted action, which is conveyed through the physiognomies and poses of the two protagonists. Here, by contrast, the action is embedded in a setting rendered in great detail; and Vermeer, in spite of his usual narrative restraint, describes the action very explicitly and even rather theatrically. The expression of uncertain surprise on the part of the lady of the house is contrasted with the determination of the maid, who turns to her, apparently awaiting some clear instruction (pp. 276/277).

It is evident that, upon entering the far room, the maid has taken off her work shoes, which can be found in the immediate foreground, and has put aside her broom. These objects are components of the narrative that also have a symbolic significance. Both literally and symbolically, the broom stands for inner and outer cleanliness.[245] The lady herself has left off her own domestic tasks – we see a basket of washing and, next to it on the floor, a sewing cushion (cf. Cat. 29) – in order to attend to her music, and then, perforce, to the letter that has just arrived. Particularly striking is the contrast between the disorder of the anteroom and the elegance of the interior beyond it. In the half-darkness we can make out, on the stain-speckled wall, a map of Zeeland and West Friesland, which is also to be found in the background of *Cavalier and Young Woman* (p. 91, Cat. 6). To the right there is a chair, and on its seat a tattered songbook. Among the pictures hanging on the rear wall of the room beyond we find a seascape and a landscape in the style of Jacob van Ruisdael,[246] although the latter is partially masked by the foreground tapestry. A similar motif to this is to be found in a painting by Gabriel Metsu: *Lady Reading a Letter* (p. 252). In that work, too, a maid is seen bringing a letter to her mistress, although at the same time she partially uncovers a seascape that was masked by a curtain: a symbol of the instability of romantic entanglements.

In *The Love Letter* Vermeer is closer than in his other genre scenes to the typical genre painting of the period. Numerous formal and thematic correspondences can be found, in particular, in a work by Pieter de Hooch: *Young Couple with a Parrot* (p. 278). This is especially so in the case of the view from a dark and disordered anteroom into an elegant interior that lies beyond. Not only is there great similarity in the silhouette of the curtain pulled to one side; the perspective construction, too, is almost exactly the same in both pictures.[247] De Hooch's *Young Couple* is dated 1668, that is to say, in all probability it was painted a little earlier than Vermeer's picture. Notwithstanding its date, Sutton proposes that both its stylistic qualities and its costumes provide good grounds for supposing that De Hooch's work was painted later than this, around 1675–1677.[248]

Situations where the observer is offered a view from one room, through an open door, into a neighbouring room were frequently found in paintings of Dutch interiors in the third quarter of the 17th century. In inventories and descriptions dating from that period such pictures are termed *doorkijkje*. Vermeer himself, in his early painting *A Maid Asleep* (p. 87, Cat. 4), made use of such a view into a second room. There, however, the principal subject of the picture is to be found in the foreground, and not in the room beyond. A further, now untraced *doorkijkje* by Vermeer is listed in the catalogue of the 1696 sale of the collection of Jacob Abrahamsz. Dissius, as "a gentleman [...] washing his hands in a see-through room with sculptures, artful and rare".[249] In addition to De Hooch, who employed the *doorkijkje* as a means of introducing striking light effects and lively narrative situations, often involving children, this device was, above all, to be found in the work of Samuel van Hoogstraten, in this case especially in the interests of illusionism. His picture *The Slippers* (p. 86), which offers a narrow view into a Dutch house afforded by an open door, is the best-known example of the entire genre. In other pictures, such as *View down a Corridor* (Dyrham Park, Gloucestershire), Hoogstraten is primarily concerned with *trompe-l'œil*. The viewer is to be deceived into believing that the painted corridor is real, and thus extends into three-dimensional space, whereas it is, in fact, painted on the wall at the end of the much shorter actual corridor. When, in 1669, Pieter Teding van Berckhout visited Vermeer in his studio (see also p. 107), he singled out for particular praise in the paintings he was shown the treatment of perspective. It is possible that he may have been referring to a composition such as *The Love Letter*.[250]

Vermeer treated the theme of receiving or writing a letter a total of six times. The three last such pictures each show a lady in the company of her maidservant. Some three years after the somewhat theatrical composition of around 1666/67 with its half-length figures, now in the Frick Collection (Cat. 24), he produced around 1669–1671 both *The Love Letter* (Cat. 30), a most unusual work, which we have just discussed, and *A Lady Writing a Letter with Her Maid* (p. 291, Cat. 31), where he once again places his protagonists in a spacious interior. Comparison with the earlier pictures of this type, however, reveals that a stylistic shift has occurred, as is detectable both in the overall compositional arrangement and in the treatment of individual details. This shift could be described as a simplification of forms. The picture is dominated by long, unbroken contours and straight lines, which create large forms: the heavy green curtain in the dark left foreground that hangs almost vertically, the parallel folds of the white curtain at the window, the narrow strip of wall beside it and the broad, black picture frame. The table, covered by a carpet, is presented as a massive block; the patiently waiting maid, in a dress falling in large, loose folds, is statuesque, almost resembling a column, and occupies the centre of the picture. The formal principle governing the composition is evident even in the details: the white blouse and the head covering of the lady shown writing appear stiff and crumpled and are composed of numerous small white and pale grey patches (pp. 280–282). At the same time Vermeer emphasizes here more strongly than in his earlier works, and possibly now under the influence of Rembrandt and of the altarpieces of the Counter-Reformation, the contrasts between light and shadow.[251]

In this picture Vermeer is telling us a story, whereby he reduces the scene to its essentials and does not lose himself in anecdotal detail. As is only rarely the case with a history painting, however, here we are not already familiar with the story being told. The letter writer appears fully absorbed in her task. She is neither hesitant nor pensive, as are her counterparts in the earlier pictures, where action tends to signify rather less than the hint

Rembrandt Harmensz. van Rijn, **Dr Faustus**, *c.* 1652
Etching and drypoint, 21 x 16 cm / 8 ¼ x 6 ¼ in. Vienna, Albertina

of a certain mood or feeling. It is at least clear that a letter has arrived: it lies folded on the floor in the immediate foreground, together with a red wax seal. It is also evident that the letter is to receive an immediate answer: the maid is now waiting, lost in thought, in order to be able to deliver the response. The empty chair in the foreground serves primarily as a formal motif, although it, too, may be assumed to have a part in the narrative. In that case the letter writer may have started by sitting here and then moved to her present position to take advantage of better light.

The large picture that occupies almost all of the rear wall depicts the Finding of Moses (Exodus 2: 1–10). The same picture, albeit on a smaller scale and more closely cropped, appears in the background of *The Astronomer* (p. 269, Cat. 27). The original of this composition, which has not survived, was possibly an early work by Sir Peter Lely (1618–1680), who had trained in Haarlem before moving, after 1640, to England.[252] A similar composition, by Pieter Fransz. de Grebber (*c.* 1600–1652/53), is now in Dresden (Staatliche Kunstsammlungen, Gemäldegalerie Alte Meister).[253] The picture shows the moment where the Pharaoh's daughter has found the child abandoned on the bank of the Nile and has decided to adopt it. When the Pharaoh had ordered that all newborn sons of the Jews be killed, the child's mother had laid it in a rush basket and left it on the bank of the Nile. The Pharaoh's daughter called the child Moses and appointed its mother to serve as its nurse. This subject, which was frequently treated in Dutch painting, was regarded as an illustration of Divine Providence, while the courageous Pharaoh's daughter was seen as a symbol of female wisdom and circumspection. It was, however, also common in 17th-century Holland for the mothers of children born out of wedlock, faced with the prospect of punishment and public censure, to abandon their infants. It is conceivable that Vermeer was here also alluding to this circumstance.[254]

On account of its immense size, the picture on the wall cannot help but seem to have a strong formal connection with the two female figures in the foreground, and this necessarily leads one to suppose that there must surely be a connection between the letter writer and the symbolic significance of the framed composition, or that the subject of the framed picture must surely supply a key to the letter writing.[255] But any solution that might be proposed would be mere speculation as we do not know the content of the letter.

The Guitar Player (p. 281, Cat. 32) has been variously interpreted in the scholarly literature. Some commentators have emphasized its compositional weaknesses, and have even questioned its authenticity; others have stressed the superb painterly technique of particular passages. Blankert views the picture as autograph, but points emphatically to

Young Woman Seated at a Virginal (detail),
c. 1672–1675 (see ill. p. 285)

the imbalanced quality of the composition, with its figure to one side and in an unnatural pose.[256] He sees in such features the unmistakable stamp of Vermeer's late style, which he characterizes, negatively, as a sort of "Mannerism". Wheelock, by contrast, regards the picture as the finest example of Vermeer's late style, offering a positive interpretation of the stylistic shift to which it testifies.[257] Schematized and impressionistic passages are juxtaposed in the *Guitar Player*. Here, we find Vermeer resorting to an abbreviated form of the sort of optical illusionism he had evolved in earlier works: this is apparent, for example, in details such as the gilt pattern of the sound opening of the guitar or the gilt frame of the picture on the rear wall, which are made up of individual dots of paint. The young woman's brightly lit, gleaming white satin dress constitutes a remarkable abstract pattern of light and shadow, and yet at the same time it brings forth the perfect illusion of silk cloth. One has the impression of greater speed of execution as the chief respect in which this picture differs from earlier works, be it in the face of the young woman, half lying in shadow, or in her hands, or in her dress, or in the background details.

The depiction of musicians shown as half-length figures is frequently encountered in Dutch painting, whether in the work of the Dutch *caravaggisti*, such as Gerard van Honthorst's *Woman Playing a Guitar* (1624; p. 280), or that of Frans Hals, such as his *Lutenist* (*c.* 1623; Paris, Musée du Louvre). Vermeer, too, made use of this type of figure, which initially arose in the first half of the 17th century. It is possible that he had been intending to paint a pendant – such as originally accompanied the aforementioned picture by Honthorst – and it could be this that accounts for the eccentric positioning of the figure and for a feature very unusual for Vermeer: light entering from the right. The framed picture in the background is based on a work by the Delft landscape painter Pieter van Asch.[258] It would also serve as a model for the painted inner lid of the virginal in the later painting *Young Woman Seated at a Virginal* (p. 285, Cat. 35). Goodman believes this idealized landscape to have a connection with the pastoral poetry of the period, which praised female beauty as a triumph of nature.[259] Moreover, the three books on the table establish a connection with erudition. The presentation of elegant young women in such a context is to be found in other Dutch paintings of this era, those of Eglon van der Neer, for example.[260]

Almost at exactly the same time, that is to say, around 1670–1672, Vermeer painted a further image of a young woman playing music. This was *Young Woman Standing at a Virginal* (p. 283, Cat. 33). Here, Vermeer once again returns to the compositional scheme that he frequently employed in varied forms between 1660 and 1665 (cf. Cat. 8, 14–18). The segment of an interior that we see shows part of the floor with black and white flagstones, a row of figuratively decorated Delft tiles running along the base of the wall and a foreshortened segment of a wall with windows. The perspectival arrangement of the picture corresponds most closely to the *Milkmaid* (Cat. 8), and thus to the earliest of the aforementioned pictures. Yet it is clear that, over the course of ten or twelve years, Vermeer's style and manner of painting – which may now be characterized by a simplification of forms – have evolved. The light now appears harsher, and the edges of objects, therefore, much sharper and more linear. Yet the degree of illusionism remains the same, as can be recognized, in this case, in the figure's clothing. This young lady in her silk dress – its vertical folds shimmering in the light, its sleeves puffed extravagantly, its blue collar decorated with red ribbons – is one of the most beautiful of Vermeer's female figures. She looks at the observer, who seems to concern her rather more than the music she is playing on her instrument, which her fingers seem barely to touch.

Young Woman Standing at a Virginal has repeatedly been considered in connection with the later picture *Young Woman Seated at a Virginal* (Cat. 35). Notwithstanding the difference between them in terms of composition and in the style of painting, or the passage of perhaps two to five years between the production of one picture and the next, these have on occasion been regarded as pendants, on account of their similar subject matter and their almost identical size. Liedtke sees the two pictures as "optional pendants", which complement each other but can also stand alone.[261] In his view the differing arrangement of the two pictures is, above all, an expression of the two very different types of women that Vermeer here intended to depict.

In *Young Woman Standing at a Virginal*, the protagonist is accompanied by no fewer than three pictures. At the centre, directly behind her, we see a large figure of Cupid, in the classicizing style of Caesar van Everdingen, with which we are already familiar from other compositions by Vermeer (Cat. 5 or 11; on its emblematic interpretation, see p. 74). To the left of it, in a gold frame, and to the lower right, decorating the inner lid of the musical instrument, appear Italianate landscapes. Both of these derive from the same composition, by the Delft painter Pieter Groenewegen (*c.* 1600–1658), dating from around 1640,[262] which Vermeer here adapts, once in a vertical and once in a horizontal format. It is possible that both original compositions had been owned by Vermeer. Among the works listed in the 1676 inventory of his estate there is mention of a landscape (albeit without further identification) and of a picture of Cupid, which may well be identical to the one depicted here.[263]

The Two Last Pictures

If the chronological sequence and the dating of Vermeer's pictures, upon which art-historical research has over the years, and with only a few exceptions, reached agreement, then the artist may be said to have painted distinctly less after 1670 than he did in the preceding years. During the last three years of his life, he appears to have produced no paintings at all, or so we must believe unless we wish to suppose that more paintings have been lost from this period than from any earlier period. The reasons for a decline in production presumably had to do with the altered political and economic situation in Holland, on account of which Vermeer stopped receiving commissions. As a visitor to his studio some years earlier had discovered to his disappointment, the artist tended not to retain a certain number of completed pictures, as his "stock" (see also pp. 104f.).

After many years of peace and of unprecedented economic growth and increasing prosperity for the Dutch Republic and its inhabitants, there occurred a catastrophic reversal of fortune. In 1672 the French king, Louis XIV (1638–1715), declared war on Holland; French troops occupied the eastern provinces and even advanced some way towards Amsterdam. It was only through opening the dykes to flood the low-lying land that William III of Orange, only just installed as General Stadtholder and Supreme Military Commander, was able to save from occupation the western part of Dutch territory, along the North Sea coast. At the same time England exploited the current weakness of Holland and launched an attack on the Dutch merchant fleet. Subsequently known as the *rampjaar* (year of catastrophe), 1672 landed Johannes Vermeer and his family in great financial difficulties, as the artist's widow was in 1676 to explain in a petition to the High Court of Holland and Zeeland: "because her deceased husband during the most recent war with the King of France, was able to earn very little, indeed almost nothing at all and was, moreover, constrained to sell at a great loss those pictures, that he had purchased in his capacity as an art dealer, in order to be able to feed his children, with the result that the family's debts increased..."[264] In 1674 came the death of Pieter Claesz. van Ruijven, Vermeer's most important patron and the man who had acquired most of his pictures, so that this secure source of income was also now lost to the artist. Vermeer's mother-in-law, Maria Thins, also suffered great losses. Because of the opening of the dykes, large stretches of land had been flooded and thereby devastated. This being the case with the lands she owned near Schoonhoven, these turned no profits, as she was not legally permitted to claim payment of the usual annual rents, which had been a substantial part of her income.

It appears that only two pictures have survived from the last three or four years of Vermeer's life. These are marked by a clear further development of his style: *Allegory of Faith*, probably dating to between 1671 and 1674 (p. 297, Cat. 34), and *Young Woman Seated at a Virginal*, possibly painted in 1672–1675, and thus perhaps Vermeer's last work (p. 285, Cat. 35). It may even be that Vermeer, in the last few years of his life, stopped painting altogether.[265]

Allegory of Faith occupies a special position within Vermeer's oeuvre. Except for *The Art of Painting*, it is the only allegory among his surviving works. But, while *The Art of Painting* gives the initial impression of being a genre scene, to the extent that its allegorical function was for a long while not recognized, in the case of the *Allegory of Faith*, the purpose of the composition is unmistakable. This most salient quality of the picture, in fact, unsettles

many observers: on the one hand because it does not correspond with the expectations they have for a picture by Vermeer, and on the other because the discrepancy between the illusionistic form of representation long associated with Vermeer and the symbolic elements of an allegory has a bewildering effect. A bloody snake that has been crushed by a stone simply does not seem to belong on the tiled floor of an upper-middle-class Dutch interior. Vermeer was, of course, perfectly aware of this dilemma; one can, therefore, only begin to approach the picture in the right spirit if one seeks to understand it in its historical context, and in relation to the probable ideas and intentions of the unknown patron who commissioned it.

A tapestry pulled to one side opens the view into an interior with a tiled floor and a beamed ceiling. Vermeer derives not only this compositional device, but also the entire perspective construction found here from his *Art of Painting* (p. 265, Cat. 26), a work produced some five years earlier. The *Allegory of Faith*, as such, is embodied in the figure of a woman in a dress of white and blue silk. She sits on a raised platform, which is covered in a carpet, her right hand held solemnly to her breast, her gaze fixed on a glass sphere suspended from the ceiling. Vermeer derived the figural motif from Italian models, perhaps the depiction of a *Penitent Mary Magdalene* by Guido Reni (1575–1642), which he may have seen in Dutch collections.[266] Vermeer here adheres closely to the account to be found in Cesare Ripa's *Iconologia*, combining the attributes of Faith with those of the Catholic Faith. The young woman places her right foot upon a terrestrial globe, while before her lie an apple with a bite taken out of it – a symbol of the Fall – and a snake crushed by a stone, rearing up and oozing blood – which embodies the Devil, conquered by Christ as cornerstone of the Church. Vermeer positions the goblet – which Ripa's allegorical figure holds in her right hand – and the book – upon which Ripa's figure, accordingly, lays her left hand – on a table, here rather resembling an altar, to which he adds a crown of thorns

Nicolaes Maes, **The Old Lacemaker**, *c.* 1655
Oil on board, 37.5 x 35 cm / 14 ¾ x 13 ¾ in.
The Hague, Koninklijk Kabinet van Schilderijen Mauritshuis

and an ebony crucifix. The gold goblet and the crucifix stand out clearly against the gilt wallcovering and the dark ground of the black picture frame, thereby emphasizing far more strongly than does Ripa the Eucharistic aspect of the allegory. The globe found here is, in fact, a literal interpretation of Ripa's description, according to which the figure of Faith has the world at her feet. The globe that Vermeer depicted had been made by Jodocus Hondius, an example of which is preserved in the Germanisches Nationalmuseum in Nuremberg (see also pp. 241f.). The book has been interpreted as a Bible; but it could also be a missal, and this would account for the altar-like arrangement of the objects on the table. Particularly striking is the glass sphere hanging by a blue ribbon from the beamed ceiling. This motif is based on an emblem of the Jesuit Guilielmus Hesius (1601–1690) that shows a winged putto, a symbol of the human soul, with a glass sphere, in which the cross and the sun are reflected.[267] The accompanying epigram, "Capit Quod Non Capit" (p. 296), compares the reflection of the entire universe in the glass sphere with the capacity of the soul to believe in God. Over and above this, Vermeer's rendering of the glass sphere bears brilliant testament to the illusionistic power of painting (p. 295).

While Ripa, in his own explanation, refers to Abraham and Isaac as symbols of Faith Triumphant, Vermeer replaces such Old Testament precursors by an allusion to the Crucifixion itself. Vermeer's model for the framed painting hanging on the rear wall was a composition by Jacob Jordaens (p. 257), which appears to have been preserved in a single version, now in a private collection. The tapestry seen in the foreground of Vermeer's picture has been interpreted as a product of Oudenaarde in the second half of the 16th century;[268] it is also possible that it was the work of François Spiering (*c.* 1550–1630), who had emigrated from Antwerp and, in 1593, had established a tapestry workshop in Delft with local assistance and encouragement. In so far as the depicted scene might be interpreted as the Wooing of Rebecca at the Well (Genesis 24), the subsequent Marriage of Isaac

Gabriel Metsu, **Lady Reading a Letter**, *c.* 1662–1665
Oil on board, 52.5 x 40.2 cm / 20 5/8 x 15 7/8 in. Dublin, National Gallery of Ireland

and Rebecca could be viewed as a precursor of the chief subject of Vermeer's painting: the union of the Church or the human soul and Christ.[269]

Such dense theological references have encouraged the assumption that Vermeer must have produced this picture in response to ecclesiastical patronage, and possibly upon receiving a commission from the Delft Jesuits.[270] However, although the relatively large size of the composition and its emphatically didactic arrangement would appear to suggest that it was conceived for the attention of a large circle of viewers, there is no secure evidence regarding such a commission. Montias has presented the counterargument that the Jesuits would have selected a more conventional subject by means of which to depict an allegory of Faith[271]; but this is not entirely convincing. Of greater significance seems to be the same scholar's observation that, in the case of an institutional commission, the painting would not have been sold on to a new owner so rapidly after its completion. The picture's first documented owner, a Protestant from Amsterdam, died in 1698. This would indicate that the original commission was not institutional. Liedtke has proposed that it may have come from Michiel van der Dussen (1600–1681), a wealthy member of the Delft Catholic community.[272]

Like the *Allegory of Faith*, Vermeer's *Young Woman Seated at a Virginal* exhibits the characteristics of the last phase of his classicizing figural style, notable for its sharp contours, rather brittle modelling and large forms. Vermeer's pictures of around 1670 (cf. Cat. 31–33) already reveal tendencies in this direction, but here we find these fully developed. Vermeer now altogether eschews features that played such a key role in his earlier work and effectively constituted his "personal style", such as the significance of the illusion of surface qualities in the rendering of various kinds of material. As a result, however, of Vermeer's sudden death, this stylistic shift was to be taken no further.

In his *Young Woman Seated at a Virginal* (p. 285, Cat. 35) Vermeer reappropriates motifs from his own earlier work. The woman looking out of the picture at the observer recalls his *Lady Writing* (Cat. 20), and the large viola da gamba reminds us of *The Music Lesson* (Cat. 13) and *The Concert* (Cat. 19). Vermeer's picture has most in common, however, with a painting produced around a decade earlier, by Gerard Dou: *Lady at a Clavichord* (p. 284). Among Vermeer's own paintings, the new work itself is, of course, stylistically closest to his *Young Woman Standing at a Virginal* (Cat. 33; see also pp. 248f.). It is clear that the differences between these two works have been very deliberately introduced by Vermeer in order to draw a distinction between the two protagonists. The young woman in the later picture flirts with the observer; she invites him, with her gaze, into what appears to be her dim-lit boudoir. This impression is encouraged by the "pictures within the picture": Dirck van Baburen's *Procuress* and the Arcadian landscape depicted on the inner lid of the virginal, which derives – albeit with altered proportions and a more elongated shape – from a work by the Delft painter Pieter van Asch.[273] A version of Dirck van Baburen's *Procuress* of 1622 (p. 182), which is also to be seen as one of the "pictures within the picture" in *The Concert* (p. 183), was owned by Vermeer's mother-in-law, Maria Thins.

Another interpretation of this composition is, however, possible. While the lute seen in Dirck van Baburens's *Procuress* represents profane love, the virginal and the viola da gamba stand for ideal, refined love. The composition as a whole would, in that case, treat the subject of choosing between the two. This would mean that *The Procuress* functions here, as a "picture within a picture", much as it does in *The Concert*. There, too, it embodied music allied to illicit love, and was set in contrast to the music being made by the company in the main picture, which is implicitly associated with proportion and harmony. Vermeer's treatment of illumination further supports this association: a bright light falls on the seated young woman and picks her out against the background. The light comes from a hidden source behind the curtain, and it also illuminates the nearest end of the virginal and the viola da gamba.

Vermeer's Death and His Estate

The last years of Vermeer's life were marked by financial difficulties and debts. In addition to his work as a painter and an art dealer, he turned to other possible sources of income; and he therefore found himself constrained to call upon the help of Maria Thins. Since 1668 she had let him have 400 florins per year from the yield of the inheritance from her aunt in Gouda, Diewertje van Hensbeeck.[274] In June 1673 Vermeer appeared before the municipality of Gouda. Here, he declared that Maria Thins had transferred to him half of the capital (that is to say, her daughter's share) bound up in the Orphanage in Gouda, and he formally requested the annual income from this sum.[275] A few weeks later, in Amsterdam, he took out two loans to the value of 800 florins.[276] In connection with the transaction in Gouda, Vermeer probably made a further journey to Amsterdam, in July 1675, in order to obtain a loan of 1,000 guilders from the merchant Jacob Rombouts.[277] The security that Vermeer offered for this loan, apparently illegal and, in any case, without the knowledge and the agreement of his mother-in-law, was the capital of the inheritance from Gouda that he had received in 1673.[278] His action in these matters is only to be explained by his despairing situation, which must have seemed otherwise hopeless to him.

Johannes Vermeer died on 13 or 14 December 1675. On 15 December his corpse was brought to the Oude Kerk in Delft, site of the family grave, which had been acquired in 1661 by Maria Thins. Already buried in this grave were three of Vermeer's children, who

The Guitar Player (detail), *c.* 1669–1672
(see ill. p. 281)

had died in 1667, 1669 and 1673.[279] Vermeer was buried on 16 December. The entry in the church's Register of Burials reads: "Jan Vermeer, art painter on the Oude Langendijck, in the church, 8 children under age."[280] The coffin of the last of Vermeer's children to die was laid on top of his own.[281] On the same day the remark "Johannes Vermeer art painter on the Oude Lange Dijck – nothing to get" was entered in the Beste Opperste Kleed Boek of the Delft Camer van Charitate.[282] Evidently, this public charity had sent a trunk to the house of the deceased in the expectation that either high-quality clothing or a corresponding donation would be provided for the poor. Montias wonders if, in this case, the failure to donate either clothes or money is to be explained not by the poverty of the family, but on religious grounds: Maria Thins and her daughter, Catharina Bolnes, Vermeer's widow, would, as good Catholics, perhaps not have wished to make donations to a foundation administered by Calvinists. But a few years later, on the death of Maria Thins, a very generous donation was made; and this would indicate that the earlier failure to donate may, rather, have lain in Catharina Bolnes's acute financial distress at the time.[283]

One and a half years later, on 27 July 1677, in a petition addressed to the States of Holland and West Friesland, Holland's highest public authority, Catharina Bolnes gave a more detailed account of the circumstances of Vermeer's death. "During the long and ruinous war with France not only had he been unable to sell any of his art but also, to his great detriment, was left sitting with the paintings of other masters that he was dealing in. As a result and owing to the very great burden of his children, having no means of his own, he had lapsed into such decay and decadence, which he had so taken to heart, as if he had fallen into a frenzy, and, in a day or a day and a half, had gone from being healthy to being dead."[284] This is to say that Vermeer, while showing no obvious signs of illness, suddenly and unexpectedly died. Montias posits that the extreme anxiety incurred by the despair he felt on account of his financial situation may have brought on a heart attack, or led him to suffer a stroke, after which he survived for only a day or two.

In April 1676, in a petition presented by Vermeer's widow to the High Court of Holland and Zeeland, as in the aforementioned petition of July 1677, the sheer number of Vermeer's dependent children is cited as a reason for his insolvency.[285] There was, however, some inconsistency in the stated number of these children. In the record of Vermeer's burial there is reference to eight underage children; but in 1676 Catharina Bolnes refers to 11 children, and in 1677 to 10 children. The discrepancy in the figures cited in 1676 and 1677 may perhaps be accounted for by the marriage of the eldest daughter, Maria Vermeer, in June 1674, after which she would have been regarded as an adult. In a further document, from 1678, two and three-quarter years after Vermeer's death, we find further details concerning his children.[286] Here it is claimed that, on his death, he left behind 10 underage children, of whom the oldest was now 21 and the youngest 4 years

old. Two were said to be ill, and a third to have been gravely injured in a gunpowder explosion on board a ship in Mechelen. We can, then, be confident in claiming that, at the time of Vermeer's death, 11 of his children were still living, and that one of these, his eldest daughter, had already left the parental home. Four children had died only shortly after birth or at a very young age. We know the names of nine of Vermeer's children.[287]

It is in all probability in connection with the financial difficulties experienced by Vermeer that we should understand the agreement that Catharina Bolnes reached, in late January 1676, only a few weeks after her late husband's death, with the baker Hendrick van Buyten (see also pp. 104f.). She sold him two of Vermeer's paintings in order to discharge the family's unpayable bills for bread, now amounting to 617 florins, although she retained the right to repay the outstanding debt in annual instalments of 50 florins.[288] Van Buyten was happy to comply with this arrangement, although this restricted his right to sell the paintings on to a third party. It is clear, however, that Catharina Bolnes was not able to make the subsequent annual repayments. Montias (1989, pp. 216 ff.) took great pains in attempting to calculate (on the basis of Dutch bread prices during the 17th century) how much bread was involved. He arrived at the figure of over 3,500 kilograms (8,000 pounds) of expensive white bread, an amount that might well have been consumed, over two or three years, by a mob of underage children as their main source of nourishment.[289] According to this speculative assumption, Vermeer's family would have been in debt to the baker from around 1672 onwards, the year the war with France started.

In the weeks and months after Vermeer's death, Catharina Bolnes endeavoured to resolve her financial problems. After settling the sum owed for bread deliveries to the baker Hendrick van Buyten, in February 1676, she sold 26 pictures to the Haarlem art dealer Jan Coelenbier for 500 florins. Taking place in Amsterdam, this transaction was made on

Jacob Jordaens, **The Crucifixion**, *c.* 1620
Oil on canvas, 160 x 121.5 cm / 62 x 47⅞ in. Private collection

behalf of, and in the name of, Jannetje Stevens, a Delft clothes and cloth merchant, and it, too, appears intended as a means of paying off debts accrued.[290] It has been assumed that the pictures sold on this occasion, which were each valued on average at 20 florins, were not the work of Vermeer, but were perhaps his stock as an art dealer. A year later, however, the sale was annulled on the instigation of Antoni van Leeuwenhoek, who had by then been appointed executor of Vermeer's estate.[291]

It was also in February 1676 that Catharina Bolnes and her mother, Maria Thins, reached a formal agreement, certified by a notary, by which the daughter formally transferred to her mother's possession Vermeer's picture *The Art of Painting* (Cat. 26), along with the income from various properties, in order by this means to settle her debts.[292] The chief reason for this undertaking would, however, appear to have been to remove this particular picture from Vermeer's estate, in order to save it from the clutches of his creditors. In connection with this donation, we should also see the division of the movable goods to be found in the house of Maria Thins into two categories, as recorded in an inventory drawn up on 29 February 1676: those that Vermeer had left behind and belonged exclusively to Catharina Bolnes and their children, and those that were the common property of Catharina Bolnes and Maria Thins. This repeatedly cited inventory, which itemized, in two columns, the contents of the house, room by room,[293] is in many respects a source of considerable importance. This is not only because it permits us an insight into the internal arrangement of a 17th-century bourgeois Dutch household – how the various rooms had been designated, how they were used and how each was furnished – but also because it enables us to learn of the items that Vermeer possessed, that he required for his work or that might feature in the depiction of domestic interiors in his own genre scenes. Of particular interest are the pictures by other painters that were to be found in the house, some owned by Vermeer, some owned by his mother-in-law. In the largest room of the house, the *groote zael* (great hall) there were family portraits: in addition to those of Vermeer's parents, there were ten portraits of ancestors of Maria Thins. There were also two *tronies* by Carel Fabritius, three further pictures from Vermeer's estate and two pictures of religious subjects: a Madonna and a "Three Kings" (in all probability, an Adoration of the Magi), owned by Maria Thins. In this room there were also numerous pieces of furniture, among them a bed, a cabinet decorated with inlay work, a large table and nine "Spanish chairs" with seats and backs of red leather, presumably the chairs with lion's head finials that feature in so many of Vermeer's pictures. Also listed in the inventory are a great many pieces of clothing, among them a "Turkish coat" of Vermeer's, an "innocent", a fashionable slashed jacket such as is worn by the painter in *The Art of Painting* (Cat. 26) and a yellow satin jacket with fur trim, belonging to Catharina Bolnes, another frequent motif in Vermeer's pictures. Near to the *groote zael* was the *voorhuis* (front room), which looked on to the street, and was imposingly decorated. Here were to be found further pieces of furniture, among which was a cabinet, four chairs and a mirror, in addition to 11 pictures, seven of them (including a large composition with Mars and Apollo) the property of Maria Thins. The remaining works, a painting of fruit, a landscape, a small seascape and a picture by Fabritius, had been the property of Vermeer. In the large house there were four kitchens, although it appears that these were also used as living rooms and bedrooms. In the *binnenkeucken*, or the "interior kitchen", there was a gilt leather wallcovering, a bed, a chest, various chairs, in addition to ten pictures on the walls, among them two *tronies* by Hoogstraten, two further *tronies* in Turkish dress, a large Crucifixion, a vera icon (a depiction of Christ's face), two still lifes (one with *vrouwentuych*, or "women's stuff", the other a vanitas with a double bass and a skull), a seascape and an unidentified picture hanging over the mantelpiece. Even in the actual kitchen, where meals were cooked (*koockeucken*), there was said to be a bed. In addition, a small kitchen was used for washing (*waskeukentgen*), and there was a small kitchen at the back of the house. On the upper floor there were two large rooms: that at the front of the house, the *voorhuis*, was probably Vermeer's studio (on its own furnishing, see pp. 233 f.).

We may reasonably assume that the inventory did not list every single item to be found in the house, either because certain items had been temporarily removed,[294] or because some belonged exclusively to Maria Thins. With regard to the objects that recur in Vermeer's pictures, it is notable that no musical instruments, neither a virginal, nor a lute, nor a viola da gamba, are cited in the inventory; nor is there any mention of Turkish carpets, china, silver jugs or bowls, nor any reference to marble floors. Above all, as observed by Liedtke, there is no reference to a camera obscura.[295]

The next step taken by Catharina Bolnes, in her endeavour to settle her debts, was a petition, presented on 24 April 1676 in the High Court of Holland and Zeeland (see also pp. 256f.), in which she formally requested a moratorium on her remaining debts, because she was unable to meet the demands of her creditors, who were themselves not prepared to make further concessions.[296] Her request was granted: Catharina Bolnes was thereby declared insolvent. She formally renounced any share in her inheritance, and she ceded the estate of Johannes Vermeer to her creditors.

In September 1676 Antoni van Leeuwenhoek of the Delft City Council was appointed executor of Vermeer's estate. This coincidental connection of the two most important creative spirits that Delft had given to the world (as they are pertinently described by Montias) – the great scientist and the truly exceptional artist – has always stirred the imagination of those who have looked into Vermeer's life and art.[297] Born in the same year, they would appear to have been the best-suited of partners. One, a cloth merchant and later a city official, received none of the usual Humanist and philological training, but was active

as an empirical scientist. Initially employing lenses with an especially short focal length, which decisively improved the functioning of the microscope, he ultimately became the leading microscopist of his era, making ground-breaking discoveries ranging from bacteria to blood corpuscles. The other was a painter who engaged, like no other, with optical phenomena, with the representation of fleeting light impressions and with illusion, and thus with sight itself, and captured these phenomena in painting. The notion that the two must surely have met each other at some point in the city, in order to exchange opinions and ideas, has proved hard to resist. It is above all the pendant pictures *The Astronomer* (Cat. 27) and *The Geographer* (Cat. 28) that have been invoked in connection with Antoni van Leeuwenhoek. It has been suggested that he not only commissioned both paintings, but is also depicted in them, although more recent research has shown this to be rather unlikely (see also pp. 240f.).

Antoni van Leeuwenhoek was, however, appointed to serve as the executor of Vermeer's estate on account of his position as Treasurer of the Delft City Council, one of whose duties it was to act as a bailiff, ensuring the compliance of debtors.[298] His activity in this function over the next few months was solely in the interests of Vermeer's creditors, and there is no evidence of a friendly indulgence towards Vermeer's widow and her family. On the contrary, he undertook to uncover every relevant detail regarding the financial circumstances of the widow and her mother. He sent a solicitor to The Hague, where Maria Thins was temporarily staying with relatives, to ask her about the estate of her son, Willem Bolnes, who had died in 1676. He had her swear, on oath, that she was not failing to declare any of the assets of her daughter and her late son-in-law *in fraudem creditorum*, to deceive their creditors. Maria Thins, by this point over 80 years old, had ensured, with great circumspection and resolve, the preservation of her inherited wealth, repeatedly rewriting and reconfirming her will (in January 1677 a fifth version was certified by a notary),[299] in order to deny her heirs any direct access to the family fortune. She named the children of her daughter as her sole heirs, but she stipulated that the property was not to be divided until the youngest grandchild had come of age. By contrast, Catharina Bolnes, the daughter of Maria Thins, received only that fraction to which she was legally entitled, that is to say, a sixth of the inheritance, out of which both her debts and the ongoing costs of bringing up the children had to be met. By this means Maria Thins sought to prevent parts of her fortune falling into the hands of the creditors of her deceased son-in-law.

Antoni van Leeuwenhoek, for his part, declared illegal the transfer, in 1676, of 26 paintings to the Haarlem art dealer Coelenbier, to settle debts owed to Jannetje Stevens.

Allegory of Faith (detail), *c.* 1671–1674
(see ill. p. 297)

He demanded the return of the said pictures and came to a separate agreement with Stevens on a payment of 342 florins of the 442 florins that were originally owed to her. He then arranged a public auction of these paintings to take place on 15 March 1677 at the Delft Guild of Saint Luke. Whereupon Maria Thins, in an *insinuatie*, registered her own protest against the sale of *The Art of Painting*, on the grounds that her daughter had transferred this picture to her, Maria Thins's, possession to settle her debts; and she insisted that legal action would follow if the picture was indeed sold at auction.[300] However, the text of this *insinuatie*, which is concerned exclusively with *The Art of Painting*, does not make entirely clear how this picture came to be added to the group of 26 transferred to Coelenbier.[301] It appears that *The Art of Painting* was, nonetheless, sold at auction along with the other paintings on 15 March 1677. It is certainly possible that this picture subsequently entered the Dissius collection, to be sold, in due course, at the 1696 auction, along with the other Vermeer paintings offered for sale there, as "'t Portrait van Vermeer in een Kamer met verscheyde bywerk ongemeen fraai van hem geschildert" ("the portrait of Vermeer in a room with various accessories, uncommonly beautifully painted by him"). Regrettably, no information on the course and results of the 1677 auction has so far come to light. This event did not mark the end of Antoni van Leeuwenhoek's duties as executor. He retained this position for a few more years. In 1678 he arranged to have sold at auction a house in Gouda and a number of properties that Catharina Bolnes had inherited from her deceased brother, Willem, and for the profits of these sales to be passed on to the creditors. He failed, however, in his attempts to have yet other parts of the inheritance seized, in the face of decisive resistance from Maria Thins. She also stubbornly refused to pay back the loan of 1,000 florins that Johannes Vermeer had taken out shortly before his death to the widow of the creditor in question, or to pay interest on it.[302]

In 1680 Maria Thins, now 87 years old, drew up her sixth and final will, in which she determined that her inherited fortune should remain untouched until her youngest grandchild reached the age of 16. Maria Thins died at the end of December 1680. Her daughter, Vermeer's widow, who had by this date moved to the predominantly Catholic city of Breda, continued to live in difficult financial circumstances and repeatedly had to take out loans. Towards the end of 1687, already gravely ill, she drew up her own will, while on a visit to her eldest daughter, Maria, and she died around New Year 1688. By this time, 13 years after the death of Johannes Vermeer, five of the couple's children were still underage.

The Art of Painting (detail), *c.* 1666–1668
(see ill. p. 265)

The Art of Painting, *c.* 1666–1668
Oil on canvas, 120 x 100 cm / 47 ¼ x 39 ⅜ in.
Vienna, Kunsthistorisches Museum, Gemäldegalerie

Pages 266/267
The Astronomer (detail), 1668
(see ill. p. 269)

The Astronomer, 1668
Oil on canvas, 51.5 x 45.5 cm / 20 ¼ x 17 ⅞ in.
Paris, Musée du Louvre

Pages 270/271
The Geographer (detail), 1669
(see ill. p. 273)

The Geographer, 1669
Oil on canvas, 51.6 x 45.4 cm / 20 ¼ x 17 ⅞ in.
Frankfurt am Main, Städel Museum

I Ver. Meer.
MDCLXVIIII

The Lacemaker, *c.* 1669/70
Oil on canvas, mounted on board, 23.9 x 20.5 cm / 9 3/8 x 8 1/8 in.
Paris, Musée du Louvre

Pages 276/277
The Love Letter (detail), *c.* 1669/70
(see ill. p. 279)

Pieter de Hooch
Young Couple with a Parrot, *c.* 1675–1677
Oil on canvas, 73 x 62 cm / 28 ¾ x 24 ⅜ in.
Cologne, Wallraf Richartz Museum & Fondation Corboud

The Love Letter, *c.* 1669/70
Oil on canvas, 44 x 38 cm / 17 ¾ x 15 in.
Amsterdam, Rijksmuseum

Gerard van Honthorst, **Woman Playing a Guitar**, 1624
Oil on canvas, 82 x 68 cm / 32 ¼ x 26 ¾ in.
Paris, Musée du Louvre

The Guitar Player, *c.* 1669–1672
Oil on canvas, 51.4 x 45 cm / 20 ¼ x 17 ¾ in.
London, Kenwood House, The Iveagh Bequest

Otto van Veen, **"Perfectus amor non est nisi ad unum" emblem** in *Amorum Emblemata*, Antwerp, 1608

Young Woman Standing at a Virginal
(A Lady Standing at a Virginal), *c.* 1670–1672
Oil on canvas, 51.8 x 45.2 cm / 20 3/8 x 17 3/4 in.
London, The National Gallery

Gerard Dou, **Lady at a Clavichord**, *c.* 1665
Oil on board, 37.7 x 29.8 cm / 14 7/8 x 11 3/4 in.
London, Dulwich Picture Gallery

Young Woman Seated at a Virginal, *c.* 1672–1675
Oil on canvas, 51.5 x 45.6 cm / 20 1/4 x 17 7/8 in.
London, The National Gallery, Salting Bequest, 1910

Pages 287–289
A Lady Writing a Letter with Her Maid (detail), *c.* 1670/71
(see ill. p. 291)

A Lady Writing a Letter with Her Maid, *c.* 1670/71
Oil on canvas, 72.2 x 59.7 cm / 28 ⅜ x 23 ½ in.
Dublin, National Gallery of Ireland

Pages 292/293 and 295
Allegory of Faith (details), *c.* 1671–1674
(see ill. p. 297)

J. C. Jegher, **"Capit Quod Non Capit" emblem**
in Guilielmus Hesius, *Emblemata sacra de fide. spe, charitate*, Antwerp, 1636

Allegory of Faith, *c.* 1671–1674
Oil on canvas, 114.3 x 88.9 cm / 45 x 35 in.
New York, The Metropolitan Museum of Art, The Friedsam Collection,
Bequest of Michael Friedsam, 1931

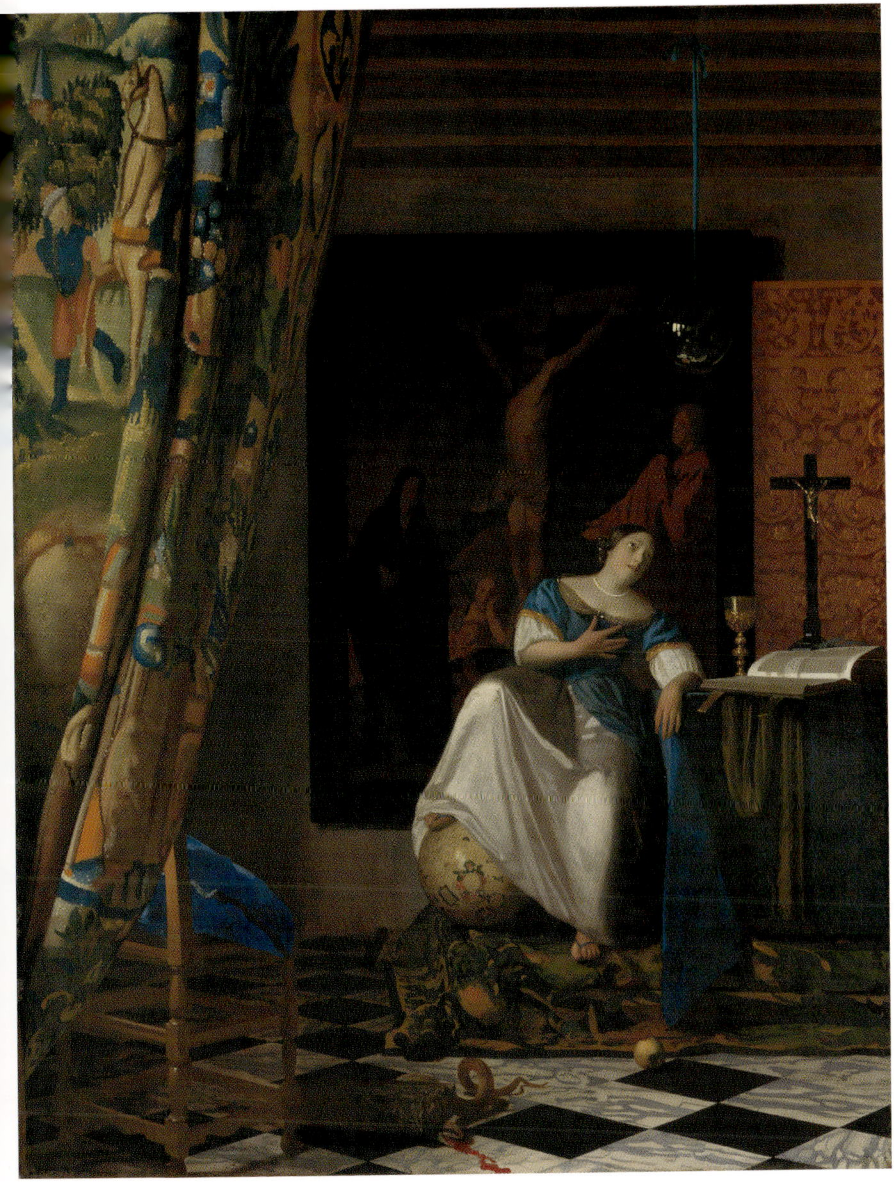

Epilogue: Vermeer's Rediscovery and Later Fame

"Vermeer was... the Dutchest of the Dutch, and verily the noblest and greatest – a classic example of Holland at one with itself."

WILHELM HAUSENSTEIN, 1924

The public perception of Vermeer's life and work is, like that of many other great artists, pervaded by clichés. In accordance with an ideal of the artist rooted in 19th-century Romanticism, the painter was long regarded as an unappreciated genius who had eked out a living in embittered poverty and whose work itself had fallen into oblivion after his death, until someone – himself surely a genius of sorts – was at last able to rescue him from this fate. It was the French art critic Étienne-Joseph Théophile Thoré who "rescued" Vermeer for posterity. The archival research carried out by John Michael Montias has, however, shown that Vermeer's work was neither unknown nor unappreciated during his lifetime. Dutch art historians have, moreover, demonstrated that Vermeer was by no means an altogether unknown figure in his homeland during the 18th and 19th centuries: this is revealed above all by the inclusion of correctly attributed Vermeer pictures in sale catalogues, and the sale prices attained by these, but also by the evidence of works painted in imitation of Vermeer's style, such as those produced around 1800 by Derk Jan van der Laan (1759–1829).[303] Very occasionally, by this time, Vermeer is mentioned in texts of a connoisseurial nature published outside Holland: the French art dealer Jean-Baptiste Pierre Lebrun (1748–1813), for example, in his 1792 compilation of engravings after paintings, *Galerie des peintres flamands, hollandais et allemands* (Gallery of Flemish, Dutch and German Painters), wrote: "This Vermeer, whom the historians do not mention, is worthy of particular attention. He is a great painter in the style of Metsu. His paintings are unusual, and in Holland they are better known, and more highly valued, than anywhere else."[304]

A number of pictures, such as *The Milkmaid* (Cat. 8) or *Woman in Blue Reading a Letter* (Cat. 16), both of which remained in Dutch collections and are now in the Rijksmuseum in Amsterdam, were known, throughout the 18th and 19th centuries, to be the work of Vermeer. In 1719, more than 40 years after the artist's death, *The Milkmaid* was designated, in the inventory drawn up by an Amsterdam collector, as "het vermaerde Melkmeysje, door Vermeer van Delft, konstig" ("the famous Milkmaid by Vermeer of Delft, artful")[305]; and around 100 years later, in 1813, the Amsterdam collector Lucretia Johanna van Winter, who was later to marry Hendrik Six van Hillegom, would acquire this picture for the enormous sum of 2,125 florins.

Somewhat over a third of the paintings by Vermeer now known to us are to be found, designated as works by him, in the inventories of Dutch collections or in the catalogues of Dutch sales compiled during the years between 1700 and 1850. This is an extraordinarily

Page 299
Mistress and Maid (detail), *c.* 1666/67
(see ill. p. 215)

The Glass of Wine (detail), *c.* 1658–1660
(see ill. pp. 166/167)

high proportion, even allowing for the fact that most of these pictures were only once cited as the work of Vermeer before his authorship was again forgotten. *A Young Woman Reading a Letter* (Cat. 5), for example, may perhaps be identified with "Een leezent Vrouwtje in een kamer, door vander Meer van Delft" ("a woman reading, in a room, by vander Meer van Delft"), cited in a sale catalogue of 1712; but in 1742, upon its sale to the Elector Frederick Augustus II of Saxony, who was also King Augustus III of Poland (1696–1763), it was thought to be a work by Rembrandt. Those pictures by Vermeer that entered princely collections during the 18th century were the first to travel beyond the frontiers of Holland, albeit as the work of other artists. It was in the early 18th century that Duke Anthony Ulrich of Brunswick-Wolfenbüttel acquired *The Girl with the Wineglass* (Cat. 10). The picture is mentioned for the first time in 1710, in the first catalogue of the ducal collection, drawn up by the painter Tobias Querfurt (*c.* 1670–1730), who served as the duke's art agent and may be assumed to have arranged the acquisition. And here, notably, reference is made to the relevant entry in the catalogue of the 1696 sale of the Dissius Collection. In 1741 the Elector Frederick Augustus II of Saxony acquired *The Procuress* (Cat. 3), which had earlier been in the collection of Count Waldstein in Bohemia (where it was thought to have been the work of Gerard van Honthorst), and in 1742 *A Young Woman Reading a Letter*, believing it to be a work by Rembrandt. In 1806, by which time this picture was in the collection of the Dresden Gemäldegalerie, it was for the first time identified as the work of "Van der Meer of Delft" in the collection catalogue complied by the *Galerie-Inspektor* Johann Anton Riedel.[306] In 1762 *The Music Lesson* (Cat. 13) was acquired by King George III of Great Britain and Ireland (1738–1820) as a work by Frans van Mieris, although it was later attributed to Eglon van der Neer. And in 1805 *The Art of Painting* (Cat. 26), complete with the faked signature of Pieter de Hooch, and heretofore in the Viennese collection of Gottfried van Swieten, entered the likewise Viennese collection of Count Czernin.

The first significant shift in the emerging posthumous celebrity of Vermeer, at least in his native Holland, may be seen to have occurred with the startling acquisition, in 1822, by the Mauritshuis in The Hague, of *A View of Delft* (Cat. 12). The picture had previously been in a private collection, although it was known through copies. In 1814 a copy made by Pieter-Ernst Hendrik Praetorius (1791–1876) had been put on display in Amsterdam, as "Een Stadsgezicht, zijnde een kopij naar een beroemd Schilderij van den Delftschen Van der Meer"("A Cityscape, being a copy after a famous Painting by the Delft Van der Meer").[307] By its very nature, however, this picture introduced an element of confusion, for it encouraged the false notion of Vermeer as an important landscape painter.

It was at more or less the same time that *The Procuress* (Cat. 3) was first recognized as the work of Vermeer. In the early 19th-century inventories of the Dresden Gallery it had been listed as a work by "Johann van der Meer", apparently on account of the signature;

but it is clear that the artist in question was primarily understood to be Johannes, or Jan, van der Meer the Younger of Haarlem, who was known as a landscape painter. The gallery's collection catalogues published after 1826 listed the picture as the work of "Jacob van der Meer van Utrecht", now probably with reference to a second painter who was both the contemporary and the namesake of Johannes Vermeer: the Utrecht artist Johan van der Meer.[308] Around 1830 the English art dealer, connoisseur and author John Smith (1781–1855), upon visiting the Dresden Gallery, was the first to perceive that the picture was the work of Johannes Vermeer of Delft, as he noted in his own copy of the gallery catalogue.[309] However, as he did not publish his discovery, Thoré-Bürger came to be seen as the first (in 1859) to have recognized *The Procuress* as a work by Vermeer. Thoré-Bürger describes how the reference to "Vermeer" in the catalogue of the Dresden Gallery drew his attention to the picture, which was then hung very high on the gallery wall, and how his connoisseurial eye revealed to him the true authorship of this work.[310] He requested, and was granted, permission to scale a ladder and examine the picture at close quarters. It was thus that he discovered the signature in the lower right corner. The similarity of this signature to others already known to Thoré-Bürger and the painting's date of 1656 established sufficient certainty, to his mind, that this was an early work by Johannes Vermeer.

Thoré-Bürger's most extraordinary achievement lay in grasping the connection between *A View of Delft* and Vermeer's genre paintings. Around 1842 he had, for the first time, seen *A View of Delft* at the Mauritshuis in The Hague, and had been fascinated by the realism and the fidelity to nature in this depiction of the city. He compared Vermeer, an artist heretofore all but unknown to him, with the greatest of all Dutch painters – Rembrandt or Frans Hals – already believing Vermeer to be their equal. During later visits to Holland he saw *The Milkmaid* (Cat. 8) and *The Little Street* (Cat. 9) in the Six

Jacobus Vrel, **Woman at a Window**, 1654
Oil on board, 66.5 x 47.4 cm / 26 1/8 x 18 5/8 in.
Vienna, Kunsthistorisches Museum, Gemäldegalerie

Collection in Amsterdam, finding also in these works by Vermeer the same spirit of truth to reality that he had so much come to value in the work of his own French contemporaries, such as Gustave Courbet (1819–1877). Thoré was especially open to the new currents in contemporary French painting; he revered Eugène Delacroix (1798–1863) and the artists of the Barbizon School, while vehemently rejecting the sort of history painting that proved so successful at the annual Paris Salons. He subsequently went on to welcome the advent of Impressionism and was to be among the first to defend Édouard Manet (1832–1883), in the face of critical disapproval and public opprobrium. As a follower of Pierre Leroux (1797–1871) and the political radicals involved in the revolutionary upheavals of 1848, Thoré had to leave France; and he spent the following years in exile, travelling in England, Holland and Germany, and publishing under the pseudonym William Bürger.

In the first volume of his *Musées de la Hollande*, published in 1858, Thoré-Bürger cited *A View of Delft* and the two pictures from the Six Collection as the work of Vermeer. In 1859, in his catalogue of the Arenberg Collection in Brussels, he added the *Study of a Young Woman* (Cat. 22) to his list. Simultaneously, Gustav Friedrich Waagen (1794–1868), Director of the Berlin Gemäldegalerie and Professor of Art History at the University of Berlin, had become alerted to the phenomenon of Vermeer, and had discovered a further work by this master in *The Art of Painting* (Cat. 26) in the Czernin Collection in Vienna. Thoré had himself assumed that this picture might be by Vermeer, but he had not had the opportunity to view it in the original. In the second volume of his *Musées de la Hollande*, published in 1860, Thoré-Bürger was able to attribute over twice as many works to Vermeer as had previously been the case. And when he brought his publications on the artist to a conclusion, with a long essay in the French journal *Gazette des Beaux-Arts* (1866), Vermeer's oeuvre, as listed there, comprised more than 70 pictures – even though over half of these were, in fact, incorrectly attributed.

The year 1866 was also to see the presentation, in an annexe to the Paris Salon, of an *Exposition rétrospective*, which presented pictures of the 15th to the 19th centuries from several private collections. Eleven of those on display here were attributed to Vermeer, among them four genre paintings: *Cavalier and Young Woman* (Cat. 6), then in the collection of Léopold Double; *The Geographer* (Cat. 28), loaned by Isaac Péreire; and two paintings from Thoré-Bürger's own collection: *Woman with a Pearl Necklace* (Cat. 17) and *Young Woman Standing at a Virginal* (Cat. 33). Of the 11 pictures supposedly by Vermeer, only these four were, in fact, his work. Two of the three landscapes on show came from the Suermondt Collection in Aachen, one of them, the so-called *Cottage rustique* (p. 311), earlier much liked by Thoré-Bürger. There were also four street scenes, likewise from Thoré's own collection. One of these we now know to have been a work by Jacobus Vrel (Los Angeles, J. Paul Getty Museum). The other three are now untraced.[311] Both the public and the critics in Paris were astonished at the thematic variety of the work of this newly discovered artist. The many incorrect attributions, in particular, those incurred through the introduction of work by Jacobus Vrel (*fl. c.* 1654–1662; p. 303),[312] confused the emerging artistic profile of the real Vermeer.

Thoré-Bürger was very much the moving spirit behind the *Exposition rétrospective*. Not only had he organized it, exploiting his good connections with private collectors in order to secure loans; he had also made available works from his own collection. On account of his publications, his contacts with other critics and with collectors, he was now the undisputed authority on Vermeer, and an expert whose assistance was also sought by museums. In 1864, for example, Sir Charles Eastlake, Director of The National Gallery in London, was considering the acquisition of a work by Vermeer for that collection, and found himself constrained to choose between three available paintings: *Mistress and Maid* (Cat. 24), *Woman with a Pearl Necklace* and *Young Woman Standing at a Virginal*, the last two then in Thoré's collection. Eastlake was, in fact, satisfied with none of the three, so that no acquisition was made at this point. The last-named picture did eventually enter the National Gallery in London, but only after the sale of Thoré's collection, in 1892. Thoré-Bürger jealously upheld his reputation as the "discoverer" of Vermeer, to the extent of openly protesting when Gustav Waagen claimed to have himself first recognized *The Art of Painting* as a work by the artist. Thoré-Bürger's outstanding achievement, the significance of which is still acknowledged, lay in having rediscovered, and then published, around half of the pictures now accepted as the work of Vermeer, on the basis of his initial knowledge of only three paintings. By comparison with this achievement, the fact that he also included in his catalogue a fair number of false attributions pales into relative insignificance. Dying in 1869, Thoré-Bürger was never to see how the fame of the artist he had rediscovered would continue to grow over the final decades of the 19th century, hand in hand with a marked rise in the sale prices achieved on the art market by the few works that emerged, one by one, from private collections.

It was also thanks to Thoré-Bürger that interest in Vermeer increased in Holland itself. On the advice of Wilhelm von Bode (1845–1929), Chief Curator of the Berlin Museums, the young Dutch art historian Abraham Bredius resolved not to study the painting of the Italian Renaissance but to focus, rather, on that of the Dutch Golden Age. Bredius made his name as a Vermeer specialist with his discovery that a landscape in the Barthold Suermondt Collection, attributed to Vermeer by Thoré-Bürger, who termed the work *Cottage rustique*, was in fact a work of the early 19th century by Derk Jan van der Laan (1759–1829; p. 311; now in the Gemäldegalerie, Berlin).[313] In parallel with his life-long preoccupation with the work of Rembrandt, the discovery of further heretofore unknown works by Vermeer and his systematic trawling of the Dutch archives for relevant documents were the central concerns of Bredius's career. The monumental end result of his research was a series of seven volumes: the *Künstler-Inventare*.[314]

The contribution of Bredius, with all his connoisseurial authority, was to prove crucial in the discovery of the two early works by Vermeer (Cat. 1, 2), and the light this threw on his beginnings as an artist. While the recognition that *The Procuress* was a work by Vermeer was rapidly made known with the publication of the Dresden Gallery catalogue of 1862, and was not subsequently called into question, the situation was quite different in the case of the even earlier work *Diana and Her Companions* (Cat. 1), not least on account of its mythological subject, which was seen as unusual for Vermeer. It was, accordingly, quite some time before a satisfactory interpretation of the available evidence was attained.[315] Acquired by the Mauritshuis in 1876, at the auction of a Dutch private collection, as a work by Nicolaes Maes, the composition with Diana was reattributed, above all, as a result of investigation and reinterpretation of the barely legible signature. Although the original monogram (correctly associated with Johannes Vermeer van Delft in the current collection catalogue produced by Victor de Stuers) had been detected beneath the faked signature of Nicolaes Maes in 1885, Abraham Bredius, since 1889 Director of the Mauritshuis, had strong – though, as it was to prove, unfounded – reservations about this attribution. In the process of preparing a new critical catalogue of the Mauritshuis collection, a number of signatures were examined, and it was thereby discovered that "the fake signature N. M. had been concocted out of what remained of the original monogram Jv. Meer" ("de valsche handteekening N. M. vervaardigd [was] uit de overblijfselen van Jv. Meer").[316] Bredius persisted, however, in his doubts, now believing *Diana and Her Companions* to be the work of the Utrecht painter Johan van der Meer, on account of the great stylistic difference between this work and the other Vermeer paintings in the Mauritshuis (*A View of Delft* and *Girl with a Pearl Earring*) and the obvious Italian influence on the composition with Diana.[317] It was not until 1895 that Jan Veth and Cornelis Gerardus 't Hooft were able firmly to establish *Diana and Her Companions* as the work of Johannes Vermeer, through their arguments on stylistic grounds.[318] In 1901, when *Christ in the House of Mary and Martha* (Cat. 2) emerged on the London art market, there could no longer be any doubt that both this and the composition with Diana were by the same artist, namely Johannes Vermeer.

On account of its signature, and through comparsion with *The Procuress*, the newly discovered picture was determined to be an early work by Vermeer.[319] In Holland the new discovery of a heretofore unknown work was found to be sensational, not least on account of the biblical theme – the revelation of a new and surprising aspect of the artist's output. It was only upon travelling to London and looking at the newly discovered work for himself that Bredius felt sure that *Christ in the House of Mary and Martha* and *Diana and Her*

The Girl with the Wineglass (detail), *c.* 1659/60
(see ill. pp. 161)

Companions must be the work of one and the same artist. But, on account of its technical virtuosity, the London picture led Bredius to believe that it could not be the work of a beginner. To his mind it remained yet to be established that the painter of these two works was identical with Johannes Vermeer. Were these pictures by him, Bredius now argued, they must surely date from a time when he was painting in a style quite different from that of his other work, and very much under an Italian influence.[320] The Deputy Director of the Mauritshuis, Wilhelm Martin (1876–1954), who saw the picture in London at the same time as Bredius, argued that all three pictures – the newly discovered *Christ in the House of Mary and Martha, Diana and Her Companions* in the Mauritshuis and *The Procuress* in Dresden – were indeed the work of one and the same artist, namely Johannes Vermeer of Delft, among other reasons on account of the similarity between the table carpets seen in both the London picture and that in the Dresden collection.

Around 1900 and in the following years it was, above all, collectors from the United States who proved especially attentive to Vermeer and who acquired his paintings at record prices. As a result of this transatlantic trade in Vermeers, there are now only seven paintings by the artist to be found in collections in Holland, while 13 are in American museums: five in The Metropolitan Museum of Art in New York, four in the National Gallery of Art in Washington, D.C., three in The Frick Collection in New York and one painting in the Isabella Stewart Gardner Museum in Boston (today lost). In other words, around a quarter of all the Vermeers we know of are now in collections in New York. The first painting by Vermeer to enter an American collection was *Young Woman with a Water Pitcher* (Cat. 14). This was acquired, in Paris, by the New York banker, and Treasurer of The Metropolitan Museum of Art, Henry G. Marquand (1819–1902). An exhibition of works from his collection, mounted at The Metropolitan Museum of Art in 1888, proved so successful that he resolved to donate the 35 pictures on display, one of them the aforementioned Vermeer, to this great New York institution. In 1892, when Thoré-Bürger's former collection was sold at auction in Paris, Isabella Stewart Gardner (1840–1924) arranged for *The Concert* (Cat. 19) to be acquired for her own collection, which was subsequently to be housed in the purpose-built Isabella Stewart Gardner Museum in Boston. A third work by Vermeer to arrive in the United States before 1900 was *Woman with a Lute* (Cat. 15): Collis P. Huntington (1821–1900) had bought this picture in Paris, and in 1900 it entered The Metropolitan Museum of Art as his bequest. Huntington had made his fortune through the construction of the first American transcontinental railway, and he later became one of the most generous supporters of The Metropolitan Museum. In the early years of the 20th century the industrialist Henry Clay Frick (1849–1919) bought *Young Woman Interrupted at Music* (Cat. 11), subsequently acquiring both the *Cavalier and Young Woman* (Cat. 6) in 1911, and *Mistress and Maid* (Cat. 24) in 1919, the year of his death. All three paintings had been sold to Frick by the New York art dealer Knoedler, and in 1913/14 they were installed in Frick's New York house, which in 1935 became the publicly accessible Frick Collection. One can say with some justification that all the great American art collectors who were active around 1900 acquired pictures by Vermeer. In addition to Isabella Stewart Gardner, Collis P. Huntington and Henry Clay Frick, this group notably included the banker John Pierpont Morgan, Sr. (1837–1913), who in 1907 acquired *A Lady Writing* (Cat. 20), a picture offered to him by the New York art dealer G. S. Hellman for 100,000 dollars, and which Morgan readily acquired even though not previously familiar with the artist and his work. Morgan loaned the picture to The Metropolitan Museum, but his son decided to sell it. It eventually entered the collection of the National Gallery of Art in Washington, D.C., in 1962, as a gift of the heirs of another prominent American collector, Horace Havemeyer (1886–1956).

The sale of pictures by Vermeer to American collectors in due course prompted a reaction in Holland. In 1905, upon the death of Pieter Hendrik Six, the Rembrandt Society hoped to acquire 39 paintings in the then publicly accessible Six Collection for donation to the Rijksmuseum in Amsterdam. The Society was, however, able to raise only 200,000 florins towards the total purchase price, and therefore sought state support in finding the remaining 550,000 florins. On this occasion the young art historian Frits Lugt issued a pamphlet arguing against the acquisition of these works by the state. Abraham Bredius, by contrast (who suspected that a plan to sell *The Milkmaid* to Pierpont Morgan lay behind Lugt's protest), sought to persuade the Dutch government to support and assist the acquisition. Public opinion in general agreed with Bredius and the Dutch Parliament eventually decided, after a vote in favour, to make available the required funds.[321]

In the years before the First World War two further pictures by Vermeer entered collections in the United States. In 1908 *A Maid Asleep* (Cat. 4) was acquired by Benjamin Altman (1840–1913), who had founded one of the first New York department stores. Like most of the pictures in Altman's collection, this was acquired through the Duveen Gallery in London. Having no children to whom to leave his collection, Altman bequeathed it to The Metropolitan Museum of Art. In 1911 *Woman with a Balance* (Cat. 18) was sold by the art dealers Colnaghi and Knoedler to Peter A. B. Widener (1834–1915) of Philadelphia, at the time one of the richest men in America, whose first fortune had been made through the sale of provisions to Union forces during the American Civil War. His son, Joseph E. Widener (1872–1943), bequeathed the Vermeer picture, along with the rest of the Widener Collection – which now also included the *Girl with a Flute* (Cat. 25), acquired in 1923 (a work discovered by Abraham Bredius) – to the National Gallery of Art in Washington, D.C.

The Girl with the Red Hat (Cat. 23) was discovered in a private collection in Paris and was published for the first time in 1925. The same year it was sold by the art dealer Knoedler to Andrew W. Mellon (1855–1937), banker, Treasury Secretary and art collector, for 290,000 dollars. In 1927 Mellon proposed that an American National Gallery be founded, with his own collection serving as its core. This plan was in due course realized, and in 1941 the National Gallery of Art in Washington, D.C., was formally opened. In 1928 the New York department store owner Michael Friedsam (1858–1931) acquired the *Allegory of Faith* (Cat. 34), a picture first identified as the work of Vermeer in 1899, by Bredius, who had acquired it for his own collection. In 1931 it entered the collection of The Metropolitan Museum of Art, as Friedsam's bequest. The last painting by Vermeer to enter an American collection was the *Study of a Young Woman* (Cat. 22). This was one of the first six pictures that Thoré-Bürger had recognized in 1859 as the work of Vermeer. At that date in the Arenberg Collection, it was in 1955 acquired by Charles Wrightsman (1895–1986), a prominent patron, over several decades, of The Metropolitan Museum of Art, to which he gave the picture in 1979.

After nearly 60 years as a recognized connoisseur of the work of Vermeer, Abraham Bredius became involved in an unfortunate art scandal. In autumn 1937 he was shown a religious composition, *The Supper at Emmaus* (p. 312, now in the Museum Boijmans Van Beuningen, Rotterdam), which had supposedly come from an old private collection in Holland. After initial hesitation, he felt sufficiently sure that this was a painting by Johannes Vermeer to publish it, as a new discovery, in the leading British art journal *The Burlington Magazine*.[322] The work was, in fact, a fake, made by Han (Henricus Antonius) van Meegeren (1889–1947).[323] The Director of the then Museum Boijmans in Rotterdam, Dirk Hannema, the first person whom Bredius told of his discovery, immediately made every effort to acquire the picture for the collection. (It was the most important art museum in Holland after the Rijksmuseum in Amsterdam and the Mauritshuis in The Hague, but it as yet owned no work by Vermeer.) Bredius and Hannema, in addition to other Dutch art experts, were firmly convinced that the newly discovered work was of outstanding national significance as part of the cultural heritage, and therefore must, at any cost, remain in Holland. Even the Rijksmuseum endeavoured to acquire the picture, notwithstanding the initial reservations of its own Director, Frederik Schmidt-Degener, on grounds of quality. But Hannema had proved quicker in raising funds for the acquisition. In his correspondence with Schmidt-Degener, Abraham Bredius made the following telling declaration: "It is frightful that Vermeer, a man capable of painting *The Supper at Emmaus*, had to paint little pictures in the style of Dou and Mieris in order to be able to support his family (he had 11 children). Those works were of course marvels of light and colour, yet where was the sublime conception and the depth of feeling in them?"[324] Not only was Bredius entirely convinced that his "new discovery" was an authentic work by Vermeer; he quite evidently believed this work, on account of its biblical subject, to be far more artistically significant than the genre scenes that typified Vermeer's output. Among other things, this demonstrates how deeply ensnared was this great connoisseur of Vermeer's

work in traditional art-historical notions of the relative importance of the various artistic categories, in particular, the belief that history painting (that is to say, work treating mythological, biblical or historical themes) was to be valued more highly than other categories (genre paintings, portraits, still lifes or landscapes). The picture was eventually acquired for the Museum Boijmans in Rotterdam by the Rembrandt Society (with the assistance of private donors, among them the ship owner Willem van der Vorm) for 520,000 florins. After restoration – the canvas was lined and the varnish refreshed – the picture went on public display, as a sensational new acquisition, in an exhibition of masterpieces from Dutch private collections.

Over the next few years further Vermeer fakes by Van Meegeren emerged in Holland, offered to art dealers and museums by a variety of middlemen.[325] In January 1941 the Amsterdam art dealer Hoogendijk – who had already been involved in the acquisition of *The Supper at Emmaus* – paid 400,000 guilders for a *Head of Christ* (now in the Museum Boijmans Van Beuningen, Rotterdam), supposedly painted by Vermeer, which he was acquiring on behalf of the Rotterdam collector Daniël George van Beuningen (1877–1955). A few months later Hoogendijk was offered, by the same intermediary, a further picture supposedly by Vermeer, though in this case much larger, at around two and a half metres in breadth: a *Last Supper* (now in a Dutch private collection). This, too, was sold to Van Beuningen – not least in order to prevent its sale to the prominent Nazi Reichsmarschall Hermann Göring (Holland being at this time under German Occupation). For this work Van Beuningen paid the enormous sum of 1,500,000 guilders. In order to raise this he had had to sell to Germany 19 pictures from his own collection, including the only recently acquired *Head of Christ*.

In 1942 there emerged a Vermeer fake of the *Blessing of Jacob* (now in the Museum Boijmans Van Beuningen, Rotterdam), and in 1943 a depiction of *The Washing of the Feet* (now in the Rijksmuseum, Amsterdam). This last picture was first offered to the art dealer De

Derk Jan van der Laan, **Cottage rustique**, *c.* 1800
Berlin, Staatliche Museen zu Berlin, Gemäldegalerie

Boer: it was in a poor state of repair, and it had no sort of frame, being merely fixed with drawing pins to a piece of plywood. De Boer showed the picture to Erhard Göpel, who had been commissioned to make acquisitions in Holland of artworks destined for Adolf Hitler's planned "Führermuseum" in Linz. But Göpel's superior, Hermann Voss, then Director of the Dresden Gemäldegalerie, and charged with special responsibility for the planned Linz museum, believed the picture to be a fake and decided against its acquisition. It was also dismissed as a recent fake by J. Q. van Regteren Altena. Other well-known art experts, however, among them J. G. van Gelder, Vitale Bloch and Max Friedländer, were convinced that the picture was the work of Vermeer. Eduard Plietzsch, who had recently published the most important German-language Vermeer biography for some time, hailed the picture as a masterpiece by Vermeer, noting in particular its affinity with Expressionist painting of the 20th century.[326] In view of observations of this sort, and the doubts voiced here and there, it is astonishing that the emergence of so many "newly discovered Vermeers" within such a short space of time did not lead to the unmasking of these works as fakes far sooner than was the case. Even *The Washing of the Feet* was acquired by the Dutch state for the Rijksmuseum, at the cost of over 1,000,000 guilders – not least so as to "save for the nation" a work of such supposed significance as part of the cultural heritage. As in all the sales taking place after 1940, this one was arranged privately and was not announced.

It was only in 1945 that the sudden emergence of so many supposed paintings by Vermeer was revealed as a massive exercise in art forgery. In late May of that year, shortly after the end of the Second World War, Han van Meegeren had been arrested in Holland as a suspected collaborator, having been found responsible for the sale, to the German banker and art dealer Alois Miedl (who had been running the Amsterdam Galerie Goudstikker), of a *Christ and the Woman Taken in Adultery* supposedly by Vermeer (now with the Rijksdienst voor het Cultureel Erfgoed, Holland), which Miedl had in 1942 sold on to Hermann Göring. Göring had had the picture taken to Carinhall, his country residence north-east of

Han van Meegeren, **The Supper at Emmaus**, before 1937
Oil on canvas, 118 x 130.5 cm / 46 ½ x 51 ⅜ in.
Rotterdam, Museum Boijmans Van Beuningen

Berlin; but at a later stage of the War his entire collection had been brought, for safekeeping, to the salt mine at Bad Aussee in Austria. The collection was discovered there in May 1945 by US Army troops. The sale to the German Occupiers of artworks deemed to be part of the Dutch cultural heritage and of great national significance was categorized as "collaboration" and incurred severe punishment. Presented with the charge of collaboration, Han van Meegeren was able to defend himself on the grounds that the picture sold on by Miedl to Göring had not, in fact, been a Vermeer, but merely one of the fakes that he, Van Meegeren, had himself produced – he had, indeed, also produced all five of the supposed "Vermeers" that had emerged in Holland since 1937, in addition to two fakes in the style of Pieter de Hooch. As a proof of his abilities as a forger, he painted, under surveillance, a further Vermeer fake: *The Twelve-Year-Old Jesus at the Temple*. As a result, the charge of "collaboration" was dropped, and in early 1946 Van Meegeren was released. He was, however, almost immediately charged with fraud and art forgery, and was tried on these counts in Amsterdam in October 1947. Meanwhile, a Commission led by Paul Coremans, Head of the Scientific Laboratory of the Musées Royaux / Koninklijke Musea in Brussels, investigated eight of Van Meegeren's forgeries – two in the style of Pieter de Hooch, six in the style of Vermeer – and discovered evidence, of both a chemical and a technical nature, that the pictures had indeed been painted in the 20th century. One key factor was the presence of bakelite. Van Meegeren was, accordingly, sentenced to 12 months in prison. But he died of a heart attack at the end of 1947, shortly before he was due to start his sentence.

When he was on trial Van Meegeren had endeavoured to present himself as a patriot, who had cheated the German Occupiers with his faked versions of Dutch art, which they had taken for masterpieces. He acquired a certain popularity among the Dutch public: for not only had he deceived the Occupiers, he had also deceived the art experts. He had, in fact, been active as an art forger since the early 1920s. He was certainly possessed of considerable artistic talent, and he had first acquired an enthusiasm for the Dutch Old Masters while still at school. But his father had refused to let him study art, insisting that he train to be an architect. In 1913, however, after six years, Van Meegeren abandoned his architectural studies and enrolled at the Art Academy in The Hague, intending to train as a painter. He won a prize for a view of the interior of the Laurenskerk in Rotterdam. Leaving the Art Academy in 1914, he held his first exhibition only three years later, at the renowned Kunstzaal Pictura in The Hague. It now looked as if the young artist had a bright future, and he found himself in particular demand as a portrait painter. His pictures drew their inspiration from the art of the Old Masters. Some of his studies of heads were painted in the manner of Frans Hals. But in the 1920s he came to see his career as an artist endangered by the frequent complaint of art critics that his work was derivative and devoid of inspiration. At the same time he discovered that his copies after the works of the Old Masters might well serve as forgeries. For he used materials "authentic" to the period of the work that he was imitating, and he also sought to give his works the appearance of age, much aided in this by the restorer and forger Theo van Wijngaarden. In 1923 Cornelis Hofstede de Groot (1863–1930) stated his conviction that a *Laughing Cavalier* by Van Meegeren was a genuine work by Frans Hals. The work was shortly afterwards revealed to be a fake: it had been painted not with oils but with a modern form of tempera. Even at that early date there were suspicions that Han van Meegeren was the forger, but it proved impossible to identify who had been responsible for this particular fake. This was also the case in 1932, when Abraham Bredius declared a *Lady at a Spinet with a Cavalier* (now with the Rijksdienst voor het Cultureel Erfgoed, Holland) to be a work by Vermeer. This picture was later generally believed to be a work by Van Meegeren, although this could not be proved.

In 1932 Van Meegeren moved, with his second wife and her daughter, to the south of France. It was there that he perfected his technique. After a total of six years of preparation, he embarked on painting his masterpiece of forgery, *The Supper at Emmaus* (p. 312). He had acquired 17th-century canvas and he employed pigments that were in use at that time. He used the artificial material bakelite as a binding agent because, upon hardening, this produced the impression of an old painting in oils. Once completed, the painting was "baked" in order to hasten the aging process, then rolled to produce an appropriate amount of surface *craquelure*. Van Meegeren had a detailed knowledge of the early work of Vermeer, and he thus knew that a history painting by a Dutch artist of Vermeer's era would be expected to evince an Italian influence. For this reason he based the compostion of his forged Vermeer on Caravaggio's treatment of *The Supper at Emmaus* (Pinacoteca di Brera, Milan).

When we now look at this picture and at other forgeries by Van Meegeren, it is hard to believe that these were not immediately recognized as the work of a contemporary, so evocative are they of the characteristics of painting in the 1930s, be it in their hint of *Neue Sachlichkeit* (New Sobriety) or even the sort of pseudo-Classicism much favoured under fascism. While the art world was devastated by the discovery of Van Meegeren's machinations (and this was immediately apparent in the paragraphs added to the Vermeer monographs published in the years that followed),[327] the scandal did not impinge upon the now well-established image of Johannes Vermeer as one of the greatest masters of Dutch painting and, indeed, one of the world's greatest artists.

The Procuress (detail), 1656 (see ill. p. 85)

Page 317
The Art of Painting (detail), *c.* 1666–1668 (see ill. p. 265)

Page 318
The Geographer (detail), 1669 (see ill. p. 273)

Catalogue

"At last he came to the Vermeer which he remembered as more striking, more different from anything else he knew..."

MARCEL PROUST, 1923

I Ver-Meer
MDCLXVIIII

Preliminary Remarks

The catalogue incorporates all 35 paintings that are generally accepted as autograph works by Johannes Vermeer. All of these are in the collections of publicly accessible museums. In an Appendix, entitled "Questionable Attributions", I discuss two pictures that have emerged in recent decades and have been attributed to the artist. Since these featured, as autograph works, in the latest monographic exhibition on Vermeer (Rome 2012/13), they are included here. In the opinion of this author, however, neither attribution is convincing.

No further early – and now discounted – attributions are mentioned. The most extensive compilation of autograph works attributed to Vermeer – comprising 42 pictures, in addition to 16 works known only indirectly, through documentation, and a further 11 questionable attributions – can be found in Bianconi 1967. For commentary on further erroneously attributed early works, see Blankert 1975 (and all subsequent editions, from 1986 to 2007, cited as Blankert/Montias/Aillaud), p. 112, note 5, and Broos 1998.

Each catalogue entry follows the same pattern: it supplies information on the provenance of the picture, and on attribution and dating, in addition to brief comments on iconography and on the settings, figures and objects depicted. Formal and thematic issues are considered at greater length in the book's main section, the relevant pages of which are cited at the end of each catalogue entry. Complete information on provenance is listed in Walter Liedtke's 2008 catalogue raisonné, as well as in the catalogue of the exhibition mounted in Washington, D.C., and The Hague in 1995/96. That catalogue (cited here as Washington/The Hague 1995/96) also supplies an extensive commentary on provenance in the entries on the pictures exhibited on that occasion, written by Ben Broos. The most complete collection of documents is provided in Montias 1989, excerpts of which are reproduced in the various editions (1975 to 2007) of Albert Blankert's catalogue raisonné (here cited, in the original Dutch, as Blankert 1992, from the second, 1992 impression of the Dutch edition of Blankert/Montias/Aillaud; see also Documentary Sources, pp. 403–414).

The bibliographical references include only a selection of the profusion of publications on Johannes Vermeer. Emphasis is here placed on the standard catalogues raisonnés published over the past four decades, the specialist literature most pertinent to each painting and the most recent exhibition catalogues.

I

I

Diana and Her Companions, *c.* 1654
Oil on canvas, 97.8 x 104.6 cm / 38 ½ x 41 ⅛ in., signed bottom left, on rock, between dog and thistle: JVMeer (VM in ligature, barely legible)
The Hague, Koninklijk Kabinet van Schilderijen Mauritshuis, inv. 406

Nothing is known of the provenance and early history of this picture. Shortly before 1866 it was purchased, from the art dealer Dirksen in The Hague, by the art collector Neville Davidson Goldsmid (1814–1875). In 1876, after the latter's death, it was auctioned in Paris as a work by Nicolaes Maes (1634–1693). It was bought at auction for 10,000 francs, for the Mauritshuis in The Hague, by Victor de Stuers (1842–1916), a Dutch Ministry of the Interior official with responsibility for works of art. The picture was first attributed to Johannes Vermeer van Delft in 1885, in response to a new interpretation of the signature, which had until then been read as "N. M.". The great stylistic differences between *Diana and Her Companions* and *A View of Delft* (Cat. 12), on display in the same room at the Mauritshuis, made it difficult, however, to believe that both pictures were by one and the same artist. In 1892 the Director of the Mauritshuis, Abraham Bredius (1855–1946), had the signature re-examined. It now emerged that the monogram "N. M." had been contrived at a later date from what remained of the poorly preserved original signature "JVMeer". It was accordingly removed. For his part, Bredius believed the picture, on account of its apparent Italian influence, to be a work by the little-known Utrecht painter Jan van der Meer (1630–1695/97; on whom see Broersma 2010). It was not until 1895 that Jan Veth and Cornelis Gerardus 't Hooft rejected the attribution to Jan van der Meer on stylistic grounds, basing their own attribution to Johannes Vermeer van Delft on the evidence of the picture's colouring and the artist's painting technique (Buijsen 2010b, p. 41). And it was only in 1901, when *Christ in the House of Mary and Martha* (Cat. 2) turned up on the London art market, that there could no longer be any

Condition before restoration in 1999/2000

doubt that both pictures were by the same artist, namely, Johannes Vermeer.

Diana and Her Companions is held by most commentators to be the earliest surviving work by Vermeer, painted immediately after his admittance, as an independent master, to the Delft Guild of Saint Luke, and thus completed, at the earliest, in 1654. Liedtke (2008, pp. 22 and 56) and, following him, Buijsen (2010a, p. 15) and Neidhardt (in Neidhardt/Kettner 2010, p. 130, cat. 1) date the painting to around 1653/54. Blankert (most recently 2010, p. 34) and Wheelock (in Wheelock/Broos 1995, cat. 3: *c.* 1655/56), on the other hand, date it to one or two years later, believing *Christ in the House of Mary and Martha* to be the earlier picture.

We here see Diana surrounded by her attendants. Vermeer does not follow iconographic tradition and shows the goddess of the moon and of hunting or her nymphs in a state of nakedness. All, rather, are fully clothed.

At an unknown date, around 12 centimetres were trimmed from the right edge of the picture. The originally dark background towards the upper right was repainted (perhaps in the mid-19th century) as a pale, overcast sky. At the time of the picture's restoration, in 1999/2000, it was ascertained that the pigments employed for this patch of sky contained Prussian blue (in use from 1704) and chrome green (known from around 1840), and that beneath these were preserved traces of the original dark background. It was resolved to cover the overcast sky with a thin, dark brown paint consistent with the traces of the original background (Kolfin/Pottasch/Hoppe 2002). The restoration of the dark background has given a new character to the entire composition.

See also pp. 50–54, *80/81*.

LITERATURE: Gowing 1952 (1970), pp. 24, 79, 91–97; De Vries 1954, pp. 40–42; Van Gelder 1956, pp. 245–248; Slatkes 1981, pp. 18f.; Wheelock 1981 (1988), p. 68; Blankert/Montias/Aillaud 1986 (1987, 1992, 2007), pp. 71–73, 171, cat. 2; Broos 1993, pp. 306–314, cat. 37; Schneider 1993 (2010), pp. 22f.; Wheelock 1995b, pp. 29–37, 163f.; Wheelock/Broos 1995, pp. 96–101, cat. 3; Rotterdam/Frankfurt

2

1999/2000, pp. 312–315, cat. 62; Liedtke 2000, pp. 191–194; Liedtke 2001f, pp. 359–363, cat. 64; Kolfin/Pottasch/Hoppe 2002, pp. 99–103; Liedtke 2008, pp. 22–24, 56–59, cat. 1; Blankert 2010, pp. 34f.; Buijsen 2010a, p. 15ff.; Buijsen 2010b, pp. 40f.; Büttner 2010, pp. 25–28; Kettner 2010, p. 58; Neidhardt/Kettner 2010, p. 130, cat. 1; Blanc 2014, pp. 194–200.

2

Christ in the House of Mary and Martha, *c.* 1655
Oil on canvas, 160 x 142 cm / 63 x 56 in., signed bottom left, on the bench: IVMeer (IVM in ligature)
Edinburgh, National Galleries of Scotland, inv. 1670

Nothing is known of who commissioned Vermeer to produce this work, nor of its early history. It is perhaps identical with a picture of this subject to be found in 1829 in the collection of John Hugh Smyth Pigott, at Brockley Hall, Somerset, where it was attributed to Raphael (1483–1520). Around 1880 it was in the Abbot Collection, Bristol; and thereafter in that of Arthur Leslie Colley, London. In 1901 it was with the London art dealer Forbes & Paterson; subsequently, it was acquired by the Scots twine manufacturer William Allan Coats (1853–1926), of Skelmorlie Castle, Dalskairth (Dumfries and Galloway, Scotland). It was presented to the National Gallery of Scotland, Edinburgh, in 1927 by his heirs, Thomas H. Coats and J. A. Coats.

In 1901, when the picture was still with the London art dealer Forbes & Paterson, it was cleaned. During this process Vermeer's signature was discovered, and its significance was immediately recognized and published (MacColl 1901). With its biblical subject, its composition with life-size figures, its intense and luminous colours, and its paint applied thickly and with broad brushstrokes, the picture was very different from the artist's later work and brought to light an entirely new and surprising aspect of his output (on the story of the picture's discovery, see Buijsen 2010b, pp. 41f.).

The composition is unanimously believed to be one of Vermeer's early works, most commentators dating it to around 1654/55 (Liedtke 2008, p. 60; Schneider 2010, p. 20) or around 1655 (Wheelock, in Wheelock/Broos 1995, p. 90).

Opinions vary, however, on its position in relation to *Diana and Her Companions* (Cat. 1). Blankert (most recently 2010, p. 33) regards *Christ in the House of Mary and Martha* to be the earlier painting because, according to him, closer inspection reveals it to be a less mature work and because *Diana and Her Companions* evinces, by comparison, an increase in Vermeer's artistic abilities. Several authors agree with this view, among them Wheelock (in Wheelock/Broos 1995, p. 90, cat. 2) and Schneider (2010, p. 20), while others, for example, Liedtke (most recently 2008, p. 60) and Buijsen (2010a, p. 17), regard *Christ in the House of Mary and Martha* as the later painting. The subject of Vermeer's picture is Christ's visit to the house of Mary and Martha (Luke 10: 38-42), prompting the two sisters to adopt opposing attitudes: while Martha proceeds to serve Christ, Mary sits at His feet.

Remarkable, in any case, are Vermeer's confident mastery of the technical aspects of painting, his swift and fluid application of paint with powerful impasto, showing no hint of the hesitancy of a beginner, as well as his independent and emphatically individual reworking of diverse stylistic models. The room in the background, sketched in with just a few paler and darker brushstrokes, consists purely of layers of a thin, brown glaze over the red ground. Here already is evidence of a later characteristic of Vermeer's representation of space, treated as a planar pattern made up of horizontals and verticals that are in themselves essentially abstract. See also pp. 54–59, *83*.

LITERATURE: MacColl 1901; Gowing 1952 (1970), pp. 79–84, no. 1; Wheelock 1981 (1988), p. 64; Blankert/Montias/Aillaud 1986 (1987/1992/2007), pp. 40, 51, 72, 74–77, 79, 98, 171, cat. 1; Buijs 1989; Schneider 1993 (2010), p. 21; Wheelock/Broos 1995, pp. 90–95, cat. 2; Liedtke 2000, pp. 194–198; New York/

3

London 2001, pp. 363–365, cat. 65; Liedtke 2008, pp. 60f., cat. 2; Blankert 2010, p. 33; Buijsen 2010a, pp. 17f.; Buijsen 2010b, pp. 41ff.; Büttner 2010, pp. 23–25; Neidhardt/Kettner 2010, p. 131, cat. 2; Blanc 2014, pp. 130, 288–292, 317.

3
The Procuress, 1656
Oil on canvas, 143 x 130 cm / 56 ⅜ x 51 ¼ in., signed and dated bottom left: ivMeer / 1656 (ivM in monogram)
Dresden, Staatliche Kunstsammlungen, Gemäldegalerie Alte Meister, inv. 1335

This work is perhaps identical to a picture from the collection of Willem Six that was sold at auction for 26 florins in Amsterdam on 12 May 1724, as "Hondhorst, De Vyf Sinnen" (Mayer-Meintschel 2004, p. 31). In 1737, by this date in the collection of Count Waldstein in Dux, Bohemia (now Duchcov, near Teplice, Czech Republic), it was first cited in a printed inventory, as "Ein Stuck mit Vier Persohnen in Lebens-Grösse von Hondhorst" / "A piece with four life-size figures by Hondhorst". In 1741 it was acquired from the Waldstein Collection by the Elector Frederick Augustus II of Saxony (1696–1763) as a work by Gerard van Honthorst (1592–1656).

In the Dresden Gallery inventories of the 18th and early 19th centuries the picture was listed as the work of Johann (Jean, Giovanni) or Jacob van der Meer, on account of the monogram, albeit without any notion of who the artist might really be. His identity was first recognized in the 1830s by John Smith (1781–1855), who did not, however, publish this insight. The picture's discovery was claimed by the French art critic Étienne-Joseph Théophile Thoré (1807–1869), who also published as William Bürger and in 1859 published it as the work of Johannes Vermeer van Delft.

Of the three dated pictures by Vermeer, this is the earliest. With its date of 1656, it establishes a fixed point for the chronological arrangement of the other early works. We see four half-length figures: a courtesan and her lover,

4

behind him a procuress and to the left a musician, here in the role of an observer, who looks at the viewer. This mediating "fictional narrator" (as he was termed by Marcus Dekiert) is dressed in black and remains largely in shadow at the edge of the composition, although he is closer to the viewer than are the other figures. The carpet, which occupies almost the entire lower half of the composition, is an accurately rendered example of the Ushak medallion type, made around 1600 in the Ushak district of western Anatolia (p. 84). Vermeer depicts only two small sections of the carpet: the corner with its red border and a lateral, secondary medallion bisected by the border, with red tendrils and white flowers on a blue background; and a small piece of the neighbouring dark blue background with yellow ornaments.

In 2004 a thorough restoration and surface cleaning of the picture was completed (Dresden 2004/05). Since then it has appeared substantially brighter and more transparent, and its colours more luminous.

See also pp. 59–66, *85*.

Literature: Gowing 1952 (1970), pp. 84–88; Wheelock 1981 (1988), pp. 15, 70–73; Blankert/Montias/Aillaud 1986 (1987, 1992, 2007), pp. 71f., 171, cat. 3; Mayer-Meintschel 1986; Schneider 1993 (2010), pp. 23–27; Liedtke 2000, pp. 188, 197–201; Liedtke 2001f, pp. 365–368, cat. 66; Dresden 2004/05; Klose 2004; Liedtke 2008, pp. 27, 62–64, cat. 3; Blankert 2010, p. 34; Buijsen 2010a, pp. 19–23; Büttner 2010, pp. 28–30; Neidhardt 2010a; Neidhardt/Kettner 2010, p. 131, cat. 3; Blanc 2014, pp. 144–148, 301.

4

A Maid Asleep, *c.* 1656/57

Oil on canvas, 87.6 x 76.5 cm / 34 ½ x 30 ⅛ in., signed left above the figure's head: I.VMeer (VM in ligature)

New York, The Metropolitan Museum of Art, Bequest of Benjamin Altman, 1913, inv. 14.40.611

The picture was in the collection of Pieter Claesz. van Ruijven (1624–1674), and in 1696 was included in the sale by auction of the estate of his son-in-law, Jacob Abrahamsz. Dissius (1653–1695), as no. 8: "Een dronke slapende Meyd aen een Tafel" (see Sources, no. 30) / "A drunken sleeping maid at a table" (trans. Montias 1989, p. 364, doc. 439). In Amsterdam in 1737 it featured at the V. Postumus auction, as no. 37: "Een slapent Vrouwtje, van de Delfse van der Meer" (cited from Blankert 1992, p. 172) / "A young woman sleeping by van der Meer of Delft".

In 1811 the picture was auctioned in Paris, and by 1881 it was in the possession of the Paris art dealer Charles Sedelmeyer. After being owned by the collector Rodolphe Kann (from 1881 until Kann's death, in 1905), then by the London art dealer Joseph Duveen (in 1907/08), the picture entered the collection of Benjamin Altman in New York (1908 until his death, in 1913), passing to The Metropolitan Museum of Art, New York, in 1913, as Altman's bequest.

A Maid Asleep is generally dated to around 1656/57, shortly after *The Procuress* (Cat. 3) and before *A Young Woman Reading a Letter* (Cat. 5), which is thought to be created from around 1657. This would make it the earliest genre scene – a scene from contemporary everyday life – to be painted by Vermeer. From both a formal and a thematic point of view, Vermeer would have been familiar with models for this sort of composition in the interiors painted by Nicolaes Maes and Gerard ter Borch (*c.* 1617–1681). In the 1650s Nicolaes Maes had notably painted a number of domestic scenes set in spaces articulated with structures of orthogonal lines, such as his *Girl at a Window* of 1654 (Rijksmuseum, Amsterdam). In Vermeer's picture a young woman has fallen asleep at a table after getting inebriated, as indicated by the earthenware wine jug and the two wine glasses. She rests her head on her right hand, a pose alluding both to melancholy and to indolence.

See also pp. 66–72, *87*.

LITERATURE: Gowing 1952 (1970), pp. 88–92; Kahr 1972; Wheelock 1981 (1988), p. 74; Ainsworth et al. 1982, pp. 18–26; Blankert/Montias/

5

Aillaud 1986 (1987, 1992, 2007), pp. 90ff., 172, cat. 4; Schneider 1993 (2010), pp. 26–28; Arasse 1994, pp. 29–31; Wheelock 1995b, pp. 39–47; Liedtke 2000, pp. 202–205; Liedtke 2001f, pp. 369f., cat. 67; Liedtke 2007, pp. 868–877; Liedtke 2008, pp. 29f., 66–69, cat. 4; Büttner 2010, pp. 67f.; Blanc 2014, pp. 152–158, 223.

5

A Young Woman Reading a Letter (The Letter Reader), *c.* 1657
Oil on canvas, 83 x 64.5 cm / 32 3/8 x 25 3/8 in., signed right centre, on wall: J Meer (fragmentary)
Dresden, Staatliche Kunstsammlungen, Gemäldegalerie Alte Meister, inv. 1336

The painting is perhaps identical to a picture included as no. 22 in the 1712 auction of the collection of Pieter van der Lip as: "Een leezent Vrouwtje in een kamer, door vander Meer van Delft" (cited from Blankert 1992, p. 182) / "A woman reading in a room, by vander Meer of Delft". In 1742, when Elector Frederick Augustus II of Saxony acquired 30 paintings by predominantly Italian artists from the Paris collection of Prince Carignan for 130,000 livres, intending these for the Dresden Gemäldegalerie, *The Letter Reader*, at that time attributed to Rembrandt, was included as an additional item by the French dealer, as reported in July of that year to Heinrich, Count Brühl (1700–1763), by Samuel de Brais, the Saxon Embassy secretary charged with organizing the sale: "Dans le nombre des tableaux que Votre Excellence recevra il y en a un de Rembrant representant une jeune fille qui lit vis à vis d'une fenêtre, il m'a été donné par dessus de marché" (cited from Spenlé 2006, p. 112, no. 9) / "Among the paintings that Your Excellency will receive, there is one by Rembrandt, which shows a girl reading at a window. It was given to me in addition to the works being sold" (trans. Neidhardt 2010b, p. 68).

Until attributed to Johannes Vermeer, the picture was held to be the work of Pieter de Hooch (1629–1684). In 1806 the Galerie-Inspektor of the Dresden Gemäldegalerie,

Johann Anton Riedel (1736–1816), identified the artist, in his catalogue of the institution's holdings, as "Van der Meer aus Delft" / "Van der Meer of Delft", probably on account of the signature. It was, however, impossible to maintain an attribution to an artist who was at that time unknown against the opinion that this was a work by the considerably better-known Pieter de Hooch. This attribution therefore soon disappeared from the Dresden catalogues, except for the note added by hand in 1826 to his own copy by the art dealer and connoisseur John Smith, who corrected the attribution to Pieter de Hooch to "Delfts van der Meer". It was not until 1858/59, thanks to the efforts of Gustav Friedrich Waagen (1794–1868) and, above all, owing to the acknowledged expertise of Thoré-Bürger, that the correct attribution gained acceptance.

This is the first of a total of six paintings (cf. Cat. 16, 20, 24, 30, 31) in which Vermeer takes as his subject the reading or writing of a letter. The picture's composition further develops the spatial arrangement found in *The Procuress* (Cat. 3) and in *A Maid Asleep* (Cat. 4), two earlier works, in both of which, as also here, a table or balustrade covered with a carpet dominates the foreground. The carpet seen in *A Young Woman Reading a Letter* is again of the Ushak medallion type, from Anatolia, in this case with a red background (cf. Cat. 3).

See also pp. 72–74, *95*.

Literature: Gowing 1952 (1970), pp. 97–103; Mayer-Meintschel 1978/79; Wheelock 1981 (1988), pp. 76–78; Blankert/Montias/Aillaud 1986 (1987, 1992, 2007), pp. 94f., 173, cat. 6; Arasse 1994, pp. 66f.; Liedtke 2000, pp. 177f., 201f., 205–210; Madrid 2003, pp. 165f., cat. 32; Liedtke 2008, pp. 32, 70f., cat. 5; Neidhardt/Kettner 2010, pp. 131f., cat. 4; Blanc 2014, pp. 116–120.

6

6

Cavalier and Young Woman, *c.* 1657–1659
Oil on canvas, 50.5 x 46 cm / 19 ⅞ x 18 ⅛ in.
New York, The Frick Collection, inv. 1911.1.127

Originally in the collection of Pieter Claesz. van Ruijven, the picture was in 1696 included in the sale by auction of the estate of his son-in-law, Jacob Abrahamsz. Dissius, as no. 11: "Een Soldaet met een laggent Meysje, zeer fraei" (see Sources, no. 30) / "A soldier with a laughing girl, very beautiful" (trans. Montias 1989, p. 364, doc. 439). The picture reappeared only in 1861, at the auction of the collection of Charles Scarisbrick, London, there attributed to Pieter de Hooch. It later entered the collections of Lee Mainwaring and Léopold Double, Paris, and in 1881 was auctioned in that city as a work from the collection of Prince Demidoff di San Donato of the Villa di Pratolino, near Florence. By 1891 it was in the collection of Samuel S. Joseph, London, and in 1911 it was sold by the New York dealer Knoedler to Henry Clay Frick (1849–1919).

The attribution to Vermeer was first made by Thoré-Bürger, who saw the picture in Paris in the Double Collection. A date of around 1657–1659 has been proposed on account of the influence of Pieter de Hooch on Vermeer, both in general and with regard to this composition in particular. In 1655 De Hooch had become a member of the Delft Painters' Guild; and his earliest dated pictures to survive from this period are of 1658 (cf. London/Hartford 1998/99, p. 15). Liedtke (2008, p. 72), who believes De Hooch's influence to be of less significance here, dates Vermeer's picture slightly earlier, to around 1657. As in all Vermeer's pictures that show a young lady in the company of a cavalier, an erotic element is only suggested, but is nonetheless unmistakable. The nature of the relationship between the figures remains ambiguous; but there are a number of hints that admit a variety of interpretations. For the perspective construction Vermeer has introduced a slight disparity between the vanishing point and the distance point, which results in a marked foreshorten-

7

ing (cf. the construction drawing in Wadum 1995, p. 70). This, in turn, produces the unusual difference in scale between the two figures, further emphasized by the lighting, the poses and, above all, the large hat worn by the figure viewed from the rear.

See also pp. 75–79, *91*.

LITERATURE: Gowing 1952 (1970), pp. 104–109; Davidson 1968, pp. 286–291; Slatkes 1981, p. 28; Wheelock 1981 (1988), pp. 82–84; Blankert/Montias/Aillaud 1986 (1987, 1992, 2007), pp. 94ff., 173, cat. 5; Nash 1991, pp. 63ff.; Schneider 1993 (2010), p. 31; Arasse 1994, pp. 49f., 79; Wheelock 1995b, pp. 55–61; Liedtke 2000, pp. 22, 145, 171f., 190f., 209f.; Liedtke 2008, pp. 33, 72, cat. 6; Büttner 2010, pp. 88–91; Blanc 2014, pp. 294–301.

7

The Glass of Wine, *c.* 1658–1660
Oil on canvas, 65 x 77 cm / 25 ½ x 30 ⅜ in.
Berlin, Staatliche Museen zu Berlin, Gemäldegalerie, inv. 912C

The picture was included in the Jan van Loon auction, held in Delft in 1736. It was subsequently in the collection of John Hope, Amsterdam, until 1784, and in that of his heirs in England until 1794. Up to 1862 it was in the collection of Henry Thomas Hope, of Deepdene, Surrey, then in that of his daughter, Henrietta Adela, until 1884, and in that of her son, Henry Francis Pelham-Clinton-Hope, London, until 1898. This collection was sold in its entirety to the London art dealer P. & D. Colnaghi and to Asher Wertheimer. In 1901 the picture was acquired by Wilhelm von Bode (1845–1929) for the Berlin Gemäldegalerie.

While in his first interiors, painted between 1656 and 1659, Vermeer suggests spatial depth by means of impeding the viewer's otherwise unhindered gaze by the interposition of various objects – a table, as in *A Maid Asleep* (Cat. 4) and *A Young Woman Reading a Letter* (Cat. 5), or a large repoussoir motif, such as the back-view figure in *Cavalier and Young Woman* (Cat. 6) – here we see right into a much larger

8

interior space than we have previously encountered. The figures and the furnishings are placed at a greater distance from the viewer and occupy the middle ground of what is now also a deeper space. It has widely been assumed (as already in Plietzsch 1911) that Pieter de Hooch's interiors of 1658 – that is to say shortly before or almost contemporary with Vermeer's painting, and which are created entirely out of the architecture of the depicted rooms – are what prompted Vermeer to embark on such a work. *The Glass of Wine* has, accordingly, been dated by most commentators to between 1658 and 1660 (Philadelphia/Berlin/London 1984, cat. 116: *c.* 1660/61; Wheelock 1995b, p. 173: *c.* 1658/60; Liedtke 2008, p. 80: *c.* 1658/59). With this picture Vermeer may be said to have moved on from the phase of his early work and to have attained his mature style.

With regard to its subject, the picture is directly related to the earlier painting *Cavalier and Young Woman*. The two figures' relation to each other is here, however, conveyed in a subtler, more multilayered fashion: an advance in psychological penetration that has its counterpart in the more sophisticated representation of space.

See also pp. 112–117, *166/167*.

LITERATURE: Neurdenburg 1942; Gowing 1952 (1970), pp. 112–119; Philadelphia/Berlin/London 1984, pp. 320–322, cat. 116; Wheelock 1981 (1988), pp. 90f.; Blankert/Montias/Aillaud 1986 (1987, 1992, 2007), pp. 101, 176f., cat. 8; Nash 1991, pp. 66, 68ff.; Schneider 1993 (2010), pp. 36f.; Liedtke 2000, pp. 150, 215ff.; Goodman 2001, pp. 75f.; Liedtke 2001e, pp. 156–158; Liedtke 2001f, pp. 376–379, cat. 70; Liedtke 2008, pp. 40ff., 80ff., cat. 8; Büttner 2010, p. 69; Blanc 2014, pp. 106, 229.

8

The Milkmaid, *c.* 1658–1661
Oil on canvas, 45.5 x 41 cm / 17 ⅞ x 16 in.
Amsterdam, Rijksmuseum, inv. A-2344

Probably in the collection of Pieter Claesz. van Ruijven, the painting was included in the 1696 sale by auction of the estate of his son-in-law, Jacob Abrahamsz. Dissius, as no. 2: "Een Meyd die Melk uytgiet, uytnemende goet" (see Sources, no. 30) / "A maid pouring out milk, extremely well done" (trans. Montias 1989, p. 363, doc. 439).

This is one of the few pictures by Vermeer with a provenance that can be traced almost without interruption, and is at the same time a picture that has always enjoyed high regard as a well-known work by the artist. In 1696–1701 it was in the collection of Isaac Rooleeuw, Amsterdam; from 1701 to 1719 it was owned by Jacob van Hoek, Amsterdam, whose inventory had it listed as "Het vermaerde Melkmeysje, door Vermeer van Delft, konstig" (cited from Wheelock/Broos 1995, p. 112, note 10) / "The famous Milkmaid by Vermeer of Delft, artful" (trans. Wheelock/Broos 1995, p. 111). It then passed through a number of other Amsterdam collections. While in that of Jan Jacob de Bruyn it was in 1781 seen by the English painter Sir Joshua Reynolds (1723–1792), who praised its high quality. In 1813 the picture was acquired, for the high sum of 2,125 florins, for the collector Lucretia van Winter (1785–1845), who in 1822 married Hendrik Six van Hillegom. It then remained in the possession of the Six family until 1908, when – following a resolution taken by the Dutch parliament – it was bought, together with 38 further paintings, by the Dutch State, with support from the Rembrandt Society, for the collection of the Rijksmuseum, Amsterdam. The acquisition was preceded by a heated debate in Dutch society and in the Dutch press, occasioned by an offer made by the American collector J. Pierpont Morgan, Sr. (1837–1913).

While there is general agreement that the picture dates from between 1657 and 1661, that is to say in the first phase of Vermeer's mature oeuvre, opinions differ on the chronological sequence of the individual pictures within this period. While Wheelock (in Wheelock/Broos 1995, p. 108, cat. 5) dates *The Milkmaid* to around 1658–1660, thus placing it after *The Little Street* (Cat. 9) and contemporary with *The Glass of Wine* (Cat. 7), Liedtke (2008, cat. 7) regards *The Milkmaid*, which he dates

9

at around 1657/58, as the earliest work of this group. As each of these three pictures embodies a distinct category of painting within Vermeer's oeuvre, permitting no assumption of a linear stylistic development, it would seem in any case to be difficult here to arrive at a firm conclusion.

The Milkmaid is the only work by Vermeer in which a housemaid in her own domestic environment is the principal figure in a genre painting. Liedtke (2008, p. 76) mentions the Dutch iconographic tradition of depicting housemaids as easily available victims of male seduction. Vermeer does, in fact, point in this direction in two details found in the lower right of his composition, neither of which he added until midway through his work on the picture. In the row of Delft tiles running along the base of the wall where it meets the floor, the figure of Cupid can be identified, and directly in front stands a small foot-warmer filled with glowing coals, of the sort that often symbolized female wantonness in pictures and texts of the 17th century (on which see also Büttner 2010, p. 50).

See also pp. 121–125, *173*.

Literature: Gowing 1952 (1970), pp. 109–112; Slatkes 1981, pp. 32–35; Wheelock 1981 (1988), pp. 86–89; Blankert/Montias/Aillaud 1986 (1987, 1992, 2007), pp. 100f., 174, cat. 7; Nash 1991, pp. 94–96; Schneider 1993 (2010), p. 61; Wheelock 1995b, pp. 63–71; Wheelock/Broos 1995, pp. 108–113, cat. 5; Liedtke 2000, pp. 207–213; Liedtke 2001f, pp. 372–374, cat. 68; Liedtke 2008, pp. 35, 43, 76–79, cat. 7; Büttner 2010, pp. 31–38; Blanc 2014, pp. 102–106.

9

The Little Street, *c.* 1658–1661
Oil on canvas, 53.5 x 43.5 cm / 21 1/8 x 17 1/8 in.,
signed below window at left: i VMeer
(VM in ligature)
Amsterdam, Rijksmuseum, inv. A-2860

Probably once in the collection of Pieter Claesz. van Ruijven, the picture was included in the 1696 Amsterdam sale at auction of the estate of his son-in-law, Jacob Abrahamsz. Dissius, as no. 32 or no. 33, respectively: "Een

Gesicht van een Huys staende in Delft, door denzelven" (see Sources, no. 30; A view of a house in Delft, by the same), or "Een Gesicht van eenige Huysen van dito" (see Sources, no. 30) / "A view of some houses, by ditto" (trans. Montias 1989, p. 364, doc. 439).

A century later this work was in the collection of Gerrit Willem van Oosten de Bruyn, Haarlem, who also owned the portrait Willem van Heythausen by Frans Hals (1580/85–1666) that is now in the Alte Pinakothek, Munich. At the auction of the Oosten de Bruyn collection in 1800, the portrait by Hals was sold for 51 florins, while *The Little Street*, listed in the sale catalogue as "wonder natuurlyk and fraai geschildert" / "painted in a wonderfully natural and beautiful manner", went for 1,040 florins (Broos, in Wheelock/Broos 1995, p. 105).

The picture was acquired by the Amsterdam collector Pieter van Winter. He, in turn, bequeathed it to his daughter, Lucretia van Winter, who also bought Vermeer's *Milkmaid* (Cat. 8). Through her marriage in 1822 to Hendrik Six van Hillegom the painting entered the collection of the Six family. In 1921, after the death of Willem Six, his brother Jan was constrained to auction it in order to pay the inheritance tax on the rest of the estate. Jan Six hoped, in vain, that the Dutch State would buy the picture for the sum of one million guilders. Eventually, Sir Henri Deterding (1866–1939), founder of, and chief shareholder in, Shell, and this company's Director, acquired *The Little Street* for 625,000 guilders, and in 1921 presented it to the Rijksmuseum, Amsterdam.

This is the first painting in which Vermeer fully departs from what had by this point become established as his usual themes. It has been assumed that this surprising choice of subject was prompted by a commission from his most important patron, Pieter Claesz. van Ruijven. In the latter's collection there were three architectural pictures by Vermeer: *A View of Delft* (Cat. 12), the present painting and a second view of houses (1696 auction, nos. 32 and 33). This is to say that at least one architectural picture by Vermeer has since been lost. There is general agreement that *The Little Street* dates from between 1657 and 1661, and thus belongs to the first phase of Vermeer's mature oeuvre; but opinions vary as to its position within the chronological sequence of works from this period. While Wheelock (most recently in Rome 2012/13, cat. 46) dates the picture to around 1658, and thus at the very start of this sequence (Cat. 7–11), Liedtke (2008, p. 89) prefers a dating of around 1659–1661, thereby placing the picture towards the end of this group, directly preceding *A View of Delft*.

Vermeer depicts the façades of two 16th-century houses, which are linked by a wall with two doors leading to their respective back yards. Their left and right extremities are cropped by the corresponding picture edges, so that their façades, positioned parallel to the picture plane, display only various large elements. This emphasizes the fortuitous character of the view. We are here not being shown a particular house or a particular street in Delft; and it is probable that, for compositional reasons, Vermeer has not even depicted two houses that did indeed stand next to one another. The picture may, rather, be assumed to be a composite view, assembled from several separate studies from life.

See also pp. 125–128, *175*.

Literature: Gowing 1952 (1970), pp. 109–112; Wheelock 1981 (1988), p. 80; Blankert/Montias/Aillaud 1986 (1987, 1992, 2007), pp. 102ff., 177, cat. 9; Nash 1991, pp. 6, 12f., 26, 29; Lindenburg 1992, pp. 680–690; Schneider 1993 (2010), p. 16; Wheelock 1995b, pp. 48–53; Wheelock/Broos 1995, pp. 102–107, cat. 4; Kaldenbach 2000, pp. 238–249; Liedtke 2000, pp. 37, 179, 184f., 195, 213, 220f., 254; Liedtke 2001f, pp. 374–378, cat. 69; Weve 2006; Liedtke 2008, pp. 89–91, cat. 11; Büttner 2010, pp. 58f.; Rome 2012/13, p. 206, cat. 46; Blanc 2014, pp. 268–274.

10

10

The Girl with the Wineglass (Young Woman with a Wine Glass), *c.* 1659/60

Oil on canvas, 77.5 x 66.7 cm / 30 ½ x 26 ¼ in., signed on lower right window pane: IVMeer (VM in ligature)

Brunswick, Herzog Anton Ulrich-Museum, inv. GG 316

Probably once in the collection of Pieter Claesz. van Ruijven, the picture was included in the 1696 Amsterdam sale by auction of the estate of his son-in-law, Jacob Abrahamsz. Dissius, as no. 9: "Een vrolyk geselschap in een Kamer, kragtig en goet" (see Sources, no. 30) / "A gay company in a room, vigorous and good" (trans. Montias 1989, p. 364, doc. 439). As Liedtke suspects (2008, pp. 108, 195), the description of no. 9 in the auction catalogue might also apply to *The Concert* (Cat. 19).

Acquired before 1710 by Duke Anthony Ulrich of Brunswick-Wolfenbüttel (1633–1714), the picture entered the Herzog Anton Ulrich-Museum, Brunswick, by way of the duchy's own Galerie Salzdahlum. Taken together, *The Glass of Wine* (Cat. 7), *Young Woman Interrupted at Music* (Cat. 11) and *The Girl with the Wineglass* form a group of similarly composed amorous scenes. All three pictures are alike in composition, featuring a standing cavalier and a young lady in profile seated directly next to him, and with the figures surrounded by similar objects: a window to the left, a table, a picture on the wall.

The present painting has many details in common with *The Glass of Wine.* The half-open window, albeit lit in a different manner, incorporates the same pane with a coat of arms, and the pattern of the tiled floor is identical. There are, however, several decisive differences between the two compositions: most notably that the Brunswick picture is of vertical format, its group of figures is much closer to the viewer and the table has been pushed against the wall. On its far side, moreover, there sits an apparently indifferent cavalier, dozing with his head resting on his right hand. The spatial relationships are thus much less clear than is the

11

case in *The Glass of Wine*, which is generally seen as the earlier work. Most commentators agree on a date for the present composition of around 1659/60, although Blankert (1986, cat. 11) argues for 1662.

The Girl with the Wineglass fails to attain the formal balance found in *The Glass of Wine* (Cat. 7); nor does it appear to be as profound in its characterization of the protagonists. The young woman, whose splendid red silk dress immediately attracts the viewer's eye and, simultaneously, marks its wearer as a girl of easy virtue, seems readier to succumb to the amorous wiles of her cavalier than does the demure lady of the Berlin picture.

See also pp. 117–119, *161*.

LITERATURE: Gowing 1952 (1970), pp. 113–117, 130–131; Brunswick 1978, cat. 39; Slatkes 1981, p. 49; Wheelock 1981 (1988), p. 92; Blankert/Montias/Aillaud 1986 (1987, 1992, 2007), pp. 109, 179, cat. 11; Nash 1991, p. 66; Schneider 1993 (2010), p. 36; Wheelock/Broos 1995, pp. 114–119, cat. 6; Hertel 1996, pp. 56–66; Salomon 1998, pp. 319–322; Liedtke 2000, pp. 217–220; Madrid 2003, p. 168, cat. 33; Liedtke 2008, pp. 41, 86–88, cat. 10; Büttner 2010, pp. 69–71; Rome 2012/13, pp. 210–212, cat. 47; Blanc 2014, pp. 224–231.

11

Young Woman Interrupted at Music, *c.* 1659–1661

Oil on canvas, 39.3 x 44.4 cm / 15 ½ x 17 ½ in.

New York, The Frick Collection, inv. 1901.1.125

The provenance of this picture can be traced back to the early 19th century. In 1810 it was sold at auction from the collection of Pieter de Smeth van Alphen, of Amsterdam, for 620 florins, being auctioned again the following year. From 1811 to 1820 it was in the collection of Cornelis Sebille Roos, until again being auctioned in Amsterdam, in 1820. It featured in a London auction in 1853, subsequently entering the collection of Francis Gibson, of Saffron Walden, who died in 1858. It then passed to his daughter, Mrs Lewis Fry, of Clifton, near Bristol, with whom it remained until 1901, when it was sold, by Knoedler in New York, to the collector Henry Clay Frick, of that city.

Two of Vermeer's earlier paintings, *The Glass of Wine* (Cat. 7) and *The Girl with the Wineglass* (Cat. 10), together with the present picture, form a group of works by the artist that were painted *c.* 1660 and that share a number of formal and thematic qualities. *Young Woman Interrupted at Music* is, however, not only distinctly smaller than the other two pictures; it also depicts a much narrower segment of an interior. In the treatment of space and the positioning of the table and chairs, the picture from The Frick Collection appears almost as if intended to be a reduced and yet more closely viewed variant of the picture in Berlin, the foreground space of that painting here being omitted and the seated lady in the present picture being shown in half-length. The New York composition is also reduced in terms of width, being compressed on both sides, so that the distance between the table and the window appears smaller than is the case of the Berlin picture.

Taking their lead from Gowing (1970, pp. 113f.), most commentators have dated *Young Woman Interrupted at Music* later than the other two pictures of this group, although Liedtke (2008, p. 84) believes that Vermeer embarked on *The Glass of Wine* – in which we may note the advent of a new phase in Vermeer's rendering of domestic interiors – after his work on the present painting, noting that it also recalls the closely viewed figures of the earlier picture *Cavalier and Young Woman* (Cat. 6). He therefore dates both the present painting and *The Glass of Wine* to *c.* 1658/59, whereas Wheelock (1995b) believes these works to date from 1660/61.

It is, nonetheless, difficult to reach a fair assessment of the present picture on account of its delicate state of preservation. The picture surface suffered in the past when it was cleaned with excessively strong chemical solutions (Davidson 1968, p. 292). Paint layers have been lost, above all, in what now appear to be large, undifferentiated planes of colour, such as the young woman's dress, the cavalier's cloak, the tablecloth and areas of the walls. Furthermore, a number of alterations were made in the past by painting over the original composition. Descriptions of the picture in the catalogues of the auctions held in 1810 and 1811 refer to a violin, rather than a framed picture, hanging on the rear wall. In 1899, in his exhaustive report on the picture, Hofstede de Groot (1863–1930) deplored its poor state of preservation, referring in particular to the violin and to the birdcage affixed to the window frame as details that had been painted in at a later date. When the picture was restored in 1907 the violin was removed and the painting with Cupid that lay beneath this was revealed. The restorers did not, however, remove the birdcage. In 1949 William Suhr carried out a further restoration. Though himself believing the birdcage to be a later addition, he did not remove it; similar, albeit simpler, cages are indeed to be found in the paintings of Gerard Dou (1613–1675). The poor state of preservation has even led some commentators to dismiss the picture as a copy. Blankert (in Blankert/Montias/Aillaud 1992, p. 204) concluded that it was not possible to determine whether it was an overcleaned original or a copy. It is, however, notable that the best preserved sections evince the artistic qualities of an autograph Vermeer.

Vermeer's composition is a variant of a subject that oscillates between amorous amusement and an attempt at seduction. The standing figure of the cavalier presents a sheet of music to the seated young lady. Both words and notes are just detectable, albeit impossible to decipher. We may, however, surmise that this is a love song dedicated to the young lady by her admirer. A lute lying on the table along with further sheets of music indicate that the two had been playing music together. But a glass of red wine and a white jug familiar to us from other paintings are also visible. The picture's traditional title, *Young Woman Interrupted at Music*, could therefore be regarded as too one-dimensional in what it tells us of the depicted scene.

See also pp. 119–121, *168/169*.

LITERATURE: Hofstede de Groot 1899; Gowing 1952 (1970), pp. 113–116; De Jongh 1967,

12

pp. 49f.; Davidson 1968, pp. 292–295; Slatkes 1981, p. 45; Wheelock 1981 (1988), p. 98; Blankert/Montias/Aillaud 1986 (1987, 1992, 2007), p. 204, cat. b2; Nash 1991, p. 71; Schneider 1993 (2010), pp. 37f.; Liedtke 2000, p. 217; Liedtke 2008, pp. 41, 84f., cat. 9; Büttner 2010, p. 77; Blanc 2014, pp. 120–126.

12

A View of Delft, *c.* 1660–1663
Oil on canvas, 96.5 x 115.7 cm / 38 x 45½ in., signed bottom left, on boat: IVM (in ligature)
The Hague, Koninklijk Kabinet van Schilderijen Mauritshuis, inv. 92

Probably once in the collection of Pieter Claesz. van Ruijven, the picture was included in the 1696 Amsterdam sale by auction of the estate of his son-in-law, Jacob Abrahamsz. Dissius, as no. 31: "De Stad Delft in perspectief, te sien van de Zuyd-zy door J. vander Meer van Delft" (see Sources, no. 30; The city of Delft in perspective, viewed from the South, by J. vander Meer of Delft). Here, it attained the unusually high sale price of 200 florins. Nothing is known of the painting's owners between 1696 and the early 19th century; but it is clear that it largely remained accessible to artists, some of whom made watercolour copies of it (Wheelock/Broos 1995, p. 126, note 17). It resurfaced in the collection of Willem Philip Kops, of Bloemendaal, near Haarlem; and, following his death, in 1805, it remained in the possession of his wife, who herself died in 1820, and of his daughter, Anna Johanna Kops, who also lived in Haarlem, under her married name, Teding van Berkhout. The picture was subsequently auctioned in Amsterdam in 1822, and on this occasion was acquired for the Mauritshuis in The Hague, for the extraordinarily high price of 2,900 florins, by the King of the Netherlands, William I (1772–1843), as: "een zeldzaam voorkomend stuk van den zoogenaamden Delfschen van der Meer […] mede een zeer beroemd meester onder die der Hollandsche school" (cited from Wheelock/Broos 1995, p. 126, note 32) / "a rarely encountered piece by the so-called Delft van der Meer […] who is also a very famous master among this Dutch school" (trans. Wheelock/Broos 1995, p. 126, note 32).

After the rediscovery of this painting in the early 19th century, and its acquisition for the Mauritshuis as an acknowledged masterpiece by Johannes Vermeer, *A View of Delft* served as the starting point for the gradual reconstruction of the artist's oeuvre undertaken, from 1859, by Thoré-Bürger. Yet, on account of this picture's uniqueness and, ultimately, the fact that it is, almost literally, "beyond compare", its chronological position within Vermeer's oeuvre, or indeed within Dutch painting of the third quarter of the 17th century, has not been easy to determine. The picture is generally believed to date from the early 1660s (Blankert 1986: 1661; Wheelock, in Wheelock/Broos 1995: 1660/61; Liedtke 2008: *c.* 1661–1663); and it is thought, in any case, to be later than *The Little Street* (Cat. 9), here dated to *c.* 1658–1661. While Wheelock dates *The Little Street* to *c.* 1658 (most recently in Rome 2012/13, cat. 46), thus implying an interval of two to three years between the two paintings, Liedtke believes *The Little Street* to date from *c.* 1659–1661, thereby placing both works at a later date.

Liedtke (2000, p. 224) surmises that Vermeer's patron, Pieter Claesz. van Ruijven, not only bought A View of Delft, but also commissioned it and proposed its subject. This opinion is supported by two considerations in particular: that Vermeer appears to have invested considerable time and effort in his work on this painting, and that his patron was interested in architectural subjects. In addition to The Little Street he owned a similar Vermeer composition, now untraced, as well as three architectural views by Emanuel de Witte (*c.* 1610–1691/92), all of which were sold at auction in 1696.

Vermeer shows us Delft viewed from the south, with its harbour in the foreground and the city itself beyond, its most prominent aspect being the fortifications and their gates: the Kethel Gate and the large Schiedam Gate, the latter with its bell tower, at the centre of the composition, and the twin-turreted Rotterdam Gate towards the picture's right edge. While the city's fortifications and their gates, as well as

13

the houses directly behind them, all lie in the shadow of the dark cloud that forms the upper edge of the picture, the more distant parts of the city are bathed in bright morning sunlight, which picks out in particular the tower of the Nieuwe Kerk, which rises high above the houses. In other artists' views of Delft, its harbour is animated with ships; but in Vermeer's picture the harbour is empty except for a few moored barges. A total of 15 figures is to be found in the composition. The six men and women in the left foreground are wearing costumes that indicate their social standing.

See also pp. 128–132, *176/177*.

LITERATURE: Gowing 1952 (1970), pp. 128f.; Slatkes 1981, pp. 40–43; Wheelock 1981 (1988), pp. 94–96; Wheelock/Kaldenbach 1982; Blankert/Montias/Aillaud 1986 (1987, 1992, 2007), pp. 102–108, 178, cat. 10; Nash 1991, pp. 6–14; Schneider 1993 (2010), pp. 15f.; Wheelock 1995b, pp. 73–83; Wheelock/Broos 1995, pp. 120–127, cat. 7; Liedtke 2000, pp. 221–226; Liedtke 2008, pp. 92–97, cat. 12; Büttner 2010, pp. 57f.; Blanc 2014, pp. 130, 259–268.

13

The Music Lesson (A Woman at a Virginal with a Gentleman), *c.* 1662–1664

Oil on canvas, 74 x 64.5 cm / 29 ⅛ x 25 ⅜ in., signed far right centre, on picture frame: IVMeer (IVM in ligature). Inscription on the virginal's lid: MVSICA LETITIAE CO[ME?] S / MEDICINA DOLOR[VM?]

London, Royal Collection, Her Majesty Queen Elizabeth II, inv. 405346

Probably once in the collection of Pieter Claesz. van Ruijven, the picture was offered for 80 florins in the 1696 Amsterdam sale by auction of the estate of his son-in-law, Jacob Abrahamsz. Dissius, as no. 6: "Een speelende Juffrouw op de Clavecimbael in een Kamer, met een toeluisterend Monsieur" (see Sources, no. 30; A young lady playing the clavecin [this should read: the virginal] in a room, with a gentleman listening). It subsequently entered the collection of the painter Giovanni Antonio Pellegrini (1675–1741), who lived in Venice but who had stayed in Amsterdam and The

Hague in 1716. In 1742 the painting was sold by Pellegrini's widow, Angela Carriera, to Consul Joseph Smith.

It then remained with him, in Venice and in Mogliano, until 1762, when it entered the collection of King George III of Great Britain and Ireland (1738–1820). When sold to the King by Joseph Smith, the painting had, on account of the deteriorated signature that was read as "FvM", erroneously been attributed to Frans van Mieris (1635–1681): "Frans van Mieris [...] A Woman playing on a Spinnet in presence of a Man seems to be her father" (cited from Wheelock/Broos 1995, p. 132). This attribution was first questioned in 1819, when Willem van Mieris (1662–1747) was proposed as the probable author. In 1869, when the painting was attributed to Eglon van der Neer (1635/36–1703), Vermeer's name was also, for the first time, mentioned. Yet it was not until 1876 that the attribution to Vermeer prevailed.

The picture is one of several spacious interiors that Vermeer painted *c.* 1660, the sequence apparently opening with *The Glass of Wine* (Cat. 7) and continuing with *The Girl with the Wineglass* (Cat. 10). *The Music Lesson* has generally been dated to a few years later than these, that is to say, to *c.* 1663–1664. Blankert (1986) assumes that *The Music Lesson* was painted in 1664, after the so-called *Vrouwtjes* (see Cat. 14–18). Wheelock (in Wheelock/Broos 1995) proposes a date of *c.* 1662–1665, and Liedtke (2008) one of *c.* 1662/63.

The picture's traditional title is largely dictated by art-historical convention and does not capture the element of erotic tension that is sensed within the composition – something, as has long been recognized, that is always present in Vermeer's work. The relationship between the two depicted individuals is established through music, that is to say, via the notion of their playing music together, but also by an emotional bond, as we are reminded by the Latin inscription on the lid of the virginal: "Music is the accompanist of joy, a remedy for sorrow." In this sizeable, imposing interior with its large windows,

14

its elaborate floor pattern of black and white marble flagstones and its select but sumptuous furnishings, the reserved bearing of the two elegantly dressed figures establishes a distinct mood of discreet restraint.

See also pp. 132–135, *181*.

Literature: Gowing 1952 (1970), pp. 37–40, 119–127; Slatkes 1981, pp. 63f., 66; Wheelock 1981 (1988), pp. 100–102, cat. 19; White 1982, pp. 143–145, cat. 230; Philadelphia/Berlin/London 1984, pp. 328ff., cat. 119; Blankert/Montias/Aillaud 1986 (1987, 1992, 2007), pp. 120ff., 186, cat. 16; Nash 1991, pp. 74, 78; Schneider 1993 (2010), p. 38; Wheelock 1995b, pp. 85–95; Wheelock/Broos 1995, pp. 128–133, cat. 8; Liedtke 2000, pp. 111, 228–232, 245f.; Liedtke 2008, pp. 104–107, cat. 15; Büttner 2010, pp. 81–84; Cambridge 2011/12, p. 204, cat. 26; Blanc 2014, pp. 64, 246–254, 320–326.

14

Young Woman with a Water Pitcher, *c.* 1662–1664

Oil on canvas, 45.7 x 40.6 cm / 18 x 16 in.

New York, The Metropolitan Museum of Art, Gift of Henry G. Marquand, 1889, inv. 89.15.21

It has so far proved impossible to trace the provenance of this picture further back than to the early 19th century. From perhaps 1801 it was in the collection of Robert Vernon, of Hatley Park, Cambridgeshire, and London, until his death, in 1849. In 1877, when it was sold in London as part of the Vernon Collection, it was attributed in the sale catalogue, where it featured as no. 97, to Gabriel Metsu (1629–1667) and described as: "Interior, with a lady at a table covered with a carpet, on which is an ewer and dish, opening a window" (cited from Liedtke 2008, p. 195). In 1878 it was sold, as a work by Metsu, to Mervyn Wingfield, 7th Viscount Powerscourt (1878–*c.* 1887), Powerscourt at Enniskerry, County Wicklow, Ireland. In 1887, however, it was sold, as a work by Johannes Vermeer, to Henry G. Marquand, of New York, who in 1889 presented it to that city's Metropolitan Museum of Art.

While Blankert (1986, p. 181, cat. 12) and Liedtke (2008, p. 98) date the picture to *c.* 1662, that is to say, contemporary with *A View of Delft* (Cat. 12) and, or perhaps even earlier than, *The Music Lesson* (Cat. 13), Wheelock (in Wheelock/Broos 1995, p. 146) proposes a date of *c.* 1664/65, that is to say, not only later than *The Music Lesson* but also later than *Woman in Blue Reading a Letter* (Cat. 16) and *Woman with a Balance* (Cat. 18). This would take account of the stylistic development that is here apparent: in the overall chromatic brightening and use of primary colours, as well as in Vermeer's skill in creating shapes out of large, coloured planes. These are important signs of the painterly economy that distinguishes this composition from his earlier pictures.

Here, Vermeer is not concerned with depicting an activity but rather with recording the presence of an idealized female figure. The young woman retains her headgear and a collar that covers her shoulders while she performs her ablutions, a situation that permits the juxtaposition of the washing utensils, jug and bowl, and the pearl necklace on a blue ribbon, which has been laid across a corner of the jewellery casket. It is, however, also possible that Vermeer intended the composition to have a further, symbolic character. Bowls and jugs are symbols of purity as well as attributes of the Virtue of Temperance (Schneider 2010); the allegorical figure of Temperantia is shown pouring water from a jug. The jewellery casket and the map on the wall, on the other hand, belong to the symbolic repertoire of the vanitas tradition, and as such allude to the transitory nature of worldly things, after the model of the biblical figure of the penitent Mary Magdalene, who did not remove her jewellery when performing her ablutions.

See also pp. 137–140, *187*.

LITERATURE: Gowing 1952 (1970), pp. 130f.; Welu 1975, pp. 534f.; Slatkes 1981, p. 50; Wheelock 1981 (1988), pp. 114–117; Blankert/

15

Montias/Aillaud 1986 (1987, 1992, 2007), pp. 109, 181, cat. 12; Nash 1991, pp. 96–98; Schneider 1993 (2010), p. 62; Wheelock 1995b, pp. 105–111; Wheelock/Broos 1995, pp. 146–151, cat. 11; Liedtke 2000, pp. 213, 226–228; Liedtke 2001f, pp. 379ff., cat. 71; Madrid 2003, p. 170, cat. 34; Liedtke 2007, pp. 877–883; Liedtke 2008, pp. 98–100, cat. 13; Büttner 2010, p. 31; Blanc 2014, pp. 130–136, 250.

15
Woman with a Lute, *c.* 1662–1664
Oil on canvas, 51.4 x 45.7 cm / 20 ¼ x 18 in.
New York, The Metropolitan Museum of Art, Bequest of Collis P. Huntington, 1900, inv. 25.110.24

It has so far been impossible to trace the provenance of this picture further back than to the early 19th century. In 1817 it was sold at the Amsterdam auction of the collection of Philippus van der Schley and Daniel du Pré, as no. 62: "Delftsche van der Meer, In een gemeubileerd Binnenvertrek zit eene vrouw in Hollandsche Kleeding, op de guitar te spelen. Frappant van licht en fraai gepenceeld" (cited from Blankert 1986, p. 204) / "Van der Meer of Delft, In a furnished room there sits a lady dressed in the Dutch style and playing a guitar, astonishingly lightly and beautifully painted". Blankert believes that this entry refers, in all probability, to the present picture rather than to *The Guitar Player* now in London (Cat. 32). By the end of the 19th century the picture had re-emerged on the Paris art market. It was acquired by Collis P. Huntington of New York (d. 1900), who, in turn, bequeathed it to that city's Metropolitan Museum of Art.

On account of similarities, in both composition and execution, with *Young Woman with a Water Pitcher* (Cat. 14), one may assume the present painting to be very close to that in date. Liedtke (2008, p. 101) dates Woman with a Lute to *c.* 1662/63, a little later than the other work, whereas Wheelock (most recently Osaka 2000, p. 20) prefers a later date, *c.* 1665. Blankert (1986, p. 203, cat. b1) proposes a date of 1662–1665; but, on account of the picture's poor state of preservation, he questions its attribution to Vermeer. Liedtke (2008) argues that Blankert sets too much store by the picture's state of preservation, while inadequately attending to its best passages.

The subdued colouring of this composition and the impact of its chiaroscuro contrasts link it with other single-figure female portraits painted by Vermeer *c.* 1663/64, on which Gowing (1952/1970) bestowed the term "pearl pictures" (see also Cat. 16–18). Within this group, *Woman with a Lute* is notable for its large, dark foreground and for the chair placed there, one of its lion-head finials standing out in lively silhouette against a paler area of the picture. Vermeer here readopts a motif to be found in his early work, for example, in *Cavalier and Young Woman* (Cat. 6).

It has been observed that *Woman with a Lute*, be it in its pictorial invention or painterly execution, is more conventional and better attuned to the taste of its era than are other works by Vermeer. An explanation for this is that it may have been among the pictures that were not painted for Vermeer's principal patron, Pieter Claesz. van Ruijven, but intended for sale. A young woman sits at a table and tunes her lute while looking out the window. In front of her on the table lie books of music, and on the floor next to the table we can see a double bass.

See also pp. 144–145, *191*.

LITERATURE: Gowing 1952 (1970), pp. 132–134; Mirimonde 1961, pp. 37ff.; Slatkes 1981, p. 60; Wheelock 1981 (1988), p. 112; Philadelphia/Berlin/London 1984, pp. 322f., cat. 117; Blankert/Montias/Aillaud 1986 (1987, 1992, 2007), p. 203, cat. b1; Schneider 1993 (2010), pp. 44ff.; Liedtke 2000, pp. 232f.; Osaka 2000, p. 20, cat. 32; Liedtke 2001f, pp. 381f., cat. 72; Liedtke 2007, pp. 328, 884–887; Liedtke 2008, pp. 101f., cat. 14; Rome 2012/13, p. 214, cat. 48; Blanc 2014, pp. 190–194.

16

16

Woman in Blue Reading a Letter, *c.* 1663/64
Oil on canvas, 46.6 x 39.1 cm / 18 3/8 x 15 3/8 in.
Amsterdam, Rijksmuseum, inv. C-251

The first record of this picture probably dates from its inclusion, as no. 22, in the 1712 Amsterdam sale by auction of the collection of Pieter van der Lip, where it was described in the catalogue as: "Een leezent Vrouwtje, in een kamer, door vander Meer van Delft" (cited from Blankert 1992, p. 182) / "A woman reading, in a room, by vander Meer van Delft." During the course of the 18th and early 19th centuries it featured in numerous further Amsterdam auctions (1772, 1791, 1793, 1801), always attributed without any doubt to Vermeer; see the thorough discussion of these in Blankert 1986 (1987, 1992, 2007), p. 182, cat. 14. In 1809 the picture was auctioned in Paris, as a work by "Van der Meer de Delft", coming up again for sale there in 1825. Between 1833 and 1839 it was with the London art dealer John Smith, who in 1839 sold it to Adriaan van der Hoop (1778–1854). The latter, who from 1811 was co-owner of the Amsterdam banking house Hope & Co. and one of the city's wealthiest citizens, possessed one of the largest collections of paintings found in Holland at the time. In 1847 he formally bequeathed this collection to the city of Amsterdam. Adriaan van der Hoop recorded the circumstances in which he acquired the Vermeer picture in the inventory of his collection titled Lijst van de schilderijen van Adriaan van der Hoop te Amsterdam (now in the Archives of the Rijksmuseum, Amsterdam): "te London met J. Smith & Sons eene ruil gedaan, hebbende van hem gekocht […] een goed schildery van den Delftschen van der Meer, vostellende eene lezende vrouw, in het blaauw gekleed" (cited from Wheelock/Broos 1995, p. 139, note 10) / "Made a trade in London with J. Smith & Sons, having bought from him […] a good painting by the Delft van der Meer, representing a reading Woman dressed in blue" (trans. Wheelock/Broos 1995, p. 138). In 1854, on the death of Adriaan van der Hoop, the 225 paintings in his collection became the property of the city of Amsterdam; but this was constrained to seek financial support from the collectors Carel Joseph Fodor and Jacob de Vos to be able to pay the requisite inheritance tax of 50,000 florins. In 1885 the painting by Vermeer entered the collection of the Rijksmuseum, as a loan from the city of Amsterdam.

Throughout the 18th and 19th centuries *Woman in Blue Reading a Letter* was regarded as the work of Vermeer. Like *A View of Delft* (Cat. 12), therefore, it demonstrates that Vermeer's name was never entirely forgotten, at least not in his native region. *Woman in Blue Reading a Letter* has largely been dated to *c.* 1663/64 (Wheelock, in Wheelock/Broos 1995, cat. 9; Liedtke 2008, p. 112, cat. 17), although Blankert (1986, cat. 14) proposes a date of 1662–1665. Gowing (1952/1970, p. 44) introduced the term "pearl pictures" for this painting and three others (Cat. 15, 17, 18). In several respects – on account of their simple compositions and their related concentration on only the most essential elements, the brilliance of their painterly realization and their thematic clarity – these pictures, in particular, Woman in Blue Reading a Letter, can be regarded as the quintessence of Vermeer's activity as an artist, as the classical high point of his oeuvre.

In terms of composition, Vermeer here returns to his picture of around six or seven years earlier, *A Young Woman Reading a Letter* (Cat. 5). Be it in the bearing of the figure, whom we view in strict profile, or our awareness of her attention directed down at the letter that she holds tightly in both hands, the two pictures are almost exactly identical. Several alterations made during Vermeer's work on *Woman in Blue Reading a Letter*, revealed by X-rays, show how precisely he calculated the compositional distribution of planes. By extending the breadth of the background map a few centimetres to the left, he was able to give exactly the same width to the patches of uncovered wall at both upper left and lower right. Further alterations were made to the outline of the blue jacket, which originally jutted out further and was trimmed with fur. By means of these

17

changes, Vermeer enhanced the figure's statuesque character.

See also pp. 138, 141–142, *195*.

LITERATURE: Gowing 1952 (1970), pp. 44f.; Welu 1975, pp. 532f.; Slatkes 1981, p. 59; Wheelock 1981 (1988), p. 104; Blankert/Montias/Aillaud 1986 (1987, 1992, 2007), pp. 114ff., 182ff., cat. 14; Nash 1991, pp. 90–92; Schneider 1993 (2010), p. 49; Wheelock 1995, pp. 6–15; Wheelock/Broos 1995, pp. 134–139, cat. 9; Liedtke 2000, pp. 238f.; Wheelock 2001, pp. 41–48; Vergara 2003, pp. 52f.; Liedtke 2008, pp. 112–114, cat. 17; Büttner 2010, pp. 42–48; Blanc 2014, pp. 81–84.

17

Woman with a Pearl Necklace, *c.* 1663/64
Oil on canvas, 51.2 x 45.1 cm / 20 ⅛ x 17 ¾ in., signed on tabletop: IVMeer (IVM in ligature)
Berlin, Staatliche Museen zu Berlin, Gemäldegalerie, inv. 912B

Probably once in the collection of Pieter Claesz. van Ruijven, the picture was included in the 1696 Amsterdam sale by auction of the estate of his son-in-law, Jacob Abrahamsz. Dissius, as no. 36: "Een Paleerende dito [i. e. Juffrouw], seer fraey van dito [Vermeer]" (see Sources, no. 30; A young lady adorning herself with pearls, very beautiful, by ditto [Vermeer]). The picture re-emerged in 1809, at the Amsterdam auction of the collection of Johannes Caudri, where it featured as no. 42 and was already correctly attributed (as it would continue to be) to Johannes Vermeer: "De Delfsche van der Meer [...] eene bevallige jonge Dame voor een Tafel, waar boven een Spiegel geplaatst is, zij is gekleed in een geel Satijn Jakje met Bont gevoerd, en schijnt zig te Paleeren [...] allertuitvoerigst gepenceelden van deze beroemde Meester" (cited from Blankert 1992, p. 182, who gives the entire quotation) / "Van der Meer of Delft [...] a beautiful young lady standing at a table, above which hangs a mirror, she is dressed in a yellow silk jacket with a fur border and appears to be adorning herself with pearls [...] very precisely painted by this celebrated master." Auctioned again in Amsterdam in 1811 and 1856, on both occasions as a work by "De Delftsche van der Meer", by 1860 the picture was in the collection of the Parisian lithographer Henri Grevedon (1776–1860). After the latter's death the painting was acquired by Thoré-Bürger and then sold by him at auction in Brussels in 1868. It was acquired by the Aachen collector Barthold Suermondt; and in 1874 it entered the Kaiser Friedrich Museum in Berlin as part of the Suermondt Collection.

This composition belongs to the group of works, each showing a single female figure and painted *c.* 1662–1664 (see also Cat. 14–18), that Gowing (1952/1970) designated as the "pearl pictures". It is difficult, however, to determine a precise chronological sequence within this group. *Woman with a Pearl Necklace* has unanimously been dated to *c.* 1663/64 (Blankert 1986, pp. 181f.: 1662–1665; Wheelock, in Wheelock/Broos 1995, p. 152: *c.* 1664; Liedtke 2008, p. 115: *c.* 1663/64). The picture is closest to *Woman in Blue Reading a Letter* (Cat. 16), and it can probably be assumed to follow *Young Woman with a Water Pitcher* (Cat. 14) and *Woman with a Lute* (Cat. 15).

We see a young lady who is just completing her toilette. Having placed a string of pearls around her neck, she holds this by its fastening ribbons while looking at her reflection in a mirror. The true subject of Vermeer's painting is the girl's direct and attentive gaze into the mirror, a gaze that penetrates the entire width of what we see of the room. It is notable that there are here no extraneous elements to distract our attention as we view the picture. The centre of the composition is occupied entirely by the large, empty plane of the white wall. During his work on the picture, Vermeer made several alterations in order to achieve this sort of concentration. A map originally hung on the now empty wall; a musical instrument originally lay on the chair in the foreground; and the large, dark blue cloth also seen here was at first intended to be smaller.

See also pp. 138, 141–142, *211*.

LITERATURE: Slatkes 1981, p. 53; Wheelock 1981 (1988), p. 110; Blankert/Montias/

18

Aillaud 1986 (1987, 1992, 2007), pp. 114ff., 181f., cat. 13; Nash 1991, pp. 101f.; Schneider 1993 (2010), p. 56; Wheelock/Broos 1995, pp. 152–155, cat. 12; Liedtke 2000, pp. 236–238; Madrid 2003, p. 174, cat. 36; Liedtke 2008, pp. 115–117, cat. 18; Büttner 2010, pp. 64f.; Blanc 2014, pp. 234–239.

18

Woman with a Balance, *c.* 1663/64
Oil on canvas, 40.3 x 35.6 cm / 15 7/8 x 14 in.
Washington, D.C., National Gallery of Art, Widener Collection, inv. 1942.9.97

The provenance of this picture can be traced back, without interruption, to the 17th century, to Pieter Claesz. van Ruijven, who is assumed to have commissioned it. In the 1696 Amsterdam sale by auction of the estate of his son-in-law, Jacob Abrahamsz. Dissius, it featured as no. 1: "Een Juffrouw die goud weegt, in een kasje van J. vander Meer van Delft, extraordinaer konstig en kragtig geschildert" (see Sources, no. 30) / "A young lady weighing gold, in a box by J. van der Meer of Delft, extraordinarily artful and vigorously painted" (trans. Montias 1989, p. 363, doc. 439). Both *Woman with a Balance* and *The Milkmaid* (Cat. 8) entered the collection of Isaac Rooleeuw, Amsterdam, and were again sold at auction in 1701. The present picture was, on this occasion, described as: "Een Goudweegstertje van Vermeer van Delft" (cited from Blankert 1992, p. 185) / "A Woman Weighing Gold by Vermeer of Delft", and was acquired by the Amsterdam collector Paulo van Uchelen; it then remained for over 60 years in the possession of three generations of his family, until it was sold at auction in Amsterdam in 1767, then again in 1777, in the latter case as no. 116: "De Delftsche van der Meer […] een vrouwtje bezig is, goud te wegen […]" (cited from Blankert 1992, p. 185) / "By van der Meer of Delft […] a woman is engaged in weighing gold […]."
In 1825 the picture was acquired by King Maximilian I Joseph of Bavaria (1756–1825), for his private art collection, through the Viennese art dealer Adamovich. At that time it was attrib-

uted to Gabriel Metsu (Munich 2011, p. 132). After the King's death part of his collection was sold at auction in 1826. It was at this point that the still visible monogram was thought to read "van der Meer": "Gabriël Metzu, et selon d'autres van der Meer. Ce tableau est marqué du monogramme GM" (cited from Blankert 1992, p. 185) / "Gabriël Metzu, and according to others, van der Meer. This picture bears the monogram GM." The painting's next owner, Louis-Charles Victor de Riquet, Duc de Caraman (1762–1839), who served from 1816 as French Ambassador to Vienna, noted in a connoisseurial spirit, in his copy of the catalogue for the auction of his own collection (Paris, 11 May 1830, no. 68), the importance of Vermeer: "Les productions de VanderMeer de Delft sont si rares, que nous ne pouvons nous dispenser de signaler celle-ci d'une manière toute particulière aux amateurs" (cited from Blankert 1992, p. 185) / "The works produced by VanderMeer of Delft are so rare that we must not fail to draw the attention of art lovers to this outstanding artist."

The picture subsequently passed into the collection of the Périer family, where Thoré-Bürger saw it in 1866, while in search of works by the artist he had rediscovered. The last member of the Périer family to own the painting was the Comtesse Ségur-Périer. In December 1910, when it was still in her possession, it was recorded and published by Hofstede de Groot, as it had not been publicly accessible since its auction in 1848. It was put up for sale by the Comtesse Ségur-Périer in 1911, when it was acquired by the American collector Peter A. B. Widener (1834–1915). According to the terms of the latter's will, his son and heir, Joseph E. Widener (1872–1943), was required to leave the Vermeer painting, along with the rest of the art collection, to the National Gallery of Art in Washington, D.C.

While described as the work of Vermeer in the Amsterdam auction catalogues of the 18th century, the picture was viewed on the art market outside Holland as the work of the then much better-known artist Gabriel Metsu. When, in 1825, an attribution to Vermeer was mooted, it is by no means clear that this was a reference to Johannes Vermeer of Delft. By 1830, however, its next owner explicitly referred to the rarity of pictures by "Vander Meer de Delft"; and in 1866 Thoré-Bürger was able to confirm the attribution.

This painting belongs to the group of works by Vermeer showing a single female figure and painted *c.* 1662–1664 (see also Cat. 14–17), which Gowing (1952/1970) described as "pearl pictures". There is little agreement regarding the difficult question of the chronological sequence of the works in this group. While Wheelock (in Wheelock/Broos 1995, p. 140) dates the present picture to *c.* 1664, that is to say, a little later than *Woman in Blue Reading a Letter* (Cat. 16) of *c.* 1663/64, and contemporary with *Woman with a Pearl Necklace* (Cat. 17) of *c.* 1664, and perhaps earlier than *Young Woman with a Water Pitcher* (Cat. 14) of 1664/65, Liedtke (2008, p. 118) posits a date of *c.* 1663/64, contemporary with Cat. 16 and 17, and somewhat later than Cat. 14 and 15. The first auction catalogues, of 1696 and 1701, include descriptions of the subject of the painting, which is assumed to be a woman weighing gold, doubtless on account of the gold coins lying on the table. From the time of Thoré-Bürger, however, the picture has also acquired the inadequate, but nonetheless popular, designation "Woman Weighing Pearls". The scales are, in any case, empty. In all probability Vermeer intended to depict the act of testing the still empty scales, to assess their precision. We watch the young woman as she herself waits for them to cease tipping back and forth. One of the picture's themes could, then, be defined as the notion of balance or the restoration of equilibrium.

See also pp. 146–147, *205*.

LITERATURE: Gowing 1952 (1970), pp. 53, 135f.; Slatkes 1981, pp. 55f.; Wheelock 1981 (1988), pp. 106–108; Philadelphia/Berlin/London 1984, pp. 326f., cat. 118; Blankert/Montias/Aillaud 1986 (1987, 1992, 2007), pp. 114–118, 184, cat. 15; Nash 1991, pp. 98–101; Schneider 1993 (2010), p. 56; Wheelock 1995a, pp. 371–377; Wheelock 1995b, pp. 97–103; Wheelock/

19

Broos 1995, pp. 140–145, cat. 10; De Jongh 1998; Schlenke 1998, pp. 55ff.; Liedtke 2000, pp. 233–237; Liedtke 2001f, pp. 383–386, cat. 73; Madrid 2003, p. 172, cat. 35; Liedtke 2008, pp. 118–120, cat. 19; Büttner 2010, pp. 65f.; Munich 2011, pp. 48–51, cat. 1; Blanc 2014, pp. 76–82.

19

The Concert, *c.* 1663–1666

Oil on canvas, 72.5 x 64.7 cm / 28 ½ x 25 ½ in., signed right centre, on picture frame: IVMeer (IVM in ligature)

Boston, Massachusetts, Isabella Stewart Gardner Museum, inv. P21w27

(The current whereabouts of this picture are unknown. In March 1990 it was stolen from the Isabella Stewart Gardner Museum along with 11 other works of art)

As Liedtke (2008, p. 108) surmises, it is possible that this picture was once in the collection of Pieter Claesz. van Ruijven. It was included in the 1696 Amsterdam sale by auction of the estate of his son-in-law, Jacob Abrahamsz. Dissius, as no. 9: "Een vrolyk geselschap in een Kamer, kragtig en goet" (see Sources, no. 30) / "A gay company in a room, vigorous and good" (trans. Montias 1989, p. 364, doc. 439). On the whole, however, this catalogue entry has been understood as a reference to *The Girl with the Wineglass* (Cat. 10).

The Concert is not again securely traceable until its inclusion in an auction in 1780. When next auctioned, in 1804, it was designated a work by "Jean van der Meer de Delft" (cited from Blankert 1986, p. 187), retaining the same designation at sales in 1834 and in 1860. At the subsequent auction, in 1869, the picture was acquired by Thoré-Bürger; and at the auction of his own collection, in 1892, it was acquired for the collection of the Isabella Stewart Gardner Museum in Boston, Massachusetts.

Gowing (1952/1970, pp. 119–127) was the first to posit that *The Concert* may originally have been painted as a pendant to *The Music Lesson* (Cat. 13). The almost identical dimensions of the two pictures, as well as their compositional and thematic similarities, seem to support the notion. Nonetheless, most commentators (Wheelock 1995b; Liedtke 2008) now reject this assumption, believing that the two pictures were each produced as autonomous works. This view finds support in the fact that both paintings appear not to share the same provenance, in as far as one can judge from the corresponding entries in the auction catalogue of 1696 (on the interpretation of these texts cf. Liedtke 2008, p. 108). Moreover, the perspective underlying the arrangement of the interior depicted in each of the two pictures is itself different, as is most clearly to be seen in the foreshortening in the pattern of the floor made up of black and white flagstones. While it is true that the horizon line lies at the same height in both compositions, the implicit degree of spatial recession differs from one to the other, with the result that the scale of the foreshortening is itself different and the figures in the present picture appear to be closer to the spectator. It would in any case be possible that Vermeer painted the second of the two pictures as a later complement to the existing one. *The Concert* has generally been seen as a work produced several years later than *The Music Lesson* (Wheelock 1995b: *c.* 1665/66; Liedtke 2008: *c.* 1663–1666). Blankert (1986, pp. 186f.) believes *The Concert* and *The Music Lesson* to be contemporary, both dating to 1664, and in any case later than Cat. 16–18.

Two ladies and a cavalier are seen making music together. In the inventories of this period this type of composition was known as "a gay company". The lady standing to the right accompanies her song with a raised right hand, although it is not clear whether her gesture is to be interpreted as an expression of the strong feeling called forth by the music, or if she is, in fact, beating time. The cavalier, whom we view from the rear, is playing a lute, of which we see only the curled finial. The seated lady to the left accompanies him on the clavichord.

See also pp. 137–138, *183*.

LITERATURE: Gowing 1952 (1970), pp. 37ff., 119–127; Slatkes 1981, p. 66; Wheelock 1981

20

(1988), pp. 120–122; Blankert/Montias/Aillaud 1986 (1987, 1992, 2007), pp. 120ff., 187, cat. 17; Nash 1991, p. 123; Schneider 1993 (2010), pp. 38f.; Wheelock 1995b, pp. 113–119; Liedtke 2000, pp. 245–247; Goodman 2001, pp. 85–88; Liedtke 2008, pp. 108–111, cat. 16; Büttner 2010, p. 81; Blanc 2014, pp. 87f., 94, 254.

20

A Lady Writing, *c.* 1665–1667
Oil on canvas, 45 x 39.9 cm / 17 ¾ x 15 ¾ in., signedon the picture frame in the background: IVMeer (IVM in ligature)
Washington, D.C., National Gallery of Art, Gift of Harry Waldron Havemeyer and Horace Havemeyer, Jr., in memory of their father, Horace Havemeyer, Sr., inv. 1962.10.1

Probably once in the collection of Pieter Claesz. van Ruijven, the picture was included in the 1696 Amsterdam sale by auction of the estate of his son-in-law, Jacob Abrahamsz. Dissius, as no. 35: "Een Schryvende Juffrouw heel goet van denzelven [J. vander Meer]" (see Sources, no. 30; A young lady writing, very good, by the same [J. vander Meer]).
The painting did not re-emerged until a century later, when the collection of J. van Buren was sold at auction in 1808 in The Hague. Here, as no. 22, it was described as: "Een bevallig vrouwtje in 't geel satyn met bond gekleed [...] uitmuntend fraai, uitvoerig en meesterlyk gepenseeld door da Delfsche van der Meer [...] zeer raar" (cited from Blankert 1992, p. 190) / "A delightful young woman dressed in yellow satin with a border [...] exceptionally pretty, carefully and masterly painted by van der Meer of Delft [...] very particular." The picture was then repeatedly auctioned: in 1816, as part of the collection of Cornelis Jan Luchtmans; in 1825 in Rotterdam, as part of the collection of E. Kamermans; and in 1827 in Amsterdam. Here, it was sold to François-Xavier Comte de Robiano (1778–1836), of Brussels; it then stayed in this collection until 1906. It was acquired in 1907 in New York by J. Pierpont Morgan (1837–1913) and exhibited on loan at that city's Metropolitan Museum of

Art until 1913. In 1940 it was sold by J. Pierpont Morgan, Jr. (1867–1943), his son, until 1946 it was in the possession of Sir Harry Oakes (1874–1943) and then of his widow in Nassau, Bahamas. It subsequently entered the collection of Horace Havemeyer (1866–1956), of New York. In 1962 the picture was donated by his sons to the National Gallery of Art in Washington, D.C.

This is one of the paintings by Vermeer that were already recognized as an autograph work in the early 19th century (cf. Cat. 16–18). It was probably painted *c.* 1665–1667 (Blankert 1986: 1666; Wheelock, in Wheelock/Broos 1995: *c.* 1665; Liedtke 2008: *c.* 1665–1667), and it seems to follow closely on the group of paintings of a single female figure that Vermeer produced in the first half of the 1660s (cf. Cat. 14–18). With its penumbral setting, it most readily recalls *Woman with a Balance* (Cat. 18), in all probability the latest work of this group. The two pictures also share the same sort of still life on a table – a box with glinting metal mounts, a string of pearls, a blue cloth – to which our attention is in both cases drawn through Vermeer's rendering of the play of light upon each object.

In addition to his two paintings of women reading letters (Cat. 5, 16), Vermeer frequently depicted women engaged in the writing of a missive. In two pictures the letter writer is accompanied by a maid, who either hands her a letter that has just arrived (Cat. 24), or waits for the letter being written to be finished in order to deliver it to its addressee (Cat. 31). In *A Lady Writing* the writer gazes at the viewer and thereby effectively dissolves the nominal distinction between a portrait and a genre painting. It is not least on this account that commentators have, from time to time, supposed that the picture might, in fact, be a portrait, perhaps of Vermeer's own wife. The yellow satin jacket with its fur border is worn by many of the women in Vermeer's pictures, among them *Woman with a Lute* (Cat. 15), *Woman with a Pearl Necklace* (Cat. 17) and the seated figure seen in *Mistress and Maid* (Cat. 24).

See also pp. 147–148, *199*.

21

LITERATURE: Gowing 1952 (1970), p. 134; Slatkes 1981, p. 70; Wheelock 1981 (1988), pp. 124–126; Blankert/Montias/Aillaud 1986 (1987, 1992, 2007), p. 189, cat. 20; The Hague/San Francisco 1990/91, pp. 456–462, cat. 67; Frankfurt 1993/94, pp. 314–316, cat. 85; Schneider 1993 (2010), p. 50; Wheelock 1995a, pp. 377–382; Wheelock/Broos 1995, pp. 156–159, cat. 13; Liedtke 2000, pp. 239–242; Vergara 2003, pp. 54f.; Dublin/Greenwich 2003/04, cat. 38; Liedtke 2008, pp. 122–124, cat. 20; Büttner 2010, p. 62; Blanc 2014, p. 90.

21

Girl with a Pearl Earring, *c.* 1665–1667
Oil on canvas, 44.5 x 39 cm / 17 ½ x 15 ⅜ in.,
signed top left corner:
IVMeer (IVM in ligature)
The Hague, Koninklijk Kabinet van
Schilderijen Mauritshuis, inv. 670

Commentators of this painting have proposed its identification with one of two pictures included in the inventory of Vermeer's estate, as: "Twee tronyen geschildert op sijn Turx" (see Sources, no. 24) / "Two 'tronien' painted in Turkish fashion" (trans. Montias 1989, p. 340, doc. 364). An alternative argument was put forward by Liedtke (2008, p. 196): that *Girl with a Pearl Earring* could be one of the three studies of heads that were in the collection of Pieter Claesz. van Ruijven. These were included in the 1696 Amsterdam sale by auction of the estate of his son-in-law, Jacob Abrahamsz. Dissius, as nos. 38, 39 and 40. The first of these was described in the sale catalogue as: "Een Tronie in Antique Klederen, ungemeen konstig" (see Sources, no. 30; The study of a head in Antique dress, uncommonly skilful). It has been thought unlikely (see Wheelock/Broos 1995, p. 168, note 9) that the painting is identifiable as either no. 39 or no. 40 at the 1696 sale.

The first secure reference to the present picture dates from 1881, when it was included in the Braams auction in The Hague, where it was up for sale as part of the Dutch collection of Arnoldus Andries des Tombe (1818–1902), and where it was acquired for the modest sum of just two guilders, even though Victor de Stuers had by this date already identified it as the work of Vermeer. As was later reported, however, Des Tombe and Stuers had reached an agreement not to bid against each other. The Des Tombe Collection in The Hague, in which the picture remained from 1881 until the collector's death, in 1902, was open to visitors.

In 1885 Abraham Bredius was the first to praise the meisjeskopje ("head of a girl") as Vermeer's masterpiece, and the picture was shown in 1890 at an exhibition in The Hague organized by the Pulchri Studio artists' association, and in 1900 for a while at the Mauritshuis. In 1903 it was bequeathed to the Mauritshuis along with 11 other pictures from the Des Tombe Collection. At this time there were reports in the press on the circumstances of the auction of 1881, estimating the value of the already celebrated picture at 40,000 guilders (Wheelock/Broos 1995, p. 168). This small composition, acclaimed as the "Dutch Mona Lisa", has become the best-known work by Vermeer. In the last 15 years, as the inspiration for the novel *Girl with a Pearl Earring* (1999), by the American author Tracy Chevalier, and then for Peter Webber's film of the book (2003), made in the United States, Great Britain and Luxembourg, it has achieved truly international popularity.

Along with the related studies of heads by Vermeer, *Girl with a Pearl Earring* is dated by most commentators to *c.* 1665–1667 (Blankert 1986: 1665; Wheelock, in Wheelock/Broos 1995: 1665/66; Liedtke 2008: *c.* 1665–1667). It would be difficult to date the painting on the evidence of its style because it has so little in common with Vermeer's genre scenes, while offering few clear connections with contemporary fashions in female attire. The attempt to identify the model as Vermeer's eldest daughter, Maria, who was born in 1654, is not convincing. In 1667 Maria would have been only 13 years old; and a later date for the painting appears improbable on stylistic grounds. The only more secure frame of reference for dating the picture is to be found in technical aspects of its execution: for example, Vermeer's use of several layers of thin, flesh-coloured glaze over a transparently modelled base so as to attain softly merging flesh tones. Vermeer evolved this technique from around 1662 to 1664, as demonstrated by paintings such as *Young Woman with a Water Pitcher* (Cat. 14) or *Woman with a Balance* (Cat. 18). In *Girl with a Pearl Earring* the additional points of reflected light in the eyes, on the lips of the slightly opened mouth and on the teeth augment the impression of a melting softness, an effect that is at its most compelling when one is able to view the picture at close quarters.

Girl with a Pearl Earring is the study of a head, a type of picture first attested in Flemish and Dutch painting of the 16th century and very common there in the 17th century. Such a picture was known as a tronie (from the Middle French term for a character head, *trogne*). Like a portrait, the study of a head captures the appearance of an individual model; unlike a portrait, however, it is intended to remain anonymous. In the case of *Girl with a Pearl Earring* the complete absence of any further characterization or definition of the figure probably accounts for the immediacy of expression and for the strong impact the picture has upon the viewer. This impact is further heightened by the unified black background, against which the girl's head stands out, removed from context.

See also pp. 151–152, *217*.

LITERATURE: Gowing 1952 (1970), pp. 137–139; Slatkes 1981, p. 69; Wheelock 1981 (1988), p. 118; Blankert/Montias/Alliaud 1986 (1987, 1992, 2007), pp. 122, 188, cat. 18; Nash 1991, pp. 19, 31–34; Schneider 1993 (2010), pp. 69–72; Wheelock/Broos 1995, pp. 166–169, cat. 15; Groen 1998, pp. 169–183; Liedtke 2000, pp. 243–245; Broos/Van Suchtelen 2004, cat. 59; Liedtke 2008, pp. 130–133, cat. 22; Büttner 2010, pp. 39–42; Blanc 2014, pp. 180–194, 239–241, 255.

22

22

Study of a Young Woman, *c.* 1665–1667
Oil on canvas, 44.5 x 40 cm / 17½ x 15¾ in., signed top left: IVMeer (IVM in ligature)
New York, The Metropolitan Museum of Art, Gift of Mr and Mrs Charles Wrightsman, in memory of Theodore Rousseau, Jr., inv. 1979.396.1

The picture can perhaps be identified as one of the three studies of heads in "antique" clothing that were included in the 1696 Amsterdam sale by auction of the estate of Jacob Abrahamsz. Dissius, as no. 38: "Een Tronie in Antique Klederen, ongemeen konstig", or as no. 39: "Nog en dito Vermeer", or as no. 40: "Eeen weerga van denzelven" (see Sources, no. 30; The study of a head in Antique dress, uncommonly skilful; Another such Vermeer; A pendant of the same). If *Study of a Young Woman* was indeed one of these pictures, this would indicate that it had originally been commissioned or bought by the father-in-law of Dissius, Pieter Claesz. van Ruijven, who had been Vermeer's most important patron. Equally hypothetical is the identification of the painting as a picture included, as no. 92, in the sale by auction of the collection of Jan Luchtmans, in Rotterdam on 20 April 1816, where it was described as: "J. van der Meer de Delft, Le portrait d'une jeune personne" (cited from Blankert 1992, p. 201) / "J. van der Meer of Delft, The portrait of a young person." Thereafter, the painting is next securely recorded in the collection of the Dukes of Arenberg at Brussels, being published as no. 53 in the 1829 collection catalogue, where it is described as: "Jean van der Meer de Delft, Portrait d'une femme affublé d'un manteau bleu" (cited from Blankert 1992, p. 201) / "Johannes van der Meer of Delft, Portrait of a woman, wrapped in a blue cloak." In 1859 the painting was described by Thoré-Bürger as one of the six works of Vermeer then known to him, in his publication on the Arenberg Collection. On the outbreak of the First World War the Arenberg family moved the painting from Brussels to their German residence, at Meppen. Its whereabouts thereafter are unknown until

23

1955, when it was acquired on the art market by Charles Wrightsman. In 1979 it was donated to The Metropolitan Museum of Art in New York by Mr and Mrs Charles Wrightsman, in honour of Theodore Rousseau, Jr.

It is probable that this painting was produced at more or less the same time as *Girl with a Pearl Earring* (Cat. 21), that is to say, *c.* 1665–1667; it also shares with that picture its format and its black, spatially undifferentiated background. Blankert (1986), however, regards the picture as a late work, dating it to *c.* 1672–1674; Wheelock (in Wheelock/Broos 1995, p. 75, fig. 134) believes it to date from 1666/67; and Liedtke (2008) proposes a date of *c.* 1665–1667. In inventories compiled in this period there are references to studies of heads both in ornamental, or "Turkish", dress and in clothing evocative of Classical Antiquity. One can well imagine that a picture such as *Girl with a Pearl Earring*, mainly because of the turban, might be described as "Turkish". On the other hand, it could just as well be regarded as an allusion to Antiquity on account of the young woman's clothing, even though this consists merely of a single gleaming white silken cloth draped around the sitter and supplied with no further distinguishing details. The subject's pearl earring, her shaved eyebrows and her high forehead do, however, fully correspond with contemporary fashion.

See also pp. 151–152, *219*.

LITERATURE: Gowing 1952 (1970), p. 138; Slatkes 1981, p. 104; Wheelock 1981 (1988), p. 132; Blankert/Montias/Aillaud 1986 (1987, 1992, 2007), pp. 148, 201, cat. 30; Schneider 1993 (2010), p. 72; Liedtke 2000, pp. 243f.; New York/London 2001, pp. 389–393, cat. 75; Fahy 2005, pp. 131–135; Liedtke 2007, pp. 888–893; Liedtke 2008, pp. 134f., cat. 23; Büttner 2010, p. 39.

23

The Girl with the Red Hat, *c.* 1665–1667
Oil on panel, 22.8 x 18 cm / 9 x 7 ⅛ in.,
signed top left centre: IVM (in ligature)
Washington, D.C., National Gallery of Art,
Andrew W. Mellon Collection, inv. 1937.1.53

Perhaps painted for Pieter Claesz. van Ruijven, this picture may be identified as one of the head studies that were included in the 1696 sale by auction of the estate of his son-in-law, Jacob Abrahamsz. Dissius, as no. 38, no. 39 or no. 40 (see Cat. 22). *The Girl with the Red Hat* is first securely recorded through its inclusion, as no. 28, in the auction of the collection of the art dealer La Fontaine in Paris on 10 December 1822. In 1823 it was acquired by Louis Marie Baron Atthalin, of Colmar, military commander with the rank of general and landscape painter, remaining in the possession of his descendants until 1925, when it was acquired, on the art market, by Andrew W. Mellon (1855–1937), of Washington, D.C. The painting remained in his possession until 1932, then was transferred to the A. W. Mellon Educational and Charitable Trust, Pittsburgh, Pennsylvania, until 1937, when it entered the collection of the National Gallery of Art in Washington, D.C.

Thoré-Bürger (1866, p. 567, no. 47: "A rechercher, à vérifier, à étudier") was familiar with *The Girl with the Red Hat* only through its description in the 1822 auction catalogue. It was not until 1925 that this picture – until that date totally unknown to art historians – was first seen in Paris, at the house of the widow of Gaston Laurent-Atthalin, by Pierre Lavallée, curator at the Paris École Nationale des Beaux-Arts. Lavallée then published his sensational rediscovery of a heretofore unknown work by Vermeer. The attribution to Vermeer has, nonetheless, frequently been questioned on account of the picture's format, the choice (unusual for Vermeer) of wood, rather than canvas, as a support and certain aspects of the painting technique here employed (Wheelock/Broos 1995, p. 165, note 3): by Swillens (1950) and Blankert (1986, p. 205, cat. b3), among others.

The Girl with the Red Hat may be dated to the mid-1660s, that is to say, to around the time of Vermeer's two larger studies of heads: *Girl with a Pearl Earring* (Cat. 21) and *Study of a Young Woman* (Cat. 22). Wheelock (in Wheelock/Broos 1995, p, 160, cat. 14) posits a date of *c.* 1655, which would place this picture at a point earlier than 1665/66, the date that he proposes

24

for *Girl with a Pearl Earring*. Liedtke (2008, p. 136) dates all three pictures to *c.* 1665–1667. The present painting differs from the two larger studies of heads in its distinct overall composition, in the extent to which the figure is closely cropped by the frame – which nonetheless also suggests a setting – and in the relatively large scale of the sitter. The implied distance between the objects shown in front of and behind the girl is so emphatically reduced as to appear to simulate a scene viewed through a telescope. The combination of this optical peculiarity and the relatively loose brushwork has been repeatedly cited as a reason for believing that Vermeer must have employed a camera obscura when at work on this picture, or must at least have intended to imitate the sort of image that would thereby be obtained (on this, cf. Wheelock/Broos 1995, p. 162; Liedtke 2008, p. 179). On the anomaly of Vermeer's painting technique here in relation to that found in his other pictures, see, among others, Wheelock/Broos 1995, p. 160. The emphatically individual facial features would suggest that Vermeer was here working from a live model, perhaps the same one who posed for his *Girl with a Flute* (Cat. 25).

See also pp. 152–155, *221*.

Literature: Gowing 1952 (1970), pp. 146f.; Slatkes 1981, p. 97; Wheelock 1981 (1988), p. 130; Blankert/Montias/Aillaud 1986 (1987, 1992, 2007), p. 205, cat. b3; Schneider 1993 (2010), p. 72; Wheelock 1995a, pp. 382–387; Wheelock 1995b, pp. 121–127; Wheelock/Broos 1995, pp. 160–165, cat. 14; Liedtke 2000, pp. 242–245; Liedtke 2001f, pp. 386–389, cat. 74; Madrid 2003, p. 176, cat. 37; Liedtke 2008, pp. 136–139, cat. 24; Büttner 2010, p. 41; Rome 2012/13, p. 216, cat. 49; Blanc 2014, pp. 240–246.

24

Mistress and Maid, *c.* 1666/67

Oil on canvas, 90.2 x 78.7 cm / 35 ½ x 31 in.

New York, The Frick Collection, inv. 1919.1.126

If this picture is understood to be identical with the item included as no. 7 in the 1696 Amsterdam sale by auction of the estate of Jacob Abrahamsz. Dissius, it may well have been in the collection of the latter's father-in-law, Pieter Claesz. van Ruijven. The sale catalogue describes the painting as: "Een Juffrouw die door een Meyd een brief gebragt word" (see Sources, no. 30) / "A young lady who is being brought a letter by a maid" (trans. Montias 1989, p. 364, doc. 439). Commentators have differed in their opinions as to whether this description refers to the present painting. Montias (1989, pp. 184, 217, 260) argues that it does not; whereas Broos (in Wheelock/Broos 1995, p. 184, note 14) and, following him, Liedtke (2008, p. 129) believe that it does. Vermeer's painting *The Love Letter* (Cat. 30) has been proposed as an alternative to which the catalogue text might refer. When included in an Amsterdam auction of 1738, *Mistress and Maid* was described in the catalogue as: "een schryvent Juffertje in haar Binnekamer die een Brief ontfangt, door de delfse van der Meer" (cited from Blankert 1992, p. 191) / "A young woman writing in her chamber who receives a letter, by van der Meer of Delft." In the early decades of the 19th century the picture was repeatedly auctioned in Paris; in 1802 it was attributed to "Van der Meer de Delft", and it was again on offer in 1818 and, finally, in 1837. Between 1889 and 1905 it was in a collection in Saint Petersburg; and at an unknown date between 1906 and 1914 at the latest, it entered a collection in Berlin. Here, in 1919, it was acquired by the art dealer Knoedler, on behalf of Henry Clay Frick. It was the third painting by Vermeer to enter Frick's collection (cf. Cat. 6, 11).

On account of its large size and the correspondingly large scale of its two protagonists, *Mistress and Maid* is something of an exception within Vermeer's oeuvre. Both figures are effectively three-quarters life-size, surpassing in this respect those found in every other painting by the artist, with the exception of the early works produced before 1656. *Mistress and Maid* is distinct from Vermeer's other genre paintings, above all, on account of its black background: apart from the suggestion of the folds of a curtain, there is nothing here to convey aspects of any sort of setting. The black background does, however, recall the example of Vermeer's more or less con-

25

temporary studies of heads (Cat. 21, 22). As his loose brushwork here also recalls what is to be found in those pictures, *Mistress and Maid* may be dated to between 1665 and 1670, and probably at the earliest to 1666/67 (Blankert 1986: 1666/67; Wheelock 1995b: *c.* 1667/68; Liedtke 2008: *c.* 1666/67). Blankert (1986, p. 140) surmises that Vermeer here failed in an attempt to bring a formal monumentality to a genre subject and, for this reason, left the painting unfinished. But, as Wheelock (1995b) has very convincingly argued, neither the painting technique nor the execution supports this conclusion.

Vermeer treated the subject of a letter being written or received in several of his paintings (see also Cat. 5, 16, 20). The present picture is, however, the first in which the letter writer is shown in the company of a maid. In his late work Vermeer twice returned to this subject (Cat. 30, 31), retaining the figure of the maid.

See also pp. 147–149, *215*.

LITERATURE: Gowing 1952 (1970), pp. 146f.; Davidson 1968, pp. 296–299; Slatkes 1981, p. 81; Wheelock 1981 (1988), p. 134; Blankert/Montias/Aillaud 1986 (1987, 1992, 2007), pp. 140, 190f., cat. 21; Nash 1991, pp. 22, 82, 94; Schneider 1993 (2010), p. 51; Wheelock 1995b, pp. 141–147; Liedtke 2000, pp. 241f.; Vergara 2003, pp. 55f.; Liedtke 2008, pp. 126–129, cat. 21; Büttner 2010, p. 62; Blanc 2014, pp. 304–310, 339.

25

Johannes Vermeer and an unidentified follower

Girl with a Flute, *c.* 1665–1670

Oil on panel, 20 x 17.8 cm / 7 ⅞ x 7 in.

Washington, D.C., National Gallery of Art, Widener Collection, inv. 1942.9.98

The early provenance of this picture has yet to be resolved, and various suppositions have been put forward regarding its first owners. We know that in 1676 the landscape painter Jan Coelenbier (*c.* 1610–1677) acquired a number of paintings from Vermeer's estate (see Sources, no. 22). It is possible that the unfinished *Girl with a Flute* was among these, and that Coelenbier himself completed the composition with a view to selling the painting. It is, however, also possible that the picture was originally in the collection of Pieter Claesz. van Ruijven, in which case it may perhaps be identified with one of the three studies of heads included, as nos. 38, 39 and 40, in the 1696 Amsterdam sale by auction of the estate of his son-in-law, Jacob Abrahamsz. Dissius (cf. Cat. 22; see Sources, no. 30). Both conjectures are, however, highly speculative and in no way verifiable.

The picture is not securely recorded until the late 19th century, when it was in the Van Son Collection in 's-Hertogenbosch. It was thereafter owned by Jan Mahie van Boxtel en Liempde and his wife, Geertruida, née Van Son. In 1876 it was sold from her estate, for a sum of 32 florins, to her daughter, Jacqueline Gertrude Marie de Grez van Boxtel en Liempde, of Brussels. In 1906, while still in the Grez Collection, the picture was discovered by Abraham Bredius, who recognized it as a work by Vermeer (Bredius 1906/07, pp. 385f.). From 1907 *Girl with a Flute* was on loan to, and on display at, the Mauritshuis in The Hague, but after 1910 it was sold, for 25,000 florins. It was subsequently in the August Janssen Collection, Amsterdam. After Janssen's death, in 1918, the Amsterdam art dealer Jacques Goudstikker offered the picture for sale at 325,000 florins. It was eventually sold to Joseph E. Widener, of Lynnewood Hall, Elkins Park, Philadelphia, Pennsylvania, who in 1942 presented it to the National Gallery of Art in Washington, D.C.

Doubts have repeatedly been voiced regarding the attribution of *Girl with a Flute* to Vermeer. Starting with Swillens (1950) and, in particular, Blankert (1975, and again in Blankert/Montias/Aillaud 1986, p. 206, cat. b4), and then Brentjes (1985), the view has been put forward that both this picture and *The Girl with the Red Hat* (Cat. 23) were, in fact, painted in the 18th century, as indicated, above all, by considerations of the history of costume. But dendrochronological and further technical examination of the wooden panel have, nonetheless, confirmed that this support was prepared in the mid-17th century, and that both the paints used and the technique of their application correspond with the practice of that period (Wheelock/Broos 1995, p. 206).

26

In both composition and execution *Girl with a Flute* is most closely comparable to *The Girl with the Red Hat* (Cat. 23). It is, indeed, possible that Vermeer shows the same model in both pictures (Liedtke 2008, p. 142); and in both we also find these figures dressed in extravagant or exotic pieces of clothing. Also common to both studies is a notably economical account of the figure's setting, of which we see only a small segment, albeit this does include clearly characterized items of furniture, such as the chairs with their lion-head finials and the tapestry hanging in the background, items familiar from other Vermeer interiors.

The two paintings are, however, markedly unalike in other ways, not least in their respective states of preservation. *The Girl with a Flute* was subsequently altered by another hand. It is now generally assumed (by, among others, Wheelock, in Wheelock/Broos 1995, pp. 204–208; Liedtke 2008, pp. 141f.) that Vermeer started work on the painting but broke off before finishing it. The picture apparently suffered serious, and by no means only superficial, damage; and it was eventually altered and completed by another painter. At a later date the surface of the painting suffered abrasions, and it was subsequently further compromised through cleaning, retouching and other efforts at restoration. See also pp. 152–155, *223*.

LITERATURE: Gowing 1952 (1970), p. 146; Wheelock 1978, pp. 242, 251–256; Slatkes 1981, p. 98; Wheelock 1981 (1988), pp. 45, 156; Blankert/Montias/Aillaud 1986 (1987, 1992, 2007), p. 206, cat. b4; Schneider 1993 (2010), p. 72; Wheelock 1995a, pp. 387–393; Wheelock/Broos 1995, pp. 204–208, cat. 23; Liedtke 2000, pp. 244f.; Liedtke 2008, pp. 140–142, cat. 25; Büttner 2010, p. 41; Blanc 2014, pp. 220, 252.

26

The Art of Painting, *c.* 1666–1668
Oil on canvas, 120 x 100 cm / 47 ¼ x 39 ⅜ in., signed on the frame of the map: I Ver-Meer; overpainted date: MDCLXVI (II?)
Vienna, Kunsthistorisches Museum, Gemäldegalerie, inv. GG_9128

This picture remained in Vermeer's possession until his death. On 24 February 1676, in order to save it from the clutches of creditors, his widow, Catharina Bolnes, transferred it to the possession of her mother, Maria Thins (*c.* 1593–1680; see Sources, no. 23). On 15 March 1677 it was sold at auction in Delft (see Sources, no. 26). It later re-emerged in the estate of Gottfried van Swieten (1733–1803), an Austrian diplomat, Prefect of the Imperial Court Library in Vienna, and the son of the Leiden-born Gerard van Swieten (1700–1772), who had been personal physician to the Austrian Empress Maria Theresa (1717–1780). Although it has repeatedly been supposed that Gerard van Swieten may himself have owned the picture, and taken it to Vienna from his native Holland, this has yet to be proved. At the 1804 auction of Gottfried van Swieten's estate the painting, then attributed to Pieter de Hooch, was acquired, for 50 florins, by Count Johann Rudolph Czernin von Chudenitz (1757–1845; Juffinger/Brandhuber 2010, p. 67). It then remained in the Galerie Czernin in Vienna, a private collection that was open to visitors, until October 1940, when the Czernin family sold it, for 1,650,000 Reichsmarks, to the then German Chancellor, Adolf Hitler (Hehenberger/Löscher 2013, pp. 105–164), who intended it for his planned "Führermuseum" in Linz (Schwarz 2004, pp. 107, 226). By 1945 the picture was to be found in the Central Collecting Point in Munich, and on 28 November of that year it was formally returned by the United States Forces in Austria to the Austrian Federal Government, in due course being transferred to Vienna's Kunsthistorisches Museum, where it was stored and eventually put on public display. Attempts by the picture's principal former owner, Jaromir Czernin, to have it returned to the Czernin family were not upheld by the Administrative Court in 1960. After the new Austrian law on the restitution of works of art came into force in 1998, the legal successors of Jaromir Czernin revived his quest for restitution. But, after exhaustive research into the matter (Hehenberger/Löscher 2013), the Restitution Committee meeting in 2011 denied their application. Until 1860 the painting had been attributed to Pieter de

Hooch. Then, independently of each other and more or less simultaneously, both Gustav Friedrich Waagen (1862, 2, p. 110) and Thoré-Bürger (1859) recognized that this was a work by Vermeer. The painting still bears the signature of Pieter de Hooch, clearly added later, on the stool on which the painter sits. The most recent examination of the picture with infrared reflectography (2009) revealed that next to Vermeer's original signature, on the map's lower "frame" (later overpainted and, at an unknown date, uncovered), there was also an inscribed date (itself overpainted but not uncovered), which could be read as "1666" or "1667/68". The space between each of the numerals and the extent of the overpainting would make 1668 the more likely date (Wald 2010, p. 196). This would also correspond with what we can learn from the stylistic evidence of the picture, and with the dating generally favoured by commentators (e.g. Liedtke 2008, p. 144: *c.* 1666–1668).

Although at first glance appearing to capture a scene from the everyday life of Dutch society, in the manner of a genre painting, Vermeer's picture is nothing of the sort. Rather, it is an allegory (cf. also the *Allegory of Faith*, Cat. 34). As such, it embodies the nobler ambitions of a history painting (on which see Wheelock 2010, p. 24). Here, it is the art of painting itself that Vermeer presents in allegorical form, as indicated by the title, "Schilderkonst", under which the picture was listed in the inventory of Vermeer's estate, and which we may assume that he himself chose. There are no grounds for believing that Vermeer intended to depict himself in this painting, as has repeatedly been assumed, nor for interpreting the interior as a rendering of Vermeer's own studio. In "turning his back" on the viewer, the painter shown here at work remains anonymous, thereby assuming a timeless and universal significance. His female model is posed and costumed as Clio, the Muse of History, as was first observed by Hultén (1949). Her attributes correspond to those given by Cesare Ripa (1555–1622), in his *Iconologia*, for the personification of History, leading us to assume that Vermeer here precisely followed this model. The painting's left edge is almost entirely taken

27

up by a tapestry, a section of which is pulled aside. This is in such close proximity to our own implied viewing position that we see neither how it is attached to the beamed ceiling nor how it is gathered and secured.

See also pp. 228–238, *265*.

LITERATURE: Hultén 1949, pp. 90–98; Van Gelder 1951, pp. 44f.; Sedlmayr 1951, pp. 169–177; Gowing 1952 (1970), pp. 139–144; Tolnay 1953, pp. 265–272; Van Gelder 1958; Badt 1961; Sedlmayr 1962, pp. 34–65; Slatkes 1981, pp. 77f.; Wheelock 1981 (1988), p. 128; Blankert/Montias/Aillaud 1986 (1987, 1992, 2007), pp. 124–126, 188f., cat. 19; Asemissen 1988; Nash 1991, pp. 119–126; Schneider 1993 (2010), pp. 81–84; Wheelock 1995b, pp. 129–139; Hertel 1996, pp. 167–170, 176–186, 200–204; Miedema 1998; Sluijter 1998; Schlenke 1998, pp. 61–75; Washington 1999; Liedtke 2000, pp. 247–251; New York/London 2001, pp. 394–398, cat. 76; Madrid 2003, pp. 178f., cat. 38; Liedtke 2008, pp. 144–147, cat. 26; Büttner 2010, pp. 99–108; Vienna 2010; Hehenberger/Löscher 2013; Blanc 2014, pp. 25–30, 166–171, 209–211, 312f.

27

The Astronomer, 1668

Oil on canvas, 51.5 x 45.5 cm / 20 ¼ x 17 ⅞ in., signed and dated on cabinet:
IVMeer / MDCLXVIII (IVM in ligature)
Paris, Musée du Louvre, inv. RF 1983–28

It appears that Vermeer was commissioned – though by whom remains uncertain – to paint *The Astronomer* and *The Geographer* (Cat. 28) as pendants. Support for this assumption comes rather less from the similarities between the two paintings in terms of composition than from their almost identical dimensions (Frankfurt 1997, p. 11), the fact that, throughout the entire 18th century the two pictures were treated as a pair and their respective subjects. For they show exponents of two interrelated scientific disciplines that were keenly cultivated in Holland. The results of technical investigations confirm that the two pictures may be viewed as a pair (Waldeis 1997, pp. 39–46). And the probability that they were commissioned is itself supported by the sudden appearance of this entirely new subject in Vermeer's oeuvre. It has been suggested that the paintings were commissioned by the celebrated Delft natural scientist Antoni van Leeuwenhoek (1632–1723), who was appointed executor of Vermeer's estate after the latter's death (Wheelock, in Wheelock/Broos 1995, p. 172; Wheelock 1997, pp. 19f.). This ostensibly very reasonable supposition has, however, been called into question by Van Berkel (1997), among others. And Liedtke (2008, p. 152), pointing to the early provenance of both pictures in the collection of Adriaen Paets I (1631–1686), Director of the Dutch East India Company in Rotterdam and, like Pieter Claesz. van Ruijven, a Remonstrant, proposes that he may indeed have commissioned these works. The collection of Adriaen Paets I was inherited by his son, Adriaen Paets II (1657–1712), after whose death it was sold at auction. On 27 April 1713, at an anonymous auction held in Rotterdam – Van Gelder supposes that this was, in fact, an attempt to dispose of all that remained unsold at the previous day's auction of the collection of Adriaen Paets II – *The Astronomer* and *The Geographer* were included, as nos. 10 and 11, and described, respectively, as: "Een stuk verbeeldende een Mathematis Konstenaar, door vander Meer" and "Een dito door denzelven" (cited from Wheelock/Broos 1995, p. 175, note 18) / "A Work depicting a Mathematical Artist, by vander Meer" and "A ditto by the same" (trans. Wheelock/Broos 1995, p. 172). They eventually fetched the high sale price of 300 florins.

Thereafter, the two pictures passed through several Dutch collections, always as a pair, until 1778 (for detailed commentary on provenance, see Maek-Gérard 1997, pp. 50–52), being owned at one point by Jacob Crammer Simonsz., of Amsterdam, whose collection also boasted two further works by Vermeer: *The Lacemaker* (Cat. 29) and a now untraced work showing a woman pouring wine. *The Astronomer* and *The Geographer* later entered the collection of Jan Danser Nijman (1735–1796), who was also a subsequent owner of *The Lacemaker*, in addition to possessing *Young Woman Standing at a Virginal* (Cat. 33). But it was at an auction that took place in 1797 that *The Astrono-*

28

mer and *The Geographer* were eventually sold to different collectors.

The provenance of *The Astronomer* can from this point be traced without interruption. During the course of the 19th century the picture passed through several English collections before, at an unknown date between 1881 and 1888, entering that of Alphonse de Rothschild (1827–1905), in Paris. Seized in November 1940, as a work intended for Adolf Hitler's planned "Führermuseum" in Linz, the picture was returned to its rightful owner in 1945. After the death of Guy de Rothschild in 1982 *The Astronomer* entered the collection of the Louvre.

From the point of view of composition, both *The Astronomer* and *The Geographer* are close to Vermeer's depictions of single female figures from the first half of the 1660s (cf. Cat. 14–18). Thematically, they function as reciprocal allegories of Heaven and Earth. In the historical context of the flowering of the natural sciences in 17th-century Holland, astronomy and geography constituted two aspects of cosmography. In each picture the depicted scholar has the same physiognomy and hairstyle, and wears the same sort of scholar's robes. This has led some to believe that the person who commissioned the works had himself portrayed in both (as outlined by Wheelock, in Wheelock/Broos 1995, p. 172). The scholar seen in *The Astronomer* is shown rising slightly from his chair as he reaches out to turn a celestial sphere. A large astrolabe lies on the table, leaning against the base of the sphere's wooden stand, and on the cupboard hangs a wall chart with a planisphere of the Heavens (Welu 1986, p. 266). The picture hanging on the rear wall depicts the biblical story of the finding of Moses.

See also pp. 238–242, *269*.

LITERATURE: Gowing 1952 (1970), pp. 147–151; Slatkes 1981, pp. 82f.; Wheelock 1981 (1988), pp. 13, 136–138; Blankert/Montias/Aillaud 1986 (1987, 1992, 2007), pp. 140ff., 193f., cat. 23; Welu 1986; Nash 1991, pp. 104, 106; Schneider 1993 (2010), pp. 75–77; Frankfurt 1997; Liedtke 2000, pp. 262f.; Van Berkel 2001; Liedtke 2008, pp. 148–152, cat. 28; Büttner 2010, pp. 91–98; Blanc 2014, pp. 158–160, 274–283, 337.

28

The Geographer, 1669

Oil on canvas, 51.6 x 45.4 cm / 20 ¼ x 17 ⅞ in., signed and dated on cupboard: Meer; above the map: I. Ver Meer / MDCLXVIIII
Frankfurt am Main, Städel Museum, inv. 1149

The Geographer is a pendant to *The Astronomer* (Cat. 27). Questions as to who may have commissioned the two works, their original appearance as a pair and their shared provenance until 1797 are addressed in the entry for Cat. 27. When the two pictures were separated *The Geographer* entered the collection of Arnoud de Lange, of Amsterdam, where it remained until 1803. It was then in the collection of Pieter Hendrick Goll van Franckenstein, also of Amsterdam, until 1833. Until 1860 it was owned by Alexandre Dumont, of Cambrai, and was there identified as a work by Vermeer and published as such, by Paul Mantz. At an unknown date between 1860 and 1866 it was acquired by Thoré-Bürger, on behalf of the banker Isaac Péreire, who owned it until 1872. In 1872–1875 it was in the collection of Max Kann, in Paris; then, until 1880, in that of Prince Demidoff di San Donato, of the Villa di Pratolino, near Florence. It was then owned, until 1885, by Adolf Josef Bösch, in Vienna, before being auctioned there by the art dealer Plach and acquired for the Kunstverein (artists' association) in Frankfurt am Main, on behalf of the Stadel Museum, for 9,000 crowns.

In contrast to Vermeer's astronomer, the figure seen in *The Geographer* is shown as if suddenly "frozen" in mid-movement. Slightly bent over a map laid out on the table, with a pair of compasses (to measure distances) in his right hand, he has raised his head to gaze contemplatively into the distance. The objects depicted around him establish numerous connections with *The Astronomer*. In both pictures the interiors are furnished in almost exactly the same way. We note especially the recurrence of a table standing below a window, covered with maps, papers and books, and with a carpet pushed to one side, and a large cupboard in the background. On the top of the cupboard shown in *The*

29

Geographer stands a terrestrial globe, which has been identified as one made by Jodocus Hondius the Elder (1563–1612) in 1618, and which is itself a pendant to the celestial sphere seen in *The Astronomer* (Maek-Gérard 1997, cat. 2). On the rear wall of the geographer's study hangs a framed map. This room also features further, rolled maps on the table and on the floor, additional books, a copper protractor lying on the stool, the aforementioned pair of compasses and a Jacob's staff hanging in the window (Maek-Gérard 1997, cat. 3). An early copy of *The Geographer* was last documented in 1937 and is now untraced (Frankfurt 1997, p. 12).
See also pp. 238–242, *273*.
LITERATURE: Gowing 1952 (1970), pp. 147–151; Welu 1975, pp. 544–547; Slatkes 1981, pp. 84f.; Wheelock 1981 (1988), pp. 13, 36, 47, 136–138; Blankert/Montias/Aillaud 1986 (1987, 1992, 2007), pp. 136, 140, 194, cat. 24; Welu 1986, pp. 263–267; Schneider 1993 (2010), pp. 75–77; Wheelock 1995b, pp. 114, 192; Wheelock/Broos 1995, pp. 170–175, cat. 16; Frankfurt 1997; Liedtke 2000, pp. 262f.; Van Berkel 2001, pp. 138f.; Kassel 2003; Liedtke 2008, pp. 148–152, cat. 27; Büttner 2010, pp. 92–98; Blanc 2014, pp. 274–283, 337.

29

The Lacemaker, *c.* 1669/70
Oil on canvas on panel,
23.9 x 20.5 cm / 9 3/8 x 8 1/8 in.,
signed top right: IVMeer (IVM in ligature)
Paris, Musée du Louvre, inv. M.I.1448

It is assumed that this picture was painted for Pieter Claesz. van Ruijven. It was included in the 1696 Amsterdam sale by auction of the estate of his son-in-law, Jacob Abrahamsz. Dissius, as no. 12: "Een Juffertje dat speldewerkt, van den zelven [Vermeer]" (see Sources, no. 30; A young lady making lace, by the same [Vermeer]). Eighty years later the painting reemerged, in the collection of Jacob Crammer Simonsz., of Amsterdam, who also owned both *The Astronomer* and *The Geographer* (Cat. 27, 28). In 1778 *The Lacemaker* was sold at auction as "Jvan der Meer, bygenaamt de Delfsche

[…] een bevallige Dame, verbeeldende een Speldewerkster" (cited from Blankert 1992, p. 197) / "Ivan der Meer, called the Delfter […] a beautiful lady, representing a lacemaker." All three Vermeer paintings later entered the collection of Jan Danser Nijman, who also owned the *Young Woman Standing at a Virginal* (Cat. 33). In 1792 The Lacemaker was again auctioned, as a work by Vermeer, eventually entering the collection of Hendrick Muilman, Lord of Heemstede (1743–1812), who himself also owned *The Milkmaid* (Cat. 8) in addition to the Portrait of Elisabeth Bas, then attributed to Rembrandt (1606–1669) – both works now in the Rijksmuseum, Amsterdam. In 1817 *The Lacemaker* was auctioned in Paris as "Vander Meer de Delft […] les tableaux de cet artiste sont extrêmement rares et recherchés" (cited from Blankert 1992, pp. 187f.) / "Vander Meer of Delft […] this artist's pictures are extremely rare and sought-after." During the first half of the 19th century *The Lacemaker* was in the collection of Anne Willem Carel, Baron van Nagell van Ampsen (1756–1851), a diplomat who until 1824 served as Dutch Foreign Minister. The picture was acquired by the Louvre in 1870.

The Lacemaker is one of the smallest surviving works by Vermeer and, in terms of format, is close to pictures such as the two small studies of heads (Cat. 23, 25). Among collectors and on the art market during the late 18th and early 19th centuries the painting was always regarded as the work of Vermeer. It must have been painted only a little later than the two above-mentioned head studies, and has generally been dated to *c.* 1669/70 (Wheelock, in Wheelock/Broos 1995, p. 176, cat. 17; Liedtke 2008, p. 153, cat. 29; Cambridge 2011/12, p. 210, cat. 29: *c.* 1670). Slatkes (1981) proposes the somewhat later dating of *c.* 1671/72, prompted by a comparison with *The Guitar Player* (Cat. 32). In any case the degree of "abstraction" to be found in that picture is substantially greater. *The Lacemaker* itself would not, strictly speaking, be categorized as the study of a head. It has, rather, more in common with Vermeer's single-figure genre paintings of the 1660s (cf. Cat. 8, 14–18, 20). This is also supported by the absence of any details

30

characterizing the figure's setting, which is reduced to a view of the white wall behind her. The woman here found working so attentively appears as if positioned close to the viewer. It is on this account that the objects in the immediate foreground – the table covered with a carpet and the sewing cushion – appear excessively large and partially blurred, a notable feature of the white and red threads hanging from the sewing cushion. Blurred details of this sort, which create an illusion of varying depths within the overall picture space and serve to direct the viewer's gaze towards the middle ground and the principal subject, are also a feature of the studies of heads (Cat. 23, 25). The canvas Vermeer used for this painting had already been affixed to a wooden panel before 1778 (see auction catalogue of that year: "op paneel"; Blankert 1992, p. 197). During this procedure, or during an earlier attempt to provide the canvas with a wooden support, so much pressure was placed on the canvas that an impression of the knots of the textile's weave was left in the uppermost layer of paint and a corresponding pattern visible in the picture surface, where it is especially apparent in the darker areas.

See also pp. 242–243, *275*.

Literature: Gowing 1952 (1970), p. 144f.; Slatkes 1981, p. 94; Wheelock 1981 (1988), p. 144; Blankert/Montias/Aillaud 1986 (1987, 1992, 2007), pp. 142, 197, cat. 26; Nash 1991, pp. 110–113; Schneider 1993 (2010), p. 62; Wheelock/Broos 1995, pp. 176–179, cat. 17; Liedtke 2000, pp. 256f.; Liedtke 2008, pp. 153–155, cat. 29; Büttner 2010, p. 38; Cambridge 2011/12, p. 210, cat. 29; Blanc 2014, pp. 127f., 240.

30

The Love Letter, *c.* 1669/70
Oil on canvas, 44 x 38 cm / 17 3/8 x 15 in.,
signed on wall, above basket: IVMeer
Amsterdam, Rijksmusuem, inv. A-1595

The provenance of this picture has so far been traced back only to the early 19th century. It was first securely recorded in the Amsterdam collection of Pieter van Lennep, remaining until the late 1800s in the possession of the Van

Lennep and Messchert van Vollenhoven families. In 1892 the painting was auctioned by the Rembrandt Society, selling for 41,000 florins, and it was in 1893 acquired by the Rijksmuseum (for a detailed discussion of provenance, see Wheelock/Broos 1995, p. 180).

The Love Letter may be dated to *c.* 1669/70 (Wheelock, in Wheelock/Broos 1995; Liedtke 2008), although Blankert (1975, 1986) proposes the somewhat earlier date of 1667. This is the only known work by Vermeer in which he employs the compositional device of the view through a doorway into a room beyond, a *doorkijkje*, so popular among painters of the Southern Dutch School of the mid-17th century. A similar composition by Vermeer, now lost, was included, as no. 5, in the 1696 Amsterdam auction of the estate of Jacob Abrahamsz. Dissius as: "Daer een Seigneur zyn handen wast, in een doorsiende Kamer, met beelden, konstig en raer van dito [Vermeer]" (see Sources, no. 30; In which a gentleman is washing his hands in an interior with sculptures and a view through to a back room, skilful and rare, by ditto [Vermeer]).

In the earlier painting *A Maid Asleep* (Cat. 4) Vermeer had already incorporated a view into a rear room, albeit there this served merely as a secondary, background element within the composition as a whole. In *The Love Letter*, however, the principal depicted action itself takes place within the rear room, while the dark foreground features an open door, a curtain and a chair, all serving as repoussoir motifs. Commentators have, on the whole, written rather negatively of *The Love Letter*, viewing it as a picture in which Vermeer seems at his most conventional and devoid of his usual sensitivity to the characterization of his protagonists and their interrelationships. Such a view was already expressed in 1892, by Bredius, who dismissed the picture as "dit mindere stuk" / "this inferior piece". Gowing (1970, p. 56) describes the composition as "a sidelong advance along a forbidden road", a view shared by Liedtke (2008, p. 156).

As *The Love Letter* was not included in the 1696 Amsterdam auction of the estate of Jacob Abrahamsz. Dissius, it has been supposed that Vermeer did not paint it for his patron,

31

Dissius's father-in-law, Pieter Claesz. van Ruijven, but rather intended it, in view of its relatively unpretentious character, for the art market. The depicted action does, nonetheless, recall that of one of Vermeer's earlier paintings: *Mistress and Maid* (Cat. 24), now in the Frick Collection. In both compositions it is apparent that the maid has delivered a letter to her mistress, which the woman of the house receives in a spirit of doubt and hesitation. In *The Love Letter* the scene is played out with rather less psychological subtlety than in the earlier picture, Vermeer's overriding concern being superficial effects. Through the exchange of glances between mistress and maid and the almost demonstratively clasped letter, the depicted action can be easily understood from a distance. See also pp. 243–244, *279*.

LITERATURE: Gowing 1952 (1970), pp. 56–60, 152; Amsterdam 1976, p. 269ff., cat. 71; Slatkes 1981, pp. 72–75, 101, 122; Wheelock 1981 (1988), pp. 140ff.; Blankert/Montias/Aillaud 1986 (1987, 1992, 2007), pp. 192f., cat. 22; Nash 1991, p. 82; Schneider 1993 (2010), p. 55; Wheelock 1995b, pp. 58, 162, 184; Wheelock/Broos 1995, pp. 180–185, cat. 18; Liedtke 2000, pp. 162f., 252ff.; Goodman 2001, pp. 76ff.; Madrid 2003, p. 182, cat. 39; Dublin/Greenwich 2003/04, cat. 38bis; Liedtke 2008, pp. 156–158, cat. 30; Büttner 2010, p. 49; Blanc 2014, pp. 110–116.

31

A Lady Writing a Letter with Her Maid, *c.* 1670/71

Oil on canvas, 72.2 x 59.7 cm / 28 3/8 x 23 1/2 in., signed on the paper hanging over the edge of the table: IVMeer (IVM in ligature)
Dublin, National Gallery of Ireland, inv. 4535

This picture remained unsold during Vermeer's lifetime and was still in his possession at the time of his death. His widow gave it, together with another work (Cat. 32), to Van Buyten, a Delft baker, as security against unpaid bills amounting to 617 florins. In the related notary's document of 27 January 1676 the picture is described as follows: "D'eene vertonende twee personagien waeroff d'een een brieff sit te schrijven" (see Sources, no. 21) / "One representing two persons one of whom is sitting and writing a letter" (trans. Montias 1989, p. 338, doc. 361). Van Buyten kept the two pictures until his death, in 1701. And the inventory of his estate, in fact, lists three pictures by Vermeer, one large composition, presumably the present painting, and two small ones (Montias 1989, p. 365, doc. 442). *A Lady Writing a Letter with Her Maid* is next recorded in the inventory of the estate of Josua van Belle (1637–1710), a Rotterdam merchant. When the estate was sold at auction in 1730, the sale catalogue described the picture as: "Een Juffrouw zittende een Brief te Schryven daer de Meid nae staet te wagten, door Vander Meer" (cited from Wheelock/Broos 1995, p. 189, note 9) / "A sitting young Lady writing a letter, next to which a Maid stands waiting, by Vander Meer" (trans. Wheelock/Broos 1995, p. 188). The picture then remained in the collection of the Slingelandt family of The Hague until the end of the 18th century.

A Lady Writing a Letter with Her Maid is not again securely recorded until 1881, when it was sold by the Austrian art collector Viktor Miller zu Aichholz (1845–1910) to a Paris art dealer. It then passed through the Secrétan Collection to that of Alfred Beit (1853–1906), an émigré from Hamburg who had made a fortune in South Africa from diamond and gold prospecting. Alfred Beit's collection passed, by way of his brother, Otto, to Otto's son, who was also called Alfred Beit (1903–1994), and who from 1952 lived at Russborough, near Dublin. In 1974 members of the IRA broke into the estate and stole 12 paintings from the collection, including *A Lady Writing a Letter with Her Maid*. The stolen pictures were rapidly traced and secured on this occasion, but in 1986 the Vermeer was again stolen, this time along with 17 further pictures. It was not until 1993, after years of negotiations, that the painting by Vermeer was returned to Alfred Beit, who then bequeathed it to the National Gallery of Ireland.

The fact that *A Lady Writing a Letter with Her Maid* was still in Vermeer's possession at the time of his death would point to a late date, in the 1670s. And, in fact, a number of its stylis-

32

tic characteristics evince a tendency towards the simplification of form that we find generally in Vermeer's late works. This is not, however, to be seen as a work from the very last years of Vermeer's career (cf. Cat. 34, 35). Rather, we may assume that it dates to *c.* 1670/71 (Blankert 1986: 1671; Wheelock, in Wheelock/Broos 1995: *c.* 1670; Liedtke 2008: *c.* 1670/71).

In terms of composition, the painting is characterized by large forms and straight lines, with a number of dominant horizontals and verticals. The heavy, green curtain in the left foreground serves a similar function to the tapestry found in Vermeer's earlier composition *The Art of Painting* (Cat. 26) or in the probably later *Allegory of Faith* (Cat. 34). Other large features include the white curtain hanging vertically at the window, the broad black frame of the picture hanging on the rear wall, the simple costume worn by the waiting maid or the sketchily painted carpet that covers the table. Vermeer's summary painting technique is also apparent in the letter writer's white sleeves. Vermeer here adds to his frequently treated subject of letter writing a new variant, which brings with it a greater narrative element than is to be found in earlier pictures with the same or related subject (Cat. 20, 24). See also pp. 245–246, *291*.

LITERATURE: Gowing 1952 (1970), pp. 153f.; Slatkes 1981, p. 101; Wheelock 1981 (1988), p. 146; Blankert/Montias/Aillaud 1986 (1987, 1992, 2007), pp. 142, 198f., cat. 27; Nash 1991, pp. 84, 86; Schneider 1993 (2010), pp. 53f.; Wheelock 1995b, pp. 157–162, 184; Wheelock/Broos 1995, pp. 186–189, cat. 19; Vergara 1998; Liedtke 2000, pp. 254ff.; Vergara 2003, pp. 57f.; Dublin/Greenwich 2003/04, cat. 39; Liedtke 2008, pp. 160f., cat. 31; Büttner 2010, p. 45; Blanc 2014, pp. 205–207, 250, 278.

32

The Guitar Player, *c.* 1669–1672

Oil on canvas, 51.4 x 45 cm / 20 ¼ x 17 ¾ in.

London, Kenwood House, The Iveagh Bequest, inv. 88028841

It has yet to be established whether this picture is one of the two that Vermeer's widow gave to

Hendrick van Buyten, a baker in Delft, as security for unpaid bills (on which see Cat. 31). In the related notary's document of 27 January 1676 one of the two pictures is described as: "Een personagie spelende op een cyter" (see Sources, no. 21) / "A person playing a cittern" (trans. Montias 1989, p. 338, doc. 361). This would mean that the picture remained unsold in Vermeer's studio. It is, however, more probable, not least on account of a more precise reference to the musical instrument, that *The Guitar Player* was in the collection of Pieter Claesz. van Ruijven and that it is to be identified with the painting that featured, as no. 4, in the 1696 Amsterdam sale by auction of the estate of his son-in-law, Jacob Abrahamsz. Dissius, where it was described as: "Een speelende Juffrouw op een Guiteer, heel goet van den zelve [Vermeer]" (see Sources, no. 30) / "A young lady playing the guitar, very good of the same [Vermeer]" (trans. Montias 1989, p. 364, doc. 439). If this were the case the painting would be one of the last that Vermeer sold to Pieter van Ruijven before the latter's death, in 1674. We are equally unsure whether *The Guitar Player* is to be identified with a picture that in the late 18th century was in the collection of Jan Danser Nijman, of Amsterdam, who owned four other paintings by Vermeer (Cat. 27–29, 33). We do, however, know that by 1794 the present picture was in England, initially in the collection of Henry Temple, 2nd Viscount Palmerston, of London, whose descendants sold it in 1888. In 1927 it passed from the collection of Edward Cecil Guinness, Earl of Iveagh, to Kenwood House, as part of the Iveagh Bequest.

The Guitar Player, as also the paintings of young women standing and sitting at a virginal (Cat. 33, 35), are dated by Liedtke (2008, p. 172, cat. 35) to *c.* 1670/72. But, as probably the earliest of these three pictures, it may also be seen as effectively introducing Vermeer's four late works, which are distinguished from his earlier output both by a change in style and by a marked shift in the choice of painterly means employed (these are thoroughly described in Wheelock 1995b, pp. 149–155). In general we may think in terms of a tendency to "abstraction", such as is also to be noted in the contem-

33

porary work of the artists traditionally known as "Dutch Classicists", such as Caesar van Everdingen (*c.* 1616–1678) or Karel Dujardin (*c.* 1622–1678). For some commentators this observable change in style has prompted doubts as to whether *The Guitar Player* really was an autograph work by Vermeer. Blankert (1986, p. 146) draws attention to the off-centre, unbalanced composition and to the figure's artificially stiff pose. Liedtke (2008, p. 172) writes of a notable equilibrium between the picture's schematic and impressionistic passages. Be that as it may the evocation of the gleaming, crisp, white silk of the dress is in fact one of the outstanding achievements of Vermeer's illusionism. A copy of the painting is to be found in the Johnson Collection at the Philadelphia Museum of Art. See also pp. 247–248, *281*.

LITERATURE: Gowing 1952 (1970), pp. 55f., 154f.; Slatkes 1981, p. 102; Wheelock 1981 (1988), p. 150; Blankert/Montias/Aillaud 1986 (1987, 1992, 2007), pp. 146, 199, cat. 28; Schneider 1993 (2010), p. 46; Weber 1994, pp. 98–106; Wheelock 1995b, pp. 149–155; Weber 1998, pp. 295–297; Goodman 2001, pp. 79–82; Liedtke 2008, pp. 172–174, cat. 35; Büttner 2010, p. 80; Blanc 2014, pp. 90, 177.

33

Young Woman Standing at a Virginal (A Lady Standing at the Virginal), *c.* 1670–1672
Oil on canvas, 51.8 x 45.2 cm / 20⅜ x 17¾ in., signed on the side of the virginal (top left of virginal): IVMeer (IVM in ligature)
London, The National Gallery, inv. 1383

The early provenance of this picture has yet to be resolved. It is possible that it was in the collection of Diego Duarte, in Antwerp. In an inventory of this collection, drawn up in 1682, a picture by Vermeer with a corresponding subject is listed as no. 182, and is described as: "Een stuckxken met een juoffrou op de clavecingel spelende met bywerck van Vermeer" (cited from Wheelock/Broos 1995, p. 203, note 13) / "A work with a lady playing on the virginal with addenda by Vermeer" (trans. Wheelock/Broos 1995, p. 202). When, in 1691, Duarte sold part of his collection, it is possible that *Young Woman Standing at a Virginal* was added to the existing collection of paintings by Vermeer in the possession of Abraham Jacobsz. or Jacob Abrahamsz. Dissius. This is indeed indicated by the description of the painting featured, as no. 37, in the catalogue of the 1696 Amsterdam sale by auction of Dissius's estate: "Een Speelende Juffrouw op de Clavecimbael van dito [Vermeer]" (see Sources, no. 30) / "A lady playing the clavecin [this should read: the virginal], by ditto [Vermeer]" (trans. Montias 1989, p. 364, doc. 439). Both descriptions, that of 1682 and that of 1696, might, however, refer to the *Young Woman Seated at a Virginal* (Cat. 35). Either at the time of the 1696 auction or probably soon after the picture had been painted, *Young Woman Standing at a Virginal* entered the collection of Nicolaes van Assendelft, being listed in 1711 in the inventory of his estate as: "Een juffr. spelende opde Clavecimbael door Vermeer" (cited from Wheelock/Broos 1995, p. 199, note 9) / "A damsel playing on the clavichord [this should read: the virginal] by Vermeer" (trans. Wheelock/Broos 1995, p. 198). By the end of the 18th century the picture was in the collection of Jan Danser Nijman, of Amsterdam, who owned four paintings by Vermeer (see also Cat. 27–29). In 1797 it was listed in the catalogue of the sale by auction of his estate as: "Een Juffrouw, staande voor een Clavecimbaal te speelen; aan de Wand hangen schilderyen; zeer fraai van penceelbehandeling" / "A Lady standing at a Harpsichord [this should read: the virginal] on the wall hang paintings; very comely in brush work" (trans. Wheelock/Broos 1995, p. 199, note 11). During the 19th century the painting was in the collection of Edward Solly (1776–1844), an English trader living in Berlin, and thereafter in that of Thoré-Bürger. In 1892, when the Thoré-Bürger Collection was sold at auction, the picture fetched 29,000 francs; but shortly thereafter it was sold, on the art market, for 50,000 francs to The National Gallery in London.

In this composition, in which Vermeer shows a young woman standing at a virginal, he can be seen to draw on his own earlier works of the period 1660–1665, in which he showed female figures in the privacy of their own domestic setting, as in the case of *Young Woman with a Water Pitcher* (Cat. 14) or *Woman in Blue Reading a Letter* (Cat. 16). By comparison with such earlier compositions the present picture is distinguished by its rendering of a scene illuminated by a form-defining cool, bright light. This stylistic evolution of *c.* 1670 in Vermeer's work has parallels in that of contemporary painters: it is to be found in the moralizing subjects painted by Cornelis de Man (1621–1706), who in 1670/71 served with Vermeer on the Board of the Delft Painters' Guild. *Young Woman Standing at a Virginal* has mostly been considered in connection with *Young Woman Seated at a Virginal* (Cat. 35), notwithstanding the stylistic differences between the two paintings. Blankert (1986, cat. 25) dates the first picture to 1670, and the latter to 1674/75. Wheelock (in Wheelock/Broos 1995, p. 196) dates the composition with the standing figure to 1672/73 and that with the seated figure to *c.* 1675. By contrast Liedtke (2008, pp. 166f.) proposes a date of *c.* 1670–1672 for both pictures, and regards them as "optional pendants", that is to say, pictures that effectively complement each other but that may also function as autonomous images. In support of this proposition he cites the almost identical dimensions of the two pictures and the complementary nature of the scenes depicted. He maintains that Vermeer deliberately introduced the formal differences to be found between the two compositions in order to point to differences of character between the two depicted protagonists. In the view of most commentators, however, the *Young Woman Seated at a Virginal* was painted several years later than the present picture.

The virginal on which the lady is shown playing here – it in fact appears that she has, rather, merely posed with her fingers placed lightly upon the keys – was in Holland regarded as a symbol of true love. Hence the significance of the larger picture hanging on the wall directly behind the young woman, which, as first observed by Delbanco (1928), depicts the naked figure of Cupid in the Classicist style of Caesar van Everdingen. The very same picture is featured, albeit rather indistinctly, in the back-

34

ground of *Young Woman Interrupted at Music* (Cat. 11) and had already been incorporated, before it was overpainted by Vermeer, in *A Young Woman Reading a Letter* (Cat. 5)
See also pp. 248–249, *283*.
LITERATURE: Gowing 1952 (1970), pp. 155ff.; Slatkes 1981, p. 88; Wheelock 1981 (1988), p. 152; Blankert/Montias/Aillaud 1986 (1987, 1992, 2007), pp. 134, 196, cat. 25; MacLaren/Brown 1991, pp. 466–468; Nash 1991, pp. 114–118; Schneider 1993 (2010), p. 44; Wheelock/Broos 1995, pp. 196–199, cat. 21; Weber 1998, pp. 295–297; Liedtke 2000, pp. 257–260, 294; Liedtke 2001f, pp. 402–406, cat. 78; Madrid 2003, p. 184, cat. 40; Liedtke 2008, pp. 166–171, cat. 33; Büttner 2010, p. 78; Rome 2012/13, p. 224, cat. 52; Blanc 2014, pp. 120–122, 211–216, 223.

34
Allegory of Faith, *c.* 1671–1674
Oil on canvas, 114.3 x 88.9 cm / 45 x 35 in.
New York, The Metropolitan Museum of Art, The Friedsam Collection, Bequest of Michael Friedsam, 1931, inv. 32.100.18

The earliest documented owner of this picture was Herman Stoffelsz. van Swoll, postmaster of Amsterdam and a Protestant. In the inventory of his estate, drawn up in 1699, alongside a number of Italian pictures, Vermeer's painting is described as follows: "Een zittende Vrouw met meer beteekenisse, verbeeldende het Nieuwe Testament […] kragtig en gloejent geschildert" (cited from Wheelock/Broos 1995, p. 195, note 23) / "A sitting Woman with deep meanings, depicting the New Testament […] powerfully and glowingly painted" (trans. Wheelock/Broos 1995, p. 194). The picture reemerged in 1718, then again in 1735 and 1749, in a number of Dutch auctions. During the first half of the 19th century Vermeer's painting, or possibly an untraced copy of it, may have been in an Austrian collection, as is suggested by its apparent presence in the background of the portrait of an unknown couple by Ferdinand Georg Waldmüller (1793–1865), *The Cartographer and His Wife* (1824), now in the Westfälisches Museum, Münster (Wheelock/Broos 1995, p. 94, fig. 4).

In 1899 Vermeer's *Allegory of Faith* was in the collection of Dmitri Ivanovich Shchukin, in Moscow, but in the same year it was acquired on the German art market, as a work by Eglon van der Neer, and for just 700 marks, by Abraham Bredius – a coup celebrated in the Dutch press as a triumph for that scholar's superior connoisseurship. The picture was on loan to the Mauritshuis in The Hague, and on display there, between 1899 and 1924, when it was loaned to the Boymans Museum, Rotterdam, and displayed there until 1928. In that year it was acquired, on the Paris art market, for US$300,000, by Colonel Michael Friedsam, of New York, who in 1931 presented it to that city's Metropolitan Museum of Art.

The Allegory of Faith was only belatedly recognized as the work of Vermeer. Until 1899 the picture had been attributed to the Dutch genre painter Eglon van der Neer. The attribution to Vermeer – soon universally accepted – was first proposed by Abraham Bredius, who himself owned this work at the time, though, in fact, described it as "een groote maar hoogst onbehagelijke Vermeer" (cited from Wheelock/Broos 1995, p. 195, note 35) / "a large but unpleasant Vermeer" (trans. Wheelock/Broos 1995, p. 194). This "unpleasantness" is in the first instance owed to the picture's subject matter. For religious allegory constitutes an anomaly in Vermeer's oeuvre. *The Allegory of Faith* and *The Art of Painting* (Cat. 26) are Vermeer's only known allegorical works. *The Art of Painting* might, at first glance, be mistaken for an example of genre painting, capturing everyday life in the artist's studio; but in the *Allegory of Faith* the allegorical content is impossible to overlook, on account of both the treatment of the setting and the character of the attributes that accompany the female protagonist.

In both the figure's physiognomy and the treatment of the drapery folds the *Allegory of Faith* is close to the *Young Woman Seated at a Virginal* (Cat. 35), which would suggest that it should be dated to *c.* 1671–1674, that is to say, in the final period of the artist's career. Such a dating would be in line with those proposed by Blankert (1986, p. 200: 1672–1674) and by Wheelock

(Wheelock/Broos 1995, p. 190: *c.* 1671–1674), while Liedtke (2008, p. 163) favours the slightly earlier date of 1670–1672.

As established by Barnouw in 1914 Vermeer in his treatment of the female figure follows precisely the recommendations of the Dutch edition of Cesare Ripa's *Iconologia* of 1644. Of the total of four allegories of Faith cited by Ripa Vermeer here devises a combination of elements of "Faith" and of "the Catholic Faith", for example, in the allegorical figure's clothing. According to the rules established by Ripa, Faith as a symbol of light and purity should be dressed in white, while Faith as a symbol of the Heavens should be dressed in blue. In Vermeer's painting the figure of Faith wears a white dress and, on top of it, a second, blue dress. Further components of the allegory as described by Ripa that are to be found in Vermeer's painting are the snake (a symbol of the Devil), which is here crushed by a cornerstone (of the Church, that is to say, Christ), and the apple with a bite already taken out of it (symbolizing Original Sin). Ripa goes on to say that the allegorical figure of Faith should hold a goblet and lay her hand upon a book. Vermeer does indeed position both of these items on the table next to his figure, adding also a crown of thorns. Also to be found within Vermeer's composition, although not mentioned in Ripa's text, are the globe on which the figure of Faith rests her right foot, a crucifix, a painting hanging on the rear wall, which depicts the Crucifixion, and a glass sphere hanging from the beamed ceiling.

See also pp. 250–253, *297*.

Literature: Barnouw 1914; Gowing 1952 (1970), p. 154; De Jongh 1975/76, pp. 69–75; Slatkes 1981, pp. 106–109; Wheelock 1981 (1988), p. 148; Blankert/Montias/Aillaud 1986 (1987, 1992, 2007), pp. 146, 200, cat. 29; Schneider 1993 (2010), pp. 79–81; Arasse 1994, pp. 17–25, 83–86; Wheelock/Broos 1995, pp. 190–195, cat. 20; Hertel 1996, pp. 205–229; Schlenke 1998, pp. 75–100; Liedtke 2000, pp. 260–262; Liedtke 2001f, pp. 399–402, cat. 77; Liedtke 2007, pp. 893–902; Liedtke 2008, pp. 163–165, cat. 32; Büttner 2010, pp. 108–112; Rome 2012, p. 218, cat. 50; Blanc 2014, pp. 314, 326–333.

35

35

Young Woman Seated at a Virginal, *c.* 1672–1675
Oil on canvas, 51.5 x 45.6 cm / 20 ¼ x 17 ⅞ in., signed to the right of the woman's head: IVMeer (IVM in ligature)
London, The National Gallery, Salting Bequest, 1910, inv. 2568

It has been assumed that this picture may once have been owned by the Antwerp collector Diego Duarte, and that it entered the collection of Jacob Abrahamsz. Dissius when Duarte sold part of his own collection in 1691. However, it is possible that the picture listed as no. 182 in the 1682 inventory of the Duarte Collection and that listed as no. 37 in the catalogue of the 1696 Amsterdam sale by auction of the Dissius estate were, in fact, identical with *Young Woman Standing at a Virginal* (Cat. 33; see that entry for the relevant commentary). The wording in both the inventory and the sale catalogue could refer to either composition.

Young Woman Seated at a Virginal is first securely recorded when it was to be found in the gallery at Schloss Weissenstein in Pommersfelden, a collection assembled by Lothar Franz Count Schönborn, Elector of Mainz and Archbishop of Bamberg (1655–1729). It is said to have been listed in the now untraced collection catalogue compiled in 1746. Thoré-Bürger saw the picture in Pommersfelden in 1866, when it was attributed to "Jacob van der Meer". The following year he was able to acquire it at an auction of part of the Schönborn Collection. The Thoré-Bürger Collection was in turn auctioned by his heirs in 1892, and *Young Woman Seated at a Virginal*, initially on the Paris art market, was acquired by the English collector George Salting (1835–1909). After the latter's death Vermeer's picture, along with many other paintings, entered the collection of the National Gallery in London (extensive details on provenance in Wheelock/Broos 1995, p. 200; in Liedtke 2008, p. 198).

Young Woman Seated at a Virginal is generally believed to be one of Vermeer's last paintings (Blankert 1986, p. 202: 1674/75; Wheelock, in Wheelock/Broos 1995, p. 200: *c.* 1675; Liedtke 2008, p. 167: *c.* 1670–1672; Cambridge 2011/12,

p. 206: *c.* 1670). In terms of its style and, above all, its subject, the painting is closest to *Young Woman Standing at a Virginal* (Cat. 33); and the two pictures have, indeed, been taken for pendants, not least on account of their almost identical dimensions (Liedtke 2008, p. 170). Differences between the two pictures as regards Vermeer's execution indicate, however, that one was not painted directly after the other. The overall simplification of forms points to a new phase within Vermeer's oeuvre: the folds of the dress, for example, create a planar pattern that conveys much less of the illusion of real cloth than is to be found in Vermeer's earlier works. We may therefore assume that this was the last painting to be completed by Vermeer: at the earliest in 1672, but in all probability towards 1675. In his depiction of certain motifs, Vermeer here looks back to some of his own earlier compositions. The painting that hangs on the rear wall of *Young Woman Seated at a Virginal* is *The Procuress* of 1622 (p. 182), a work by Van Baburen. Awareness of this painting had been among the factors prompting Vermeer to paint his own *Procuress* (Cat. 3); and an imitation of Dirck van Baburen's version was included by Vermeer in the background of *The Concert* (Cat. 19). There, as in *Young Woman Seated at a Virginal*, the "picture within a picture" provides a significant contrast to the scene depicted in the foreground. In the later painting debauchery and vice, accompanied by the light and frivolous music supplied by a lutenist, is set in contrast with the moderation and harmony of the ideal, refined love represented by the virginal and the viola da gamba.

See also 253–254, 166, *285*.

LITERATURE: Boström 1949, p. 24; Gowing 1952 (1970), pp. 155ff.; Slatkes 1981, pp. 91f.; Wheelock 1981 (1988), p. 154; Blankert/Montias/Alliaud 1986 (1987, 1992, 2007), pp. 148, 202, cat. 31; MacLaren/Brown 1991, pp. 468f.; Nash 1991, pp. 114ff.; Schneider 1993 (2010), p. 44; Wheelock/Broos 1995, pp. 200–203, cat. 22; Weber 1998, pp. 295ff.; Liedtke 2000, pp. 257–260, 294; Liedtke 2001f, pp. 402–406, cat. 79; Liedtke 2008, pp. 167–171, cat. 34; Büttner 2010, p. 79; Cambridge 2011/12, p. 206, cat. 27; Blanc 2014, pp. 211–220, 223.

Questionable Attributions

36
Saint Praxedis, 1655
Oil on canvas, 101.6 x 82.6 cm / 40 x 32 ½ in., signed bottom left: Meer 1655;
bottom right: Meer N R […] o [.] o
Private collection

Between 1943 and 1969 this picture was in the collection of Erna and Jacob Reder, of New York, and in 1969–1987 with the New York art dealer Spencer Samuels & Co. It remained in the Barbara Piasecka Johnson Collection from 1987 to 2014, when, on 8 July, it was auctioned at Christie's in London.

The work is an exact copy of a composition, presumed to date from *c.* 1640–1650, by the Florentine painter Felice Ficherelli, called Il Riposo (1605–1660), which is now in a private collection in Italy (Rome 2012/13, p. 204, cat. 45b). The only significant difference between the original and the copy is that Vermeer's saint holds a crucifix in both hands while squeezing a martyr's blood from a sponge.

The picture was on public display for the first time in 1969, when it featured in an exhibition at The Metropolitan Museum of Art in New York on the theme of Baroque painting from Florence to be found in American collections. At that time Kitson proposed a possible attribution to Johannes Vermeer on account of the signature.

In 1972, in the context of an investigation into the pigments used by Vermeer, Hermann Kühn, of the Dörner Institut, Munich, announced that "it is probable that the picture [Saint Praxedis] was painted in Holland". Blankert (1975 and 1987) rejected an attribution to Vermeer, on account of the formal irregularity of the signature and the crude execution of the work itself.

The second signature was interpreted by Egbert Haverkamp-Begemann as reading "Meer naar Riposo". In 1986 Wheelock proposed an attribution to Johannes Vermeer, following a careful analysis of the technique employed and in view of characteristics shared with Vermeer's later work. Wheelock also saw

a possible connection between this painting, with its emphatically Catholic subject, and Vermeer's own conversion to Catholicism on the occasion of his marriage. It remains to be discovered where Vermeer might have seen Ficherelli's original painting. Wheelock assumes that this work, or a copy of it, was to be found in Holland at the appropriate period, though he also mentions the entirely hypothetical possibility that Vermeer may even have travelled to Italy in the early 1650s. Weber (1993, p. 300) believes the painting to be the work of the Utrecht painter Johan van der Meer, who is known to have been in Rome in the mid-1650s.

The picture was included, as the work of Vermeer, in the 1995/96 exhibition held in Washington, D.C., and The Hague and, most recently, in that of 2012/13 held in Rome, where it was shown alongside Ficherelli's original.

LITERATURE: Kitson 1969, p. 410; Blankert 1975, p. 112, note 5; Blankert/Montias/Alliaud 1986 (1987, 1992, 2007), p. 163, note 5; Wheelock 1986, pp. 71–89; Weber 1993, p. 300; Wheelock 1995b, pp. 21–27; Wheelock/Broos 1995, pp. 86–89, cat. 1; Rome 2012/13, pp. 200–202, cat. 45a; Blanc 2014, pp. 314–326.

37

Young Woman Seated at a Virginal,

c. 1670–1672

Oil on canvas, 24.7 x 19.3 cm / 9 ¾ x 7 ⅝ in.

Private collection

There have been attempts to link this painting with the collection of Pieter Claesz. van Ruijven, and thus also with the 1696 Amsterdam sale by auction of the estate of his son-in-law, Jacob Abrahamsz. Dissius, where the sale catalogue described no. 37 as: "Een Speelende Juffrouw op de Clavecimbael van dito [Vermeer]" (see Sources, no. 30) / "A lady playing the clavecin [this should read: the virginal], by ditto [Vermeer]" (trans. Montias 1989, p. 364, doc. 439). This text could, however, also refer to Cat. 33 or 35.

Until 1814 the picture was owned by Wessel Ryers, of Amsterdam. From *c.* 1890/1900 it is presumed to have been in the collection of Alfred Beit, Sr., in London, then in that of his heirs until 1960. By 2004 it was owned by Baron Frédéric Rolin, of Brussels, and thereafter by his own heirs. It was sold at auction at Sotheby's, London, on 7 July 2004, as no. 8, a work in the collection of Steve Wynn, of Las Vegas, Nevada. It was acquired by its present owner in 2004.

The picture is comparable, both in its composition and as regards individual motifs, with Vermeer's late paintings of female figures playing musical instruments (Cat. 32, 33, 35). It was first attributed to Vermeer by Hofstede de Groot (1907–1927), who was followed in this by Gowing (in the second, 1970 edition of his Vermeer monograph), Goldscheider (1967, p. 133) and finally by Liedtke (2008 and 2012). Liedtke proposes a date of *c.* 1670–1672. De Vries initially believed the painting to be an autograph work, but in 1948 categorized it, rather, as a work made *c.* 1800 in imitation of Vermeer's style. Blankert (1975–2007) makes no mention of the picture, Wheelock (1981) believes it to be the work of a contemporary from the circle of Vermeer, and Broos (1998) rejects the attribution to Vermeer. It is clear that the yellow shawl was added by another hand, painting over the original composition. Examination of X-rays has brought forth evidence of a carefully executed dress beneath this later addition. Precise technical analysis (Sheldon/Costaras 2006; Liedtke 2012) has established, among other things, that the canvas used for this painting comes from the same bolt of cloth as the canvas used for *The Lacemaker* now in Paris (Cat. 29). At the time of Vermeer's death, however, ten pieces of canvas (presumably already primed and ready for use) were to be found in the artist's studio (Montias 1989, p. 341, doc. 364, no. 11); so this latest discovery is not a sufficient argument for Vermeer's authorship of the present work.

The picture went on public display for the first time since 1907 when it was included in the New York and London exhibition of 2001: Vermeer and the Delft School. It was not, however, included in the catalogue. The picture was again to be seen in the 2012/13 Rome exhibition entitled *Vermeer: Il secolo d'oro dell'arte olandese*. Here, the attribution to Vermeer was upheld.

LITERATURE: Hofstede de Groot 1907–1927, I (1907), pp. 592f., no. 24; Gowing 1970, p. 157; Wheelock 1981, p. 45; Liedtke 2000, p. 294, note 252; New York/London 2001, p. 403, note 11; Sheldon/Costaras 2006, pp. 89–97; Liedtke 2008, pp. 175ff., cat. 36; Liedtke 2012; Rome 2012/13, p. 220, cat. 51; Blanc 2014, pp. 160, 250.

Notes

1 Proust *Correspondances*, vol. 20, p. 226.
2 5th vol., published in 1923.
3 Princeton 1989.
4 Source, no. 1.
5 Montias 1989, pp. 8–16.
6 Montias 1989, pp. 17–34.
7 Montias 1989, pp. 55f. and 279f., doc. 94.
8 Montias 1989, pp. 55–84.
9 Montias 1989, pp. 60, 284, doc. 118.
10 Montias 1989, p. 284, doc. 124.
11 Montias 1989, p. 284, doc. 122.
12 Delft 2002, pp. 62 and 157, no. 12.
13 Cited from Montias 1989, pp. 63 and 285, doc. 133.
14 Cited from Montias 1989, p. 290, doc. 156.
15 Cited from Montias 1989, p. 290, doc. 157.
16 Source, no. 2.
17 Montias 1989, p. 305, doc. 240.
18 Source, no. 3.
19 Montias 1989, p. 329, doc. 324.
20 Montias 1989, p. 332, doc. 330.
21 Montias 1989, p. 332, doc. 331.
22 Montias 1989, p. 332, doc. 336.
23 Source, no. 16.
24 Montias 1989, p. 333, doc. 340.
25 Het Schilder-boek, 1604, fol. 191r.
26 Rotterdam/Frankfurt 1999/2000.
27 New York/London 2001.
28 Source, no. 6.
29 Ibid.
30 Most recently in 2012, in the context of the discussion of a doubtful early work; cf. Cat. 36.
31 Thoré-Bürger 1866, p. 312.
32 MacColl 1901, pp. 9–11.
33 Cited from Blankert/Montias/Aillaud 1992, p. 211; trans. Montias 1989, p. 326, doc. 315.
34 Cited from and trans. Blankert/Montias/Aillaud 1992, p. 211.
35 Broos 1998, p. 19: "it seems that Houbraken accidentally forgot to turn page 853".
36 Source, no. 24.
37 Source, no. 4.
38 Source, no. 5.
39 Montias 1989, p. 103.
40 Montias 1989, pp. 106f.
41 Begheyn 2008, pp. 42–44.
42 Liedtke 2008, p. 16.
43 Montias 1989, pp. 105 and 308f., doc. 249–252; cf. Source, no. 4 and 5.
44 Montias 1989, pp. 108–128.
45 Montias 1989, pp. 154–170.
46 Source, no. 4.
47 Montias 1989, pp. 129f.
48 Montias 1989, pp. 129.
49 Buijsen 2010a, pp. 14f.
50 Buijsen 2010a, p. 15.
51 Montias 1989, pp. 139f. and 312, doc. 269.
52 Cited from Montias 1991, p. 46, no. 7.
53 Wheelock, in Wheelock/Broos 1995, p. 90.
54 Blankert, in Rotterdam/Frankfurt 1999/2000, p. 15ff.
55 Blankert, in Rotterdam/Frankfurt 1999/2000, p. 26.
56 *Metamorphoses*, II, pp. 453–462.
57 Blankert 2000, p. 193.
58 Liedtke 2008, p. 57.
59 Blankert 2010, pp. 31ff.
60 Liedtke 2008, p. 27.
61 Liedtke 2008, p. 60.
62 Blankert 2010, pp. 33f.
63 Renger 1970.
64 Montias 1989, pp. 122 and 292, doc. 167; Blankert/Montias/Aillaud 1992, p. 208.
65 Bok 2001, pp. 205–209.
66 Neidhardt 2004/05.
67 Slatkes 1998, p. 82; Neidhardt 2010a, p. 51.
68 Dekiert 2003, p. 265.
69 De Winkel 1998, p. 334.
70 Liedtke, 2001a, pp. 10ff.
71 Liedtke 2000, p. 199, fig. 260.
72 Neidhardt 2004/05, p. 19.
73 Gaehtgens 2002.
74 Blankert 1995, pp. 31ff.; Gaehtgens 2002, pp. 202–206.
75 *Groot Schilderboek*, III, ch. 1, p. 130, cited from the first English edition, *The Art of Painting*, trans. John Frederick Fritsch, London 1738.
76 Gaethgens 2002, pp. 212–217.
77 Blankert 1995, p. 31.
78 Blankert 1995, p. 32.
79 Ibid.
80 Source, no. 30, no. 8.
81 Liedtke 2008, p. 67.
82 Wheelock 1995, pp. 39–47; Schneider 1993 (2010), p. 27.
83 De Winkel 1998, p. 328.
84 *Natural History*, XXXV, 65.

85 Mayer-Meintschel 1978/79.
86 Antwerp 1608.
87 Gaskell 2000.
88 Liedtke 2000, p. 143ff.; 2008, p. 33.
89 Liedtke 2008, p. 72.
90 Wheelock 1995b, pp. 55ff.
91 Cf. the construction drawing in Wadum 1995a, p. 70.
92 New York/London 2001, p. 62, fig. 65.
93 Gowing 1952 (1970), pp. 105ff.
94 Slatkes 1981, p. 28.
95 Welu 1981, p. 107.
96 Wheelock 1995b, p. 61.
97 Liedtke 2008, pp. 72ff.
98 Source, no. 8.
99 Montias 1989, p. 311, doc. 268.
100 Montias 1989, pp. 154–170.
101 Montias 1989, pp. 133f.
102 Montias 1989, pp. 110, 310, doc. 258.
103 Montias 1989, pp. 85–97.
104 Montias 1989, p. 310, doc. 262.
105 Source, no. 9.
106 Montias 1989, p. 171.
107 Source, no. 7.
108 Montias 1987 and 1989, pp. 246–262.
109 Source, no. 30.
110 Montias 1989, pp. 322ff. doc. 301.
111 Source, no. 11.
112 Montias 1989, p. 251; Source, no. 13.
113 Montias 1989, pp. 251f.
114 Montias 1989, pp. 253f.; Source, no. 29.
115 Source, no. 30.
116 Montias 1989, pp. 184 and 265ff.
117 Montias 1989, p. 312, doc. 269: "Een graft besoeckende van der Meer 20 gulden" – "A picture of the visit to the grave by van der Meer, 20 guilders"; see Bredius 1915–1921, vol. 1, p. 233.
118 "In the front hall / Firstly a painting in a black frame by Jan van der Meer"; cited from Blankert/Montias/Aillaud 1992, p. 210.
119 Montias 1989, p. 316, doc. 284.
120 Montias 1989, p. 318, doc. 298.
121 Source, no. 21.
122 Montias 1989, pp. 184ff.
123 Source, no. 22.
124 Montias 1989, pp. 185f.
125 Montias 1989, p. 347, doc. 375.
126 Montias 1989, pp. 180f.; Source, no. 10.
127 Source, no. 12; cited from Wheelock/Broos 1995, p. 180.
128 Wheelock/Broos 1995, p. 162, fig. 1 and 2.
129 The arguments are most recently summarized in Liedtke 2008, pp. 179–189.
130 Delsaute 1998, p. 112.
131 Ibid.
132 Huygens 1971
133 Hoogstraten 1678.
134 Mills 1998.
135 Wadum 1995a, pp. 67f.
136 Wadum 1995a, p. 69.
137 Plietzsch 1939; Fleischer 1997; London/Hartford 1998, p. 38; most thoroughly Liedtke 2008, pp. 40ff.
138 Büttner 2010, p. 71.
139 Ibid.
140 Hoogstraten 1678, p. 90.
141 Goodman 2001, p. 76.
142 Neurdenburg 1942.
143 Brunswick 1978, p. 166.
144 Arnheim 1611.
145 Weber 1998, p. 303.
146 Liedtke 2008, p. 87.
147 Gowing 1952 (1970), pp. 114–118.
148 Naumann 1981, no. 28.
149 De Jongh 1967, pp. 49f.
150 Cited from Wheelock 1995b, p. 67.
151 Gutruf 1998, p. 66.
152 Blankert/Montias/Aillaud 1992, p. 174.
153 Wheelock 1995b, pp. 63f.
154 Source, no. 24.
155 Rand, 1998.
156 Source, no. 30; trans. Montias 1989, p. 364, doc. 439.
157 Swillens 1950, pp. 93–96.
158 Rome 2012/13, p. 206, cat. 46.
159 Kaldenbach 2000.
160 Gutruf 2000, p. 16.
161 Liedtke 2008, p. 92.
162 "Dit kapitaalste en meest-beroemde Schilderij van dezen Meester"; cited from Wheelock/Broos 1995, p. 126, note 30.
163 Thoré-Bürger 1866, pp. 297–330, 458–470, 543–575.
164 "C'est ainsi que j'aurais dû écrire"; Büttner 2010, p. 8.
165 Plomp, in New York/London 2001, pp. 429ff.
166 Schneider 2010, p. 15.
167 Swillens 1950, p. 92.
168 Wheelock 1995b, pp. 122f.
169 Wadum 1995a, p. 69 and note 10.
170 Liedtke 2008, p. 105.
171 Wheelock 1995c, pp. 129f.
172 Wheelock/Broos 1995, p. 130.
173 Gowing 1952 (1970), p. 124.
174 Goodman 2001, p. 87.
175 Montias 1989, p. 122.
176 Gowing 1952 (1970), p. 42.
177 Liedtke 2008, pp. 99f.
178 Wheelock 1995b, pp. 108–110.
179 Blankert 1995, p. 39.
180 De Winkel 1998, pp. 330f.
181 Welu 1975, pp. 532f.
182 Mirimonde 1961.
183 Slatkes 1981; Philadelphia/Berlin/London 1984, p. 323, fig. 10.
184 A. Poirters, S. J., *Het Masker van der Wereldt afgetrocken*, Antwerp, 1659.

[185] Büttner 2010, p. 65.
[186] Rudolph 1938.
[187] Source, no. 30.
[188] Liedtke 2008, p. 123.
[189] Boström 1951; see Wheelock/Broos 1995, p. 159, note 2.
[190] Source, no. 24.
[191] Source, no. 24 and 30.
[192] Liedtke 2008, p. 134.
[193] Liedtke 2008, p. 136.
[194] De Winkel 2006, pp. 246–248.
[195] Wheelock/Broos 1995, p. 165, note 1.
[196] Seymour 1964, pp. 323–331; see also Wheelock/Broos 1995, p. 162.
[197] Wheelock/Broos 1995, pp. 204ff.; Wheelock 1995a, pp. 387–393.
[198] Montias 1989, pp. 173, 310, doc. 260.
[199] Montias 1989, p. 329, doc. 324.
[200] Montias 1989, p. 330, doc. 325.
[201] Source, no. 13.
[202] Montias 1989, p. 204.
[203] Source, no 16.
[204] Source, no. 17.
[205] Wheelock 2010, p. 24.
[206] Sluijter 1998, pp. 265f.
[207] Source, no. 23.
[208] Arasse 1993 (1996).
[209] Sedlmayr 1951 and 1963; Badt 1961; Mengden 1984; Hertel 1996, pp. 18–21.
[210] Hultén 1949.
[211] Gelder 1951, p. 44.
[212] Wadum 1995a, p. 67; Wald 2010, p. 197.
[213] Wadum 1995a, p. 67.
[214] Sluijter 1998, p. 266 and note 13.
[215] Hoogstraten 1678.
[216] Büttner 2010, p. 109.
[217] De Winkel 1998.
[218] Source, no. 24.
[219] Pénot 2010.
[220] Schilder 2010.
[221] Biemond 2010, p. 167.
[222] Eiche 1982, p. 203.
[223] Schmitz von Ledebur 2010, p. 96.
[224] Pénot 2010, p. 53.
[225] Büttner 2010, p. 104.
[226] Pénot 2010, p. 53.
[227] Liedtke 2008, p. 150.
[228] Waldeis 1997, pp. 39–46.
[229] Thoré-Bürger 1866, p. 559.
[230] Wheelock/Broos 1995, p. 172.
[231] Van Berkel 1997, pp. 225f.
[232] Liedtke 2008, p. 152.
[233] Welu 1975.
[234] Welu 1975, p. 544.
[235] Welu 1975, p. 543.
[236] Frankfurt 1997, cat. 4.
[237] Frankfurt 1997, cat. 3.
[238] Welu 1986; Frankfurt 1997, cat. 11.
[239] Welu 1986, pp. 266f.
[240] Nash 1991, pp. 110–113.
[241] Liedtke 2008, p. 153, fig. 29b.
[242] Cf. Munich 2003, pp. 90–93, cat. 37.
[243] Liedtke 2008, p. 153.
[244] Wheelock/Broos 1995, p. 178.
[245] Cf. De Jongh 2000, pp. 193ff.
[246] Stechow 1960.
[247] Wheelock/Broos 1995, p. 180.
[248] Sutton, in London/Hartford 1998, cat. 40.
[249] Trans. Montias 1989, p. 364, doc. 439, no. 5; Source, no. 30, no. 5.
[250] Source, no. 12.
[251] Liedtke 2008, p. 160.
[252] Blankert/Montias/Aillaud 1992, p. 193.
[253] Cf. Wheelock/Broos 1995, p. 189, note 2.
[254] Schneider 1993/2010, p. 54.
[255] Vergara 1998, pp. 235–255; cf. Liedtke 2008, p. 160.
[256] Blankert/Montias/Aillaud 1992, p. 146.
[257] Wheelock 1981, p. 150; Wheelock 1995b, pp. 149–155.
[258] Weber 1998, pp. 295–297.
[259] Goodman 2001, pp. 80f.
[260] Liedtke 2007, pp. 513–516.
[261] Liedtke 2008, pp. 166f.
[262] Weber 1998, pp. 295–297; New York/London 2001, p. 402, fig. 293.
[263] Source, no. 24.
[264] Source, no. 25; trans. Montias 1969, pp. 344f., doc. 367.
[265] Liedtke 2008, pp. 163–177.
[266] Wheelock/Broos 1995, p. 192.
[267] De Jongh 1975/76, pp. 69–75.
[268] Liedtke 2008, p. 165.
[269] Büttner 2010, p. 110.
[270] De Jongh 1975/76, p. 75.
[271] Montias 1989, p. 202.
[272] Liedtke 2008, p. 165.
[273] Weber 1998, pp. 295–297.
[274] Montias 1989, p. 327, doc. 318.
[275] Montias 1989, pp. 209, 334, doc. 342.
[276] Montias 1989, pp. 209, 334, doc. 344.
[277] Source, no. 18.
[278] Montias 1989, pp. 211f.
[279] Montias 1989, p. 213.
[280] Trans. Montias 1989, p. 337, doc. 357.
[281] Source, no. 19.
[282] Source, no. 20; trans. Montias 1989, p. 337, doc. 358.
[283] Montias 1989, p. 216.
[284] Source, no. 27; trans. Montias 1989, p 212.
[285] Source, no. 25 and 27.
[286] Source, no. 28.
[287] Montias 1989, pp. 213ff.
[288] Source, no. 21.
[289] Montias 1989, pp. 216ff.
[290] Source, no. 22.
[291] Montias 1989, p. 348, doc. 377.
[292] Source, no. 23.
[293] Source, no. 24; Montias 1989, pp. 220ff.; Liedtke 2008, pp. 17ff.
[294] Montias 1989, p. 222.
[295] Liedtke 2008, p. 20.
[296] Source, no. 25; Montias 1989, p. 223.
[297] Montias 1989, p. 225.
[298] Van Berkel 1997, pp. 23ff.

[299] Montias 1989, pp. 277, 437f., doc. 376.
[300] Montias 1989, p. 229; Source, no. 26.
[301] On this cf. Montias 1989, pp. 229f.
[302] Source, no. 18.
[303] Bredius 1882; Broos 1995; Broos 1998, pp. 22f.
[304] Cited from Dresden 2010, p. 10.
[305] Wheelock/Broos 1995, p. 111.
[306] Neidhardt 2010b, p. 67.
[307] Trans. Wheelock/Broos 1995, p. 124.
[308] Weber 1993, p. 300.
[309] Neidhardt 2004, p. 7.
[310] Thoré-Bürger 1858/60, vol. 2, p. 79.
[311] Suzman Jowell 1998, pp. 34ff., fig. 1–7.
[312] On whom see Mai 2003.
[313] Bredius 1882; Broos 1998, p. 22, fig. 3.
[314] Bredius 1915–1921.
[315] Broos 1993, pp. 306–314.
[316] Cited from Broos 1993, p. 309.
[317] See Broersma 2010.
[318] Buijsen 2010b, p. 41.
[319] MacColl 1901.
[320] Bredius 1901.
[321] Buijsen 1990.
[322] Bredius 1937.
[323] See, most recently, Lammertse 2011.
[324] Cited from Blankert 2010, p. 30; see also Blankert 2006.
[325] Lammertse 2011, pp. 23–41.
[326] Plietzsch 1939.
[327] E. g. Swillens 1949, or Gowing 1952.

Documentary Sources on Vermeer's Life and Work

1.
31 October 1632
Johannes Vermeer is baptized, as "Joannis", at the Nieuwe Kerk in Delft
Dito [1632 October 31] *'t kint Joannis, vader Reynier Janssoon, moeder Dingnum Balthasars, getuijgen Pr. Brammer, Jan Heijndricxz., Maertge Jans.*
(Delft, G.A., Doopboek Nieuwe Kerk, no. 12)
First published in Obreen 4, 1881, p. 291; Ruurs, p. 208; M 136

2.
23 April 1641
Vermeer's father, Reynier Jansz. Vos, purchases the "Mechelen" tavern on the Groote Markt in Delft
Willem Jansz. Sloting and Pieter Willemsz. Van Vlijet sell to *Reijnier Vosch* a house with yard (*huys ende erve*) on the marketplace by the name of *Mechelen*, for the sum of 2,700 florins. The local land tax (*deut op de gulden*) levied by the Camer van Charitate amounts to 16 florins, 17 stuivers and 8 pence. (Delft, G.A., Archief van de Camer van Charitate, no. 237, fol. 40r and 40v; this undated document is to be found among records of transactions effected during the first half of 1641. The precise date is provided by the notary's document concerning an attempt, on 2 January 1669, to sell the building [M 324])
First published in Montias 1989, p. 291, doc. 161; M 161

3.
12 October 1652
Vermeer's father, Reynier Jansz. Vermeer alias Vos, is buried at the Nieuwe Kerk in Delft
[1652 October 12] *Reinier Jansz. Vermeer op 't Marctvelt*
Reinier Jansz. Vermeer [formerly resident] on the marketplace
(Delft. G.A., Begraafboek Nieuwe Kerk)
First published in Van Peer 1959, p. 240; Ruurs, p. 209; M 243
On this occasion no donation of clothing is made to the Opperste Kleed of the Camer van Charitate, as would usually have been the case.
(Delft, G.A., Camer van Charitate, Opperste Kleed Boek, no. 73)
First published in Montias 1989, p. 306, doc. 243

4.
5 and 20 April 1653
Vermeer's marriage to Catharina Bolnes
The painter Leonaert Bramer and Captain Melling serve as witnesses, on 5 April 1653, before the Delft notary Johannes Ranck, at the request of Johannes Vermeer (*Jan Reijniersz.*) and Catharina Bolnes (*Trijntgen Reijniers*), the youngest daughter of Maria Thins and Reynier Bolnes, to the fact that Maria Thins, with the support of her sister Cornelia, refused, on the previous evening, 4 April 1653, to give her formal consent to the marriage of these two persons, and yet had formally stated her consent upon the notice of their intention to marry.
Op huijden den 5den april 1653 compareerde voor mij Johannes Ranck, openbaaer notaris, bij den Hove van Holland geadmitteert, binnen der stad Delft residerende, in presentie van den ondergeschreven getuijgen, Capiteyn Melling, out ontrent 59 jaeren, ende Leonart Bramer, schilder, out ontrent 58 jaeren, beyde burgers alhier, die verclaerden ende attesteerden ten versoucke van Jan Reijniersz. ende Trijntgen Reijniers waerachtich te weesen, dat sij getuijgen neffens mijn, notaris, gisteren avont, sijnde den 4den deser sijn geweest ten huijse aen ende bij de person van Joffrouwe Maria Tints woonende alhier, als wanneer bij den voornoemden notaris Ranck in onser presentie is versocht off de voorseyde joffwrouwe Tints (geadsisteert met Cornelia Tints, haer suster) gelieffde te teijckenen de acte van consent van het aenteyckenen van de huijwelijcks gebooden van haer joffrouw Maria Tints dochter, genaemt Trijntgen Reijniers, met

Jan Reyniersz, mede woonende alhier, beyden voornoemt, om deselve gebooden te doen vercondigen naer gebruijck deser stad; die wij alsdoen tot antwoort hebben hooren geven, niet van meninge was te teijckenen ende haer hant bekent te maken, maar wel mochte lijden, dat de gebooden gingen ende hetselve soude aensien, ende tot verscheyde maelen seyde, dat sy die niet soude beletten off verhinderen.

(Delft, G.A., prot. not. J. Ranck, no. 2112)

First published in Obreen 4, 1881, p. 292; Van Peer 1959, p. 242; Ruurs, pp. 209f.; M 249

Johannes Vermeer and Catharina Bolnes marry on 20 April 1653 in Schipluiden, a village outside Delft.

Den 5den Apprill 1653: Johannes Reijniersz. Vermeer, jongeman op 't Marctvelt. Catharina Bolenes jongedochter mede aldaer. As a marginal note: Attestatie gegeven op Schipluij den 20en April 1653.

(Delft, G.A., Legger van de persoonen, die haer begeven in den H. echten staat binnen de Stadt Delff, begonnen metten jare 1650 ende eyndigende den lesten December 1656)

First published in Obreen 4, 1881, p. 292

Goudappel 1977, pp. 20–26; M 250

5.

22 April 1653

Johannes Vermeer and Gerard ter Borch serve as witnesses

Johan van den Bosch, a captain in the service of the States General, formally confirms that he will pay to Dido van Treslong a sum of 1,000 guilders, to which she is legally entitled as part of her inheritance from the estate of the deceased Mr Van Treslong, as soon as such a sum is shown to be necessary. Witness to this formal assurance are the two painters *Monsr Gerrit Terburch* and *Johan van der Meer*. These sign, respectively, as *Geraerdt Ter Borch* and *Johannis Vermeer*.

(Delft, G.A., prot. not. W. de Langue, no. 1695)

First published in Montias 1977, pp. 280f.; Ruurs, p. 210; M 251

6.

29 December 1653

Johannes Vermeer is formally enrolled as an independent master in the Delft Guild of Saint Luke

Schilder. Den 29 December 1653 Johannis Vermeer he[e]ft hem doen aanteijkenen als meester Schilder, sijnde burger en heeft op sijn meester geldt betaelt 1 gul. 10 stuyv. rest 4 gul. 10 st.

As a citizen of Delft, Vermeer is required to pay the enrolment fee in full. But he pays on this occasion only part of the fee due: 1 guider and 10 stuivers. He will eventually pay the remaining amount, a sum of 4 guilders and 10 stuivers, on 24 July 1656.

(Delft, G.A., Archiv der Lukasgilde, Register van alle de nieuwe meesters en winckelhouders [behoorende onder Ste Lucas gilde], Tsedert den Jare 1650)

First published in Obreen 1, 1877, p. 56; Ruurs, p. 210; M 256; M 265

7.

30 November 1657

Vermeer and his wife borrow 200 florins from Pieter Claesz. van Ruijven

Johannis Reyniersz. Vermeer, schilder and *Catharina Reyniers Bolnes [sijne huysvrou]* (the square-bracketed words are crossed through on the original document) formally confirm that they owe to *Pieter Claesz. van Ruijven*, or his legal representative, the sum of 200 guilders, which they have today received. They promise to repay, within a year, the sum itself, in addition to the interest due on it, at the rate of 4 ½ per cent per annum, and to pay all further interest that may become due if the entire sum is not repaid after a full year has elapsed, and to do so until the entire debt is discharged.

(Delft, G.A., prot. not. J. van Ophoven, no. 1952, fol. 99)

First partially published in Bredius 1885, p. 218; Ruurs, p. 210; M 271

8.

27 December 1660

One of Vermeer's children is buried at the Oude Kerk in Delft

Een kint van Johannes Vermeer aen den O. Langedijck.

Johannes Vermeer is cited as the deceased child's father and as resident on the Oude Langedijck.

On 10 December 1661 Vermeer's mother-in-law, Maria Thins, will purchase a grave in the same church (M 289). Vermeer's other children who die in infancy will be buried in this second grave. (Delft, G.A., Begraafboeken, no. 40, fol. 40, Oude Kerk)

Discovered by H.W. van Leeuwen, and first published in Montias 1980, p. 49; Ruurs, p. 210; M 279

9.

Between 14 August and 31 December 1662, and between 12 November and 31 December 1663
In 1662/63 Vermeer is elected as headman of the Delft Guild of Saint Luke

An entry made between 14 August and 31 December 1662 in the Guild's Register of Newly Enrolled Masters and Shopkeepers names those serving as its officiating headmen for 1662 as follows:
Regerende Hooftmans deses Jaers waren Cornelis de Man, Arent van Sanen, Aelbrecht Keijser, Johannes Vermeer, Jan Dirckse van der Laen, Ghijsbrecht Kruijck. The sequence of the names indicates that Cornelis de Man is serving in his second year as headman, while Johannes Vermeer is serving in his first year. The others listed were glassmakers and fayence artists.
The entry made between 12 November and 31 December 1663 lists the officiating headmen for 1663 as follows: *De regerende Hooftluijden deses jaers waren Joannes Vermeer, Arent van Saenen, Gijsbrecht Cruick, Anthonij Pallemedes, Frans Jansz. van der Fijn, Jan Gerritse van der Houven.* Here, Vermeer is serving in his second year as headman, while Anthonie Palamedesz. is serving in his first year.
(Delft, G.A., Archiv der Lukasgilde, Register van alle de nieuwe meesters en winckelhouders [behoorende onder Ste Lucas gilde]. Tsedert den Jahre 1650)
First published in Obreen 1, 1877, p. 68; Ruurs, p. 211; M 291; M 296

10.

11 August 1663
Balthasar de Monconys visits Vermeer's studio in Delft

Vermeer is not able to show his visitor any of his own pictures, but Monconys sees one of these on calling at the house of a Delft baker, who claims to have paid 600 livres for it, even though it depicts only a single figure, and Monconys himself would not have paid for it six pistoles [a pistole was a gold coin equivalent in value to 10 livres].
A Delphes ie vis le Peintre Vermer qui n'avoit point de ses ouvrages, mais nous en vismes un chez un boulanger qu'on avait payé six cens livres, quoyqu'il n'y eust qu'une figure, que i'aurois creu trop payer de six pistoles.
Monconys 1666, 2, p. 149; Ruurs, p. 211; M 294

11.

19 October 1665
Vermeer is a beneficiary of the will of Pieter van Ruijven and his wife, Maria de Knuijt, receiving a bequest of 500 florins

The will comprises three separate documents: a joint instruction from the married couple, by which each appoints the other his/her sole heir; an instruction concerning the guardianship of any surviving children; and Maria Knuijt's own will, which would have taken effect only if she was predeceased by her husband. The Delft notary Gerrit van der Wel is appointed guardian of any surviving children. Should he die, the administrators of the Delft Orphanage are to appoint another guardian, with the stipulation that Jan Claesz. van Ruijven, a relative, is not to be considered for this role. The appointed guardian is to preserve all items of value in the estate until such time as the surviving children come of age. Particular instructions regarding the collection of paintings (*de schilder konst*) are contained in a codicil, which has not survived. In her own will Maria de Knuijt names her children as her own sole heirs. Should all her children predecease her, their originally intended inheritance is to be divided into three equal parts: one third of this is to go to the Delft Orphanage, one third to the public charity for the poor (the Camer van Charitate) and one third to the priests of the Reformed Church of Delft, who are in turn to distribute the sum among priests who have been expelled from Catholic lands. In addition, several bequests are stipulated (the sums concerned to be paid out before the aforementioned tripartite division of the inheritance): 6,000 guilders to each of the children of her late brother, and to her husband's nephew; 1,000 guilders to *Johannes Dircxz. de Geus* (it is unclear as to whether this refers to a further relative); and 500 guilders to *Johannes Vermeer*. The initial remark that, should this last-named beneficiary die before receiving the bequest, then this is not to be passed on to his children or to their own children, has been crossed through on the original document and the deleted words replaced by the phrase: *sall 't voors. Legaet te niet zijn* (the aforementioned bequest shall be annulled). By this means, Catharina Bolnes is to be excluded from Vermeer's succession. The bequest to Vermeer is the only such instruction in this will to be restricted expressly to its named beneficiary.

(Leiden, G.A., prot. not. N. Paets, no. 676, document no. 99); M 301

12.

14 May and 21 June 1669

Pieter Teding van Berckhout visits Vermeer's studio in Delft

Pieter Teding van Berckhout, in his diary entry for 14 May 1669, concerning a visit to Delft, records that he has seen an outstanding painter by the name of Vermeer, who showed him a number of remarkable works of his own (*un excellent peijntre nommé Vermeer, qui me monstra quelques curiosites de sa main*). He subsequently writes of a second visit to Delft, on 21 June 1669, when some of the works shown to him by Vermeer were notable for their effects of "perspective": *ie sortie ensuite et fus voijr un celebre Peijntre nommé Vermeer, qui me monstra quelques eschantillons de son art dont la partie la plus extraordinaijre et la plus curieuse consiste dans la perspective.*

(The Hague, Koninklijke Bibliotheek, inv. 129 D 16, vol. 1)

First published in Montias 1991, p. 48; Montias 1993, p. 377, doc. 325* bis; Washington/The Hague 1995/96, p. 50, fig. 4

13.

11 February 1670

Will drawn up by Vermeer's sister, Gertruy, and her husband, Anthony van der Wiel

Johannes Vermeer's older sister, *Geertruyt Reijnersdr. Vermeer* and her husband, *Anthony van der Wiel*, draw up their joint will before the notary G. van Assendelft, with *Arent van Pynacker* and *Pieter Ruyven*, Lord of *Spaleand*, serving as witnesses. Husband and wife appoint each other his/her sole heir. It is also stipulated that, should Gertruy predecease her husband, he is, within six years, to surrender all her clothes and her personal effects, together with the sum of 400 guilders, to her relatives and heirs *ab intestato* (this refers exclusively to Johannes Vermeer, he being Gertruy's only sibling and she being childless). On 18 July 1671 (see doc. 16) Johannes Vermeer will receive the sum of 148 guilders. Montias assumes that the difference between the sum specified in the will and the sum that Vermeer received is explained by the debts incurred by Digna Baltens, the mother of Johannes and Gertruy Vermeer, the amount of which exceeded the payments still owed to her, with the result that Gertruy's estate was smaller than originally expected.

(Delft, G.A., prot. not. G. van Assendelft, no. 2128, fol. 311)

First published in Montias 1980, p. 56; Ruurs, p. 212; M 329

14.

13 February 1670

Digna Baltens, widow of Reynier Vermeer, and the mother of Johannes Vermeer, is buried at the Nieuwe Kerk in Delft

Begraven in de Nieuwe Kerk 13 Februarij 1670 Dyna Baltens weduwe van Reynier Vermeer in de Vlamingstraet. (Delft, G.A., Begraafboek)

First published in Obreen 4, 1881, p. 291; M 330

Donations made on 26 August 1670 to the Delft Camer van Charitate are to the value of 6 guilders and 6 stuivers.

(Delft, G.A., Beste Opperste Kleed Boek, no. 74, part II, fol. 8)

Ruurs, p. 212; M 330, M 333

15.

28 October 1670 and 28 October 1671

In 1670/71 Vermeer serves a second period of office as headman of the Delft Guild of Saint Luke

The entry in the Guild's Register for 28 October 1670 names those serving as its officiating headmen for the year 1670 as follows: *De Hooftmans waren Louijs Elsevier, Michiel van den Houck, Gijsbrecht Kruyck, Joannes Vermeer, Jasper Serrot, Jacob Kerton.* Of the painters named, Elsevier was here serving in his second year as headman, and Vermeer in his first year.

The Register's entry for 28 October 1671 lists the officiating headmen for the year 1671 as follows: *De regerende Hooftmans waren Joannes Vermeer, Jasper Serrot, Jacob Corton, Cornelis de Man, Cijbrant van der Laen, Claes Jansz. Metschert.* Of the painters named, Vermeer was here serving in his second year as headman, and Cornelis de Man in his first year.

(Delft, G.A., Archiv der Lukasgilde, Register van alle de nieuwe meesters en winckelhouders [behoorende onder Ste Lucas gilde]. Tsedert den Jahre 1650)

First published in Obreen 1, 1873, pp. 77f.; Ruurs, p. 212; M 334; M 339

16.

18 July 1671

Vermeer receives his inheritance from the estate of his late sister, Gertruy

Vermeer, confirming his profession as *konstschilder*, declares, before the notary G. van Assendelft, that he has received from *Anthonj van der Wiel*, the widower and sole heir of *Geertruyt Vermeer*, his late sister, that part of the inheritance due to him from the estates of his sister and of his mother, Digna Baltens, and that he has no further claims, except the sum of 148 (*een hondert acht ende veertich*) guilders, which the said Van der Wiel has declared himself ready to pay at any time. Cf. doc. 13 Bredius (1885) and, following his reading, Blankert and others, interpret the stated sum as 648 (*ses hondert acht ende veertich*) guilders. According to Montias (1989, p. 332), while the first documentary reference to the sum permits such an interpretation, this is not the case with the second, which clearly reads 148.

(Delft, G.A., prot. not. G. van Assendelft, no. 2131, fol. 368)

First published in Bredius 1885, p. 218; Ruurs, p. 212; M 337

17.

24 May 1672

Hans Jordaens and Johannes Vermeer deliver their expert opinion on pictures displayed for their assessment at the Painters' Guild in The Hague

Johannes Jordaen and *Johannes Vermeer*, in their capacity as esteemed painters from Delft, appear before the notary Pieter van Swieten in The Hague, and formally confirm that, at the request of Mr *Hendrick van Formanteau*, they have viewed and examined 12 pictures displayed for them in the Guild's Assembly Hall, which are described in the following list or catalogue as extraordinary Italian paintings and valued at the sums indicated:

Op huyden den 23 Mey 1672 compareerden voor mij Pieter van Swieten Openb. Notaris ... d'Heeren Johannes Jordaen ende Johannes Vermeer uytmuntende Kunstschilders tot Delft en verclaerden sy deposanten te saemen ter instantie van Sr. Hendrick de Formanteau voor de oprechte waerheyt getuycht, verclaert en gedeposeert waer te syn dat sy deposanten op haere Confrery Camer alhier op data gesien en gevisiteert hebben 12 stucks Schilderien d'welcke op de lijste ofte cathalogus die de requirant hen deposanten heeft geexhibeert, gestelt ende genaemt staen voor uytmuntende Italiaense schilderien, mitsgaders getaxeert soodanigh als achter yeder stuck uytgetrocken Staet namentlych:

een Venus en Cupido, beelden grooter als het leven van Ryxdaelders
Michiel Angelo Bonarotti, Hollants gelt 350: 320
een Conterfeytsel van Giorgion del Castelfrancko van Titiaen, naer het leven geschildert 250: 240
een harder ende harderinnetje van Titiaen 160: 150
Weergadingh van deselve groote van Titiaen 120. 110
een dans van naeckte Kindertjenslevensgroote van Iacomo Palma 250: 240
een Venetiaense Dame van Paris Pordinon 160: 150
een Conterfeytsel van een Prelaet van Hans Holbeen 120: 110
een Ceres met overvloet, met veele naeckte Kindertjes van Giorgion del Castel Franco 120. 110
een out mans confeytsel van Raphael Urbin 150: 140
een St. Paulus, halfbeelt, levensgroote,van de Oude Jacomo Palma 80: 70
een Schoone Venetiaense vrouw van Titiaen 200: 185
een lantschap van Titiaen met een Satierdie de nimphe Caresseert 240: 230

Each of the pictures bears the seal of his Serene Highness, the Great Elector of Brandenburg. But not only are they not the extraordinary Italian works they are claimed to be. They are, on the contrary, merely a lot of great rags and bad pictures. They are by no means worth even a tenth of the stated prices; and they could not be assessed in terms of value by the witnesses, for they were of no value at all.

sijnde de voorsz. Schilderien gecachetteert met het signet van syne Ceurvorstelycke Doorluchticheyt Van Brandenburgh, welcke Schilderiën niet alleen niet en syn uytmuntende Italiaense Schilderiën, maer ter contrarie eenige groote vodden ende slechte schilderiën, die op verre nae te tiende part van de voorsz. uytgetrocke prysen niet weerdich en sijn, ende sy deposanten die niet en connen estimeren, dewijle deselve niet geacht en konnen werden.

First published in Bredius 1916a, pp. 89–91; Ruurs, p. 212; M 341

18.

20 July 1675

Vermeer borrows 1,000 florins from the Amsterdam merchant Jacob Rombouts

Nearly three years later, on 2 April 1678, Maria Thins formally declares herself willing to pay to Johanna Kiest, wife of Jacob Rombouts, the remainder, or the

as yet unpaid portion (*restant ofte defect*), of the sum loaned by Rombouts to Johannes Vermeer, because Johanna Kiest will receive nothing from the estate of the said, now late Johannes Vermeer. Maria Thins will not, however, pay any earlier or subsequent interest due on the original sum (M 389).
(Amsterdam, G. A., prot. not. Jacob Hellerus)
Document of 2 April 1678 first published in Bredius 1910, p. 64; Ruurs, p. 215 (re. document of 2 April 1678); M 356

19.
15 and 16 December 1675
Death of Johannes Vermeer and his burial at the Oude Kerk in Delft
In the Register of Burials at the Oude Kerk in Delft, the entry for 15 December 1675 includes: *Jan Vermeer*, painter on the *Oude Langendijck*, in the church (*Jan Vermeer kunstschilder aen de Oude Langedijck in de kerk*). There is a marginal note: 8 underage children (*8 Me: J: kind*).
(Delft, G. A., Personen die binnen deser Stad Delft overleden ende in de Oude Kerck als oock daer buijten begraven sijn tsedert den 19 Julij 1671)
First published in Obreen 4, 1881, p. 294
A further register relating to places of burial records that on 16 December 1675 *Johan Vermeer* is laid to rest in a grave, and that the coffin of the child initially buried on 27 June 1673 (M 343) is placed on top of his own. Here is also to be found a list of all those who are buried in the Oude Kerk grave purchased by Maria Thins on 10 December 1661:
On 10 July 1667 a child born to *Johan Vermeer* who had died very shortly after birth was placed in this grave as its first occupant
On 16 July 1669 a child of *Johan Vermeer*
On 27 June 1673 a child of *Johan Vermeer*
On 16 December 1675 *Johan Vermeer* was laid to rest in this grave, and the coffin of the last mentioned child was placed on top of his own
On 23 March 1676 *W[ille]m Bolnes* [bachelor] was buried here
On 27 December 1680 [there followed] *Maria Thins*, widow of *Reijnier Bolnes*, and the grave is now full.
10 julij 1667 is in dit graf geleijt een baerkint van Johan Vermeer, uijtgesondert dat baerkint is het graff ledigh
Den 16 julij 1669 een kint van Johan Vermeer
Den 27 junij 1673 een kint van Johan Vermeer
Den 16 dec. 1675 is in dit graf geleijt Johan Vermeer ende het bovenstaende baerkin op de kist van de voorn Vermeer geset
Den 23 maart 1676 is hier in geleijt Wm. Bolnes j. m.
Den 27 december 1680 Maria Thins wed. van Reijnier Bolnes, ende is nu vol.
First published in Van Peer 1968, p. 223; Ruurs, p. 213; M 357

20.
16 December 1675
After Vermeer's death no donation is made to the Camer van Charitate
The entry in the list of donations (Beste Opperste Kleed Boek) of the public charity for the poor, the Camer van Charitate, reads: nothing to collect from *Johannes Vermeer*, painter on the *Oude Lange Dijck (Johannes Vermeer kunstschilder aen de Oude Lange dijck niet te halen)*. (Delft, G. A., Camer van Charitate, Beste Opperste Kleed Boek, no. 24, part II, fol. 50v)
First published in Montias 1980, p. 57; Ruurs, p. 213; M 358

21.
27 January 1676
Catharina Bolnes sells two pictures by Vermeer to the baker Hendrick van Buyten
Catharina Bolnes declares, before the notary G. van Assendelft, that she sold to Hendrick van Buyten, a master baker in Delft, two pictures by Vermeer: one depicts two people (one seated and writing a letter), the other depicts one person playing a cittern. Catharina Bolnes declares that she received 617 guilders and 6 stuivers for the pictures, a sum equivalent to what she had owed to Van Buyten for bread delivered to the Vermeer family, which debt Van Buyten now regards as fully discharged.
Catharina Bolnes, Wed. van za: Johannes Vermeer, in sijn leven kunstschilder binnen Delff, ende bekende aen Hendrick van Buyten, Mr. backer alhier vercoft ende getransporteert te hebben twee schilderijen bij den voorn: Vermeer geschildert, d'eene vertonende twee personagien waeroff d'een een brieff sit te schrijven, ende d'ander mede een personagie spelende op een cyter. En bekende daervoor voldaen te zijn met de somme van ses hondert seventien gulden en ses stuyvers die sij comparante aen gelevert broot aen den voorn. van Buyten schuldig was en welcke reeckening, door desen gehouden wert voor geannulleert ende vernieticht.

Catharina Bolnes reserves the right to buy back the pictures, which Van Buyten agrees to allow her upon her particular urging. She undertakes to pay Van Buyten an annual sum of 50 guilders, starting on 1 May 1677. After the full discharge of the 617 ½ guilders, in addition to a further 109 guilders and 5 stuivers owed to Van Buyten for further bread deliveries, he is to return the two pictures to her. Should Catharina Bolnes's mother die before the entire sum has been repaid, however, the sum still owed will have to be repaid at the rate of 200 guilders per annum, in addition to 4 per cent interest. In the case of repayment made in an irregular fashion, an annual interest payment of 4 per cent will also be due.
(Delft, G. A., prot. not. G. van Assendelft, no. 2132)
First published in Bredius 1885, pp. 219f.; Ruurs, p. 213; M 361

22.
10 February 1676
Catharina Bolnes sells 26 pictures from Vermeer's estate to the painter and art dealer Jan Coelenbier in Haarlem
On 30 November 1676, at the request of *Jannetje Stevens, Sr. Jan Colombier* declares that, on 10 February 1676, he bought from the widow of *Johannes van der Meer*, at the apothecary "At the Three Lemons" in Amsterdam, 26 paintings of diverse sizes for a total of 500 guilders, in the name and on the account of Jannetje Stevens. The sale price was equivalent to a sum that the widow of Johannes Vermeer still owes to the said Jannetje Stevens for various goods supplied (*voor rekeninge en in de name van de voorsz. requirante heeft gekocht 26 stucks, soo groot als cleyne Schilderyen te same nom en voor de somme van 500 guldens welke somme soude strekken tot betalinge op tgene de voorsz. Wed. van Johannes van der Meer aen de voorn. requirante wegens winckelwaren schuldlich was*). Catharina Bolnes handed the pictures over on the spot to Colombier, who took them to Haarlem and brought them to his house, where they are still to be found, because he himself has certain financial claims on Jannetje Stevens, which he intends to settle either with goods or in cash (*hebbende hij deposant de 26 stuks schilderijen naer dese Stadt Haerlem laten vervoeren en tsijnen huyse brengen, alwaer deselve schilderijen gebleven sijn, omdat hij deposant tot laste van de requirante eenige praetensie had en t'resterende aen haer regte off met gelt off met waren soude voldoen*). (Haarlem, G. A., prot. not. P. Baes)
First published in Bredius 1916b, p. 161; Ruurs, p. 214 (under the date 30 November 1676); M 362

23.
22 or 24 February 1676
Catharina Bolnes formally transfers Vermeer's *The Art of Painting* to the ownership of her mother, Maria Thins
[The date on the original document appears to read "22 February", yet the subsequent *insinuatie*, of 12 March 1677 (doc. 26), refers to a document drawn up on 24 February 1676] *Juffr. Catharina Bollenes*, widow of the deceased *Sr. Johan van der Meer* [*Ver* crossed through], appears before the notary and declares that she, in partial settlement of her debts (*in minderinge van 'tgeene sy schuldich is*), both in her own right and in her capacity as a widow, as administrator of her late husband's estate and as guardian of their joint children, has ceded to her mother, *Juffr. Maria Tins*, widow of the late *Reynier Bollenes*, full and free possession of a picture painted by her aforementioned late husband, depicting the "Art of Painting" (*haer moeder in vollen en vrijen eygendom over te geven een stuck schilderie, geschildert bij den voorn. haeren man za: waerin wert uytgebeelt "de Schilderconst"*), as also her right to the income from her property *Bon Repas* near *Schoonhoven*, inherited from *Cornelia Tin* and the subject of a *fideicommissum* [which, as determined by Cornelia Thins, should pass, after the death of her sister, Maria Thins, to the latter's daughter, Catharina Bolnes], in addition to claims that she has on just over five acres of land in *Oud-Beyerland*, and other annual income from the inheritance of Cornelia Thins, which, together, amount to 200 pounds [i. e. guilders] per annum. She renounces her claim to all these assets, retaining none for herself, in order thereby to reduce the debts owed to her mother. (The Hague, G. A., prot. not. J. Vosch, no. 3561, fol. 28)
First published, in several sections, in Bredius 1885, p. 220; Ruurs, p. 213; M 363

24.
29 February 1676
Inventory of the personal effects in the estate of Johannes Vermeer
The items in the inventory of personal effects in

Vermeer's estate are listed by the rooms in which each was to be found. The list is divided into two parts, arranged in the original document into left- and right-hand columns. The two columns are here reproduced one after the other, and numbered 1. and 2. The first list features those items that are now the property of Catharina Bolnes; the second list those items that belong in equal part to Maria Thins and Catharina Bolnes. Only the works of art and objects directly related to Vermeer's activity as a painter are listed here. The original Dutch text follows the form in which it was first published in full, in 1957, by A. J. J. M. van Peer.

1. Enumeration of the personal effects that are now the property of *Catharina Bolnes*, widow of the deceased Mr *Joannes Vermeer*, resident on the *Oude Langendijck* at the corner of *Molepoort*, and that are now to be found in the aforementioned house (*Specificatie van alsulcken huysraet ende meubile goederen als Catharina Bolnes, wede wijlen Sr. Joannes Vermeer, wonende aenden ouden Langendijck op den hoeck van de Molepoort in eygendom sijn toecomende, ende inde opgemelte huisinge berustende*).

In the front hall (*In 't Voorhuys*):

– A painting of fruit (*Een freutschilderytje*)
– A small seascape (*Een zeetje*)
– A landscape (*Een landschapie*)
– A painting by Fabritius (*Een stuckie schildery door Fabritius*)

In the great hall (*Inde groote zael*):

– A painting representing a peasant's barn (*Een schildery uytbeeldende een boere schuyr*)
– another painting (*nog een schilderij*)
– Two studies of heads by Fabritius (*Twee schilderyen Tronyen van Fabritius*)
– One [painting] with three pumpkins and other fruits (*Een daerinne drye pompoenen ende ander freut*)
– Portraits of Mr Vermeer's late father and mother (*Twee conterfeitsels van Sr. Vermeers zalr. vader ende moeder*)
– Three small drawings in black frames over the mantelpiece (*Drye kleyne teekeningentiens voorde schoorsteen met swarte lijsten*)
– A drawn coat of arms of the aforementioned Mr Vermeer in an ebony frame (*Een getekent wapen vande voorn. Sr. Vermeer, met een ebbe lijst*)
– A suit of armour and a helmet (*Een yser harnis met de stormhoet*)
– Linen and wool (*Linne en wolle*)
– A Turkish coat of the aforementioned late Mr Vermeer (*Een Turxse mantel vande voorn. Sr. Vermeer zal.*)
– An "innocent" [short, close-fitting jacket] of the same (*Een ditto inocent*)
– A yellow satin jacket with white fur trim (*Een geele zatyne mantel met witte bonte kanten*)
– An old green coat with white fur trim (*Een oude groene mantel met een witte bonte kant*)

In the small room adjoining the great hall (*Int Camertie aende voorz. groote zaal*):

– A large painted wooden trunk with iron fittings (*Een groen geschilderde houte koffer met yser beslagen*)

In the interior kitchen (*Inde binnenkeucken*):

– A large painting representing Christ on the Cross (*Een groote schildery, uytbeeldende Christus aen 't cruys*)
– Two paintings of heads by Hoogstraten (*Twee trony schilderyen gedaen by Hoogstraten*)
– A painting with every sort of women's stuff (*Een schildery daerinne allerley vrouwentuych*)
– A vera icon [depiction of Christ's face] (*Een van Veronica*)
– Two "tronien" painted in Turkish fashion (*Twee tronyen geschildert op sijn Turx*)
– A seascape (*Een zeetgen*)
– a painting hanging over the mantelpiece (*een schilderij hangende voorde schoorsteen*)
– A still life with a double bass and a skull (*Een waer in geschildert staet een bas met een dootshooft*)
– approximately seven yards of gilt leather wallcovering (*omtrent seven ellen goutleer aende muyr*)

In the basement room (*Op de keldercamer*):

– a painting of Christ on the Cross (*een schildery uytbeeldende Christus aent Cruys*)
– a painting with a woman wearing a necklace (*een schildery vertonende een vrou met een ketting aen*)

In the front room (*Opde voorkamer*) [this room, overlooking the street and presumably on the upper floor, would appear to have served as Vermeer's studio]:

– two Spanish chairs (*twee spaense stoelen*)
– a cane with an ivory knob (*een rotting met een yvooren knop daer op*) [this was the painter's maulstick, but was not recognized as such by the inventorist]
– two painter's easels (*twee schilders eesels*)
– three palettes (*drye paletten*)
– 6 unpainted panels (*6 paneelen*)
– ten painter's canvases (*tien schilderdoucken*)

– three bundles of diverse prints (*drye bondels alrehande slach van printen*)
– a desk (*een lessenaer*)
– here and there a jumble of diverse items that are not worth listing separately (*voorts soo hier ende daer eenige rommeling niet waerdig om yder bysonder gestelt te worden*)
2. Enumeration of the personal effects, half of which now belong to *Maria Thins*, widow of *Reynier Bolnes*, and half of which now belong to her daughter, *Catharina Bolnes*, widow of *Joannes Vermeer*, and which are to be found in the latter's house in Delft, on the Oude Langendyck (*Specificatie van alsulcken huysraet ende inboel als Juffr. Maria Thins wed.e wijlen Sr. Reynier Bolnes ende haer dogter Juffr. Catharina Bolnes wede van Joannes Vermeer elx voor de gerechte helfte in eygendom sijn toecomende, ende sijn berustende ter woonhuyse van de voorn. wed.e staende aenden ouden Langendyck alhier opden houck van de Molenpoort*).
In the front hall:
– a cabinet with joinery work (*een schrijnwercktkasie*)
– a large painting of Mars and Apollo in a bad black frame (*een groot stuk schilderij van mars ende Apollo in een slechte swarte lijst*)
– two somewhat smaller paintings (*twee schilderijen wat kleijnder*)
– four more paintings with bad frames (*nog vier schilderijtgens met slechte lijsten*)
– a mirror with an ebony frame (*een spiegel met een ebbe lijst*)
In the great hall (*Inde groote Zaal*):
– an ebony cabinet with inlay work (*een schrijnwerckt kasie met ebbenhout ingeleyt*)
– nine chairs with red Spanish leather seats and backs (*negen roo spaensleere stoelen*)
– an ebony crucifix (*een ebbenhout cruys*)
– ten portraits of ancestors of the aforementioned Mrs Tins, all in bad black frames (*tien conterfeytsels van de voorn. Juffr. Tins geslacht alle met slechte swarte lijsten*)
– A painting of the Madonna in an oak frame (*Een schilderey uytbeeldende de moeder Christi in een eyke lyst*)
– another painting of the Three Kings [Adoration of the Magi] (*nog een schildery vande drye koningen*)
In the small room adjoining the great hall (*Int camertgen aende voorsz. zaal*):
– two paintings (*twee stuckiens schildery*)
In the basement room (*Op de kelderkamer*):
– a painting with a gilt frame (*een schildery met een vergulde lyst*)
– a painting with an oak frame (*een met een houte eycke lyst*)
In the little hanging room (*Opt hangkamertgen*):
– 5 or 6 old books (*5 a 6 oude boecken*)
– three small paintings in black frames (*drye kleyne stuckiens schilderij in swarte lysten*)
In the back room on the upper floor (*Boven opde agterkamer*):
– six paintings (*ses schilderijen*)
In the attic (*Boven op de solder*):
– a table with a stone top, on which to grind colours (*een steene tafel om verruwe te vrijven, met de steen daerby*)
(Delft, G.A., prot. not. J. van Veen, no. 2224)
Excerpts first published in Bredius 1885, p. 219; first published in full in Van Peer 1957, pp. 98–103; Ruurs, pp. 213f.; Vienna 2010, p. 133, cat. 2, 3; M 364

25.
24 and 30 April 1676
Catharina Bolnes petitions the High Court of Holland and Zeeland for permission to be formally relieved of her debts
Catharina Bolnes declares that she is burdened with the care of eleven children [these words are underlined in the original document] because her deceased husband, during the most recent war with the King of France, was able to earn very little, indeed almost nothing at all, and was, moreover, constrained to sell at a great loss those pictures that he had purchased in his capacity as an art dealer, in order to be able to feed his children, with the result that the family's debts increased to such an extent that she, the petitioner, is not in a position to pay her creditors. These, in turn, are unwilling to make exception for her, on account of the great losses and the general misfortune occasioned by the aforementioned war. On the contrary, they demand immediate repayment, which she, the petitioner, is not in a position to supply (*hoe dat sy Suppliante belast synde met elf levende kinderen vermits de voorn. haere man geduerende desen oirlogh met den Coninck van Vranckrijck nu eenige jaren herwaarts seer weinich ofte bynae nietwes hebbende konnen winnen, oock die Kunst, die hy hadde ingekocht ende waermede hy*

was handelende, met seer groote schaede heeft moeten ujit sijn handen smijten tot alimentatie der voorsz. sijne kinderen daerdoor dan soo verre is geraeckt in verloop van schulden, dat sij Supplte. niet machtich is alle haere crediteuren [die geen regard willen nemen op het voorsz. haer groot verlies en quade fortuijn door den voorsz. oorloogh gecauseert]). As petitioner, Catharina Bolnes begs the Great and Mighty Lords of the High Court to sanction the issuing of documents that will bring about the relief of her debts (*cessie met committimus*). Catharina Bolnes accordingly testifies to her inability to discharge her debts, an admission intended to set in train the appointment of a responsible third party to administer Vermeer's estate. The High Court grants this petition and orders the Court of Law in Delft to issue the appropriate documents (*fiat mandemant ende cessie met committimus op den gerecht van Delft*).

The following are listed as creditors:
Maria Tins
N. Hoogenhouck, brewer
N. Rombouts
N. Dirckx
N. Van Leeuwen
Heindrickie Dircks
Tanneken
Heindrick van Buijtenen
Emmerentia

[The clerk charged with writing out this list placed a letter "N" where a creditor's forename was unknown to him]

(The Hague, Algemeen Rijksarchief, Hoge Raad van Holland en Zeeland, no. 80A)

Excerpts first published in Bredius 1910, p. 62; list of creditors first published in Van Peer 1957, p. 96; Ruurs, p. 214 (under date 30 April 1676); M 367

26.

12 March 1677

Maria Thins protests against the proposed sale of *The Art of Painting*

Maria Thins informs *Anthony Leeuwenhoek* that Vermeer's picture *The Art of Painting* had been ceded to her possession by her daughter, Catharina Bolnes, in February 1676 (doc. 23), as one of several measures undertaken to reduce the latter's debts to her mother. Maria Thins alerts van Leeuwenhoek, in his capacity as administrator of the estate of her deceased son-in-law, Johannes Vermeer, to the fact that (as she has learnt) the aforementioned picture is to be included in an auction of the paintings in Vermeer's estate publicly advertised as due to take place on 15 March at the premises of the Delft Guild of Saint Luke, where it will be sold to the highest bidder (*...mijne dochter Catarina Bolnes in mindering vant geene sij aen mij schuldich is... in vollen en vrijen eygendom heeft overgegeven, opgedragen ende getransporteert seeker stuck schilderije, geschildert by den voorn. Vermeer, waerinne wert uitgebeelt de Schilderkonst, van welcke voorsz. acte van overgifte ende opdracht Monsr Anthony Leeuwenhoek,... als Curateur over den boedel ende goedere van voorn. Vermeer ende Catharina Bolnes, visie en copie is gegeven. Ende dat des nietttegenstaende de voorn. Sr Leeuwenhoek in de voorsz. qualiteyt by affixie van gedruckte billietten (waervan mij een is toegezonden) by publicque opveylinge aen den meest biedende op den 15 Meert toecomende 1677 op St Lucas Gildecamer binnen deser stadt Delft presenteert te vercoopen de voorsz. schilderije, aen mij opgedragen als voorschreven is*). She commissions the notary to visit Leeuwenhoek personally and, with all urgency, to inform him that she does not wish the picture transferred to her to be sold, because this transfer had been effected expressly so as to reduce the amount by which her daughter was indebted to her. Should the picture nonetheless be sold, the notary is to insist upon the fact that Maria Thins is still legally permitted to seize it, and that the sum for which the picture is sold should not be borne by her [that is to say, paid out to the creditors], but should, rather, be deducted from the amount owed to her by her daughter (*Soo sal den eersten nots, hiertoe versocht, zich hebben te vervoegen aen den persoon, van den voorn Sr. Leeuwenhoek ende denselven uyt mijnen naem te insinueren ende aen te seggen, dat ick niet en verstae, dat de voorschreven aen mij opgedragen schilderije bij hem sal werden vercocht, als moetende coomen in minderingh van mijn achterwesen, off wel dat hij, de selve vercopende sal stipuleren dat bij mij genaest sal mogen werden ende dat de penningen daervoor de selve schilderije soude mogen werden vercocht byj mij niet en sullen werden uijtgekeert maer affslaech sullen strecken in minderinge van mijne voorn. dochter ende swagers boedel*). Should Leeuwenhoek ignore her warning, he will be held responsible for all costs and damages arising. (Delft, G.A., prot. not. Oudendijck, no. 2211, fol. 23)

Excerpts published in Bredius 1885, p. 221; Ruurs, p. 215; Vienna 2010, p. 134, cat. 4; M 379

27.

27 July 1677

Petition addressed by Catharina Bolnes and Maria Thins to the States of Holland and West Friesland

The petitioners inform the States that Johannes Vermeer, during the long and ruinous war with France, was not only unable to sell his own works (*van sijne kunst niet was hebbende kunnen vercopen*), but also found himself, to his great distress, saddled with the pictures by other painters, in which he dealt (*van andere mrs. daermede hij was handelende*). Burdened, moreover, by the great number of his children, he finally had nothing more (*niets van sijn selve hebbende*) and lapsed into such despair and took this all so to heart that he fell into a sort of frenzy and, within just one or one and a half days, went from a state of complete good health to death (*tot soodanigen verval ende decadentie was gekomen, 't welck hij soodanich ter harten hadde getrocken, dat hij gelijck als in frenesie vervallende in een dach of anderhalff was gesont ende doodt geweest*). They state, furthermore, that the first petitioner [Catharina Bolnes] is now piteously saddled with the care of ten underage children, the youngest of these being around two years old (*met tien onmondige kinderen waervan het jongste omtrent de twee jaren ont was*), she has never been able to do more than attend to her household and to her children (*haer noyt verders ofte anders als met hare huyshouding ende kinderen hadt bemoeyt*) and, only a little later, learnt of the poor condition of the estate. And, as she has been burdened with large debts, she has had to seek refuge in the miserable benefit of ceding control of the estate (*miserabele benefitie van cessie*), as a result of which she has lost everything she once owned to the benefit of her creditors. As her ten children would have nothing to live on, and as none of them is as yet able to earn his or her own living, she has been forced to seek assistance not only from relatives, but also from strangers, which has not been at all easy for her, she being of good family (*sulcx sy dan genootsaeckt soude wesen assistentie te versoecken niet alleenlijck bij hare vrunden, maer oock bij vreemden waertoe sy supplicante, als gekomen sijnde van eerlyke luyden, niet geerne en soude vervallen*). According to the will drawn up by Dieuwertge Hensbeecq, the great-aunt of the first petitioner [Catharina Bolnes], a sum of 2,900 guilders was deposited in the form of interest-bearing investments, in the Orphanage in Gouda, the principal sum of which was to be paid out to the petitioner and her children, while Maria Thins, in accordance with the *fideicommissum*, was granted a lifetime right to draw the revenues from and interest on this principal. As there are now good reasons for this sum to be used to assist in the upbringing of the first petitioner's underage children, both petitioners beg the States of Holland and West Friesland to remove the restrictions associated with the *fideicommissum*, so that they may have access to the capital of 2,900 guilders.

The petitioners' request is granted by the States of Holland and West Friesland: Catharina Bolnes is empowered to access the 2,900 guilders deposited in the Orphanage in Gouda.

(Gouda, G. A., Orphan Chamber, Weesboek 9, fol. 277)

Excerpts published in Matthijs 1976, p. 43; M 383

28.

1 September 1678

Maria Thins and Catharina Bolnes bring a petition before the municipal authorities in Gouda

Maria Thins and Catharina Bolnes bring the following petition before the Lord Magistrates of the City of Gouda: Maria Thins intends to renounce her rightful lifelong usufruct on a sum of 1,200 guilders deposited in the Orphanage in Gouda, which sum belongs to her daughter, Catharina Bolnes, in favour of the said daughter. The reason for this decision is as follows: of her daughter's children – the eldest is now 21 years old and the youngest still only 4 years old – two are at present very ill and another was gravely injured during a gunpowder explosion (*dat daer buskruijt in waer, 't welck aengingh*) on a ship in Mechelen. Their mother, Catharina Bolnes, is thus no longer in a position both to feed the aforesaid children (none of whom is yet able to earn his or her own living) and to pay the high cost of medicaments and the services of physicians.

(Gouda, G. A., Orphan Chamber, Weesboek 10, fol. 179)

Excerpts published in Matthijs 1976, p. 43; M 393

29.
April 1683
Inventory of the personal effects of Jacob Abrahamsz. Dissius derived from the estate of his late wife, Magdalena van Ruijven

Here are listed only the pictures by Vermeer.
Inventory of the estate and the personal effects due to *Jacobus Abrahamsz. Dissius*, inherited upon the death of his late wife, Magdalena van Ruijven, on 16 June 1682 (*Inventoris van den boedel ende goederen toecomende Jacobus Abrahamsz. Dissius uijt syn eijgen hoofde aen hem aenbesturven door't overlyden van Juffr. Magdalena van Ruyven*).
In the front room (*op de voorkamer*):
– Eight paintings by Vermeer (*Acht schilderijen van Vermeer*)
– Three ditto by the same ["with" crossed through] in cases (*Drie dito van denselven in kasies*)
In the back room (*Op de achterkamer*):
– Four more paintings by Vermeer (*Nogh vier schilderijen van Vermeer*)
In the kitchen:
– a painting by Vermeer
In the basement room (*op de kelder kamer*):
– 2 paintings by Vermeer
In addition to the aforementioned objects there are also:
– Two paintings by Vermeer
(Delft. G.A., prot. not. P. de Bries, no. 2325, fols. 31ff.)
Excerpts first published in Bredius 1885, p. 222; Neurdenburg 1951, pp. 37f.; Ruurs, p. 215 (under 20 June 1682); M 417

30.
16 May 1696
Catalogue of the pictures from the Dissius Collection sold at auction in Amsterdam

Catalogue of pictures sold on 16 May 1696 in Amsterdam (*Catalogus van schilderyen. Verkogt den 16. May 1696 in Amsterdam*)
[English titles as supplied by Montias (1989, p. 363, doc. 439) are given at the end of this list when these differ slightly from those supplied here]
1. A young lady weighing gold, in a box by *J. vander Meer of Delft*, extraordinarily artful and vigorously painted (*Een Juffrouw die goud weegt, in een kasje van J. vander Meer van Delft, extraordinaer konstig en kragtig geschildert*) 155–0
2. A maid pouring out milk, extremely well done, by ditto (*Een Meyd die Melk uytgiet, uytnemende de goet van dito*) 175–0
3. The portrait of Vermeer in a room with various accessories, uncommonly beautifully painted by him (*'t Portrait van Vermeer in een Kamer met verscheyde bywerk ongemeen fraai van hem geschildert*) 45–0
4. A young lady playing the guitar, very good of the same (*Een speelende Juffrouw op een Guiteer, heel goet van den zelve*) 70–0
5. In which a gentleman is washing his hands in an interior with sculptures and a view through to a back room, skilful and rare, by ditto (*Daer een Seigneur zyn handen wast, in een doorsiende Kamer, met beelden, konstig en raer van dito*) 95–0
6. A young lady playing the clavecin ([this should read: a virginal] in a room, with a gentleman listening, by the same (*Een speelende Juffrouw op de Clavecimbael in een Kamer, met een toeluisterend Monsieur door den zelven*) 80–0
7. A young lady who is being brought a letter by a maid, by ditto (*Een Juffrouw die door een Meyd een brief gebragt word, van dito*) 70–0
8. A drunken sleeping maid at a table, by the same (*Een dronke slapende Meyd aen een Tafel, van den zelven*) 62–0
9. A gay company in a room, vigorous and good, by ditto (*Een vrolyk geselschap in een Kamer, kragtig en goet van dito*) 73–0
10. A gentleman and a young lady making music in a room, by the same (*Een Musiceerende Monsr. en Juffr. in een Kamer, van den zelven*) 81–0
11. A soldier with a laughing girl, very beautiful, by ditto (*Een Soldaet met een laggent Meysje, zeer fraei van dito*) 44–10
12. A young lady making lace, by the same (*Een Juffertje dat speldewerkt, van den zelven*) 28–0
[Catalogue nos. 13 to 30 are pictures by other painters]
31. The city of Delft in perspective, viewed from the South, by J. vander Meer of Delft (*De Stad Delft in perspectief, te sien van de Zuyd-zy, door J. vander Meer van Delft*) 200–0
32. A view of a house in Delft, by the same (*Een Gesicht van een Huys staende in Delft, door denzelven*) 72–10
33. A view of some houses, by ditto (*Een Gesicht van eenige Huysen van dito*) 48–0

35. A young lady writing, very good, by the same (*Een Schryvende Juffrouw heel goet van denzelven*) 63–0
36. A young lady adorning herself with pearls, very beautiful, by ditto (*Een Paleerende dito, seer fraey van dito*) 30–0
37. A lady playing the clavecin [this should read: a virginal], by ditto (*Een Speelende Juffrouw op de Clavecimbael van dito*) 42–10
38. The study of a head in Antique dress, uncommonly skilful (*Een Tronie in Antique Klederen, ongemeen konstig*) 36–0
39. Another such Vermeer (*Nog een dito Vermeer*) 17–0
40. A pendant of the same (*Een weerga van denzelven*) 17–0
[English titles as supplied by Montias for nos. 5, 6, 12, 31, 32, 35, 36, 38, 39 (Montias 1989, p. 363, doc. 439):
5. In which a gentleman is washing his hands in a see-through room with sculptures, artful and rare, by ditto
6. A young lady playing the clavecin in a room, with a listening gentleman by the same
12. A young lady doing needlework, by the same
31. The Town of Delft in perspective, to be seen from the South, by J. van der Meer of Delft
32. A view of a house standing in Delft, by the same
35. A writing young lady, very good, by the same
36. A young lady adorning herself, very beautiful, by ditto
38. A tronie in antique dress, uncommonly artful
39. Another ditto Vermeer]
(Hoet 1, pp. 34–36)
Ruurs, p. 216; M 439

Abbreviations

G.A.	Gemeente Archief
prot. not.	notary's protocol
M	reference to entry in Appendix B, List of Documents, in Montias 1989, pp. 268–368

Literature for Documentary Sources

Bredius, Abraham, "Iets over Johannes Vermeer", *Oud Holland* 3, 1885, pp. 217–222.
Bredius, Abraham, "Nieuwe bijdragen over Johannes Vermeer", *Oud Holland* 28, 1910, pp. 61–64.
Bredius, Abraham, "Italiaansche schilderyen in 1672 door Haagsche en Delftsche schilders beoordeeld", *Oud Holland* 34, 1916, pp. 88–93 (Bredius 1916a).
Bredius, Abraham, "Schilderyen uit den nalatenschap van den Delftschen Vermeer", *Oud Holland* 34, 1916, pp. 160–161 (Bredius 1916b).
Goudappel, C. D., "Ondertrouw en huwelijk van Jan Vermeer", *Delftse historische sprokkelingen*, 1977, pp. 20–26.
Hoet, Gerard, *Catalogus of Naamlyst van Schilderyen met derselven pryzen zedert een langen reeks van Jaaren zoo in Holland als op andere Plaatzen in het openbaar verkogt*, vol. 1, The Hague 1752.
Matthijs, C. J., *De takken van de dorre boom: Genealogie van de Goudsefamilie Van Hensbeeck*, Gouda 1976.
Monconys, Balthasar de, *Journal de voyage de Monsieur de Monconys*, 2 vols., Lyons 1666.
Montias, John Michael, "New Documents on Vermeer and His Family", *Oud Holland* 91, 1977, pp. 267–287.
Montias, John Michael, "Vermeer and His Milieu: Conclusion of an Archival Study", *Oud Holland* 94, 1980, pp. 44–62.
Montias, John Michael, *Vermeer and His Milieu: A Web of Social History*, Princeton 1989.
Montias, John Michael, et al., "A Postscript on Vermeer and His Milieu", *The Hoogsteder Mercury* 12, 1991, pp. 42–51.
Montias, John Michael, *Vermeer en zijn milieu*, Baarn 1993 (ed., in Dutch trans., of Montias 1989).
Neurdenburg, Elisabeth, "Nog einige opmerkingen over Johannes Vermeer van Delft", *Oud Holland* 66, 1951, pp. 31–44.
Obreen, F. D. O., *Archief voor Nederlandsche Kunstgeschiedenis*, 7 parts, Rotterdam 1877–1890.
Peer, A. J. J. M. van, "Drie collecties schilderyen van Jan Vermeer", *Oud Holland* 72, 1957, pp. 92–103.
Peer, A. J. J. M. van, "Rondom Jan Vermeer van Delft", *Oud Holland* 74, 1959, pp. 240–245.
Peer, A. J. J. M. van, "Jan Vermeer van Delft: Drie archiefvondsten", *Oud Holland* 83, 1968, pp. 220–224.
Ruurs, Rob, "Documenten", in Blankert/Montias/Aillaud 1987, pp. 207–216.

Bibliography

Arasse, Daniel, *L'Ambition de Vermeer*, Paris 1993; English ed.: *Vermeer: Faith in Painting*, Princeton 1994.

Asemissen, Hermann Ulrich, *Jan Vermeer: Die Malkunst: Aspekte eines Berufbildes*, Frankfurt am Main 1988.

Badt, Kurt, *"Modell und Maler" von Jan Vermeer, Probleme der Interpretation: Eine Streitschrift gegen Hans Sedlmayr*, Cologne 1961 (2nd ed., with a postscript by Lorenz Dittmann, Cologne 1997).

Bailey, Anthony, *Vermeer: A View of Delft Then and Now*, London 2001; 2nd ed. 2002.

Bailey, Martin, *Vermeer*, London 1995; latest ed. 2011.

Begheyn SJ, Paul, "Johannes Vermeer en de jezuïten te Delft", *Oud Holland* 121, 2008, pp. 40–55.

Bianconi, Piero, *L'opera completa di Vermeer*, Milan 1967; English ed.: *The Complete Paintings of Vermeer*, London and New York 1967.

Binstock, Benjamin, *Vermeer's Family Secrets: Genius, Discovery and the Unknown Apprentice*, London 2008.

Blanc, Jan, *Vermeer*, Paris 2014.

Blankert, Albert, with contributions by Rob Ruurs and Willem van de Wetering, *Johannes Vermeer van Delft, 1632–1675*, Utrecht and Antwerp 1975 (English ed.: *Johannes Vermeer of Delft, 1632–1675*, Oxford and New York 1978).

Blankert, Albert, John Michael Montias and Gilles Aillaud, *Vermeer*, Paris 1986; Dutch ed. Amsterdam 1987; 2nd, rev. ed. 1992; English ed. New York and London 2007.

Blankert, Albert, "The Case of Han van Meegeren's Fake Vermeer *Supper at Emmaus* Reconsidered", in *In His Milieu: Essays on Netherlandish Art in Memory of John Michael Montias*, ed. Amy Golahny, Mia M. Mochizuki and Lisa Vergara, Amsterdam 2006, pp. 47–57.

Bleyswijck, Dirck Evertsz. van, *Beschryvinge der Stadt Delft*, 2 vols., Delft 1667–1680.

Boström, Kjell, "Peep-show or case", *Kunsthistorische Mededelingen van het Rijksbureau voor Kunsthistorische Documentatie 's-Gravenhage* 4, 1949, pp. 21–24.

Boström, Kjell, "Jan Vermeer van Delft en Cornelis van der Meulen", *Oud Holland* 66, 1951, pp. 117–122.

Brandhof, Marijke van den, *Een vroege Vermeer uit 1937: Achtergronden van leven en werken van de schilder / vervalser Han van Meegeren*, Utrecht 1979.

Bredius, Abraham, "Iets over Johannes Vermeer", *Oud Holland* 3, 1885, pp. 217–222.

Bredius, Abraham, *Künstler-Inventare: Urkunden zur Geschichte der Holländischen Kunst des XVIten, XVIIten und XVIIIten Jahrhunderts*, 7 vols., The Hague 1915–1921.

Bredius, Abraham, "An Unpublished Vermeer", *The Burlington Magazine* 61, 1932, pp. 144f.

Bredius, Abraham, "A New Vermeer", *The Burlington Magazine* 71, 1937, pp. 210f.

Broersma, Geerte, "Vermeer, Vermeer en nog eens Vermeer" / "Vermeer, Vermeer and Vermeer", in *De jonge Vermeer / The Young Vermeer*, exh. cat., The Hague, Mauritshuis, and Edinburgh, National Galleries of Scotland, ed. Edwin Buijsen, The Hague and Zwolle 2010, pp. 73–87.

Broos, Ben and Ariane van Suchtelen, *Portraits in the Mauritshuis, 1430–1790*, ed. Quentin Buvelot (with contributions by Rudi Ekkart, Quentin Buvelot, Guus Sluiter, Petria Noble, Peter van der Ploeg, Hans Vlieghe and Frederik Duparc), The Hague and Zwolle 2004.

Buijs, Hans, "Voorstellingen van Christus in het huis van Martha en Maria in het zestiende-eeuwse keukenstuk", *Nederlands Kunsthistorisch Jaarboek* 40, 1989, pp. 93–128.

Buijsen, Edwin, "Music in the Age of Vermeer", in *Dutch Society in the Age of Vermeer*, ed. Donald Haks and Marie Christine van der Sman, The Hague and Zwolle 1996, pp. 106–123.

Büttner, Nils, *Vermeer*, Munich 2010.

Cambridge 2011/12: *Vermeer's Women: Secrets and Silence*,

exh. cat., Cambridge, Fitzwilliam Museum, ed. Marjorie E. Wieseman with H. Perry Chapman and Wayne E. Franits, Cambridge, New Haven and London 2011.
Davidson, Bernice, *The Frick Collection: An Illustrated Catalogue,* vol. 1: *Paintings, American, British, Dutch, Flemish and German,* New York 1968.
Dekiert, Marcus, *Musikanten in der Malerei der niederländischen Caravaggio-Nachfolge: Vorstufen, Ikonographie und Bedeutungsgehalt der Musikszene in der niederländischen Bildkunst des 16. und 17. Jahrhunderts* (doctoral dissertation, 2000, Universität Bonn), Münster, Hamburg and London 2003.
Delft 1996: *Delft Masters, Vermeer's Contemporaries: Illusionism through the Conquest of Light and Space,* exh. cat., Delft, Stedelijk Museum Het Prinsenhof, ed. Michiel C. C. Kersten and Danielle H. A. Lokin with Michiel C. Plomp, Delft and London 1996.
Delft 2002: *Schatten in Delft: Burgers verzamelen, 1600–1750 / Treasures in Delft Burghers' Collections, 1600–1750,* exh. cat., Delft, Stedelijk Museum Het Prinsenhof, ed. Ellinor Bergvelt, Michiel Jonker and Agnes Wiechmann, Delft and Zwolle 2002.
Dresden 2004/05: *Johannes Vermeer: "Bei der Kupplerin",* exh. cat., Dresden, Gemäldegalerie Alte Meister, ed. Uta Neidhardt and Marlies Giebe (with contributions by Albert Blankert, Christine Klose, Annaliese Mayer-Meintschel, Uta Neidhardt), Dresden 2004.
Dresden 2010: *Der frühe Vermeer,* exh. cat., Dresden, Gemäldegalerie Alte Meister, ed. Uta Neidhardt (with contributions by Albert Blankert, Edwin Buijsen, Michael Franses, Jasper Kettner, Uta Neidhardt, Christoph Schölzel et al.), Berlin and Munich 2010 (Buijsen 2010a / Buijsen 2010b / Neidhardt 2010a / Neidhardt 2010b).
Dublin/Greenwich 2003/04: *Love Letters: Dutch Genre Paintings in the Age of Vermeer,* exh. cat., Dublin, National Gallery of Ireland, and Greenwich, CT, Bruce Museum of Arts and Science, ed. Peter C. Sutton, Lisa Vergara and Ann Jensen Adams, London 2003.
Düchting, Hajo, *Jan Vermeer und seine Zeit,* Stuttgart 2011.
Eiche, Sabine, "'The Artist in His Studio' by Jan Vermeer: About a Chandelier", *Gazette des Beaux-Arts,* 6/99, 1982, pp. 203–204.
Fahy, Everett (ed.), *The Wrightsman Pictures,* New York and New Haven 2005.
Fink, Daniel A., "Vermeer's Use of the Camera Obscura: A Comparative Study", *The Art Bulletin* 53, 1971, pp. 493–505.
Fleischer, Roland E., "Ludolf de Jongh's *The Refused Glass* and Its Effect on the Art of Vermeer and de Hooch", in Roland E. Fleischer and Susan Clare Scott (eds.), *Rembrandt, Rubens and the Art of Their Time: Recent Perspectives* (Papers in Art History from Pennsylvania State University 11), University Park, PA, 1997, pp. 251–266.
Franits Wayne E. (ed.), *The Cambridge Companion to Vermeer* (with contributions by Klaas van Berkel, Wayne Franits, Marguerite Glass, Elise Goodman, Valerie Hedquist, Christiane Hertel, Walter Liedtke, H. Rodney Nevitt Jr, Lisa Vergara, Arthur K. Wheelock Jr), Cambridge 2001.
Franits, Wayne E., *Dutch Seventeenth-Century Genre Painting: Its Stylistic and Thematic Evolution,* New Haven and London 2004.
Frankfurt 1997: *Johannes Vermeer: Der Geograph und der Astronom nach 200 Jahren wieder vereint,* exh. cat., Frankfurt am Main, Städelsches Kunstinstitut und Städtische Galerie, ed. Michael Maek-Gérard (with contributions by Klaas van Berkel, Michael Maek-Gérard, Jørgen Wadum, Peter Waldeis, Arthur K. Wheelock Jr), Frankfurt am Main 1997.
Gaskell, Ivan and Michiel Jonker (eds.), *Vermeer Studies* (with contributions by Daniel Arasse, Marten Jan Bok, David Bomford, Ben Broos, Nicola Costaras, Jean-Luc Delsaute, Ivan Gaskell, E. Melanie Gifford, Karin Groen, Eddy de Jongh, Koos Levy-van Halm, Hessel Miedema, John Michael Montias, John Nash, Irene Netta, Nanette Salomon, Leonard J. Slatkes, Eric Jan Sluijter, Frances Suzman Jowell, Lisa Vergara, Jørgen Wadum, Gregor J. M. Weber, Marieke De Winkel), New Haven and London 1998.
Gaskell, Ivan, *Vermeer's Wager: Speculations on Art History, Theory and Art Museums,* London 2000.
Gelder, Jan Gerrit van, "Jan Vermeer's Clio", *Oud Holland* 66, 1951, pp. 44–45.
Gelder, Jan Gerrit van, "Diana door Vermeer en C. de Vos",

Oud Holland 71, 1956, pp. 245–248.

Gelder, Jan Gerrit van, with commentary by Jan A. Emmens, *De Schilderkunst van Jan Vermeer*, Utrecht 1958.

Goldscheider, Ludwig, *Jan Vermeer: The Paintings*, London 1958 (2nd ed. 1967).

Gowing, Lawrence, *Vermeer*, London 1952; 2nd ed. London and New York 1970.

Greub, Thierry, *Vermeer oder die Inszenierung der Imagination*, Petersberg 2004.

Grimme, Ernst Günther, *Jan Vermeer van Delft*, Cologne 1974.

Gutruf, Gerhard, and Hellmuth Stachel, "The Hidden Geometry in Vermeer's 'The Art of Painting'", *Journal for Geometry and Graphics* 14, 2010, pp. 187–201.

The Hague 1996: *The Scholarly World of Vermeer*, exh. cat., The Hague, Museum Van Het Boek and Museum Meermanno-Westreenianum, ed. Ton Brandenbarg and Rudi Ekkart, The Hague and Zwolle 1996.

The Hague/Washington 2008/09: *Dutch Cityscapes of the Golden Age*, exh. cat., The Hague, Mauritshuis, and Washington, D.C., National Gallery of Art, ed. Ariane van Suchtelen and Arthur K. Wheelock, Jr, Zwolle 2008.

Hammer-Tugendhat, Daniela, *Das Sichtbare und das Unsichtbare: Zur holländischen Malerei des 17. Jahrhunderts*, Cologne, Weimar and Vienna 2009.

Hedinger, Bärbel, *Karten in Bildern: Zur Ikonographie der Wandkarte in holländischen Interieurgemälden des 17. Jahrhunderts*, Hildesheim, Zurich and New York 1986.

Hehenberger, Susanne, and Monika Löscher (eds.), *Die verkaufte Malkunst: Jan Vermeers Gemälde im 20. Jahrhundert* (Schriftenreihe der Kommission für Provenienzforschung 4), Vienna, Cologne and Weimar 2013.

Hertel, Christiane, *Vermeer: Reception and Interpretation*, Cambridge, New York and Melbourne 1996.

Hoet, Gerard, *Catalogus of Naamlyst van Schilderyen met derselven pryzen zedert een langen reeks van Jaaren zoo in Holland als op andere Plaatzen in het openbaar verkogt*, vol. 1, The Hague 1752.

Hoogstraten, Samuel van, *Inleyding tot de hooge schoole der schilderkonst*, Rotterdam 1678.

Houbraken, Arnold, *De groote schouburgh der Nederlantsche konstschilders en schilderessen*, 3 vols., Amsterdam 1718–1721.

Hubschmitt, William Evan, *The Art of Painting: An Iconographic Examination of De Schilderconst by Johannis Vermeer of Delft*, Binghamton, NY, 1986.

Hultén, Karl G., "Zu Vermeers Atelierbild", *Konsthistorisk Tidskrift* 18, 1949, pp. 90–98.

Huygens, Constantijn, *De jeugd van Constantijn Huygens, door hemzelf beschreven*, Dutch trans. (from original Latin of *c.* 1630), ed. A. H. Kan, Rotterdam 1971.

Jongh, Eddy de, *Zinn- en Minnebeelden in de schilderkunst van de zeventiende eeuw*, Amsterdam 1967.

Jongh, Eddy de, "Pearls of Virtue and Pearls of Vice", *Simiolus* 8, 1975/76, pp. 69–97.

Kahr, Madlyn Millner, "Vermeer's Girl Asleep: A Moral Emblem", *Metropolitan Museum Journal* 6, 1972, pp. 115–132.

Kaldenbach, Kees, "Het Straatje van Johannes Vermeer: Nieuwe Langendijk 24–26?", *Bulletin van de Koninklijke Nederlandse Oudheidkundige* Bond 99, 2000.

Kassel 2003: *Johannes Vermeer – Der Geograph: Die Wissenschaft der Malerei*, exh. cat., Kassel, Staatliche Museen Kassel, Gemäldegalerie Alte Meister, ed. Thorsten Smidt, Kassel 2003.

Kitson, Michael, "Current and Forthcoming Exhibitions: Florentine Baroque Art in New York", *The Burlington Magazine* 111, 1969, pp. 409–410.

Kleinert, Katja, *Atelierdarstellungen in der niederl. Genremalerei des 17. Jahrhunderts: realistisches Abbild oder glaubwürdiger Schein?*, Petersberg 2006.

Kolfin, Elmer, Carol Pottasch and Ruth Hoppe, "The Metamorphosis of Diana: Changing Perceptions of the Young Vermeer's Painting Technique", *Art Matters: Netherlandish Technical Studies of Art* 1, 2002, pp. 99–103.

Lairesse, Gérard de, *Groot Schilderboek*, 3 vols., Amsterdam 1707; rev. ed. Haarlem 1740; English ed.: *The Art of Painting*, London 1738.

Lammertse, Friso, Nadja Garthoff, Michiel van de Laar and Arie Wallert, *Van Meegeren's Vermeers: The Connoisseur's Eye and the Forger's Art*, Rotterdam 2011.

Lefèvre, Wolfgang (ed.), *Inside the Camera Obscura: Optics and Art under the Spell of the Projected Image*, Berlin 2007.

Leonhard, Karin, "Vermeer's Pregnant Women", *Art History* 25, 2002, pp. 293–318.
Leonhard, Karin, *Das gemalte Zimmer: Zur Interieurmalerei Jan Vermeers*, Munich 2003.
Liedtke, Walter, *A View of Delft: Vermeer and His Contemporaries*, Zwolle 2000.
Liedtke, Walter, *Dutch Paintings in the Metropolitan Museum of Art*, 2 vols., New Haven 2007.
Liedtke, Walter, *Vermeer: The Complete Paintings*, Ghent and Amsterdam 2008.
Liedtke, Walter, et al., "Canvas Matches in Vermeer: A Case Study in the Computer Analysis of Fabric Supports", *Metropolitan Museum Journal* 47, 2012.
Lindenburg, M. A., "Het 'straatje' van Vermeer", *Delfia Batavorum Jaarboek*, 1992, pp. 680–690.
London 2013: *Vermeer and Music: The Art of Love and Leisure*, exh. cat., London, The National Gallery, ed. Marjorie E. Wieseman, London 2013.
London/Hartford 1998/99: Peter C. Sutton, *Pieter de Hooch, 1629–1684*, exh. cat., London, Dulwich Picture Gallery, and Hartford, CT, Wadsworth Atheneum, New Haven and London 1998.
Lopez, Jonathan, *The Man Who Made Vermeers: Unvarnishing the Legend of Master Forger Han van Meegeren*, San Diego 2008.
MacColl, Dugald Sutherland, *A Note on Vermeer of Delft and the Picture "Christ with Martha and Mary"*, London 1901.
MacLaren, Neil, rev. ed. Christopher Brown, *The Dutch School, 1600–1900* (National Gallery Catalogues), London 1991.
Madrid 2003: *Vermeer y el interior holandés*, exh. cat., Madrid, Museo del Prado, ed. Alejandro Vergara and Mariët Westermann, Madrid, Museo Nacional del Prado, 2003.
Mai, Ekkehard, "Wer war Jacobus Vrel? Hypothesen zum sogenannten 'Vermeer der Armen'", *Kölner Museums-Bulletin*, 2003, pp. 42–71.
Mayer-Meintschel, Annaliese, "Die Briefleserin von Jan Vermeer van Delft: Zum Inhalt und zur Geschichte des Bildes", *Jahrbuch der Staatlichen Kunstsammlungen Dresden* 11, 1978/79, pp. 91–99.
Mayer-Meintschel, Annaliese, "Vermeers 'Kupplerin'", *Jahrbuch der Staatlichen Kunstsammlungen Dresden* 18, 1986, pp. 7–18.
Mengden, Lida von, *Vermeers De Schilderconst in den Interpretationen von Kurt Badt und Hans Sedlmayr: Probleme der Interpretation*, Frankfurt am Main, Berne and New York 1984.
Mills, Allan A., "Vermeer and the Camera Obscura: Some Practical Considerations", *Leonardo* 31, 1998, pp. 213–218.
Mirimonde, A. P. de, "Les Sujets musicaux chez Vermeer de Delft", *Gazette des Beaux-Arts*, 6/57, 1961, pp. 29–52.
Monconys, Balthasar de, *Journal de voyage de Monsieur de Monconys*, 2 vols., Lyons 1666.
Montias, John Michael, "Vermeer's Clients and Patrons", *The Art Bulletin* 69, 1987, pp. 68–76.
Montias, John Michael, *Vermeer and His Milieu: A Web of Social History*, Princeton 1989.
Montias, John Michael, et al., "A Postscript on Vermeer and His Milieu", *The Hoogsteder Mercury* 12, 1991, pp. 42–51.
Munich 2011: *Vermeer in München: König Max I. Joseph von Bayern als Sammler Alter Meister*, exh. cat., Munich, Alte Pinakothek, ed. Marcus Dekiert, Munich 2011.
Nash, John, *Vermeer*, London 1991.
Netta, Irene, *Das Phänomen 'Zeit' bei Jan Vermeer van Delft: Eine Analyse der innerbildlichen Zeitstrukturen seiner ein- und mehrfigurigen Interieurbilder*, Zurich and New York 1996.
Netta, Irene, *Vermeer van Delft: Ein Maler und seine Stadt*, Munich 2001.
Neurdenburg, Elisabeth, "Johannes Vermeer: Eenige opmerkingen naar aanleiding van de nieuwste studies over den Delftschen Schilder", *Oud Holland* 59, 1942, pp. 65–73.
New York 2009: *The Milkmaid by Johannes Vermeer*, exh. cat., The Metropolitan Museum of Art, ed. Walter Liedtke, New York 2009.
New York/London 2001: *Vermeer and the Delft School*, exh. cat., New York, The Metropolitan Museum of Art, and London, The National Gallery, ed. Walter Liedtke with Michiel C. Plomp and Axel Rüger (with contributions by Marten Jan Bok, Walter Liedtke, Michiel C. Plomp et al.), New Haven 2001 (Liedtke 2001a– 2001g).
Osaka 2000: *The Public and the Private in the Age of Vermeer*, exh. cat., Osaka, Municipal Museum of Art, ed. Arthur K. Wheelock, Jr, Osaka and London 2000.
Philadelphia/Berlin/London 1984: *Masters of Seventeenth-Century Dutch Genre Painting*, exh.

cat., Philadelphia, Philadelphia Museum of Art, West Berlin, Gemäldegalerie SMPK, and London, Royal Academy of Arts, ed. Peter C. Sutton et al., Philadelphia 1984.

Plietzsch, Eduard, *Vermeer van Delft*, Munich 1939.

Pops, Martin, *Vermeer: Consciousness and the Chamber of Being* (Studies in the Fine Arts, Criticism 16), Ann Arbor, MI, 1984.

Rambach, Christiane, *Vermeer und die Schärfung der Sinne*, Weimar 2007.

Rand, Harry, "Wat maakte de 'Keukenmeid' van Vermeer?", *Bulletin van het Rijksmuseum* 46, 1998, pp. 275–278, 349–351.

Raupp, H.-J., "Ansätze zu einer Theorie der Genremalerei in den Niederlanden im 17. Jahrhundert", *Zeitschrift für Kunstgeschichte* 46, 1983, pp. 401–418.

Rome 2012/13: *Vermeer: Il secolo d'oro d'arte olandese*, exh. cat., Rome, Scuderie del Quirinale, ed. Sandrina Bandera, Walter Liedtke and Arthur K. Wheelock, Jr, Rome 2012.

Rudolph, H., "'Vanitas': die Bedeutung mittelalterlicher and humanistischer Bildinhalte in der niederländischen Malerei des 17. Jahrhunderts", in *Festschrift Wilhelm Pinder*, Leipzig 1938, pp. 405–433.

Runia, Epco, *Vermeer in het Mauritshuis*, Zwolle 2005.

Schlenke, Hubertus, *Vermeer, mit Spinoza gesehen*, Berlin 1998.

Schneider, Norbert, *Jan Vermeer, 1632–1675*, Cologne 1993 (2nd ed. 2010).

Schütz, Karl, *Das Interieur in der Malerei*, Munich 2009.

Schütz, Karl, "Von Pieter de Hooch zu Johannes Vermeer: Zur Beurteilung der Malkunst im 19. Jahrhundert", in Hehenberger, Susanne, Monika Löscher (eds.), *Die verkaufte Malkunst: Jan Vermeers Gemälde im 20. Jahrhundert* (Schriftenreihe der Kommission für Provenienzforschung, vol. 4), Vienna et al. 2013, pp. 263–270.

Schwarz, Birgit, *Hitlers Museum: Die Fotoalben "Gemäldegalerie Linz": Dokumente zum "Führermuseum"*, Vienna, Cologne and Weimar 2004.

Schwarz, Heinrich, "Vermeer and the Camera Obscura", *Pantheon* 24, 1966, pp. 170–182.

Sedlmayr, Hans, "Der Ruhm der Malkunst: Jan Vermeer 'De Schilderconst'", in *Festschrift Hans Jantzen*, Berlin 1951, pp. 169–177.

Sedlmayr, Hans, "Jan Vermeer 'De Schilderkunst'", *Hefte des Kunsthistorischen Seminars der Universität München* 7–8, 1962, pp. 34–65.

Seymour, Charles, Jr, "Dark Chamber and Light-filled Room: Vermeer and the Camera Obscura", *The Art Bulletin* 46, 1964, pp. 323–331.

Sheldon, Libby, and Nicola Costaras, "Johannes Vermeer's 'Young Woman Seated at a Virginal'", *The Burlington Magazine* 148, 2006, pp. 89–97.

Slatkes, Leonard J., *Vermeer and His Contemporaries*, New York 1981.

Smith, David R., "Vermeer and Iconoclasm", *Zeitschrift für Kunstgeschichte* 74, 2011, pp. 193–216.

Snow, Edward, *A Study of Vermeer*, Berkeley and London 1979; 2nd, rev. ed. Berkeley and Oxford 1994.

Steadman, Philip, *Vermeer's Camera: Uncovering the Truth behind the Masterpieces*, Oxford 2001.

Stechow, Wolfgang, "Landscape Paintings in Dutch Seventeenth-Century Interiors", *Nederlands Kunsthistorisch Jaarboek* 11, 1960, pp. 165–184.

Stoichita, Victor Ieronim, *L'Instauration du tableau: métapeinture à l'aube des temps modernes*, Paris 1993; rev. ed. Geneva 1999; English ed.: *The Self-aware Image: An Insight into Early Modern Meta-painting* (Cambridge Studies in New Art History and Criticism), Cambridge 1997.

Stone, Harriet, *Tables of Knowledge: Descartes in Vermeer's Studio*, Ithaca, NY, 2006.

Sutton, Peter C., *Pieter de Hooch: Complete Edition*, Oxford and New York 1980.

Swillens, Pieter T. A., *Johannes Vermeer: Painter of Delft, 1632–1675*, Utrecht and Brussels 1950.

Thoré, Étienne-Joseph Théophile (as William Bürger), *Galerie d'Arenberg à Bruxelles avec le catalogue complet de la collection*, Paris, Brussels and Leipzig 1859.

Thoré, Étienne-Joseph Théophile (as William Bürger), *Musées de la Hollande*, Paris 1858–1860.

Thoré, Étienne-Joseph Théophile (as William Bürger), "Van der Meer de Delft", *Gazette des Beaux-Arts*, 21, 1866, pp. 297–330, 458–470, 542–575.

Thoré, Étienne-Joseph Théophile (as William Bürger), "Meisterwerke der Braunschweiger Galerie in Radierungen von William Unger, III. *Das Mädchen mit dem Weinglas.* Ölgemälde von Jan van der Meer", *Zeitschrift für bildende Kunst* 3, 1868, pp. 262–263.

Tokyo 2008: *Vermeer and the Delft*

Style, exh. cat., Tokyo, Metropolitan Art Museum, ed. Peter C. Sutton, Tokyo 2008.
Tolnay, Charles de, "L'Atelier de Vermeer", *Gazette des Beaux-Arts* 6, 41, 1953, 265–272.
Vander Auwera, Joost, "Taking Local History Seriously: The Case of the Chandelier in 'Saint Luke Painting the Virgin' by Abraham Janssen van Nuyssen and in 'The Art of Painting' by Johannes Vermeer van Delft", in *Liber amicorum Raphaël de Smedt*, ed. Joost Vander Auwera, Leuven 2001, 317–338.
Vienna 2010: *Vermeer, "Die Malkunst": Spurensicherung an einem Meisterwerk / Vermeer, "The Art of Painting": Scrutiny of a Picture*, exh. cat., Vienna, Kunsthistorisches Museum, ed. Sabine Haag, Elke Oberthaler and Sabine Pénot (with contributions by Christoph Brandhuber, Dirk Jan Biemond, Jaap. J. Boon, Roswitha Juffinger, Eva Mongi-Vollmer, Elke Oberthaler, Sabine Pénot, Günter Schilder, Katja Schmitz von Ledebur, Robert Wald, Arthur K. Wheelock Jr), Vienna and Salzburg 2010.
Vries, Ary Bob de, *Jan Vermeer van Delft*, Amsterdam 1939; German ed. Basle 1945; English rev. ed. London 1948.
Vries, Ary Bob de, "Vermeer's Diana", *Bulletin van het Rijksmuseum* 2, 1954, pp. 40–42.
Wadum, Jørgen, "Johannes Vermeer (1632–1675) and His Use of Perspective", in *Historical Painting Techniques, Materials and Studio Practice*, ed. Arrie Wallert et al., Leiden 1995, pp. 148–154 (Wadum 1995b).
Wagner, J., *Der junge Vermeer in der Zeit der Entscheidung: Ein Beitrag zur Historienmalerei des Delfter Vermeer*, Alfter 1993.
Washington 1999: Arthur K. Wheelock, Jr, *Johannes Vermeer: The Art of Painting*, exh. cat., National Gallery of Art, Washington, D.C., 1999.
Washington/The Hague 1995/96: *Johannes Vermeer*, exh. cat., Washington, D.C., National Gallery of Art, and The Hague, Mauritshuis, ed. Arthur K. Wheelock, Jr (with contributions by Albert Blankert, Ben Broos, Jørgen Wadum, Arthur K. Wheelock Jr), Zwolle 1995 (Wheelock 1995c / Wadum 1995a).
Weber, Gregor J. M., "Antoine Dézallier d'Argenville und fünf Künstler namens Jan van der Meer", *Oud Holland* 107, 1993, pp. 298–304.
Weber, Gregor J. M., "Johannes Vermeer, Pieter Jansz. van Asch und das Problem der Abbildungstreue", *Oud Holland* 108, 1994, pp. 98–106.
Welu, James A., "Vermeer: His Cartographic Sources", *The Art Bulletin* 57, 1975, pp. 529–547.
Welu, James A., *Vermeer and Cartography*, Ann Arbor, 1981
Welu, James A., "Vermeer's Astronomer: Observations on an Open Book", *The Art Bulletin* 68, 1986, pp. 263–267.
Westermann, Mariët, *Johannes Vermeer* (Rijksmuseum Dossiers), Amsterdam 2004.
Weve, Wim, "Noogmals het 'Straatje'", *Delf (Cultuurhistorisch Bulletin Delft)* 1, no. 8, 2006, unpaginated.
Wheelock, Arthur K., Jr, *Perspective, Optics and Delft Artists around 1650*, New York and London 1977.
Wheelock, Arthur K., Jr, "Zur Technik zweier Bilder, die Vermeer zugeschrieben sind", *Maltechnik Restauro* 4, 1978, pp. 242–257.
Wheelock, Arthur K., Jr, *Jan Vermeer*, New York 1981; 2nd ed. 1988.
Wheelock, Arthur K., Jr, and C. J. Kaldenbach, "Vermeer's View of Delft and His Vision of Reality", *Artibus et historiae, rivista internazionale di arti visive e cinema* 6, 1982, pp. 9–35.
Wheelock, Arthur K., Jr, "*Saint Praxedis*: New Light on the Early Career of Johannes Vermeer", *Artibus et historiae, rivista internazionale di arti visive e cinema* 14, 1986, pp. 71–89.
Wheelock, Arthur K., Jr, "Pentimenti in Vermeer's Paintings: Changes in Style and Meaning", in *Holländische Genremalerei im 17. Jahrhundert: Symposium Berlin 1984*, ed. Henning Bock and Thomas W. Gaehtgens, Berlin 1987, pp. 385–412.
Wheelock, Arthur K., Jr, *Dutch Paintings of the Seventeenth Century* (The Collection of the National Gallery of Art Systematic Catalogue), Washington, D.C. (Wheelock 1995a).
Wheelock, Arthur K., Jr, *Vermeer and the Art of Painting*, New Haven and London 1995 (Wheelock 1995b).
White, Christopher, *The Dutch Pictures in the Collection of Her Majesty the Queen*, Cambridge 1982
Wolf, Bryan J., *Vermeer and the Invention of Seeing*, Chicago 2001.
Wright, Christopher, *Vermeer*, London 1976.

Index

W/Z

Photo Credits

Agenzia Fotografica Scala, Antella, Florence: pp. 182, 266–267, 269 372.; Archive of the publisher, collectors or author: pp. 90, 126.; © ARTOTHEK: pp. 20, 154.; bpk | Gemäldegalerie, SMB | Jörg P. Anders: pp. 80, 204, 210, 311; bpk | Gemäldegalerie, SMB | Christoph Schmidt: p. 144; bpk | Gemäldegalerie, SMB | Volker Schneider: pp. 162–167, 206–209, 211, 300, 330, 350.; bpk | Hamburger Kunsthalle | Elke Walford: pp. 15, 240.; bpk | Staatliche Kunstsammlungen Dresden | Herbert Boswank: pp. 49, 56, 85, 92–93, 95, 315, 324, 327; bpk | Staatliches Museum Schwerin | Elke Walford: p. 35; bpk | The Metropolitan Museum of Art, New York: pp. 76, 87, 115, 148, 184–185, 187, 188–189, 190, 191, 219, 260, 292–293, 295, 297, 325, 344, 346, 362, 387, 398; Bridgeman Images: pp. 25, 140, 160, 183, 355, 393, 397.; Collection Centraal Museum, Utrecht: p. 71.; © Dulwich Picture Gallery, London: p. 284.; © The Frick Collection, New York: pp. 88–89, 91, 136, 143, 168–169, 212–213, 215, 299, 329, 337, 367; © GDKE – Landesmuseum Mainz (Ursula Rusischer): p. 59.; Grafische Sammlung Albertina, Vienna: p. 245.; Herzog Anton Ulrich-Museum Braunschweig, Kunstmuseum des Landes Niedersachsen / Fotograf: Claus Cordes: pp. 51, 64, 158–159, 161, 307, 336.; Koninklijke Bibliotheek van Nederland, Den Haag: pp. 282, 296.; © Koninklijk Kabinet van Schilderijen Mauritshuis, The Hague: pp. 31, 80/81, 153, 217, 251, 303, 320, 340, 359; The Kremer Collection: p. 216.; Kunsthistorisches Museum, Vienna: pp. 16, 55, 60, 120, 147, 172, 232, 239, 263, 265, 315, 369.; © MAK, Vienna: p. 84.; © Musée du Louvre, Dist. RMN-Grand Palais, Paris / Georges Poncet: p. 86.; Museum Boijmans Van Beuningen, Rotterdam / Photographer: Studio Tromp, Rotterdam: pp. 37, 312.; Museum Prinsenhof Delft, the Netherlands: pp. 19, 101, 130, 133, 139.; Museumslandschaft Hessen Kassel: p. 220.; © The National Gallery, London: pp. 26, 246, 255, 281, 283, 285, 382, 384, 390; © The National Gallery, London/Scala, Florence: pp. 43, 44, 47, 79.; © National Gallery of Art, Washington D.C.: pp. 98, 106, 117, 157, 174, 200–202, 205, 196–197, 199, 221, 223, 352, 357, 363, 365; © National Gallery of Ireland, Dublin: Cover, pp. 225, 226, 252, 286–288, 291, 380; © National Galleries of Scotland, Edinburgh: pp. 69, 83, 322.; Österreichische Nationalbibliothek, Vienna: pp. 109, 229.; © Photo RMN-Grand Palais, Paris / Jacques Quecq d'Henripret: p. 63; Photo RMN-Grand Palais, Paris / René-Gabriel Ojéda: p. 82; Photo RMN-Grand Palais, Paris / Jean-Gilles Berizzi: p. 119; Photo RMN-Grand Palais, Paris / Gérard Blot: p. 275; Photo RMN-Grand Palais, Paris / Franck Raux: pp. 280, 376; © Rheinisches Bildarchiv Köln: pp. 257, 278.; Rijksmuseum, Amsterdam: pp. 6, 13, 94, 105, 129, 170, 173, 175, 180, 192–193, 195, 235, 279, 331, 333, 348, 378.; The Royal Collection © 2009, Her Majesty Queen Elizabeth II, London: pp. 110, 178–179, 181, 342.; © Royal Museums of Fine Arts of Belgium, Brüssel: p. 125.; Städel Museum – U. Edelmann, Frankfurt a. M./ARTOTHEK: pp. 270–271, 273, 318, 375; © The State Hermitage Museum, St. Petersburg: p. 198.; Stedelijke Musea Mechelen: p. 236.; © Margareta Svensson, Amsterdam: Vor- und Nachsatzpapier, pp. 1–5, 9, 176–177, 276–277.; © Wallace Collection, London, UK / Bridgeman Images: p. 40.; Worcester Art Museum, Massachusetts, USA / Bridgeman Images: p. 75.

Acknowledgements

Author's acknowledgements

It would have been impossible to produce a new text encompassing Vermeer's work in its entirety had it not been for the many years of research and publication on the part of other scholars. Above all among these I would mention John Michael Montias, Albert Blankert, Arthur K. Wheelock and, not least, Walter Liedtke, whomlost his life in tragic circumstances in 2015. For their contribution – be it through enlightening discussion, valuable advice, bibliographical assistance or answers to specific questions – I am especially indebted to Beatrix Kriller-Erdrich and the staff of the library of the Kunsthistorisches Museum, Vienna, as also to Gerhard Gutruf, Rudolf Hopfner, Peter C. Sutton and Angela Völker. My particular gratitude is due to Brigitte Beier for her editorial expertise and her enormous commitment to this project.

Publisher's acknowledgements

We are much indebted to all the museums, archives and other institutions cited in the picture captions and in the photo credits for their kind assistance in the publication of this volume. A great many curators, collectors, photographers and photo agencies have contributed decisively to the success of our undertaking. We should like to acknowledge: Keith Christiansen (The Metropolitan Museum of Art, New York), Ryan Clee (Scottish National Gallery of Modern Art, Edinburgh), Faye Cliné (Koninklijk Kabinet van Schilderijen Mauritshuis, The Hague), Claus Cordes (Herzog Anton Ulrich-Museum, Braunschweig), Penelope Currier (The Frick Collection, New York), Kenny Daragh (The National Gallery, London), Emilie Gordenker (Koninklijk Kabinet van Schilderijen Mauritshuis, The Hague), Peter Huestis (National Gallery of Art, Washington, DC), Ilse Jung (Kunsthisthorisches Museum, Vienna), Jerzy J. Kierkuc-Bielinski (Kenwood House, London), Iris Labeur (Rijksmuseum, Amsterdam), Bernd Wolfgang Lindemann (Gemäldegalerie, Berlin), Louise Morgan (National Gallery of Ireland, Dublin), Alan Newman (National Gallery of Art, Washington, DC), Wim Pijbes (Rijks-museum, Amsterdam), Steffi Reh (Staatliche Kunstsammlungen Dresden), Christoph Schmidt (Gemäldegalerie, Berlin), Volker Schneider (Gemäldegalerie, Berlin), Margareta Svensson (Amsterdam), Steffen Wedepohl (Bridgeman Images, Berlin), Angela Weihe (Herzog Anton Ulrich-Museum, Braunschweig), Arthur K. Wheelock (National Gallery of Art, Washington, DC), Astrid Winde (bpk, Berlin) and Fabian Wolf (Städel Museum, Frankfurt on the Main). Equally fruitful has been our collaboration with the photo-lithographers Giuseppe Brisotto and Silverio Zanotto (Fotolito Brisotto, Tezze di Piave).

The Book of Bibles

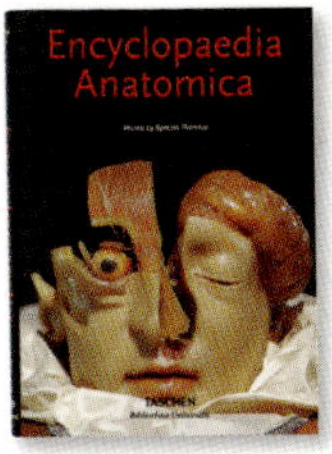

Encyclopaedia Anatomica

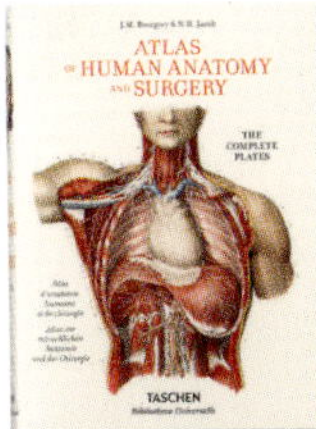

Bourgery. Atlas of Anatomy & Surgery

Alchemy & Mysticism

Basilius Besler's Florilegium

A Garden Eden

Martius. The Book of Palms

Piranesi. Complete Etchings

Seba. Cabinet of Natural Curiosities

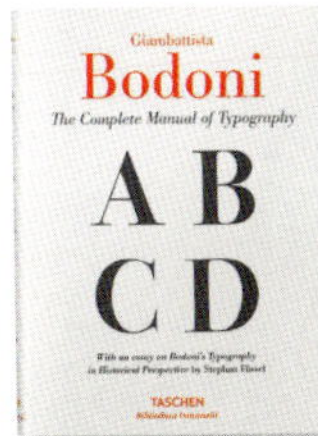

Bodoni. Manual of Typography

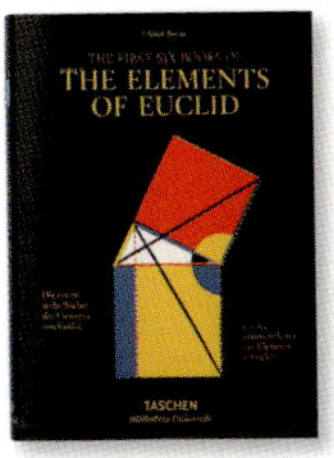

Byrne. Six Books of Euclid

The World of Ornament

Racinet. The Costume History

Karl Blossfeldt

Eugène Atget. Paris

Curtis. The North American Indian

Stieglitz. Camera Work

20th Century Photography

New Deal Photography

A History of Photography

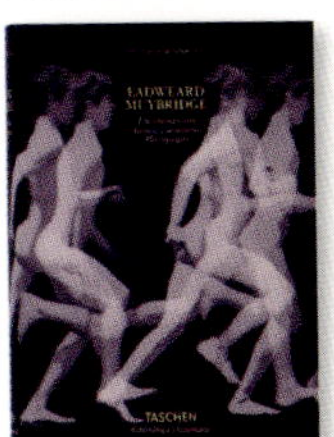

Eadweard Muybridge

Film Posters of the Russian Avant-Garde

Bauhaus

Modern Architecture A-Z

Architectural Theory

Renaissance radical

The haunting visions of Hieronymus Bosch

Only 20 paintings and eight drawings are confidently assigned to Netherlandish painter Hieronymus Bosch (c. 1450 – 1516) but in their fantastical visions they have secured his place as one of the most renowned cult artists in history. 500 years on from his death, his works continue to inspire scholars, artists, designers, musicians, death metal band names, and designer dresses. Through full spreads and carefully curated details, this book surveys the artist's compositional scope as well as his most compelling, if disturbing, inventions, from horse-skulled harp players to devils on ice skates.

"Bosch in breathtakingly unearthly depth of field."

— *Die Welt*, Berlin

Hieronymus Bosch. The Complete Works
Stefan Fischer
520 pages

The deftness of da Vinci

The drawings of art history's master genius

One of the most accomplished human beings who ever lived, Leonardo da Vinci remains the quintessential Renaissance genius. Creator of the world's most famous paintings, this scientist, artist, philosopher, inventor, builder and mechanic epitomized the great flowering of human consciousness that marks his era.
This book features top-quality reproductions of 663 of Leonardo's drawings, from anatomical studies to architectural plans, from complex engineering designs to pudgy infant portraits. The overwhelming majority of the drawings, more than half of which were provided by the Royal Collection at Windsor Castle, are presented in full-page format and show the delicate finesse of one of the most talented minds, and hands, in history.

"There's no legal way of approaching Leonardo's work more closely."

—*The Financial Times*, Hamburg

Leonardo da Vinci. The Graphic Work
Frank Zöllner, Johannes Nathan
776 pages

YOU CAN FIND TASCHEN STORES IN

Berlin
Schlüterstr. 39

Beverly Hills
354 N. Beverly Drive

Brussels
Place du Grand Sablon / Grote Zavel 35

Cologne
Neumarkt 3

Hollywood
Farmers Market, 6333 W. 3rd Street, CT-10

Hong Kong
Shop 01-G02 Tai Kwun, 10 Hollywood Road, Central

London
12 Duke of York Square

London Claridge's
49 Brook Street

Miami
1111 Lincoln Rd.

Milan
Via Meravigli 17

Paris
2 rue de Buci

"If browsing is considered an art form, the TASCHEN store is a masterpiece."
— Dwell

Frontpapers and endpapers:
A View of Delft (detail), *c.* 1660–1663
Oil on canvas, 96.5 x 115.7 cm / 38 x 45 ½ in.
The Hague, Koninklijk Kabinet
van Schilderijen Mauritshuis

Pages 1–5:
A View of Delft (details), *c.* 1660–1663
Oil on canvas, 96.5 x 115.7 cm / 38 x 45 ½ in.
The Hague, Koninklijk Kabinet
van Schilderijen Mauritshuis

Page 398:
Allegory of Faith (detail), *c.* 1671–1674
Oil on canvas, 114.3 x 88.9 cm / 45 x 35 in.
New York, The Metropolitan Museum of Art,
The Friedsam Collection,
Bequest of Michael Friedsam, 1931

Page 441:
Diana and Her Companions (detail), *c.* 1654
Oil on canvas, 97.8 x 104.6 cm / 38 ½ x 41 ⅛ in.
The Hague, Koninklijk Kabinet van
Schilderijen Mauritshuis

EACH AND EVERY TASCHEN BOOK PLANTS A SEED!
TASCHEN is a carbon neutral publisher. Each year, we offset our annual carbon emissions with carbon credits at the Instituto Terra, a reforestation program in Minas Gerais, Brazil, founded by Lélia and Sebastião Salgado. To find out more about this ecological partnership, please check: www.taschen.com/zerocarbon
Inspiration: unlimited. Carbon footprint: zero.

To stay informed about TASCHEN and our upcoming titles, please subscribe to our free magazine at www.taschen.com/magazine, follow us on Twitter, Instagram, and Facebook, or e-mail your questions to contact@taschen.com.

Hohenzollernring 53, D–50672 Köln
www.taschen.com

Original edition:

Project Management: Petra Lamers-Schütze,
Meike Nießen, Cologne
Editing: Brigitte Beier, Hamburg;
Mahros Allamezade, Cologne
Translation: Elizabeth Clegg, London
Design: Sense/Net Art Direction /
Andy Disl, www.sense-net.net;
Birgit Eichwede/Claudia Frey, Cologne
Production: Ute Wachendorf,
Tina Ciborowius, Cologne

ISBN 978-3-8365-6510-3
Printed in China